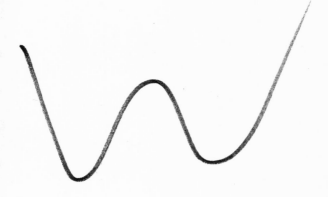

FLOATING WORLDS

Also by Cecelia Holland

FICTION

Great Maria (1974)

The Death of Attila (1973)

The Earl (1971)

Antichrist (1970)

Until the Sun Falls (1969)

The Kings in Winter (1968)

Rakóssy (1967)

The Firedrake (1966)

FOR CHILDREN

The King's Road (1970)

Ghost on the Steppe (1969)

FLOATING WORLDS

CECELIA HOLLAND

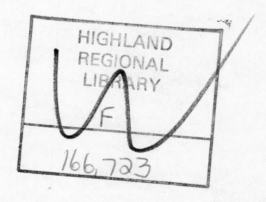

LONDON
VICTOR GOLLANCZ LTD
1976

ISBN 0 575 02202 7

Printed in Great Britain by
Lowe & Brydone Printers Limited, Thetford, Norfolk

For my sisters,
Deborah and Jennifer,
minds like music, and
hearts of glass

FLOATING WORLDS

THE EARTH. January, 1852–January, 1853

"These people were giants," Tony said. He waved up at the towering ruin before them. "They built on such a scale, their ideas were so absolute and universal—"

Paula said, "They were Fascists."

"You can't have everything."

She scuffed her feet over the pavement, two thousand years old, seamed with moss. She had never been good at history. Down the wide, straight street, a man in a white hat leaned back to take a snapshot of the ruins. Paula went down the steps and turned to look up at the building. On the frieze above the doors stone masks hung, labeled. She tried to make out the lettering. BRA—

"Haven't you ever been here before?" Tony said. He came up behind her, his hands in his pants pockets.

"Once. When I was little. My mother brought me. We had ice creams afterward." Why was everything so large? She shaded her eyes to see the letters. MANTE. She would have to look it up.

"What was it used for?"

"A museum. A library. Something like that."

She looked around them. Both sides of the street were lined with ruins. Opposite, a wall still stood upright, the windows worn soft and round with age.

"I don't like it," she said. "It's arrogant."

"You're very provincial."

She grunted at him. They went along the street. Her footsteps rang noisily after her off the ruined walls. The pavement was hard and her legs hurt. Other people strolled around, their heads tilted back.

On the street corner a woman sat painting at an easel. Tony went straight toward her. Paula ambled after him. Opposite the museum, green vines swallowed the last remaining wall of another building. The yellow tongues of sweet Mary reached out to the light. She veered across the pavement and picked one flower and sucked it for the trace of honey. She would have an ice cream on the way home. Voices here traveled far, perhaps the stone carried them; she could hear people talking in the next street. She went up beside Tony.

He stood next to the painter, his face pursed. Amused, she watched him put his head this way and that to see the picture from different angles. He was really a critic, not a writer at all; he knew every pose.

"The lighting presents an interesting problem," he said.

The woman wiggled her brush in a muddy cup of water. "The domelight changes from day to day. Almost from hour to hour."

Paula looked straight up overhead. The light was diffuse. It fell in pale sheets through the height of the dome, here blue and there definitely more yellow. It was hard to realize that the ocean covered them. Tony was discussing Art with the painter. He sounded knowledgeable but Paula did not understand anything he said. She went across the street. From here she could see through the broken walls to the next row of ruins, and through them to the next, all huge, the biggest buildings she had ever seen. The people who had built this city had dominated the Earth for three centuries, by money, by force, and by guile; they had colonized Mars, reached as far as Uranus, cracked atoms and made whole cities out of polymer, and Manhattan had been the heart of that empire.

"You know a lot about art," the woman said to Tony. "Do you paint?"

He smiled at her. "I'm a writer. My name's Tony Andrea."

"Oh, really." They shook hands. She had read his first book. Paula circled behind them to look at the water color. She did not like it. Cramped onto the square paper, the buildings looked small, like broken boxes. She put her hands in her jacket pockets, raising her eyes back to the ruins.

"Are you a writer too?" the painter said.

Paula shook her head. "I'm—"

"We haven't figured out yet what Paula is," Tony said.

They walked off down the street. A thick tarry slab of the concrete had buckled up the pavement in the middle. The street ran off straight to the shining wall of the dome in the distance, bordered on either side by raised strips of poured stone. Paula stepped up onto the border.

"Why is this part higher than the other?"

Tony walked along the lower level, beside her. She could see the balding crown of his head. Maybe when he was asleep she would draw an ivy wreath on it. He said, "They drove their cars on this part, and the people on foot walked up where you are. Out of the way, see?"

"They drove their cars on the ground?" No wonder the street was so broad. "Were they horse-drawn?"

"They were a little more advanced than that, kitch."

Ahead of them the angle of the light changed. They were coming to the wall of the dome. A jagged shell of a building rose up from the street, hundreds of feet high, catching the light like glass. She put her hand up between her eyes and the dome. "It's glass." The domelight shone green as leaves along the edges of the walls. "That's a dumb thing to make a building out of."

Tony laughed. He swung her off the border and down to the street beside him. "You really are a narrow-minded little materialist."

"Did they live here? In glass buildings?" Some fable moved elusively at the edge of her memory.

"No. They lived somewhere else and came in here during the day."

"Now tell me the truth."

"I'm sorry, kitch, that is the truth."

She stood looking up at the glass. Maybe in those days glass had been more common than it was now. Waves of stain crossed it, traces of dry dust like tracks from the time when the ruins had been under water.

"Atlantis."

"That's a different place entirely," Tony said. "That's in Aegea."

They went on to the port. The covered boat waited in the brackish water of the dock, empty. Paula went down between the benches to the back, next to the steering box. Tony sat down beside her.

"The doctor says he won't do the operation unless you sign a paper saying you know I can get you pregnant."

"What?"

"I know it's ridiculous, but he's an old bastard, he says he's tired of naturalizing the men and then six months later sucking out the women."

Paula leaned on the wall of the steering box, looking in at the controls. "It's not up to him." The long handle coming from the floor was probably the brake. She was surprised that having a baby would be so complicated. The boat rocked; people crowded on board.

"Are you having dinner with me tonight?" she asked.

"I have to work," Tony said. "I've been with you all day."

He was writing a metaphysical novel, of which she had already read three drafts. He was endlessly inventive without being especially creative, which made his books easy to read. He told her how he was changing Chapter Three, where the hero murdered his wife. She wondered if he had made up the doctor's demand. Maybe he did not want a baby after all. The painter was maneuvering her easel through the door into the boat. Behind her the boatman came in and pulled up the ramp. He got into the steering box beside Paula.

"Hang on, we may bump going through the locks."

The deck shuddered under Paula's feet. She heard the rumble of an engine. She turned to the window. The rubberized walls of the lock closed around the boat and slipped with a wet slick plop past the window. The interior lights came on, making everything white. The boat rose straight up. Outside the window the ocean was lit dark green from the dome wall they were passing. So close to New York, the sea was filthy. Flakes of garbage floated around the window. There was supposed to be an ancient dump here someplace, still leaking after hundreds of years. Tony was talking to the boatman about nautical design. The water outside the boat filled slowly with sunshine. She pressed her cheek against the clammy plastic of the window. Half a mile below, the Manhattan dome glowed like a moon in the ocean.

The boat surfaced. They flew across the choppy open water. Paula sat back. The other passengers talked in low voices. Tony sat absently licking the hairs of his mustache into his mouth and biting them off. Ahead, the southern end of the New York dome reflected the late sunlight back across the water in a coppery trail. In the western sky, rank with pollution, swirling with smoke, three images of the sun sank toward the horizon. Half the sky was brilliant ruddy orange. The boat yawed in the wind off the seacoast. They sank into the water again. The boatman steered them through the underwater lock and up to the surface of the terminal pond.

Tony helped her down the ramp, steering her by one hand on her arm. They went into the terminal building and took the crowded vertical car to the roof bus stop. Dark was falling. The winking white light of an air bus was coming above the trees. Tony stood beside her, rocking back and forth on his heels.

"Write something down I can show my doctor, so he can take the plug out."

"I think you ought to go to a doctor who minds his own."

The bus settled down onto the roof. She went up the steps beside the driver. She hadn't paid for a bus ride in days; she put a dollar into the box. Tony came after her, crowding her in. The bus was full, all the side benches taken. She went down the aisle to the back.

"Do you like the name Jennie?" Tony asked.

"I like Jennifer better."

"Jennifer Mendoza sounds terrible."

She looked up at him, drawn by his earnestness. His eyes were blue, unexpected against his chocolate dark skin. Their baby would not have blue eyes.

"Andrea is a girl's name." It was a fad to name babies for their fathers.

"I've been thinking about that," he said.

The bus slowed and settled down on a rooftop, and the lights blinked on and off. "Hobold Building," the driver called. "Change for crosstown. Next stop the university."

"What if it's a boy?" Paula said.

Tony shrugged. "I have no preference in boys' names."

The bus flew off in a giddy curve. She clutched the railing to keep from falling. Out the window, beyond the fat woman on the bench, the blue night domelight shone on the surface of the lake. The bus crossed a hilly stretch of trees and lowered again. She slid between Tony and a row of knees toward the back door.

She got off the bus near the turret of the Biochemistry Building. There was an arrow-shaped sign pasted to it: *Celestial Mechanics Conference.* She went across the campus. Most of the university was underground. On the silo of the Technology Building was another arrow-shaped sign. She liked the phrase, "celestial mechanics." Maybe she would name the baby that. She went through the park. It was dark under the trees and she stayed in the open. An owl hooted. She stopped and waited but heard nothing more.

The top three stories of her building were above ground. She went in the front door, past the crowds of bicycles, and up to the third floor. In the circular middle room of the commune a small knot of people already waited at the big table for the dinner rice. She stopped at the videone for her messages. There were no messages. She went to her room, in the back hall, threw her bag on the unmade bed, and went next door and knocked.

"Who's there?"

She opened the door and went into a tiny, crowded room. An Chu was standing at her drawing table sketching. Paula took off her jacket, dropped it on the bed, and stretched herself out on top of it and the other woman's stacked clean sheets and towels.

"We went to Manhattan. Have you ever been there? The undersea dome."

An Chu's beaked Aztec nose was an inch from the paper. "I can't stand being under water. The job list is there on the bed."

Like Paula, An Chu was out of work. Paula sat up. She piled the clean laundry up into a single stack against the wall and found the long sheet of paper advertising jobs. Outside in the hall, someone called, "The rice is out." An Chu took the bowl and went to get their dinner. Paula toed off her shoes. She got up to see the long sleeveless dress An Chu had been drawing. The walls of the little room were papered with sketches of clothes. An Chu brought the nutty fragrance of rice into the room.

"Here's one," Paula said, sitting down on the bed again. "Swamper for an all-night bar. Prefer non-drinker."

An Chu located her cutting board and a knife and began to chop vegetables. "You drink." A piece of celery sailed into Paula's lap and she ate it.

"I could quit. What's a bramante?"

"I think it's a place in Lisbon."

"I think it's a man. I'm glad I can't type." Rows and rows of uninteresting jobs required typing. She watched An Chu pile up the green and orange vegetables at the side of the chopping block. An Chu's skin was golden, her lips full, her long eyes like jet. She swept the vegetables into the pot, where they sizzled.

"I have to get up early tomorrow," Paula said. "Make sure I wake up, will you?"

"Why?"

"For the oral exam. For the Committee."

"Oh, lord. You aren't still doing that?"

"It's a job. They pay better than anything else except the Martians."

"If you ask me," An Chu said, stirring the vegetables, "there's no difference between the Committee and the Martians. They're all a power train."

Paula folded the job sheet and stuck it into a crack in the wall. She sat down on the floor, ready to eat. An Chu was right about the Committee. A worldwide company, it negotiated contracts and ran diplomatic errands for the rest of the Middle Planets. She had applied out of curiosity, and the tests had become a kind of joke; they asked for some training in interplanetary law, which she did not have, and gave aptitude tests in mathematics and science, which she knew she had flunked. It was amusing to answer tongue-in-cheek to all their solemn stupid questions. The other woman spooned up rice and vegetables into a bowl, and Paula reached for it, hungry.

The Committee for the Revolution had its New York office in a gulley between the campus and the lake. The building was one story, with three or four air cars parked on the roof. When Paula got there, the waiting room was already full of people. She crossed through the crowd, conscious of the stares, and read down the schedule on the bulletin board. Her name was third on the list for the oral exam. She could not leave to get her breakfast as she had planned. There was no place to sit. She stood by the wall next to the desk.

She had seen most of the other people at the written examinations. Nearly all were younger than she was by five or six years. They bent over their notebooks studying, or stared into space, book plugs in their ears. They took it all terribly seriously. The room was warm. She could smell her own body. She wondered why she was scheduled so early. Her stomach fluttered. It was easy to be facetious and irreverent to a piece of paper.

The inner door opened, and a tall redheaded girl came out. Behind her was a man in a white cotton pullover with NEW YORK LIBRARY stenciled on it in green. That was Michalski, the Committee secretary. Everybody in the waiting room came to attention. He said, "Carlos

Sahedi?" and a boy with pimples left the couch and went in. Michalski shut the door.

The redheaded girl let out her breath in a loud shoosh. "Well, I'm glad that's over."

"What did they ask you?" Half the people waiting began to call questions. Paula crossed her arms over her breasts. Someone brought the redheaded girl a paper slip of water.

The girl drank. "Don't bother studying, it's not like that, it's why-do-you-bite-your-fingernails?"

Paula bit her fingernails. She closed her hands into fists.

"Who's on the panel?"

"Sybil Jefferson. Richard Bunker. Three or four others. I didn't recognize them all. Where did this water come from?"

The people around the water cooler moved away to let her reach the spigot. Paula sighed. She stared across the room at the split-sphere projection of the Earth on the far wall.

After a long while, Carlos Sahedi came out, Michalski behind him. "Paula Mendoza."

She went after him into the corridor. The cooler air brushed her sweating face and neck. Michalski said, "Are you thirsty? I can bring you some coffee."

"No, that's all right," she said. "Thanks." Her voice sounded scratchy. He nodded to a door on her right. Voices came through it.

"Go on in," Michalski said. He went down the corridor.

Paula stood still a moment, listening to the people inside the room argue. A woman's voice said, "Why hasn't anybody learned it?"

"Who could use it?" said a voice she thought she recognized. "They aren't exactly the likely people to have an anarchist revolution, are they?" Paula pushed the door in and entered the room.

Ranged behind a shiny table, the six members of the panel turned to face her. She shut the door and went straight up toward them, itching with nerves.

"I'm Paula Mendoza," she said.

The six faces stared blankly back at her. The fat woman in the middle was Sybil Jefferson, her cheeks powder-white. She flipped over a page in the loose-bound book before her.

"Your father was Akim Morgan, the behaviorist, wasn't he?"

"Yes," Paula said, startled.

"I met him once. He was very didactic."

"He was strong-minded," Paula said, angry. Her father was dead. "He wasn't didactic."

The slight dark man on Jefferson's right leaned forward over the table. "Why do you want to work for the Committee?"

That was Richard Bunker, and it was his voice she had recognized. "I'm not sure I do," she said.

"Sorry. I'll rephrase it. Why did you apply?"

She made herself stare straight at him. "Because the Committee has forgotten its purpose. It was formed for the sake of revolution. Now it's just a vestigial government. I wanted a chance to tell you you've failed."

The six faces did not change. Nobody seemed outraged. Bunker leaned back. He was as dark as Tony, slight and short. His hands on the table were thin-boned like a woman's. He said, "The general idea is that the Committee protects the condition of anarchy, and within the anarchy people have the freedom of their own lives. What do you think we should do—smuggle revolutionary propaganda to Mars and Venus? Form cadres? Blow up Crosby's Planet?"

"No. I—"

At the other end of the table a man called, "Under what circumstances would you advocate the use of force?"

"Be brief," someone else muttered. "Twenty-five hundred words or less."

"Force is inefficient," Paula said. A trickle of sweat ran down her side. She wished she had accepted Michalski's offer of coffee. "I'll reserve the remaining 2497 words."

"You didn't answer the question," Sybil Jefferson said. She smiled at Paula. Her eyes were china-blue.

"It's meaningless. If you'd rationalize force in one circumstance, you rationalize it all the time."

Bunker said, "I still want to know how you'd promote the revolution."

"Disband the Committee," she said. "Any time there's trouble, now, people just depend on you to negotiate it out. If you disbanded, people would have to find their own solutions."

Michalski came in with a tray. She smelled coffee. He transferred the pot to the table in front of Bunker and a plate of sugar-nuts to the table in front of Jefferson, put two stacks of cups between them, and started out. Paula said, "Michalski, could I have some too, please?"

"There's an extra cup."

The six Committee members were clustered around the coffee pot. Jefferson bit into a sugar-nut. When she talked she sprayed white frosting across the table. "The anarchy has to have some means to defend itself. The rest of the system isn't as advanced as you are."

"Nobody can take anybody else's freedom away," Paula said. The other people were going back to their chairs. She poured coffee into the remaining cup. "Not unless you give it up."

The broad breast of Jefferson's red tunic was snowy with

frosting. "I suppose you know about that. You were in prison once, weren't you?"

"On Mars," Paula said. "For six months."

"What for?"

"For trying to take something out of Barsoom illegally." Barsoom was the capital of Mars.

"A camera," Jefferson said. "Did you forget about the export duty?"

"No. I didn't think the Martian government had any right to charge me for taking my own camera with me." She drank her coffee. They were watching her as if she were performing. She supposed she was. Bunker pushed his cup away across the table. He had a reputation for double-dealing; "Mitchell Wylie," Michalski had called him once, behind his back, the folk name for Machiavelli.

Someone else said, "I thought you had connections on Mars, Mendoza?"

She put the cup down on the table. They did know everything about her. "I worked for Cam Savenia, when she ran for election to the Martian Senate, but when I was arrested, she fired me."

"Cam Savenia." Bunker's head snapped up, wide-eyed. "Dr. Savenia? You worked in a Martian election?"

"I wanted to see what it was like."

"That's suspect."

"It wasn't my Planet."

"Well, well, well."

"What was it like?" asked the woman who had mentioned her connections.

"Hocus pocus," Paula said, and the other people laughed. She looked at Bunker. "Why is that a well-well-well?"

"Dr. Savenia and R.B. do not get along," Jefferson said. "You're twenty-nine, Mendoza? You've never had a full-time job before?"

"Just with Dr. Savenia, that time."

"But not on the Earth? How do you live?"

"I substitute with the university orchestra, I do a little pick-up work with the recording studios. That's all the money I need."

"What do you play?"

"Flute."

"Oh, really?" The old man at the end of the table tilted himself forward over his fisted hands. "Do you like Alfide? Why didn't you make a career out of that?"

"I'm not good enough. Alfide is my favorite composer. And Ibanov. And me."

"What do you know about the Styths?" Jefferson said.

She drank the rest of her coffee. Obviously they had even

discovered that. "They're mutants. They live in artificial cities in the Gas Planets—Uranus and Saturn."

"We all know that much." The old woman pulled a sugar-nut apart with her hands. The edge of the table indented her fat stomach. "Don't you know anything else?"

"Well," she said, "I speak Styth."

They all moved slightly, inclining toward her, their eyes intent. Bunker said smoothly, "So we're told. You learned it in prison?"

"Yes. There were three Styths locked up in the men's unit. The warden needed somebody to teach them the Common Speech."

Jefferson ate the sugar-nut. "But instead you learned Styth. Why?"

"I couldn't very well pass up the chance. Styth is the only other language still being spoken." She stopped; that seemed enough, but they all stared at her as if they expected more. She said, "The warden was driving me crazy."

"You don't really expect us to hire you, do you?" Jefferson said.

"I'm not sure I want the job."

"Well," Bunker said, "we are offering you a job. The Interplanetary Council wants us to negotiate a truce between the Middle Planets and the Styth Empire. Unfortunately, none of us speaks any Styth."

"Oh," Paula said. "Well, get some tapes. It's not hard. Lots of little rules and things. Genders."

Jefferson was eating the last of the sugar-nuts. Paula saw why she was so fat. "Take the job, Mendoza. We don't have time to scour the system looking for an anarchist who speaks Styth."

"All right," she said. Meanwhile she would find something else.

Tony said, "You're selling your soul."

"I don't have a soul. And if I did, they're paying me a fortune for it. Eight hundred dollars a month." That was more than he made.

"You are an inveterate materialist." He picked up a black pebble. On the grid between them, broken lines of black and white stones faced each other, shaping the space of the game. Tony's hand hovered over the board. "You can always come here and live with me." He put the black pebble down, watching her face.

"It's educational."

"Working for the Committee? Being a cop?"

Most people played Go in silence. Tony had developed the tactic of distracting conversation to the point where he could not play without talking. On the grid between them, she could close two positions with a single crucial play. Tony had to keep forcing her to play elsewhere, which he was doing. She sat back, taking a deep breath. Tony put his head forward.

"Look at what the Committee does. They leech off the anarchy. It's in their best interests that people fail. Are you going to play or not?"

She played. "Aha," he said, and with a click put a stone down on the grid, rescuing his men. "You just don't have the stamina. I'm way ahead of you, you know."

"Is wanting to win so much that you pant, a sign of materialism?"

His apartment was on the ground floor of an old stone building near the edge of the wood. The five rooms were stacked with books and manuscripts: he taught Style. They made dinner in his kitchen, arguing about the Committee, and went to bed, where he also attempted to teach.

A crash woke her up. She sat straight, the hair on her neck standing on end, and nearly fell out of the bed. They were sleeping on the porch of his apartment, and the bed sloped. Tony scrambled across her, reaching for his trousers.

They went down the hall to the bedroom, where there was a convenient window. She heard no more loud noises, but voices rose in the stairwell of the building, and someone shouted outside. Wrapped in a robe of Tony's, she climbed after him out the bedroom window to the ground.

Between his building and the wood a meadow stretched flat and open in the domelight. Several people were running across it toward the trees. By the time she and Tony reached the wood, a small crowd had gathered. The night bus was parked on the flat ground at the edge of the trees and its few passengers were standing around outside it. A little two-seated car had crashed into the top of a tree and turned over. It rested like a strange hat in the branches. Paula went forward to see and Tony caught her arm.

"It might fall."

The people around her milled about. One man was walking up and down saying, "I don't even have insurance." She looked up at the car. It was wrecked. A big branch had run through the side window and come out the top, and the front end was pushed in.

"Was anybody hurt?"

"That one doesn't look too good to me. He was the passenger."

She looked where these people were looking. A man sat under a tree, his head in his arms, a coat thrown over him, or a blanket. Paula wondered if she could do anything to help. Her feet were cold and she picked them one at a time off the ground.

"Watch out!"

Two men were pulling the air car down by ropes. The bigger man wore a jacket with *NIGHT BUS SERVICE* on the back in white script.

The wreck slithered down out of the tree, breaking branches and scattering leaves onto the people below. Paula jumped back away from it. The car hit the ground with a crunch. Tony appeared beside her.

"The car ran into the bus's air buffer," he said. "The driver must have been drunk or something."

The car's driver was bent over the wreckage, moaning that he had no insurance. Tony and a woman bystander got into an argument about how fast the car had been going. Paula looked around for the car's passenger. He was still sitting under the tree. Someone was offering him a drink from a half-liter bottle of whiskey. He ignored it, and when the other person pushed it at him, he raised his head and shouted, "Go away!"

The busman tramped around the car, coiling a rope. "Somebody ought to come down tomorrow and prune the tree." He walked up face to face with the car driver. "Is he hurt?" He gestured toward the passenger.

"I don't know." The driver had half a papercase in his hand. He looked at it and threw it back into the wreck.

"What are you going to do?" the busman asked. "I have to leave, I have my run to finish."

Tony called, "Take him to the hospital. Take him in the bus."

The driver made a little gesture with one hand, his gaze on his passenger. "I don't have any insurance."

"I can run you by the Asclepius," the busman said. He and the driver went to the hurt man under the tree and helped him to his feet.

"Hey—that's my coat." A tall woman trotted out of the crowd and retrieved the coat wrapped around the hurt man. He walked stiffly between the other two men toward the bus. The reflector strips on the sleeves of the busman's jacket gleamed red and white. None of the other people moved to get back on the bus. The inside lights came on, shining across the grass. Through the big windows, Paula could see the lines of empty benches, the driver of the wrecked car and his passenger slumped together on the last seat. The horn tooted sharply three times. No one in the crowd paid any attention. The bus's engines hummed and the long machine rose into the air and sailed away.

On Paula's left, the tall woman folded her coat over her arm. With the rest of the crowd she moved down toward the wreck. A man climbed over the smashed front end.

"Here's a radio—I'll share it with anybody who helps me get it out."

Paula and Tony went back across the grass toward his place. She turned to look back. There was a whoop of triumph from the crowd clustered around the car. Two men dragged a seat out of the ruin.

"Vultures," Tony said.

Paula hurried on her cold feet toward the light of his hall. "What's wrong with salvage?"

"That's a euphemism. The word is theft."

"If nobody took anything, the dome would be littered with junk." She pushed the window in and slung one leg across the sill. By morning every relic of the car would be gone, even the plastic, which brought 1.5 cents a pound at the recycling plant. She and Tony went onto the porch.

Her first meeting in the matter of the Styth Empire was in the same room where she had had her oral examination. When she let herself in, Jefferson sat at the table rummaging through a handbag like a satchel. "Mendoza," she said. "Richard is late, as you can see. How do you like your office?"

"It's terrible. The window looks right out on the gulley bank." She pulled out a chair and sat across the table from the fat old woman. "I have a terrific view of roots and yellow clay." That was not entirely true, since a spindling tree grew between the window and the bank. So far it had no leaves. She hoped it was dead. Jefferson was peeling the wrap off a roll of mint candy.

"What did you do for Dr. Savenia?"

"Speechwriting. She had two kinds of speeches, personal attacks and issues. I wrote the attacks."

Jefferson chortled. Her face was papery white and looked soft, like dough. "Were you good? And here comes Richard."

A flat papercase under one arm, Richard Bunker walked in the open door and shut it behind him. He put the case on the table. "Hello, Mendoza. Sybil." He had a windbreaker over his shoulder and he hung it on the back of the chair beside Paula. He clicked up the lid of the papercase.

"Where have you been?" Jefferson said. "You know, I do have other things to do now and then besides wait for you."

"I've been in the copying room trying to get the film transcriber to work." He dropped a thick file onto the table in front of Paula. It was more than an inch thick, held together with plastic clips. She picked it up while Bunker and Jefferson traded jibes on the state of the machines and people of the Committee.

"You can read that later," Jefferson said to her. "Dick, give her a brief, so we can get on with it."

He sat down in the chair beside Paula's, and she shut the file. Bunker said, "In the past thirty-six months there have been twenty-one reported shooting incidents between ships of the Styth Empire and ships from either the Council Fleet or the Martian Army. All these shootings have been below the asteroid Vesta. Eight have been below

Mars. The Council wants us—" his voice rose to a singsong, "to negotiate a truce and any other permanent or semi-permanent arrangements necessary to maintain the peace." He was slumped down in the chair, his head against the back. "The Council never asks us to do anything possible."

"Shooting incidents," Paula said. She had heard nothing about any shootings. "Is it serious?"

They both laughed, humorless, and she heard how stupid she had sounded. Jefferson put a candy into her mouth. "More serious is that we can't seem to reach the Styths."

"They keep to themselves," Paula said. Most of the mutant race lived in Uranus, billions of miles away.

"Not any more," Bunker said. "Do you have any idea why they might be coming here now?"

She shook her head. The Styths had always seemed in a different Universe from the Middle Planets, living in their floating cities far from the Sun. Bunker said, "Do you know what an Akellar is?"

"The chief officer of a Styth city. They have a central council called the rAkellaron. That's just the plural of Akellar."

"Yes. We've been trying to make contact with the Prima Akellar, a man named Machou."

"Machou," she said. "The Vribulo Akellar."

"You've heard of him."

"One of my teachers was from Vribulo. Machou's city. If it's the same Machou." She frowned, trying to remember everything the three Styth prisoners had said. "Has anybody been killed?"

Jefferson fingered the roll of candy. "Yes, about twenty Martians that they're admitting. We don't know about Styths. We don't even know if all this action constitutes a systematic policy by the Styths or just random piracy. You said one of your Styths was from Vribulo. What about the others?"

"They were both from Saturn-Keda. The chief city of Saturn." Saturn-Keda was usually the closest Styth city to the Middle Planets. She reached for the thick file and thumbed down the pages. "What's in this? What do you know about them?"

"Nothing immediately useful," Bunker said. "Nothing at all."

"The Saturn Akellar was the Prima Akellar before Machou," Paula said. "Apparently a very . . . a great man. He built six or seven new cities and reformed the fleet. Cleaned up the laws. Outlawed infant marriage, that kind of thing. Kind of a liberal. For a Styth."

"Infant marriage," Bunker said, in a titillated voice.

"Don't you know who the rAkellaron are?"

Jefferson shrugged. "A few names. Did you keep notes from your prison meetings?"

"The warden took all my notebooks. Maybe there are some Styths still in the joint."

Jefferson fed herself another candy. Her cheeks sucked in around it. "I checked when we found out about your episode. The Martians very efficiently executed them all. What was the name of this paragon?"

"The Saturn Akellar? Melleno. I don't know if he's still in the rAkellaron."

"Can we reach him?" Bunker said.

"I'll try," Paula said.

Her new office was a bare white box with a desk and chair, another chair, and a file. The window let in no direct sunlight because of the high wall of the gulch just outside. She had already decided not to put anything on the walls since she was keeping this job only until she found other work. She sat down beside the desk and opened the file on the Styths, but before she had read more than a paragraph, two men came into the office.

"We have a case for you," the shorter of the two said.

Paula shut the file. She looked from one man to the other. "Yes, what?" Immediately she disliked them: they were smiling. She opened the deep drawer in her desk and stuffed the file in on top of a pile of multicolored forms.

The shorter man sat down. He wore a brown sweater with the initial R in red on the right breast. "We live in a building in the south dome that's owned by a Mister Roches, and we want something done about it."

"We've been writing him letters of complaint for a year," the other man said. "Without even the grace of a reply."

The man in the chair crossed one leg over the other. Carefully he straightened his trousers. "We aren't the only ones who are complaining. The place is infested with mice, it smells of mildew, the verticals are usually broken, none of our flats has been painted or refloored in more than two years, and the old fellow is a dreadful gossip. The piping is absolutely antique, you can't get an air filter installed—"

She put her elbows on the desk. "What do you want me to do?"

Their faces slid down out of their smiles. Intense, she leaned forward, looking from one to the other. "Why the hell do you come in here with something like this? You're supposed to be anarchists. You're supposed to take care of yourselves. If you don't like it, move. If nobody likes it, get everybody to move, open the gas cocks and throw in a match. Get away from me."

The shorter man popped up out of his chair. "You're supposed to be here to help people."

"If you need help for something like that, go someplace where there's a government. Like Mars." She yanked the drawer open and put the Styth file on the desk in front of her.

"No wonder everybody hates the Committee." The taller man rushed to the desk. She ignored him, pretending to read. He and his friend strode out of the office.

She leaned back in her chair, pleased. Outside the window the sunlight was at last reaching the ground, where a green sprinkling of grass grew near the tree. In places the claybank was yellow as lemons, in places orange. She sat thinking of the Styths in the Martian prison. The man from Vribulo had been waiting to be gassed for murder. Lonely and angry and homesick and frightened, he had shouted at her and tried to attack her and talked, when she had finally begun to understand him, talked in a desperate flood. That had been five years ago. She had not thought of him in a long while. She had liked him and his death had hurt; she had made herself go to witness it. She turned over the first page of the file.

Overwood's Import Shop was in the Old Town of Los Angeles, between an optometrist's and an astrologer's. When Paula went in, a bell rang in the back of the store. It was so dark she ran into an air fern hanging from the ceiling in a bucket. The air smelled of marijuana. At the back of the shop a little man in an apron leaned on a counter.

"Help you?"

"Are you Thomas Overwood?"

"That's right, honey. Call me Tom."

She went up to the counter. "I understand you deal in crystal."

His round face settled. "Call me Mr. Overwood."

"I'm from the Committee."

"Oh." He reached his hand out to her, smiling again. "Whyn't you say so? Sure, I traffic in crystal. But it'll cost you."

"Where does it come from?"

"Uranus. Farmed in the White Side." Overwood ducked down behind the counter and brought up a stack of black and white holographs. "One thousand dollars the ounce."

She lifted off the top photograph. Against the black background the crystal polyhedron looked like a jewel. Overwood tapped the photograph.

"That's Relleno. There are five grades, all I deal in are the premier grades, Relleno and Ebelos. Sixteen O-Z's of Ebelos would power the whole California dome for six months."

Paula leafed through the photographs. "I don't believe you."

Overwood muttered something.

"How do you get it?" she said.

"Oh, now—"

She put the holographs down. "We have a message for someone in the Styth Empire. Can you arrange to deliver it?"

His wide eyebrows rose. "I see. That will cost you, too."

"Can you guarantee?"

"Who do you want to reach?"

"Melleno. The Saturn Akellar."

Overwood leaned his forearm on the counter. "Maybe."

"For a maybe, you'd better not ask much."

He gathered up the photographs and put them away under the counter. Even here on the Earth, where there were no laws and no police, he was cautious. She wondered who his enemies were. Maybe other smugglers. He said, "My connection can get into Saturn-Keda."

The doorbell jangled. She turned to watch a woman with a white dog cross the dark shop. Overwood went from behind the counter.

"Help you?"

"I'm looking at your splendid glassware."

Paula strolled around the display cases along the wall. They showed rows of incense jars, plates, figures of animals. Amulets and books on Zen. She admired an old ivory and ebony chess set. On the wall above it was a corkboard, with bits of paper pinned to it.

Commune share 25/mo. Drugs check, one kid check.

Overwood sprayed foam around a dish of Venusian glass. While the casing dried, he took the woman's money and gave her change. She tucked her white dog under one arm and the foam case under the other. The bell rang her out.

"Cost you fifteen hundred dollars to send a message to Saturn-Keda," Overwood said. "In advance."

Paula glanced at him over her shoulder. "For a maybe?"

"For certain. He'll deliver."

"One thousand. When we know it's delivered."

"No chance. My connection is a busy man."

"I don't doubt it. Where does he go? Does he go to Uranus?"

"Vribulo. Matuko. Flying around in a Gas Planet isn't something I'd do, for instance. These spacemen are crazy."

Overwood took a tray out of the counter. "Direct from Saturn." With a little flourish he turned back the lid. "Genuine reproductions."

There were five big medals inside the box. Paula lifted one out by the chain. "What are they?"

"When a Styth warrior goes into military orders, you see, he wears a medal with his sign, here." He pointed at the design cut into the medal's face. "That's the Fish. They're very superstitious people."

She reached for another. "What's this one mean?"

"Unh—"

"Twelve hundred. Seven in advance, five when we know it's delivered."

"Now, my connection is a busy man."

"So are we."

He pursed his lips. "For the Committee." He offered his wide hand, and Paula shook it.

The SoCal dome reached out to the deep water. The surf was too dirty to swim in. She walked along the beach, watching the waves break sluggishly over, brown with dirt. Garbage encrusted the sand. The filth lowered her mood, or maybe she had come here because her mood was already low and needed celebration.

The poet Fuldah had thought that all societies contained a finite number of persona, and the people left over from this cast could only wander around outside making trouble. She felt herself being forced into a role. Her life was closing in on her. She hated the Committee job, even the Styth case bored her, but it paid well and she kept putting off quitting because she liked the money. Tony would make her pregnant which would determine the next eighteen or twenty years while she raised her child. She felt as if her life were over.

The beach was studded with black rocks. Ahead, the brown cliffs rose, cut with gulleys. The edge of the water was strewn with purple and white jellyfish. A sea carrot, alive with flies, lay rotting along the high-tide line. She swerved away from its stink toward the cliffs, took her clothes off, and sat on a warm rock.

In spite of her restlessness she could not think of anything to do. *Free as a bird,* her father would have said. Free to do what every other bird did. She picked at the white scale on the rock. Out past the surf, the dome wall shone in the sunlight. It was not solid: a gas dome, held by a magnetic field, because of the earthquakes. Two boys came down the beach looking for rocks. She waved; they waved. After a while she put her clothes on and went back to the rooming house to eat.

Bunker was coming in on the underground train; at ten in the evening she went to meet him. He came across the platform toward her, putting on his sweater. "I thought it never got cold here." Paula turned to walk beside him. They climbed the stairs to the ground level. She handed him an envelope.

"That's the message to Melleno."

They went out of the tube station and the cold wind struck her in the face. The paper flapped in Bunker's hands. He turned to shelter it. Although the night had fallen long since, the domelight was bright enough to read by. Paula looked up at the hills. The wind was roaring out of the canyon behind them. The SoCal dome was huge; they were proud of their winds.

Bunker nodded. "I hope he can read it." He gave her back the paper and they walked along the flat desert, their backs to the wind. The tall palm trees that marked the path milled their broad leaves like arms. "Do you suppose anybody there speaks the Common Speech?"

Paula shrugged. "Overwood does business with them. Overwood thinks crystal is some kind of super-battery."

"I take it from your tone of voice that that shows his ignorance."

"He's more like a transformer than a battery."

The path took them in toward the flank of the steep hills, where the houses clustered like a colony of barnacles above the bare dusty desert floor. A bike was wheeling toward her and she moved out of the way. They went up a steep path into the Old Town. The wind had blown weeds and leaves up against Overwood's door. It was locked and the shop was dark. Paula stood looking in the window. Bunker turned.

"He must live around here somewhere."

"I called him," Paula said. "He said if he wasn't at the shop, he'd be in the bar." She pointed down the street. Two men were just going in a bright doorway. "I'll bet that's it."

As they went through the doorway a bell clanged. There were three tiltball machines against the far wall, half-hidden behind a crowd of players. The room smelled of beer. Overwood was sitting in a booth in the back, behind a potted jacaranda tree, his hands laced over his little round stomach. Paula went up to him.

"Hello, there," he said. "Have a seat. I'll sit you a drink."

Bunker shook his hand. "My name's Richard Butler."

"Whatever you say. Thomas Overwood here."

Another chorus of bells rang out behind her. She slid between the jacaranda and the wall into the booth across from Overwood and held out the envelope to him. "For the Saturn Akellar."

"Seven hundred dollars," Overwood said.

Bunker pulled a chair around to the end of the table between them. He took a wallet out of his hip pocket and sat down. A waiter brought them a pitcher of beer and glasses. Bunker counted out money into a stack before him: fourteen fifty-dollar bills. The fifteenth he gave to her. "Sign that."

It was an expense chit. She signed it.

"How long will this take?" Bunker said.

"Maybe four months." Overwood put the money in one pocket and the message in another. "Maybe less. That's a long way away, that." The waiter poured the bright beer. "What's the Committee's interest in Styth?"

Paula reached for a glass. "Who supplies you with crystal?"

Overwood smiled at her. "Now, now."

Bunker pushed the money over to him. "We want information. The Committee's favorite food. We need good sources of information, first-generation, on the politics of the rAkellaron."

"That's funny." Overwood laughed; his bushy eyebrows went up and down. The laughter rumbled on steadily, like a motor. "That's very funny. I've been told they'll buy information about the Earth."

Paula put her elbows on the table. "I'll send you a price list."

"What have you told them?" Bunker asked.

"All they're interested in is military stuff."

"Our interests are a little broader."

"I can't help you." Overwood nodded at her. "I don't know anything about Styths. Ask her, she stepped on me twice today, trying to fake it. Venusian glass, maybe, or chess, or smuggling, but Styths—" He spread his hands.

"Do you buy the crystal directly from them?" Bunker said.

Overwood shrugged elaborately, smiling, his eyebrows arched. "I can't talk about that."

"We'll pay."

"Sorry."

Paula watched Bunker's face. There were deep creases marking the corners of his mouth, but otherwise he looked bored. She lifted her glass. The tiltballs bells rang like a carousel. Lights flashed.

"If I hear anything," Overwood said, "I'll let you know."

"Call me." Paula wrote down her name and extension number for him. With Bunker she left the bar.

They went to the end of the street, where the ground pitched off sheer to the desert below, and stood in the shadows of the trees. From this height she could see the even furrows of the cropfields on the desert below. Two circles of lights burned on the dark flat land. Bunker was looking back down the street toward Overwood's shop.

"Come on." He went at a swinging walk across the street. Paula followed.

"Where are you going?"

He led her down the alley between Overwood's shop and the astrologer's. When she came up beside him he was trying to open the back window.

"Do you have a knife?"

"No. I'll go keep Overwood busy." She went down the alley to the street again.

Even from here she heard the jangle of the tiltball bells in the bar.

Two women walked unsteadily out of the bar and went off down the hill, their arms around each other. Paula strolled back to the doorway of the bar. The domelight drove her shadow to a puddle around her feet.

Overwood was standing up beside his booth, paying the waiter. She crossed the crowded room toward him. "Overwood."

He looked up, his hands full of money. She went around beside him. "I want to talk to you."

"Oh? Where's the other fellow?"

"That's what I want to talk to you about. Let me buy you a beer."

Overwood let her buy him a beer, two beers, and a third. She impressed him with the necessity of dealing with her and not Bunker, even though Bunker had the money, asked him if anybody in Saturn-Keda could read the Common Speech, and finally talked him into going out with her to show her the fastest way down the hillside. He took her to the end of the street, right past his shop, and pointed out three different trails, white as thread down the slope, among the aloes and manzanita.

"You'd better be careful. If you fall and hurt yourself, you could lie there all night." He beamed at her. "To say nothing of the coyotes."

"I like dogs." Over his shoulder she saw Bunker coming down the alley by his shop.

He let out a rumbling laugh. "You wouldn't like a coyote."

She was looking out across the vast dome. The bracelets of lights on the desert floor held her gaze. "What are they doing down there?" She pointed. Each of the circles seemed to be made of a dozen little fires.

"Trance circles," he said. "They sit around and chant and watch the fires and throw themselves into trances. Kids, bums, people like that."

"Why don't they just take drugs?"

"That's too easy."

"Well," she said, "maybe I'll try it. Thanks." She started down the nearest of the paths he had shown her.

The hill was steep. She was inching across a narrows, her clothes snagged on the brush, when Bunker caught up with her.

"What did you find?"

"Nothing," he said.

She glanced at him over her shoulder. He was watching his feet on the thin trail. The hillside was studded with spiky plants. Ahead the trail widened, tame.

"Nothing at all? I don't believe you."

"He's smart. Nothing's written down."

"I don't believe you."

"Frankly, junior, I don't give a damn."

"Why do you call me that?"

Beside her, his hands in his pockets, he smiled at her. "You don't like it, do you?"

"No."

"Junior," he said, "you have a lot to learn." He went off ahead of her down the trail. Burning, she stood still and let him walk up a good lead before she started off again.

Paula took the midnight train to New York. Walking up the aisle of the car, she saw Bunker sitting next to the window on a forward bench. After a moment she put her bag on the rack over his head and sat down opposite him. He had a book plug in his ear; he ignored her. She stretched her legs out before her. The train was almost empty. The lights flashed on and off, and the bench under her jerked forward. She braced herself. The train bounded forward, stopped cold, and started up again. They rolled off into the dark.

The windowless walls of the car were covered with graffiti. Gaining speed, the train swayed from side to side. She rocked with it, sleepy. Los Angeles was two and a half hours from New York; it would be nearly dawn when she reached her home. On the bench across from her, Bunker sat with the tape purring in his ear. He was spare and lean, even his kinky hair close to his head. He could have been forty, or fifty, or her age. She knew he was older than she was.

"The Styths don't know much about us, either," she said.

"Not if they want to know about our military."

The train sailed wide around a curve. She flung her arm across the back of the seat. He was staring at the wall. Obviously he would say no more than he had to. She aimed her eyes at the figure-covered wall.

Her flute was gone. She kept it under her bed. Nothing else in her disordered room had been touched, so she knew as if he had signed his name who had taken it. She went next door to An Chu's room.

"Shaky John has crooked my flute again."

An Chu looked up. "Are you sure it was him?"

"I will be." She tipped up the lid to the other woman's sewing box. An Chu kept her sequins and sparkles in little plastine bags. Paula shook one empty.

"You shouldn't accuse people when you aren't sure."

"Hunh." She took the little bag and went across the common room to the kitchen.

Three people stood at the sink, singing an obscene round and washing dishes. Water puddled the floor. She opened the cupboard over the stove and filled up the plastine bag with baking soda. The boisterous singing followed her out again. She went down the other hall to the third door on the left and knocked.

"Go away."

She tried the latch. The door was locked. John's plaintive voice called, "Go away." She felt in her pockets, found her pay envelope, slid the edge through the seam in the door and lifted the hook on the inside.

"Hey!"

She went into a dark, stinking room. The floor was caked with rotting food. The mattress against the far wall smelled of piss and mildew. John sat huddled on it, his arms crooked up to his chest.

"Why you coming in here?"

"Why you stealing my flute? Where is it?"

He was trembling. He curled up on the mattress. "Let me alone."

Paula crouched before him. At her feet was an apple core fuzzy with mold. She kicked it away. She took the plastine bag out of her jacket pocket and waved it at him. He straightened slowly out of his curl. His face was broken out and his nose dripped. He scratched around in his crotch, his eyes on the bag.

"Where is it?" she said.

"Don't have it. You can look. Let me—" He reached for the bag. She drew back, holding it in the air above her head.

"Where is it?"

"Don't have it. Pl-please, Paula. I'm sick. Look how sick I am." He held his shaking hands out. "You can't be mad at me, Paula."

"Where's my flute?"

"Sold it. I sold it. Don't have it any more."

She clenched her teeth. "Who bought it?"

"I'm sick." His fingers dug into his armpits, his hair. His clothes stuck to him. "I'm real sick."

"John! Who bought my flute?"

"B-Barrian. Barrian."

"How much?"

"Please—"

She shook her head. He was playing sick, mostly; if he whined enough, people gave him money to score just to be rid of him. There were several running bets in the commune on how long it would take him to die. She said, "John, how much?"

"Forty dollars."

She muttered, "Forty dollars." Of course he had none left. She threw the plastine bag down on the stinking mattress. He lunged for it.

"John, if you do this to me once more, I'll make your life miserable. Even more miserable. You hear me?"

He was scrambling around, looking for his works. "Sure, Paula.

You're a good girl." With his shaking hands he lit a candle to cook the soda he thought was morphion. She went out.

Barrian's was a music store in the underground mall south of the campus. She stood looking at a violin in a glass case while the shopman talked to another customer. The violin's body was burnished to a chestnut glow. A small sign identified it by a Latin name and the date A.D. 1778. It was nearly four thousand years old. She went up to the counter.

"A loadie came in here over the weekend and sold you an ebony flute."

The shopman had white hairs growing out of his ears and nose. "That's right," he said. "And a beauty it is, too."

"It's mine."

"Not any more." He tapped the glass counter. She looked down. On the velvet-covered shelf, her flute lay in its open box. A small sign on it gave it a Latin name, an age of fifty years, and a price of six hundred dollars.

She said, "If you look under the lip with a magnifying glass, you'll find my name. Paula Mendoza."

"We bought it in good faith."

"For forty dollars."

The shopman smiled at her. "Of course, if you pay our price—"

"I'll give you back the forty dollars."

"Sorry."

She drew in a deep breath. Paying out forty dollars would reduce her to eating rice for the next week, until she was paid again. Six hundred was impossible. She tapped her fingers on the counter.

"I want my flute."

"I can see that. The price is six hundred dollars."

"I work for the Committee."

"I'm very happy for you."

"Give it back, or I'll go through our files and find something on you."

"You'll be looking a long time, we're honest."

She went off around the shop. On the wall, in plastic clips, hung swatches of paper music. She could try to steal the flute, but the shop, being underground, was tight against thieves, and the glass case was probably locked. She could borrow the money. Save it over weeks. Maybe Tony would loan it to her. A fat boy with frizzy blond hair down to his waist came into the shop, a guitar over his shoulder.

"Wait." She intercepted him. "Please let me talk to you a minute."

The boy swung the ax down between them. "Sure."

"Please don't buy anything here. A junkie stole my flute and sold it to them for a ridiculous low price and they won't sell it back to me."

The boy's blue eyes looked past her. The shoulder of his shirt was ripped. He swayed the guitar gently against his knees. Finally, he said, "Check," and left.

The shopman came around the counter at top speed. "You can't do that."

She showed him her teeth. "Watch me."

"Get out."

She went out the door, into the dark subway walk, and loitered under the red sign marking the shop. A man in a plaid shirt started in; she talked to him, but he went in anyway. For half an hour she walked up and down before the door, until the shop closed.

The next day she called Michalski at the office and told him where she would be, and she sat down in front of Barrian's and told everybody who would listen that the shop was stealing her flute in collusion with a junkie. Most people ignored her. Some argued. A few turned away. Barrian's people tried to chase her off. An Chu brought her lunch. The day following, when she called the Committee, Michalski said she had been given a week's unpaid leave. She took a chair to Barrian's. A man from the hourlies came and interviewed her. Every half hour the shopman from Barrian's threw buckets of water on her. She talked to everybody who went into the store. Two out of three did business there anyway.

Tony was unsympathetic. "You shouldn't own something you can't afford to lose. You're a hostage to your possessions. Property is theft."

Shaky John was still angry with her for burning him, but she gave him five dollars, and he sat in front of Barrian's for a day and fired himself up, hour after hour, with morphion, aspirin, barbiturate, horse-downer, distilled water, plastic blood, and milk. Without even talking he turned more people away from Barrian's in one hour than she had in four days. That evening, the shop sold her back her flute for fifty dollars.

The little tree outside her window put forth pink flowers. Michalski told her it was a dogwood. She spent hours in her office watching the progress of its bloom.

She had dinner with Tony and they went to a reading of Aeschylus at the university. Tony insisted on leaving at the intermission because the translation was so bad. They sat in a booth in the campus bar and he explained to her that the heart of Greek tragedy was ritual appeasement and no anarchist could ever fathom that because ritual was meaningless to anarchists.

"How can you say that?" she said. "You can understand something without committing yourself to it, can't you?"

"Only in the head, Paula. Not in the gut." He folded his napkin into quarters. He had already lined up the sauceboats, both their glasses, and the salt and pepper dishes and match-lighter. "You miss the whole absoluteness of the thing. The whole sense that there is nothing else. The self-punishing aspect of nonconformity."

Paula set her chin in her hand. She wondered if Tony ever enjoyed anything. It occurred to her that she had heard all this before from him, that he had already told her everything he would ever say to her. She got up and went through the dark barroom toward the door.

She cut across the park toward the round house of the Biochemistry Building. When he shouted at her, behind her, she stretched her stride. She thrust her hands deep into her jacket pockets. The domelight silvered the grass. Tony galloped up beside her.

"I'm sorry." His arm slid around her waist. "Maybe you're pregnant and that's why you're so sensitive lately."

"I'm not pregnant."

They walked down a slope through the birch trees. A deer bolted away from them. She heard low voices in the dark bushes ahead of them and swerved off to avoid the people there.

"Tony," she said. "Good-bye."

"What?"

He stopped, and she turned to face him; she could not see him in the dark, but she knew how he looked, she knew him far too well. She said, "Good-bye, Tony," and went away through the trees.

The open room of her commune was dark. She stepped across a man asleep on the floor to reach the videone and took a slip of paper out of her box. She stuffed it into her pocket and went down the hall to An Chu's room. The girl was a long still shape under her bedclothes.

Paula sank down on the narrow bed in the darkness. "Wake up." She shook her by the shoulder. "I just broke with Tony."

An Chu murmured, still half-asleep, wrapped in blankets, warm against Paula's hip. In the quiet Paula could hear water dripping in the bath across the hall. Tony would take her back, if she asked him. But she did not want him. She would end up like her mother and father, alone all her life.

"Paula?"

"I'll talk to you in the morning." She went next door, to her room, turned on the light, and remembered the message.

"Paula Mendoza," it read. "Meeting room tomorrow at 10:30. Melleno has answered. RB."

When she went into the Committee office, half a dozen people were packed around the videone in the corner. She stopped to see what they were looking at.

The screen was off; the newsband was on. "—Damage estimated in the millions. Thus far the reports list no dead and thirteen injured, with eighty-seven missing. Both attacking Styth ships escaped apparently without damage. Repeating the lead line: the Martian-ruled asteroid Vesta has sustained the first space-to-surface attack by Styth ships against the Middle Planets. This is a—"

She went down the corridor to the meeting room in the L. She was early. Only Michalski was there, sorting mail into stacks. Rubbing her sweating palms together, she went around the book-covered room.

"What's the message?"

"Bunker has it. He was on night duty when it came in." Michalski shook the papers before him into neat piles. "I don't know anything, I just work here."

"Have you heard any jabber about the raid on Vesta?" She took off her jacket and dropped it across a chair. "There must be two brands of Styths, ones who shoot and ones who talk." Or they were turning down the negotiation.

Bunker came into the room, his papercase in one hand. He swung it flat onto the table and unsnapped the clasps. "I don't follow all these large gestures." He took out a transparent page. Paula reached for it and he held it away from her.

"Don't be grabby, junior." He gave the page to Michalski. "Transcribe this."

Michalski left the room. Bunker sat down, his eyes on Paula. "I don't know what it says, except that it's relatively long. You heard about the attack on Vesta?"

"Yes. What does that mean?"

"Emphasis, I guess."

Talking behind her, Jefferson backed in the door. She wore a red suit that made her look massive. Michalski followed her in, his cheeks ruddy. He had a tape plug in one hand. He dropped it into the socket in the table and pressed a button.

A sexless computer voice said, "By Melleno, in Saturn-Keda. We have received your message. We know what the Committee for the Revolution is and what your request really means. Since the beginning the Sun-worlds have robbed us and lied to us. Now when the Empire is great, you beg for our friendship. Nothing you can say will change the course of justice. If you want to talk, you must show the good faith. You submit the names of your people and the places you can meet us, and we will choose your agent and the place and moment. Answer by this light band. Ended. Melleno."

Paula bounced in her chair. The tape shut off with a double click. Jefferson settled herself in her chair. "Congratulations," she said to Paula. She opened her purse and took out a hard-cooked egg and a paper twist. "I missed breakfast."

Bunker shook his head. "Curious."

"How many ships attacked Vesta?"

"Two. One lured the patrols off and the other got in and out in eighty-five seconds, shooting all the way."

Paula stood up, excited. "Then Melleno must not be connected with the raiders."

"Not necessarily," Bunker said. "At the moment, Vesta happens to be directly in line with Uranus and the Earth. It could be a warning."

Jefferson opened out the paper twist and rolled the egg in salt and pepper. "The message came from Saturn."

He slid down in his chair, his hands on his flat stomach. "Uranus is the brain of the Empire."

"He didn't say anything about the rAkellaron," Paula said. Michalski was still standing at the foot of the table. "Give me a copy of that." He bent over the recorder.

"He said '*we.*' "

"He also said 'Answer by *this* light band.' " She dropped back into her chair. "The rAkellaron meets in Vribulo."

Jefferson said, "I favor Mendoza's interpretation. Obviously Melleno dissents from Machou's authority." She ate part of the egg. "Didn't you say Melleno was once the Prima Akellar? What was that about the course of justice?"

Paula made circles with her fingertip on the table. The recorder paid out a long tongue of paper, and Michalski ripped it off, like taking an hourly out of the dispenser. She grabbed the page away from him. Another copy was rolling out of the table. She put the letter down flat in front of her.

"Hurrah," she said.

"What shall we answer?" Jefferson said. "The three of us as possible negotiators—"

"Start with a preamble on the purity of our motives," Bunker said. He reached across the table for the next copy.

"Where can we meet them? Mendoza, what do you think?"

"What about Titan? It's more like the Earth than a Gas Planet. And we could see more what they're like."

Bunker wrote on his copy of the letter. "That's probably their idea, to look at us. I don't think they'll want a look at Titan."

Michalski brought Jefferson a pad of paper, and the old woman busied herself in her purse. Looking for a stylus. *Nothing will change the course of justice.* Paula traced a line under the sentence. Maybe they were the raiders. She could not see how it all fitted, Machou's indifference, the raid on Vesta, Melleno's offer to talk. Except if Bunker was right, and they wanted to take a reconnaissance.

"Let's see where they want to go," she said. "Give them a choice of Mars or the Earth."

Jefferson was writing. Her pen jigged across the yellow paper. "Where on Mars?"

"What about the Nineveh Club?" Bunker said.

Paula laughed. Jefferson put her forearms on the table. "Isn't that some kind of sex club? Wine enemas and trained dogs?"

"I've never been there."

"The Styths won't negotiate a walk to the door with a woman," Paula said. "They'll certainly choose him." She glanced at Bunker. "You mean you do have fun sometimes?"

Jefferson hooted in a piercing voice. "I think she's warming to us, Richard. Good. The Nineveh Club. Where shall we have them on the Earth? Tahiti?"

"That's fine with me," Bunker said.

"I'll give them New York. If they have the good sense to come here, they should see us at our most confusing."

"We have an added starter." He put his head back against the back of his chair. His glance flicked toward Paula. "Has either of you ever heard of the Sunlight League?"

Paula turned her gaze toward Jefferson. The old woman said, "A political club, isn't it? Fairly recent."

"An anti-Styth political club," Bunker said. "With some important members. Martian, I think, most of them. Also anti-Committee."

"Naturally," Jefferson said. "Where did you hear about the Sunlight League?"

Bunker flicked at the papers in front of him with his finger. "Around."

"When?"

"A while ago."

Paula said, angry; "Four months ago. In Los Angeles. When he broke into that smuggler's shop. Isn't that right?"

He never even looked at her; he said to Jefferson, "Any time, Sybil."

"I don't like to see you taking candy from babies," Jefferson said.

"You lied to me." Paula's cheeks burned hot. She pushed her

chair back loudly from the table. "You told me you didn't find anything there."

"Tsk," Bunker said. "I have another meeting. Is there anything else important?"

Jefferson groped in her purse. Paula stared at the far wall. After a moment the man across the table from her rose, closed his papercase, and went out.

"Damn him," Paula said. "I feel like a fool."

"You look like one," Jefferson said. "Have a mint."

The commune bath was filthy. On Paula's day off, she took off her clothes, filled a bucket with soapy water and ammonia, and started to scrub the walls of the shower room. Turning on the nearest shower, she twisted the head around to rinse off the section of tile she had cleaned.

"Do you mind if I wash?"

She plunged her arm into the bucket, holding her nose against the ammonia. "Just stay in the end I haven't done yet."

The young man stood at the last spigot, soaping himself in the spray. "It's about time somebody cleaned up in here." Paula glanced at his brown back. She hardly knew him; he lived in the other hall. The faucets and showerheads were rough with scale. She stood scrubbing at them with all her strength.

"Aren't you on the Committee?"

"Yes."

He turned in the shower. The soap washed white down his body. "I just lost my job."

There were a lot of people out of work. She picked at the grit on the faucet. Stay out of this. "That's too bad."

"Charmichael has laid about fifty people off on the job in the past week."

"Charmichael? The Moneyer?" She glanced at him, interested. Stooping, she dunked the brush into the bucket. The shower behind her was on full heat. The steam billowed around her. Her skin was pebbled with condensation although she was nowhere near the water.

"What did you do?" she asked.

"Media analyst."

Which was a fancy name for file clerk. She stood and washed the wall. "Did they offer to retrain you?"

He turned off his shower. "Just a second, while I get a towel." He went out to the next room. Paula washed grime off the wall. Where she had scrubbed, the white wall shone like china.

. . .

"I'm sorry." The man from Charmichael Money & Credit spread his hands. His face was cheerful as a sun. "We aren't retraining anybody any more. It's too expensive. We have statistics to prove it."

"Oh, god, don't rain numbers on me." She swiveled her chair back and forth. The dogwood was losing its leaves. She studied the man from Charmichael, who smiled back at her.

"Andressen," she said. "Richard Bunker is bringing an action against you for double-billing. How would you like a copy of his file on you?"

The man's smile broadened by six teeth. "Very much."

"Enough to retain my clients?"

"Yes."

"At full pay."

"At half pay. You're talking about fifty-two people, Mendoza."

She nodded. "I accept." She opened her desk drawer and took out three thick file folders and a paper for him to sign.

The dogwood tree was completely bare. She pruned off the dead branches and raked up the leaves. She saw nothing of Tony, not even a call. There had been no more incidents with the Styths since the raid on Vesta. Jefferson went to Crosby's Planet, where the Council met. Thomas Overwood called from Los Angeles. He had information for Paula, and he had found a Styth living on the Earth.

The Styth was somewhere in Alm'ata, in Central Asia. Overwood soured when she pushed him for an address. "I found his dome for you, isn't that enough?" Reluctantly she called Dick Bunker, who went to Alm'ata, while she took the tube across the continent to Los Angeles.

Overwood gave her a thin paper pamphlet. The title on the cover was *The Mutant Menace.* She held it under the light and turned the pages. "This is propaganda. This is no good." On the last page was printed THE SUNLIGHT LEAGUE.

The shopman looked disappointed. He would not say how he had gotten it. She gave him two hundred dollars, took the pamphlet, and went by rocket to Alm'ata.

In flight over the ocean, she read through the booklet. It was a collection of fact and lie and mixtures of the two, all written like slanders. The print was perfect, an expensive production, on high-quality paper. Near the end was a piece of thinner paper, folded in half and stuck into the binding. She worked it loose.

It read:

Merkhiz	SIF 4	*Ebelos*	
Matuko (Saba)	SIF 6	*Ybix*	Vesta
Lopka	SIF 13	*Kundra*	Vesta

Merkhiz and Matuko were cities of the Empire; saba meant "he knows." *Ebelos* was a grade of crystal. She turned the paper over. There was nothing else. SIF looked like an acronym. Styth Imperial. Styth Imperial Fleet. She bounced up and down in her seat. The old man across the aisle gave her a look of disapproval. She spread the paper flat on her knee. Then *Ebelos*, *Ybix*, and *Kundra* could be the names of ships.

The rocket was descending. She folded the paper and put it in her pocket. Below, through the little window like a gun-slot in the wall, she saw the crumpled surface of the Great Asian Lake. Alm'ata was the Earth's primary surface harbor; the long narrow dome, open at both ends, enclosed half the water. Her seat faced the back. She twisted around to watch the approach. The floor thumped under her feet. The secondary engines had come on. The jet skimmed over the surface of the lake. Scum rolled in patches on the water. Greenish threads of pollution trailed by the window. The flared round tunnel of the dome swept up around them. Abruptly the air was clear, the water sparkled and broke in white curls of foam. The rocket circled once and set down on the spiral runway.

Bunker was not at the terminal to meet her. She seethed all the way down the ramp. Outside, she put down her bag and put on her jacket. The air was icy cold. She walked across the city park, asking directions here and there. Little children in brilliant orange coats raced in a game under the bare trees. She came to the Lenin Hotel, an old-fashioned above-ground building in an orchard of fruit trees leafless in the winter cold.

When she let herself into the hotel room, Bunker was lying naked on his back on the couch under the vitamin lamp, a tape plug in his ear, wet balls of cotton on his eyes, and a pink napkin tented over his crotch. Paula shut the door. He did not move.

"This place looks like the University of Barsoom," she said. The room was white, the boxy chairs and tables painted in black lacquer. The carpet was dark red. She put her bag down and went through to the kitchen. The carpet skidded slightly under her feet, treacherous.

"I hope you're doing the cooking," she said. "I can't boil water." She took a beer out of the cold drawer.

"Mendoza, what can you do?"

She swallowed the nasty remark in her throat. The kitchen smelled of must. She opened the window and let in the cold wind. Something mewled overhead, and a gull sailed by. Its wings were black-tipped. She went out to the white and black room again. The vitamin lamp glared on the wall.

"Did you call Jefferson?"

"Don't unpack." Bunker switched off the lamp. "The Council is balking, they may null the case." He threw the tape jack across the room.

"Oh, shit."

He put his shirt on. "Did Overwood have anything?"

She took the paper out of her shirt pocket and gave it to him. He went into the bedroom. A drawer slammed open. She sat on the couch, still warm from the lamp, and pulled off the paper tab on the can of beer.

He came back into the room, pulling his pants on, the paper in his hand. "What is this?"

Paula tucked her feet up under her on the couch and sipped the beer. One-handed, he fumbled the tongue of his belt through the buckle. He said, "What does *Ybix* mean?"

"I don't know the word."

He sat down beside her, taking a pencil off the end table. "So, SIF 4 *Ebelos.* That's the ship, and Merkhiz is her base. *Ybix* and *Kundra* attacked Vesta." He wrote on the paper.

Paula grunted. "You got more than I did."

"Where did you find this? Overwood? How much did you pay him?"

"Two hundred dollars."

"Mendoza. You're improving. Let's go talk to my Styth."

They went up three flights of stairs to the roof of the hotel, to catch the air bus. Bunker said, "He's a local celebrity, Kary is. It took me fifteen minutes to find him, every bum knows him."

Paula walked to the edge of the roof. In the gray trees below her a child in a red coat dashed about, singing in a breathless voice. The cold made her face tingle. The air bus was coming. She went over to the square of paint on the roof and stood with Bunker waiting. The bus driver let down the ladder for them.

They flew back across the city toward the beach. Paula looked out the window. They passed over the Central Market. Piles of fruit covered the stalls, Hessian sacks of almonds and cashews. Tightly packed together in a pen, the white backs of goats looked like fish in a net.

"What's this mean?" Beside her on the bench he was looking at the note again. "Say-ba."

"Saba. Long a's. It means 'he knows.' "

"He. Who?"

"You're the genius."

The air bus was settling down to park before the terminal. They went down the back ramp to a stone pier. The lake stretched before her. She could hear the crash of the surf on the beach. The wind sliced across the open harbor.

Bunker led her along the pier to a line of shops. They went into a drugstore and he bought two quarts of red wine for fifty cents each.

Single-file they descended the steps of the pier to the beach. Her feet sank into the wet sand. Bunker walked into the shade under the pier. A man was lying in the dark between two stone uprights. He was black as soot, and stretched out across the sand he looked ten feet long.

"Kary," Bunker said. "Remember me?"

The Styth sat up. "You again," he said, in a deep alcoholic rasp. Bunker gave him a bottle of wine, and he tore off the paper cap and drank deeply.

Paula sank down on her heels beside an upright. Kary's shaggy hair was frizzy with malnutrition. His mustaches hung thin as string down over his chest. Around his eyes and mouth, his skin was graying. He was old, past mere grandfather old, ninety, perhaps over one hundred. She said, "Where are you from, Kary?"

He glanced at her around the bottle. "What's this?" He looked her over, leisurely. "Skinny little cow, isn't she?" he said to Bunker.

"Where are you from?" This time she said it in Styth.

Kary had the bottle midway to his mouth. He put it down again. "You speak Styth?"

She looked at his hands. "Yes." His right thumb was missing at the first joint. The rest of his fingers ended in blunted nubs. "What happened to your claws?"

He held up the stub of his thumb. "This one was bitten off in a fight in Vribulo when I was a —" She missed the word. Sadly he folded his fingers into his palms. "The others just don't grow any more."

"You're from Vribulo? How did you get here?"

He blinked at her. His eyes were round as carbuncles. To Bunker he said, "Your cow speaks Styth."

Bunker shook his head. "I don't know the language."

Kary emptied the bottle of wine. His head wobbled. Paula said, "How did you get here?"

"I got in a fight. Real bad fight. I killed somebody who had a lot of relatives. One the Prima's lyo." He tried the collapsed bottle again and dropped it to the sand. "Just enough to get me thirsty."

Bunker took the other bottle out of his jacket. Kary's two hands reached for it. "Ah, you're a kindly little people," he said, in the Common Speech.

Paula laughed. She could not judge his height. Probably he was a couple of inches over seven feet, tall even for a Styth. He smelled of stale clothes. Carefully he set the bottle in the sand and wiped his mouth. "You speak Styth," he said to her. His gaze moved over her, and he turned toward Bunker. "Don't you feed her?"

Bunker said, "I like them skinny. It keeps them eager."

Paula looked around her. The stone pillars that held up the pier stood solid in the dark. Kary lay down on the sand, one hand protectively on his bottle.

"I'm going to sleep now."

The two anarchists laughed. "Good-night."

They walked back to the hotel, and she unpacked her bag. Bunker was right. If the Council aborted the case, they'd have to go home again, but she wanted to stay awhile to talk to Kary. She hung up the long white dress, which wrinkled easily. There were two beds, covered in the same dark red as the slippery carpet. On the wall above them was a woven hanging, Turkoman, or Uzbek. A sweet spicy odor made her sniff. She went across the sitting room to the kitchen.

Bunker stood by the counter cutting peaches into a big stew pot. She went in behind him and took a beer out of the cold drawer. Neither of them spoke. She swallowed a cold mouthful of the beer. The sun was going down, and the kitchen lights were coming on in the ceiling. She turned the dial on the wall to brighten the light. Bunker put the lid on the stew pot. He ran the spoon and knives through the washer spray and wiped off the counter.

"You're certainly tidy," she said.

"I don't like to leave tracks," he said.

The pot buzzed. He turned it off and ladled out the flavorsome stew into bowls and handed one to her.

They went into the living room. Sitting on the floor, she blew across the top of the stew to cool it. Bunker crossed to the couch.

"I take it the Styths live in families."

She ate a sweet stewed peach. "Big families. They're polygynous." She thought with sympathy of Kary, family man, alone in an anarchist world. "This is pretty good chicken."

"I'm glad you approve."

"Maybe you missed your real art. When you went into burglary."

He went to the massive antique videone behind the door and dialed through the range of the local radio. At last he settled on progressive music. She spooned up the last juices in her bowl. He flopped down on the couch, cradled his bowl in his lap, and began to eat.

"Actually burglary is only a hobby. How well do you know Cam Savenia?"

"I traveled with her for eight weeks. That was a long time ago."

"She's ambitious."

Paula lifted one shoulder and let it fall. "She's a Martian. And a woman."

"I've never noticed women are more ambitious than men." His spoon clicked on his bowl.

"I meant being a woman on Mars she has a lot to make up for," Paula said.

The videone buzzed. Paula leaped to her feet, dropping the empty bowl. She reached the cabinet one step ahead of Bunker, got between him and the controls, and flipped the switch from radio to intercom. The camera swung on a flexible arm. She yanked it down to her level. The face on the screen belonged to the desk clerk.

"I have a message coming through for you from Crosby's Planet."

"Jefferson," Bunker said.

A flicker rolled across the screen. Paula rapped her fingers on the cabinet. The message was in block letters; it appeared slowly on the yellow ground, at first too dim to read, and she reached for the adjustment knob and Bunker caught her hand. Slowly the print darkened.

Jefferson to Bunker. Council voted 270–265 to continue the case.
Zed.

Paula screeched. She backed away from the videone and spun in a circle. Bunker said, "Five votes. Nobody handles the Fascists like Roland."

"Do you think she had to negotiate the vote?"

"Any time it's that close, she doesn't leave it to their goodwill."

He switched the videone back to the music. Paula sat down on the floor again. "What did you call her? Roland."

"Madame Roland," he said. "Always meddling." Rolling to his feet, he went into the kitchen. She heard the hiss of the washer.

Paula took a shower. While she was drying herself off, Bunker came into the bathroom doorway. "What's this?" He had the propaganda leaflet in his hand.

"Overwood gave it to me. It's supposed to be by the Sunlight League." She shook the damp towel and hung it up on the back of the door. "Some of it's true." She glanced at herself in the mirror. Little drops of water glistened in her puffed coppery hair. She went out to the bedroom.

"The bed on the left is mine," he called.

She pulled back the red cover on the right bed and climbed in. Limp, her eyes shut, she stretched out, and the fluid mud-filled mattress gave softly beneath her. Bunker came in, reading the pamphlet.

"Listen to this. *The Styth is incapable of culture. Like all the dark races. The cities of Uranus were designed and built by technicians of the Earth of the Pre-Contention Period. Most of the ships in the Styth Fleet are Martian. At least 75 per cent.*" The paper crackled in his hand. "Are broken sentences the product of a broken mind? Also remark what goes for culture to the Sunlight League."

"What's the Pre-Contention Period?" Paula asked.

"I guess the Three Planets Empire."

The mud bed gave in waves beneath her whenever she moved. Bunker lay down on the other bed. She had to admire his ability. She yawned, drowsy.

Kary unstopped the bottle of wine. The armchair was too small for him, and he hitched himself awkwardly up straight in it again, his legs braced on the floor. He drank once, looked around, and drank again. "Nice trap you have here."

"Thank you. The Lenin Hotel thanks you. Do you mind speaking Styth? I need the practice." Paula sat down sideways on a straight chair in the sunlight. "What does '*Ybix*' mean?"

"Ybix." He put the bottle down on the arm of the chair, keeping fast hold of it. "That's a fish. In the lakes in some places in Uranus." Without letting go of the bottle, he formed a square of his thumbs and forefingers. "Kind of that-shaped. A little fish, but it bites." The bright sunlight behind her was making him squint. She got up and pulled her chair into the shade.

"What is '*Kundra*'?"

"That's a spell-caster. A witch."

"A man?" 'A' was a masculine ending.

Kary shook his head. "All witches are women."

"How did you get here? After the fight in Vribulo."

"Shipped out. Some friends of mine were running a load of crystal down to meet somebody in the Trojan Asteroids. A couple of us kept on going down toward the Sun. Just to see, you know. Got in trouble in Mars, because in fucking Mars being the wrong fucking color is a fucking crime—"

He stopped to drink, and she watched the level of the liquor fall in the bottle. He wiped his mouth on his hand.

"So when I got out of prison they said *Where do you want to go*, and I'd heard there weren't any police in the Earth. I've been here ever since."

"You haven't had any trouble here?"

"Not me. You won't catch me picking trouble with an anarchist. They always get you in the end."

Bunker was coming in, with more wine. They worked with Kary the rest of the morning. He drank three bottles of red wine and ate some of Bunker's stew, taught them a children's song, and told them his life story. He had been on the Earth at least twenty-five years; he remembered the riots of the thirties, water rationing, and Noah Mataki, who had been on the Committee until 1829.

Kary told them that the Styths had been born of the wives of the first Uranian colonists—Moon-people, he called them, "because they left the Planet and went up to the moons to live, when the strange babies were born. But they sent the Styths into the crystal farms and made them slaves, and if a Styth fought back, the Moon-people caught him and chained him, hand to hand and foot to foot, and threw him into the farm to starve, in the dark and the cold. That's why the Prima wears a cuff, to remind us where we came from."

He drank another bottle of wine. In the middle of a long sad monologue on the beauties of Vribulo, he fell off the armchair. Bunker took his shoulders and Paula his feet, and they dragged him in and put him to sleep in her bed, which she had not made anyway.

"You're as much of a slob as he is," Bunker said.

"If it bothers you so much, make it yourself."

They went up to the roof. Below, in the gray trees, several people were shooting their bows. The wind flapped her jacket. They sat on the low rail at the edge of the building and watched the sunset light flash on the dome wall. She taught him Styth grammar.

"It's like a game. All those rules."

Darkness settled over them, so cold the air hurt her lungs. The blue domelight flickered overhead. She thought of Tony, wondering what he was doing. If he had another friend yet.

"What do you make of the Sunlight League?"

She bundled her hands into her sleeves. The domelight ran in ripples across the darkness high overhead. "The Styths are black. You know how Martians are about skin color. They're harmless."

"Fascists are always harmful in mass. And they don't come any other way."

"I'm freezing. I'm going inside."

He slid off the rail to his feet. They went down the stairs together.

"By Melleno. We will take Richard Bunker for a hostage. Paula Mendoza will meet at the Nineveh Club with the Matuko Akellar, by your time the ten mid-days of April 1853. You arrange safe-conducts for the Styth Fleet ship *Ybix* and fifteen men. Ended. Melleno."

MARS. April 1853

Paula walked down an accordion tunnel from the rocket. Every few yards, there was a sign on the pleated wall reading "Terminal," with an arrow pointing ahead, like encouragement, since there was nowhere else to go. When she walked out of the mouth of the ramp into the expanse of the waiting room, a tall blond woman stepped forward to meet her.

"Hello, Madame Diplomat."

"Cam," Paula said. She switched her bag to her left hand. "How did you know I was coming? I was going to call you when I got here."

Cam Savenia's handshake was cool and white. "Oh, I have ways. How long has it been?"

"Five years," Paula said. She was tempted to say, Four and a half years and six months in prison. Cam was much taller than she was. "You came here just to meet me. I'm flattered."

They started across the waiting room, cutting through the rows of molded plastic benches. The flooring was rippled for traction. Cam said, "This is a pretty important mission. When did you join the Committee?"

"A year ago."

"I always thought you had too much brain to waste your life sitting under a tree. You'll go far with them, if you're as smart as I think you are."

Paula followed her up an ascending ramp. The other passengers from the rocket went on before them. They passed a videone screen showing times of arrival and departure. In spite of the crowd, the place looked barren. Nobody lived here, they just came and went. The walls were papered with the drawings of schoolchildren: giant birds, and people like monsters in space helmets and uniforms. Cam led her to the rooftop parking lot.

"I'll take you out to the Nineveh." She steered Paula down a lane between a wall and a rope. Ahead, a row of air cars waited under a sign that read INTERDOME TRANSPORT.

"Doesn't your term end this year?" Paula asked.

"Yes. The Senate is impossible. Really small beer. I'm announcing for the Council. I have three party endorsements, how do you like that? Want to write my speeches?"

Paula laughed. "Write your own. Mine were awful." She slid into the back seat of a cab.

"Oh, no. I know my limits. I can think and I can do, but I can't express." Cam leaned across the back of the front seat. "Driver, the Nineveh Club." Sitting down, she slid the door closed and locked it.

The cab rolled forward, its engine sputtering, and leaped up in a rush that turned Paula's stomach over. They sailed away across Barsoom. Paula looked out the window. They were entering a stream of traffic, three or four lanes deep and a dozen lanes wide. Below the clutter of cars streamed the puffed heads of the palm trees that lined Cleveland Avenue.

"Do you know what's ahead of you?" Cam said. "Incidentally, I've met this Styth."

"You have?" Paula swiveled around, her arm on the satchel between them. "When?"

"Yesterday."

"He's here already?"

"He's at the Nineveh. Him and eight bodyguards. Turning the place into a zoo."

Just beyond the cab window a private air car flew. Inside it, the old woman driving hunched forward over the steering grips, her teeth set. Below them the land was cut into perfect squares of green, each framing a tilted roof, set with the blue jewel shapes of swimming pools.

"He's at the Nineveh. What's he like?"

Cam shook her head. "Impossible." She took a cigarette from her purse and set it into a long black holder.

"Does he speak the Common Speech?"

"Yes. He's not stupid. I didn't realize they're so big."

They were coming to the lock. The driver swore softly. The traffic was packed around the entrance to the lock, and far ahead a red light flashed. The driver turned his head.

"Be a little while, ladies."

Cam leaned forward. "Go around by the auxiliary."

"I'm not supposed—"

The Martian woman flashed a badge under his nose. "My authority."

"Yes, Senator." The driver pulled the car straight up, out of the traffic jam, and swung it off to the side, and Cam sat back, smiling. She puffed on her cigarette.

"How old is he?" Paula said.

"I can't tell. Older than I am." Cam was thirty-two. "God, they are black, too."

Paula stiffened. She looked out the window again. They passed through the auxiliary lock in the wall of the dome and went into the dark Martian day. Barsoom was at the edge of a line of craters. They flew above the hollow hills. For miles around them the surface of the

Planet was heaped up with red dust, the wastes of the water bears, the native organisms that mined out the minerals and water. There was no wind. They flew above a crater. The dust lay in geometric cones among the steep red walls. She wondered if Cam were here to pitch to her or just to spy. The smoke from the Senator's cigarette hurt her nose. Now they were flying over the virgin Planet. They crossed a rill like a seam in the red crust. Paula knew Cam was watching her. Ahead, the sunlight glanced off the shining dome of the Nineveh.

"What do you think of the Committee?" Cam asked.

"It's a job."

"Sybil Jefferson has the morals of an ax-murderess. As for that rat Bunker—"

"The guts of a burglar," Paula murmured, looking out the window.

"Right. And to prove it they send a green girl in to take their beating for them."

"Thanks for the confidence."

"Damn it, you don't know what you're into."

Paula stared out the window at the dark world. "I learn."

"These people are animals."

"You're so civilized, Cam."

"You're damned right." Cam sucked intently on the last of the cigarette. Her fingernails were shaped to points. "I believe in law and order and authority, right and wrong, little old-fashioned things like honor and responsibility and morality. Why did you bring him to Mars? He's interested as hell in the dome, I'll tell you that." She pushed the butt out of her cigarette holder. "I guess to a primitive, Mars must be mind-swamping."

Paula cleared her throat. They passed through the wall of the dome, from the subdued natural light to the brilliant green of the Nineveh Club. They flew over an arm of a golf course, a patch of dark trees, another long strip of lawn. She sat up straight, looking forward over the driver's shoulder. Surrounded by lakes, the hotel stood in a long white wedge among the trees in the distance.

"There's the river," Cam was saying. She pointed past Paula's shoulder. "Every drop of water manufactured in Barsoom."

The car circled once and lowered toward the front of the hotel. They swooped over a swimming lake, formed into round coves and little inlets framed in trees.

"How long has he been here?" Paula said. Probably Cam had pitched to him, too.

"The Akellar? Since yesterday. His ship is parked in orbit. If he's taking a look at Mars, I can tell you we're taking a good look at *Ybix*. It's an old Martian Manta destroyer, which proves something, I guess."

Savenia pointed to a flock of yellow birds flying off toward the golf course. "They even sing." Every feather manufactured in Barsoom.

"What has he been doing?"

Cam gave Paula an oblique look. "You're single-minded." The cab was parking. Trim as a bugle boy, a man in a wine-red uniform rushed up to open the door. When Paula slid out to the pavement, he reached for the satchel, and she held it around behind her out of his range.

"Take the luggage to Room 2017," Cam said. "Pese-pese."

"Yes, Dr. Savenia."

Paula let Cam marshal her through the hotel's main doors. The lobby spread out around her, hushed and elegant. The walls were set with glass boxes, back-lit, displaying hats and jewels. A woman and a man in golf knickers passed her.

"Straight ahead," Cam said. "You have to register. The Styths don't do much, except at night. Then they want everything in the place. They beat up a waiter who made the mistake of talking back to them."

Paula said, "The light here is much brighter than they're used to." She went between two rubber plants to the registration desk.

"So they maul people? Why didn't the Committee send a man?"

"The Styths requested me." Which meant they weren't serious about negotiating, a minor obstacle. The desk clerk approached her, his gaze directed over her head, as if he didn't quite see her.

"May I help you?"

"This is Paula Mendoza," Cam said, behind her.

"Yes, Miss Mendoza." The clerk snapped like a soldier to his work. He put a voice box down in front of her. "Your suite is ready. Second floor overlooking the gardens, near our other interplanetary guests." Paula said her name and the Committee's name into the flat box. It whirred and a pink card popped up from the top. The clerk said, "Now, if you'll give us your thumbprint—"

She pressed her thumb against the patch on the card.

"Come on," Cam said. "I'll buy you a drink."

Paula followed her across the lobby, the satchel in her left hand. "Come up to my room. I have a bottle of Black Label."

"I never pass up an invitation like that."

They went up a flight of steps. On the second-floor landing, the corridor branched off in three directions. Cam led her off down the middle. Two old people crept toward them, the woman leaning on two canes. She gave Paula a look focused three feet beyond her. Cam took her by the arm again.

"I think you're—"

A Styth was walking down the corridor. Paula stopped, and Cam bumped into her. The Styth ignored them. He sauntered past, black as a stone in the white plastic Martian world. He disappeared out the door to the stairs, ducking his head to miss the lintel.

Cam said, "They walk like a bunch of women. It's funny to see all those huge men pussyfooting around." She strode across the corridor to a door. "Try the lock. It ought to be working by now."

Paula set her thumb on the white patch on the door, and it slid back into the wall. The lights in the ceiling in the room beyond came up bright as sunlight. She walked into a room as big as the public room in her commune. At one end was a bar with three stools; at the other end a massive brick hearth, set up with logs and a revolving phony fire. She went around the couch to the long draped wall opposite the door and pulled at the curtains until she found an opening and looked out at a broad garden, laid out in curves and squares of hedge.

"Do you like it?" Cam said.

"It's fantastic," Paula said. She turned around again. The wall beside the door was an aquarium four feet square. She went toward it, drawn by the flight of red fish.

Cam said comfortably, "You pride yourselves on your poverty." She opened the door behind the bar. Paula followed her into the next room. Her suitcase lay open on the rack at the foot of the bed. She put down the satchel and stepped out of her shoes. The carpet was deep enough to sleep on.

"Here." She took out one bottle of the Scotch and gave it to Cam. "Go pour while I take a fast shower."

"Fine."

Cam went back to the opulent front room. Paula looked quickly around. The cushioned furniture and draped blue walls offered a dozen hiding places for spy devices. Cam had always been fond of gimmicks. She peeled off her clothes, stiff from travel, and found the washroom.

There was a sheet of fancy paper tucked into the mirror. "For Our Single Guests." While she was turning in the dryer, she read it. "The Nineveh provides a wide range of excitement and self-discovery for the man or woman with sophisticated tastes." Call girls, call boys. Press a button and we'll send up an amputee. She remembered this had been Dick Bunker's idea.

"Paula?"

"Yes?" She went out to the bedroom.

Cam turned, brisk, saw her, and averted her eyes. She scratched quickly at her upper lip. Naked people made her nervous. "The Akellar is on the videone. Not literally, they've disconnected the camera. He wants you to come up there now." She glanced shyly at Paula's body.

"I don't want to do that," Paula said. She took her long robe out of the suitcase. "Tell him my respects and I'd like to get some rest first."

"Right-o." Cam went out. Paula put the robe on and dug around in the suitcase for the belt. She heard Cam's voice in the next room, rising with temper, and started through the door.

Cam stood over the videone in the far corner by the hearth. Her face was stained pink across the cheekbones. "Now, you listen to me, tough guy—" Paula went up to the videone and shut it off.

The Senator stepped back, her face smooth. They stared at each other a moment. Finally Paula went past her toward the bar.

"Tell me why you're here, Cam."

The bottle stood on the countertop, unopened. She circled the bar and squatted to take a glass from the shelf below the cold drawer. The bar was stocked with mixers and soft drinks.

"I don't think you understand what this confrontation is all about," Savenia said.

Paula straightened up. She poured Scotch into her glass. "Tell me."

"The Styths are our enemies, Paula. They can never be anything else. They're mutants. They're genetic pollution."

Paula took a bracing sip of the Scotch and licked her lips. She had heard that phrase before. Cam stalked across the room. "I can help you. I know a little bit about Styths, and about this Styth in particular. You are a sacrificial lamb, baby. Jefferson and Bunker have set you up." She was a gifted speaker, all fire no matter what she was saying. She marched up to the bar. "He isn't really human, Paula. Sometimes I don't think the Committee is human either."

"Have you ever heard of the Sunlight League?" Paula asked.

Cam's face twitched. She put her white hands on the bar. "Are you listening to me? Because—" She backed up in a rush, startled, her eyes aimed beyond the bar.

Paula turned around. Her bedroom door was opening. A big Styth walked through it, not a tall man, for a Styth, massively built. He was staring at Cam. He said, "You think you're a man, I'll treat you like a man. You have until the light comes back to leave."

Cam stood straight as a flagpole. She said, with great dignity, "This is my Planet, Akellar."

Paula set her glass down. "Cam, you made your speech, now go."

"I'm sorry for you, baby, but you'll get what you deserve." She went to the door. Her white face appeared over her shoulder. "You know, breaking and entering is against the law on Mars."

The Styth took two steps toward her, and Cam went out. The sliding door sighed closed. Paula rested her hands on the edge of the bar. The big man wheeled toward her and looked at her down his long Styth nose. He said, "When I come into the room, you stand up."

"I am standing up," she said. "I'm very short. How did you get in here?"

"I walk through walls."

"That must be hard work. Would you like a drink?"

He picked up her glass and swirled the dark amber liquor and drank the whole two fingers straight down. "Give me some of this."

Paula filled up the short glass to the top. The sliding door whisked back into the wall, and Cam Savenia came in again. Three men followed her, identically dressed in gray jackets. One carried a weapon with a trumpet muzzle. Paula started around the bar.

Savenia pointed at the Akellar. "Him." She touched the wall switch and the ceiling lights burst up, dazzlingly bright. The Akellar reached for the glass of Scotch. The air smelled of hot copper. Paula sniffed, puzzled. The three policemen stopped midway across the room, and the gun disappeared.

"Dr. Savenia, we've been told not to interfere with the Styths."

Paula stopped at the end of the bar, relieved. Cam said, "Do you know who I am?" in a voice that squeaked.

The guards backed to the door. "Yes, sir, Dr. Savenia."

Paula went around behind them to the light switch and dimmed the lights. The policemen filed quickly out. Cam stood where she was, staring at the Akellar. Paula said, "You must be tired, Cam, after all your labors. I'll call you tomorrow."

Cam said, "When the Council hears this, there will be hell, I can tell you." She left. The door slid closed behind her.

Paula laughed. The Styth rubbed his eyes. She put the bar between them again and poured another three fingers of Scotch into his glass. Maybe she could get him drunk.

"Do you think you're a man?" he said.

"I'm not a Martian. I don't have to be a man." The stink of copper was coming from him. She opened the cold drawer. "Do you want some ice?"

"Ice."

She used the tongs to put two ice cubes into his glass. He fished one lump out with his fingers and put it in his mouth. She made herself another drink. His mustaches hung down past his collarbones, so Cam was right, he was her age, or a little older, thirty-five or forty. The ice crunched between his teeth.

"Do you want to see my credentials?" she said.

"I know who you are. What is this stuff?" He drank his glass empty.

"Scotch whiskey."

"It's not bad."

She poured his glass full again, remembering Kary's capacity. He ate the other ice cube. She stooped behind the bar, found a bowl in the back, and filled it with ice cubes and put it down on the counter next to him.

"From now on," he said, "when I send for you, you come."

"What did Cam tell you about us?"

"Nothing I didn't already know." He laid his forearms on the bar. "We know all about the Committee." He stared at her a moment, eating ice. She busied herself neatening up the bar. The coppery stink was gone. He reached for the bottle and topped off his glass.

"This is Earthish, this drink?"

"Whiskey? Yes. It's distilled in Scotland."

"Is that where you live?"

She shook her head. "I grew up in Havana. Now I live in New York. You speak the Common Speech very well."

His chest swelled; he was proud of that. "I taught myself. Reading engine manuals. Do you speak Styth?"

"Not very well."

"Say something to me in Styth."

She did not want him to know she was fluent. Ungrammatically, she said, "I hope you have a good time on Mars."

"We'd better keep to the Common Speech." He put his glass down with a thunk. His voice dropped half an octave under the weight of authority. "The Earth is an anarchy."

"Yes."

"No government. No laws. No army."

"That's right. No taxes, either."

"I don't believe you."

Paula rolled whiskey on her tongue. It was late; she was tired, and she had to call Jefferson. She said, "Well, it won't be the last time."

His black eyes glinted. He folded his arms on the bar top. "Aren't you supposed to be convincing me to trust you?"

"You'd be a fool to trust anybody. You don't look like a fool to me."

He stared at her a moment. Finally he slid off the stool and walked across the room. The back of his shirt was dark with sweat. His black hair was pulled down and knotted at the nape of his neck. She put her elbows on the bar. She did not want to talk much in this room before she had taken out any relics of Cam Savenia.

He said, "I can understand Savenia. She's ambitious. She's just hauling her own freight. What's yours? What do you want in this?"

"It's my job."

He spun around, his hands on his hips. "Where I come from, women don't have jobs—they stay home with their families where they belong." He walked back up to the bar and leaned on it, bending over her. "Savenia says I shouldn't believe anything the Committee tells me—you're all thieves and liars."

"Say flexible. It's a nicer word."

"Are you? What do you want? Money?"

She raised her head. "Are you offering me a bribe?"

"Yes."

"To do what?"

"As you're told."

She burst out laughing. "How much did you pay the Nineveh not to interfere with you? I'll bet it was too much. You should have come to the Committee. They're good at negotiating bribes."

He sat down again on the stool and reached for the ice. She caught a whiff of the coppery heat. "You're saying no?"

"That's right."

He mashed an ice cube in his teeth, his eyes on her. Paula smiled broadly at him. He was embarrassed; he pulled on his mustaches, getting his face in order.

"Are you married?"

"No. Anarchists don't usually get married."

"But you do breed."

"Sometimes."

"Do you have any children?"

She shook her head. He was leaning forward across the bar, attacking. "Why not? What are you waiting for? You're already past the best age."

"I'm too busy to have a baby."

"Too busy doing what?"

"My job. My own life."

"That's not much of a substitute."

She finished her drink and put the glass down. "Well, I like it." His hands lay flat on the bar. His long fingers were tipped in heavy black claws.

He said, "If somebody tried to bribe me, I wouldn't laugh," and the claws flexed.

"Aren't you glad I'm a pacifist?"

He stood up. She raised her head to follow him. He was over six and a half feet tall. Short, for a Styth. She said pensively, "I guess it wouldn't matter."

"You're damned right it wouldn't. I'm going. You come up to my place tomorrow. Five o'clock. What do I call you?"

"Paula."

He was on his way to the door. "Will these—Martians sell me that whiskey?"

"It's expensive. Don't let them give you the Martian version, it's wholly other."

His big head bobbed once. "My name is Saba." He sounded as if he were granting her a favor. The door opened for him, and he left.

The small hinged window in the shower was unlocked. He was burly, a tight fit through the window. She turned off the light, locked the bathroom door, and went back to the sitting room to call Jefferson.

The old woman's face was grooved with irritation. "How long have you been there?"

"I'm sorry, Jefferson, I've been busy." She swung out the stool and sat down in front of the camera. "I've met him."

"You have. What's he like?"

"Remember that list of ships? Saba is his name. He's very defensive. I think he's scared. He seems to have made up his mind that the best protection is to attack first. Cam Savenia is here, by the side."

"Dr. Savenia? The Senator?"

"She and the Akellar have fallen in love." She told Sybil how he had broken into her suite.

Jefferson cackled with laughter. "Yes, that's the trouble with law. What is she doing there?"

"Trying to wreck the meeting. If he talked to her the way he talked to me, I can see why she's angry." She scratched her chin. "He tried to bribe me."

"He did. How much?"

"He never said."

Jefferson's mouth screwed up thoughtfully. "Do you get along with him?"

"Better than Cam. He read me the sermon on woman's place, and the way he told me his name I should use it sparingly. He's all right. He ate half a drawer of ice the first ten minutes he was here."

There was a ripple of interference across the screen. Jefferson glanced away. Paula fiddled with the image focus.

"Is he intelligent?"

"He's no genius. He speaks the language like a don." Another wave rolled slowly over Sybil's image. "You know someone is getting onto us."

"I'm aware of that. I'll deal with it. You have a scanner, don't you? You'd better look around your suite."

"I will."

In the morning, when she tried to call Cam, the computer told her Savenia had checked out. Paula sent down for breakfast. She carried the electronic scanner all over the suite and uncovered two small listening devices. She put them in her suitcase to take back to the technicians in New York. The page who brought her breakfast hovered around her, pouring her tea, and setting out butter and jelly and kefir.

"If you expect a tip, Charley, you're hanging around the wrong woman." Her eggs were sprinkled with paprika. She reached for the fork.

"Dr. Savenia gave me a fifty to make things easier for you." The page set out a dish of sausage. He stepped back, his hands behind him, smiling. He wore a little round cap at an angle on his fair hair.

"Do you see much of Mr. Black?"

"Mr.—" his blank look went suddenly to a broad grin. "Mr. Black. Yes, ma'am. You mean the Styths. They broke up the club last night, up on the roof—did you hear about that?"

"Which Styths?"

His hand flew out toward her, palm up. "Ten dollars."

Paula ate a link of sausage. Her stomach was still queasy from the space flight. "Charley, I'll pass."

The page stiffened. He tucked his arms behind him again. "Yes, ma'am." He waited until she was finished and took the table away without a word.

She went up to look at the club on the roof of the hotel. The floor was covered with broken glass, and the piany had sat down, its hind legs broken. Three men in aprons were sweeping up. Paula walked through to the back, where a bald, tired Martian sat eating a roll and drinking coffee.

"Hello," she said. "Did you see the performance?"

The Martian raised his head. "One of them. Who are you?"

"Paula Mendoza. I'm from the Committee."

"Forget it." He took a bite out of the roll. "I don't want to get involved."

"Do you work for the hotel?"

The bald man chewed, silent. She said, "Last night a Styth broke into my bedroom and the hotel police didn't see fit to ask him not to do it again."

His jaw moved steadily. She stood there while he ate the rest of the roll. He pushed the plate away.

"Sit down."

She sat in the chair across the table from him. "You said you saw one fight. There was more than one?"

"Three." He held up three fingers. "The first two were nothing. Some regular person bumped into one of those big black bastards, or said something, you know, just funny, and got decked, I didn't even call Security for the first." He shrugged. His eyes were puffy with fatigue. "The late-night fight was the all-black wrecking crew. They had some of the cats with them, you know, the working women, and there was some competition, and—"

"Who? Did you hear any names?"

"The names all sound the same. One of them, he's got a brush cut—" He ran one hand back and forth over the crown of his head. "He's the high muck-muck's son, he says, you know, loud. He was the loser. One with a scar—" he gestured at his cheek, "he was the champ." The Martian's pale eyes blinked at her. "One of them broke into your room. You know, honey, you're in trouble."

She looked around at the rooftop. A sweeper tipped his dustpan over the trash barrel and broken glass rained down into it. "Do you think your troubles are over?"

"That's right. Because I'm closing. If Security won't protect me, I'm going on vacation." A sweeper brought the coffee pot and filled his cup again. "Give this young lady some coffee."

"No, thank you," Paula said. "You said they had some of the whores with them?"

"The braver ones."

"Who?"

"Try Lilly M'ka. She'll take anything on." He stirred his coffee, his head turning. What he saw of his club made his face sag. "I wouldn't go near one. That's a mean pack. I'd like to see one matched up against something like a little more, you know, natural armament. A wolfdog. Or a leopard."

Jolted, she said nothing. She watched him drink his coffee down. When she left, she went down to the sportshop in the lobby and bought a hand torch with an intense beam.

In the afternoon, she met Lilly M'ka in the lounge on the second-floor mezzanine. They sat near the windows. A steady parade of models sauntered through the tables, showing off fur clothes. The whore was dark, almost as dark as Paula, and several years younger, in her early twenties. She said, "Funny you should ask. Dr. Camit Savenia asked me the same question."

"I'm happy to hear it. How well do you know Cam?"

"Not very. I thought you were interested in the Styths."

A tall model in mink pants strolled past their table, reversed, posed a moment, and went off. "Did you talk to her much?" Paula said.

"Just once, since the Styths came."

On the far side of the room the Martian guests applauded in a patter of gloved hands. Paula took the straw out of her soda and licked cream off it. "How long was she here?"

"Two or three days. She's easy to get to know. She likes an audience."

"I'll say."

Lilly's eyes were dramatically painted, like a butterfly's wing. With her dark skin, she was probably not Martian-born. Paula said, "Who's your client with the Styths?"

"The main one? Saba. The Akellar."

"Oh, really."

"He thinks he's a rocket."

"Is he any good?"

The whore made a little languid gesture. "Not as good as he thinks he is."

"Who is?"

Lilly laughed. She put her forearms on the table and leaned forward, her voice softer. "Are you interested in the fact one of them is gone?"

"Gone." Paula glanced at the clock. It was four-thirty. "What do you mean?"

"A real tall one with yellow eyes. I haven't seen him since the first night they were here."

"Yellow eyes."

"That's how I remembered. All the others have those big round black eyes."

Paula stuck her straw back into the soda glass. "I'm interested."

"I thought so." Lilly gave her a broad wink and walked away.

Paula went to her room and put on her fancy black dress. She stood at the mirror combing out her kinky red-gold hair. Her chin was pointed, and her eyes tipped up at the outer corners. Cat-faced, Tony had called her. That reminded her of the clubman's euphemism for the whores: working women. She got the package out of her satchel and unsnapped the lid.

The short jeweled knife inside had come from Persepolis. There was a listening device in the handle, which would tune itself to the first voice it heard after the knife was drawn out of its brocaded sheath. She put it back in its satin bed and took it down the hall to the Styths' suite.

The man who answered her knock was short, his face broad across the cheekbones. A round of thin gold wire pierced his left nostril. He backed off a step and called, in his own language, "It's not one of the whores, so it must be the anarchist." He looked down at the box in her hand. "What is that?" To her he used the Common Speech.

"It's a present for the Akellar."

She went into a long room full of Styths. The lights were dimmed and the window drapery pulled. Half a dozen men sprawled in the chairs or stood along the walls, all watching her. They were dressed in identical long gray shirts, leggings, and soft boots. The bar was broken into two pieces, and the rug was stained. She blinked, trying to adjust her eyes to the half-light. A young man came toward her, his homely face misshapen with bruises. The inch-long spikes of his mustaches ran straight across his upper lip, and his hair grew in a fur over his skull. He did not look like the Akellar, especially battered.

"What's that?"

The man with the gold wire in his nose went to a door on the far side of the room and opened it. "In here," he said to her.

The boy said, "Wait—what if that's a bomb?" and all the men laughed. She went into the next room.

It was much smaller than the one she had just left, although the blank walls and the absence of furniture made it seem big. The outdoor light was pouring in the windows. The Akellar sat in front of them, so that to face him she had to look into the dazzling light. The only furniture was the desk in front of him and the chair he sat in. She put the package down on the desk.

"What's that?"

"It's a present from the Committee," she said. "Kind of an earnest of our intentions." With the light behind him she could not see his face. He turned the box over.

"These people have been yapping at me since I got here," he said. He found the spring catch and opened it. "And they keep jumping my men." He raised the lid of the box.

His hands paused. Paula moved around the desk to stand by the window, so she could watch his expression. He took the dagger out of the white lining and drew the knife from the sheath.

"What is this?" he said.

"It was made in Damascus for a Seljuk prince. When there were still princes on the Earth."

He turned it over in his hands, admiring it, and held it so that the emeralds glittered. Abruptly he rammed it back into the sheath, stuck it into the box, and pushed the box away.

"I have nothing for you."

"I don't care."

"Take it back."

"If you want."

She made no move to pick it up. He pulled on his mustaches. "I guess you are a woman. A man wouldn't give me a present without getting something in return."

"Why not?"

"Because all systems equalize." He got out of the chair and pulled the curtains closed across the window. A gloom fell. It was dark in

Uranus, cold and dark. She was comfortable enough in the light dress but he was sweating.

"If it bothers you so much that I'm a woman, why did you pick me?" she said. "There's a man in the case."

"Very little of this was my idea." He pulled his chair around and sat down. "There is only one thing we have to say to you. Styth will rule everything, sooner or later. We have a saying: 'One Sun, one law, one Empire.' We are your natural masters. If you submit to us, we will rule you justly. If you don't, then you'll have to suffer the consequences."

Paula sat down on the floor. "That's amazing. Did you make that up?" she said, and he flared.

"I don't make things up. Do you think I'm a child? I know how the Universe works. Are you calling me a liar?"

"No," she said.

"You are a liar."

"When have I lied to you?"

He slapped his hand flat on the desk. "The other watch, when I was in your place. You said there's no government in the Earth."

"There isn't. Why don't you think people can take care of themselves?"

"Because it's not human nature."

He was sweating heavily, and the chair was too small for him, pinching him between its round arms. "Nobody does anything he doesn't have to do. Who takes care of the city, for instance? People don't see that large—all most people see is the tunnel of their own little lives."

"The dome is owned by a private company. When you pay for your heat and water, you subscribe to the dome maintenance."

His round black eyes were unblinking. He made a disbelieving noise in his chest. Picking up the case on the desk, he took the dagger out of it again. "This is a beautiful thing."

"Yes."

"What if it was yours, and someone stole it?"

"I'd do what I could."

"What about credit? Who issues your money? Do you use money?"

"Yes. Those are private companies, too. Like the Committee."

"You mean anybody can go down there and make any amount of money?"

"Nobody would use money unless they knew it was worth something. Moneying is a very conservative profession. There's only twenty-four companies on the whole Planet and they have big conventions about the future of credit-mongering and they all wear the same clothes. Very dull."

"Are you making fun of me?"

"No. I'm sorry. I was making fun of us."

He drew the dagger and turned it and laid the flat of the knife against his cheek. They stared at each other awhile. His head turned toward the door.

"Ketac!"

The brush-headed boy came in: his son. The Akellar said to her, "He'll take you back. I'll send for you when I want to talk to you again."

She got to her feet, pulling the skirts of the black dress straight with her hands. In their own language he was telling the young man to escort her back as if her room were a million miles away. She started toward the door, and the big man said, "And when I call, you come. You understand?"

She took hold of her temper, enough not to say anything, and gave him a long look down the room. He flicked the dagger back into its sheath. She went out after his son.

In the corridor, Ketac watched her the whole way back to her room. She avoided meeting his stare. He made her uneasy. At her door, she stopped and pressed her thumb into the key patch and the door slid open.

"Thank you."

He put his hand on the doorjamb, so that his arm blocked her way. "I want—" He swallowed. With a jerk of his head he indicated the room beyond. "Go in. I go in."

"No." She backed into the middle of the corridor. "Get out of my way."

"I hear—anarkisto—"

"Ketac, get out of my way."

He moved aside. She went past him into the safety of her suite and pulled the door closed.

"It doesn't sound promising," Jefferson said.

"I don't know. He's that curious." Paula touched the frame of the videone. "They're tearing the place apart."

"What? Who? The Styths?"

"Not deliberately. They don't get along with the Martians. Mr. Black here bribed the security, so nobody is putting the arm on them."

"Are you all right?"

"So far."

Sybil wiped the corner of her eye with her forefinger. "I have an idea. Two ideas. He's throwing money around as if he believes in it, maybe we can throw some at him. Not ours, naturally. I'm sending you a book on interplanetary trade relations."

"I don't know anything about economics."

"This is politics, dear girl. Your weapon of choice."

"I don't think you know me very well."

Jefferson cackled. Someone knocked on the door. Paula went to answer it. Outside was the short Styth with the gold wire in his nose. He gave her a heavy object wrapped in a piece of black cloth. "Paulo Mendoz'," he said. "With the—the compliment of the Matuko Akellar." He nodded down at her and went away.

Inside the soft black cloth was a clear crystal the size of a peach. When she put it on the screen for Jefferson to see, the old woman grunted. The crystal was cut in perfect octagonal facets and caught light like a diamond.

"Balancing an equation," Paula said. "I guess he's keeping the dagger." She picked up the crystal and measured it in her hand.

"That belongs to the Committee," Jefferson said swiftly.

"He gave it to me." The crystal weighed at least a pound.

"We paid for the knife. That thing is worth a fortune."

Paula wrapped the crystal back up in the black cloth. A thousand dollars an ounce, on the Earth; how much would it cost in Uranus? She began to see a way to use Jefferson's trade paper.

"What else?"

"Hmmm?"

"You said you had two suggestions."

"Oh." Jefferson fingered the flabby skin of her throat. "Bring him to the Earth."

Paula opened a drawer and put the piece of crystal inside. That would be easy, with his curiosity already hot. "If you want, Sybil."

She sat on the couch watching the fish zigzag back and forth through the wall aquarium. The big Styth's arrogance tempted her. He had weaknesses; he could be had. She switched off the lights and went to the bedroom. Just into the darkened room, she caught a whiff of a coppery odor.

Her nerves tingled with warning. She backed up into the front room again. The little pocket torch she had bought was in the bar, and she took it in her left hand and went into the bedroom again.

Halfway across the room to the bed, she was engulfed in the coppery reek. She whirled around. A hand closed on her right wrist. She switched on the hand torch and shot the bright beam straight up into his eyes.

He released her. His arms crossed over his face, he staggered back from her. It was Ketac. She ran around the foot of the bed and turned the torch off. She heard nothing and saw only a flicker of movement in the dark but when she reached the bedside lamp and lit it, he was gone.

The window in the washroom was open. She slammed it shut. There was no way to lock it. She closed the washroom door, moved the bedtable over against it, and went to bed.

The following morning, when she took the receiver down from the closet shelf, about two inches of the wire had been run off. She wound it back to play. The device bleeped, to show it was working. It was designed to pick up only voices. She listened to their talk about the Sun, the law and the Empire. Her own voice always sounded strange to her, deeper than she expected.

"Pop," Ketac said, "Tanuojin is back."

The Akellar uttered a low, indefinite sound. Keyed to his voice, the device would pick up every vocal noise he made. She plunged her face into a steaming hot towel.

"What's the matter with you?" a deep, musical voice said.

"I drank too much. There's some liquor here, like fluid explosive, the Earthish woman told me about it."

"Naturally. What is she like?"

The Akellar laughed. "She's this big. She's mouse-brown, her eyes slant like a snake's, her hair is like gold wire all on end. She looks as if she has one toe stuck in a charge socket."

She put on a pair of overalls and took the recorder into the front room. A breakfast cart was standing alone by the couch. The page had abandoned her. She poured hot water into a china teapot with a decal of the hotel on its belly. While the tea was steeping, she buttered toast.

"Did you get to Barsoom?" the Akellar said, and she dropped the butter knife on the floor.

"Yes," the deep voice said. "It's impossible to see it on foot. It goes on and on, and even when it's turned away from the Sun, it's all lit up, every little corner."

She ate the toast. Had he walked to Barsoom? She imagined the uproar if he had been caught. But he had not been caught: amazing.

"What about this anarchist? What have you found out?"

"Oh, she comes down with the same story, no government, no army, nothing. I offered her money and she laughed. She's a liar, like every other nigger in the Universe."

Paula took the teacup across the room to the windows and pulled the drapes half-open. It was another splendidly sunny day, manufactured in Barsoom. Two men with a cart were pulling up the blue delphinium below her window and installing daffodils, yellow and white.

"Tanuojin," the Akellar said, "I don't think this was one of your better ideas."

"We're in the wrong place, that's all."

Before she could find out the right place, the wire ran out. She reloaded the receiver and put it up on the top shelf of the closet, behind her shoes. The name Tanuojin, like all Styth names, was made up of word particles; it meant "the ninth boy" or "the new boy," she was unsure. She went down to the lobby.

The headline on the current hourly read: BARSOOM SUPERS REACH CUP PLAY-OFFS. She went across the lobby. In a side room, the small Styth with the nose wire was shooting pool. Two Martian men played dik-dakko at the opposite end of the room, three other game tables between them and the Styth. There was a tiltball machine against the wall. She put her paper down, got out ten cents, and started the machine. The lights came on in the multicolored cube. She pushed the trigger and a ball fell into the top. She used the handles to shake the ball down through the maze.

"Hello," the Styth said, beside her.

"Hello."

"I am supposed to watch you. It will make it that much easier if you help."

She pushed the trigger button. "What's your name?"

He leaned against the wall. At her eye-level, a chain hung around his throat, inside the wide collarless neck of his shirt: an order medal. He said, "My name is Sril. What is this engine?"

She turned back to the tiltball machine. This time she had drawn two balls. They careened off in opposite directions. She kept the cube moving. The balls reeled through the levels of colored plastic. With two it was easy: she held one in a cul-de-sac while slipping the other past the traps. When the two balls rolled through the gate, lights flashed, a bell jangled: FREE BALL.

"I will try." Sril pushed her out of the way.

"I'm in the middle of—"

"What do I do? This?" He pushed the button. He was lucky: the machine was random-loaded, and only one ball fell into the maze. He touched the handles. The ball dropped like a stone down the center trap. The machine went dark.

"What happened?" he cried.

"You lost. Try it again. You see the holes, there, you're supposed to avoid them."

"No—you do. I watch."

She fed the machine another dime and pushed the trigger. Five balls rolled into the chute at the top of the maze. She teased them to the last level, hardly moving the cube at all, and then turned one handle too far and lost the middle and the last down a side trap.

Sril groaned in disappointment. Paula said, "That's good, for me. You play it."

Another Styth was coming across the room toward them, a big man with a scar on his cheek. In Styth, he said, "You're supposed to be on watch. Where is the Man?"

"I am on watch," Sril said. "I'm on squaw-duty." He turned back to the tiltball machine. "Saba is upstairs." He reached for the trigger.

Paula stepped back. A ball fell with a ping into the maze. Sril fought it, cursed it, and pleaded with it down to the third level, where it dropped through.

"Let me try." The big man shoved at him. Sril thrust him off. They crowded into each other, swearing and laughing. The steady patter of the dik-dakko ball across the room stopped; a man said, "What's that stink?" This time, getting three balls, Sril managed to take one successfully through the maze. When he lost the next ball down the central chute, he let out a yell, grabbed the tiltball machine, and tore it off the wall.

A dik-dakko player shouted. Paula dodged a flying tiltball. The machine sagged over onto its side. Steel balls cascaded out of the bin across the floor.

Sril backed off, looking apprehensively around. The other Styth grabbed his arm. "Let's get out of here."

"Too late," Paula said.

A tall white man was moving toward them at top speed, his body at an attacking angle. She wondered nervously if she had broken any Martian law. He walked straight up to her. His gaze raked the Styths.

"Are you all right, Miss Mendoza?"

"I'm fine," she said, relieved.

The two black men were standing on the far side of the wreckage of the machine. Tiltballs rolled around on the floor, clicking into each other. The Martian turned on the Styths, fierce.

"Which one of you did that?"

Paula stepped back to the wall. That was the wrong approach. The doorway to the lobby was packed with the curious faces of guests.

Sril said, "We do n-nothing. He just falls off." He still smelled strong.

The manager fisted his hands. "You don't expect me to believe that."

"Is something wrong?" said a musical bass voice. A rangy Styth sauntered across the gameroom, his eyes on the Martian. Straw-thin, he towered four or five inches over seven feet. His eyes were light brown. Yellow eyes. The Martian rounded on him.

"Are you their superior officer?"

"That's right." Tanuojin slid his long hands under his belt. "What's wrong?" He nodded to Sril and the other man. They bolted out the door, the guests jumping out of their way.

"Hey!" The hotelman wheeled.

Tanuojin stood over him. For an instant, looking up, the Martian lost his breath. He regained it in a rush. "You must take me for a fool!"

The tall Styth snorted. He walked off, away from the hotelman. The Martian puffed up. His lips curled. He headed for the door to the lobby.

"All right, everybody—" He herded people out of the doorway. "Show's over. Move along." He turned back toward the Styth. "You're a bunch of stinking savages. They ought to run you right out of the Universe." He left.

Paula stood still. Tanuojin had not noticed her. He strolled across the room to the outside door, where he had come in, and went away. Loose tiltballs rolled around the floor at her feet. The copper smell was fading in the air. Thoughtfully she went out of the gameroom.

Wherever she went, Sril followed her. She walked around the hotel garden, bought photo-cards in the card shop and wrote them out in the lounge and posted them. The Nineveh had its own photo-relay projector, so they would reach the Earth in a few hours. The trade paper arrived from Jefferson in Barsoom and she took it out to the garden to read. The Styth followed her everywhere, looking bored.

Paula read half the paper and skimmed the second half. She went back into the hotel, her Styth shadow close behind. As she passed the restaurant off the lobby, she caught sight of the Akellar, sitting at the bar.

The bar stools on either side of him were conspicuously vacant. She went to the one on his left. In the antiqued mirror behind the bar she saw everybody else in the room watching them. The Akellar put his glass down. He beckoned and the barman hurried toward them. The Styth with the nose wire, Sril, stayed about ten feet away.

Paula said, "Why is he following me around?"

The man behind the bar poured whiskey into his glass. The Akellar gestured to Sril, who left. "You're here alone, I wouldn't want something happening to you. Somebody might blame it on me." His gaze caught on something in the mirror. She looked; he was watching a girl come into the bar. While the girl crossed the room, met other people, took off her coat and sat down, the Styth looked her over inch by inch. The barman turned to Paula.

"Can I get you something, dear?"

If she had been a Martian he would have called her *miss*. She said, "Do you have ice cream?"

"Sure."

"A brandy float."

He sauntered off behind the bar. The Akellar, with nothing else to look at, was watching her. He said, "I haven't seen that other—that white woman around. Your friend."

"My friend. You mean Cam Savenia? She left."

He liked that; he made an approving sound in his chest. "You know her, don't you?" he said, and stopped, his eyes on the mirror again. Another pretty woman was coming into the bar.

Paula sat back. The barman put a bell-glass of brandy and ice cream in front of her, and she paid him. The Styth ignored her; he was staring at women. She smothered her irritation. She saw a way to use what he was giving away about himself. She took the spoon out of the glass and sipped the creamy brandy. The object of his stare had disappeared out of the room and he turned back to her.

"What's that you're drinking?"

She spooned up ice cream and brandy and held it out to him. He put his head back to look at it, suspicious, and finally opened his mouth and let her feed him. She said, "I worked for Cam once. We don't know each other very well."

He savored the ice cream. "That's good. What is it?"

"Ice cream." She took another sip of the brandy, cooled and sweetened with the melting milky dessert. He turned sideways on the stool, facing her, his elbow on the bar. She said, "I—," and broke off. She had lost his attention again to a woman leaving the bar.

"I can't get used to all these women going around with their faces uncovered," he said. He reached for his glass. Paula spooned up another bite of the ice cream. She started to eat it, but his eyes followed it, and she offered it to him. He ate it eagerly.

"Mars is a strange place," she said. She swirled the brandy in the glass. "I have these fish in my wall, swimming around. Of course, this being Mars, they're probably plastic." She drank the last of the liquor and pushed the glass away across the bar. "Come up and look at them and tell me if they're plastic."

Now his eyes were fixed on her, and he smiled. The smile made him look much younger. He said, "Do you have any of that whiskey left?"

"I have another bottle."

He got up off the bar stool. They went out the door.

. . .

The sun was going down. Long hazy light struck across the garden and penetrated in shafts into the room. She pulled the curtains closed and poured them each a glass of whiskey. They sat on the couch opposite the aquarium.

"What is the Earth like?" he asked. "Like this?"

She shook her head. She was sitting in the curved limb of the couch. "The Earth is the original of which Mars is the copy."

"Then it is like this."

She put her glass down on the table, untouched. Toeing off her shoes, she folded her legs under her. "No. You'd have to go to the Earth to see the difference. Do Styths kiss?"

"I don't know. I don't recognize the word."

She knelt beside him, facing him, and leaned forward and put her mouth against his. His mouth was unresponsive. She touched his lips with her tongue, her hand on his shoulder, and his arm went around her waist. A rush of his heavy metallic scent surrounded her. He twisted, pushing her down under him on the couch.

"You're hurting me." She could not breathe. Her face was smothered against his shoulder. "You're too heavy."

He straightened up on his arms. She could scarcely breathe in the dense fragrance he was giving off. When she kissed him again, his skin was warm, almost feverish. They got up and undressed. His body was perfect. Dressed, he simply looked massive. His broad chest swelled into his back, the muscle and bone smoothly shaped down to his long waist. He had an erection. They lay down side by side on the couch. His skin warmed her. While she explored him with her hands and her mouth she tried to get used to his scent. All in silence they joined together. His eyes closed, as if he were doing it alone. She rubbed herself down on his thick stalk, her hand on his hip, intent on the swelling tension in her groin.

The couch was too narrow. They went down to the floor and handled each other, moving around each other almost without speaking. He was so tall she could not kiss his face when he was inside her. The watery light from the aquarium rippled over his chest. She touched him all over, to see what he liked. Her body swelled closed around him. He took her hips in his hands and drove himself into her, gasping.

"Oh, Jesus."

She sat back, pleased, her legs across him, and gave him the full tumbler of whiskey. His arms stretched out over his head. For a long while they stayed as they were, the man lying on his back on the floor, and Paula beside him, without saying anything. She felt revenged on him for his condescension. The videone buzzed. She ignored it and it buzzed again.

"Aren't you going to take that?" he said.

"It's just my boss."

"What would he do if he knew we were here like this?" His hand slipped over her thigh.

"Not he, she. Sybil Jefferson."

"How many men have you had?"

"You aren't a personal friend."

His fingers pressed and stroked over the inside of her thigh. His claws grazed her. "Which means what?"

"That I won't answer a personal question."

"A lot." Patterns of light from the aquarium lay across his face like a mask. "How did I do?"

"You didn't talk," she said, "which I liked."

He turned his face toward the aquarium. He was cooling off, and she swung her legs across his body and sat beside him. His cock had drawn back inside the sheath of his foreskin. With her fingers she traced the heavy muscles of his chest. He had no hair on his chest. He wasn't perfect after all. He put his hand on her hand and pressed her palm against him.

"So it's not personal, this—" He caressed himself with her hand. "Then it's business? Are you trying to sell me something?"

"Sell you something?"

"I've heard an anarchist can sell anything to anybody."

"What do you want?"

"The only thing you have that interests me is that whiskey." He folded his arms behind his head. His scent had disappeared.

"Good," she said. "I'll send you a case every aphelion for the rest of your life. Courtesy of the Committee."

His teeth flashed in a white smile. "Are you serious?"

"I'll make it two cases."

"Do it."

She touched his stomach. His skin was velvet black. "Do you believe in god?"

"I believe in Planck's Constant and the speed of light. Truth at 186,000 miles per second. What else are you going to sell me? A little philosophy?"

"The Council wants to establish permanent embassies with the Empire."

"We don't treat with other governments. The only law in the system is Styth, the rest of you are all outlaws. There's nothing you can offer us except to submit to us."

"You didn't listen to me."

He pushed her hand away from him. "I don't have to listen to you—you listen to me."

"I said that was what the Council wants, not what I want."

Between his round black eyes two short vertical lines appeared. He rolled smoothly onto his feet. "You think you can talk around me." His clothes were scattered about the room, and he collected them. Paula sat watching the fish. He sat on the couch and pulled his leggings on. Instead of underwear he wore a kind of cup to protect his organs. He hung a medal on a chain around his neck. The marking in the heavy disk was the sign of the fish.

She said, "Actually, what I want is to make you rich."

He was putting his shirt on. His head emerged through the neck, and he stood up and tugged the shirt down over his body. He sat back down on the couch. She turned her gaze away from him, back to the red stream of fish in the wall.

"How are you going to do that?" he said.

"There's no trade now between the Middle Planets and your city, is there?"

"No. You have nothing I want."

"But there is a lot of smuggling."

"Not much."

"Whatever you say." She watched the fish reverse direction, perfectly aligned. "I could get you a report on it. We estimate about forty to fifty thousand dollars' worth of goods come and go between Matuko and the Earth every Earthish month."

"That's exaggerated."

"Suppose you brought the smuggling inside the law and controlled it yourself, you'd make that money, instead of the smugglers getting it all."

He said nothing. She turned around to face him. He had his belt in his hands; after a moment he seemed to remember it was there and rose and slung it around his waist.

"You're brave," he said, "offering me a bribe."

"That's your word."

"Why would I sell my people for a couple of thousand nigger dollars?"

She leaned on the couch. "We can negotiate you a contract that would guarantee you one million dollars the first year, a caesium year, climbing to ten million a year by the fifth year."

There was a long silence. She drew with her fingernail in the yellow plush of the couch. He sat down again to put on his boots.

"It's still a bribe."

"Whatever you want to call it. Why don't you go think about it?"

"I don't have to think about it," he said, and walked out. In his wake the door slammed shut, rebounded, and bounced off its track. She tried to shut it but it was stuck halfway open. She took a shower, wrapped herself up in her robe, and went out to the front room again. Jefferson had worked him out, sight unseen: his key was money. She turned out the lights, barricaded the bedroom door with chairs, and went to sleep.

Tanuojin's bassoon voice said, "You mean she seduced you?"

"I wouldn't have thought of it myself, looking at her—she's nothing to look at, is she? What do you think they're trying to do?"

"They're trying to buy you."

Paula was washing her hair in the bathroom sink. The soap smelled of egg. The Akellar's voice came up from the recorder on the floor by her feet. "How long is a caesium year?"

"It's a lie. She's lying. Why do you go soft-headed over any woman who sleeps with you?"

"Ah, shut up."

"Can you keep her out of her room long enough for me to search it?"

Paula rinsed her hair and turned on the dryer in the ceiling. The Akellar said, "I can think of something to do with her. And she doesn't cost me fifty dollars an hour, either."

A strange voice said, "Jesus, it's hot." "Jesus" was their favorite expletive. They pronounced the J like a hard g.

"You think it's hot in here, stud, stand out there in the radiation." That was Sril, the small one with the wire in his nose. His voice grew louder. "Akellar, I see you get along better with that Earthish woman now." Several men laughed.

"No," the Akellar said. "She gets along better with me."

She took the recorder into the sitting room and listened to it while she collected everything she did not want Tanuojin to find: the wires from the recorder, the devices Savenia had left. The men talked about their ship and the Martian food, which they loved.

"How long is a caesium year?"

"Saba, don't listen to her!"

"I asked you a question."

Sulky: "Around twelve hundred watches."

The Akellar and Tanuojin puzzled her. They talked like equals, intimately, not the way the Akellar talked to the other men, but now and then he leaned over Tanuojin, and Tanuojin always yielded. Now the deep, surging voice said, "I called the ship, while you were down there letting that woman make use of you."

"Ah?"

"Kobboz says they—"

The wire ran out. She loaded the recorder again, packed everything she was removing from the suite into her satchel, and took it down to the lobby.

"My door is broken," she said to the clerk.

He was bent over the desk doing the anagram in the ten o'clock hourly. He did not look up. "Did it involve a Styth?"

"Unh—"

"We'll have to move you to another room." He circled an answer in red ink. "We're leaving all that damage for the underwriters' inspector."

"Never mind." She put the satchel on the desk. "I want this kept in the vault."

He took it away. She went into the restaurant to eat her lunch. While she was sitting at a table near the windows eating a minji and drinking coffee, Lilly M'ka came up and took the chair opposite her.

"The one with the yellow eyes is back."

"I know that," Paula said.

"Yes, I guess you have your own ways of finding things out." The whore straightened the ruffles on her halter top. Paula envied her tiny waist. "I hope you don't plan on taking any more of my clients."

"Do you have any more like that?" Paula bit into the minji.

"He's good, isn't he?"

Paula swallowed a mouthful of bread and sausage and hot sauce. "He has a beautiful body."

"He's a very handsome man. Or haven't you looked that far?"

Over the girl's shoulder, at the far end of the room, Paula saw the Akellar coming in the door. "You sound as if you're in love with him."

"I have a thing for men who pay cash."

He had seen them; he was coming toward them. Lilly said, "Besides, he—" and Paula jabbed her chin at him, and the whore turned and saw him. She sat back. The Styth stood beside the table, between them, looking from one to the other.

"Hello, Saba," Lilly said. She got up, taking her shoulderbag off the back of her chair.

"Hello, Lilly."

"See what I mean?" Lilly said to Paula, and went off across the bar to the door. The Akellar sat down in her place.

"Comparing things?"

Paula drank her milk. "What do we have in common? I thought you were giving up on me." She pushed her plate out of the way. Lilly was wrong: his features were too coarse to be handsome.

"I may give you another chance," he said. "After all, you're just a woman."

"You broke my door."

"One of my crew will fix it. Come outside with me. It's like a hot-box in here."

She went with him out to the park. She had gotten up well after noon, and the sun was falling toward the horizon, the domelight was coming on. He stayed in the cool and shade of the great deodar trees that lined the golf course. The ground was deep in spongy grass, even where the trees' cloaking branches kept the light out all day long. Paula lagged behind him. On the far side of the path he stopped to let her catch up. Two Martians in knee-length pants, a man and a woman, were coming toward her. Another man in the hotel's livery pulled a cart full of golf clubs after them. She paused to let them pass.

"Stunning little negress," the woman said.

The man had seen the Akellar, standing in the deep shadow on the far side of the path. He hurried the woman on. Paula went up beside the Styth, and the Martians gave her another, harder look.

"They hate us together," he said. "They don't like us one at a time but they hate us together."

The sun had gone down. They went into the cool open ground of the golf course. Paula walked fast and he walked slow. He bent to take her hand.

"Are you married?" she said.

"Four times. Two of them are back with their fathers where I should have left them in the first place."

Holding his hand made her uncomfortable. They were coming to a bridge and she used the chance to free herself. She went ahead of him across the bridge.

"How many wives are you allowed?"

"As many as I can keep." He kicked at the ground, tore up a piece of turf, and bent to touch it. "My father had twenty-three wives. He was a greedy son of a bitch." He pulled apart the bit of turf in his hands. "This isn't real, is it?"

"Nothing here is real, Akellar."

There was no wind; the Nineveh dome was too small for wind. The golf course swept off before them, blue-white in the domelight, toward the white three-story block of the hotel. The yellow glow of windows studded it. He said, "We want to go to the Earth."

"We. Who's *we?*"

"I. *Ybix*. My ship."

She went off down the smooth lawn, her back to him. "What's a ybix?"

"It's a fish." He caught up with her. His cold fist closed around her hand again. "It's one of my family emblems." His fingers were cold. His grasp held her too close to his side; she felt like a child next to his height and bulk.

"What was your ship's Martian name?"

"Martian? My father built *Ybix.*"

"I thought your ship was Martian."

"The hull was Martian-built. Metal is scarce, in Styth. My father captured the original ship off Jupiter and tore out her guts and rebuilt her." The golf course dipped away. She scrambled down the grassy bank beside him. He said, "Martian ships are fuel-driven. Laser-imploded hydrogen plasmas. My ships are crystal-driven. There isn't a ship in the Council Fleet that could stay in the same space with *Ybix* for five minutes."

She tugged on her hand in his grip. He tightened his hold on her. In the dark sweep of grass, the sand trap in the embankment glinted white and blue. They sat down in the cool sand.

"Why don't you like me to touch you?"

"Please let go of my hand."

At last he did. She clasped her fingers over her knees. He said, "You weren't faking—back in your room. You liked it then."

"I just don't favor being dragged around, that's all."

He kissed her. She showed him a few more ways to use his tongue and his lips. He began to shed his scent. That reminded her of the night before, which excited her; she enjoyed the smell. They lay back in the sand. She fingered his shirt. It was heavy, some kind of armor.

He said, "Are you going to take me to the Earth?"

"I can try. It would help if it looked as if you were cooperating."

"By taking your bribe?" He unfastened her blouse down the back. She let him peel her clothes down. His body heat kept her warm. "Are all Earthish women this little?"

She laughed. Unbuckling his belt, she tugged on his shirt. "Take this off."

"What was your mother like?"

"Flat-chested." She watched him strip himself. His body was magnificent. "My mother is an architect. She has all the best qualities of an I-beam." She propped herself up on one elbow.

"What about your father?"

"He was crazy. He collected skulls. And slept in his clothes. I think he was flat-chested too, but I never saw him with his clothes off."

They kissed again, lying in the sand, their arms around each other. Behind them, down the golf course, there was a long shrill whistle.

He rolled away from her, sitting up, and said an obscenity in his own language. She asked, "What was that?"

"Marus. One of my crew." He reached for his shirt. "Cover yourself up." She dressed. Putting two fingers into his mouth he whistled so loud she winced at the pain to her ears. A man she did not know jogged up to them.

"Akellar, there's a fight in the public room."

"Shit." He turned to her. "Stay here." He ran off, Marus on his heels, down the long dark fairway.

Paula stood up. The two men disappeared in the trees. She went after them at a trot. The light gravity filled her with energy. She stretched her legs, running as fast as she could, and ran herself off-balance and fell rolling. When she sat up, her head seemed to turn around in circles. Maybe that was why the Styths moved so slowly. She walked down through the gardens.

At the end of a row of hedges was the entrance to the Ninus, the club's blue-sash restaurant. She pushed the door open and went in. The small lobby was massed with people, men in black velvet tunics and women in long white gloves. They were staring down a short flight of steps into the restaurant. She could not see what they were looking at. She went into the narrow lobby. The cushioned red flooring yielded under her feet. Behind the crowd, next to a double door, was a placard on an easel:

Readings from Marlowe's *Tamburlaine*
and Ravishavanji's *The War Bride*

She went between two fancy-dressed men to look where the crowd was looking.

"So help me, I'll shoot."

The people around her murmured in excitement. They were crowded around the head of the stairs. A woman blocked Paula's way, bare white shoulders above a low white dress. She went by to the carpeted steps.

Three steps led down to the restaurant. The tables near the bar had been shoved up against the wall, the white linen rucked up, and the crystal knocked over. On the far side of the room, a young man, a Martian, was standing on a chair, a gun in his hand.

"Don't come near me—"

The gun was aimed at the four Styths ranged along the bar to Paula's left. The Akellar was among them. In his own language, he said, "Somebody has to get behind him and distract him. Sril—"

"Any of you come near me," the man with the gun cried, "I'll kill you." He was very young, no more than twenty, and his face glistened with sweat.

The crowd shifted around Paula. More people were coming down into the lobby to watch. Crowded, she went down the two steps to the level of the restaurant. Plaintive, a woman behind her said, "I can't see."

The Styths were moving. Sril went across the restaurant, through the scattered tables, and the others spread out between him and the Akellar like a cordon. The young man on the chair followed them with his gun, pointing it now at one and now at another. He was too frightened to shoot.

"This I have to see," a man in the crowd murmured. "They'll hash the poor kid." Paula licked her lips. She went down the steps into a miasma of coppery Styth temper. The big Styth with the scar on his cheek stood in front of her, his back to her. She passed him, and he jumped.

"Akellar."

The man with the gun had seen her. He jerked around. His foot slipped on the chair seat and he caught at the back to hold himself still. The gun was shaking, aimed at her. She walked slowly toward him, her eyes fixed on his face. The art was to keep moving. If she stopped to talk it would be hard to start toward him again. "Paula," the Akellar said, and she waved at him to be quiet.

"Stop right there," the young man cried.

"I'm from the Committee," she said. She was only five feet from him. His mouth opened, red and wet, and his eyes shifted past her toward his audience. In the silence she heard someone behind her smother a cough.

"Don't come any closer—"

"You'll be a real hero, won't you, if you shoot an unarmed woman?"

He shifted the gun to one side, to aim past her at the Styths, and she moved to stay in front of it. She reached out her hand for it, her eyes on his face. "Give me the gun," she said, almost whispering, so that no one else could hear her. "You are interfering in a Committee negotiation, and you're making me angry." She took hold of the gun behind the wide bell-shaped muzzle. He pulled back, and she let go.

"I'm not going anywhere."

"Oh, yes, you are. If you stay here, the police will be here, with gas and spray and probably dogs."

She took hold of the weapon again. He was shaking so hard she was afraid the gun would go off by accident. He swallowed, his gaze fixed on hers, and let go of the gun.

With it in her hand, she sighed, relaxing, and felt the quiver in her knees. She looked around them. In the back of the dark restaurant, past Sril, a red sign shone marking the exit. She said, "Come on," and took him by the arm and led him on a crooked course through the tables.

"Where do you live?" she said. They passed tables left in the middle of the meal and reached the door under the red light.

"Barsoom. I only came for the—" His face was deeply lined, like a wax mask. "You're really from the Committee?"

"I'll send you a bill." She pulled open the door and let him go out ahead of her. The crowd was streaming back into the restaurant. The Akellar watched her over their heads. She went after the young man along the concrete walk toward the front of the hotel. His gun was in her hand. She held it carefully, afraid of setting it off. They went up a flight of steps. At the top was the curved parking apron at the main entrance.

"There. I'll get you a cab."

They went along the walk past the lobby. He said, "I could have taken them."

"Are you crazy? They have inch-long claws. A couple of them weigh over three hundred pounds."

"That's why I brought the gun." He reached for it in her hand. "Let me have it back."

"No." She went ahead of him toward the line of cabs parked along the edge of the apron. He followed her, talking.

"I have to have it. It's my father's. He'll kill me if he finds out I took it."

She stopped beside the cab at the head of the line, and the driver came around to open the door. She said to the boy, "Get in there and I'll give it to you. Go on. And don't come back, or you'll get hurt."

"I can—"

"Get in there."

He climbed into the back seat of the cab. She shut the door on him and gave the gun to the driver. "He lives in Barsoom. Make his father pay you."

The driver held the gun by the barrel. "What am I supposed to do with this?"

"Give it to his father." She went into the lobby.

In the dark by the stairs, in the warm dry air, she stood wondering what to do. He had come just to fight a Styth. Bringing a gun he was afraid to shoot. She climbed the stairs. If she were the Akellar she would break off the talks for violations of the safe-conduct, fly away in a righteous huff, and demand all kinds of apologies and sureties before she came back. The door was still jammed half-way open. She went into the dark room. Something moved behind her. Before she could turn, a blow struck her in the head, and she fell.

. . .

She woke in the dark, her head ringing, and sat up. After a moment she dragged herself up to her feet. She could have been lying there for hours. Her head boomed like a drum, and she sat down heavily on the arm of the couch and tried to pull her mind together.

"Go get yourself a drink," the Akellar said, behind her.

She jerked around. He was sitting on the end of the couch; she could just make out his shape.

"Did you hit me?"

"No. You were out when I came."

It had been Tanuojin. She went to the bar and felt out a glass and ice and the bottle of whiskey, without turning on the light. While she was pouring the whiskey, he settled himself on the stool opposite her.

"Whoever it was gave you grace," he said. "Because I had a chance to cool down. If you'd been awake when I got here, I'd have killed you."

"Me. Why?"

"Because you made me look bad."

She gulped down a steadying jolt of the whiskey. Her head pounded, spinning, in an alcoholic rush. She put the glass down. "Well, maybe you are."

He moved, and she tried to elude him, but he was too fast. His grip fastened in her hair. She whined through her teeth. He pressed her face down toward the counter of the bar. She shut her eyes. With her nose against the counter, he said, "You talk too much. You think you're so damned smart, but you don't know about me." With a wrench that burned her whole scalp, he let her go.

She sagged against the bar, tears streaming down her face; her head was stitched with pain. She wiped her eyes. "I learn fast."

"Here." He pushed her glass toward her.

"That makes you feel better?"

"Shall I do it again?"

"No. No." She drank from the glass; it nearly fell out of her fingers. Her eyes were still watering. Her elbows on the bar, she wiped her hands over her face.

He went to the videone and called his suite. She turned the ceiling lights on half-bright. Sitting down on the couch, she stared at the red fish schooling across the wall.

He said, "I want to go to the Earth."

"Maybe you'd better leave me alone for a while."

"I'll decide what I do." He sat down on the other end of the couch and put his feet up on the magazine table. "I've been thinking about this contract you want for me. The only way you could guarantee that much money is if you're talking about trading in crystal. Is that what you mean?"

"Get out."

"Come on. You're such a tough little bitch, are you sulking about getting your hair pulled?"

The fish performed a mathematical turn. She refused to look at the Styth. "All right. Yes, crystal."

"You don't understand what you're getting me into. There's an imperial law in Styth against selling crystal off the Planet. I can't stand against the whole rest of the rAkellaron."

"We can arrange contracts for them too. They can all get rich." She put her head back against the couch and shut her eyes.

He grunted. "I don't know if I want that. But it makes it easier. Except that everybody's going to ask why we should supply you with crystal so you can fill the Council Fleet with ships that are as good as ours."

"The Council Fleet has about eight ships. The people you are fighting is the Martian Army."

"Is there a difference?"

Sril appeared in the doorway, made a salute to his master, and knelt down to look at the foot of the door. He opened a little roll of tools across the floor. The Akellar said, in his own language, "Where is Tanuojin?"

"Back in the trap."

The Akellar turned back toward Paula. "I can't promise anything. If you take me to the Earth, I'll try to arrange this contract." He put his feet on the floor and rose. "That's fair, isn't it?"

"Whatever you say, Akellar."

"You come down to my place at seven and have dinner with me and we'll talk about the fine points. There's somebody you have to meet." He stepped wide past Sril and out the door.

Paula was holding her breath. She let it out in a little sigh. Sril stood up, lifted the door, and set it down carefully, watching the foot. With one hand he pushed it in and out of the wall. He stooped to put his tools back into the roll.

"Who do I have to meet?" she asked.

He made a vague gesture. "I no—I know not." When he struggled with the Common Speech his voice was pitched higher than when he spoke his own tongue. He said, "That you did, in the—the feed place—you are brave, Mendoz'."

"Your boss didn't think so."

"He thinked so," Sril said. "Good leave." He went.

It was Tanuojin she was supposed to meet. When she went into the Akellar's bedroom his length was arranged across an oversized inflated chair, his back to the window, and his legs reaching halfway across the room. The Akellar gestured at him.

"That's my lyo."

"Hello," she said, and got no answer. The room was freezing cold. She was glad she had worn her jacket. The other Styth's yellow eyes stared at her, unfriendly. The balloon chair looked too small for him. The Akellar took her by the arm and maneuvered her to another chair.

She sat down. "I just spent half an hour on the videone with my boss. When do you want to go to the Earth?"

The two men exchanged a quick look, and the Akellar smiled. "We have a rendezvous to make first. Where are you taking us?"

Ketac and another young man brought in a hotel cart full of bottles and glasses. She said, "Anywhere you want. New York is as much of a capital as we have."

Tanuojin said, "What about the ship?" He wore the same long gray shirt, the boots and leggings and slot-buckled belt as the Akellar. He had no order medal. One of the young men took him a glass of ice-water.

Paula said, "You'll have to leave the ship parked in orbit around Luna. That's going to be a kind of a problem. The government of Luna—"

The Akellar's head flew up. "I thought you didn't have governments."

"Not on the Earth. Luna is ruled by a military clique. They're paranoid about their security."

The two men looked at each other once again. Ketac brought her a glass full of sparkling cider. He avoided her eyes. Although she was tempted to make some remark to him about their previous meeting, she did not want to embarrass him in front of his father. The cider was cold and delicious and she drank half of it before she put it down.

"What about when we're in your Planet?" the Akellar said. "What about security there? It must be a pretty damn dangerous place, all you people doing whatever comes into your heads all the time."

She crossed her legs at the ankles and folded her hands on her stomach. "You'll be safe as babies, believe me."

"How can you promise that? You've seen what's happened here. Like that boy in the restaurant."

"He was a Martian." Now the two young men were bringing in a cart of steaming food. She said, "The Martians admire force, so do you, naturally you'd get in trouble."

"But you don't use force," Tanuojin said.

"No. We're very peaceful people."

Behind the drooping strings of his mustaches his mouth curled into a sneer. "I don't believe you."

"If you knew anything about it, you wouldn't have to rely on faith, would you?"

That made him angry; his off-color eyes glittered. The Akellar was watching him, amused. Ketac brought his father a dish, and he picked through it, eating neatly with his claws. Tanuojin said, "If you won't use force, you can't defend yourselves. You'd be slaves. And you would deserve it."

"We don't use force, we don't submit to it, either. It isn't easy, living on the Earth. Most people can't do it." Now Ketac was serving Tanuojin, or trying to serve him, but the tall man ignored the dish offered to him.

He said to her, "If it's true, then it's vile."

"No," she said. "If it's true, then you're wrong, and that's vile. To you."

"Are you trying to offend me?"

"I'm just talking." Ketac brought her the dish. She shook her head at him. She did not want to look stupid trying to eat like a Styth. Tanuojin's face was rigid with bad temper. Abruptly he got up and walked out of the room.

The Akellar sent the boys away with a gesture. Fishing a spoon out of the cart, he brought her a dish of lamb and sat on the floor beside her chair with another dish. He said, "I knew that would happen. He hates women."

"I'm glad it's not personal."

He laughed. They ate in silence; when she had done, he took her bowl, still half-full, and finished it, and went back to the cart for more. She watched him eat that, amazed at his appetite.

"He isn't married? Your lyo."

"No. His wife is dead. Actually I think he hates everybody, except me. But he's brilliant, he's read all kinds of books." He chuckled under his breath. "And he hates to be wrong."

She watched the big man chew his way through another bowl of the lamb. He had enjoyed setting her against Tanuojin. Finally he put the bowl down and belched and patted his stomach.

"Give me one hundred fifty watches between now and when we come to the Earth."

She divided in her head. "All right. That's about six weeks, our time."

"I promise I won't shoot anybody in the meanwhile." He went over to the serving cart for a towel to wash his hands. "Sleep with me," he said.

"I have to work," she said to the cart. She followed him and drank the last of the cider from the bottle.

"Do it next watch."

"I don't have the time."

He pushed her away. "Go."

Her door was open. Heavy synthetic music blared through into the hall. She stopped in the doorway. Sril was cross-legged on the floor, inhaling smoke through a tube from a small bowl on the floor in front of him. Ketac sat on the couch. The air was sweet with opium. Ketac looked asleep; his cheeks fluttered. She took her clothes off in the bathroom and went into the shower.

The Styths' taste in music was distinct and narrow. When the synthesizer gave way to something more complex, they hunted through the radio and found some hard rock. The music reached her clearly even in the washroom. While she was drying off, the music stopped and a shocked Martian voice said, "What's going on in here?"

Pulling on her robe, she went to the threshold of the front room. The music blasted on again. The big scarred man was standing in front of the videone, protecting it from the Nineveh's manager. The Martian's face was furred with a night's beard. He looked about him, aghast. Paula wrapped her belt around her waist and tied it. The booming music hurt her ears. Sril and Ketac stooped over the opium heater. The Martian wheeled on Paula.

"I'm holding you responsible for this." He shook his finger in her face. "You brought them here—"

The scarred man said, in Styth, "Don't let him turn the music off."

The manager strode out the door. Paula looked after him down the corridor, worried. Narcotics were illegal on Mars. Sril raised his head. He was hunched over the opium bowl; he held the long tube in his fingers like a paintbrush. "Ketac," he said, in his own language, "find out what that was all about."

Ketac was slumped on the floor, his forehead resting on one raised knee. He made no response. Paula knelt beside Sril. The music was so loud she had to shout.

"Sril. You have to get out of here. He's gone for help."

Sril laughed. The whites of his eyes were stained with red. "He needs help."

"You don't know them. He'll bring a security team—"

Ketac lifted his head. His eyes were only half-open. His mouth hung slack. "You think we can't take their whole army—"

She shook her head. "I can't understand Styth in this racket."

Sril said, "We fight two Martians each. Guns too." He held up two fingers. "Maybe three." With effort he added another finger.

"I'm sure you can. That only makes it worse, don't you see?" She took his hands, trying to make him pay attention to her. "Sril, they'll throw us all in jail."

"We can fight anybody," Ketac said. "Anybody."

Sril straightened up. "Yes, but we shouldn't make trouble for her. Come on. Bakan—"

Beneath the thunder of the music there was a pounding on the door. "Open up in there! This is Security!"

Paula looked around for some place to hide them. Ketac started to his feet and sat down hard. Sril bent to help him.

"Open this door!"

"In here." She pointed to the bedroom door.

Bakan and Sril lifted Ketac up by the arms and hauled him away. She went around the couch to turn off the videone. The bedroom door shut, and the front door crashed open. The Martian hotelman and three policemen in gray bugle-boy uniforms charged in a wedge into the room. Paula went between them and the bedroom. Three bell-shaped pistols veered toward her.

"Where are they?"

She looked up at him. "Who?"

The red furred face of the hotelman puffed up fat with rage. "You have twelve hours to get yourself and those animals—those—" He was shouting in her face. She blinked.

"Mr. Lanahan, this is opium!"

The Martian's windy voice rose to a shriek. "You'll get thirty years in prison for this, if it takes me that long to put you there."

"What is this?" The Akellar came in the broken door behind them.

Lanahan swung around. The Styth walked into their midst. The three guns swiveled from Paula to the bigger target. He ignored them. To Lanahan he said, "You're bothering her. Leave her alone."

The Martian said, stiff, "I don't exactly think you—"

"Put your hands up!" a policeman cried.

The Akellar got Lanahan by the wrist and swung him around between him and the gunman, one hand on his collar and one on his arm. Paula stood where she was. She glanced at the bedroom door. The police backed up, their guns pointed at their chief's belly.

"Mr. Lanahan—"

"Do as he says—" Lanahan stood up on his toes, his arm twisted up behind him.

"Out," the Akellar said.

The police backed out the door. The Styth lifted Lanahan in big steps toward the threshold. He said, "Don't talk back, nigger, it's painful, see? See?" Lanahan screeched. The Akellar thrust him out the door. Paula went up beside the Styth to look out to the corridor. Lanahan sagged down on his knees, cradling his hand to his chest. He sobbed, his face gray with pain. The policemen stood around him. The Akellar lifted the door back onto its tracks and slammed it shut.

Sril came up to them. "I'm glad you're here. Ketac has fallen out in her bed." Bakan stood in the bedroom doorway.

"Go back to the trap. We'd better leave. I was getting a little tired of this Planet anyway."

Paula went into her bedroom. Ketac lay sprawled on his face on her bed. The Akellar came after her.

"You can't free slaves, you see? They just forget who they are and make trouble." He sat on the edge of the bed and shook his son. "Wake up, crumb."

"They aren't slaves. We don't keep slaves."

Ketac was limp as rope. If he was awake, he gave no evidence. The Akellar said, "They talk like slaves. They work like slaves. The difference is when they get old and sick you don't take care of them." He heaved his son up across his shoulders.

She followed him out to the front room. Ketac's head and arms hung down his father's back. She gathered up the opium heater and the straw and piled them into the crook of the big man's arm. "You have a diplomatic license and I don't."

"Will you be safe here?"

"Yes."

"I won't leave you here if you're going to have trouble."

She raised her head, smarting. "How did I ever get along without you?"

He started to say something. Instead he left, angling his child's long legs through the door.

The cruise ship's corridor was just wide enough for one person. Paula held her suitcase awkwardly before her, reading the numbers on the brown sliding doors on either side. At 113, she knocked.

"Who is it?" Bunker called, inside, and she pushed the door back and went in.

Two stacks of beds filled the little stateroom. Bunker sat on the end of the near lower shelf, his shirt off. A medic in a white coat was pasting sensors to his chest. Paula threw her bags on the upper bed. The phony gravity held her feet down to the floor as if she had glue on her shoes. She looked curiously at Bunker.

"How was it?"

The medic said, "Breathe in, Browne."

Bunker inhaled. She wondered if he ever told his real name to strangers. "Interesting. I've never been in a deep-space ship before." The medic made notes in a notepad.

"Are you Paula Mendoza?"

"Yes."

"I'm supposed to give you a physical."

Paula sat down on the lower bed opposite Bunker. She took off her jacket, unsnapped the pocket, and pulled out a piece of paper, which she gave to Bunker. She said, "You look pale."

"He's anemic," the medic said. "Free fall and rich atmosphere."

"You were in free fall on *Ybix*? What was it like?"

Bunker was reading the rough draft of the agreement. "This is solid check. Mendoza, I don't know how you did it." He folded up the paper and gave it back to her.

"He's getting what he wants."

"He's getting what he thinks he wants."

Paula looked around the room. There were no ports. The walls were covered in textured beige plastic. It was smaller than the bath at the Nineveh. The medic put his computer on the bed and gave Bunker a towel to wash the sensor paste off his chest. Paula pulled her shirt off over her head. She turned her back to the medic.

"Did you get to know any of the crew?"

"All the ones inboard." Bunker put on his shirt. He stood and pulled a ring in the beige wall, and a panel opened out. The medic held something cold against her back. Bunker said, "Some of them are real compulsives."

"Is he honest?" She glanced over her shoulder at the medic.

"Yes. Breathe in."

She breathed deep. Bunker took a small film can from the shelf in the wall. Paula reached for it. The medic thumped her back. The end of a strip of film stuck out of the can. She pulled out half a roll of pictures. The first several frames were exteriors of a kite-shaped spaceship. On its metal back was painted a black three-pointed star.

The door rattled under a rapid knock. "Who is it?" Bunker said, and Jefferson came in, squeezing sideways through the door.

"Well, Richard, you look fit."

Paula held up photographs of a spherical room. "What's this?"

"The bridge."

"They let you go all over the ship? Hello, Jefferson."

Jefferson slid between the medic and Bunker and sat down on the bed beside Paula. The medic's fingers pressed gently under Paula's jaw. He felt along her shoulder.

"You're tense, relax."

Jefferson unbuttoned the front of her suit. The frilly blouse underneath made her breast look a yard wide. "Mendoza was run out of the Nineveh Club," she told Bunker. "After only five days."

"The food was awful," Paula said.

Bunker said, "Mendoza, for six days I've had nothing to eat but chalk buttons and water."

She looked at film of a winding tubular corridor. Jefferson said, "I gained five pounds sitting in a hotel room waiting for Mendoza's infrequent calls. I think we all suffered appropriately."

Paula gave her the film and the draft of the treaty. The medic was writing in his notebook. She turned to Bunker.

"You went all over *Ybix*? What's it like?"

"A Mylar wormhole. And *all over* isn't very far."

The old woman covered her right eye with her hand. She held the single typed page of the agreement out to read it. "My. What's this scrawl here?"

"That's his signature."

Jefferson's head wagged. "Fair, for a first draft. In five days."

The medic stabbed Paula's finger with a metal clip. He picked up the blood in a long glass straw. She said, "It doesn't mean much. He talks for his own city, and that's all. There was another man down there, Tanuojin—"

Bunker lay down on his back along the narrow bed. His shirt was unbuttoned. His bony chest looked hard as a carapace. "I heard all about him. *Ybix*'s second officer. They call him The Creep. Not exactly the most popular man with the crew. Is he the Akellar's brother?"

"His lyo. It's a sworn friendship. Remember, Kary said something about it."

"And is he an Akellar himself?"

"I think so."

The medic straightened. "That's all, Mendoza." He sealed up his computer. "He's anemic." He turned to the door. "And she's pregnant." He went out. Paula stared stupidly at the dark panel shutting in the wall.

Bunker and Jefferson burst out laughing. Paula said, "No," and they roared.

Jefferson said, "Paula, you'll have to apply for a bonus for hazardous duty." Bunker howled. He gasped for breath; tears ran down his face.

Paula put her hands up to her cheeks. Jefferson said, chuckling, "I'm sorry, Mendoza, but it's terribly funny. Here, have a mint."

Bunker wiped his eyes. "So that's how you did it."

She bared her teeth at him. "You take over. I'd like to see you handle him, rat."

"I wouldn't get pregnant." He smirked at her, and Jefferson burbled again with laughter. He propped himself up on his elbows. "I've always wished I could, actually. Give it to me, Mendoza, if you don't want it."

Paula leaned against the wall. She put her hand on her stomach. "What would you do with a baby?"

"I'd be very loving. The perfect parent."

She grunted.

"Then when he got to a nice size, I'd cook him and eat him."

Jefferson said, "You did get pregnant at the Nineveh."

Paula's stomach fluttered. She counted days on her fingers. It was only ninety-six hours. The medic couldn't be sure. "That bastard. He didn't even warn me."

Jefferson patted her shoulder. "I'm glad I'm not young. You can have the bottom bunk." She climbed onto the deck above Bunker's head.

"You should have warned him," Bunker said. He folded his arms behind his head. "But you were so busy taking advantage of the poor dumb chump—"

"Shut up," Paula said, between her teeth.

LUNA. Averellus 26.5, 1853

All Luna was built below the surface, thirty decks of halls and rooms cut from the rock. Its only important industry was cryogenics. The natural gravity was weaker even than on Mars. The floors were treated with plastograv. The officer who met the three anarchists at the space port took them through customs, where they changed out of their own clothes into blue and white striped coveralls with their names and photographs on the left breast. With the officer they rode the fast track of the moving sidewalk past blocks of living rooms. Here and there, the walls were painted with flowers and bushes and grass. Most of the people they saw on the sidewalk wore uniforms: the black and white of the Lunar Army, the tan of the Martian Army, now and then the dark blue tunics and white pants of the Interplanetary Police. The ceiling and walls shed an even light. There were no shadows.

Paula rubbed her face. She was tired. The trip from Mars had taken 135 hours. She was space-sick and she could not eat. Bunker tapped her arm. She went after him and Jefferson down a step to the middle track and onto the slow track and to the motionless floor. The officer took them down ten levels in a vertical car.

"We're coming to a security area," he said, smiling. "We'll try to keep the inconvenience to a minimum." The vertical settled to a stop and the doors whirred open. They went out to a small room; the lights came on automatically. Paula looked up at the ceiling. She walked beneath a round lens like an eye that moved to keep her in its field. Jefferson sat down on the sofa. She crossed her legs.

A tall redheaded girl came in, carrying a box. She said, "My name is Karene, I'm your technician." Her voice was meaninglessly intimate, like a nurse's. She took a small box off the bigger box and showed it to them. "A simple radiation detector." One at a time, she ran the device over them, an inch from their bodies. Cleared, they all went down a corridor, single-file, and through a narrow door. When Bunker stepped across the threshold the door buzzed.

"You must be carrying something metal," Karene told him.

"I have two gold fillings," he said.

"That would not register. Oh. It must be your ring."

He took the ring off his little finger and gave it to her. Without it the door passed him. Karene put the ring in her bag. "I'll just hold this for you. Now, if you'll come this way—"

They were in a corridor painted glossy white. Jefferson was already standing on a red dot in the floor. "Oh," Karene said. "You've been here before. Look straight ahead, please."

Paula turned to the slight man beside her. "Gold fillings?"

"I meant it in a lighter spirit than it was taken." The corners of his mouth were stressed in deep lines. She knew that meant he was trying not to smile.

"Next," Karene said, and he took Jefferson's place on the dot. The redheaded girl stood by the wall, pressing buttons.

"Next."

"If that's an X-ray," Paula said, "I'll pass."

"I'm sorry. We can't change our procedures."

"I'm pregnant."

"Oh." Karene's face fell. She stood still a moment, staring at Paula. Nobody said anything. Finally the girl said, "I'll have to ask. Please wait here." She went to the end of the corridor. A door clanged open and shut. Almost at once, a young man in a black uniform came in. He smiled at the three diplomats and stood with his hands clasped behind him. They waited a long while, in silence, until Karene returned.

Her cheerful smile was back. She sent the soldier away. "If you'll come this way, please."

They went down the corridor. Every few steps they passed through a sensor ring built into the walls. Cameras watched them from the ceiling. Paula walked along behind Jefferson.

"If you'll wait in here, General Gordon will see you soon." Karene stood beside an open door. "I hope you enjoy your visit to Luna."

Paula went through into a wood-paneled room. The bulky furniture was made of leather and wood. She crossed the room to a white window frame opposite the door. Beyond lay a green meadow, flecked with yellow and red flowers. The three-dimensional effect was perfect, even to the puffy clouds in the sky. When she looked down, she could see over the outer sill. She touched the window: plastic.

"General Gordon," a mechanical voice announced.

The Luna tyrant came in a side door. He was short and balding. His uniform looked padded. He went behind his desk.

"My apologies if I've kept you waiting. I've been in my chapel."

Jefferson lowered herself into a corner of the overstuffed couch. "Do you know my associates, General? Richard Browne—"

"I know who you are." Gordon did not offer to shake hands.

"And Paula Mendoza."

Gordon gave her an instant's glance and sat down. She rubbed her upper lip with her forefinger. This would not be easy. Gordon fussed with the styli and pencils on his desk blotter while Jefferson made talk. The photograph on the wall behind him was of Marshal David King, the first tyrant of Luna. Between it and the state emblem was a large tau cross.

Jefferson said, "Now we need your cooperation, General."

Bunker was sitting down on the couch beside her. Paula glanced at the window again. Gordon said brusquely, "I do not cooperate with gross immoralism, Miss Jefferson."

"That's a highly subjective comment."

"No, it isn't. You were hired to negotiate a truce with the Styth Empire, not flaunt your godless anarchist immorality all over the Middle Planets."

"General," Bunker said, "from certain perspectives there's no difference."

Gordon jabbed his sharp chin at Paula. He talked almost without moving his lips. "You don't deny she became the mistress of a Styth pirate."

Paula frowned at Bunker. "What's a mistress?"

"What you think."

Jefferson said, "The Matuko Akellar is one of the most powerful men in Styth. If he's a pirate, General, so are you."

Gordon stood up, turning his back on them, his eyes on the cross on the wall. He jammed his fists into his pockets. "My tolerance for insult is very low, Miss Jefferson."

"The Styths are there," Jefferson said. "The interface between them and us will only grow with time. We'd like to develop a relationship that will give everybody a reasonable stake in keeping the peace."

"By seducing them?" Gordon sat down again. His hands danced over his collection of pens. "God is not mocked, Miss Jefferson. The future won't belong to those who suck tit with the devil, but to those who serve god."

Paula thought of the Akellar, flying away into space, sucking tit with Planck's Constant. She raised her eyes; the ceiling was pocked with sensors and cameras.

"Is that his baby?" Gordon barked.

She leveled her gaze at him. "It's my baby." Taking the treaty out of her pocket, she went up to his desk and put the paper down on the blotter. "We have two objectives, a truce and a workable trade agreement. We have the trade. If he comes to the Earth, we'll get the truce."

"A piece of film."

Jefferson said, encarameled, "The Council is enthusiastic."

The general's sharp face was stiff. His cheeks sucked in. To Paula, he said, "What guarantee do you have he'll keep this?"

"He signed it," she said. "He'll keep it. Which is the kind of devil you like to deal with."

"The devil's always handsome to a whore."

Thinking of Lilly M'ka, she had to laugh. His mouth pinched to a slit. He snapped the paper around and read it. She moved away from him. Bunker slid down on the couch, his hands in his lap.

Gordon said, "If this ship comes here, she'll spy on every facet of our operations. Luna is the chief harbor of the Middle Planets. You want to bring in this damned pirate—"

"We'd like you to take a look at the ship, if you can," Bunker said.

"The Martian Fleet's scan failed."

"They looked in the wrong places for the wrong things. I just spent six days inboard *Ybix*, I have some ideas." He crossed the room, past Paula, to the desk. "This ship has accounted for three out of the five patrol craft lost so far in the war. Including both ships lost below Vesta." He dropped the packet of photographs on the blotter.

Gordon took out a laser cutter and opened the envelope. He spilled the photographs onto the desk. "Unh." His white hands held the strips of film up to the ceiling lights. "That's certainly a Manta hull. How do they make it go so fast?"

Jefferson said, "We've been running into static from some of the Martians, General. If they've been talking to you—"

"I don't listen to the Martians." Gordon sprang up again. His hands disappeared in his pockets. "I'll keep these photographs. You can park that ship here for ten days Earth. Send me your recommendations for a scan." He pressed a button on his desk. "Escort these people out." He gathered up the strips of film and left the way he had come.

"That's the kind of devil you don't like to deal with," Bunker said.

"Richard," Jefferson said, "park your mouth."

They were escorted back the way they had come. On the moving sidewalk none of the anarchists spoke. The officer who had brought them took them through customs again. They got back their clothes, sealed into clear plastic bags. Bunker's ring was attached in its own little sack.

With the hundred-odd other passengers they boarded the Earth–Luna shuttle. The benches in the coach section were just wide enough for two people, and they found a pair in the back where no one else was sitting and Bunker and Paula turned one to face the other. Bunker sat down.

"You know, Gordon's cracked. They'll pick him up someday in sackcloth and ashes announcing the Second Coming."

Paula took off her jacket. The bus was stifling hot and smelled of antiseptic. "He seems reasonable to me. So he's a little paranoid." She watched Jefferson fish inside her purse.

"We could sell him a report on his security system," Bunker said. "That would make him even more paranoid."

Jefferson popped out her right eye and split it between her fingers like an egg. She picked out the sensor inside. "They're looking for weapons." She took her false eye from her purse and slipped it into the socket. Paula swallowed, her stomach quivering. On the armor-gray wall of the bus, next to her, was a face drawn in black ink. During the fifteen-hour shuttle flight a graffist could take time on a piece. The hair swirled away in ringlets, which turned into curlicue words.

This floating world is but a phantasm
It is a momentary smoke

She turned her head almost upside down to read it. It sounded like Zen. She would have to look it up. She sat thinking of the thousands of things she had always meant to look up.

"What have you done with that crystal?" Jefferson asked.

Paula straightened on the bench. Bunker said, "What crystal?"

"The Styths gave her a huge energy crystal," Jefferson said.

"Oh?"

"It's in my luggage," Paula said. She glanced over her shoulder. The other passengers were sleeping, or singing; no one was within hearing. She turned back to Jefferson. "He gave it to me. It's mine."

Bunker was frowning at her. The old woman said, "We paid for the knife."

"Why did they give you something that rich?" Bunker said. "The knife is a bauble."

"What do you think—that I took their bribe?" She looked from Jefferson to him. "Because he wanted to keep the knife. Therefore he had to give me something, or he'd have stood in my debt. Crystal isn't worth that much to them."

"Exactly," Jefferson said. "He gave it in return for the knife, which we gave him, not you."

Paula crossed her arms over her chest. She was already resigned to giving up the crystal. She thought of the baby, the Akellar's other little present. She would rather have the crystal. Morose, she stared at the wall.

NEW YORK. April–May 1853

"If he won't do it," An Chu said, "you can go to the women's center. They give you a pill and you go to sleep and when you wake up there's no more baby and you hardly bleed at all."

They walked down a flight of steep gray stairs into the doorway of the building. The corridor beyond was lined with doctors' offices. Paula rubbed her palms on the thighs of her trousers. Her father had hated doctors. *If you go in with a hangnail you have a fifty-fifty chance of coming out alive.* On each door they passed, a white rectangle told the doctor's name, followed by several letters. At *Thomas Adena*, M.D., O.B., GYN., she and An Chu went in.

The waiting room was divided in half. Three women sat on one side, all pregnant, so huge they could hardly sit up straight. Four little children climbed and screamed in the bright-painted bar-gym beyond the railing down the middle of the room. Paula sat on the couch and leafed through a magazine full of pictures of babies. An Chu told the enormous women a web of lies about her sex commune, her thirty-three friends, their fourteen mutual children. They shared recipes for baby food.

The doctor was a man. He took a blood sample and made her lie on her back on a white table so that he could feel around through her insides. An Chu followed them patiently from room to room until they reached his office again. The office walls were painted with sunflowers. On the shelves behind his desk were several models of human guts.

"How do you feel?" the doctor said.

"Awful. I can't eat, I throw up all the time, my breasts are sore, I go to sleep in the middle of dinner. I feel terrible. Maybe I'm just sick."

The doctor shook his head. He was almost as dark as a Styth. His trim little beard reminded her of Tony. "You're two weeks' pregnant. I gather this is unplanned?"

She nodded. Counting back on her fingers, she came to the Nineveh Club.

"Your friend didn't warn you he was natural? He might not know, sometimes the valve opens spontaneously—"

She said, "The father is a Styth." She was on the verge of a hot temper, for no reason, although the sudden hilarity on the doctor's face was a reason.

"A Styth. Where did you find a Styth?" He reached for a long yellow notepad and a pencil.

"On Mars. I'm on the Committee."

He scribbled. "Well, well. And this conception was in the course of a normal relationship?"

"What do you mean by that?"

"I mean he didn't attack you, or—"

"No." She glared at him. "Would you ask that if he were Earthish?"

He smiled at her behind his prim little beard. "He isn't Earthish."

Behind her, An Chu whispered, "Let's get out of here. Let's go to the women's center."

"Are you planning an abortion?" the doctor asked. He rolled his pencil in his fingers. His eyes reflected two little sparks of lamplight.

"Yes."

"Then let me offer you an alternative. I can transplant the fetus into an artificial uterus." He got up. The back of his white coat was wrinkled from the chair. He took a clear plastic model down from a shelf over his head and put it on the desk. "This is constructed to allow the fetus to develop as normally as possible outside the mother. We can observe it at every stage."

The model was threaded with tubes and chambers like a tiltball maze. An Chu whispered, "Come on, Paula, let's go."

The doctor sat down, one hand resting on his plastic mother. "I realize it's a little hard to accept at first—"

Paula said, "What about when it's born?"

"We'll find a suitable foster home and continue observations." His hand patted the uterus, which resounded softly. "You could be saving the lives of hundreds of babies. The first being your own."

They were both watching her. After a while she looked up. "Is it alive?"

"It was alive from the moment of conception. I'd like to examine the father—"

She sat up straight. "He's gone. He's in space."

"Oh. Is he a diplomat too?"

"No, he's a pirate." She was getting angry again, her mood boiling over. She could not look away from the chambered shell under the doctor's hand. An Chu was tapping her foot on the floor. Paula said, "I'll keep it."

The doctor leaned back. His chair creaked. "That's a risky—"

"I don't care. If you can raise it, I can."

"It might be a better idea to transplant it anyway—as it develops, it may—"

"No. I'll keep it."

His mouth crooked behind his mustache, and he took his hand off the plastic uterus. Standing, he put it up on the shelf again. "Do you want me to deliver it?"

"No," An Chu said.

Paula said, "Yes."

"Very well." He sat. "My fee is three hundred fifty dollars."

Paula leaned on the arm of the chair, her gaze on his face. "Why don't you do it for free? After all, you'll be able to observe it almost as well in me as in that thing."

The doctor was writing on his yellow pad. "I'll have to do a lot of tests. There will be some inconvenience."

"Fine."

"Half price. One hundred seventy-five dollars."

"Fifty."

"One hundred."

"Seventy-five."

"Agreed." He nodded at her. "Come into the lab again and let me have a few more blood samples."

"Does Daddy know yet?" Sybil asked. She was driving.

"No," Paula said.

"When are you—"

"I'm not." She crooked her arm over the back of her seat. Jefferson drove at an elephantine pace just above the trees. Other cars swerved in and out around them, barely missing them. In the back seat, Bunker was staring fixedly out the window. Paula had been watching Jefferson since they left the Committee building; the old woman had traveled three miles without referring to any of the side-view mirrors. They were lowering down over the park. Ahead was the beehive shape of the entry port. Sybil beat a long green taxi into the entrance to the parking lot.

Paula sighed. Sybil seesawed the car back and forth, trying to fit it into a parking space large enough for a bus. At last they got out of the car. They crossed the dark parking lot to the door to the outside ramp.

Paula walked along the rail. Gradually the city appeared, spread out below her. All the trees were springing with green leaves, burying the above-ground houses and offices. The lawn below her was spotted with dandelions.

Jefferson said, "Dick thinks you should resign the case."

Paula swung around toward him. "Oh? Why?"

He gave her an oblique, feline look. Jefferson said, "Some of your techniques are rather original, Mendoza."

"Pah."

"The Council is not happy."

"The Council loves it," Paula said. On the curved wall of the building was the door to the Committee's reserved port. She followed the other diplomats into the waiting room, and Jefferson turned the lights on.

"What you really mean is you think I might sell you out," Paula said to Bunker.

He dropped into a molded plastic chair against the wall, sliding down, sitting on his spine as usual. "That's exactly what I mean." He wore a thin shirt, plain dark pants, cloth shoes, nondescript, like a disguise. She braced her shoulders against the clear wall between the waiting room and the dock.

"Take him," she said. "Go on, you do it."

Jefferson was watching them from the far side of the room. Bunker put his head back. "Your career with us hasn't been a raging success, junior. The only other case you've even accepted was one where you took a personal interest. Right?"

So he had found out that she had stolen his files. Before she could answer, a light flashed on the wall over her head. They all went out onto the dock platform.

The air wall roared. The big car was sinking down into the cradle of the dock. Paula rubbed her sweating hands on her pants legs. When she touched the railing she got a shock. The Styths poured out of the bus.

The Akellar tramped up the steps. She had forgotten how big he was. Jefferson spoke to him, but he brushed her off. When Bunker approached him the Styth sidled toward him and would have knocked into him if Bunker had stayed where he was. The Akellar reeked; he stood over Paula.

"I told you to come alone."

"What's wrong? Did you have trouble?"

"Yes." He snarled at the other men, crowded onto the platform, and they spilled into the waiting room.

"You've made your point," Bunker said into her ear. He and Jefferson disappeared. The Styths towered around her. Ketac's wild brush of hair bobbed among the trim heads of the men. Most of the others were strangers to her. There was a brief, fiery argument, which the Akellar resolved by knocking someone down.

Paula opened the door to the ramp. The Akellar shouted his crew into order. Tanuojin came out past her, nearly scalping himself on the top of the door, and made for the railing. The rest followed him. The Akellar took her arm and started off at top speed. She stopped, resisting him, and he turned.

"What's the matter with you? Look, I'm warning you—"

"Don't tow me around."

He opened his hand. His men were packed against the rail. "Look!" They leaned out to stare at New York.

"What happened?" she asked. She had to tilt her head back to meet his eyes.

"I had a long talk with General Gordon."

"Oh." The spring breeze touched her face. Panicked, she remembered that Gordon knew about the baby. At her pace they went on down the ramp. The other Styths were strung out along the railing, pointing and laughing at what they saw.

"Did you go to surface-Luna?"

He shook his head. Bad-tempered, he shed a harsh rush of his odor. She went ahead of him into the dark parking lot. The hot bright scent had certain connotations for her. The parking lot stretched off into the dark, scattered with air cars, the pavement marked into stalls. The three Committee cars were lined up near the exit. Their drivers leaned against the fender of the big bus, passing a cigarette around.

"We have a house out in the New Haven dome," she said. "It's the only place where you could all stay together." She slid into the back seat of the small car. The Akellar folded himself into the space beside her. If he knew about the baby he would have said something by now. He took her chin in his hand, and she kissed his cool mouth.

The driver said, drawling, "You two want to get going sometime today?"

They pulled apart. Paula touched her mouth. She looked out the window. The driver rolled the door shut and put the plastic divider across the seat between him and them.

"Gordon gave me a whole long sermon on how I ought to behave," the Akellar said. He was cramped into the narrow seat, his arms and legs folded up to his body. "With a lecture on the side on the sanctity of women."

The car rolled forward. She said, "He's an ass." He leaned forward to watch the driver shift and steer. The car rose off the ground. Below them, the green heads of the trees rolled in the wind. The lake glittered, down toward the south.

"You're right," he said. "This isn't like Mars."

Above the wood a flock of daws circled and fought. The driver circled over the lake, lined with naked and half-naked bathers. Out the back window she could see the two cars following them. The Styth shaded his eyes from the light.

They left the dome. The stretch of coast between New York and New Haven was heaped with ancient slag. The torrential summer rains had eroded the hills into canyons and cliffs white with the droppings of wild birds. The sun was setting behind them. Sharp against the smoky sky, the ridge ahead poked up its two round humps. She pointed it out to him.

"That's called the Camel."

"What's a camel?"

"A big animal. There's an old proverb that it's easier for a camel to pass through the eye of a needle than for a rich man to enter the Kingdom of Heaven." They passed to the south of the Camel and the slag pinnacle just beyond it came into view. "That's the Needle." Through the long eye in the spire the sky showed rosy from the setting sun.

"What's Heaven?"

She sat back. "Forget it." The sunset streaked the sky with red and orange. "It used to be that the cities were polluted and the air out here was clean. A long time ago."

A blackbird flapped by them. He said, "How do the birds live here?"

"They adapted. Some of them. Some birds can only live in the domes, some of them go in and out. It's called the gas-mask effect." She nodded toward another shape in the gray slag. "That's the Throne. If you can sit there for twelve hours, you'll rule the Earth."

"Oh?"

"The pollution would kill you in six."

"You people have a strange sense of humor."

They came to the dome. The Akellar stretched his neck to see all around them while the driver took them through the curved plastic wall. They flew over black earth spiked with green. Night was rolling over them. The domelight came on, blue as a flame in the clear air. A sheer red cliff ran like a barrier along the east. The hillside below them was covered with trees. A clearing opened and the car drifted down toward the two buildings below.

The Committee House was a square two-story wooden block, a replica of a pre-Atomic Federalist house, complete with a broken pediment over the front door and a carved eagle on the bannister. Before all the Styths were out of the cars, Ketac was climbing into the apple tree, and two other men were chasing the cook's terrified white cat. Paula went into the front hall. The house smelled of cinnamon and ginger.

"This isn't the Nineveh," she said to the Akellar. "There's a cook, but that's all. You have to look after yourselves."

He felt of the eagle's chiseled wing feathers. There was a door at the foot of the stair; he reached down to the knob, pulled it, pushed it, and finally turned it, and the door opened. She led him up the stairs. The front upstairs hall was full of rubber plants and morning star. He pulled a white blossom off a geranium and ate it. Out the window she could see his crew running around in the woods. She brushed through the curtain of beads into the back hall and opened the room on the end.

"Paula!" he shouted, in the hall.

"I'm down here." She took off her jacket and hung it on the knobbed bedpost and began to unbutton her shirt. He came in the door. "What are you waiting for?" she said. He shut the door.

"Have you been on your ship all this time?"

"My ship and a couple of others." He was still half-dressed. Sitting up, he peeled off his leggings and his shirt. Paula lay on her side, glutted from the hard sex. The blanket was wet; she threw it back over the foot of the bed. He lay down beside her.

"Did you miss me?" He slid his hands over her. His knee pressed between her thighs. "You didn't go with anybody else, did you?"

She wondered why that mattered to him. His lust reassured her. As long as he wanted her, she could deal with him. Above his collarbones smooth hollows formed. She touched him, remembering him.

"I thought you'd like to go to Manhattan tomorrow. That's an ancient city, under the ocean—the same people who built it built the first Styth cities."

"What's the ocean?"

"You'll see."

"And why should I want to see something those people made? They were monsters."

"They were your ancestors."

His hair had come half-unknotted, and he pulled it loose. Wavy from being bound up, it hung over his shoulders down nearly to his waist. He said, "Not really. They were the medium, perhaps, but it was Uranus who made Styth. Uranus and the Sun."

She played with his hair. He lay on his back, his eyes half-shut, while she fondled him. The Committee would drop her as soon as they could do without her. She had to keep him her property. Bending, she licked his breastbone, and he draped one arm around her shoulders.

. . .

Across a smashed inlaid floor, fluted columns stood up into the dark. Deep inside the ruin, something rained down slowly from a great height. Paula climbed over a block of stone down into the vast room. The Akellar came in behind her.

"Look at this place." He leaped across the broken stone of the steps down to the floor. "It's bigger than the rAkellaron House." He was speaking Styth.

Tanuojin came after him. Their voices echoed in the pitch of the ceiling, invisibly far above them in the dark. "There are hundreds of them. Who could have lived here?"

"She says the Moon-people."

"She's lying. They never built anything like this."

Paula put her hand out to the wall, covered with scale and dry moss. She had thought of telling him about the baby; she knew she should tell him, since it was his baby, but she was afraid of what he might do. Kill her. She imagined him scooping the baby out of her belly with his hands. At her touch the patina over the wall crumbled. There were letters under it carved into the brown marble.

hn Jaco

Some kind of incantation. She climbed up a pile of square stones to the door and went back to the street.

The two men followed her, talking. Ketac raced down the middle of the street toward them. "Pop! How big is that one? Fifteen hundred feet? What ruined them? Was there a war?" He rushed across the street to the foot of a towering wreck of a building. Paula stood with her hands in her pockets, watching the Styths. Tanuojin at the foot of the tower was so small she could not make out his face. She walked up the street away from them.

When they reached New Haven again, the Federalist house was empty. It was long after dark. A turkey was browning in the oven, but even the cook was gone. The Akellar swore. He went out to the backyard and whistled and got no answer. Paula opened the cold box. Ketac walked into the kitchen and she took out a beer for each of them.

"Where are they?" The back door banged open. The Akellar walked in. On his heels Tanuojin hit his head on the ceiling lamp and let out a gross obscenity.

"Where's my crew?" the Akellar snarled at her.

"I don't know. I've been with you, remember? Ask him."

The cook was coming in the back door. He was a small man, tree-dark; under his arm he carried two gallon sacks of milk and a package of sweet potatoes. He said, "Thought I'd make a sweet potato pie," and went to the cold box to put the milk away.

"Where's my crew?"

"Halstead's, I think." The cook stooped to look through the oven window at the turkey.

Paula said, "That's a roadhouse. Sweets, how did they get there? All the cars are here."

"Walked." The cook took the sweet potatoes to the sink to wash them. His white cat trotted in and leaped onto the counter.

"What's a roadhouse?" the Akellar said. "Where are they?"

"It's a bar," Paula said. "Come on—we can go pick them up."

"Come on." The Akellar pushed her ahead of him toward the door.

She went out the back door into the dark. The wind blew in a low moan over the meadow. She climbed into the driver's seat of the big bus. The cab was colder than the outdoors. The Akellar slid into the passenger seat. She thumbed the starter button. The engine growled sluggishly and she reached down under the seat for the choke.

Halstead's was toward the southwest. She took the car up to 150 feet, watching the compass on the dashboard. "If you see a sign, tell me. I've never driven to this place before."

She flew down the hill, over the woods, toward the long barrier hill in the east. The trees thinned. The fields below them were planted in strips of corn and marijuana. They flew over the farmhouse and barn.

"This place is much more beautiful than Mars."

"That's because everything is alive."

"There." He pointed. "Is that a sign?" On the roof of a cattle barn ahead were white letters. She swerved to fly over.

Halstead's, the roof said, *Cave-cooled Beer*, and an arrow pointed off to the right. She turned the wheel and pulled back on it to ease the car around the curve. Ahead, a light shone in the blue night. She drifted down on it, holding the air car slightly into the wind. The three buildings below were Halstead's. She settled down on the roof of the biggest.

"Let me fly back," he said.

She slid out of the car. "Don't you like the way I drive?"

"Not particularly."

She went across the parking lot to the head of the stairs. "You don't want your crew to see a woman driving you around." The stairs were steep. She held on to the rail. He came after her down into the warm lamplight.

"I don't want you to get used to it."

At the foot of the stairs they went into the short end of an L-shaped room. There were people crowded around the open hearth in the middle and in the booths along the walls. The Styths were scattered at random among them. Paula went into the long part of the room to the bar. Behind it, a man with black wooly whiskers stood talking to two of the Styths.

"Hup!" the Akellar said, loud, behind her.

All around the room, the Styths bounded to their feet. The anarchists, turning their heads, stayed in their chairs.

"What are you doing here?" the Akellar said, in Styth. "Line up at the stairs. Who said you could come over here?"

Paula turned to the barman. "How much did they drink?" The Styths hurried to the stairs. The Akellar was cursing them individually and in mass.

The barman scratched busily in his whiskers. "Military discipline." He took a piece of paper from his apron. "You owe me eighteen dollars and thirty-six cents."

The Akellar crowded her off to one side. He dropped a plastic disk on the bar. "I've got a rating at the Luna Credit Bank." He sidestepped into her again, shoving her away, and leaned over the man with the whiskers. "Well? What are you waiting for, a tip?"

The barman took the credit disk off the bar. He tossed it up high and caught it. "It's on the arm, captain." He flipped the disk to the big Styth. In his wooly beard his teeth showed yellow in a smile. "Part of the tour." Along the bar, other people laughed.

The Akellar stiffened. Paula said, "Come on, the turkey will be done by now." She went toward the stairs. He put his hand on her shoulder and steered her up the steps to the parking lot, where his crew was roaming around in the dark.

"I thought you said they wouldn't fight."

"Who fought?" She pulled open the air-car door and climbed up into the front passenger seat. The other men crowded into the back. There was sitting room for only four of them and the others crouched on the floor, their arms and legs all at angles. The Akellar got behind the steering deck. Paula showed him how to run the seat back.

He started the motor and took hold of the wheel. The car rose steeply off the roofs. Halstead's sailed away. Paula found herself clutching the seat, her breath stuck in her lungs. He circled once, climbing steadily up into the domelight, and raced back up the tree-covered ridge. A creek glittered a hundred feet below, winding between two fields. Horses drowsed in a pasture.

"Is this your car?"

"The cars belong to the Committee. I can't afford one. Please don't crash it."

"All the Martians have air cars."

"The Martians are rich."

He went straight across the ridge and swooped in a long

descending spiral toward the Committee House. His sense of direction was perfect. She wondered if he were using the compasses. Ketac ran out across the yard, yelling and waving his arms. The Akellar set the car down on its skids at the edge of the meadow.

The men piled out through the side doors. Ketac cried, "You should have seen where we went!" The Akellar sat behind the wheel, his hands moving uncertainly over the lighted dashboard. The engine hummed, overchoked. "How do I turn it off?"

She turned the switch on the steering column. He caught her hand. The last of his men went inside, and quiet fell. Hissing through the meadow, the wind bent the high grass and rustled the leaves under the oak tree. His fingers tightened on her hand.

"This is not what I expected," he said.

She had to smile. She liked him, even if he had made a fool of himself at Halstead's.

"What's funny?" he said, his dignity still tender.

"Nothing. You're a nice man."

"Am I. I never thought I was that ordinary." He leaned toward her to kiss her. His mouth tasted pleasant. She slid her fingers down the nape of his neck. They nuzzled and caressed each other, moving around on the broad seat. The steering grips gouged her in the ribs. Her hand slid over his thigh and he parted his legs. His fingers rolled and pulled at her nipple. They kissed again hotly. Abruptly he put his head back. His hand pressed exploring over her breast.

"Are you pregnant?"

She jumped. The steering grip dug into her side. "How—what makes you think that?"

"I've had some experience. You are, aren't you. Is it mine?"

She put her hand up to her face. Her fingers smelled of him. They moved apart; now she was behind the steering panel, her back to the door.

"You people are so damned smart," he said. "Don't tell me you don't know how to prevent things like that. Did you do it on purpose?"

"No!" Pulling her shirt closed, she fastened the clips. "Here all the men are—you don't have babies by accident here. A boy has an operation. To close the duct. If you want a baby, the man has to go have another operation." She raked her fingers through her hair. "It never occurred to me you'd be natural. It was just once."

"That's all it takes. Why didn't you tell me before? I can probably arrange an abortion."

"If I wanted an abortion I'd have gotten my own."

Behind her, in the yard, the rhythmic crunch of footsteps came nearer. She twisted to see through the window in the door. Ketac stood there, stooped to look in, and she swung the window open.

"Sweets wants to feed you," he said past her to his father.

"I'm talking to her. Serve Tanuojin without me."

"Yes, sir." Ketac went away. Through the open window the wind blew cool. She turned her hot face to it.

"Why didn't you tell me?" he said.

"I didn't know what you'd do."

"What should I do?"

"Nothing. Forget you know."

"You're going to have it and bring it up, all by yourself? Can I ask you a delicate question? Are you sure it's mine?"

His tone of voice grated on her feelings. She swung toward him. "I've had about two hundred different tests. It's half-Styth, a boy, and you'll be gratified to learn that claws and scent glands and probably hot tempers are dominant. I didn't plan this, you didn't plan it, so why don't you forget the whole thing?" The domelight lay in a bar across his shoulder. His face was invisible in the dark. She turned her face back into the wind.

"A boy. He'll go mad here. How can you tell that it's a boy?"

"They have a test for it." She drew a deep breath. Clear light poured over the meadow. The shadows lay black and sharp under the elm tree and the wheelbarrow tipped up against the side of the barn. "I was going to have an abortion. I went to a doctor and he tried to talk me into letting him transplant the embryo into a—a kind of a plastic mama. So he could study it. It was grotesque. I guess it was funny, too. I realized the baby was there, and alive, and mine."

"It's impossible. A Styth, in this place."

"He won't be a Styth here, he'll be an anarchist."

He took her hand and turned it over in his fingers. "Do you have enough money? I could send you money." He held her hand against his cheek.

"I'll do all right." She stroked his face. That was how Styths kissed. "I'm hungry."

"Let's go eat."

She woke up shivering. The window was open and the curtains blew in; the room was freezing. She burrowed down under the covers. She was alone in the bed, and she began to doze off again, warm under the covers. The door creaked, and the Akellar sat down on the bed beside her.

"Are you awake?"

"Ummmm."

"What did you dream about? You were moving around."

"I don't remember."

"Get up." He poked her through the covers. "I want to go out. It's dark now, I can see better."

"Out where?"

"In the trees. Get up." He pulled the blankets off her.

She put her clothes on. She remembered the dream: the baby had been born in two halves, and they had lost one half. The Akellar had been there in the delivery room, which had looked like an observatory. It would have been simple to sew the two parts of the baby together if they could have found the other half. Dressed, she went down with the Akellar to the kitchen and made them coffee. He strolled around the darkened room eating bread and cheese and apples.

"Turn the light on, if you want," he said.

"I don't mind. I spent half my childhood in the dark. My father never turned the lights on. He read somewhere that artificial light induces early puberty in girls."

When he laughed his teeth flashed in the dark. "I'd like your father."

"You're too late, he's dead."

They walked up the hill, through old meadows. A line of white beehives stood under the trees at the edge of the open grass. A small dark beast loped away toward the trees, brush-tailed. The place was called Fox Hill. Paula stopped at the head of a slope and looked off to her left. The high meadow rolled down steep toward the valley, flat in the distance, ending at the foot of West Rock. She followed the Styth into the trees.

He stopped to look at everything; it was easy to keep up with him. The floor of the wood gave soft under her feet. White birch grew in clumps among the dark trunks of bigger trees. They circled the broken foundation of a long ruined house. Part of an old fireplace still stood at one end. Climbing a wall of piled stones, they started across another meadow.

A dog raced toward them through the grass. Paula froze. She could hear its growls. It charged past her toward the Styth and burst into a volley of barks. It was huge, some kind of mastiff. A chain collar glittered in the rolls of its neck.

"What's that?" the Akellar said. The dog circled him, barking, and Paula went in between it and the man.

"Are you protecting me?" He sounded amused. The dog's lips snarled back from its teeth. Paula flinched. The animal charged, not at her, at the Styth.

He pushed her out of the way. She fell onto one knee. The dog sprang at him and he swiped at it, one-handed. In mid-air the snarl broke into a ki-yi-yi-yi, and the dog bounced into the grass. It scrambled onto three legs, one forefoot curled up near its body. Down its fawn side welled four long stripes of blood.

Paula got up, cold, and shaking all over. The dog hobbled in a circle around the big man. Its throaty snarling raised the hair on her neck. She had never seen a dog act like this before. The Styth's teeth showed white, like a smile. Under his breath, he said, "Want some more, little thing?" He moved back, stooping, and the dog lunged after him. The man wheeled around with an animal's fluent grace and slashed out. The dog gave a single cry. When it hit the ground it lay still. Paula took a step toward it. Its forepaws were twitching, trying to run. Blood ran from its belly. Its eyes were like blue glass in the domelight.

"Are you all right?" the Akellar said, amiably.

"Oh. I'm fine," she said. "Just lovely." She started on toward the trees, her legs unsteady.

"Do you have a rag—something I can wipe my hand on?"

There was a scarf wadded up in the pocket of her jacket. Under the trees, she stood watching him clean the blood off his fingers and claws. He said, "It jumped on me. I have a right to protect myself."

"Yes," she said.

They went on, now going downhill, skirting thickets of thorny vines and steep rocks. An old dirt road cut over the flank of the hill. Dry puddles of cow dung spotted it. They followed the road down to the creek, curving off between two pastures, lined with willow. Frogs and night insects made a racket its whole length. Paula led him down the bank a hundred feet from the road and sat down and took her shoes off.

"You said he'll have claws. Our son." He dropped on his stomach and put his face down to the water to drink.

"That's what the doctor says."

"He'll go out of his head here when they start to grow in."

She stuck her feet into the icy water. In the open pasture beyond the stream, six or eight black and white cows lay sleeping, all facing the same way. "When he gets old enough maybe I can send him to visit you."

"Don't do that."

"Why not?"

He sat on the bank digging stones out of the ground. "Because somebody from this world would have the shit torn out of him in Styth."

"Oh, really? It's that bad."

"No. That's just the way we live." He piled white river stones before him on the flattened grass.

"An anarchist can live anywhere."

"Not in Styth."

Almost in front of her a frog plopped into the water. A moment later its eyes bumped above the surface. "You don't expect much of a future for this baby, do you? He'll go crazy here and be killed there."

"That's right."

She frowned across the river at the cows. His certainty sawed on her temper. Around her the capes of willow branches rustled in the light breeze.

"About this treaty."

"Un-hunh," he said.

"We need a truce."

"A truce!" His head flew up. "You mean I have to stop fighting?"

"That's the accepted definition."

"No. Impossible. That's my only money. I have to support my crew. I have fourteen children, and the way my wives expect to live—and *Ybix* costs me more than a wife." He took one of his stones and threw it down the creek. It splashed into the water a hundred feet on, and several other splashes echoed it: frogs.

"You'll have all that money from the trade agreements, remember?"

"I'm going to use that for something else."

"Oh? What?"

"That's none of your concern. No truce. Get me the rest of it without a truce."

"I can't. No truce, no money."

He bounded onto his feet. "I should have known there was a hook in it somewhere." He walked off into the pasture behind her. She waggled her feet in the water. He came back and squatted beside her. "No truce."

"What about just with the Council?"

"The Council only has a couple of ships."

"I know."

"Then it's a sham. Forget it. I don't traffic in lies."

"No truce, no money."

He took another white stone from the pile and threw it with a scythe motion of his arm. This splash sounded much farther away than the first. She reached for his hand. Down the backs of his fingers the tendons ran like wire. She remembered the dog; she had not realized how strong his hands were. She remembered how he had tricked the dog into attacking him. He closed his hand over hers and held her.

"All right," he said. "With the Council, for a definite length of time. Not too long."

She let her breath out. "Ten years, I thought." Jefferson would settle for seven.

"Ten years. But that had better be everything—the trade agreements, the truce. Nothing more."

"One more thing."

"What?"

"I want to go with you. Back to Uranus. To Matuko."

He released her hand. Bending over his collection of stones, he fingered one after another, choosy. "Why? To be with me?"

Her feet were dry. She put her shoes on again. He said, "Not for me. You aren't very flattering, you know."

"Do you want me to lie?"

"You could rub me up a little, you know, I mean, cater to me a little." He cocked his arm back and fired a stone across the stream. On the grass opposite them a black and white cow jerked up her head out of a drowse, turned suspiciously toward her flank, heaved herself first to her hindfeet and then to all fours and trotted away. The Akellar swore.

"I thought that was a rock. What is it?"

"A cow. They make the milk."

They walked back up the stream to the road. The Akellar said, "It's a different kind of life, in Styth. It won't be easy, even with me there to take care of you."

She ducked her head and shoulders through two rails of the fence along the road. "I don't want to do things that are easy. I want something hard."

"It'll be that."

Down in the pasture, the cows were moving in their leisurely pace up toward the gate. The big man vaulted the fence and took her hand.

"Sure," he said. "I'll take you. Do you want me to marry you?"

"No."

"That way the baby would be legitimate."

"No."

The road led steadily upward. Dawn was coming. The wood looked strange, clogged with shadow, while the road grew lighter. They crossed a cattle guard and went down the brick path toward the Committee House.

"You'll have to insist on it," she said. "On me going. Or Jefferson and Bunker will get suspicious. Maybe even null the treaty."

"You don't trust them."

"Well, I trust them." She scratched her nose. "They don't exactly trust me." She glanced at the Akellar, curious. She had expected him to balk at taking her. She should call him by his name now, stop thinking of him by his title, and as an instrument. In the yard, he let go of her hand and veered over toward the air cars. She went inside.

All the spice cake was gone; the sweet potato pie was gone. She poured a glass of milk. The Akellar did not come in. She opened the back door. He was sitting on the steps, his legs out before him. She said, "Come inside, it's about to rain."

"Rain?"

"Every morning after the sun comes up it rains here. It has something to do with the shape of the dome. Look." She pointed. The oncoming rain was shaking the trees on the far side of the meadow. The downpour swept in across the grass. He went out to meet it. He held his face up to the rain and opened his mouth. The rain streamed over him. It drummed on the air cars and beat on the roof and went on busily off across the dome. The Akellar came up to her, his mustaches plastered to his jaw and neck, laughing, his arms spread.

"What was that? Can I come in like this?" She put her hand on the nape of his neck and pulled his head down to kiss him.

"You have fourteen children?"

"Fourteen and a half," he said. He patted her stomach. A crosswind struck the car and she braced herself while he pulled the car up and turned it back on course. They were crossing a rare clear pocket. Below them the slag heaps spread out gray as ash, gouged with rivers that branched and coiled toward the sea. In the north she could make out the worn red hills. She tried to imagine having fourteen children.

"Is Ketac the eldest?"

"No. My oldest is Dakkar, my prima son. Then there's a girl, she's married, you won't meet her. Then Ketac."

"You must have married young." She gripped the seat in both hands as a draft took them straight up and dropped them down again. He flew at the limit of the car's speed, and very high. If they crashed—

"I was a neophyte. Ketac's age. My father came back from space and found me in jail in Vribulo. He went on a panic program. Called 'straightening out Saba's life.' In about thirty watches he had me clubbed, commissioned into the fleet, and married to Boltiko. Do you know what a watch is?"

"About ten hours on the Earth. Why were you in jail?"

"I don't remember. I was put up a lot when I was a neophyte. Probably for buying morphion."

The car swooped into a long descending turn. Ahead a bank of yellow cloud lay along the river that divided New York from the slag. She could not see the dome. The sweeping curve knotted her stomach.

"For buying morphion. How much did you load?"

"Plenty. I was addicted most of the time I was a neophyte."

"You couldn't have done that much or you'd have died."

"I nearly did."

She caught herself pulling up on the arm of the seat. He was lowering to circle the dome. They flew into the fog. She could barely see the great smooth shape of the covered city off to their left. He pulled out the sensor panel from under the dash; the car made a red dot crossing it.

"I was in jail once," she said. "For smuggling. On Mars."

"You really are a low-life, aren't you?"

On the black sensor plate, ruby-red lines formed a schema of the dome in intersecting parabolas. Carefully she let go of the handgrip. "Are you reneging?"

"No. I have plans for you." He pushed the steering grips forward, and the car sank down in an even descent. "I'm going to civilize you."

She put her head back, offended. He said, "Do you want to renege?"

"Not after that remark."

"Good."

Paula jumped gratefully to the solid ground of the East-Lock parking lot. "Oh," she said. "I never thought I'd make it alive." She crouched and patted the concrete with her palms.

The parking lot was surrounded by woods. They walked side by side down the slope. It was mid-afternoon. From high on the hillside she could see the lake but as they walked down the trees swallowed it.

"I hold eight free-space speed records, and you don't trust me to drive that slug."

"It's me I don't trust. I don't trust myself to bounce when we hit the ground." She circled a thicket. The soft earth gave under her feet. She stopped and took off her shoes and stuck them in the crotch of a tree to pick up on the way back.

"What's that?"

She went down the steep hillside so she could see what he was pointing at: a round gatehouse. "That's the entrance to a building." The sun streamed over the meadow. She walked toward its green warmth.

"Where's the building?"

"Under the ground." She held her arms and face up to the sun. He stayed back under the trees, out of the direct light. At the far end of the meadow, a dozen people sat in a circle. Maybe it was a school. They went on toward the lake.

"What's that?"

She was going through her pockets for a dime to buy an hourly. "That's a swan." The narrow mud beach of the lake was striped with the bodies of sunbathers. The swan was feeding in the eelgrass in the shallows. A girl in a yellow swimsuit walked by, and the Akellar watched her, his head turning to follow her course.

They walked up under the trees. The ground smelled moist. The crozier heads of ferns were poking up through the rotting leaves in the deep shade. She read the hourly's headlines.

"Hunh."

"What?"

"Cam Savenia was elected to the Council seat for Barsoom. By fifty thousand votes."

He took the paper from her. They went north, passing through another sunny meadow. "Is it fair?" he said. "An election?"

Paula shrugged. "Depending on the definition of fair. The trick is to be nominated. Do you have hourlies in Styth?"

"We live much closer together than you do." He bent and picked up a fragment of blue eggshell. Paula took the hourly from him. "Anybody who wants to know anything can just come ask me."

"You know that Cam's a member of the Sunlight League?"

He crushed the eggshell in his fingers and sniffed the residue. "Yes, we got that idea." They were cutting across the campus. A deer grazed beside the turret of the Biochemistry Building. At their approach it bolted away.

"A cow?" he said, uncertainly.

"A deer."

He took her hand. She was getting used to that; she guessed the touch gave him some kind of comfort. The Styths touched each other constantly. The square mouth of the underground shopping mall opened in the hillside before them. They went down the steps.

Bicycles lined either side, and the walls were covered with graffiti. They passed a boy and a girl drawing in red and blue swirls over a clear space of tile. Three doors on past Barrian's, the music store, they came to The Circle, a shop that recycled toys, among other things. It was brightly lit. The Styth winced and put his hand up over his eyes. She took him by the arm. Plants and banners and china bells hung down from the ceiling. The shelves were made of planks and bricks. In the back, under a big sign, they found three boxes of toys.

"Here."

He squatted down on his heels and reached into the nearest box. She watched him sort through the tops and dolls and wooden models, putting what he wanted on the floor by his feet.

"Ah." He untangled a pull toy from the heap and held it up. "A camel."

She laughed. "Right."

He put it on the floor and rolled it back and forth on its wheels. The head bobbed up and down. "Are there live ones? How big are they?"

"Tremendous."

"Bigger than cows?"

"I think so." She sat cross-legged on the floor. He was taking other model animals out of the box, inspecting each one.

"What's this?"

"A mouse."

"Mouse. We have something—*mus*. Little things. Brown."

"Sure," she said. "Mouse."

"Aha." He put the mouse back into the box, uninterested.

He bought a dozen little toys; he also bought a music box and an hourglass. The shop clerk took his credit chit, put everything into a box, and tied it fast with string. She wondered if he traded in crystal. Before long, everyone would, because of her.

"I guess I'll have to carry this myself," Saba said. He picked up the box in his arms. They went through the jungle of hanging plants and banners to the door.

Most of the shops in the mall were dark, closed for the night. In the walkway they passed a man wrapped in hourlies, asleep against the wall. Ahead were the bright windows of the Optima, the Martian store. Behind the glass the mannequins walked and turned in a glare of backlighting. The Akellar started.

"Jesus. For a minute I thought they were real."

"This is a Martian store. Nothing is real."

He looked in the door. It hissed open, and he took a step toward the vast bright store inside. "How much time do we have?" Paula followed him into the store. He put the box down to turn a rack of book plugs. When he went off he left the box on the floor and she carried it. He led her up and down the aisles; he looked at everything, the stacks of shoes, a three-color animation selling vitamin lamps, boxes of buttons, wrapping paper and ribbon. She picked up a child's striped shirt. It looked too small to fit anything human. Next to the counter of children's clothes was a counter of bright little sweaters and boots for dogs. When she looked around, the Styth was gone.

"Saba?"

"Here."

She went into the next aisle. Three illusion helmets were sitting on a display shelf; he was reading the price tags. He said, "Everything here costs about twice as much as it's worth. How do these things work?"

The counter behind them was piled up with cut-rate illusions. She took one at random and stuck it into the slot on the back of a helmet. "These knobs adjust the size. Put it on your head."

He stuck his head into it, stood a moment clutching the plastic bubble, and yanked it off. He held the helmet out in front of him and tried to see the illusion without putting his head into it.

"It won't go on unless your head's inside."

"It feels—" He looked around, taking a reconnaissance, and put the helmet back on. Paula set the box down on the counter. Illusion helmets always made her feel locked in a closet. He took it off again and studied it.

"I want one of these." He put it back over his head and played with the knobs. She looked up at him, dismayed.

He bought the illusion helmet and six cartridges, drew on his hand with red lip-slicker and blue eye color and bought several boxes of that. He bit a cheap necklace and lost interest when he realized it was plastic. He flicked his claws at a headless mannequin wearing a bra and a girdle. "That's disgusting—putting that up for people to look at."

She laughed. "We ought to go. I think we're late already." Her arms ached from carrying the box. She shifted it elaborately, to draw his attention, but he ignored it. They went toward the door. A mechanical female voice was talking out of the ceiling; she said, "Have you bought your Optima card yet? Remember, every month, card-holders receive special low prices on a wide range of needed items." The door opened itself for them.

The mall was cool and dark. Paula boosted up the big package in her arms. They went up the wide steps to the surface. He slung the bag with the illusion helmet over his shoulder.

"I went all through there looking for something I could give you but there wasn't anything I thought you'd want."

They walked along a wide graded path. On either side of it were dogwood trees. She could not make out his expression. "You're very smooth."

"You suspect everything I do."

"Everything you do is suspect."

"No—you're just a suspicious bitch." They went across the dark grass to the Committee office.

Jefferson and Bunker were in the meeting room. The woman sat at the table, eating candy, while the man sat in a chair by the wall and argued with her. Paula went into the room, taking her jacket off. She turned to Michalski, who had followed them in.

"Can you dim the lights down?"

"Sure."

Jefferson said, "You're improving, Mendoza, you're only an hour and ten minutes late. Good evening, Akellar."

He turned a chair around, its back to the table, and put one knee on it.

The ceiling lights dimmed to half-strength. The Akellar looked up.

Paula went off to the end of the room, past Bunker, who was watching the big Styth. They had only met once before, at the entry port. Jefferson was explaining how the transcribing equipment in the table worked.

"Is it on now?" the Akellar asked.

"No," Jefferson said.

"Then turn it on, because I have an offer to make you."

Paula swung around, and Bunker took his hands out of his pockets. The big man faced the three anarchists. He rocked his weight forward; he looked cramped in the room, his head and shoulders confined under the low ceiling. He said, "I don't pretend I understand you people, but I know what you want. I'm willing to sign a truce with the Interplanetary Council, and I'll sell licenses to trade in Matuko and sell Matuko crystal to the rock-worlds. I want that money, in metal, iron if you can get it, and I want my rights with her and her baby."

Paula went up to the table. Her mouth was dry.

Jefferson said, "How much money?"

"It comes to twenty-six million dollars over five years," Paula said.

Bunker kicked at the floor. "What rights with her?"

"She goes with me," the Styth said. "Now."

"To Uranus?"

Paula sat down. Jefferson's mouth was pursed, her thin gray eyebrows arced like bows. The Akellar rocked back and forth on his knee on the chair, staring at Bunker.

"It's my baby."

Jefferson said, "How long a truce?"

"One hundred thousand watches."

"Ten years," Paula said.

"Good," Jefferson said. "That's a good length."

"You aren't serious?" Bunker shot a furious glance at Paula and went the length of the table to Jefferson. "What the hell are you doing? She set this up with him. She's trading us off."

"Do you agree to go?" Jefferson asked Paula. She put a mint into her mouth. Paula nodded. The old woman sucked on her candy, her hard blue eyes going to Bunker. "I like it. It's practical, it might work, and I can sell it to the Council."

The anarchist circled the table. "You Fascist," he said to her. He went past the Styth and out the door. It slammed behind him.

Paula sat down. Jefferson said, "He's getting narrow, Richard, in his dotage." She tipped up the lid of the recorder in the table and pushed buttons. Above her head, Paula met the round black eyes of the Styth, triumphant.

. . .

An Chu spread out the skirts of the black dress and folded them carefully in layers of tissue. "Can I write you?"

"I don't see how you'd post it."

"Maybe it would be easier for you to write me."

Paula was packing her books into the pockets of a flannel cloth. She rolled it up and tied the tape. The room was stripped to the walls and floor. She had sold her bed and given away everything else she was leaving behind. She put her flute into the satchel bag with the books.

"Help me," An Chu said, sitting on the suitcase. While they were buckling the straps there was a knock on the door.

It was Dick Bunker. Paula bent over the suitcase again. "What do you want?"

"Junior, why are you doing this?"

"It's my treaty." She closed the satchel. "I can manage it better in Styth than here." She stood up. The naked room looked smaller, like a cage. An Chu glanced from her to Bunker and lugged the suitcase out. He tipped himself up against the wall.

"You won't be much use dead, or locked up in a harem, or in a slave market, which is where you'll be."

"You certainly know a lot, for somebody who spends all his time talking."

They faced each other. His eyes were black as a Styth's. After a moment, he said, "I apologize for losing my temper yesterday."

"It doesn't bother me if you get emotional. Do you have something you want to say?"

"The Lunar Army blotted the scan of *Ybix*."

"Oh. That's typical."

"Will you take a sensor inboard with you?"

She snatched her jacket off the doorknob and thrust her arms into the sleeves. "He'd kill me. I'm not that stupid. Get out of my way." She grabbed the satchel. He backed up, and she went out the door after An Chu.

YBIX. Watch logs H11, 523–L11, 674

The hatch clanged open over her head. Paula reached up and drew herself through into a long silver tunnel. She bumped into the soft wall. The light was dim as twilight. She floated in the cold air, helpless. The Akellar shot up through the hatch. In mid-air he twisted around head-first like a fish and went the other way along the corridor.

"Come on."

She followed him, pushing herself along the yielding wall. On one wall was a double-barreled black arrow pointing the way she had come, and on the other a white arrow pointing the way she was going. In the free fall, without gravity to help her, she could hardly move. They passed a round hatchway marked with a black symbol. The corridor veered upward. They came to another tube, twisting away like a soft metallic hose, marked with double red stripes. The Akellar stopped and she bumped into him and knocked him down the corridor.

He came back toward her; he moved so fast she could not see how he did it. "You'll learn. There's a kind of a knack, it's nothing like walking." He went into the red corridor.

She struggled after him, banging into the walls. The surface was slippery. She began to shiver in the cold. Ahead, Saba had stopped to open a hatch. She flung her arms out, trying to stop, and ran into him again.

"You'll learn." He pushed her head-first through the hatch. "Just keep trying."

The room beyond was oval. Two lines of bulbous monitor screens dimpled the wall below her. She drifted to the side of the room. A handle stuck out of the wall. When she pulled on it she pulled herself into the wall. The Akellar turned over in mid-air. He flicked up a switch below a round screen near the monitors. She saw that he braced himself with the other hand.

"Bridge," he said.

"Yes, Akellar," a voice said through the screen. She thought it was Sril's.

"I'm inboard. What's our course?"

"Orbiting Luna at thirteen hundred miles, belt plus 2 ellipse, making ninety-three leagues. Our attitude is 0-0-2. Perimeter clear. The whole crew is inboard." It was Sril. She put her feet against the soft wall and pulled on the handle.

"Turn it," Saba said.

She turned herself slowly around by the handle. He said, "What's the watch?"

"High watch, Akellar," Sril said.

With one hand he held her body still against the wall. The handle was stiff and took all her strength to open. It clicked.

"Ah." She pushed herself back from the wall, and a long hatchway opened up before her. The space was covered by heavy white rubber, like a membrane. The Akellar was talking to Sril. She stuck her arm into the pleated rubber. It gave way and fit around her arm. Suddenly it gushed cold water over her hand and wrist. She lunged away, startled.

"That's a wetroom," he said. "That's where you wash."

Her sleeve was sodden. She turned around, drifting, and he came up to her. They were face to face; she was eye-level with him. She pulled his floating mustaches down.

"Are you cold?"

He went smoothly away past the hatch. In the double row of monitors on the wall, the other Styths floated in other silvery rooms, like fish in tanks. She watched him pull open a door in the wall. He used his foot to brace himself; when he put his hand on the wall to hold the door open, he dug his claws into the fabric. In the compartment in the wall her satchel floated above her suitcase. Straps held them fast. She took the satchel out.

She struggled with the buckles, and he started to help her. "No. I'll do it." She held the satchel between her knees. He went off. The half-light bothered her eyes. She opened the satchel and took out her jacket.

"I'll teach you to speak Styth," he said. He peeled off his clothes and stuffed them into a hole in the wall.

"I speak it better than you think. I understand everything you say." To prove it she spoke Styth. He was pulling on a suit of heavy gray overalls; he turned toward her, surprise on his face. She closed the satchel again and tried to take it back to the compartment. It was easier to move herself around by holding on to the satchel than to move the satchel. The speaker in the wall clicked.

"Yes," Saba said.

"Akellar, there are three Lunar Army hammerheads coming up on our perimeter."

"I'll be right there. Call Tanuojin. Saba."

She maneuvered the satchel into the compartment and strapped it down. Below her suitcase was the box of toys and the foam shell of the ullison helmet. If the trip turned boring she could always take that out. Saba came up behind her.

"Why did you lie to me?"

"I didn't lie to you."

"You told me you couldn't speak Styth." He was getting angry. She moved away from him, one hand on the wall.

"I didn't tell you that, you decided that."

He fastened up the front of his overalls. On the forearms of his sleeves were five diagonal stripes. He turned away from her; there was a black three-pointed star on his back. It was a uniform. Her hackles rose.

He said, "Did you hear what he just said? About the Lunar Army?"

"Yes."

"What do you know about that?"

"Nothing."

"If you're lying to me again—"

"I'm not. I don't know what's—" She sucked in her breath, thinking of Dick Bunker's scan. "Or maybe I do."

"What?" He lunged at her, his arms spread. She floundered in the air. The cold half-light confused her. He shouted at her, "What are you trying to do to me?"

"Not me, Dick Bunker. He tried to get me to bring a sensor in with me." She put her hand out to him. "Why else would the Lunar ships show up now? We must have brought something in with us."

His face clenched tight. "What? Where is it?"

"I don't know."

"You lie."

"I don't know." She fought to keep her voice steady. He wheeled away to the wall speaker; now it was above them.

"Bridge."

"Yes, Akellar."

"Send Tanuojin to my trap. Where are the hammerheads?"

"One on either wing and one behind us, Akellar. They're matching our course and speed."

She rubbed her hands together. Bunker could have hidden something in her bag during that uncharacteristic apology. If she had brought it on, the Styths would probably kill her. She went back to the compartment and took the satchel out again.

"If you're lying to me, so help me, I'll break everything in your body."

Behind the satchel was the illusion helmet in its protective coat of foam. She pushed the bag out of the way and took out the helmet. She looked around for a knife or clipper to cut the foam. He took the white ball from her. His claws sank into the foam and he tore it in half. Something sealed into the casing broke with a ping.

Saba growled in his chest. He ripped at the shard of foam, pulling out yards of thin plastic wire. The crumbs of foam sailed off thick as snow. The hatch burst open. Tanuojin came in, sinuous as rope in the free fall. On the sleeves of his overalls he wore one less stripe than Saba.

"Look at this," Saba said. He thrust a handful of looped wire at her. "What is it?" Tanuojin snatched it away from him.

"It's a sensor." His yellow eyes aimed at her. "I told you she's a spy."

She scrambled back away from them. The slick soft walls glinted in the low light. Her heart banged in the pit of her throat. She looked at Saba.

"Where did you have that wrapped up?"

"At the Committee office."

Tanuojin's head snapped around. "You said she didn't speak Styth."

"I don't think she had anything to do with this."

Paula slid along the wall. Tanuojin's lips pulled back from his teeth. "I do." He struck at her, backhanded. When she tried awkwardly to avoid him she ran herself into his stroke.

She gasped. Saba thrust in between them. Her jacket was in ribbons from sleeve to sleeve. She saw a cloud of fine red bubbles floating out before her. Her chest began to burn. She clenched her teeth at the swelling hot pain. Saba pulled her into the curve of his arm.

"Look what you did to her."

"I didn't hit her that hard."

"She's not Styth. She'll die. Heal her."

"Saba, she's just a nigger."

"Heal her!"

She panted. The long gashes down her breast hurt when she breathed. Tanuojin came toward her. She backed away from him. Numb, she fought to stay conscious.

"Hold her hands, or she'll scratch my eyes out."

Saba caught her wrists. He said, "Be good, Paula." The pain made her sob.

"This won't hurt," Tanuojin said. He put his hands flat to her torn skin.

At his touch she felt nothing, not even the cold. She gulped a deep breath. Saba held her tight against him. Tanuojin moved away from them. His hands left her. Her breast began to throb. Saba let go of her. She curled forward. Four long scabbed wounds ran like seams across her left breast and her stomach. They looked days old. She touched the scabs and they peeled off, the wounds healed in pale new flesh.

"Let me see." Saba's fingers slid through the shredded jacket. Tanuojin went out. She flinched from the touch on her skin. "He did it," he said to himself.

She pulled his hand out of her clothes. "What did he do?"

"Don't tell anybody." He took her by the arms and looked her in the face. "Don't talk about it to anybody, do you hear me?"

She nodded. Her numbed mind refused to work. What had he done? She was cold; her teeth began to chatter.

"I have to go to the bridge." He took her by the chin. "Don't ever lie to me again." Taking the sensor wire with him, he went out the hatch.

She hung suspended in the air. The blood and scraps of foam drifted around her in clouds. Slowly they were sucked into the filters in the wall and the air cleared. As the evidence disappeared her belief in what had happened disappeared. The Creep. She had paid no attention to that. The cold drove her to the effort of moving. She wrestled her suitcase out of the compartment and pulled out a shirt and a heavy sweater.

In the back of the compartment was the square box of toys for Saba's children. She took it out and used a nail file from her bag to hack open the foam wrapper. There were two more wires strung through the white plastic. One had a cube on the end the size of her thumb. She floundered around the room to the little wire mesh speaker and pushed the lever beside it and ran herself head-first into the wall.

She recoiled. Tears of frustration filled her eyes. She felt as if she were stuck in a pocket, in a prison. Her mind was jammed. She forced herself to relax. This place was strange because she did not know it; when she knew it she would understand. She put one hand on the wall and the other hand on the speaker lever and pushed it up.

"Bridge," she said.

A startled Styth voice said, "Who's this?"

"Tell Saba I found another one and a transmitter." She pulled the lever down again.

She did not know how to change her clothes without gravity. Her arms were too short. While she stuffed her legs into trousers she floated around the room. Every motion pushed her in a new direction. She put the shirt on over her head and fought with the sleeves. The hatch wheel clicked over.

She turned her head, and her whole body turned. Saba came feet-first into the hatch, coiled around in mid-air, and came down beside her. She pointed to the compartment door. She had tied the wires to the handle. He untangled them. She put another pair of trousers on, struggling with the legs.

Tanuojin came through the hatch. She stopped what she was doing. He pretended not to see her and went to his lyo. Floating over their heads, she straightened the legs of her trousers.

"Look at this," Saba said. "Have you ever seen anything like this? This wire in here must be some kind of recorder."

"We have to get it off the ship."

"We have to get the ship away from here."

Tanuojin wrapped the wire around his hands and tried to break it. "Do you think it's talking to those hammerheads?" He yanked the wire so hard the plastic hummed.

"She said—" Saba looked up over his head at her. "You said there was a transmitter."

She scrambled down toward him and took hold of the cube on the end of the wire. "This."

He turned the cube over in his claws. His head rose, and his body drifted up past her, following. "What about our supplies?" he said to Tanuojin.

"The package is ready, it's on the lighter, the lighter is on the far side of the Planet."

"Shit."

"We need the package. We're red-lined on oxygen and water." Tanuojin glanced at her. His mustaches curved back over his shoulders. "The lighter isn't due in this sector for six hours."

Saba rubbed his jaw. He was studying the little transmitter. "Call them and see if we can pick it up."

"I did. They'll put the package on a towsled, we can pick it up any time."

"Good. I'll take *Ybicsa*. You stay here and keep Gordon busy and those ships away from us." Saba took the other man by the arm. They turned together in a circle, orbiting each other. "Convert him."

Tanuojin produced a nasty thin fish-smile. "If you say so. What about her?"

Saba went to the hatch. "Leave her alone." He cranked the wheel over. Paula struggled after him. She banged into the wall and rolled helplessly over. When she dragged herself out the hatch to the corridor, he was disappearing around the bend.

"Saba, wait."

He turned back toward her, his arms spread out, sculling. She pushed herself along the wall to him.

"Where are you going?"

He towed her by the arm around the curve. "I'm taking the sidecraft to pick up our supplies. What's the matter—are you afraid of him? Think you're a little out of your range?" They went out to the corridor of the black and white arrows and down it a few yards to another tunnel. This was banded in blue stripes. He pushed her ahead of him down to a closed hatchway and banged on it with his fist, holding himself still against the wall with his free hand. "Ketac!"

Inside the hatch, a voice called, "Not here."

"Go find him, send him to the docking chamber." The Akellar shoved her ahead of him back to the arrow tunnel and they went down along the black arrow. She fisted her hand in his sleeve.

"I didn't know about that—the sensors."

"I believe you." He wheeled around her, stopping them both, and reached up over his head to a hatch. "You see this light?" He tapped a bulb in the oblong rim of the port. "When that flashes, this hatch has to be sealed, or the dark will come in faster than we could stop it." His free hand was flexed in the soft wall by his head. He pulled the hatch down.

She rose into a long chamber. A small needle-nosed spaceship filled it from wall to wall, anchored by struts in a wheel around its waist. She went along its pale metal side. On the nose cone was a three-pointed star and four rows of Styth lettering. She put her hand on the cold hull. Saba was folding back the accordion door of a locker in the wall. The space within was hung with limp black headless bodies. She went up to him.

"Are you going alone?"

"Ketac is coming with me." He took a suit out of the rack. She picked up the sleeve in her hand. The fabric was slightly greasy. Five yellow stripes decorated the forearm of the sleeve. The suit opened down the front. He doubled up to put his feet into the legs. The hatch banged open. Ketac came in, his hair streaming behind him.

"Put your suit on," Saba told him. "We're taking *Ybicsa* over to the dark side of this rock, and we might run into the Lunar Army on the way."

"Yes, sir." Ketac gave off a burst of hot copper. She watched him reach into the rack of suits. Saba was poking his arms into the sleeves of the suit.

"We'll launch hard, run toward the Earth to pick up some speed, and swing back on the polar axial. All right?"

"Yes, sir."

Paula turned toward the hatch. Her face was cold.

"Do you remember how to get back to my trap?" he asked her.

"Yes."

"Stay there. If Tanuojin gives you an order, do it."

"Why?"

"Because I told you to." Foreshortened below her, he looked all head and shoulders. He thrust a pair of gloves under a strap on his sleeve. She went out the hatch. When she shut it, the bulb on the rim began to flash red. She turned the wheel as far as it would go. The corridor was warmer and darker than the chamber she had just left. She wandered along, kicking and flapping her arms around and crashing into the wall. Somewhere behind her a bodyless voice said, "Kobboz, to the bridge." A round hatch popped open and a Styth in overalls dove out. He rolled over.

"Mendoz'." It was Sril. He came up to her, smiling wide. In the Common Speech, he said, "Now you come to our world."

"I speak Styth." She looked into the room he had just left. "What's this?"

"The galley. Are you hungry? I'll show you." He took her by the arm and pushed her into the narrow little room. The walls were covered with ring-pulls and levers. There was just enough room for the two of them, side by side. He flipped down a lever in front of her nose and the slot below it tongued out a clear packet with a big red tablet inside.

"Not like your food," he said. "They say I should have gone to the

Earth instead of Mars, the food was even better." He pulled down another lever and a tube of water came out of the wall. She put the red tablet into her mouth. It tasted like raw starch. He ripped the top off the tube of water for her, solicitous. "Do you like *Ybix*?"

"I haven't seen very much. Is there much to see?" The water tasted gluey. Tanuojin had said they were low on water. "Maybe I shouldn't drink it all."

"There's no way to put it back. You speak good Styth. I thought you probably did, back on Mars, you always knew what I was talking about. I—"

A voice came out of the wall over their heads. "Sril, to the bridge."

"Later." He touched her arm and went out. She drank the rest of the water. He had been friendly, and she liked him; she began to feel better. The rings in the wall pulled out flat drawers of knives and tools. She went out to the corridor again. Two men passed her, giving her curious sideways looks. Each of the hatches she passed was marked with a symbol in red. The living space was fitted into the crevices between the giant crystal systems that ran the ship, and every few feet the corridor twisted like a rabbit hole. *Like a Mylar wormhole.* She was learning to move, but she still could not stop very well, and she ran into a man coming the other way along the tunnel.

He lunged at her. She did not know him; she dodged out of his way, but he got her by the sleeve and towed her into a branch corridor. She looked around for a way to escape. He spun a wheel over and stuffed her in through a hatch.

She tumbled into a huge hollow ball. The bridge. The curved wall was solid with the glass faces of instruments and decks strung with wires. Sril caught her by the arm. He was sitting on a strut sticking out from the wall. When he turned, his stool revolved with him.

"Akellar, here she is."

Upside down over her head, Tanuojin sat in a cage footed against the wall. He dove out of it. "Come here." His hand closed on her wrist.

Over a loudspeaker, General Gordon's voice said, "*Ybix*, your time is running out."

Tanuojin pulled her around to the cage. She turned over, her feet toward the wall. He thrust her at a screen in front of the cage. "There she is, General."

Paula took hold of a hooped rib of the cage. On the screen was General Gordon. She said, "Hello, General. Doing the lord's work?" She could smell a strange bitter scent, maybe Tanuojin.

Gordon said, "Miss Mendoza, are you there of your own free will?"

"Are you?"

"Don't duel with me, young woman. Tell them I want to talk to the Akellar Saba."

Tanuojin pushed her out of the way. "He's asleep."

"Then wake him up."

The wall beside her was covered with dials. All the needles were swinging, twitching, at random. Besides Sril, two other men sat on stools along the curved wall. The scarred man, Bakan, headphones over his ears, was directly above her.

Tanuojin said, "Why am I to wake up the third-ranking Akellar of the Styth Empire just because you tell me?" He spoke much slower in the Common Speech than in Styth.

"Akellar," Bakan said, "*Ybicsa* is launching."

On the far side of the cage from her was a holograph. She let go of the rib and scrambled through the air toward the green cube of light. Someone above her laughed at her. In the hologram, an image of *Ybix* sailed along through clear green space. Two smaller ships flanked her and a third flew after her, an inch from her long whip-tail. Paula recognized the T-shapes of the Lunar Army's patrol craft. A small green image streaked out of *Ybix*'s side and flew off the map.

"I want to see your captain," Gordon was saying.

"*Ybicsa* is launched, Akellar," Bakan said.

Paula lifted her head. Gordon's pinched face looked tired. Tanuojin leaned over the screen. "You don't talk to Saba. You take your ships away, or I start to shoot."

An arm moved over the screen before Gordon. He glanced down and up again. "*Ybix*, you have launched another ship. We have regulations—"

Tanuojin turned his head. "Where is Saba?"

"Halfway back to the Earth," Bakan said, "and going like hell."

Paula looked up. She was drifting. Now Sril was above her on the curved wall, and Bakan was off to her right. The hatch opened and two men came in.

"What's going on?"

Gordon was saying, "I want to talk to your captain. If you don't produce him in five minutes, I'll assume he's on the ship you just launched and I'll proceed accordingly."

Paula looked down at the holograph. *Ybix*, manta-flat, was the size of her hand, the Lunar hammerheads the size of her thumb. Other ships sailed along in orbits below and ahead of her. The patrol ship behind *Ybix* seemed to draw up on her. Tanuojin and Gordon were arguing. Suddenly an alarm shrieked in her ears.

She started all over, her skin cold. The warning horn whooped again. Tanuojin jumped out of the cage. "Sril!"

"I have him on one, Akellar."

The hammerhead slid back, away from them, and the alarm rang silent. Paula was shivering. She glanced up at the men massed in the bridge above her. Sril had his hands on a lever in the wall beside his stool. He was watching Tanuojin.

He wheeled back to General Gordon. "God damn you, if you break my perimeter again, I'll shoot."

Gordon never blinked. "Even the devil knows the name of the lord. I'll give you ten minutes to leave before I blow you to hadrons." The screen went dark.

Paula rubbed her finger over her cheek. They were just playing with each other, and they both knew it. The hatch was directly above her. She rose toward it.

"Where are you going?" Tanuojin said. "You stay here."

"You don't need me here."

"Akellar, that hammerhead is drifting up again," Bakan said.

He flew down to the cage. "Bring her along thirty leagues."

"Mendoz'," Sril said. He leaned down, his hand stretched toward her. "Catch on." She took hold of his hand. The ship was gaining speed. Paula was falling toward the wall. She held on to Sril with both hands. In the holograph, *Ybix* moved out ahead of the three hammerheads. Her arms ached. Slowly she grew lighter again.

"Making one hundred twenty-six leagues, Akellar."

"The patrol ship is speeding up, Akellar," Bakan said. In the hologram another vessel showed, ahead of *Ybix*: the next ship in orbit.

"Good. Brake her down thirty leagues."

Sril said, in her ear, "Hold on." She put her arm around his waist. The ship slowed. She was dragged in the other direction, stretched out like a flag in the wind.

"Meet her, Marus," Tanuojin said. "You're dropping her."

The siren whooped. The hammerhead behind them was running up on them. "Sril!"

"Ready to fire, Akellar."

"Fire."

"Fire one."

The scream of the alarm made her ears hurt. Her weight lessened. She was floating again. *Ybix* flew backward through the green map into the following wedge of the hammerheads. A light flashed just behind the tailend ship, and the Styths groaned. A miss. The hammerhead bent its course, rising up over *Ybix*'s broad back. The siren stopped. Paula's ears rang like brass.

"Take us back to station," Tanuojin said. "Keep Gordon happy."

The helmsman said, "Braking ten leagues."

Paula slid gently against Sril's side. *Ybix* drifted backward through the map cube. The hammerheads were scattered across the space, out of order.

"Akellar, *Luna* is signaling."

"Didn't I say the little man was bluffing? What's our course?"

"We're on station, Akellar."

She let go of Sril and floated free in the air. The hatch was below her now, and Tanuojin inside the cage was above her again. The videone lit up: General Gordon.

"You can count yourselves lucky that maneuver failed. Your ten minutes is almost up. I'm warning you, I'm not a generous man."

Tanuojin put one arm through the cage bars. Paula glanced at the holograph. The hammerheads were again flying on either of *Ybix*'s wings and just behind her. The Styths around her were utterly still.

"I'm not taking this ship anywhere until my commanding officer gives me an order," Tanuojin said, "and he's asleep." He was waggling the hand outside the bars. Beside Paula, Sril bent over a deck of wires.

"Yes, Akellar." He pushed the deck like a drawer back into the wall.

Tanuojin waved at him. His arm withdrew into the cage. He and Gordon debated waking up Saba. She looked up at the hatch. There was no reason to stay here. Sril was turning slowly away from her, his hand on the lever on the wall, and his eyes on Tanuojin.

"You don't have to shake your superstitions in my face," Tanuojin was saying to Gordon. He thrust his arm out of the cage and waved at Sril. "I've already noticed that you're ignorant."

General Gordon's face thinned. Paula could not see his hands, only his shoulders and head. Was he signaling too? She drifted down toward the hologram. Bright green, *Ybix* sailed on her even course. The three smaller ships skirted her. The hammerhead on *Ybix*'s tail was flying higher than the Styth ship. She supposed they were creeping in to try to catch the transmission of the sensor wire. Tanuojin raised his hand.

"As long as you're here, you're subject to our law," Gordon said.

"I don't need your laws, I have my own."

"If you—"

The alarm wailed up so hard in Paula's ear she flinched. Tanuojin held up one finger. Sril pulled the lever down. "Shoot one." He glanced at Tanuojin and reached for the next lever. "Shoot two."

On either side of *Ybix* points of light sparkled, like firecrackers. The hammerhead off the left wing tumbled over like a wheel. Part of the hull broke off. The Styths roared a cheer that thundered off the curved bridge wall. The men around him reached out and clapped Sril on the shoulders.

Tanuojin shouted, "Quiet!" Paula grabbed hold of the strut of

Sril's perch. Now certainly Gordon would shoot back. Her sweating hands slipped on the plastic strut.

"Akellar, Saba is calling on the ship-to-ship!"

They thundered up another cheer. The bridge stank of their excitement.

"Break this contact with *Luna*. Where is Saba?"

Bakan read off a series of numbers. The videone went dark. Sril pulled the wire deck out of the wall and leaned over it. Paula looked up at the holograph. A hammerhead sailed along on *Ybix*'s off wingtip, another behind her tail. Suddenly they sheered away.

"Akellar, the surface has launched a missile."

Paula turned; she bumped her head on the strut. Tanuojin said, "Clear the bridge. Secure to speed." He charged out of the cage and went up to Bakan's post. The men gathered to watch crowded toward the hatchways. Paula pushed herself after them. Tanuojin shot toward her.

"You stay here, where I can watch you." His fingers closed on her arm. Her spine shivered at his touch. He thrust her at Sril. "Hold on to her."

"Akellar, she can't—"

"Akellar," the helmsman called. "I have a course to intercept *Ybicsa*."

Over his shoulder, Tanuojin called, "Ready to break orbit." He leveled his pale eyes at Sril. "You keep your mouth shut, bang-boy." He dropped away toward the cage. The hatch was just over her head, and she reached for it. Sril pulled her by the arm against his side.

"Hold on, Mendoz'."

"Launch on point." Tanuojin was climbing into the cage. Behind the voices of the other men, talking in numbers, ran the beep and mutter of the machines along the wall. A red light came on near her face. Sril turned her around, her back to his chest.

"Akellar, the missile is firing a cluster. Make it five minutes behind us. Heat-chasers. Four minutes thirty-one seconds."

The sound level rose to a low mechanical rumble that made her ears itch. She moved against Sril's chest. The ship was sliding away from her. She sank back against the man behind her. He spoke to her. The roar drowned his voice. The pressure hurt her eyes. She could not move, wedged against Sril's side. Painfully she strained for breath. Like footsteps her pulse beat louder and louder in his ears.

"*Ybix, Ybix,*" Saba's voice shouted, above the racket.

She turned her head. Her mouth was sticky. Through a pink blur she saw the Styths sitting on their perches, doing their work. They bore the pressure without effort. It hurt her to breathe. She closed her eyes.

"Saba, hold your course. We'll run over you. Can you dock at this speed?"

"I've got this sled in tow." Saba's voice was coming from inside the cage.

Bakan said, "Akellar, four rockets are still tracking us."

"What rockets?" Saba cried, alarmed.

"Akellar," Sril said loudly, "she can't breathe."

She could breathe. Her eyes hurt, and her ears ached as if needles were run through them. Saba said, "What's your pressure?"

"Eight plus," Tanuojin said.

"Compensate. What missiles?"

She fought for air. Her chest lightened. She felt her lips pulled back from her teeth, and her hands rose. She blinked her pink blurred eyes clear.

"Akellar, there's a hammerhead coming up fast on *Ybicsa*."

"Sril, fix him."

"He's out of range—"

"Fix him!"

Paula moved around to Sril's back, her arms around him. If she fell she would land on the cage. She wiped her eyes on her shoulders.

"Two rockets still tracking, two minutes back. I read fission warheads."

When she leaned her head on Sril's back she left a smear of blood across his shirt. She touched her mouth. Down past her feet, *Ybix* sailed through the green map. At the edge of the hologram another image was forming, a needle-shape: *Ybicsa*. The smaller ship fell back into the green field around *Ybix*. Now she saw a third ship, T-shaped, flying up toward *Ybicsa* from the bottom of the hologram. The three flights converged. *Ybix* flew over *Ybicsa*, covering her with her flat shape. The hammerhead veered, running behind them, and exploded.

The men roared. Tanuojin said, "I couldn't have done that better if I'd planned it." Against her face Sril's back bounced in a soundless laugh.

"Saba. Can you dock?"

Ketac's voice came through the cage, high and rapid with excitement. "Akellar, we'll dock. We'll need three men in the chamber to inboard this sled."

Paula was floating. She let go of Sril and put her hands to her face. The holograph light glowed on her rumpled trouser legs. Sril said, "If Ketac is flying, I'll wait back at Luna." He twisted toward her. "How do you feel?"

The hatch was over her head. She stretched her arms up toward it and went out to the corridor.

. . .

She stayed in the wetroom while the ship accelerated to cruising speed. That took fifteen hours. She woke up once, in the dark in a roar of noise. She could not move at all. The wetroom held her in its supporting membranes. She was afraid but there was nothing she could do. The weight of the air against her face hurt her nose. Her eyes were shut and she could not raise the lids. The metallic ring in her ears went on and on like something heard in a seashell. She was losing consciousness. She passed into a noisy dream.

The next time she woke she could move her head, open her eyes, and turn over. She was back in free fall. Someone was banging on the door below her feet. That had wakened her.

"Who is it?" Her stomach was clenched with hunger.

"Paula," Ketac said. "You can come out now."

She tried to push herself backward, fumbling with her bare feet for the door. "No," he called, "go forward, go through the dryer. Do you have any clothes on?"

"No." She crawled head-first through the dark.

"I'll be out in the corridor."

Her head poked up into the open air. With a click a blower fired a gust of warm wind into her face. She drew herself out of the wetroom into a closed dark space. Her arms and legs were painfully cramped and her back had kinked up like a rope. She turned over, working her stiff muscles. Below her a disk of light showed pale in the dark. She dove through it into the cabin.

After the wetroom the oval cabin was huge. She tumbled across it, somersaulting, rolling in the air, her arms and legs flung out. She crashed into the soft wall and rebounded. It was wonderful to move. Her skin tingled in the cold air.

"Paula," Ketac called.

"Yes." She brought herself up against the wall, dizzy. "What is it?"

"Are you dressed yet? Can I come in?"

"Wait." She went around the room, looking for the compartment with her clothes. She put on two pairs of trousers and a shirt and a jacket and two pairs of socks. The cold air was delicious. She opened the hatch and went into the corridor.

Ketac's hair floated like an aureole around his face. "Why didn't you talk to me in Styth, before? All that time I could have been talking to you."

"I don't speak it very well." She reached the corridor of the arrows. She could not remember which way the galley was. Ketac came up beside her. Below her a man dove out of a hatchway, and she went in that direction.

"Pop says I'm supposed to show you around the ship." He came after her into the narrow galley. The rows of levers on the wall were tagged in neat handwritten Styth labels. She pulled one and ran herself straight up into the ceiling. Ketac jeered at her. One hand on the wall and the other on the tab, she pushed in opposite directions. Out the slit-mouth below came a water tube.

"Where is Saba?"

"In the bridge. He's on watch."

She stowed the water tube in mid-air and worked another lever, which produced a strip of protein. The dim light strained her eyes. Her hands and face were cold.

"All right." She drank the water and took a bite of protein bar. "Show me around the ship."

"Actually, I think The Creep is right, for once. This is a warship. You ought to stay in my father's cabin."

She went along the tunnel. Ketac glided along beside her. They turned into the blue corridor. "What's this, for instance?" She put her head into a big open hatchway. Inside was the largest room she had seen, including the bridge. The round wall was plastered with posters, most of them of naked women. There was no one in the room. The lights were out at the far end. She went in. The lights rose.

Ketac followed her. "You shouldn't be in here." He cast a look of horror around at the beaver shots on the wall. "This isn't any place for a woman."

"Don't be silly." She went back to the hatchway. "What's up there that you think I haven't seen? Where do you sleep?"

He led her on down the curving tunnel. He traveled effortlessly beside her; she had to struggle to keep up with him. He brushed his thick hair back with his hand. "That's the Tank—where we just were. The off-duty room." Scooting off ahead of her, he spun the wheel on the next hatch and pulled the cover open. "This is the library."

The deep narrow room was dark. The light from the corridor reached in across the round honeycomb wall of books. Ketac was already scooting off, and she followed him.

"This is the aft bridge hatch—" He struck in passing at a doorway. Beside it was a bank of meter faces like clocks. "And that's the aft engine hatch." Paula went after him in short energetic dashes.

"How many watches are there?"

"Pop's, Tanuojin's, and Kobboz's. You don't know anything, do you?"

They went down the black and white corridor again. "No," she said. "Not a thing."

"There are five men in each watch—the watch officer, the helm, the gunner, the sparks—you know, communications—and the greaser. That's me. I just do what everybody else says." He scooped his wild hair back with his hands. His feet milled steadily to keep him upright. "Pop's is the high watch, The Creep is the middle watch, Kobboz is the low watch."

"Where is Tanuojin now?"

"Asleep, I guess. He has the cabin up beside the library." He dropped away from her into the twilight. "Ask me anything. Go on, ask me something."

"How fast are we going?" She was learning how to move, and she kept up with him all the way down to the next hatch. He looked at her sideways, as if it were a trick question.

"About one and a half miles an hour."

"I mean the ship, Ketac."

"Oh. Thirty-two hundred leagues above course point. Plus six acceleration. That's not very much, we were up to plus 185 in the low watch. Uniform hyperbolic course. Ask me something else."

"I didn't understand the first one." They went into another tunnel, marked with yellow stripes, so there were three: red, blue, and yellow, curved, meeting the black and white corridor at each end. Ahead, the metal tube jogged, and in the dim light someone moved. She started violently all over. A strange Styth raced around the bend and brushed between her and Ketac.

"Ask me something."

"How long will it take us to reach Uranus?"

He stopped at a hatchway. "This is the crew's quarters. The Hole. We're going to Saturn first."

"Let me see." She pulled on the wheel in the hatch. He opened it, and she put her head inside, into a long dim room in which the Styths slept wrapped in their bedrugs like bats in their wings, attached by their feet to the wall.

"When we get there," Ketac said, "we use the Planet's fields to brake and fall into orbit, so we can supply up." He pushed the hatch closed. She turned toward him. "Then we use the fields to boost back to cruising speed and head for Uranus. My father calls that a counter-inertial equivalency system."

"Oh."

"My father is the best engineer in the fleet. Ask me something else."

She led him along the corridor. "Ketac, I don't understand anything you're saying. I wouldn't understand it in the Common Speech." They came to another hatch: the supply room, lined with computers, their checkerboard faces blinking in three colors. He refused to take her into the men's toilet. While she was still hunting for arguments, a bell rang somewhere down the corridor.

"That's the end of my watch," Ketac said. His hair floated on end around his head. "You'd better go back to Pop's cabin now."

She backed away from him. Backing up was easier than moving forward. "Go on, do as you please. I'll be all right."

"Paula, this is a warship. You can't wander around—"

"Thank you." Head-first, she went into the black-white corridor, twisted to change direction, and flew down through the cool dim tunnel.

Ketac had not shown her all the ship. There was a tiny observation room in the nose of the ship, just big enough for two people. Saba took her there, shut the hatch, and pushed a button in the wall. The black wall over her head split down the middle and folded back on either side, and she was looking into the depthless black of space.

"Oh." She put her hand out. Her fingertips grazed the cold plastic of the window.

He stretched his legs out past her, along the foot of the window. His shoulders packed the end of the little pyramidal room. She looked out at the clouds of stars. With difficulty she made out the rectangular constellation Gemini.

"Can I see Uranus?"

"Uranus is on the other side of the ship. Scorpio sector." For navigating the sphere of the stars was divided up into sectors according to the major constellations. He pointed with his little finger at a bright white spark in the long box of Gemini. "That's Jupiter." His claw ticked on the plastic. "Castor and Pollux." He pointed out the two bright stars at one end of the rectangle and the fainter pair at the other end, butting against the Milky Way. "The Star Gate. The Mouth of Hell. Gemini is called the House of Hell. Half the time Uranus's pole axis points to the Sun, but when the Sun enters Gemini the pole slips and starts to wander."

On Uranus the polar axis lay close to the plane of the ecliptic. The star shell was the same, but their astrology would be totally unlike hers.

"I used to dream about space," he said. "Before I ever saw it. I dreamt I crawled up and up through the Planet, until I came to the surface, outside of everything, and I floated away."

"A nightmare?"

"No." He said a word she did not know. "It was a good dream. It was a good feeling. My father was space-drunk. He used to say he could bring his body back to Matuko but his heart stayed in deep space."

The starlight shone on his face. She took hold of his sleeve, fingering the thick material. There were thin dark gray stripes in the light gray ground. "What do these mean?" She ran her thumb down the diagonal stripes sewn on his forearm cuff.

"Rating stripes. Subtenant, lieutenant, commander, master commander, master." He put his hand on her stomach. "Then there's general and master general, which nobody ever gets."

Directly below her Tanuojin's voice said, "Saba, call the bridge."

She rolled out of the way. He reached for the speaker tab in the wall. "Bridge."

"Akellar, Ketac is tearing up Uhama in the Tank."

"Damn him." He left. Paula shut the hatch to keep out the light. She lay in the air staring out at the black fields of space. The stars eased her mood, scattered thick past counting over the window, unimaginably distant. After a while she found the switch that hooded the window again. She went out to the ship's glossy tunnels.

There was another place Ketac had not shown her: the brig, off in a corridor of its own above the number six engine, in the tip of one wing. Saba threw his son into this jail for fighting with Uhama. Two bells rang: the beginning of the middle watch. She wrapped herself in a blanket and Saba rolled them both in the thick rug of his bed, and they slept, attached to the wall by a ring near their feet. The shag fur made her nose feel dusty. The big Styth slept with his arms around her. She wondered what Matuko would be like and shut off her curiosity. If she went with expectations she would only confuse herself. She put her face against the sleeping man's bare shoulder.

At three bells he went to the bridge. The Tank was crowded and she did not go in. She went to the library, but Tanuojin was there. She wandered around the halls, bored. At the end of the black and white corridor, under a storage hatch, she found three little fish swimming behind a round window in the hall.

She searched around the ship and found five more fish bowls. The little fish were dull gray, with spines on their backs. She went into the blue corridor and down the short wing tunnel to the brig.

The pounding of the engine below vibrated the air. The heat was terrific. At the blind end of the tunnel, Ketac hung upside down, his eyes closed. His skin was oily with sweat. She went back out to the arrow tunnel and down to the galley.

Two men crowded it. One was Marus, Tanuojin's helmsman. She watched outside for them to leave.

"One thing about Sril," Marus said. "He does all his fighting in the ship, where it doesn't matter he isn't big enough to see over his old woman's ass." He came out past her, ignoring her, as all Tanuojin's men did. She got a tube of water from the galley wall and went back to the brig.

Ketac was staring at the wall. The side of his face was deeply scratched. There were rings set into the wall, but he did not seem to be tied.

"Here," she said.

He jumped, his hands flying up. "Paula." His voice croaked. He tore open the tube and sucked out the water. Soaked dark with sweat, his overalls were open down to his crotch. The racket jangled her; she felt gritty.

"Thanks, Paula." He squeezed the last of the water into his mouth.

"I'll bring you another."

He followed her around the bend to the hatch. "Stay here—don't leave me alone here."

"The hatch isn't locked. You can leave."

He scrubbed his face with his hands. "I promised my father I'd stay here." His voice was raw. "He'd tie me if I left."

"I'll bring you something to eat." She went out to the cool, quiet tunnel beyond.

When she came back, he was floating in the blind end again. He beamed at her, relieved to see her, and grabbed the tube of water.

"Thanks. Nobody else has even come in here."

The vibration set her teeth on edge. The boy hung sidewise in the air. The tip of his forefinger was bloody and scabbed over, the claw broken off deep in the quick.

"What are those fish for?"

His teeth mashed through a mouthful of food tablets. "They're scouts. If the hatches leak they die." He drank the rest of the water. Bits of plastic wrapping floated around him.

"How long will you be here?"

"Until he lets me out." He kicked, knocking himself back into the wall. "Nobody cares about me—I'm going crazy—" He banged around the end of the tunnel. She moved away from him, wary.

"Paula, don't go—"

"I can't even hear you." The heat made her face itch. "I'll come back later."

"Paula! Stay here—please—"

"Ketac—" A bell sounded, muffled. "I'll come later." She left him alone.

She went to the bridge, to meet Saba coming off watch. He had already gone. Kobboz was sitting down in the cage. She looked in the Tank and in the library, and turned on the monitors in her room and hunted through them. He was nowhere. Neither was Tanuojin; they were together. She stopped looking.

She went to bed. The rug folded around her like a great loose skin. Drowsily she wondered why they fastened up the foot instead of the head. It was pleasant to float free in the air. She yawned.

The hatch opening woke her. Saba swung himself in through the oval doorway. She started to call to him but she heard Tanuojin's voice.

"Come down to the library. I'll show you."

"I'm tired." Saba was stripping off his overalls. "Next watch."

"Jesus." The deep voice rasped. "All your off-time now you spend with her."

"What's the matter with you?"

The hatch slammed. Tanuojin went away. She heard Saba give a low laugh.

Halfway through the middle watch, she thought of Ketac again and took him a dozen food tablets and two tubes of water. When he saw her his face split in a broad smile. "Paula."

She wiped her face on her sleeve. He ripped open a water tube.

"Talk to me. Stay here and talk to me."

"Ketac, it's hot in here."

"Nobody else has even come to see me—all my so-called friends—" He ran himself into the wall. "Nobody but a nigger squaw. Oh, Jesus, I have to get out of here."

"Do you know who Jesus was?"

He stroked his hair back. His sprouting mustaches were pointed, like feathers. "I don't know. It's just a curse. It sounds like a curse. It feels good to say it." His eyes glinted. "Like fuck."

The corridor was littered with bits of white wrapping. She gathered them up. Around the bend, the hatch banged open. She spun. Saba came feet-first toward them. "Paula. What are you doing in here?" He took her by the arm. "Hot, isn't it?" he said to Ketac.

"Pop, let me out—please—"

"You sound pretty lively yet to me." He pulled her off along the tunnel. "One more watch, Ketac."

"I'll die!"

"I'll miss your company."

In the corridor, the cool air bathed her face; her shirt was stuck to her arms and she pulled her sleeves free. Saba pushed her along ahead of him.

"Stay away from him."

"He was hungry."

"He's supposed to suffer. He isn't your crumb."

The computer in the supply room made her several sets of overalls, like the uniforms of the men, with the black three-pointed star on the back but no rating stripes. She wore two sets at a time to keep warm. In the dim light she learned to use her other senses more than before. Quickly she lost track of time. The high watch, the low watch, the middle watch ran after each other like clock gears. The time didn't seem to change at all, any more than the ship seemed to move, suspended in the dark, the stars unchanging before the window. In the Asteroids near Pallas three Martian ships ambushed them, but *Ybix* outran them in fifteen minutes. Paula was starved for real food. The chewy protein strips sometimes satisfied her need to eat but she dreamt of gingerbread and whipped cream and sugar candy. As if she were gorging herself, her stomach began to bulge.

Sril played a ulugong, a sheet of metallic plastic that he held on his lap and struck with his knuckles, like a drum with bell tones. She brought her flute to the Tank and they played duets. The other men threw darts and made models and argued the various merits of the posters on the wall. Occasionally they got into a fight over the paper women spreading their legs on the curved wall. She read, and she worked on the first draft of the trade contract, but the music kept her mood light. The low mellow voice of the ulugong went well with the flute. They made up songs, she and Sril, by the hour.

They clubbed Ketac. All the crew but two men left to mind the bridge packed into the Tank. Ketac knelt down in the air before Saba, who took his hands and stretched his arms out before him. Behind him Tanuojin pulled the young man's hair back.

"Who is the man?" Saba asked.

"Styth," Ketac answered. His voice trembled, passionate.

"Which is the way?"

"To the Sun."

"Keep faith." Saba slapped him hard across the cheek.

The other men cheered. His face glowing, his hair fastened neatly down, Ketac whooped in their midst. Behind them all, Paula tucked her hands into her sleeve. It was such a simple ritual. She wondered uneasily why they could not do without it altogether. Saba brought out a bottle of Scotch. Ketac tried to drink out of it, while the other men laughed and pounded him on the back. She picked up her flute and withdrew into the music.

Saba steered her down the arrow corridor, past the mouth of the blue tunnel. After 121 watches she moved as easily as he did, faster sometimes, but he still maneuvered her around whenever he could. They went into the Beak, the room in the nose of the ship. The window was shut. While she felt around the rim for the switch, Saba came in beside her and closed the hatch. She pressed the switch, and the window cracked and light spilled through the widening gap into the little room. In half-phase, banded in cream and gold, wrapped in the curved blades of its rings, Saturn filled the window.

Paula lay back in the air. The brilliant golden light dazzled her. The rings were tilted down away from her, like thin dust veils.

"The first time I ever came here," he said, "it was my third voyage into space. Tanuojin's first. My father brought the ship down on the trade lane and we stopped everything that came by. Melleno was the Prima then. After we'd held up about a dozen freight ships going to Saturn, he sent his Saturn Fleet out and chased us off. My father howled so hard, you could hear him all over the ship."

"Why?"

"The Prima wasn't supposed to have any rights in deep space. My father didn't approve of other people breaking the law. Just him. Jesus, that was an awful voyage. My father took such a hate to Tanuojin—Tajin had worked for Melleno. Then when we got back to Uranus, Tajin went to Melleno and they mended their quarrel and he wrote a law for Melleno putting a 100 per cent tax on goods stolen from Styth hulls and sold in Styth markets. They took all the profit out of piracy. It almost ruined the fleet."

She looked out the window at the ringed Planet. The shadow of one of its moons lay on the golden surface of the clouds. "What was your father's name?"

"Yekaka. It fitted him, too." The name meant loudmouth. "Do you want to go down to Saturn-Keda?"

"Oh. Yes. Can I? Will you take me?"

"If you promise to keep quiet."

She looked out at the Planet. The surface was patterned in whorls and streamers of clouds, changing shape while she watched, changing hue. "I promise."

"Good. It'll give you an idea what Matuko is like."

The yellow light shone over the side of his face. She put her hand on his legs, lying beside her. "I want to name the baby David."

"David. What kind of a name is that? It sounds like a girl's name. Call him Vida. It's the same thing. Vida—David."

"Then you call him Vida, and I'll call him David."

He played with her fingers. His claws tapped her palm. "What else?"

"Does there have to be more?"

"Most shirt-names are a little more elaborate. Nobody ever uses it." He manipulated her fingers.

"What's a shirt-name? Ouch."

He pulled her hand up and kissed her palm and rubbed his cheek over the flat of her hand. Her palm stung where the claw had pricked her.

"When the baby is born I wrap him up in my shirt and take him outdoors, so that people can see I accept him as mine, and I give him his name."

"What's your shirt-name?"

"Takoret-aSaba. 'He knows the right way.' My father liked righteous names. He was always telling me to live up to my name." He laughed, his hand up to his chin, his face painted in Saturn's yellow light. "I knew all the wrong ways."

"Does the name have to mean something?"

"No."

"Good. Then David Mendoza." She put her hand on her rounding body. "What's Tanuojin's shirt-name?"

"He hasn't got one. He's an orphan. The people who brought him up found him in the street when he was barely old enough to walk. They already had eight boys, so they named him 'the ninth boy.' " His voice broadened with pride. "He started from point. He had nothing."

"He still has very little."

Someone banged on the hatch below her. She moved out of the way. He opened the hatch, and Tanuojin's head and shoulders rose through the round entry. He gave Saturn a glance and ignored Paula.

"Here." He thrust a watchboard and a stylus at Saba. "Did you call Melleno?"

"I will now." Saba wrote on the board. He took a slide calculator out of his sleeve. "She is going with us."

Paula moved back against the wall, out of their way. Tanuojin took the board again. "Why?"

"Make sure you clear that orbit with Titan. You're in my way."

Tanuojin backed out of the hatch. Saba went out. Paula started after him and the other man blocked the hatch.

"No, Saba, let me talk to her."

Paula withdrew into the darkness, her back to the giant Planet. Through the hatch came a short laugh. "Talk all you want."

Tanuojin came into the cramped space after her. She stayed as far away from him as she could. Her fingers went to her breast. "What do you want?"

"I'll ask the questions. Look over there." He gestured to one side and put out his other hand. She recoiled.

"Don't touch me."

The Planet glared over his long face, his catfish jaw. The hatch was below him. She could not escape. He said, "Do as I say. Look over there. I'm just going to touch you."

"No."

He lowered his hand. "What are you afraid of?" His voice was unsettlingly deep. "Are you afraid of me?"

"Yes."

He spun over the hatch wheel and pushed the cover away into the corridor. "Get out. You stink like pig."

She went out the hatch and down the corridor; she did not stop until she was in the red tunnel, two hatches from her room.

She spent ten minutes in the wetroom, scrubbing herself on the walls. Washing her face was fun, although the soap stung her eyes. Thinking about Tanuojin made her uncomfortable. When he had healed her she had been so groggy she could hardly remember what had happened. She rubbed soap into her hair and rinsed it in the water streaming along the wall.

"Are you in there?" A fist banged on the watch below her feet.

"Yes."

"Come out and get dressed, if you want to go to Saturn-Keda."

She crawled into the gusty warmth of the dryer and went out to the room. The cold roughened her skin. She took out a fresh pair of overalls.

"Put on something fancy. You can't go like that."

She got her suitcase out of the long compartment in the wall. "Why are you taking me, anyway?"

"I told you. I'm civilizing you." He was stripping off his uniform.

It would be cold in Saturn-Keda. She put on overalls and the long black dress An Chu had made for her, which had a coat that went with it. The layers of skirts floated around her, glinting with silver threads.

"How do I look?" She turned around, and the many layers of the dress swirled around her. She put the coat on.

"You look fine. One more thing." He floated in front of her, standing up the collar of the coat. "Decent women don't go out in public in Styth with their faces uncovered."

She slid back away from him. "What do you mean?"

"I mean you go veiled."

"No."

"Do you want to go or not?"

She watched him, angry, while he opened a bin and got out a length of black cloth. He wrapped it around her head and draped it over her face, tucking the excess down under the collar of the coat.

"Good," he said. "That will do fine."

She turned away, humiliated.

They went through the tunnels to the docking chamber. He let her take the veil off while they flew to Saturn-Keda. Tanuojin was already in the chamber, pulling on a black pressure suit. Saba led her to the rack in the wall. He helped her put on a space suit. It was Sril's, who overstood her by fourteen inches. She pulled the thick leggings up until her feet reached the bottom, and he tied the slack around her knees.

"I did some tuning on this suit, and we'll launch soft. You ought to be comfortable most of the time." He showed her the helmet, a smoky plastic cylinder. "You wear this until I say you can take it off."

She took the helmet in her arms. He gave her a pair of gloves. "Tanuojin! Plug her in."

Ybicsa's hatch was wide open. Paula poked her head through into the narrow cockpit of the ship. Three tandem seats took up most of the space. Tanuojin came around the last, took the helmet away from her, and pushed her into the middle seat. He reached past her and pulled a shoulder harness around her. Floating sideways, he uncoiled a white tube from under the seat and fixed it to a socket in the suit leg behind her knee.

"Put the gloves on."

She put her hands into the enormous gloves. Saba came into the ship, massive in his suit. He dropped into the front seat. Its high back hid him from her. Tanuojin tugged the gloves down over her wrists and strapped them tight. She looked him in the face. His yellow eyes were notched with brown. He put the helmet over her head. The smoked plastic darkened her sight.

Saba said, "I'll take her down the A-39 chute at a 28-degree attitude, level off at minus 100M, and underfly Saturn-Keda. All right?"

"Fine," Tanuojin said.

She floated in the huge padded seat. When she turned her face up, the helmet struck the back. There was an ax strapped to the wall beside her, and below it a long tube that looked like a gun. The cab lights went off. She sat in the dark, in the mid-air, the harness holding her six inches above the seat.

"Bridge," Saba said.

"Yes, Akellar." The voices came through the helmet above her ears.

"Start a count from twenty-five."

Her seat had no arms. She put her hands under the harness and pulled herself down to make contact with the seat. In the top of the helmet an uninflected voice was counting backward. She put one hand on the wall. Even through the glove she could feel it tremble. A green light shone in front of the cab; Saba had turned on the holograph beside his knee. Leaning forward, she could see it and the side of his head.

"Sixteen, fifteen, fourteen—"

The two men talked in a litany of orders and replies. Paula slid her hand under the harness, down to the round bulge of the baby. This might hurt him. He's a Styth, he can do anything.

"Five, four, three, two, one, point."

There was a roar that hurt her ears. She was slammed back into the seat. Her eyes streamed. The pressure suit had failed. Her chest felt caved in. Her heartbeat pounded in her ears. She lost consciousness.

"Paula."

"Uuh." She opened her eyes. She was floating. Something bounced off the top of her helmet, and it lifted away. The green light of the holograph shone brilliantly in her face. Saba stooped beside her, wedged between the seat and the wall.

"How do you feel?"

She put her hand up to her head. "That's a jolt."

He laughed. He looked beyond her, at Tanuojin, who did not laugh. Her left hand, still thrust under the harness, smarted rhythmically. She pulled her gloves off. The harness straps had imprinted the backs of her hands in deep purple welts. He took her fingers.

"Don't do that." He pointed up over her head and went back to his seat.

She raised her eyes. The ceiling was clear, a wide window. The stars shone in a broad swath above her. Near the edge of the window two crescent moons shone, one the size of an orange, the other the size of a pea. Her helmet was fastened to a clamp in the ceiling, obscuring the middle of the sky.

"That was a damned dead perfect launch," Saba said, ahead of her. "We're plus or minus one for the chute."

She could hear the cluck of a radio in the back with Tanuojin. She leaned around her seat to look. Twisted in his seat, he was bent over a deck of instruments, earphones over his head. A red light on the panel flashed on his cheek.

"Get me some temperature readings," Saba said. She turned straight. Enormous, splendid, Saturn was rising into the window, spilling its light into the cab. In the holograph's green cube *Ybicsa* like a pin dropped into a thickening yellow radiance.

"About this new ship," Saba said. "Maybe if I tuck her in a little at the waist, she won't tail up so much at launch."

Tanuojin said, "You have that ship half-built already, and you don't even have the money to buy the model plastic."

Saba reached awkwardly around the back of his seat and patted Paula on the knee. "I've got it right here. I just haven't converted it yet."

The cab was filled with the Planet's light. At the edge of the holograph the green thickened to a yellow like cheese. *Ybicsa* shot toward it. They were passing over the rings, now resolved into a flood of particles, sparkling in the sunlight. She could see only the innermost stream. The curve of the Planet showed through it.

"Temperature readings. Rim: 300. Thermolayer 1137. Ten M, 350. Twenty M, 152."

The Planet glared in the window. Red and yellow plumes of gas ran past them. They thickened to a light-filled cloud. The ship plunged through a yellow fog. The holograph showed *Ybicsa* nosing into a pale stream that backed and curled like a river through the Planet's substance. Ahead, a darker loop bulged into the stream, pressing it out on either side.

"Braking," Saba said. "Paula, put your helmet on."

She stretched her hands up over her head toward the ceiling. The helmet was beyond her reach. She wrestled with the harness. She was heavy; she weighed enough to hold herself down in the seat, and the clamps on the harness were too stiff to open. She pulled at the straps holding her down.

Tanuojin leaned across the back of her seat, took the helmet off the ceiling, and rammed it down over her head. "Put your gloves on!" he shouted.

She found her gloves and fitted her hands into them. Her mouth was dry. The ship rocked violently and she slid forward into the harness.

"Reef," Tanuojin said. "Coming fast."

"I see it."

A thick dark stream wound along the holograph. The ship bucked down, lurched to the left as if she were sliding down a wave, and heaved herself straight again. The suit was rigid. Paula could move her fingers inside the fat gloves but the gloves were immovable. The light was fading. They passed into a deep dusk, into a midnight darkness. The pressure suit had hardened like a shell around her. She looked up overhead. The darkness was complete. Suddenly a fragment of coherent light appeared, a long streak that melted away while she watched.

"What's that?"

"False image," Saba said. "Döppelganger."

There was a scream of noise like an alarm going off. A mechanical voice said loudly, "A-39, A-39. This is Saturn-Keda, identify."

Ybicsa bucked upward again and fell off sheer to the left. Paula gulped down the nausea in her throat. Dizzy, she fixed her eyes on the seat before her. Tanuojin was saying, "SIF 16 *Ybicsa*, armed scout from SIF 6 *Ybix*. Barkus-rating H. Check white records. Automatic clearance rAkellaron confirmed."

Paula moved her fingers. The suit was beginning to soften. *Ybicsa* sailed into a long curve, and she fell against the harness. She braced herself on her arms. The ship swung around again, faster than Paula's stomach.

"*Ybicsa*, this is Saturn-Keda, we read an unregistered person in your craft."

"No registry. Female mixed blood."

"Status."

"No status. Saba's property."

"Paula," Saba said, under his breath in her ear, "Look up."

She raised her head. Over them, in the dark, was a vast slimy roof, festooned with scum and feathery crystalline growth. The underside of Saturn-Keda. She straightened to see the holograph. The scale had changed; *Ybicsa* was four times as large as before. She was flying along below a glob like an Idaho potato, trailing long strings like roots down into the magma. The bubble was too large for the map, and only a patch of it showed.

"*Ybicsa*, this is Saturn-Keda, we will dock you from here. At point you will lock your control system into—"

"Stop," Saba said. "I dock my own ship."

"We do not allow—"

"Stop. Call Melleno. This damned dumb computer."

She looked up again at the encrusted skin above her. They were passing a root trailing down into the dark. Spidery outgrowths sprouted like hairs from it, barely visible in the dark.

"There's a lot of radiation, Saba," Tanuojin said. "All the dials are white."

"It's always hot around here this part of the spin." Saba wheeled out of his chair. He pulled off his helmet and turned to help Paula. He stood with one foot braced on the sloping side of the ship.

"I thought you said she's smart," Tanuojin said. "She couldn't reach the helmet, back at the brake. She's too stupid to ask for help."

The helmet lifted off her shoulders. Stiffly she said, "Thank you."

"You stupid pig."

She started up. Saba pushed her down into the seat again. He said, "The suits are all on one line, if one isn't sealed, none of them seals."

"Oh." She glanced at Tanuojin. "Then I take it back." She sat straight in the curved seat.

"*Ybicsa*," a live voice said, in the radio speaker, "this is Saturn-Keda. You may dock under manual power. Use XM-7. Please do not race. If you stall in the tunnel, remain where you are and we will guide you in."

Tanuojin got up. He stood in the narrow aisle beside Saba's seat, one long arm braced on its back. She leaned to one side to see the hologram. *Ybicsa* floated in a green soup. The ship's wake showed clearly in the shifting light of the map. She nosed forward into the mass of the bubble. Its skin, overgrown with rough crystalline, seemed to thicken out of the magma around it. *Ybicsa*'s needle-snout disappeared into it, and a new hologram wiped diagonally onto the map. *Ybicsa* flew into a narrow tunnel. Light flashed blinding through the window. Tanuojin raised one arm to shield his eyes.

"What was that?" she asked.

"The dock is leaking," Saba said. "Read off the speed, will you?" His voice deepened; he was talking to his lyo.

"One-two," Tanuojin said. "One-two. You're going too fast. Three-four. Three-four."

"*Ybicsa*," the radio said urgently, "you're coming in too fast. Please do not race. You'll stall—"

"Turn that off," Saba said, and Tanuojin leaned back and shut the volume down; she could still hear the tiny voice complaining behind her.

Ybicsa glided smoothly as a dream through the series of short jogs. Paula held herself in place, her hands on the harness. After the free fall she felt heavy and dull in the gravity.

"One-four," Tanuojin read. "Three-sixteen. Saba, you could fly a piece of silk. One-eight, one-eight."

She raised her heavy head like a bulb on her neck. *Ybicsa* crept through the utter dark. Paula blotted out Tanuojin's voice reading their speed. They hardly seemed to move. Then light flashed on ice, and *Ybicsa* burst up through the surface of the water and shot through the city, and Paula jumped, startled.

Tanuojin sat down again behind her. The ship settled, turning a slow corkscrew. Saturn-Keda flew past the window, striped with bushy green foliage. It was dark, like twilight. She looked down through the window over her head into streets lined with little square buildings. She was too high above them to make out the people save as a coiling swarm in the street. *Ybicsa* rolled slowly over, and the city curled around her, covering the inside surface of the bubble. They passed beneath an inky river stitched over with bridges. Abruptly *Ybicsa* was swallowed.

Paula gave a violent start. But they had only flown into a dock. The engines roared. She was sliding forward into the harness. The ship slowed around a curve. A string of other ships was parked along the inside wall of the dock. Saba eased the ship up to an empty platform. Something thudded against the outside of the hull under her feet: maybe an anchor. She pulled off her gloves. Tanuojin climbed past her and thrust the hatch up and out. The ship rocked slightly under his step. She struggled with the clips of her harness. Saba leaned down to help her.

"Remember, no talk." He unplugged her suit and fastened the veil across her face. She clambered after him out the hatch. The suit was heavy as chain over her shoulders. She could barely stand upright.

The platform was bare and cold. The wall was papered over with torn posters. The veil closed off her side vision. Tanuojin stood talking to a big graying man. The sleeves and front of his shirt were embroidered in metallic thread. He swung around, looking over her head.

"Saba, why do I spend a fortune training pilots?" They shook hands.

"Your pilots don't fly my ships."

Another man brought a board and a stylus up to him. "Akellar, I need your full engine rates—" Saba took him off to the stern of his ship.

The old man looked down at Paula. "Who is she?"

"Saba's latest moral aberration," Tanuojin said.

She glanced up at him, and the old man laughed. He smacked Tanuojin on the back with his open hand. "Tajin, you've made yet another enemy. Let's go, it's cold."

They took off the black pressure suits in a locker room near the platform and went down a stair to the inner surface of the bubble. The three men talked about people she had never heard of. They walked along a street crowded with Styths. She had to trot to keep up with Saba. The buildings on either side were one and two stories, plain stone houses. Strips of green separated them: the grass that helped circulate the air. It even grew on the roofs of some houses. The buildings, the people around her, everything dwarfed her. She felt shrunk to miniature, like a toy. They went down a huge step in the street. She took Saba's hand to negotiate it. In the twilight, the street ran straight off before her to the curve of the bubble in the distance, ran up the side, and turned and came back over her head. When she looked straight up she could see the busy streets and buildings of the other side of Saturn-Keda, two or three miles over her head, upside down. A strong odor of fish reached her nose. She looked around at the sheets of nets hanging from the eaves of the houses they passed. The street glistened with fish scales. A furry brown beast, cat-sized, was eating something in the gutter.

They went through an open gate into a yard. Three children were chasing each other around at the far end. Their heads were bald as onions. Her arms and legs ached with fatigue. Her face sagged. Saba took her hand and helped her up three high steps. They went into a blue hall.

"Here." Saba planted her firmly in the middle of the room. "Stay here. Melleno, let me use your photo-relay."

Melleno took him out of the room. Paula looked around her. The blue light rippled through the room, constantly changing color. It was like being under water. This was what Matuko would be like, dark and cold. There was no ceiling: she looked up across Saturn-Keda, into the distant web of streets. Tanuojin was at the far end of the room, ignoring her. Melleno came back.

"Well? Tell me about the Middle Planets."

"You're right," Tanuojin said. "It's a lot more complicated than we thought."

"Tajin. Tell me something new."

She went to the table against the wall. It was strange to walk. Even the crepe dress felt heavy. The table was Styth-sized and her chin just cleared the top. A bowl stood on it heaped up with little red beans, or perhaps fruit.

"The Martians have the guns and the money," Tanuojin was saying, "but the anarchists do all the thinking."

"Where did he get her?"

"On the Earth."

"Is she an anarchist?"

"Melleno, she is a pig. You know how he is about women."

Her back was to them. She pulled the veil aside. He had been enraged, in *Ybicsa*, because he had had to help her. She took a handful of the beans out of the bowl and put one in her mouth. It was soft and sweet with a hard pip in the center.

"What do you think of Saba's treaty?"

"I like the economics. That's a lot of money. What about this truce?"

"It's just with the Council, not with the Martians."

"Is there a difference?"

She went along the wall to a window. The sill was a foot wide. She stood eating the fruit. The Styth children were playing before her in the yard. They were bigger than she was. They looked very young, their cheeks still round, like babies'. Now the air in the room was green. She took a seed out of her mouth and flicked it out to the courtyard. Maybe it would grow: her mark on Saturn-Keda.

"Can we take them?" Melleno asked.

"Yes, we can take them. We have to think of how, that's all, but there's a way. You used to tell me we could take anybody. Don't you believe it any more?"

"Well, an old man sees short. What do you want to drink?"

"Nothing. Water."

Melleno's voice softened with amusement, even affection. "You know, Tajin, if you allowed yourself the occasional vice, you might find life more pleasant."

"Why is it such a crime not to get drunk?"

Paula leaned on the window sill. A woman had come out of a door nearby. Her hair was piled up on her head; her fringed sleeves hung down almost to the ground. She called angrily to the children to stop screaming.

Behind Paula Saba came into the room. She yanked the veil across her face again. He went up to the other men, and Tanuojin slung one arm around his neck.

"I feel as if I'm going to put my foot through the floor."

"What was the Earth like?" Melleno said.

Saba raised his head. "Beautiful. Even the natural parts, outside the cities. Every place you look there's something you've never seen before. They don't just have two or three kinds of trees, they have hundreds. They have insects there that look like flowers and flowers as high as your head. And the strangest people I've ever met."

Several small pale men in white coats brought a little wagon into the room. They were the first people of her own race she had seen in six weeks. Swiftly and silently they opened the lid of the cart and took out cups. Her spine prickled up. They were slaves. One was obviously part-Styth, like her baby.

"I've never done so many strange things in my life," Saba said. "Maybe it was just being so far from home."

"It was hot and bright," Tanuojin said. "And every time I went through a door I cracked my head."

The slaves went among them, bringing cups and a platter. The three rAkellaron ignored them, probably did not notice them, would notice them only if the slaves made mistakes. Paula turned back to the window. Across the courtyard the children were throwing sticks at each other.

A trickle of feeling ran quickly down her side. She straightened, astonished, and put her hand on the fat hump of the baby. She had never felt him move before.

"They have no standards, Earthish people," Saba was saying. "Except themselves."

She turned to watch them. Melleno's sleeve glittered. He raised his cup. "The Earth is the only place outside Styth I've ever wanted to see."

She watched his hands. He wore a thick bracelet around each wrist. He had been the Prima, a great Prima. His strong action against piracy had forced the Styth Fleet to raid down below Jupiter, into the Middle Planets, since they could no longer rob their own people. He was an old man, his claws whitening, and his mustaches hanging down over his embroidered shirt.

Tanuojin came in again. Paula turned away from them. In the window, looking out at the city, she tried to judge how much energy they needed to maintain all this, to make life possible here. Of course they had Saturn itself, an inexhaustible supply of energy, yielding up radiation like a little sun. People like her had come here to take that energy, and the Planet had made them into Styths. *Home is where the heart is,* she thought, and laughed.

Ybix flew on through the dark, away from the Sun. After the journey to Saturn, the ship closed around Paula like a shell. The baby moved inside her body, energetic. He woke her up sometimes, kicking. Her stretching skin itched intolerably. She scratched herself until she bled. Saba threatened to tie her hands behind her. All her overalls were too tight and he changed the settings in the computer and made her new ones.

One of the fish died in a tank in the transverse corridor. She scooped it out of the water and took it off to Saba. The number four engine was missing timing, and he paid no attention to the fish. His hands already shining with grease, he plunged head-first down a hatch into the engine room. She took the fish to the computer room and sealed it into a plastic folder for the technician to analyze.

In the high watch, while Saba was on duty, she worked in the library, writing out a master contract to allow off-worlders to trade in Matuko. The sketches clipped to the wall were parts of Saba's new ship, *Ybicket*: the more he worked out the designs, the more he nagged her to finish the contract. While she was busy with this work, Tanuojin's voice said, behind her, "If you want to see how that fish died, go look now."

She wheeled; he was gone. She switched off the file projector and went down the blue tunnel to the black-white corridor. The hatch was open. Cold air streamed down on the fish. She put her head through the hatch into the dark.

In the back of the storage compartment, beyond a row of exygen tanks, a blue light shone. She went toward it. A man was curled over the glow of a small lamp, heating a bottle of Saba's Scotch. It was Uhama, the greaser on Kobboz's watch.

She spun toward the way out. He had seen her. She lunged away but he caught her by the ankle.

Twisting, she broke free. The big man moved between her and the hatch. She was already shivering in the cold. She said, "Uhama, listen to me." Her lips were stiff.

"If you tell him, he'll lock me in the hot closet," he said, and came toward her.

"He'll do worse than that if you hurt me—" She backed away, banging into the tanks. His arms spread to corral her, the big man followed her into the back of the compartment, into the dark.

"Nobody knows but you."

"Tanuojin knows—"

His hands closed around her throat. She clutched his wrists. A white light burst in her eyes.

"Paula!"

Uhama thrust her away, wheeling around, and she bumped into the wall. She gagged for breath. Locked together with someone else, Uhama banged into the tanks along the wall and caromed toward her. The other man was Ketac. She slipped past them toward the shaft of light coming through the hatch. Her throat hurt so much she could hardly breathe. In the corridor she flew down to the nearest call screen and pressed the lever up.

"Bridge." Her voice wheezed.

"Yes—who's this?" Bakan said.

"Ketac and Uhama are fighting in the number four storage bin." She looked back that way. The hatch flew wide open and Uhama tumbled out. He started in her direction, saw her, and whipped around to go the other way. Ketac shot out to meet him. He caught the fleeing man by the shoulders and slammed both feet into Uhama's back. Uhama clawed at him, grunting with effort, his eyes white-ringed. Saba raced around the bend in the corridor. Ketac sprang back. Uhama hung still in the air, half-conscious.

"What's going on?" Saba asked.

Ketac's chest heaved. He pointed to Paula, ten feet down the corridor. "I was coming around here, and I saw the hatch open, and he was in there strangling her."

Saba raised one arm across his body and struck Uhama. The other man hit the wall face-first. "Take him to the brig."

"Yes, sir." Ketac towed Uhama away by one foot.

Paula touched her throat. She was alive by seconds. Her bruised muscles refused to swallow. Saba lunged at her, bad-tempered.

"What were you doing in there with him?"

In a croaking voice she told him about the fish, Tanuojin, the bottle of whiskey. He went into the compartment and came out again, the lamp in one hand, and shut the hatch.

"That son of a bitch," he said. "He knew you'd go in there alone." He herded her down the tunnel. One bell rang: the end of his watch. He pushed her into his cabin. She felt of her throat. In a rising temper, Saba circled once around the little room. He stopped at the call screen.

"Bridge."

"Yes, Akellar."

"Call my watch into the Tank." He wheeled around and pushed her, hard. "I warned you. You stay with me from now on. Or in here with the hatch locked." He flew to the hatch. His wake was heated with his rage. She gave a quick glance around the room and followed him.

They went through the warren of the ship into the yellow

corridor. One of the men from Tanuojin's watch was coming the other way, and Saba attacked him. The other man never tried to fight back. He rolled to one side, his arms up to protect his face, and Saba slashed at him. Tanuojin's man dodged behind the blow and raced away. Saba let him go. Paula went after him through the curtain of their scents. He swerved up into the Tank.

Sril and Bakan were at the far end of the long dim room. Near the hatch, Saba's helmsman was talking to Marus, Tanuojin's helm. Without a word, Saba flew at Marus. All three of the men of his watch charged at the man they had just been tolerating and clawed at him. Paula flinched back to the wall. Marus burst free and fled out the hatch, leaving a smoky trail of blood behind him in the air.

Sril came up to her. The gold wire winked in his nose. "Mendoz', this is how innocent sailors die in space."

Saba circled in the middle of the room, below the posters of naked women. Ketac had come in; he floated over beside Paula.

"Thank you," she said, low.

"You helped me," he said. "I pay my debts."

"Listen to me." Saba looked around at his men. "My lyo thinks he can run around me in my own ship. I'm going to kick him into shape, so stay away from him, unless you want some extra stripes." He lunged at Ketac and got him by the shirtfront. "That means you, clothead." He pushed his son backward away from him.

Paula sidled down the wall. Bubbles of Marus's blood bobbed in the air around the hatch. It was the low watch, when Saba and Tanuojin were both off-duty. She looked both ways into the tunnel. A few yards away on either side, its kinks took it out of sight. She went out the hatch.

There was nowhere she could go to hide from them. The ship was like a maze. She flew down toward the red corridor. A sound ahead of her made her stop sharp. Tanuojin came around the next bend.

He flew at her, and she raced back the way she had come, into the S-curves below the Tank. Just out of his sight, she flattened herself against the wall. He sailed past her. She went back the other way. He struck at her and missed her by inches, his claws like knives. She was faster than he was. At the mouth of the red corridor she paused and looked back and saw him stopped ten feet up the tube, watching her. She went down to her cabin and locked herself in.

She was too jittery to play her flute. She prowled around and around the room. The cold and dark closed over her. The Styths on watch swam through the monitor screens. Her throat was still sore. She was tired. Her eyes burned in their sockets. Taking out the bedrug, she clipped the ring to the wall and wrapped herself up in the thick shag.

Saba woke her, banging on the door. She let him in. He came past her into the room. When he turned she saw four deep scratches down the side of his jaw.

"What happened?"

"Nothing."

The wounds were marked in dried blood. She put one hand on his shoulder, holding her blanket around her with the other. "What happened to your face?"

"There's nothing wrong with me." He brushed her off. Unbuckling his belt, he peeled his overalls off. She backed away from him.

"Was that Tanuojin?"

"No. I can't find him."

They rolled the bed around them. The wings overlapped and clung to one another. She squirmed until she was comfortable. He ground the heel of his hand into his eyes.

"I'd like to wrap his damned dirty tongue around his neck."

They lay quiet a moment. The floating bed rocked slightly back and forth. His fingers moved in her hair. Usually he was asleep before she was even settled enough to close her eyes.

"Why does he do this to me?" he said.

"How long have you known him?"

"Since we were neophytes."

"Then you know what he's like."

He barked a flat laugh. "Yes. He knows what I'm like, too, which is why he's staying out."

"How did you meet him?"

"I don't remember." He squirmed around in the bedrug. "It was while I was loading. He was always around, being creepy. I couldn't stand him. He has that nasty mouth—Anyhow, I got sick, and my friends decided I was dying and left me in an alley. He found me and took me to his trap. When I had the fits, he put his hands on me and I stopped kicking. He kept me alive all the time I was shedding my joe. As soon as I could stand up, we swore the irelyon."

He yawned. The wounds down his face were ridged with dried blood. Grouchy, he said, "Now he thinks I'm his sole property." She watched him fall asleep. For a long while, she lay in the air beside him, thinking of Tanuojin.

At three bells she went after him down the winding tunnel to the bridge. The rest of his watch was gathered around the hatch. Saba pushed the hatch open, and she followed him into the hollow bridge.

The other men streamed in behind them. On the perches along

the wall, Tanuojin's watchmen started up, intent. Saba dropped feet-first toward the cage. Tanuojin circled around it. His yellow eyes were fixed on his lyo. Saba ignored him. Tanuojin shot up to the hatch and plunged out. His watch followed him.

Paula settled down to the space of clear wall before the holograph. *Ybix* sailed thin as a blade through the green void. Saba was in the cage. He sat unmoving, his shoulders bowed. She watched him through the bars. He rubbed his hands together; at the tips of his fingers the claws clicked together. Sril brought him a watchboard and hung there holding it out for half a minute before Saba noticed him. Paula fixed her eyes on the holograph.

The watch dragged along. Saba would not let her leave the bridge. She went around to the other stations to watch what the crew did. Bakan let her wear his headphones while he made up his log. His little finger stuck out crooked from his hand, swollen like a sausage. All she could hear in the headset were beeps and squeaks, half-animal noises.

Finally she said, "I'm hungry."

"Wait." Saba was writing on a watchboard. He did not look up.

"I'm starving."

"Ay. Sril. Go with her."

She thrust herself up through the bubble of the bridge toward the hatch, not waiting for Sril. He met her in the corridor just beyond, and they went side by side down to the black-white tunnel.

"How long will this last?" she said.

"Until it stops."

The tunnels were empty. They flew along looking over their shoulders, furtive. In the slot of the galley, she breathed a trace of a scent, like a feather from a peacock's tail. Peeling off the wrapper, she ate a food tablet. Sril was braced in the hatch, keeping guard.

"Does this happen often?" she asked.

"Depends on the ship. On the ship's master. Yekaka used to start watch wars just to keep his crew in shape."

"Did you serve under Yekaka too?"

He shook his head. "My father was his prima gunner. My grandfather was gunner under Yekaka's father. Hurry up and eat."

She took a protein strip and a tube of water and followed him out along the corridor. A head popped through a hatch before them and ducked back out of sight. Sril grabbed her arm.

"Move!"

He pushed her along through a bend in the tunnel. Just in front of her she smelled someone coming, and she pulled back out of his grip. Marus shot toward her. Sril lunged between them. The two men tangled together, their claws fixed in each other's faces, their legs milling. One of them whistled. She ducked away from them. Beyond Marus, another of Tanuojin's men appeared. He and Marus flung themselves on Sril. Their locked bodies packed the tunnel. Sril's face was ripped. She wanted to help him but she could not think how.

Ketac raced around the bend past her. He pulled Marus off Sril's back. Paula started forward and shrank back again. Tanuojin was coming. He cut through the tangle of men like a knife, the other men giving way to him, all but Ketac. The young man wheeled to meet him. Tanuojin hit him shoulder first and knocked him down the corridor.

Ketac bounced off the wall. Dazed, he swung around, and Tanuojin went at him again. Paula pushed away from the wall. Abruptly Saba raced in between his son and his lyo.

Tanuojin backed off. Paula was behind him; she saw his raised hands, the fingers spread, and the hooks arched. He and Saba faced each other a moment. Saba lunged forward and Tanuojin flinched back away from him. She moved, giving them room. They paused again, face to face. Saba feinted, and Tanuojin yielded to him again, his arms up to protect himself.

"This is my ship," Saba said.

"Please," Tanuojin said, so low she could hardly hear him.

"This is my ship."

Tanuojin's back was still to her. The other men were watching, their faces rapt. Slowly Tanuojin dropped his hands, leaving himself open. He closed his yellow eyes. Saba lifted his head.

"Get out of here." He gestured to his crew, and the men turned and flew away. Paula floated quiet in the tunnel, watching. Saba put his hand out, and Tanuojin took it and they embraced. Tanuojin put his head down against Saba's shoulder. Paula went away up the tunnel.

She had taught Ketac the rules of Go, but she could not teach him the art. They played in the Tank, on a grid floating between them, with little magnets. He always tried to control the entire board, winding up with nothing.

"Tanuojin is an Akellar, isn't he?" she said.

The young man's head bobbed. "He was Melleno's pitman. You met Melleno, didn't you? In Saturn-Keda."

"Yes. What's a pitman?"

"He's the man who does an Akellar's work for him in the House when he's not there. The rAkellaron House, in Vribulo. The pitman goes around and talks about the laws and makes deals. Like that. Tanuojin was that for Melleno. Then when Melleno built Yekka, he made Tanuojin its Akellar."

She shook a handful of magnets, watching him play a white one onto the grid. Sril and Bakan were throwing darts at the end of the Tank. In eighteen watches they would reach Uranus. She played, and Ketac ignored her move and put a white magnet down in another corner. He refused to defend himself. But he never actually lost: he had developed a technique for avoiding that. Now he glanced at the other men and lowered his voice to keep them from hearing what he said.

"I could whip Tanuojin. If—"

"If you could only get your face off the floor."

"He can't fight. He's a coward. Everybody knows that. Didn't he come after you?"

Sril called, "You're talking about the only known saint in the Styth Fleet, boy. Be reverent." He sailed a dart through the air toward the target.

Paula set another pebble on the grid and gathered up six of Ketac's stones. His neck swelled.

"Hey!"

"I keep telling you—"

"You can't do that." He sucked in his breath, glaring at the board. He struck it with his fist and knocked it flying, bringing the game to its usual end. A magnet tapped her in the mouth and rebounded.

"Hey, boy," Sril said. He and Bakan glided down the room toward Ketac. "You're out of hand again, boy, you know what the Man said about that."

Ketac rolled over backward and made for the hatch. Sril and Bakan plunged through the litter of pebbles after him. She gave them room. Ketac sprayed a warning scent at them.

"Stay away from me—"

The two men were maneuvering him between them. Sril's face was wide with his grin. Ketac charged for the hatch and they chased him out. In the corridor a high yelp of pain sounded. Paula went around the Tank gathering up the magnets. Saba had told her that they would break the air filters if they got into the screens. Sril came in again, beaming.

"Don't believe Ketac. Whatever The Creep is or isn't, he can fight like a red snake when he has to." Sril went to the wall, where the darts stuck up in a clump like feathers. "Come here. I'll teach you to hit."

MATUKO. Saba's Akellarat. The White Season

She woke up surrounded by Styth children. She lifted her head, and they burst into giggles and disappeared out the door. A small lamp burned on the table beside the bed, giving off a gentle warmth. She swung her feet over the edge of the bed and slid off. The drop to the floor jarred her. She looked around at a huge room. The bed was eight feet long and so high off the floor she doubted she could climb back up without help.

The room was dim and except for the little lamp's heat it was cold. She took the lamp and went off to explore. A sliding door covered a rack in the wall full of her clothes, all neatly hung on arms and hooks attached to the wall at arm's length above her head. Her shoes were on a shelf completely out of reach. Her flute was on the floor next to her valise and the big suitcase. She had slept a long time, while all this was going on around her. She could remember being in *Ybix* orbiting Uranus; she could remember being in *Ybicsa* and starting down to the Planet, but nothing more.

Outside this room was a short hall. She crossed it to another room, bare of furniture. When she went in, a brown furry animal raced to the window, jumped to the sill, and dove out. She put the lamp up on the sill of the window and tried to pull herself up to see out but even when she stood on tiptoe she could see no more than the wall of a building across the way. She went back to the room where she had wakened and dragged a chair across the hall to stand on.

Kneeling on the seat of the big chair, she looked out the window to a wide, open yard, ringed around with white one-story houses. A few feet away from her stood a strange kind of post, silvery gray, with several short stumps like branches coming out of the top. At its foot the small brown animal crouched. Its long tail twitched and one ear swiveled to listen to her. The window swung open wide at her touch. She leaned out, looking up, and saw Matuko. The city closed over her head three or more miles away, veined with crooked streets. It was dark, like an Earthish middle twilight, almost colorless, brown and dark brown and gray. Above her, nearly hidden behind the roof, she could see part of the black ribbon of a lake. Streaks of white lay here and there. In the dull brown it looked like frost on a wintery field.

Children giggled again. She looked about in time to see half a dozen round heads sticking out past the corner of the house. They shrieked and hid. The brown animal raced away. It paused halfway along the wall of the house to turn a pop-eyed monstrous face to her and ran on.

Somewhere inside the house a door slammed. "Paula?"

"I'm in here." She turned around. Saba came in from the hall.

"What are you doing, running around like this?" He picked her up and put her on her feet on the floor. "You should stay in bed until you get used to the gravity." He patted her belly. She had to look up at him again. He fit this vast room, the huge furniture. She turned back to the window, uneasy.

"What's that white stuff?"

He looked out where she was pointing. "That's grass."

"White grass? What's that?" She pointed to the post.

"That's a bilyobio tree."

"It's not really a tree."

"No. It's not organic. Nobody knows what they are, they grow all over Styth, everywhere there are Styths. Except the moons. They're good luck. They say if you live near a bilyobio tree, you'll live to die of old age."

"What's little and brown and has a long tail and pop-eyes?"

"Why don't you stop asking questions and come over and meet my wives? As long as you're up. I—" He raised his head. Someone was walking down the hall. "Hup!"

"It's me, Pop."

A tall young man appeared in the doorway. Older than Ketac, he was in Saba's image, slenderly built. Red jewels glittered in the furls of his ears. He said, "I have to talk to you. I didn't want to do it in front of Mother. There's been a lot of trouble about this treaty."

They looked at her, and she turned away from them and went to the window and pretended to be watching out. She guessed this was his prima son, whose name she had forgotten. The young man said, "There's been a lot of dirty talk, and some fighting and a bomb went off in the Lake market—"

"How did the news get around?" Saba asked.

"I don't know. We had to close the Peak Farm, there was a threat to bomb it, too."

Saba let out a string of swearwords. "Who's behind it?"

"I can't find out. Nobody, I think—it's just streetwork, you know—spontaneous."

"Dakkar," his father said, "nothing like this is ever spontaneous. Somebody is back of it."

An edge crept into Dakkar's voice. "I think I'm looking at him. Sir."

"Oh, you do?"

"Everybody is saying you sold us out. This treaty—"

"Sir."

"I'm serious about—"

"Sir."

Paula frowned at the wall. If the treaty failed, she was finished.

"Yes, sir," Dakkar said, behind her.

"That's right," his father said. "And you don't close my crystal farm."

Raising her eyes, she looked around the barren room. The gravity dragged at her, drawing the burden of her pregnancy down, so that she had to stand with her hips thrown forward to support it. She put her hands on the small of her back.

"Yes, sir," Dakkar was saying stiffly.

"Go find out who's trying to knock us. You can leave."

His son left. Saba said, "Paula, let's go."

She went after him up the hall. They passed through a formal room, massed with huge furniture. A swing couch hung from the ceiling by chains. She felt too small to be noticed, a mouse in a rat world.

They crossed the yard toward the next house, cat-corner on the wall on the compound. On the eave of its roof, the brown animal sat washing its face with its forepaws.

"What's that?"

"A kusin." He still sounded angry. "They're harmless, except to the dog-mice and snakes."

"It was in my house."

"It won't come back, now that somebody is living there. They don't like people." His hand dropped to her shoulder and aimed her at the door into the house ahead of them. "Go in there. I have something to do. Boltiko knows who you are. I'll see you later." He walked off across the yard toward the biggest building in the compound, against the wall opposite her little house. She stopped and looked back the way she had come, to see what the house looked like. A white box. She thought of going back there. But she had to face his wives sometime. She went on toward Boltiko's house.

His prima wife was years older than he was. Her body was lost in rolls of fat. Necklace creases indented her neck. Paula sat uncomfortably in a chair in Boltiko's kitchen while children dashed in and out screeching and the wife cut bread and cooked meal.

"Were you married in the Earth?" Boltiko asked.

"We aren't married."

"Oh." Boltiko turned and swatted a passing child on the backside. "Didn't I tell you not to run in the house?" She smacked him again.

The little boy scurried out the door, his spread hands protecting his rump. Paula knew he was a boy because his head was shaven; the girls all wore their hair in braids. Boltiko looked Paula over covertly while she stirred the meal.

"Will you be married here?"

"No."

"Oh."

Another woman came in, this one very young, tall, and extravagantly beautiful, like an advertisement. The sleeves of her dress were of silver lace.

"Illy," Boltiko said, "this is Paula."

"Hello," Paula said.

Illy stared at her, unfriendly. "Hello," she said, after a moment. Her voice had the same musical quality as Tanuojin's. She sank into a chair down the table from Paula.

"Where is he?" she asked Boltiko.

"He went somewhere with Dakkar, into the city."

"What did he bring you?"

"A timepiece, the same as usual. Quaint."

"He gave me skin-color. Gold, can you imagine?" Illy turned toward Paula. Her hair was gathered on the crown of her head in an aureole of perfect curls. She was the most beautiful woman Paula had ever seen, Styth or other. "Where did he meet you?"

"On Mars," Paula said.

"Mars," Illy said, astonished, and Boltiko said, "Mars," as disapproving as her reaction to the news that Paula and Saba were not married. Illy said, "I thought you were Earthish."

"I am. But we met on Mars." She looked from one black face to the other. "At a very fancy sex park."

Illy's lips parted. Boltiko said, "I don't know what manners are in the Earth, but in my house we don't use words like that around the children." She poured something liquid into the meal and set the covered pan on the back of the counter.

"I don't understand," Illy said. "What were you doing there? Were you alone?"

"Yes. I was talking to him. Politics."

"Oh." Boltiko wiped the already spotless table. "Was that how you got the baby? Talking?"

"That was where. How was the usual way."

To her surprise, Boltiko laughed. The back door burst open. Saba came in, with his son Dakkar, and behind them Ketac. Paula glanced startled from Ketac to Boltiko; under all that fat, her face was shaped like his. Illy raised one hand delicately over her mouth, veiling herself before the young men. To Boltiko, Saba said, "I'll eat in the Manhus.

Hurry up, I'm starving." He went out again, trailing his sons, without looking at the other women. Illy lowered her hand.

"I'll show you the timepiece he gave me," Boltiko said.

They went down a hall, past rooms full of children and children's things, to a large dim room. The furniture was packed into it like hoardings under a ceiling painted with an abstract design. The chairs and hanging lamps were shielded in clear plastic bags. The three women made a winding course through the clutter to a corner cabinet. On the shelves were several little clocks. The sandglass Saba had bought on the Earth stood among them.

"Oh," Illy said. "Isn't that clever."

"This cabinet is so pretty," Boltiko said to Paula. "I had nothing to put here, so I asked Saba to bring me something when he goes on his trips."

Paula reached for a watch with a clamshell case. She found the spring catch and opened it. Boltiko said, blankly, "Why—it has an inside."

Paula showed her the open watch. In one half was a picture of a white baby, with wisps of fair hair and a stupid babyish smile, and in the other half a fancy scrolled initial T. Boltiko took it.

"Illy, look."

The other woman glanced at the watch. "Ugh. What an ugly baby."

Paula backed away from them. She realized Boltiko had no notion of what Saba did on his trips. She went around the room looking at the heavy furniture, protected in its wrap of plastic.

On the far side of the room, Illy said, "She's a slave! He didn't marry her!"

Paula raised her head. The furniture hid her from the other women.

"No," Boltiko said. "But he says we're supposed to treat her like a wife."

"She's ugly. He'll get tired of her. He'll sell her."

"Sssh, she'll hear you."

Paula was behind a chair. She leaned against it, staying out of their sight. Illy said, "She's gone."

"If you ask me," Boltiko said, "he's already tired of her—he just feels responsible for getting her that way." Her skirts swished. She and Illy went to the door into the hall. "That's all the more reason to be nice to her."

"At least he didn't marry her."

They left, and Paula let them get down the hall before she followed. The baby rolled up in her body anchored her down. Her back hurt. Slowly she waddled back toward the kitchen.

Boltiko was putting covered dishes on a tray. Illy sat in one of the big chairs inspecting her beautiful hands. Paula lowered her eyes. For a moment she hated them both; she burned to say something to wither them. She climbed up into the chair beside Illy's.

"Pedasen," Boltiko called, out the back door.

A dark man came in from the yard. He wore a loose white quilted tunic. For an instant he and Paula stared at each other. He was of her race, with Tony's coloring, and he had pale eyes like Tony's. Boltiko tapped the tray.

"Take this to the Akellar. See I get all the dishes back this very watch."

"Yes, mem." His voice was satiny. He kept his eyes away from Paula and took the tray out. Paula watched him go.

"Pedasen will help you fix your house," Boltiko said.

"He isn't—" Paula wet her lips. "I don't want him."

Illy giggled. "He is an it."

The nerves crawled in the backs of Paula's hands. She sat rigid in the chair that did not fit her, that held her far away from the table. That was why Pedasen's voice was so smooth: he had been gelded. The two women talked about things she did not understand, in words she did not know. She closed her eyes.

When she had been there long enough to have her walking strength back, she told Saba she wanted to go out, to look at the city. He refused. They were sitting on the swing couch in her front room, reading through the trade contract, and she let him go on two or three paragraphs before she said, "When can I go out?"

"The street is no place for a woman. If you want something, send a slave for it. On this bond, here—" he tapped the page, "I wanted you to make that forfeit if they break the law, remember?"

"That's the next paragraph."

He read the next paragraph. She watched his face. The baby was kicking her hard up under the ribs. The baby's father sat back, holding out the page to her.

"You've spelled it out too much—I want it vague, so I can get rid of somebody I don't like."

Their eyes met. She said, "Do you think I'm going to stay locked up in here the whole ten years?"

"Boltiko and Illy never go out." He put the contract on her lap. "Finish the contracts and I'll talk to you about things like that."

Paula grunted at him. She reached for the thirty close-printed pages of the contract. "I'm getting bored. Sril could go with me."

"I just told you. I won't discuss it until you finish the contract. And if you try to sneak out, I'll use my belt on you."

She threw the contract onto his lap, slid off the couch, and went down the hall to her bedroom. She heard him go out of the house through the front door.

When she went into labor, Boltiko called the midwives. Paula lay in her bed, wrapped in a heavy blanket. The women held her hands and stroked her hair back. There were three of them, all very old: one was slave, but the other two were Styth. The pain made her whimper and bite her lips. She clung to the slavewoman's hands, afraid.

Saba came in. He had been away in the city. The woman moved back and he sat on the bed beside her and put his hands on her body.

"Does it hurt?"

She nodded; she could not talk.

"It's supposed to hurt. Don't be frightened. I'll be in the next room." He left.

She shut her eyes. The women moistened her lips with a sponge. They murmured to her, crooning, and sang her songs and said little charms. When she curled up they made her lie straight. A bell rang. The low watch had begun. She panted, trying to catch her breath. Her body knotted around the baby. She screamed, and Saba came in again.

"Akellar," a woman said. "She is too small. We have to open her."

He leaned over her, one hand on her belly. "No. It's moving. Let her kick. She'll get it out." He stroked her face. "Don't worry, Paula. They think every birth is the first."

She closed her eyes, terrified. She clutched his fingers but he disengaged himself and went out of the room. She lay in a web of pain. The baby was tearing her apart. She heard two bells ring. Her throat was raw from screeching, she was so tired she could only moan.

"She is too small. She'll die if we don't cut her open and take it that way. The baby will die."

Saba had come in again. Dopey with pain, she had not noticed him, and she could not care. He handled her. "No. Give her time. It's a big baby. She's getting it out."

The pain was blinding. She lay in its grip for two watches more. At last David was born. The women took the howling baby away. Paula lay in a dazed feverish half-dream, blood pooling under her hips.

"You can't bring a strange man in here," Boltiko said.

Saba lifted the blankets off Paula's body. "She trusts me. I have to do something."

"It's disgusting. Hasn't she suffered enough?"

"Get out if you don't like it."

Paula's mouth and throat were papery dry. Her strength was gone. She could barely turn her head. She wondered where the baby was. A man she had never seen before sat down on the bed beside her.

"There," Saba said. "Over her womb." He threw the blankets back. She whimpered in the cold.

"Saba—" The stranger bit his lip. "I—"

"Damn you, she's bleeding to death." Saba got the man's hand by the wrist and slapped his palm down on Paula's belly. She shut her eyes. She was cold. Saba pulled her legs out flat on the bed, her feet apart.

"Mikka. Let off, let me see what happens."

The hand left her belly. Saba said, "She's bleeding like a river. Here." The cool hand fell on her body again. Saba was bending over her. She saw him in a mist. She could not breathe deep enough to fill her lungs.

"Massage her. Rub her, hard." He stooped over her and rammed his fist up through the torn channel of her body into her womb and put his free hand over the other man's.

She cried out. The deep pain burned like salt. He squeezed her into another hard contraction.

"Good girl. That's a good girl. One more."

He massaged her, his arm buried in her halfway to the elbow. "Come on, girl, damn it, break the law and live." She whined. Her body clenched. He drew his hand out of her. "Good. Good." Her womb tightened again of itself, and she whimpered.

"I'm cold."

"A little longer," he said. "Just a little longer and you can rest." He was sitting on the bed between her spread legs. In his hand was a tool with jaws, like a staple gun. "Don't worry. I've clipped together men with wounds a lot worse than this. Mikka, stay there."

The stranger stared off in the opposite direction. His hand was spread over the soft empty hill of her belly. She shivered in spasms, in fits. Distinctly she felt the grip of the stapler in her skin. The tool clicked steadily. She was too tired to cry. Finally he put her legs together.

"Let off, Mikka."

The hand left her. Saba murmured, "Good. Stay in the next room, in case she starts to bleed again." He lifted her up and wrapped her in a clean dry blanket. Her groin throbbed, zippered up with plastic teeth. "You're a good little lawbreaking bitch." He kissed her forehead. She yawned, sinking into sleep.

. . .

"Mikka is my brother," Saba said. "He's a blood-stauncher. His one gift, aside from getting thrown out of drinking docks."

"Like Tanuojin." Paula braced her shoulders up on her elbows, watching him take the clips out of her crotch. He bent over her, his head and shoulders framed between her raised knees. One by one the clips dropped into a bucket on the floor.

"Tanuojin is a little more than a blood-stauncher. I told you not to talk about that." Another clip rang into the pail. "If I ever lose my call, I think I'll take up midwifery. That's not a bad job."

"How is David?"

"Vida is fine. Boltiko has him. I shirted him the watch after he was born. He looks like me." He sat back and put the pliers down. "Thirty-four clips. Those were three long wounds, sweet."

She moved painfully over to the edge of the bed. When she sat up her head felt swollen. "Have you heard anything from the Committee?"

"Nothing. Stay in bed for a while." He went over to the door. "I'll tell you if anything happens."

"I want my baby." Carefully she raised herself up on her feet, gratified by her strength. She went toad-legged to the clothes rack on the wall.

"Boltiko knows all about babies. Let her take care of him."

"I want him."

"You aren't the mothering type."

"How do you know what I am?" She took a pair of her *Ybix* overalls, to keep her warm, and a long dress.

"I know you. He's my son too. I won't let you mistreat him."

She glanced at him, standing by the door with his hand on the latch, and pulled the overalls up over her shoulders. "What do you think I'm going to do to him, whip him?"

"I won't let you turn him into some freak anarchist."

She put the dress on. Her body was still thick, sway-backed from the baby. Saba went out; she heard the front door slam.

The baby's eyes were not round, like a Styth's, and not black. They were long and slanted, brown like hers, set far apart in his round chinless face. Boltiko gave her heaps of clothes for him, showed her how to mix his food and how to feed him, and called in the slave Pedasen to carry everything over to her house for her. "He's a fine, strong baby," the prima wife said, "although he's so small. Saba doesn't breed weaklings. If you need help, send for me." She put the baby into Paula's arms. He was heavy. Paula shifted his weight against her shoulder. Looking down at him, she felt a sudden wild surge of love.

Pedasen carried the basket of clothes and food after her out to the yard. She slowed down so that he could catch up with her, and he stopped behind her. She went back to his side. His face was smooth, like a child's; he had never shaved his beardless cheeks.

"Is that your whole name?" she said.

"Mem," he said, blank.

"Don't you have another name?"

She had been speaking Styth. Now he turned his gaze on her, his arms wrapped around the basket, and said, "Why did you come here?" in a slurred, liquid version of the Common Speech. "Why didn't you stay where you belong?"

"Come on," she said. "Standing up makes me dizzy." She went off toward her house. He followed her, and she stopped, irritated, and said with force, "Come on," and made him walk beside her. They went into her house.

He spoke only enough Styth to take orders. While they put away the baby's things, she talked to him in the Common Speech, and he answered in the dialect. He had no other name, just Pedasen, which had been his mother's name too. Somewhere out in the compound a bell rang, and he hurried away to answer it.

Most of the time the baby slept. Boltiko sent another slave to bring Paula her high watch meal. When she had eaten and slept, she took the baby and went out to walk in the yard. The biggest building in the compound was the Manhus, on the wall opposite her house. Long and low, it ran the length of the yard, its door like a mouth and its front porch like a jaw. She had never been there, and she went in there now.

The door led her into a wide dark hallway. Sril was standing in the back, reading from a message board on the wall. When he saw her, he grinned all across his wide face.

"Mendoz'. Let me see." He came up to look at the baby.

"You don't live here, do you?" she said.

He was bent over the baby, cooing. "No—up the curve. Ah, he's pretty. I like little babies." He straightened up, his eyes on her. "Are you supposed to be in here?"

"Probably not." Three doors opened off the hall on either side, and she went to the nearest and went through it.

It was crowded with Styths, their backs to her, so that no one noticed her. The baby slept heavily in her arms. She moved to one side to see what was happening. At the head of the room Saba walked up and down past a broad table. A lone man faced him, his hands behind him fastened together with a white plastic yoke. Paula stood back near the wall. The twenty-odd men packing the rear half of the room were watching intently, silent.

"My family has dominated Matuko for eighteen generations," Saba was saying. "For the blood we've lost for this city, the least we could get is trust." He circled the table. The men watching him were utterly silent. "I don't care what you call it," he said to the man on trial, "I say you started a riot."

No one moved. The bound man said, "You can put me up for the rest of my life, Akellar, but you can't make me believe you haven't betrayed us."

"I know what's right for my own city." Saba walked up and down before the table, his hands on his hips. "I haven't betrayed anybody. This treaty will give us a kind of life none of you has ever dreamed of, and all you can do is squawk at me. I'm risking my back and my rank in the Chamber to make my city great, and all I get is hysteria."

The baby stirred, flinging out his arms. Paula went back to the hall. He had opened his crystal farm again and his slaves were refusing to work. Pedasen brought her wild rumors from the street about fires and riots. She carried the baby across the yard to her house to feed him. Saba told her nothing. In fact, she had seen him little since David's birth. He was busy. She knew he still wanted her. She fed the baby and rocked him on the swing until he fell asleep. She was strong again, and her body had healed. She knew he would come to her.

"Boltiko is much older than he is," she said.

"The blacks do that," Pedasen answered. He carried an empty pack on his shoulders that flapped with each step. "If a boy's wild, they marry him to some old mare who steadies him." They were coming to the market. In the open lot above the lake shore, Styths and slaves in white milled around bright-painted open stalls. She looked back over her shoulder. On the perpendicular wall of the city Saba's compound was an open square, head-on. She could just make out the roof of her house.

"How long have you been here?" she asked.

"I was born in Yekaka's Manhus," Pedasen said. "My mother came from outside the Planet."

"Do you know where?"

"No." He stopped and pointed through an alley. "Down there is the Varyhus. That's the district where the plastics factory is—it's a terrible place, full of thieves and murderers. Don't ever go there."

She stood looking down the alley. It dipped along a short hill. On either side were low red buildings, brick-colored, peeling posters hanging off the walls. The air smelled bitterly of resin. She trotted after the eunuch, who was going into the market.

There were many more slaves than Styths. Pedasen led her through the thick stream of people to a booth piled with fish. There was an awning spread under the table to protect them from the radiation coming from the ground. Paula reached for a fish. Its belly was slit open from head to tail; inside, the flesh was translucent pink. Pedasen smacked her hand and she put the fish down again. A slave in a blue apron came up to the far side of the booth to serve him. Fish scales glittered on his sleeves and the round scaler was stuck in his cuff.

Paula wandered away through the crowd. The next line of tables was stacked up with live chickens. Styth chickens: they had no wings, their feathers were like silky white hair. They huddled mute on the counter, their long red feet tied together. She went along the street, her hands in her sleeves to keep them warm.

The city was large enough that the ground under her feet seemed flat and the street rose and fell in little hills, but whenever she lifted her eyes she saw the vast bubble around her, closed over her head, like a tremendous cave. The slaves around her chattered in their liquid speech. The few Styth women among them were veiled to the eyes. She felt the vast drone of the city around her, oppressive. In the next lane were slaves hanging cloth from the eaves of their booths, red and white striped canvas, black silk, the heavy gray cloth Saba's shirts were made of. In the alley beyond she found beer vendors. She turned a corner and came into a narrow street where they sold people.

She stopped in the middle of the street. Her hackles rose. On the side of the street, three women sat, their knees drawn up, and their feet yoked together with white plastic yokes. A card over their heads told their ages and use. None of them seemed to notice her. One was fair-skinned, almost Martian white. Beside them, in a little cage, a child slept curled on the ground.

"Paula!"

She turned away from the slaves. Pedasen hurried up to her. "What are you doing in here?" In one hand he held a brace of chickens by the feet. The bag on his back was stuffed with his purchases, and the string of credit around his neck was almost naked of its coins. He gripped her arm and rushed her out of the street. "This place gives me the chills."

She went beside him back through the market. He held her arm as if she might run away. He was taller than she was, and he walked fast, so that she had to stretch her legs to keep up. The chickens swung from his free hand.

"You won't get in trouble, will you?" she said. "For bringing me here."

He shook his head. "All the trouble will land on you."

She looked up ahead of them. In their passage across the city, the ground seemed to flatten away from her, and now Saba's compound was sinking down slowly into the clutter of large buildings along that part of the wall. They were passing the head of the lake. Boats rowed over it in lines, like soldiers.

"What are they fishing for?" She saw the nets in their wake, swollen fat with the black lake water.

Pedasen shook his head. "You ask too many questions. You're just going to have to learn not to be so curious."

She looked up at him. He was staring at the street just ahead of his feet. His silken cheeks were darker than hers, his eyes startlingly pale. Certainly his mother had been Earthish. In the street ahead of them, between high walls, Styth children were throwing a curved stick back and forth. She followed Pedasen down the grassy lane that led along the back wall of Saba's compound and in the little slave door.

Boltiko's house was full of screaming children. Paula let herself in the front door to the cluttered sitting room. Down the hall the prima wife's voice sounded, shrill: "I don't care what he did, I've told you again and again—" There followed the smack of a hand on a child's bottom. In the hall a knot of five or six children packed the kitchen door, their backs to Paula. She went unseen into Boltiko's bedroom, where David lay asleep on the bed, and took him away out the front door.

He woke while she was changing his clothes, and she lay on her bed nose to nose with him. His arms and legs flailed aimlessly and he heaved himself onto his side, as if he were trying to roll over. She kissed his head, capped in thick black hair. After a while, she realized there was someone behind her.

Saba was in the doorway. He said, "Where did you go?"

"Out." She slid off the bed to her feet.

"I told you what I'd do if you did that." He took off his belt. She wet her lips. He came around the bed, took her by the scruff of the neck, and whipped her with the doubled belt, six or eight times. It hurt. When he let her go she grabbed the bed to keep from falling.

"This isn't the Earth," he said. "You can't do as you please around here. That was for your own good—if you go out in the street you'll just be hurt."

She sat on the bed, her hands in her lap. Standing in front of her he buckled on his belt again. He said, "I told you when you wanted to come here it wouldn't be the kind of life you were used to." His voice sounded above her head. She refused to look up at him. "You'd better get off your high branch. I won't take your selfish anarchist act too long. Are you listening to me?"

"I hear you."

"Why don't you learn how to sew and make yourself some decent clothes? You look like a street-pig, you act like a street-pig, and I won't take it. Understand? I have enough trouble. I won't take any more from you."

He walked out of the room. She put her head back and shut her eyes. She did not belong here. She had come here by mistake, by accident. The baby whimpered. She got up and took him down to the kitchen to feed him.

She put off leaving the compound again. Boltiko mixed little bowls of mush to feed David. "Just give him a little at first, in case it makes him sick." The prima wife dipped up a bit of mashed fruit on her finger and ate it. She sighed, all her fat quaking. "I don't know what I'm to do with Ketac. I hope he didn't behave like this when he was in your world. Dakkar is such a perfect son."

Pedasen came in, and the three cleaned Paula's house. She told herself that was why she was not going out into the city again: the baby needed her, the house was dirty, Boltiko wanted to talk.

"Why don't you use this room for a nursery?" Pedasen said. He looked in the door to the empty room across the hall from hers. "There's furniture over—yeow!"

She rushed after him into the room. "What's wrong?"

"There was a kusin in here!" He pulled the window closed. She went up beside him and opened it again. Pedasen's pale eyes were popping with excitement. He shut the window. "You can't leave this open—it comes in through the window."

She opened the window. "It comes in here to drink."

"It will eat the toes off the baby."

"It's very shy. It won't go near the baby."

Pedasen muttered something. He rubbed his nose with his forefinger. She left the room, and he came after her to help her move the big cabinet in the sitting room.

The doors of the cabinet were divided into eight panels, inlaid with metal under a thick shiny glaze. "That's the story of Capricornus," he told her. "He was a hero—" He reached up to touch the top panel. "See? Here he is wrongfully accused and his father exiles him, and he goes on his wanderings. But he returns home in the end."

She wiped the glossy surface of the door with her sleeve. In the panel at her eye-level a tiny man fought a lizard with a round badge on its breast. "What's this?"

"That's the dragon Jupiter." His finger traced the blossom of the beast's flaming breath. Now she recognized the planetary symbol on the disk. The figures were in low-relief under the glaze, realistic in the detail, even the little image of the man.

"I'm not keeping you from anything, am I?"

"Oh, no," the eunuch said. "If the mem wanted me, she would ring the bell."

"You're hiding out," she said.

"Not really."

"Really."

"You don't mind, do you?" he said.

"No."

"I'd work for you, if there was anything to do."

"I know. It's all right."

"When the Akellar gets back," he said, "he'll probably put everybody to work."

She leaned on the back of the swing couch. The chains skreed under her weight. "Where is he?" The couch swayed away from her, and she lifted her feet off the ground and swung with it.

"Half a block of the Tulan was blown down last watch. There was an awful riot." Pedasen caught the swing. "He's out looking it over. Next they'll be breaking down the compound door."

The baby cried, and they turned their heads to listen. Paula waited to see if David would quiet by himself, and after three or four yells he subsided. She leaned on the couch and swung back and forth. She felt like a ghost in this world, something these other people imagined for their own use: Pedasen to escape work, David to feed him, Saba to deal with the Committee. She had to stop leaving her life up to accident.

"The Tulan," she said. "What's that?"

"The rich district, across the city."

"Take me there."

Pedasen found her slave's clothes: baggy white trousers and a white quilted tunic. They walked down to the lake and along the street that followed the shore. The watch was high. Lines of boats rowed across the black water, drawing their nets after them. Three oars to a side they crawled on the still lake surface. The street was busy with slaves going to and from the market on the city wall to her right. Pedasen led her down a steep lane between rows of tall old houses, smelling of fish.

"You're asking for worse than a whipping," he said once.

They cut through a part of the Varyhus, along a stretch of the factory fence, and came to the Tulan. Here it was quiet. Banks of white grass grew on either side of the path and in the lanes between the walled houses. She saw no one else, not even children, until they turned a corner and came to a broad stretch of rubble.

For two or three acres, broken concrete and plastic covered the ground. A cart stood in the street, half-full of debris. Two slaves were shoveling in the mess that littered the street. Other white slaves stooped and picked through the ruins. A bilyobio tree grew up at the edge of the street. Paula went over to it, watching a single file of Styths on the far side of the blown-up place. The rubble crackled when she stepped on it, gave way, and nearly dropped her. Pedasen grabbed her elbow.

"Paula." He nodded at the Styths two hundred feet away. "That's him."

She stepped carefully over a broken wall, high as her knees. There was a puddle of melted plastic on the far side, still warm. The sharp edges of the trash cut her shoes. She saw something bright in the blackened crumbled concrete and picked up a metal buckle.

"Paula!" Pedasen hissed, behind her.

She showed him the buckle. The etched design was laid in with soot. "I'll bet you this I can walk right up to him and he won't even see me."

"You'll get your back peeled off." His lips were pressed together, like Boltiko's when somebody swore. She rolled the buckle into the cuff of her sleeve. Watching for things she could salvage from the junk, she crossed the ruin. A sweetish stench of acetone came from the burned ground. Pedasen followed her. At a big two-headed bilyobio tree in the middle of the place, three slaves had gathered to pass a jug of water around. She stopped near them.

"Give that over here," Pedasen said, and the strange slaves handed him the jug. They were all watching the Styths.

"Find anything?" one said, low.

Pedasen shook his head. He jabbed his chin at Saba and his men, who were cutting across the rubble toward the next street. "How long has he been here?"

"Since the half-watch," another slave said. They were all talking in murmurs. Paula looked up at the bilyobio. One stubby upper branch was split, but otherwise it seemed untouched by the explosion. The jug came around to her and she sipped the cool water. Saba was scanning the ground, his hands on his hips, and his face gripped with bad temper.

"Have they found anything?" she said.

"Two bomb casings," a strange slave told her.

Another man took the jug from her. "They'd have found plenty, but Tssa's men were here last watch cleaning up." He grinned; he had no teeth in his upper jaw.

"Who is Tssa?" she asked.

Pedasen's elbow slammed into her ribs. "Don't ask questions." To the others, he said, "She's fresh, she still talks too much."

Saba was coming closer, his men strung out behind him. His son Dakkar was among them. The slaves moved away from the bilyobio tree, hurrying in their quick stride, bending to search in the trash. Paula drifted over toward the Styths. She circled them once, coming within five feet of Saba. He kicked at the ground and black char flew in a spray. He looked straight at her without seeing her. She went slowly back toward the street, casting around on the ground for salvage, met Pedasen, and they started home.

She reached the compound, left her slave clothes with Pedasen in the slaves' room of the Manhus, and retrieved David from Boltiko. When she went in the kitchen door of her house she could hear the sawing of the swing chains in the front room. She went down the hall to the archway. Saba was sprawled on the couch, her flute in his hands. He was trying to play it, but as hard as he blew over the mouthpiece he could not draw a note from it. Seeing her, he put the flute down.

"You're lucky I don't lose my temper easily."

She laid the baby on the floor by the Capricornus cabinet and tucked his blanket around him. "This seems to be the only way I can get your attention."

"I've been busy." He took a strip of green recording tape out of his sleeve, and she went to the foot of the swing. "This came from the Earth while you were out running around like a whore."

She took the tape and sat down on the swing with it in her hand. "Have you had it transcribed?"

"I've listened to it. There are about fifty questions on details and they're complaining about something in the bond clause."

She wound the tape into a coil. That was why he was keeping his belt on. She said, "You never come near me any more."

He stirred. His eyes shifted away from her. "I don't want to get you pregnant again." He fussed with his mustaches. In her imagination she heard something stop, like a song stopping. She made herself admit that she had lost him. She looked quickly away before he saw it in her face.

"What are you going to do about that?" he said.

She put the tape on the couch. "I can't tell until I read it. There's no sense in worrying about it anyway before you stifle this street action against the treaty."

"That's not your business."

"It is my business. If you can't put this treaty over here, I might as well go back to the Earth. Do you know who's doing it?"

He scowled at her. She faced him, expressionless. "Is it Tssa?"

On the floor by the cabinet the baby squealed. She went to look. He had wakened; he seemed happy enough staring at the shining cabinet door.

"What do you know about Tssa?" his father said.

"Not me. The slaves. The slaves see everything that happens. None of you ever notices them, but they're everywhere."

"What do they say about Tssa?"

"His men were there in the Tulan, before you saw the ruin. Is this attack on you or just the treaty?"

"Me. Do you know how I received my call?"

She shook her head. He stood. Relieved of his weight the couch swayed off in a parabola. She went to catch her flute before it fell.

"I had two older brothers. They murdered my father. I and Tanuojin came after them and killed them." His back was to her. Soot powdered his sleeves. "It was the hardest time in my life. We were outlaws here, nobody could help us. For forty watches, whenever one of us slept, the other had to be standing guard. That was when I knew I was called to follow my father. To be the Akellar."

"Why did they kill him?"

"With Yekaka there was always some reason."

She looked down at the flute in her hands.

"Anyway, my oldest brother left two sons, both young, very young, and like a fool I let them stay in Matuko. Tssa is the elder. I'm almost sure he's engineering the trouble, but if I take him on suspicion and I'm wrong, it will only make the thing worse, and I can't get a grip on him. He's too cautious." He made an impatient gesture. "Or he's innocent."

She took the flute apart. The box was on the table under the window. "I look like a slave. I could go right into Tssa's house. Find out whatever you have to know."

"Don't be a fool. I need you for this other work, and he'd catch you. He's not stupid."

She took the buckle out of her sleeve and held it out to him. "I saw you there, last watch, in the Tulan. Did you see me?"

His mouth opened. He took the buckle and turned it over. She snapped the lid of the flute's box closed. Finally he tossed the buckle down on the couch.

"Not his house. You'll have to follow him."

"I'll need Pedasen," she said.

Tssa lived in the Tulan. For six watches she and Pedasen followed him wherever he went. He went nowhere interesting. Saba had set Bakan to spy on his nephew as well; Bakan stayed away from Paula. In the seventh watch, the low watch, Tssa came out of his rambling walled house, started off along the street, and lost all three of them.

Paula circled through the narrow grassy lanes of the Tulan and found him again, with three other men, in an alleyway watching the street. She guessed he was looking out for Bakan, who was there to be dodged. When Bakan did not appear, Tssa and his men went away at top speed into the Varyhus District.

Paula and the eunuch stayed about a hundred yards behind them. They took her around the factory, squat and stinking behind its high mesh fence, to a long house blackened with grime. The building was one story for most of its length but a narrow second-story annex was stacked up along the right side, with a stair running up the outer wall to its door. rUlugongon and drums pounded inside the windows of the ground floor. From the corner of the lane Paula watched the last of Tssa's men go into the upper annex.

"Stay here," she said to Pedasen. She went down the street to the stairs and climbed them. The stairs were worn sway-backed in the middle. On the landing at the door, a black and white kusin hissed at her, its long whiskers bristling, and jumped to the roof and ran away over the peak. She looked behind her. Pedasen was sitting on the ground at the corner watching her. She went into the building.

In the dark hallway she was blind a moment. The music boomed up from below, making the floor vibrate. She struggled with her fear. In the white slave clothes she felt conspicuous. Her eyes began to see in the gloom and she went down the hallway. Through an open door on the right she saw an empty room, a table, a window scummed opaque with dirt. The next door was shut. She put her ear against it but heard nothing except the pounding tuneless music. Under the banging another sound reached her, growing louder: feet coming up the stairs. She went into the empty room.

The footsteps passed her and stopped before the next door, and a knock rattled on it. She went across the little room to listen. The music drowned the words of the two voices. The plank wall between the room was so thin that it yielded when she touched it, but she could hear nothing but a loud laugh in the room beyond.

She had found Tssa's meeting place, or one such, and she tried to convince herself that was enough. Saba would not think it was worth very much. She searched along the wall for a chink or a hole she could see through.

A voice bellowed in the hall. "Is there a nigger up here?"

She ran out the door. A big man leaned out of the next room: Tssa's man. "Bring us a tank, and hop." He ducked back inside and slammed the door.

She dashed down the outer stairs to the street. Pedasen stood up when he saw her, but she waved him down again and ran around to the front of the building and in the door.

The whole long ground floor was one room. In a corner six men played the deafening music. A few other scattered men sat around on the floor. Apparently it was the off-watch. There were no tables or chairs. On one side wall, beside a flight of stairs, was a big barrel with a tap faucet in the bottom and a row of jugs on a shelf beside it. The floor was deep in sand. She crossed to the barrel and took down the biggest jug on the shelf. Opening the tap, she filled the jug with the thick yellow beer.

"Hey!"

She nearly dropped the tank. A fat man in a smock blocked her way. He held out one huge hand. "Pay."

"It's for Tssa," she said. "Upstairs."

"Just the same, you pay now."

She gave him the jug to hold and took the string of credit from her neck. The fat man said, "So now he's bringing his own slaves. He won't escape paying me that way." The jug tucked under his arm, he snatched the string away from her. "He can pay what he owes me, too." The credit jangled. He counted off more than half. Paula glanced around. A man near the door was watching and she looked hastily away from him. It was Mikka, Saba's blood-stauncher brother. She took the jug and the raped credit string and hurried up the stairs.

Mikka had recognized her. She wondered if he worked for Tssa. The stair took her out at the end of the annex. She knocked on the closed door and it sprang open.

Tssa sat at a table under the window, counting out credit into stacks. Of her age, he was slightly built, with Saba's marked sensual features. She put the jug down on the table. The room was crowded with men. She backed up to the wall, trying to memorize their faces. They ignored her. She was trembling, not from cold.

"Here comes Kolinakin," said a man by the window. He nodded down into the street.

Tssa was drinking beer. He put the cup down and beckoned to another man. "Go make sure nobody is following him." The man left. Saba's nephew frowned at Paula. "What's that doing here?"

"I'm supposed—" her dry voice squeaked, and she coughed. "I'm supposed to ask to be paid."

"Paid!" Tssa looked around at his men. "He thinks I'm a street vendor. Or that this slop is worth money; which is it?" The other men laughed. There were cups on the shelf beside the door, and the Styths took them down and passed the tank around. Tssa stretched his back, his hands behind his head. "Go," he said to her.

"Please. He'll beat me." She was ruining her usefulness; he would certainly recognize her after this, but she wanted to see the man he was here to meet: Kolinakin.

"Maybe he likes beating you," Tssa said, amiably.

The door banged open. A huge man stamped into the room. He walked flat-footed, his toes out, his knees bent; he was the tallest Styth she had ever seen, inches taller than Tanuojin. Tssa stood and they shook hands.

"That's what I came for," the giant said. He flicked one finger at the credit piled on the table.

Tssa sat down again. "You'd better be careful. My uncle is having us all watched." He put his elbows on the table on either side of the money.

Kolinakin snapped his fingers with a crack that made Paula start. Quickly a man took a cup from the shelf and blew into it to blow away the dust and poured him beer. The giant said, "I know every man in Saba's crew. He doesn't even suspect I'm in this. I'm having him watched. You aristocrats." He took the beer. "You think with your blood instead of your brains." The cup vanished into his enormous hand.

Tssa's eyes were half-closed. He studied Kolinakin. Paula licked her lips. Whoever the big man was, he was pushing Tssa, and not the other way; he was the master. Tssa said, "Girl." When she looked up he tossed her a small credit. "That's yours, for the whipping. Tell the slop-tender he can wait for his."

She went to the door, glad to be leaving. Just as she reached it, the door flew open. Mikka stumbled into the room. She shrank back, her heart jumping into her throat. The air was suddenly charged with metallic heat. Behind Mikka came Saba.

Tssa stood. Kolinakin turned, and someone swore in a choked voice.

"Now, look who's here," Saba said. He faced Kolinakin. Behind him, his crew jammed the hall. "The Akellar of the Varyhus."

Kolinakin lunged for the door. Paula reached it a step ahead of him. Saba's men charged in. They ran her off her feet and carried her deep into the room, and the brawl broke out around her. She scrambled toward the door. Two men backed into her from opposite directions. She squeezed out of the press of bodies. On hands and knees she crawled between men thrashing and fighting and curled up underneath the table, as close to the wall as she could get, her arms over her head, while the annex rocked and the walls broke all around her.

She kept the heat in her house low, for David's sake. While she was bathing him, Pedasen came into the steamroom behind her.

"The Akellar wants you in the Manhus."

She glanced at him. David yawned; the inside of his mouth was pink as a cat's. She wrapped him in a towel.

"What I'd like to know is why you let him go in there when I was still in the middle of it," she said to Pedasen.

"I didn't do anything. He just came. I think he was following us, on top of all the rest. Here, I'll take him." He reached for the baby.

Pedasen could dress David and put him to bed. She crossed the yard to the Manhus. During the brawl she had been stepped on twice and fallen on once and her ribs still hurt. Sril was standing just outside the maproom door, in the hall of the Manhus.

"Mendoz'," he said. "You got us all blood-pay. I'll buy you a cup sometime." He opened the door for her.

The oval room beyond was lined with maps, set in frames along the wall like windows, green maps of Uranus and blue and white maps of the solar system. Saba sat on a pedestal chair in the middle of the room. He waved to her to stay where she was. The two men before him had their backs to her, but she recognized Tssa and Mikka.

"There is such a thing as family loyalty," Saba said. "Honor, and regard for your own blood. Although anybody who would put his head together with a thug like Kolinakin—"

Kolinakin was dead. They had dragged him into the street and broken his neck. She put her hand to her sore ribs. Neither of the two bound men noticed her. Saba made a gesture with his left hand. A plastic glove sheathed his right to the elbow; he had broken three fingers in the fight. Sril brought him a pair of shears.

"I'm giving you a choice," he said to Tssa. He nodded at the broad-bladed shears in the gunner's hand.

Under his shirt Tssa's shoulders were rigidly straight. "You never gave my father any choices. What are you trying to pay for, uncle?"

Saba nodded at her, where she stood in the doorway. "Look over there, Tssa."

His nephew's head turned. When he saw Paula his round eyes narrowed. Saba said, "That's how I caught you. That slavewoman caught you for me. Your father was stupid but he would never have let a nigger trap him, and a woman at that."

The younger man's gaze fell. Mikka was staring at the far wall. Saba swiveled his chair back and forth in tiny rhythmic squeaks. "Take your choice. It makes no difference to me."

Tssa's head was bowed. The room was silent a long moment while he thought. At last he reached for the shears in Sril's hand. He hacked off his own hair, just above the club, and dropped the knot of hair and the shears on the floor. His eyes looked blind. He came toward Paula, long-striding, and she moved out of the doorway and he brushed by her without looking at her. The door shut.

Saba tapped Sril's arm. "Make sure he leaves Matuko."

"Yes, Akellar." Sril hurried out after Tssa.

Saba turned to Mikka. "Now, what about you?"

His brother took a step toward him. "I didn't have anything to do with it. Ask her. I was just there having a jar." He put his hand out to Paula. "Tell him. I saved your life, didn't I?"

She looked from him to Saba. "He was Tssa's lookout. He saw me, but he was too drunk to come upstairs."

"I saved your life!"

Saba pushed at the hair knot on the floor with his foot. "Go get drunk in somebody else's city."

"I don't have any money." Mikka wiped his hand over his mouth. "Tssa owed everybody." He tramped out of the room, grumbling.

Saba rotated the chair back and forth. Paula said, "I'm not a slave."

"When you go out, you'll use the slave door, and you'll wear slave clothes. I won't have people thinking I'd let my wife run around in the street." He waved his plastic hand at her. "You can go."

Boltiko sat down, pulling her skirts smooth over her knees, and sighed. "Sometimes I think I'll just die. I can't eat anything any more without getting sick." She fanned her vast face, smooth with fat. Illy's slave poured kakine, the sweet green Matukit liquor, into three glasses on the table before her.

Paula's chair was a sling of white shaggy fur, big enough to sleep in. She curled her legs under her. Illy's whole house was done in white, chrome, and glass. The young wife came in from the sleeproom. Against such a background, her beauty was riveting: there was nothing else to look at. Boltiko glared at her.

"That boy of yours is incorrigible."

Illy had three children. Paula could never pick out which of the horde they were. Illy sat down in the chair between the other women. "I'm sure I can't be blamed."

Boltiko snorted. She reached for a glass of kakine. "That baby is tiny," she said to Paula. "You aren't feeding him enough."

"If he were any bigger I'd have to put wheels on him to move him around."

"He cries. That's a sign he's hungry."

"I think he's just bad-tempered," Paula said.

"He cries all the time."

"All you ever talk about is children," Illy said. She sent the slave away with a wave of her hand. "He's in a good mood now."

All she ever talked about was Saba. Paula rubbed her hand over the long white nap of her chair. The treaty had come back, signed, and the trade contracts had been covered by a syndicate of fifty-two Martian traders.

Boltiko said, "Nobody is blowing down Matuko, that's why. Dakkar says the city is very peaceful."

The house slave came in again with a tray of cut fruit. Like Pedasen, he was a eunuch. In his whispery voice, he said, "Mem, Pedasen is in the back. The Akellar will see Mem Paula in the Manhus."

"In the Manhus," Illy and Boltiko said, in one voice.

"I wonder what he wants," Paula said. She slid down from the chair.

Pedasen waited in the back doorway of Illy's house, David in the crook of his arm. When the baby saw her he burst into an enormous smile. She took him from the slave. With Pedasen beside her she crossed the yard to the Manhus door.

"Boltiko says it means he's hungry when he cries," she said to Pedasen.

He shrugged. On the steps, he reached for the baby again. "She thinks that's all that can be wrong with people, that they're hungry."

Paula laughed. He loathed the Styths. She watched him take the baby back toward her house, then went into the Manhus.

Saba was in the maproom, staring at a green map of the Planet, his hands on his hips. She went into the oval room and shut the door. He turned his head; the light whitened the side of his face.

"How is Vida?"

"He's fine. He cries a lot."

"That's good, that means he's strong-minded." He turned off the map and she could no longer see his face. "I'm going to Vribulo. Do you want to go with me?"

"Yes, of course." She sat down in the pedestal chair, her gaze on his solid featureless shape among the maps. He sauntered around the room and came up behind her.

"I got a record slip from a bank in Luna. They're holding a million dollars in iron at my order." His hand rumpled through her hair.

"What about my commission?"

"That isn't how we do things here." His fingers worked in her hair. His voice was smooth. "I'll take care of you and Vida. I give you everything you want, don't I?"

"I suppose so." She could not help but smile.

"Then what do you need money for?"

"Nothing, I guess."

"You're a very reasonable woman," he said.

. . .

VRIBULO. Machou's Akellarat

Vribulo was darker than Matuko, almost like full night, and bitterly cold. The air smelled rancid. The streets swarmed with people. They walked faster here than in Matuko, hurrying along in a continuous crowd. She stayed close by Saba. If she got lost here she would have to find her own way back. Ketac had come with them, together with Sril and Bakan. The young man walked along beside her, looking around him, his bed slung over his shoulder.

The buildings of the ancient city, the oldest city of the Empire, were blackened with time. The upper stories overhung the streets and in places closed above the street into arches. A siren started up behind her. She glanced back. The street threaded away through the dark, picked out with the blue-white of crystal lamps. There seemed to be a million people walking after her. At a run she went back among her own Styths.

The slaves here wore white, like in Matuko, which made them show up in the dark among their dark masters. She heard another siren. High above them, she could just make out the far side of the city: the square shapes of buildings, the dim sheen of water. They came into a street with a lane of thick blue grass down the center.

Sril touched her shoulder. "Look up there, Mendoz'."

They were coming to the end of the bubble. Something covered it that she thought at first was a natural formation, some kind of Stythite rock laid down in ledges that ringed the blunt end of the bubble. Sril said, "That's the rAkellaron House."

Now she could see the windows, the jutting balconies, and a torrent of steps running down from the high open porch. People walked there, so small she overlooked them, her eyes taken by the building. Sril laughed at her as she stood gaping at it. He took her by the arms and lifted her up a step onto the floor of a covered arcade. Saba and the other men had gone on ahead of her along the front of the building.

"This is the Barn," Sril said. "All the rAkellaron have offices here." He waved in passing at a door. The arcade stretched along the long front of the building, cut with a door every fifty feet. Over some of them shone blue lights. She went to the edge of the arcade and looked up at the rAkellaron House.

"That must be heavy."

"Heavy as the Empire," he said: some proverb. He opened a door for her. They were nearly to the end of the Barn, only two more doorways between them and a black wall. Sril said, "The Creep isn't here yet. That's his office, the last." She went past him into a room full of men.

Saba stood in the middle of everything, talking to a little ring of faces. She circled them to the window on the far wall. Ketac was there, one hip braced on the sill, his rolled bed tipped against the wall beside him. She glanced into the street outside the window, now much below them.

"Nervous?" she asked Ketac. He was staying here, on Saba's staff.

"I'm fine," he said.

"Don't worry. You'll get used to it."

"I said I'm fine!"

She laughed. The young man grew hot. His fingers plucked fiercely at his short mustaches. Like his face, his hands were all knobbed bones. In the street below a pack of men was passing by, wearing dark blue shirts with red chevrons on the upper sleeves. Seeing Ketac in the window, one called, "Hey, socks."

Ketac's head snapped around. He leaned across the window sill. "Watch what you're saying, sitdown-sailor." Sril elbowed him out of the way.

"What are you looking for, pouchy," he shouted at the chevrons. "Flying lessons?"

The men in the red chevrons were crowding toward the window. Their voices rose in a chorus of insults. Inside the room, Saba called, "Sril, front up." The little gunner went out from between Paula and Ketac. The men in the street were drifting away.

"Uranian Patrol," Ketac said. "The first thing they learn is deep breathing. That's so if their ship's wrecked they can hold their breath until they get home." He scratched his nose, not looking at her.

A big desk took up one side of the office; a square paper flag hanging on the wall behind it was marked with Saba's kite-shaped emblem. Behind the desk was a door. She went through it, through a narrow room lined with analog decks that chuckled and flashed lights, and through another door into a smaller room. Her satchel lay on the low bed along the wall. She sat down in a chair by the window and kicked her shoes off. Through the window came the mechanical roar of the great dark city. She began to shiver. There was a blanket folded on the bed; she wrapped it around herself, over her head and under her feet, and sat in the chair with her knees drawn up and her arms around them, watching the people going by in the street.

After a while Saba came in, looked all around, and started out. He saw her and stopped. "There you are." He sat down on the bed, opened her satchel, and took out a bottle of whiskey. "You don't like it, do you?"

"It isn't very pretty."

"We'll go eat in a few minutes, you can see a little more." He drank deeply of the dark red liquor. At the rate he was drinking it two cases would not last him an Earthish year. She would have to arrange for more. He said, "We're going to the Akopra, too."

"Oh." The Akopra was the Styth theater. "You never go to the one in Matuko."

"Matuko is a third-rate Akopra. The Vribulo company is the best in Uranus."

"Where do I sleep?"

"Here. With me." He lay back on his elbow across the bed, smiling. "You can seduce me, like the first time. I liked that."

She pushed back the hood of her blanket. "I'll sleep in the chair."

He frowned at her. "What's the matter with you?"

"Nothing. I just like things the way they are."

The whiskey sloshed in the bottle. In a crabbed voice, he said, "I don't care, you know. I'm—I was just trying to do you a favor, that's all."

"I appreciate it." She leaned forward, reaching for the bottle, and he gave it to her.

He said, "I mean, it's been a long time for you."

She drank a small warming mouthful out of the bottle and stretched to give it back to him. "When are we going to eat?"

"You'd better not be taking on someone else behind my back."

"I'm hungry. Let's go eat."

He stoppered the bottle and put it on the floor under the bed. She could tell by the way he moved that he was angry. There was a narrow rack in the wall opposite the window, and he took out a clean shirt and stripped himself, all in the same hard, short gestures, his back to her.

"Come on," he said, and yanked the door open.

They went a short way down the street to a drinking dock called Colorado's, after a Vribulit Akellar who had been Prima some long while past. Paula's coat had a veil attached to the hood, which she kept fastened across her face under the eyes. The place was huge, the floor deep in sand, and gloomy as an old church. There was nowhere to sit except on the floor. The Styths stood in clumps drinking and talking. The face-cloth narrowed her vision and as soon as Saba had gone off somewhere she lowered it.

There were plenty of other women, and none of them was veiled. Their faces were painted in figures of red and white, yellow, green, as concealing as veils. Their clothes were spectacular. A woman passed her in a dress of ribbons that fluttered around her while she walked. Paula watched them all, fascinated.

"He did bring you," Tanuojin said.

Paula looked up; she had not seen him come in. "I think he's still trying to civilize me." He stood with his hands flat under his belt, his gaze moving slowly over the room. She had forgotten how tall he was. She said, "He's over there someplace."

"I know where he is," he said, as if she had insulted him. He crossed his arms over his thin chest. She moved away from him. She was hungry; she cast around for something to eat. Saba was coming toward her, a woman beside him. Her eyes and mouth were traced in three colors. He and Tanuojin met like lovers, their arms around each other. Paula went in among them.

"I told you to wear that veil," Saba said.

"I can't see. And I'm hungry."

The painted girl was looking down at her. The rings of color glowed faintly in the dark, accenting her huge black eyes. "Aren't you from someplace strange?"

The two men were talking. Paula nodded her head. "From the Earth. My name is Paula."

"Mine is Tye. Why did you come here?"

"Dumb, I guess."

The girl laughed. Her dress covered her from throat to feet; the supple cloth moved like water over her body. "I've heard a lot about you, and none of it makes you sound dumb."

"Look," Saba said. "Do you want to eat or not?"

There was a slave beside her with a tray, holding it by habit up at the level of his head. She pulled it down to her range and took a plate off it. The plate was divided into sections and held beans and soup and leaf. Tanuojin went off somewhere into the gloom. Saba and the painted girl stood face to face talking. She laughed at something he said and reached out and started to unbuckle his belt. He caught her hand.

A pair of strange boots tramped up, scattering sand into Paula's lap. She raised her head. The boots belonged to a tall young man in a shirt much decorated with chips of metal. He was staring down at her. She went back to her half-eaten dinner, now liberally salted with sand.

"Leave her alone, Ymma," Saba said.

She put the plate down beside her. The young man swung toward Saba. "Oh, is she yours, Matuko? You've always had strange tastes. But now the Prima thinks it's time you came back inside the border."

Saba had the painted girl by the hands. "Tell him to draw me a map." He smiled at the girl.

Tanuojin came up behind Ymma, a plate in his hand. "Running messages, Ymma?" He fed himself, his eyes on the dish. The younger man swung around to face him, his head thrust forward, belligerent.

"I have a couple for you, any time you want to take them. What your friends do could hurt you, you know."

"Talk, talk." Tanuojin turned away. He spoke without missing a bite.

"Are you sure you're getting enough to eat?"

"Yes. Want some?" Tanuojin palmed the dish and pushed it into Ymma's face.

Paula stood up. Across the room someone yelped with laughter.

Everybody turned to watch. Ymma gobbled wordlessly through a mask of thick soup and vegetables. Paula circled around to Saba's far side, out of their way if they fought. Tanuojin leaned over him.

"If you want to fight me, Ymma, do it in the pit, where it matters." He walked off toward the gate.

Dripping food, Ymma started after him, and Saba got in his way. "Maybe you should wash your face, Akellar." Ymma backed up a step, pawing at the mess on his face, and Saba pushed him. The younger man retreated from him.

"Paula," Saba said, "let's go." He turned to the painted girl, Tye. "Come to the Akopra with us."

"I can't," Tye said. "I'm meeting someone else. I'll get rid of him at one bell, if you want."

"I'll meet you here." He gave her a piece of paper credit out of his sleeve. "Get something to drink." He herded Paula before him toward the door.

In the street, she remembered the look on Ymma's face. "Who is he?"

"The Lopka Akellar." Saba was looking around them. "He sits under Machou's arm. Something's cooking." He threw his hand up over his head and shouted, and went off down the street. She had to run to keep up with him. In the street ahead of them, with people passing by on either side, Tanuojin stopped to wait for them.

"Are you coming to the Akopra with us?" Saba said.

Tanuojin hunched his shoulders. "You see what's happening, Saba. They're setting us up over that damned treaty. Only it isn't you they'll start into, it's me."

They were walking at their regular pace. Paula fell behind them. She broke into a run to keep up.

Ahead, along the side of the street, a line of people was forming. The head of the line disappeared around the next corner to the left. Saba led her alongside it. The waiting line thickened. On the far side of the street was another, all in white: slaves. The lines led up the steps of a round building with a dome roof. Bright paper banners hung from the eaves. Saba took her around the head of the line of Styths to a side door.

"The rAkellaron get in free," he said. They went into a lobby. "A privilege we pay for by making up the house deficit." A fat man rushed across the lobby toward them.

"Yes, Akellar—it's been quite some time since we had the honor of entertaining you." He ushered them up the flight of stairs, breathless with compliments. The carpet over the steps was worn. The hallway at the top of the stairs was dark. Drapery cushioned the walls. The fat man waddled ahead of them to pull back a section of the hanging.

Saba's hand on her back pushed her through the gap. She went into a little balcony. Tanuojin sat in one of the four chairs, his back to the curtain. Paula went by him to the rail of the balcony. One story down, the open theater was filling with people. She stood on her toes to see over the railing to the round stage. The lights above it came on. Saba lifted her up from behind like a child and put her down in a chair so deep she felt swallowed.

"Can you see?" He sat down on her left; she was between him and Tanuojin.

"Yes. Thank you."

"Are you warm enough?"

"Yes."

"Why do you fuss over her?" Tanuojin said, in his deep musical voice.

"She's making me rich," Saba said.

"Did you tell her how? Look over there. Machou is here, and Ymma is with him."

Saba's head turned, his eyes aimed across the theater at the balcony directly opposite them. Three or four people were milling around in the little space. Saba stood up. On Paula's right, Tanuojin swore and slouched down and put his feet up on the rail. In the far box, a big man sat, and Saba took his seat.

"You've got slave manners," he said to Tanuojin.

"I stand up for him in the pit. That's all he's worth."

Saba put his elbows on the arms of his chair, his hands on his belt. "Neither of you has any breeding."

"You are all virtue. Tell her how she's going to make you rich." Tanuojin's hand struck the side of her head so hard she was dazed a moment, blinking and stupid. He said, "If any of the rAkellaron want off-world markets arranged, we have to do it through you, don't we?"

"Don't hit me," she said, through her teeth.

"He's charging us each ten per cent of our advances for the use of what I suppose you call your mind."

Unsurprised, she gave Saba an oblique look. What Ymma had said about his strange tastes came back to her. In Styth he was probably a dangerous radical. He nodded over the rail.

"Watch."

The Akopra began. She could make no sense of it. Four men, wearing huge painted masks, moved in stylistic gymnastic poses around the bare stage. The performance was short. At the end, the audience roared and clapped, enthusiastic, the applause lasting for minutes after the four men had left the stage.

"He's pretty good," Saba said.

"He's terrible. They all are." Tanuojin propped his long legs up on the rail. "It's supposed to be an art, not a contest."

Another Akopra was beginning, or perhaps another scene of the same one: the same dancers came back, two in different masks. Tanuojin was not watching. She looked across the theater at Machou, dimly visible in the far balcony.

They watched a third performance, and Tanuojin said, "This is awful. Let's go."

Saba rose. "Are you worried about Ymma?"

"I wouldn't mind if he broke his leg getting down to the street."

They went back along the quiet hallway toward the stairs, going at a Styth pace. Just as they reached the door, a harsh voice said, "Saba."

He stood back, taking his hand off the door pull. Paula was between him and Tanuojin. A file of men was walking toward them. Ymma was third in the line. The man in front walked up to Saba. His face was rutted with scars around the eyes. His hair was streaked with white and his ropy gray mustaches hung down over his chest. Paula glanced at his hands, fisted on his hips. On his left wrist was an iron manacle. He said, "Open the door for me, Saba."

Tanuojin hissed. Machou drew his gaze slowly from Saba to stare over Paula's head. His chest looked wide as a wall. He radiated confidence. Saba pulled the door open, and they stood there while Machou and his whole crew filed out. Tanuojin swore. He charged through the door behind them.

Paula followed in the hot wake of his temper. Saba came after her. She stopped. Machou and his men were just going out the door to the street.

"That's what having a father accomplishes." Tanuojin came up to Saba. "Every time you see a gray hair you back off."

They went out to the street. The men walked along arguing. Paula looked up over her head. The streets were thick with traffic. The air smelled bad, like grease. Rancid. Nearby a siren began to whine. A man tore past her. Two steps behind him, another man ran after him, the siren screeching on his belt.

They went back to the Barn, the long building at the foot of the rAkellaron House. In the arcade Ketac came to meet them. He had a long knife in a sheath on his belt.

"What happened? We heard you were in a fight at Colorado's." He turned to walk beside them, down the arcade.

Tanuojin said, "What's the watch?"

"About thirty minutes to one bell."

They went through Saba's office, across the narrow filing room, and into the little sleeping room. There was a crystal lamp burning and the place was relatively warm. She took off her coat.

"Ymma and Machou just backed us off over at the Akopra," Tanuojin said.

"Backed you off?" Ketac wheeled toward his father.

Saba sat down on the bed and reached under it for the bottle of liquor. "He's the Prima Akellar. I don't see how I can pick a fight with him over precedence. What are you so hot over?" He was talking to his lyo; his voice was genial. "If Ymma challenges you and you start to lose, I'll step in. And Machou will step into me, and we'll get the teeth kicked out of us. But I won't close that market."

There was a cup on the table by the bed. Paula took the bottle from him and poured a slight two fingers of whiskey into the cup and took it over to the window. Outside, the noisy, filthy city stretched away like a vast tunnel. Sirens roamed in the gloomy streets.

Ketac was saying, "You're going to fight in the pit." His voice was thin with excitement. Tanuojin came up to the window, ignoring her beside him.

"Well, maybe," Saba said.

Tanuojin looked the same as he always did, flute-thin, his gray shirt undecorated, his black slot-buckled belt and leggings like anybody else's. Paula cast a glance back into the room at Saba. She put the cup on the window sill. "Machou is afraid of him," she said to Tanuojin.

He stared out the window, his long dished profile toward her. "You've blown your tubes. Machou hasn't even had to fight in sixty or seventy sessions."

"I take it if Ymma is losing, Machou can jump in and help him?"

"Step in. Yes."

"That's why he played that farce at the Akopra. Now he can stay out and nobody will say he's afraid of Saba. Therefore he's afraid of Saba."

The corners of his mouth rolled down; he still refused to look at her. He pulled his mustaches between his thumb and his forefinger. "You don't know what you're talking about."

"What is Ymma to you?"

"My cadet. One rank below me. If he beats me he takes my place."

Saba came up behind him and put his arm around the other man's waist. He was half-drunk. "Why are you heating up? You can handle Ymma."

"I can't handle Machou."

"I'll take Machou." He glanced behind him at Ketac, who was going out of the room. The door shut, and Saba turned to Tanuojin again. Saba's voice fell to a murmur. "Just don't show off. If you get hurt, stay hurt."

"I can't make myself bleed."

"They know you're a blood-stauncher. That doesn't matter. Just don't let them find out about the rest of it." He slapped Tanuojin's ribs. "Go get some sleep."

"I'll call you at two bells." Tanuojin went to the door. Saba had the whiskey bottle with him, which he raised to his mouth. Paula reached for her cup. Machou was old, and Saba was young, strong and young. She thought over the display at the Akopra. Machou had known that Saba would not defy him over a courtesy. Another ritual.

"Can he beat Ymma?" she said.

"Oh, sure," Saba said. "He's just panicked. He ran into a hammer the last time he fought in the pit. Bokojin tore him up." He dribbled liquor into her cup. "I wouldn't like to be Ymma. Tajin has a lot to prove. Drink that, don't waste it."

One bell rang, in the next room, and in the city other bells rang, tuneful and cracked and clanking, all over Vribulo. She said, "You'll be late to meet Tye."

"Oh. I forgot." He put the bottle down empty and strode out. Paula dragged a chair over to the window and climbed onto it to reach the window shade. A siren started up in Machou's smoky crowded city. She leaned against the frame, her hand above her head, looking out there. Saba was third in the rAkellaron order. With work and some luck, he would be Prima. Work, luck, and money. She pulled the shade down over the window, undressed in the dark, and went to bed.

At two bells Saba and Tanuojin went into the rAkellaron House for the session of the central council of the Empire. Paula wanted to go out to the city, but Sril refused to let her out of the office.

"I'm hungry," she said.

"I've got orders," he said. He was sitting behind the desk in the front office, one leg crooked over the arm of the chair. "One thing I never do is disobey orders."

Bakan came in, bear-sized. "Any word yet?"

"No," Sril said. "They have to wait until Machou finishes his own business—it won't be until the mid-third of the watch. She's hungry."

"Take her to Colorado's," Bakan said.

Paula started back through the filing room; she would go out the window of the bedroom. Sril reached ahead of her and shut the door before she could leave the main office. He said, "The Man told me not to let her out."

"Did he tell you to let me starve? You can come with me, I won't run away."

Sril's hand stayed on the latch of the door. To Bakan, he said, "Bokojin offered him fifty thousand dollars for her. You can see what he's afraid of."

The hulking man crossed the room to the other side of the desk. "Here, Mendoz'. If you're hungry, try this."

"Who is Bokojin?" she said. She took a flat orange strip from his hand. It did not look like food. She bit into the end. The stuff was of the texture of strip protein and as hard to chew. The bitter taste screwed her face up. She spat it out.

"Ugh!"

The two men were laughing; Bakan slapped his thigh with amusement. He chewed a mouthful of the stuff like a cud. "Mendoz', you aren't as tough as you think you are." He turned his head and fired a gob of spit into the wastebin in the corner.

She worked her lips to get rid of the horrid taste. Her tongue was numb. Sril's face danced with amusement, but he left the chair and went into the next room and came back with a cup of water for her. Gratefully she drank it.

Sril sat down again, his hands behind his head. "Bokojin is Saba's cadet. Vice captain of the Uranian Patrol. Machou's favorite. He's a comet, he's been in the rAkellaron about the same time as Tanuojin, but he whipped up the rank—"

Bakan spat again. "Until he came to Saba."

"What is that stuff?" she asked.

"Laksi."

"Did he fight Saba?"

Sril said, "The Man let him know what he was going to do to him for Tanuojin's sake." His gaze went to Bakan, sitting on the corner of the desk. "Do you think The Creep can take Ymma?"

"That lady," Bakan said. "My opinion, since you asked. The Creep is under-ranked. He'd be eighth or ninth if he'd fight more."

Paula wandered around the room. The two men talked about fighting. She could not sit still; she was trying to imagine what was happening up in the House—what a pit fight was like. She wondered if she were right about Machou. Being Prima was its own defense. If Tanuojin would fight more, he would be hurt more, and they would all see that he was not just a blood-stauncher. What was he? His touch had healed her wounds in seconds.

"I'm still hungry."

"Go get her something to eat," Sril said to Bakan.

"Why should I go?"

"Because I'm on duty. Go on, just go to Colorado's."

A shout sounded in the arcade. Paula wheeled around. The door burst open, and Ketac rushed into the room, his face shining.

"Tanuojin just beat Ymma down in seventy-three seconds."

Sril whooped, throwing his hands up over his head. Bakan spat. "I knew it. It's just surprising it took him so long."

"What about Saba?" Paula said.

Ketac turned on his heel in the center of the room. "It was The Creep's fight from the beginning. Machou never even stood up." He looked at Bakan. "The Creep worked on him a little. Once he saw that Machou wasn't stepping in, he tore Ymma's face off." Ketac clapped his hands together. "I've never seen anybody fight like that. Smart like that."

Paula went to the door. The arcade was filling up with men. Their voices rose, jubilant. She reached for the door, but it sprang out of her hands. Tanuojin shouldered in past her. His shirt was splattered with blood and his hair hung down over his shoulders. His face was scored with half-healed scratches. He was hot and he stank and his rare smile showed. Paula moved away from him. Marus and Kany and others of his men flooded in the door behind him. He shouted, "I wish I could afford it, I'd buy for the whole city of Vribulo." His hands were covered with blood. The other men slapped him on the back. Saba came in behind him and draped one arm around him. Paula lowered her eyes.

MATUKO

Before she had her coat off, Boltiko and Illy burst in the door. "What did you think of Vribulo? Where did you go?" They closed around her. Illy took her coat and Boltiko hustled her into the kitchen of her house.

"Did you go to the Akopra? Where did you stay?"

"In the Barn." She sat on the curved bench at her kitchen table. There were cushions on it, to lift her up to a Styth level. "We went to the Akopra and saw *The Dragon*." Boltiko put a steaming cup before her on the table. Illy sat beside her.

"*Dragon*. Was it good? But you wouldn't know."

"Tanuojin said it was terrible."

"Tanuojin," Boltiko said. "Was he there?"

"Where is David?"

"Where did you go to eat?" Illy said. "Did he buy you anything?"

Boltiko said, "The baby is asleep. He was so sick before, I walked him up and down all last watch, but he's better now."

Paula sipped the sweet tea. Boltiko worried over every cranky cry. "We ate at Colorado's. What was wrong with him—his stomach again?"

"Colorado's," Illy said, blank. "What's that?"

"A dock," Boltiko said. "You should have made him take you somewhere nice, Paula."

The tea was gone. Paula sat back, her hands on her warm belly. "I liked it. All the women were painted up; I felt like a mouse. I guess they're whores, aren't they? Saba had some trouble with the Prima—Tanuojin was in a fight in the pit."

"I hope Saba didn't get involved?"

"What was wrong with David?"

Boltiko sat down in a chair across the table from Paula. "His tum-tum. Poor baby."

"Little glutton."

"Who fought Tanuojin?" Illy said. "Did he win?"

"Oh, yes. It was Ymma, the Lopka Akellar." Paula watched Boltiko sip from a cup, dainty as a nun. "You don't like Tanuojin?"

"That man will ruin Saba," the prima wife said.

"I don't know him," Illy said. "My brother hates him." Her brother was the Merkhiz Akellar, the Prima Cadet, whose cadet was Saba.

"Do you like him?" Boltiko asked Paula.

"No."

"I knew him—before Saba's father died, sleep deep, when we lived in Vribulo, Tanuojin practically lived with us. After Melleno fired him." Boltiko took her cup across the kitchen to fill from the jug on the counter. "He's low-born, he's ambitious, and he is evil. I can feel it."

"How do you know he's low-born? If nobody knows who his parents were."

"With those nigger-eyes," Illy said, "he's slave-bred. Tiko, me too."

Boltiko brought the hot jug and filled each of their cups. "He is no slave. He's deviant. He should have been destroyed at birth. That's the law." She sank into her chair. "Instead, some soft-hearted woman protected him. She suffered. Everybody who ever helped him has suffered. Melleno gave him work and a respectable position and he seduced his daughter. Yekaka took him in and he betrayed him to Melleno."

"Seduced his daughter," Paula said. "Whose daughter?"

Illy gulped her tea. "Melleno's. When he was the Prima, and

Tanuojin worked for him. Here. I'll show you how to tell your future." She turned her empty cup over on the table.

Paula leaned toward the prima wife. "Tiko, you've known him longer than I have, but I can't see Tanuojin seducing anybody."

"He drugged her." Illy lifted the cup. A wet ring showed on the tabletop. "See? It's unbroken, that means my love is true. If it's broken, that means lovers."

"He drugged her," Paula said to Boltiko. The story fascinated her. And Tanuojin would have been much younger, just clubbed, a creepy adolescent.

Boltiko's round shoulders rolled in a shrug, her eyes watched Illy's cup, her mouth was pursed. "She was very young, Diamo. Why would a girl like that, sweetly bred, defy her father for a man like Tanuojin?"

"Diamo." It was a pretty name. I-love-you, it meant. Which seemed a possible answer.

"Drink your tea," Illy said. "We'll tell your future."

In the lake shore market place, the people of Matuko were pressing thick around the open stall selling illusion helmets. Paula went through the mob, David slung on her hip. A roar of laughter went up. Like a flag a pair of white lace underpants waved above the crowd at the end of a long black arm. Paula glanced around her. Sril was waiting in a line to buy Martian cloth. In another direction, she saw three more people she knew coming out of a shop, packages in their arms. She would have to risk being spied on. Going down a lane between two shops, she went through a back door and into a room filled to the rafters with crates.

"Hello, junior."

A window in the far wall half-lit the narrow open space between the rows of boxes. She went sideways, into the dark. "You're taking a chance. You're lucky you gave that message to the right slave."

He shut the door behind her and switched on a light. "Not exactly. I understand he's your property." He crossed the room to pull a shade across the window. Paula sat down on a crate, putting David on the floor at her feet. Bunker looked thin. Neatly he settled himself across from her on a heap of quilted padding.

"Just the same," she said, "don't come here. I can get in touch with you if there's anything I need."

"How are you getting along?" He folded his arms over his chest. His gaze went to the little boy on the floor. David passed a bit of rope from his right to his left hand. His head was covered with a thin fuzz of hair; in a few days he would be shaved again. He raised his head, looking for Paula, and beamed at her.

"I just can't connect that with you, junior," Bunker said.

She laughed. "Look at his eyes." The crate under her was hard, and she shifted to a pile of packing foam. "What do you want?"

"There's a difficulty with the Council over the treaty."

"Why? Saba is keeping the truce."

"We have trouble convincing people that what isn't happening is good for them."

She looked around the crowded storeroom. The sides of the boxes were stenciled with the word BARSOOM and a long number. She flicked at a bit of packing foam on the skirt over her knee. "In one hundred fifty watches they are taking *Ybix* down past Jupiter. I'm sure if they know he's coming they can protect themselves."

"He confides that much in you? Poor chump."

"He doesn't confide anything. Is that all you want to know?"

Bunker scratched his chin. His black eyes glinted. "There's the incident at Luna."

"Pah. That was your fault."

"Let me finish. That little exercise ushered General Gordon into the rose garden. Luna is now suffering under General Marak, whose itch is money, not god. The Council says if the treaty works, we should be able to bring Matuko to answer for two ships and eight crewmen and a government."

"Two ships," she said.

"*Ybix* destroyed two patrol ships at Luna, didn't she?"

David had taken hold of her skirt and was dragging himself up onto his feet. She watched him, remembering what had happened at Luna. "What did you have in mind?"

"The Council says if the Styths are dedicated to peace and law, they'll be willing to put the case before the Universal Court."

She put her hand down, and David took it, wobbling on his widespread legs. "Well, maybe they will."

Bunker's folded arms unlocked. He put his hands in the pockets of his heavy jacket. "Are you serious? Can you get them there?"

"Can Crosby's Planet handle a visitation? Send them a subpoena." She watched her son lower himself down to the floor again. "Not to Saba. He wasn't even inboard during the shooting. Send it to Tanuojin." She smiled at David, delighted by a new thought. "Send it by way of Machou." David let go of her hand and landed with a thump on the floor.

"Will it work?"

"Maybe." She stood up, stooped, and lifted the little boy up into her arms. "If it doesn't I'll try something else. How is Jefferson?"

"Fat Roland is getting old." He shook his head. "We'll be in trouble when she leaves the Committee."

"You're always in trouble. Send the subpoena." She went out to the lane between the shops.

She sat on the hard shore of the lake playing her flute. Behind her were the tenements where the fishermen lived. Their ten-foot oars were propped up against the walls and their nets hung off the eaves in loops of mesh. The lake spread out before her like a sheet of carbon. The edge rippled against the flinty shore. She wondered what stirred the water: maybe the motion of the Planet.

Saba was coming along the shore toward her. She stopped playing to warm her hands in the sleeves of her tunic. Although she saw him often enough in the street, he had never seemed to notice her before. He came up beside her.

"What are you doing?"

"I'm just sitting here." She picked up her flute again. "I like it here."

"I want to talk to you."

"Talk." She blew six quick rising notes on the long black flute.

He sat down on the ground beside her and stared across the lake. She played the dream sequence from Alfide's *Spanish Anarchist*. In the lake shallows, fish schooled, no longer than her fingers. They fed on waterbugs, invisibly small. Where the water was deeper, a flat shape stirred off the bottom—a ybix, which fed on the fish.

"Look," he said. "I want you to do something for me."

"What?" She lowered the flute.

"If you do I'll take you to Vribulo."

"I can go to Vribulo by myself whenever I want."

"I'm in love with this girl who lives in there." His head jerked back toward the tenements behind them.

"Oh."

"I've never felt like this about a girl in my whole life." His hands rose off his knees. "But I can't even talk to her. Her husband keeps her locked up. I've only seen her face three times. I'm going crazy."

"Oh." She turned to look back at the tenements, draped in nets. "Is he a fisherman—her husband?"

"Yes."

"What is she like?"

"She's beautiful. And she's so young, and soft, and—" He rubbed his hands over his eyes. "Ive never felt like this before. Take a message to her for me. You can talk to her without anybody noticing."

"What message?"

He sat back straight, smiling. "I knew you'd do it. I'll buy you anything you want."

"You don't have to do that," she said.

. . .

In the middle watch she went to Illy's house, where Boltiko was fitting a dress to the young wife. Paula sat in the fur chair drinking kakine while Illy turned slowly around, her arms out, and the prima wife tacked up the hem. The dress had three sets of sleeves, one snug to the wrist, one slit to the elbow, one open to the shoulder, in three different kinds of cloth. The rest of the dress was black.

"How does it look?" Illy asked Paula, high-spirited.

"It's beautiful. Tiko, it's stunning."

Boltiko said, "Neither of you thinks I can do anything." Kneeling, she sat back on her calves to look, her moon-face placid with a smile.

"Wait until he sees it," Illy said.

The prima wife held out one hand, and Paula got out of her chair and helped her stand, her fat hanging in layers off her bones. "He won't be seeing too much at home, unless I miss the signs."

Illy's hands paused, unfastening the clips down the front of the dress. "What?"

Paula curled up in the soft white chair again, her head on the arm. Boltiko said, "He won't be sleeping with any of us for a while, that's what. Here, let me have it." She removed the dress from Illy.

Surprised, Paula watched the young wife's face drop open with alarm. "He has another woman."

Boltiko was folding the new dress. Smoothing the cloth under her hand, she laid her gaze a moment on Illy. "Put your clothes on." She turned to Paula. "Am I right?"

Paula nodded. Illy turned away, one hand out for her yellow robe. Boltiko stood watching her back, her vast face soft with sympathy.

"Child, you will never learn." Her hand stroked and stroked the dress hanging over her arm. "Well. I have work to do." She went heavily out the front door.

Illy sat down in the other sling chair. There were tear slicks down her cheeks. "Who is she?"

"A girl in the Lake District."

"How can he do this to me?"

Paula sat up and filled her little cup again from the jug of kakine. Illy said, "Is she young? Have you seen her? Is she younger than me?"

"Yes. She's very young."

The Styth woman's eyes overflowed with tears. The bright robe hung open. Under it she wore white underclothes like harness. Her body was beautiful, like her face, even crying.

"How can he do this to me?"

"Come on," Paula said. "I'll rub your back."

Illy took her into her sleeproom. The windows were screened off with long panels of silk embroidered with rose-flies, their wings edged in gold. The room was dim as a cave. Illy lay down on the broad bed; while Paula stroked her back, she opened most of the tight white underclothes. Illy wept as if she enjoyed it. Quieting, she lay still and Paula ran her fingers up and down the soft skin of her back.

"He'll come back to me. He always does."

Paula bent and kissed her neck. "I think you're beautiful. Don't cry." Paula pressed her mouth to the soft black cheek. "You're much more beautiful than she is." Illy turned toward her. Paula put her arms around her and kissed her mouth. "Don't cry."

The Styth woman's lips parted. Saba had taught her how to kiss. The two women lay side by side, their mouths touching. Illy's skin warmed, her breath came fast. She had no scent. When Paula touched her breast, Illy rubbed against her hand.

"Let me go get the kakine," Paula said.

She locked the front door, brought the jug of liquor back to the sleeproom, and took her clothes off. Illy watched her.

"I've never done this before."

The room was freezing. Paula climbed onto the bed and pulled the thick cover over her. She touched Illy, who lay down again on her back.

"This is bad, isn't it?"

"It's the same as with him." Paula gave her the jug. She dipped her finger into the thick sweet liquor and drew in green kakine on Illy's breast and licked it off.

"I never did that with him."

They painted each other with kakine and sucked and kissed and licked it off. Illy's skin softened and warmed. Her voice fell, husky.

"I wish he was here now. Don't you want him?"

"We don't need him."

Illy's thighs stroked together. Her pubic hair was shaved. Her hips were smooth, full arches. Paula spread kakine over her slit and the tiny nub at the top. Illy opened her legs.

"Please—"

"Do it to me." Paula ran her tongue over the soft folded flesh.

"It tastes bad."

"It tastes fine."

"Oh." Illy moved, offering herself. Her hands slid down over Paula's legs and rump and her claws worked. Paula drew back.

"Oh," Illy said. "Don't stop."

"Do it to me."

"I can't—I—"

"Do it. Use the kakine, if you don't like the taste." Paula fingered Illy's body, and the Styth woman reached for the jug. Paula put her head down between the other woman's legs again.

Illy balked twice more. Paula thought she liked pretending to be forced. In the end she did so well that Paula sobbed and clung to her through a pulsing climax. Illy lay on her side, shaking the empty jug.

"That's nothing like with him. He would never do that for me."

"You can suck him. He might learn."

Illy called her house slave in to give him the jug. Paula covered herself in the bedclothes, her head near Illy's knees and her feet on the pillow. The eunuch avoided looking at them. He might tell Pedasen, but he would tell no Styths.

"Could we get drunk like that?" Illy laughed. The slave brought back the jug, full. "I think I'm drunk, a little. Did I do it right? Did you like it?"

Paula smiled at her. Illy moved over and cradled her head on Paula's thigh. "I liked it." Paula touched the long black hair. Against Illy's black skin her skin looked warm: red brown. She put her head down, pleased to be in bed with such a beautiful woman.

In the high watch, Paula went to the rack in her bedroom and found her clothes hacked to pieces with scissors. Pedasen was with her. He picked up a bit of a sleeve. "That low nigger," he said, under his breath.

"Who did it?" She wheeled on him. He stooped, gathering up the shards of her dresses, the back of his head to her, and mumbled something inaudible. She squatted beside him. "Who?" she said into his face.

"I don't know, mem."

He took the rags away. She followed him down to the kitchen. "Why, then? I don't even know any of the other slaves."

Pedasen fed the scraps of cloth into the shredder. "Because you keep with the blacks. Going to her like that." His face was guileless. She realized he was destroying the evidence before Boltiko found it. She watched a long black ribbon disappear between the lips of the shredder.

"How can they hate me when I don't even know them?"

"You stay with the blacks against your own people."

Angry, she went away down the hall.

"You're pulling my hair out by the roots."

"Everything that makes you beautiful hurts a little." Illy brushed hard at Paula's hair. David was in his new crib, in the room across the hall from Paula's bedroom, and he let out a wail. Pedasen came down the hall from the kitchen to the child's room. In the mirror Illy's hands fluffed the bush of Paula's hair. Illy stooped and kissed her shoulder.

"There. Doesn't that look better, darling?"

"It looks fine. Can I get dressed now?"

"You're impossible," Illy said, and kissed her again. "I guess all intelligent people are a little odd in some way."

Pedasen was singing to David, in the room across the hall. Paula strained to make out the words in the low voice. While she was dressing, Saba shouted in the front room. Illy clutched her shoulder.

"What is he doing here? You told me he didn't come here."

"That isn't what I said." Paula poked her feet into her shoes and slid off her bed. She had told Illy that Saba never slept with her. Saba came in the doorway.

"Do you have any more questions? I'm leaving in three hours."

Dakkar appeared behind him in the hall. His prima son would rule Matuko in his absence. Illy withdrew across the room, veiling her face with one long black hand.

Paula said to Saba, "No—as long as I can use your computer I can figure everything out, I think."

"Get the contract advances as high as you can," he said. He ignored Illy as if she were not there. "Remember, one-tenth of it goes to me. Where is Vida?"

"He's asleep." She could still hear Pedasen singing to him.

Saba waved his hand at Dakkar, standing in the doorway with one hand on the frame. "I've told him to keep watch on you. Make it easy for him, like a good girl." He turned and walked out of the room, and with a backward glance at her Dakkar followed him.

Illy said, "All those instructions. You must be important." She ran her hands down Paula's arms. Her voice turned wistful. "He never once said how pretty you look."

The collar of Paula's new dress itched. David lay heavy in her arms. Boltiko stood directly before her, and the mob of younger children before her, blocking Paula's view of the yard. She knew Saba was somewhere near the bilyobio tree because the steady murmur of voices came from that direction. This ceremony was obviously important, since Ketac had come all the way from Vribulo for it.

This was her family now, these people around her. David made her belong to them, to Boltiko and Illy beside her, the little children, the older boys having part in the ceremony, and the man taking ceremonious leave of them all. She felt no kinship with them. Sometimes she wondered how else she ought to see herself, an alien intruder, a guest, or a glorified slave. Maybe, like the man who rode across Lake Constance, if she saw what she really did, she would die of fright.

Illy turned her head slightly. Her face was covered, like Boltiko's, only her beautiful eyes showing. Through the tail of her eye she glanced at Paula, and she moved a step backward and took Paula's hand. Paula squeezed her fingers.

Saba took *Ybix* away to the Asteroids. Half the rAkellaron wanted contracts to trade with the Middle Planets, and they could not understand why Paula needed more time than a watch to draw them up. She began with Melleno, thinking that he would be easier to deal with because he was Saba's ally. She was mistaken. He refused to give her information she needed and ignored some of her questions entirely. At first it made her angry, until she realized that he was not being arbitrary. He was simply acting like a man who could recite his pedigree back fifty-three generations to a mythical hero. To get his attention she had to assure him of his family's glory and remind him of his duty to maintain it, and to convince him that trading with the Middle Planets was the way to do that.

With five cities and four million people under his rule, Melleno could demand three times the advances Saba had gotten, but the mention of money made him very short-tempered. She guessed he was afraid of seeming to be bribed; and anyway it was ignoble to need money. The payments had to be disguised as gifts and tribute, incidental to the real purpose of the contract which was to glorify Melleno among the fifty-three generations of Mellenos.

Tanuojin's contract was much easier. Yekka was the newest city in Uranus and the biggest bubble in Styth. Only a hundred thousand people lived there, mostly small farmers. Although Tanuojin had been married to Melleno's daughter, he himself had no family at all. Paula worked with his pitman and the man left behind in Yekka to rule in Tanuojin's absence and they wrote a contract in plain language and straight terms.

The politics of the rAkellaron were actually simple: they bullied the weaker and obeyed the stronger; but they went about it with the formality of an Akopra. At first she thought that, if she could only find the right key, she could talk directly to the sense; but there was no key. The Styths responded only to the forms. She had to learn their diplomatic language phrase by phrase.

Slowly she grew confident in it. Matuko no longer seemed such a strange place. She walked in the city, she talked to Boltiko and Illy and slept with Illy, and she and Pedasen took care of David. The child was her clock in the timeless city. He walked, he ran, his babbling began to sound like words. She took him around the city with her, but once three or four slaves in the market threw street shales at her and chased her halfway home, and after that she left him in the compound.

"What did you bring for Paula?" Boltiko asked.

Paula looked up; Illy stopped pulling on her new gloves. The three women faced him across the little round glass table of Illy's sitting room. He fussed with his mustaches. "I forgot."

"Oh, Saba."

"I'll get her something in the White Market."

Paula folded her legs under her. She sat deep in one corner of the sling chair. She was glad he had forgotten to bring her a present, which put her apart from the other women and the bawling horde of children. He had gotten everything in the Off-World Market anyway, before he left. Illy tugged the gloves off her hands.

"You can have these." She thrust the soft leather handful at Paula.

"Don't be silly," Paula said.

Her arm extended toward her, Illy gave her husband a slashing look. "Take them."

"Illy, they won't fit me." Paula tucked her hands in her sleeves. She glanced quickly at Saba, afraid he would suspect them. Illy's eyes were liquid with tears. Slowly she put on the fawn-colored gloves. With a low cry she rushed into the sleeproom and shut the door.

"What's the matter with her?" Saba said. Between them, Boltiko turned toward Paula. Her face brimmed with understanding. Paula stared at the prima wife a moment. Illy's eunuch brought in a tray of cakes and fruit and set out the little dishes on the table. Boltiko turned away.

"Go ask Illy what she will drink," Paula said to the slave. Saba was picking up a handful of cakes. Just after one bell he had come back from six hundred watches in *Ybix;* he had spent the whole low watch in bed with Illy. Boltiko caught Paula's eye. Her small mouth was clamped shut, as if she bit on something foul. The slave poured whiskey for Saba and Paula and kakine for Boltiko.

"I have something for you," Paula said to Saba. "A lot of money."

"I saw Tanuojin's contract in Saturn-Keda." She had sent a copy of it with Melleno's contract, since they were related. Saba swallowed a mouthful of cake. He picked up a white pala fruit. "He's a little salty you know so much about Yekka."

Illy came in and sat between them, her face stony. Saba ignored her, intent on the sweet juices of the pala fruit. Paula buried her fists in her lap.

"What does he expect—I can't go to the Martians without knowing what I'm talking about."

"If you brought him the five moons in a net he would call you a thief. He thinks you're the kundra in the Akopra."

Illy was staring at the table, her profile to Paula, her beautiful mouth swollen, her eyelashes tipped in gold. I use her the same as he does, Paula thought. As kindless as him. She said, "It's amazing how much you find out—drawing up a contract like that." Her voice sounded brittle. She cleared her throat.

"Are you keeping everything you learn?"

"Naturally. What happened on your mission?"

"Everything bad. The Martians were all running in convoys. We didn't take a ship." He picked up Illy's hand in the soft skin glove and laid her palm against his cheek. To Boltiko he said, "Come feed me something that isn't sweet." She heaved quaking off the chair and followed him out.

Paula sighed. She smoothed her hair back from her face. Illy took off the gloves, her gaze on her hands.

"I nearly let him know about us, didn't I?"

"Boltiko knows."

"She won't tell him."

"Maybe we should—" Paula tried to judge what he would do if he found out about them. Unpredictable. She would not risk it. "Now that he's back, we should break it off."

Illy lurched around to face her. "No. You're staying with me." She flung the gloves down on the table.

Paula emptied her cup and put it down. She scrambled forward off the chair. Illy grabbed her sleeve.

"You can't leave me."

"You're worse than a man."

"If you leave me, I'll tell him." Illy gripped her arms. "I'll tell him, and he'll take your boy away."

Paula wrenched loose. She brushed past her to the door and went out to the yard. Behind her Illy screamed her name. She ran back to her own house.

Saba gave David a robot that talked in pidgin Styth when it was wound up. After two watches of its screechy little voice Paula broke off the key. None of the women was talking to any of the others. Saba noticed it and made several remarks to Paula he obviously thought were the fine edge of wit. Everything he said convinced her that he knew about her and Illy. Whenever Paula was in sight, Illy hung on him. Paula could barely eat. Finally he went down to Yekka, and she went limp with relief, and the next watch woke up with a piercing pain in her belly.

The cramps bound her guts so that she could not straighten. She sent David for Pedasen. Certainly Illy had poisoned her. But the eunuch poked at her stomach and shook his head.

"No, it's just slave-gripe." He went down to the kitchen and came back with a pot of boiling water and the box of tea.

David climbed onto the bed. "Mama, I help you." He pulled on her arm. Pedasen steeped the tea in a cup.

"I'm surprised you haven't had it before," he said. "Maybe because you spend all your time with the blacks. They never get it."

"Pedasen," she said, "don't lecture me." She doubled up, groaning.

"Here." He pulled David away and gave her the strong bitter tea to drink. "You'll feel better when you have the shits."

She gulped the tea. Her forehead burst with sweat. David scrambled up beside her. "Mama, get up." Pedasen lifted him away.

Feet hurried down the hallway, and Boltiko and Illy rushed into the room. They consulted with the eunuch. Paula lay on her side, breathing with pain. Illy sat down beside her.

"It's all right, my darling, I'm here."

Pedasen was right. Her guts loosened in a stinking, burning flux. The relief lasted only a few moments. Her body knotted up again. All the rest of the watch she went between her bed and the washroom. Pedasen and Boltiko left, but Illy stayed the whole time. She held Paula's hand and talked to her, even while she squatted over the hole in the steamroom and gave up her insides in a flood.

She began to feel better. Illy washed her face with scented water. Paula moaned in the new luxury of being free of pain. She felt guilty for suspecting Illy of causing it. She took Illy's hand and kissed it, and Illy hugged her.

Boltiko watched her hands in her lap. She was weaving a shawl. She sat on the swing in Paula's sitting room; she had claimed as she walked in the door that she wanted to get away from the children. Paula stood by the window, her back to the window, and folded her arms over her chest.

"All right. You want to talk about Illy."

The prima wife's gaze remained on her hands. "I'm very disappointed in you. You know you're betraying Saba?"

"Saba has other women all the time."

"He's taken you into our home."

"That's because he needs me. We have work together."

"I know that," Boltiko said. "You've changed him, you've made him think differently about almost everything. I admit I'm jealous of you." She turned the work in her hands, smoothing the intricate design between her weaving needles. "We all have our lot in life." She nodded down the hallway. "You are the only person I've ever known to tame a kusin."

The little animal was coming out of the baby's room. It ran down the hall in the opposite direction, to the kitchen to drink. Paula's eyes followed it. She had done nothing to tame it.

"That's a compliment, Tiko. It won't come in when Illy is here."

"I still think you're betraying him," Boltiko said. "He'll forgive you, because you're his friend. Illy he will not forgive."

YEKKA. Tanuojin's Akellarat.
The Black Season

The bus stopped in Yekka's city gate, and she and Sril got off with the other passengers in the public section. The little open platform outside the docking tube was loud with their footsteps and voices and the people come to meet them. She unfastened the veil and pushed her hood back. Most of the people around her were farmers who had taken their produce to sell in Vribulo and Matuko. They went off, carrying their baskets. She went to the edge of the platform, blinking in the unexpected bright light.

The gate stood in a green field. The grass was knee-high, like a meadow, and the air rang with the thin voices of insects. The men and women who had just left the bus were walking away along a narrow path. The bubble was so big she could not make out the far ends; she had a sudden feeling of being released into its vast space. Sril came up behind her and shouted, and on the path leading to the gate two men broke into a run toward them.

One was Marus. The other was a boy, a neophyte, his shaggy hair unclubbed, who gave Paula a strange, piercing look. Sril handed Marus her satchel, and the third watch helmsman passed it on to the young man.

"This is Kasuk, Mendoz'. The Akellar's son."

"Hello," Paula said.

"Hello." The boy stared over her head, avoiding her eyes. Sril went back into the closed part of the gate, to take the bus back to Matuko, and Marus and Tanuojin's son led her off into a pathway that crunched under her feet.

The city seemed wild, without people. The meadows were fields, cut into long furrows and planted with green. Insects soared from leaf to leaf. They passed through an orchard of little trees. The naked branches were thin and knobbed like arthritic fingers.

"Pala trees," Marus said to her. "More pala trees in Yekka than people."

"What are those insects?"

"Krines. You should hear them during the hot time, they really shout." They were coming to a bridge, humped over a stream, and he took her arm. "Be careful. It's slippery." There was no rail.

The green city curled around her, bright as an afternoon. She wished she had brought David. Kasuk was watching her. When she saw him, he jerked his gaze away. They went through a high white wall into a compound yard. The low white buildings on either side were trimmed with red under the eaves and around the windows and doors. Marus took her into the house on her right and along a narrow dark hallway to a room in the back.

Saba and Tanuojin were bent over a long table on the far side, under a window. Their backs were to her. Marus left. She went across the room to the table, whose slanted surface was papered with sheets of clear plastic held fast by clips. Each of the pages was a line drawing of a spaceship. The two men ignored her. She stood on her toes, her arms on the edge of the table, to see the sketches.

"Here." Tanuojin thrust a folded paper at her. "What is this?"

Her heart quickened. She opened out the paper in her hands. "This must be a first. It's a subpoena to the Universal Court." At the head of the clear computer stock was the Court's wing-and-balance insignia.

"What does that nigger treaty say we have to do about it?"

She was reading through it, delighted. The list of charges ran half the page: two counts of grand piracy, one count of theft, one count of harassment, six counts of refusing a directive, three counts of contempt of authority. She said, "I don't think they expect you to do anything, or they wouldn't have thrown in all these bogus charges."

"Forget it," Saba said. He straightened, his arms braced on the drafting table on either side of the sketch, and bent and gave her a fast kiss on the forehead. "That was almost before the treaty, anyway."

Tanuojin came around him and took the paper from her. "This is a lie." He sounded outraged. He shook the subpoena under her nose. "It's a biased, prejudiced frame-up. The whole print job is a fraud."

Paula looked away from him. The walls were chambered with bookracks. Charts and black and white recognition posters of spaceships hung above them. Saba stuck his pen in his hair.

"I like the scoopnose better."

"That damned Machou. How did he get this?" Tanuojin read through the subpoena again. "They blew up their own ship and they're hanging it on me. And what's this theft charge? We should have stolen everything they had. What's contempt of authority?"

"Do you remember telling General Gordon he was ignorant and superstitious?" Paula said.

"He is."

"Contempt of authority." She tapped the paper. "That's a sieve, those charges. You can't be held for that, it's only a crime on Luna."

"So the damned treaty only works one way, you see? They keep us in line, but they do whatever they please."

Saba tore the top sheet of his drawing off the pad. "Forget it. Report the kill, maybe the fleet will vote you your fifth stripe." He bent over the sketchpad. "They can't do anything to us."

"Call you nasty names," she said. "Stop payments on your contracts."

Tanuojin went to the window. Paula watched him through the corner of her eye. Through the window came the rhythmic ringing strokes of an ax, or maybe a hammer.

"How was the bus ride?" Saba asked.

"Not bad."

Tanuojin said, "Where is this nickel-dime court?"

"In Crosby's Planet. The man-made planet at Venus's aft lagrangian."

He put his hands on the red window frame, his eyes aimed out toward the sound of the hammer. Beside her, Saba said, "What did you have in mind?"

"I'd like to shove the thing down Machou's throat." He turned. "Come on."

They followed him out to the hall. Paula skipped every few strides to keep up with them. Saba said, "Are you thinking of going down there?"

"Why not?" Tanuojin opened a door, and they went out to the yard. "You said yourself we could use another reconnaissance down there. Here they are sending us an invitation. And that's deeper than we've ever been, that's as far down as they go."

They walked across to another white building. At the far end of the yard, his son was striking at something on the ground with great full strokes of a sledgehammer. Paula went after the two men into the house. They turned a corner and led her into a room stacked around with boxes. Against the wall, under a window, was a bed covered with a gray blanket, the only piece of furniture there.

"Look at this place," Saba said to her. He flung his hand out at the piles of crates. "Do you know how long he's been living here? It looks as if he's still moving in. Even you unpacked your clothes. He's lived in this room since he entered the rAkellaron."

Tanuojin sprawled across the bed. Saba went around the small, barren room. He took a bottle of his Scotch out of the box at the foot of the bed and pulled the stopper out.

"He used to fire it up," Tanuojin said. "Now he just drinks it." He twisted around to shout out the window. "Kasuk!"

The hammer stopped. His son's shaggy head appeared in the open square of the window. Tanuojin said, "Stop for a while. You're driving me crazy."

"I'm almost done."

"Stop for a while."

Kasuk slung the hammer over his shoulder and went away. Paula sat down on a box. The walls of the room were bare. He had lived here more than five years without making one personal impression on the place.

"Tell me about this court," Saba said.

"It's very simple. There's one judge, drawn by lot out of a pool of three hundred, most of whom for one reason or another are anarchists."

"Why?" Tanuojin said.

She shrugged her shoulders. "Most of the people in the pool are so anarchistic they don't even call themselves anarchists. Sybil Jefferson is a judge of the court."

He was staring at her, his yellow eyes unblinking. His hard look put her nerves on end. He said, "Let me touch her."

Saba turned, on the opposite side of the little room, and Paula backed up a few feet. "Touch me?"

"Do you want to do that?" Saba said.

"She already knows enough about me to get me killed."

"Touch me how?" she said.

"Come here." Saba sat down on the bed's foot, his hands out. She faced them both, wary.

"What are you going to do?"

"Do you have something to hide?" Tanuojin said. "I won't hurt you."

Saba got her by the skirt and drew her over against his knees. "Don't be afraid." He put his arm around her waist. She had no way to escape. Tanuojin sat up and took her by the wrists.

"Look over my shoulder."

She stared into his face, her arms stiff in his grasp. Saba held her uncomfortably tight. Tanuojin said, "Look over my shoulder, damn you, you're distracting me." She turned her head, aiming her eyes past him, at the blank white wall. Her arms were warm. She felt a warmth and a pleasant lassitude climbing through the muscles of her arms, across her shoulders, and into her back. Her neck felt hot. He let her go; Saba let her go.

"She had the Committee send that paper to Machou," Tanuojin said. He lay down on his elbows again. "She's been meeting somebody from the Committee behind your back."

She went cold down to her heels. "How did you know that?"

"I know everything you know."

Saba gripped her shoulder. Her mind refused to work. She stared stupidly at Tanuojin, who had read her mind. He said, "I told you she was a spy."

"How often has she met him?" Saba asked. His hand clutched her painfully hard.

"Only once. She'll do it again."

She said, "If you know—everything, you know I told him not to come back."

Tanuojin's yellow eyes gave her a flickering glance. He said, "Lock her up."

"She's useless if she's locked up." Saba's free hand landed on her other shoulder. He stood up, holding her fast.

"Then kill her."

"She wouldn't be much good then, either, would she?" He held her between them, his hands so tight she bit her lower lip, resisting the pain. "She's not like us. She doesn't know better. You can't expect her to change all at once."

"You have to do something with her, she's dangerous."

"Is it true? Did she tell him not to come back?"

Reluctantly Tanuojin said, "Yes, she did. But just to keep out of trouble."

Saba pushed her away toward the door. "She'll learn."

"She works on the worst things in you," Tanuojin said. "All your vices."

"We can't all be pure and holy like you. Throw that paper away." He steered Paula out to the hall.

"What is that—how did he do that?" She looked up at him while they walked. "Did he read my mind? What did he do?"

His hand slipped off her shoulder. They went along the corridor at his speed. She jogged beside him. "He has a gift—he healed you, that time, remember? It's a gift he has, an influence."

They turned a corner and he stopped and opened a door. Paula went ahead of him into a room like Tanuojin's. This one was flooded with signs that Saba lived here. His dirty clothes lay piled on the floor and three empty whiskey bottles ranged along the window sill. At the foot of the long narrow bed was her valise.

"Whom did you meet from the Committee?"

She turned by the bed. He was taking his belt off. Her skin crept with alarm. "What are you doing?"

"You have to learn," he said. He held her by the back of the neck and whipped her half a dozen times with the doubled belt. Through the layers of her coat and dress and overalls she hardly felt the blows. He put his belt back on. She stood with her back to him, her jaw clenched. She hated him so much she could have wept.

He sat down on the bed, watching her. "I think there's hope for you," he said. "When you can still get that angry."

"Do I have to sleep here?"

"Yes."

"There isn't enough room."

"Everybody here thinks you're my wife. It would look strange."

She knelt on the bed and pushed the liquor bottles out of the way so she could see out the window. Green and unpeopled, Yekka stretched away from her, hazy with distance. She could revenge herself on him. She knew all his weaknesses. She folded her arms on the broad sill of the window. She could not risk the indulgence. She depended on him; he was her weakness. The wafting breeze smelled of dry grass. She put her head down on her arms.

They slept together in the bed, side by side, not touching. When she woke up, she was alone. The hammer clanged and clanged in the courtyard outside the window. She put on a pair of overalls and the long green dress Boltiko had made for her. Two bells rang.

She went out through the hall. Marus, Kany, and the rest of Tanuojin's watch were gathered beside the door to read a paper posted on the wall.

"Mendoz'." Kany grabbed her arm and hauled her into their midst. "What's this about another trip to the Middle Planets?"

She pried up his fingers, releasing herself. "You gentlemen have been touring the galaxy lately."

"Now, Mendoz'." They crowded around her, bumping into her, pulling her hair and breathing down her neck. "You can tell us." She maneuvered through them and went out the door to the yard. In the doorway the crew moaned and hissed at her.

At the opposite end of the yard, Kasuk was swinging the hammer hard, his body twisting from the heels with each stroke. His hair flew. She went up behind him to see what he was doing. The hammer was pounding at the base of a little bilyobio tree. Every time he hit it the short stump threw off a cloud of silvery dust. She liked the bilyobio trees; she felt as if he were hurting it. Her nose began to itch and she sneezed.

Kasuk wheeled around. "Oh. I didn't see you."

"What are you doing?"

He gestured at the half-destroyed stump. His eyes slid away from her. "My father—the bilyobios disturb him." He picked up the hammer again and hit the stump a terrific whack that broke it off at the base.

"Where are they?"

"Gemini? They're down by the Akopra." He kept his back to her. She went around in front of him, irritated, and he turned away.

"What do you have against me, anyway?"

He pulled at his shaggy hair. "I'm not supposed—my father—my father says you'll corrupt me." Shyly he looked at her.

She let out a peal of laughter. He straightened, leaning on the hammer. His eyes were black, like an ordinary Styth's. She said, "I'll do my best. Where is the Akopra?"

"Just across Koup Bridge. It isn't built yet." He swung the hammer up over his shoulder and led her toward the gate in the wall. Dust streamed out of his clothes. In the gateway, he stood pointing across the fields. "There's Koup Bridge, on the curve. The market used to be there but he moved it so he could put the Akopra there." Just beyond the humped bridge, half a mile from her, was a circle laid out on the ground in scaffolding.

"Maybe someone should go with you," he said.

"No, thank you." She started away down the path.

The whole of the bubble was laid out in long narrow fields, what the Styths called cold-farms to distinguish them from the hot-farms where they made crystal. She passed an old woman coming the other way with a basket on her back. She wondered how much Tanuojin knew, and how he would use it, and when. Before, she had disliked him; now she was frightened of him. She stepped out of the path to let a flock of chickens pass, herded by a little boy with a stick.

At first the Koup Bridge seemed to be on the perpendicular wall before her, but as she walked the ground flattened out, and she saw the bridge and the round wall beyond it not from above in Egyptian perspective but sideways, straight ahead of her. The fields on this side of the stream were flooded. Dark gray tentacles sprouted up out of the water. She went to the edge of a paddy. The water was only four inches deep. Under it the soil was covered in layers of dark cloth. The vines were leafless, mottled gray.

She went over the bridge. The slats of the round scaffolding reached higher than her head. The grass around it was trampled flat. The yellow roots showed. She walked around the circular building, searching for a way in. A pile of dark gray plastiment bricks and long strips lay in the grass on the side of the building away from the stream, before a gap in the circular wall. She went into the round building.

Saba and Tanuojin were walking along the inside of the curve. Tanuojin was pointing off across the building and talking, but Saba saw her, elbowed him to be quiet, and they turned and watched her come up to them. Saba waved one hand at the building.

"Look at this theater he's building with the money you got for him. He hasn't even thanked you, has he?"

"She's getting what she wants." Tanuojin slid his hands under his belt, looking down at her. Uneasily she wondered again how much he knew of her conversation in the White Market with Dick Bunker.

"He says you have some idea we can use this subpoena against Machou." Saba's hand on her shoulder steered her across the hard-packed dirt toward the opening in the curved wall. Tanuojin went ahead of them through the gap. He looked back over his shoulder at her, his eyes yellow as bile. He knew everything. Saba shook her. "Tell me."

She shrugged against his grip, and he let her go. They went out of the theater. Tanuojin was some way ahead of them. She said, "They have no case against you on any of those counts except the one. You'll make them look very stupid, if you go down there and prove it."

"How does that help me against Machou?"

"Machou can't deal with the Middle Planets. Show you can, and who will the others listen to, you or Machou?"

On the far side of the bridge, Tanuojin stopped beside a paddy, sank down on his heels, and thrust his hand into the water. She slowed her walk. Saba was staring at the ground in front of him. He fell to her pace.

"Jesus, you talk well." He thrust his head up, toward Tanuojin, on the far side of the bridge. "He wants to do it. Not for your reasons. He's afraid of losing that money. Did you guess that, too? I don't trust you, Paula, you're running me again, like at the Nineveh."

She led him onto the bridge. If Tanuojin wanted to go, he could talk Saba into it. "What are those vines?"

"Rellah vines." He went down the slope of the bridge to the paddy. Kneeling, he pulled the end of a vine out of the water. He pierced the thick dark skin with one claw and pressed his thumbs on either side of the wound. A trace of pale sap oozed out. "When they mature, they're transplanted into a dry bed and staked up, and a tube is grafted into the body to tap off the gul. The milk. Most of the plastic in Styth is made out of rellah gul."

"What's the cloth for?" She pointed through the standing water.

"They're tender babies. They have to be in the shade or the radiation burns them."

The rellah vine sank back into the water. Tanuojin's reflection floated on the still surface. "Was he finished? My son?"

"Yes." She stood up. They went along the path toward his compound. Saba cast a sharp look at his lyo.

"Are you going to try it again?"

Tanuojin nodded.

"Let her watch it," Saba said. Paula raised her head.

"It will frighten her," Tanuojin said.

"Just the same, let her watch."

"Let me watch what?" Paula asked. "What are you doing?"

Tanuojin shrugged his shoulders. His gaze was directed straight ahead. "If you want. Maybe she'll learn something."

They reached the compound. In the front hall of his main house, his younger son came up to him with a message, and she and Saba went on down a side corridor to Tanuojin's room. Paula opened her coat. She had seen no other woman in Tanuojin's compound, even among the few slaves.

"What was his wife like?"

He dropped onto the bed and reached for a pad of sketchpaper covered with drawings of ships. "She wasn't very pretty. Kasuk looks like her." The pages turned under his hand. "She had an opinion of everything, Diamo."

"Did he love her?"

"She wanted him, I think, more than he wanted her."

Paula sat on a box against the wall. Out the window she could see the green wall of the city in the distance. "How did she die?"

"Bearing the younger boy. We were in space, we couldn't get back in time. The midwives hacked her to pieces."

"Oh." Her hands made fists. That would not have been here; Yekka had not been made then. She remembered Tanuojin's pleasant touch. He had drugged her. He had touched her. He came into the room, shutting the door behind him.

Saba was bent over the sketchpad, a stylus in his hand. Tanuojin said, "Do you think you can leave that miracle ship alone for ten minutes?" He leaned past Saba and drew the window screen down.

Paula crossed her legs under her. Putting down the sketchpad, Saba stood up beside the bed, and Tanuojin lay down on his back on it. Saba glanced at her.

"You're sure of this?" he said to his lyo.

"Yes. The tree is gone now, we can do it now."

Saba's head turned toward her again. "Watch." He brushed his mustaches back, put one knee on the edge of the bed, and stooped to kiss Tanuojin on the mouth.

She started. Her scalp prickled up unpleasantly. Tanuojin's hand slipped off the cot and hung limp over the edge. Saba rose. He staggered a step and flung out his arms to balance himself. His eyes looked strange, like a pale reflection in the wide black pupils. His face was gaunt. She glanced at the man on the cot, asleep, dead, gone. She bit her fingers.

"You and I have something to talk about," he said, in a voice deeper than Saba's.

He crossed the room toward her, Saba's body, Saba's face: not Saba. She pressed against the wall behind her. He came between her and the door.

"Tanuojin, stay away from me."

He crouched over her, his breath in her face, and caught her wrist tight. His touch made her wince. "You gave us to the Martians."

She could say nothing. Tanuojin's expression floated in Saba's face like an image in water. His voice sounded in Saba's voice. He wrenched her arm, and blood filled her mouth: she had bitten her tongue.

"I ought to tear out your witch-heart."

The pain and the threat stiffened her. She ducked her shoulder, trying to ease her arm in his fingers. "If I wanted to hurt you I would have done it a long time ago."

"You couldn't hurt me."

"If the wrong people found out about you, they'd give you to the Planet. Wouldn't they?"

His grip loosened on her arm, and he raised her wrist up between them, letting the pressure off her elbow. "You're going to talk yourself into being killed."

"You won't do that."

He stared at her, Saba's eyes, Tanuojin's look. She turned her head and spat blood onto the floor. Her tongue hurt in pulses. She said, "You've tried before, a couple of times, but I've never tried to pay you back, have I?"

"That's a woman's argument. 'Don't hurt me, I'm harmless.' "

"That isn't what I said."

Out of the haunted face before her a different voice spoke. "Let her alone." It was Saba.

Every porpentine hair on her head stood on end. He rose and walked away from her, slouching like a tall man in the short man's body. She spat out more blood and wiped her mouth on her hand. He prowled around the room. Now his way of moving was Saba's: the straight back, the solid step. On the bed the empty body looked like a corpse. She should fix in her mind everything that she was seeing. The inhabited body stood by the window, and she could hear their low voices talking back and forth.

He sat down on the bed and put his mouth on Tanuojin's mouth. Tanuojin's long hand rose. For a moment Saba stayed bent over him, his hands on the bed on either side of the other man, protective. They spoke. She could not hear the words. Saba stood erect, turning toward her. Her shoulders slumped with relief. He gestured at her.

"We're going to Crosby's Planet—the three of us. You call the Committee."

"We won't need the Committee," she said.

YBIX. Watch logs M15, 432–L15, 434

They went to Crosby's Planet. From a feeling she did not analyze, she insisted that David come with them. He loved *Ybix*, the free fall and flying, and got into everything and into everybody's way. He sneaked onto the bridge, where he was not allowed, and nearly blew up the ship. Unfortunately he chose Tanuojin's watch for this experiment, and Tanuojin took him into the cage, where there was gravity, and spanked him until David's throat and backside were raw.

For the next several watches he stayed within arm's length of Paula. Whenever he saw Tanuojin, he hid behind her, which made the men laugh. She took him to the Beak, the little pyramidal room in the nose of the ship, while she talked to Saba about the court.

Tanuojin was going to argue the case for *Ybix*. Saba was not convinced of it. She said, "He was there. His memory is perfect, and he knows more law than any three other people." She looked beyond him at the field of stars in the window.

"Styth law."

"Law is law."

David pressed his nose to the window. Saba drew his floating mustaches down. "Who argues against us? The—what did you call him?—the adversary."

"I don't know."

"Somebody from the Committee?"

"I doubt it. I don't think anybody from the Committee would get involved in this dubious a case."

"You think they'll fake the evidence?"

"They have to. I have three computer graphs to prove *Ybix* never fired at the second ship. They'll have General Gordon to swear to their version, and we have you and Tanuojin."

David flattened his cheek against the window, trying to see behind the stars. The blazing Sun in the lower corner of the glass streamed its fiery hair. The hatch opened, and Tanuojin squeezed up into the little room. David shrank back, circled behind Paula, and dove head-first out the hatch.

Paula nodded at Tanuojin. "The problem will be to break Gordon. That's why he's the best defenser. He was there, it's first-hand for him."

Tanuojin spread himself out horizontally in the cramped space, his back to the stars. "Can we bribe the judge?"

Paula laughed. She moved around Saba, trying to give them all enough room. "Maybe. If we can, so can the adversary."

"Hunh."

Saba said, "Ask her."

She turned her head. "Ask me what?"

"I want you to do something with me," Tanuojin said.

"What?"

"That—what Saba and I did, in Yekka."

When she shook her head, her whole body turned from side to side. "No. I told you before. Do it with Saba."

"I want to try it with somebody else. To see if I can do it with somebody else."

"You can't. Not me."

Saba got her by the arm and pulled her around in front of him. "You want us to do some strange things, sometimes. It's not dangerous for you, it's dangerous for him."

She made a sound in her throat. Now she was between them. Saba's hands cupped her shoulders. Tanuojin said, "Besides, I have to know about this court. It would take you hours to tell me everything, and then you might garble it, knowing you."

That made sense to her. She wondered why she was afraid, anyway, perhaps just of the novelty. She looked over her shoulder at Saba.

"You stay here."

"I will. Look, there's nothing to it. I've done it six or eight times."

Tanuojin's long hands reached for her. She flinched from his touch. He put one hand on the back of her neck and fit their mouths together. There was no sensual interest in the pressure of his open mouth. She tasted copper on her tongue. Her throat numbed downward. She went blind.

"Saba!"

She flung her hands out. Her arm struck something floating in the air. Saba seized hold of her. She said his name again, but no sound came from her mouth. She could hear nothing. Saba held her tight. His arms around her. His breath against her cheek. Then she felt nothing at all: her sense of touch, her body was gone, he was gone; she was alone.

Her mind stuck. A brilliant passage of colors rolled through her imagination. Orange and green stretched in rays infinitely away. She struggled to feel. She had forgotten how. The colors began to spin.

"Paula."

A very small voice somewhere in her mind. She fought to see. She could not think without some sense to feed on, someplace to start from. The colors wheeled faster, in streamers. She was exploding. Not me: I am not here. Something was here. What? What is I? False. False. The colors pinwheeled brighter and brighter. False.

"Paula!"

Confused, she stopped struggling. The colors faded to black, like space, like a Styth.

"Good, that's better."

It was Tanuojin's voice. She waited for him to say something else. Where is he? In here with me. Abruptly Saba stood in front of her. In an instant he was gone. She had imagined him. Gone. Stray music came into her mind. Flecks of color, odd smells. My wool-gathering imagination. Saw hands plucking fat apples of wool from trees.

She thought of Mella Square in Havana, blue twilight, walking home. The pavement was checked with seams. Step on a crack and break your mother's back. She stepped on all the cracks. Years of no result made it no less satisfying. Reciting Yeats and Fu Sheng at the top of her lungs. *Toil and grow rich*—

I wish I had an ice cream.

May I buy you an ice cream?

O thank you.

She ate ice cream, changing the flavor with each bite. Plum. Vanilla. Mint chocolate. Chocolate made her skin break out. When she was a little girl, afraid no one would ever want her. She rode a horse bareback along a country road. The sun was bright and the horse stretched out, it hurtled along the road like a rocket. The trees streamed past in a blur. The triple beat of the hoofs pattered faster. The horse stumbled and threw her. She flew in a tremendous arc through the blazing blue sky and fell softly (it is only a dream) into the grass.

She sat up. She was bored, and slightly disoriented: where was she? Wherever you want to be. In rising panic she blundered through a series of random images until she remembered that she was in *Ybix*, in the Beak, and Tanuojin possessed her. She thought, *I don't like this.*

She strained to see. Saba was able to see when he did this, hear and even talk to the other creature in his mind. She concentrated on what she knew was out there: the Beak, Saba, and the stars. Her skin burst with feeling. She was kissing Tanuojin again. She began to hear again, the constant low throb of the ship sprang into her ears. A coppery taste flooded her mouth. She saw Tanuojin as if through gauze, and then clearly, and he moved away from her, his eyes turned away.

She stroked her hands down her sleeves. Her body was vigorous with sensation. Saba took her by the chin.

"You looked so different. You looked like him. It didn't hurt, did it? You weren't afraid?"

"I'm going to find David." She opened the hatch and went out to the corridor.

CROSBY'S PLANET. Maye–Juine 1857

Saba announced he would take six of his crew down to Crosby's Planet. The crew drew lots. Then the high-ranking losers fought the low-ranking winners in the corridors and the Tank and the galley, until the four men of Saba's watch and Marus and Kany from Tanuojin's watch wound up with the red tickets, strictly in order of their rank.

"Why hold a lottery at all?" Paula asked, when they were on the space bus.

"Because then nobody can say I keep pets."

Beneath the window, the cone-shaped mechanical Planet rolled its pitted surface into the sunlight. Its silver skin was a solar battery, gleaning energy for the interior. Saba moved around on the seat beside her, David on his lap. She knew the bench was too narrow for him. The gravity bound her down. She wondered how David felt.

The men behind her were arguing loudly about the conical Planet ahead of them. Sril insisted a gunshot would pierce the skin. Paula sat back, her hands in her lap. She had heard that a solid missile would dissolve in the Planet's fields long before it reached the surface. They were the only passengers on the bus. David stared open-mouthed out the window. She glanced over her shoulder at Tanuojin, two benches back and across the aisle. He sat with his arms folded, a book tape in his ear, his eyes on the floor. She turned straight again. She was sick with anticipation; Crosby's Planet was the first terrestrial Planet she had seen in nearly four years.

"Mama!" He stood up in Saba's lap, pointing out the window. Saba dropped him down again.

"Sit still for once. You have the manners of a white anarchist." Paula laughed.

The mouth of the entry port opened round and dark before them, marked with red lights like a wreath. The interior lights in the bus came on. Paula set the edge of her hand on the window to shade the glass. The entry port was a shaft running down the Planet's axis. On the curved metallic walls, a red arrow flashed. Although she could see nothing she pressed her forehead against the sour-smelling plastic window. The bus slowed, turned, and ran into a slip against the wall.

"Please remain seated until the spacecraft is anchored."

Paula took David by the hand. His crew moved up around them. The driver opened the hatch. They filed out through an inflated tunnel. At the far end they came into a brilliantly lit white room.

Saba flinched from the light. David wheeled and hid his face against Paula's body. The other men stopped around her.

"Jesus, it's like a furnace."

A phalanx of people approached them, small, light-skinned people. Licking their smiles. They introduced themselves to Saba: a welcoming party from the Politburo of Crosby's Planet. Hands pumped. Tanuojin went up beside his lyo, and everybody began talking insincerely in the Common Speech. They were in a cell along the edge of a vast white terminal. Paula went up to the rope that cordoned them off from the rest of the place. A crowd was gathering to stare at the Styths.

"What are they? Are they real?"

"That one must be almost eight feet high."

David clung to her, his arms around her thighs. She blinked. It was warm here, and she unbuttoned the front of her coat. The people pressing up against the rope were pale and dark and brown, all short, like her. None of them even noticed her, their eyes on the Styths, the freaks. Their weight on the rope knocked over one of the standards.

"Mendoz'," Sril said.

She let him take her back in among the crew. Someone murmured, "Here, little boy," and Kany picked David up. They started off through the terminal. A string of policemen escorted them. In the midst of the Styths, Paula went along unnoticed. They took a moving stair down one level, to the Styths' raucous amusement.

"You must be Paula Mendoza."

A toothy man smiled at her, walking along beside her. Sril barged in between them. Before she could speak he had forced the white man away out of sight. She frowned up at the little gunner.

"I'm just doing my job," he said, injured. "Don't blow your rack at me."

Paula clenched her teeth. She could hear an important voice up at the head of the herd, telling Saba how the Planet had been built. Past the men around her she caught glimpses of the lighted display windows of shops. The air smelled like wintergreen.

They came to a moving sidewalk, and the police were shoving back the crowds for them. People already massed the fast track of the sidewalk. With the Styths Paula stepped up from the curb onto the slow belt. The traveling band carried her along above the covered street, swarming with traffic. She looked up over her head. The white ceiling was pocked with lights and air vents and the speakers of the public address system. Tanuojin was behind her. He pushed her, and she went across the middle track to the fast one, passed Saba who was still in the middle, and dropped down beside him. Tanuojin had come along behind her. David was asleep in Saba's arms.

The dark man who had met them made a dapper bow at her with his head. "Welcome to Crosby's Planet, Mrs. Mendoza." He had a robotic perfection of voice and mannerism.

"What did you call me?" she said.

"My wife is an anarchist," Saba said. He took her by the shoulder, his favorite handle. "All thorns and no bloom."

The robot released a peal of genuine-sounding laughter, as if Saba had made some witticism. Ahead, the moving sidewalk passed through a narrow gateway. On either side, in glass booths, men in uniforms stood facing them. The robot took a billfold from his neat black tunic and flipped it open to show a badge. They went through the gate without even stopping.

"What is that?" Tanuojin said. He looked back.

"A checkpoint," she said.

"You mean they even tell these people where they can travel?"

"It isn't that bad. It's all done by statistics."

Tanuojin laughed in a flash of shark-teeth. She wondered what he thought was funny. He said, "You know, I'm beginning to think we lead a very quiet life in Styth."

They crossed a large open plaza, studded with trees in planters. The leaves were pale yellow. On the far side was the building where the Universal Court was held. The dapper man said, "We've arranged for you to stay at the Palestine Hotel, just around the corner—you'll probably never have to leave this sector." His voice was edged with warning. The moving sidewalk carried them past the plaza and they got off.

Inside the glass doors of the Palestine, a swarm of little men in red and gold jackets surrounded them. Saba passed out liberal amounts of money and signed many papers. Paula walked around the hotel lobby. The tile floor was inlaid with a stylized map of the Levantine Coast, the ancient cities marked in stars. A gold trireme sailed in the rippled sea.

They crowded into one car of the vertical train. Paula heard someone's head strike the ceiling, and Marus swore, behind her. The car took them down six levels, very fast.

Tanuojin said, "I hope there's some other way out of this place."

"Stairs," Saba said. "At either end of the hall."

The robot had come with them. In the Common Speech, he said, "While you're here, Akellar, consider our office at your disposal." He gave Saba a plastic card. "We have copiers, a deaf-room, workrooms, taping rooms, guaranteed phones—" He led them out of the vertical and across a short corridor. "There are two other suites on this floor, but they open on the other side of the stack." He opened the door before them with a little flourish. "I'm sure your privacy will be undisturbed."

Paula went into the room beyond. The air smelled of freshener. The Styths poured noisily after her. David gave a sleepy wail. The big room was shaped like a half-moon, decorated all in black and white and clear acrylic. The mirror over the couch was curved to fit the wall. The men around her were reflected all along the wall, made taller and denser by the concave mirror. She went across to a door and opened it.

The lights came up in the room beyond very bright. There were two twin beds against the far wall of the room. She went back to the half-moon sitting room and opened the next door. This was a narrow kitchen. The tap leaked. She tried the third door off the sitting room and found the master bedroom.

Three hanging lamps like lanterns shone on when she crossed the threshold. The wide bed was covered in a tufted spread. She kicked her shoes off. The mirrors on two of the walls made the room seem even bigger than it was. A buzz sounded behind her. She pulled out a drawer in the wall and found a videone.

A pale face mouthed at her from the screen. She turned the volume up.

"—Messages here for you, if you'd like me to send them down."

"Messages. From who?"

Tanuojin crowded her out of the way. "What's this?"

She wandered off across the room. The light drenched her, the warmth, the richness of the carpet under her feet, the softness, as if the dark cold of Styth had dried her to a husk. David came in, yawning.

"Mama, I'm hungry."

She looked through a side door into a dark bathroom. There were already footprints on the thick pale carpet. Her son pulled on her skirt.

"Mama!"

Tanuojin crossed the room toward her. "Who is Sybil Jefferson?" His face was bland.

Paula grunted at him. "You know damned well. Did she call? I wonder what she's doing here."

Saba walked in the doorway from the sitting room. His shirt was stained dark with sweat. "I'm hungry. Get us something to eat. And make them turn the heat down."

Paula went over to the videone. When she pushed the top button, the screen lit up, off-white. She said into the phone, "Room service."

"Yes. That is number 833. I'll connect you." The screen switched to an advertisement for hairsuds.

Sril was standing just behind her. "Mendoz'. Do they have women here?"

"You mean like the Nineveh? No."

He made a face. The advertisement cut away to a rolling menu: roast beef, red pork, pilaf and mikambu and salmon mousse. She ordered it all.

"And a couple of gallons of chocolate ice cream." The kitchen clerk was typing the whole order onto a computer terminal. "And a case of champagne."

"Yes, ma'am," the clerk said. "Real ice cream?"

"Yes. Where can he get laid?"

The clerk's fingers never broke rhythm. "MH-111-1-15-77-3. Ask for Elsie." He rolled the bill out of the machine. "Six roast beef, six ham, six—"

"Don't read it, send it. Room 1017. Thank you." She called the front desk and had them turn the air conditioning down to 50 degrees.

Saba and Tanuojin stood at the foot of the bed talking. David was asleep again on the floor. She dragged him out of the way of the men. Sril went out, repeating rapid-fire the address the kitchen clerk had given him. She hoped Elsie was cosmopolitan. She went up beside Saba.

"What about Sybil Jefferson?"

Saba glanced at her. He turned to Tanuojin, his chin thrust out. "See if you can raise the ship."

"Tell her," Tanuojin said. "What are you trying to do, Saba—you know if she takes to it she can escape. Do you want her to fly out when we're in this up to the hairline?"

"Go raise *Ybix*, stud—leave her to me." Saba poked him in the chest.

"You know so much about women, big man, I know more about her than you ever will." Tanuojin headed for the door. In passing he knocked a hanging lamp swinging.

Saba turned on her. "What did he mean by that?"

"How would I know? He's your friend."

He charged out toward the sitting room. She followed, shutting the door so they would not wake David if they fought. In the black and white room, the rest of the crew was scattered around. Tanuojin tramped through them to the bedroom on the end and disappeared. Saba kicked at the baggage piled in the middle of the floor.

"Stow this. Bakan. Call the ship."

Bakan passed Paula into the bedroom. Sril said, "Akellar, we were hoping we could get a leave." The other men watched him hopefully. There was a knock on the door.

"Room service."

In the next room, David cried, tearful, "Mama?" She went to answer him. His face was bleary with sleep. He held out his hands to her.

"Mama, I want to go home."

"I know, David. I have a surprise for you."

"I'm hungry." Holding her hand, he went into the front room.

Three shining white hot-carts stood just inside the door. Styths ringed them. A lid clanged to the floor. She smelled the meat and her mouth sprang with water. Saba was in the doorway paying the waiters. Tanuojin came out of the far room and cursed his way through the thick of the other men. Paula crowded in between Sril and Marus. Someone stepped on her foot. She got a spoon, stooped, and reached between legs for a drum of ice cream.

David stood by the couch, rubbing his eyes. Grouchy, he looked around him. "I want to go *home*."

"I know." She sat him down on the couch and fed him a spoonful of chocolate ice cream.

He mouthed it, his face still caught in its fret, and swallowed. His eyes widened. He opened his mouth, and she gave him another bite. At the expression on his face she burst out laughing.

"Here." She put the spoon into his hand. "Don't make yourself sick."

He hacked at the ice cream with the spoon. She stood up. The Styths were scattered around the room eating. She found a plate on the bottom shelf of a cart and forked up the last slice of beef. Saba came over beside her, flipped back another lid, and reached into a fruit salad.

They stood side by side, eating. One bin was half-full of succotash. He ate the beans and she ate the corn. After a while, he said, "Sybil Jefferson is at the Interplanetary Hotel."

"Akellar." Sril came around the carts, facing him, and stood at respect. "We'd really like a leave."

"Just a second." Saba raised his head, looking around at his crew. "You stay out of trouble. You remember that gate we came through, on the trudgeway? They have those all over this place. They can tell where you are within a five-hundred-yard radius, anywhere." He ate fruit. "Go on."

"Thank you, Akellar." The room emptied of them. The door shut.

Saba was chewing something. "Pine—" he frowned, trying to remember. "Pinefruit?"

"Pineapple."

"Pineapple." He speared cubes of the yellow fruit on his claws.

Bakan put his head out the bedroom door. "Akellar, Kobboz has to talk to you."

Saba went into the bedroom. Paula stuffed a leaf of crisp lettuce into her mouth, ate a radish, and looked in the small bins for dressing. Tanuojin stood next to her.

"I wish he'd take the cork out of his ass."

Paula swallowed a dripping artichoke heart, slippery as a raw egg. "That was a sharp remark you made, before."

"Yes. But true." He chucked her under the chin and went off to his room.

When she had stuffed herself full, Saba was in the shower. She took off David's chocolate-covered clothes and sent him in with his father. There was a directory in the videone panel; she called the Interplanetary Hotel.

A young man with an intense bushy mustache answered Jefferson's extension. "Look, it's two o'clock."

"I'm sorry. I'm not on your time yet. Is Roland there? I'm Paula Mendoza."

"Oh. Hold on."

She stood listening to the rattle of the shower. The suite was quiet. Saba's clothes hung over the edge of the bed.

"Mendoza."

She turned back to the screen. Jefferson was putting herself into a garden-print kimono. Her face was barded with fat. "Sybil," Paula said. "What are you doing here? You look awful."

"I'm here on Council business, which is probably why. How are you?" Jefferson did up the hooks over her shelf of breast.

"I get along. Who's our judge in the court?"

"Wu-wei. Do you know him?"

Paula pursed her lips. "Yes. This will be interesting." She looked around the room, wondering if the place were tapped.

"Are you arguing the Styths' case?" Jefferson asked.

"No. Tanuojin is. Saba's lyo."

"And the adversary is Chi Parine."

Paula shook her head. "Blank."

"I guess he's too recent for you. He's a Martian. In the past few years he's been quite a little firebrand. He's a member of the Sunlight League."

"My my. What's their case?"

"I don't know." Jefferson took a lace-edged hanky from her pocket and dabbed at her bad eye. "There's been more show than law in it, so far. Frankly, nobody expected you to answer the subpoena. They were taken rather aback when you did."

"I think we'll take them all the way back to the ape," Paula said. She glanced behind her at the shower. David was laughing. "I'm sorry I woke you up. I'll call you tomorrow."

"Fine, Mendoza."

Paula turned off the videone. The hiss of the shower half-drowned David's giggles. She had met Wu-wei once, on the Earth; they had talked about music and ritual circumcision. She took off her clothes and went into the shower with Saba and David.

"We're late."

"They won't start without us." Tanuojin turned over the single long sheet of the hourly. "Where did they get these pictures of us?"

Saba led them down the corridor. "I don't think it's a good idea to be late."

Paula broke into a trot to keep up. The rest of the crew was strung out along the corridor behind them. Painted apple-green, the inside of the court building reminded her of a school where her mother had sent her before she grew big enough to run away. They went through a set of double doors into the courtroom.

Spectators filled the back two-thirds of the room, which was also apple-green. All the heads turned. The racket of conversation hushed. Paula moved in between Saba and Tanuojin, where she would not be noticed. A railing separated the gallery from the Bench. To the right front of the judge's table was a small crowd of seated people: the adversary. They were all Martians.

The Bench was vacant. Wu-wei wasn't a man to wait in public. Saba bent to swing open the gate in the railing, and they went in to the left side of the court.

Paula took her coat off. The courtroom was warm even for her. She glanced at the adversary side and met five sets of unfriendly eyes. She recognized Chi Parine from his picture in the hourlies. He was a small man, in early middle age, his hair thinning back from his forehead. His clothes were flamboyant, a green tunic, yellow shoes.

"Why are all these people staring at us?" Bakan asked, behind her.

Saba pointed at the wall, and the five Styths lined up along it. Tanuojin sat down carefully in a straight chair. It was much too small for him. Saba half-sat on the railing.

A woman in a short dress came out the door behind the judge's table. She knocked with her knuckles on the tabletop.

"Please rise for the Bench."

Paula was still on her feet. Behind her, the gallery got noisily up, and the Martians stood, but Saba and Tanuojin stayed as they were. Wu-wei came in. He took his seat behind the table. Folding his hands in front of him, he aimed his yellow epicene face at Tanuojin. The audience slapped down into their chairs, and the Martians all sat but one.

Wu-wei said, "I assume you gentlemen are registering a protest of some kind. Would you care to express it now?" His velvet tenor voice reminded her of Pedasen.

Tanuojin sprawled long as a whip across the chair. "I don't know what you're talking about. I'm an Akellar of the Styth Empire. I only stand up for an Akellar who outranks me."

"No," Wu-wei said. He opened his paper file. "You're just bad-mannered." He turned to the bailiff. "Read the case."

The woman who had announced him stood and read off the charges and the names of the people involved. She managed to mispronounce both the Styth names and the name of the ship. Paula went over beside Tanuojin's chair and sat on her heels. She glanced at Chi Parine, who was watching her narrowly. To Tanuojin, she said, "Ask them for bigger chairs." Surprised, she sniffed at the metal taint in the air. "Tanuojin. You're afraid."

He twisted to look back at Saba. Slumping forward again, he whacked her in the side with his elbow. "Get away from me."

Parine was up on his feet, his chest thrown out. He reminded her of Machou, displaying in the hall of the Akopra. "Your Excellency, I want to protest the defenser's churlish behavior. This is a civilized proceeding. If these—" he waved at the Styths—"people don't intend to abide by our laws, they shouldn't have come here."

Several spectators clapped. Wu-wei banged his knuckles on the table.

"I think I've already noted that the defenser is being defiant and hostile. Perhaps as he comes to know us, he'll take to us a little more. I understand you have some bills, Parine."

"Indeed we do, Your Excellency." Parine strutted up to the Bench. "We are bringing a bill to disqualify Paula Mendoza from the defense."

Paula went back to the railing and sat on it, beside Saba. The spectators murmured. They sounded eager. Saba looked around at them.

"That's an unusual bill," Wu-wei said.

"Your Excellency, this is an unusual case. The charges have been brought against these two men." Parine gestured toward the Styths. "They have chosen, wisely or not as time will tell, to argue in their own defense. Miss Mendoza works for the Committee for the Revolution. The laws of the court require that third parties to a case declare their interest before the case opens. The Committee has declared no interest in this case—"

Tanuojin was unfolding himself out of the chair. He rose up to his full height, and Parine faltered, distracted. He wheeled back toward the Bench.

"The Committee hasn't declared any interest. Therefore Miss Mendoza has no right in the case."

Wu-wei was writing on his worksheet. Paula stared at Tanuojin's back. His shirt was sticking to him. She expected him to come over to the rail, to talk it over, but he watched Parine. The little lawyer put his hands on his hips, his arms sticking out, and swaggered back toward his chair.

"Defenser, do you have an argument?" Wu-wei said.

"I don't need an argument." Tanuojin walked along the midline between their side of the room and Parine's. "He needs the arguments. He hasn't proved she still works for the Committee."

Parine bellied up to him. "She's never resigned. The first person she called in Crosby's Planet was Sybil Jefferson."

Paula muttered, under her breath. So their suite was tapped.

"Ask her if she works for the Committee."

"The Committee is accustomed to operate sub rosa—"

Wu-wei tapped his knuckles on the table. "Parine, I'll ask her myself."

Sulky, Parine said, "Request permission to withdraw the bill."

Wu-wei nodded and bent to mark his worksheet. Tanuojin sauntered across his side of the court. He slid his hands under his belt. He was warming to it. Parine turned to the Bench again.

"Your Excellency, we have another bill—"

Tanuojin went to his chair and put one foot up on it. Parine was arguing to set a time limit on the trial. With many fine gestures he laid out a dozen reasons for his bill. At the height of his discourse, Tanuojin leaned on his chair and broke it.

The people sitting in the gallery behind Paula gasped. Wu-wei threw his head back, and Parine wheeled. Tanuojin said, in the silence, "Bring me something I can sit on."

Parine's face flushed bright red. "Your Excellency—"

Wu-wei said, "Parine, this is my courtroom. The bailiff will supply the defenser with a suitable chair. Two suitable chairs." He looked at Tanuojin. His soft, ageless face was expressionless. "I'll call a recess until fourteen while we arrange the furniture." He rapped on the table. "Akellar, come here, please."

Saba slid off the railing. He took Paula's hand. "Let's go—I'm hungry."

Tanuojin got her by the other arm. "No, leave her with me, I need her."

Saba's jaw clenched. Without a word he vaulted the rail and went down the aisle toward the door, brushing aside the people in his way. Sril, Bakan, and Trega followed him. Paula watched him go.

"I think the Man is jealous," Tanuojin said, under his breath.

Paula glanced up at him. She went toward the Bench, passing Chi Parine, who was putting away notebooks in a papercase. When her back was to him, Parine said, soft, "Where do you hide the puppet strings?"

She pretended not to hear him. Wu-wei was smoothing his worksheet down with the flat of his hand. Tanuojin came over beside her, facing the judge.

"You wanted me?"

"No," Wu-wei said. "But I have you, by the jug-luck." He looked at Paula. "I'm an easy man, as long as I'm amused. I don't mind slack manners but I won't stand violence. If that happens again, I will pack and leave, and none of us will get what we came here for." He got up and went out the side door.

Paula snorted. She turned to go. Tanuojin said, "The she-man thinks you're the master mind."

"They don't seem to respect your intelligence."

The last of the spectators were leaving out the door. Marus and Kany came up on Paula's free side. They walked along the green corridor. She skipped a stride to keep up with them. The long hall streamed with people.

"What do you think of Parine?" Tanuojin asked.

"He'll probably sharpen up."

They went out the doors and across the plaza. Her heels clacked on the pavement. She was still unused to the gravity and walking was a chore. She looked around the broad plaza for Saba. A man loped along a few feet away, a camera up to his face. She jerked her head straight.

When they returned to the courtroom, there were two oversized padded armchairs on their side of the rail. Saba and Tanuojin did not stand for Wu-wei's entrance, and the audience booed them. Parine argued an obscure point of evidence supporting his bill for a time limit to the trial. His four assistants sat in a line along the rail, two young men, two young women, their legs crossed right over left. Halfway through the lecture, the redheaded woman on the end of the line rearranged her legs left over right, and the others copied her, one after the other.

Parine said, "Because whatever euphemisms the radical fringe might employ, the friction between Mars and the Styth Empire amounts to a war. To stretch out this trial as long as the defense cares to would make this courtroom another battlefield of that war, which is surely not the court's or our intention." When he sat down several people scattered through the gallery clapped with vigor.

"Defenser?" Wu-wei said.

"Just a moment." Tanuojin swung around toward Paula, who

was leaning against the railing behind the two Styths. "What is he talking about?"

He spoke the Common Speech, and he did not lower his voice. Paula folded her arms over her chest. "I don't know. I think he's just shoveling dirt."

Tanuojin straightened around in his chair. "I don't care," he said to Wu-wei. "Make it as short as you like. You'd make it even shorter if that little niggerman wouldn't use six times the words he needs."

Parine's pale Martian cheeks went ruddy. The crowd erupted into boos and catcalls and stamped their feet on the floor. Saba turned to look them over, his face pensive. Paula gave a little shake of her head. Tanuojin was determined to make everybody hate him. Wu-wei nodded at the bailiff, who rang a handbell until the people in the gallery quieted and sat down.

Wu-wei raised his silky voice. "The trial will also run a good deal shorter if the gallery will not take the defenser's baits. I accept the bill."

Parine locked his hands behind his back. He fixed Tanuojin with an icy look. "We will now introduce a bill for a declaration of evidence."

Paula straightened, unfolding her arms. The Martian lawyer paraded around his side of the court, his eyes on Tanuojin. "In the interests of the time limit, we are offering to submit an outline of our case, provided defenser is as forthcoming, and reduce the points of controversy."

Tanuojin got out of his chair. He put his back to Parine and bent, his hands on the arms of Paula's chair, to talk into her ear. "What is this?" Now he was speaking Styth.

"It's usually done the other way," she said. "The defenser offers to limit the case to one or two points of controversy." She tapped her fingers on her knees. "Don't accept it. Make them talk about it, maybe we can find something out."

He glanced at Parine. Straightening, he flexed his long hands at his sides, unsheathing his claws. He sauntered around their side of the courtroom. Everybody was watching him, even Wu-wei, his hands folded neatly before him.

"If you want," Tanuojin said. "There were two ships killed at Luna, that watch. I ordered the shooting from *Ybix*, and the rest of the charges are false. That ought to limit the points of controversy."

Parine sat down in his chair. He plucked at the knees of his doe-gray trousers. "You're in advance of yourself, aren't you? The question isn't one of issues yet, just procedure."

"Oh." Tanuojin circled past the Bench. "I'll try not to confuse the case with the facts. How do I know we need your evidence declared?"

Parine turned his head away, insouciant. The young redheaded woman stood up before her chair. She spoke to the Bench. "We are not offering evidence itself, but an outline of our case. Of course, if the defenser is so willing to admit to the crimes as charged—"

"Object," Paula said. "That isn't what he said."

Tanuojin shook his head at her. He walked slowly down the midline of the room, patrolling his boundary. He swayed to keep from hitting the white china lamp hanging from the ceiling, and the crowd murmured. Saba frowned.

"I don't need your case," Tanuojin said. "I know my evidence." His bassoon voice was softer than before, as if he were uncertain.

Wu-wei said, "The defenser is obviously not familiar with the procedure. I'll ask the adversary to restate his bill."

The redheaded woman started toward the Bench. "Your Excellency, our evidence is exclusively documentary. If the defenser's case is compatible, we can dispose of the adversary presentment in a matter of hours."

Tanuojin strolled up between her and the judge's table. Still talking, she backed away from him, and he took a step toward her. The redheaded woman braced herself. "Bench, tell this man not to chase me around."

Paula put her hand over her mouth. Tanuojin walked away from the Martian woman, veering around the lamp. His back to the Bench, he said, "I don't need his case. I know what happened at Luna. If he says something else happened, he's lying. I don't have to know the substance of a lie."

Wu-wei knocked on the table. "Decline Parine's bill of declaration." He looked irritated.

Another of Parine's staff bobbed out of his chair. His voice was high-pitched with indignation. "Bench, we object to the defenser's behavior. Defenser is resorting to the coarsest tactics, including physical intimidation." His voice quivered. "We'd like the Bench to state that he will use contempt procedures to control behavior in this courtroom."

Saba leaned toward her across the arm of his chair. "I thought you said they'd have General Gordon."

She shrugged one shoulder, her gaze on Parine, who was inspecting his own trim little hands. "That's what I thought."

Wu-wei was watching them. His face was smoothly expressionless again. Tanuojin went off on another tour of their half of the courtroom. Wu-wei said, "I have my doubts about the contempt citation, as I'm sure you know, but if the defenser agrees to it, I'll consider the use."

Tanuojin came up behind his chair and leaned on the back. "Against me only, or them too?"

"Against the offense," the little judge said.

Parine bounced onto his feet. "We're people of principle, sir, we don't—"

Tanuojin said, "I've never met but one nigger with principles, and her principle is she has no principles."

The audience roared. A voice in the back called, "Throw the black bastard out." Marus and Kany left the wall and came up along the rail, between their chief and the crowd.

"I can assure you, Tanuojin," Wu-wei said, "I am a man of no principles whatsoever." The corners of his mouth tipped up in a V of a smile.

Parine had gone back to consult with the redheaded woman and another aide. He returned to the Bench. "Your Excellency, we have a bill of—"

Wu-wei leaned forward. "Parine, it's almost seventeen hours. Before we get involved in another of these choreographs of yours, I'll recess until nine tomorrow, so you won't be rushed for time." He knocked on the table. The rest of the courtroom, all but Tanuojin, heaved to its feet, and the judge went out through the back door into his office.

Paula rubbed her hands together, glad to be finished for the day. Parine's staff was putting away papers. Tanuojin stood frowning at the floor.

"Why don't you go back where you came from?"

Paula went to the gate in the railing. A dozen spectators were crowded along it, yelling at Tanuojin. When she went through the gate, a fat woman turned on her. "You, too." And raised her purse and struck her.

Marus went sideways into the fat woman, who fell hard, screeching. "He attacked me!" Three men in dark gray uniforms hustled her away. Paula turned her back. The police cleared out the courtroom.

Saba came through the railing. "You're supposed to be watching her, too," he said to Marus.

Paula went off down the aisle toward the doors. Saba and Tanuojin ranged up alongside her. The Styths came after her. Marus said to both of them, "I'm sorry, Akellar, I didn't think—"

"Don't try," Tanuojin said. He went ahead of them all out the door.

Saba and Tanuojin started to argue on the way back to the hotel. Paula dropped behind them to stay out of their way. The other Styths trailed her. In the lobby, crossing the map in the floor, the two men kept still, but when she and Saba and Tanuojin were alone in the vertical car Saba swung around, his eyes flattened, and said, "You're supposed to be a lawyer. You're handling this like a hack."

"Could you do it?"

"Better than you." Saba crowded against her, pushing her toward the other man. "Tell him." She stared straight ahead, uncomfortable in the heat of their tempers.

The vertical door opened and they went into the black and white sitting room of their suite. David ran to meet them. Saba snarled at Tanuojin, and the little boy veered away from him. His smile wilted.

"This snappy little stud lawyer is making fools out of us because of you."

Paula led David by the hand into the big bedroom. His hands were grimy; he said something about a green yard where he had played in water. Sril had taken him to the park. Saba tramped in behind her.

"What are you fighting about?" she said to Saba.

"He's botching the case." The big Styth dropped flat across the bed. "This place makes me feel crazy. Trapped."

She had spilled something on the front of her dress at lunch. She scraped at it with her fingernail. "It's all the people."

"What's that whore's address?"

"One-one-one something. Ask Sril." She crooked her arm up behind her to unhook the back of the dress. "I think he's doing well. He doesn't know the court, he has to see how much the Bench will let him get away with." She pulled the dress down over her hips, shivering in the cold, and turned to the closet for her robe. Saba was still lying on the bed, staring at her body. She turned her back to him. In the mirror she watched him roll up to his feet and stride out of the room.

She called Sybil Jefferson, to find out about General Gordon. Jefferson looked sleepy. Paula said, "What, did I get you up again?" and the fat woman shook her head.

"I haven't been to bed yet."

"Oh." Paula wondered what her business was with the Council. "I'll keep it short. Where is General Gordon?"

"Dead," Jefferson said. "A heart attack. Electrically inspired."

"Hunh. When was this?"

"Just a few months ago. The information isn't in general release. I don't really know much about it, dear girl, why don't you ask Wylie?"

Paula grunted. That was Richard Bunker. "Where is he—on the Earth?"

"No—he's here. You know he has an interest in you and the Styths."

"How can I get in touch with him?"

"Don't try. I'll have him call you. Is that all?"

"That's all." Paula turned off the videone.

She took a shower. Without General Gordon, Parine had no case. They had misjudged the Styths. It would be instructing to see how long it took the Martians to adjust their prejudices. While she was standing in the hot mist of the shower washing her hair, David climbed into the stall with her. She washed him and dried them both off with a white towel. The child's body was round and sweet. She hugged him, and he put his arms around her neck.

In the bedroom, Tanuojin stood at the videone, talking to someone on the screen. She put on her robe and got David into his shorts, but he refused to wear a shirt. Tanuojin shut off the videone.

"That was your friend Bunker. He's meeting us at the Committee office at twenty-one hours. He says this place is wired."

"Probably." She found clean clothes. "You've met him, haven't you? You know who he is."

"Yes. The man who sent that listening device inboard *Ybix* at Luna and started this." He paced around the room, his hands under his belt. David was struggling with the latch of the door. Tanuojin said, "Your friends are as bad as you are."

"Don't call them my friends. When anarchists are friends it means they fuck each other."

"You're the only people in the Universe who could make 'friend' into an obscenity."

Her arms roughened in the cold. She put on her clothes, shivering. David finally realized he had to turn the door latch; he darted out to the next room.

"Where did Saba go?" Tanuojin said.

"To the whorehouse."

"Damn him."

She put on a sweater and a jacket. In the mirror his image paced across the room, swerving to miss the lamps. His long hollow face was gnawed with bad temper. She reached for her comb.

"I'm not doing that bad. In the court," he said.

"You're doing fine."

"Who's listening in on us? Parine? Do you think he speaks Styth? Somebody there must."

He never stopped moving; his restless pacing took him around the room. She felt the burden of the Planet around them, the pressure of its millions and millions of lives. She kept her eyes on her own face in the mirror and combed out her bush of brass hair.

"Damn him, he's totally irresponsible," Tanuojin said. "When I need him he goes off to an orgy."

"Let him alone," Paula said. She veered across the low-ceilinged street to read the markings on the corner building. Above the address, a plaque set into the wall read

WARNING: This building protected
by Sentry Security—guard your home—
hire a Sentry

They turned the corner. The street was empty of people. It was lined with people's homes, what in Crosby's Planet they called a dormitory area. Every few feet down the gray walls on either side was a door or a window, alternating, identical, except for the changing numbers.

"Let him alone," Tanuojin said, sneering. "If I let him alone, do you know what he'd do? Do you know what he was like when I met him?" They went up a moving stairway. Through the gap between the step and the rail, she looked down into another stairway, on the next level below.

At the top of the stair was a gate, beside the gate an enclosed booth for the guards. Tanuojin passed their identification in through the little revolving door in the window. The guards were staring at him. Paula hung back by the grillwork of the gate. Tanuojin would not let her carry the little plastic card Saba had made up for her on the ship's computer. The gate clicked, and they moved into the street beyond. They went down a trunk street, empty like all the others, reading the numbers of the doors, and crossed a white line into a sector darkened for the artificial night. The only light came from the display windows of shops in either wall, where pale-skinned mannequins showed off clothes of feathers, of green plants, and metal.

"He's a whore," Tanuojin said. "He'll lie down for anybody."

"Maybe he enjoys it."

"You won't be so broad-minded when he catches you with his wife."

She swerved over to the side of the street. In the wall white letters marked the office of the Committee for the Revolution. The door was locked.

"Don't tell him about that," she said. Bunker was nowhere in sight.

"Then keep sweet with me. What are we supposed to do, wait outside?"

"No. Give me that card."

He gave her his fleet card and she used it to shim the lock. She reached for the latch. His hand caught her wrist. Startled, she looked up at his face, and he flung her off into the street and dodged back.

A muffled crack sounded. The door shook. Waist-high in the middle panel a ragged hole appeared. Paula rolled over to her hands and knees. Tanuojin launched himself shoulder-first at the door and through it into the office.

The door slammed against the wall with a splintering crack. A Martian voice cried, "Watch out!" The inside ceiling lights came on bright as sunlight. Paula got up, breathing a coppery stench that made her heart gallop. Shots like sticks breaking crackled inside the office. A bloody man staggered across the threshold and fell on his face in the street. He had a gun in his hand, and she stooped and took it. His shredded Martian tunic was dark with blood. Suddenly his body flew backward feet-first into the office. She whirled.

"Come in here," Tanuojin said. "Turn these lights down."

She went into the waiting room of the Committee office. Under a glaring ceiling, three other men lay on the tawny carpet. Tanuojin's hands and the forearms of his sleeves shone with blood. She found the light switch and turned off all the lights but one.

"There's one more," Tanuojin said, shutting the door. "Down the hall. He has your friend Bunker, but he'll probably shoot at me first. Are you all right?"

She nodded. Bent double, she went from one Martian to the next; they were all dead, all their eyes were open wide. When Tanuojin faced her, she saw a ragged hole in his shirt over his chest.

"You were hit."

"I'm fixing it." He went to the door behind the desk and opened it.

She watched him go into the corridor beyond. She knew what would happen. Three shots banged out from the end of the hall. Tanuojin went toward the gun, his hands at his sides. Paula went into the hallway behind him. The Martian crouched in the doorway at the end of the hall let out a screech and shot once more, and the Styth reached him.

Behind him, on the floor, Dick Bunker lay tied up like a market hen. Paula brushed by Tanuojin, who let the Martian drop.

"Richard." She knelt by the bound man. "I didn't think you fell into things like this."

She picked out the knot with her fingers and teeth. Tanuojin said, behind her, "Is he hurt?" His voice was thick, as if with pain. Still on one knee, she twisted to face him. The door beside her was open and the light spilled out, glittering on the side of his face. His cheek was laid open down to the white bone. The wound was healing so fast she could see the meat growing. There was no blood.

"No," she said. She glanced at Bunker. "He's sound."

Bunker was untangling himself from the rope. His eyes never left Tanuojin. The stink of blood was heavy over the fading coppery taint. Tanuojin's face had healed to a thin gray scar. His eye above it looked swollen and he pawed at it with his hand. He was splattered with blood. None of it was his.

"We have to get out of here," she said. "You can't walk around the streets like that, there must be a washroom." They found a washroom at the end of the hall. The ceiling lights came up.

"He's going with us," Tanuojin said. Just inside the door, Paula stopped to dim the lights. Bunker walked in a circle around the blind end of the room, his hands in his hip pockets.

"Where?"

"To Uranus," Tanuojin said. He unbuckled his belt and stripped off his shirt and gave them to Paula. Leaning on his arms on the washbasin, he slumped a moment, his head hanging. She realized he was tired. She turned his shirt inside out, to hide the blood. Bunker was watching from the dim back of the room.

"I'm not going to Uranus."

"You're her friend." The water pounded into the basin. Tanuojin scrubbed his hands. "Otherwise I'll kill you."

"Tell us about General Gordon," Paula said to Bunker.

The water ran pink down the drain. Tanuojin said, "I don't care what he says. He knows about me. I won't let him go."

Paula looked across his bent back at the other anarchist. Their eyes met. Tanuojin put on his shirt and she handed him his belt.

"Are you all right?" she said.

"Yes." He got Bunker by the shoulder again and steered him out the door.

They went down to the rail bus. There was a train in the platform; they went through it until they found an almost empty car. The lights glared on and off. At the far end of the car, a man sat staring at his hourly, ignoring the Styth twenty feet away. Tanuojin yawned.

Beyond Tanuojin, Bunker raised his head. "General Gordon," he said, staring across the car. "After you shot up Luna, he was kicked down and jailed. Where he seems to have jellied." He was using Styth, which he spoke badly. "A writer disguised as a priest got to him and encouraged him to, unh, confess. The priest recorded the whole thing on a pocket tape, which he managed to smuggle out of Luna."

Tanuojin transferred his grip from Bunker's shoulder to his wrist. Bunker jumped, and his mouth shut. His glance licked at Paula.

"Keep talking," Tanuojin said.

Bunker looked away down the car. "Anyhow, the priest converted back to a writer, and sold the tape to a publisher in London, who decided it was entirely too ripe for the masses and sold it back to Luna—General Marak—for three and a half million dollars in virgin iron. General Gordon caught a buzz. The writer overdosed. The publisher's air car crashed outside the dome, and the pollution killed him."

Tanuojin thumbed down his mustaches. The bright lights made

him squint. Paula leaned forward to see Bunker. "But Marak has the tape."

"Apparently there are copies. I've never seen one, I don't know anybody who has."

Paula glanced at the man at the far end of the car. Now he was watching them from behind his hourly. Tanuojin said, "Now that interests me," and yawned again.

"I don't know anything more," Bunker said. He slid down slumped on the bench, his wrist caught in the Styth's grasp. "This is the first time I've heard that Gordon said anything about the *Ybix* incident. The bomb was his version of the '49 coup. And the things he knew about people still in power. Not the least being Cam Savenia."

The bus lurched around a curve. Paula looked up at the ceiling. The glaring lights hurt her eyes. "Maybe we can find a copy of the tape." The checkpoint was coming, and the bus slowed.

"That might take time," the Styth said. He let go of Bunker and fingered his fleet card and Paula's out of his left sleeve. The lights flickered. Bunker sat relaxed on the bench, his eyes down, showing no interest in escape.

The bus stopped. The police came into the car and walked toward them: a young man and an old one. "Badges?" Tanuojin gave them the cards. The two men handed them back and forth between them. When the young man gave them back to Tanuojin, he saluted.

"Master commander. Hope you enjoy your stay here." He turned to Bunker. "Badge."

The anarchist rose, taking a folder from his hip pocket, and held it out. Paula said, "That badge is forged."

Tanuojin shot to his feet. The old man snatched the folder from Bunker, and the young one drew his gun. The old man ran the badge through a pocket scanner.

"It is a forgery!"

"Hold it," Tanuojin said. "He's mine."

The young man's gun jabbed at Bunker. "Spreadeagle. You're under arrest. You're responsible for everything you say or do henceforth." His partner took out his gun and aimed it at Tanuojin.

"You stay out of this, Commander."

Bunker moved down the car and put his hands on the wall. Tanuojin said, "I'm warning you—" Paula pulled on his sleeve.

"Be careful."

He struck her arm away. One policeman was groping down Bunker's sides. The old man pointed the bell-shaped muzzle of his gun at Tanuojin's stomach. "You keep out of this, or I'll be forced to shoot."

The young man turned around, his nose wrinkling. "What's that smell?"

Tanuojin took a step toward Bunker. Paula got in his way. "If they shoot you," she said, "everybody on Crosby's Planet will know about you."

His face gleamed with sweat. He stood rigid while the policemen took Bunker out of the car.

"Don't worry," Paula said. "He won't say anything. Who would believe him?"

His look made her flinch. He sat down beside her on the bench. All the way back to the hotel, he said nothing to her at all.

Saba was not there when they reached the hotel. He had not come back when they left the next morning for the courtroom. Tanuojin cursed him all the way there. Paula bought an hourly from a stand just outside the court building. The *Ybix*–Luna Case was still in the right top headline. They went into the courtroom. Tanuojin sat down in his chair, scowling.

"Do you know where he is?" Paula asked.

"Yes."

"Is he safe?"

"Yes."

She took the hourly out of her pocket and unfolded it. There was no sense worrying about Saba. Below the story about the Styths was a headline in lighter print. The Council had voted to send a peacekeeping force to Venus 14, to settle the civil war there. Maybe that was why Jefferson was in Crosby's Planet. Meddling Roland. She looked over the top edge of the hourly at Chi Parine's aides, sitting in their row opposite her. Now the little lawyer himself came out of Wu-wei's office, behind the courtroom, and took his place on the adversary side. He wore a yellow vest, bright as a daffodil.

Wu-wei came in, and everybody stood but Tanuojin. The audience howled until the bailiff rang for order. Chi Parine advanced swaggering toward the Bench.

"Your Excellency, there is a very serious charge being made against one party of this court."

Paula straightened her face. She put the hourly into the pocket of her jacket. Wu-wei glanced at Tanuojin and said, "Parine, I hope you aren't about to use my time and space for a hyde-park."

"Your Excellency, this is entirely relevant." Parine gestured with an outstretched hand, and an aide hurried forward with two sheets of paper. He gave one to the Bench and brought the other across the room to Paula. Parine said, "I am giving you a record of a heinous crime. A horrible crime. Of which the defenser is certainly not ignorant."

The paper was a list of four names, addresses, ages, and causes of death. Parine spoke with relish. His voice boomed through the room.

"These four men were murdered last night. They were slaughtered, brutally and efficiently, at the office of the Committee for the Revolution." The rapt crowd murmured. "They were slashed to pieces, as if by the claws of a powerful animal." The crowd gave up its breath in a sensuous gasp.

"Bench," Paula said, "would you mind requiring the adversary to show how all this is relevant?"

Wu-wei smoothed down the worksheet on the table before him with the flat of his hand. "I'll accept that request. Parine?"

Parine stalked toward Tanuojin, who sat moveless in his chair, his head propped up on his fist. "The guards passed at least one Styth into that sector and out again, at times bracketing the time of the murder. Are you willing to surrender that man for questioning?"

"If you like," Tanuojin said. His voice was mild. "It was me."

The audience fell silent. Parine's forehead creased into a frown. Tanuojin unfolded himself out of the chair. "I'm an Akellar of the Empire. I don't savage people in alleyways."

Wu-wei's lips were curved into a pensive bow. His gaze went to Tanuojin's hands. Parine said, "I don't believe it was you. Your—colleague isn't here. Why not? Because he's recovering?"

Paula leaned forward in her chair. "Parine, do you have any actual evidence of any of this?"

"Your Excellency." Parine rushed forward toward the Bench. "These four men were murdered in a manner that only a Styth could employ. One of the defense panel is missing, obviously another casualty. Since it happened at the Committee office, and these people are so well connected with the anarchists, we have no hard evidence—"

Tanuojin said, "If there really is a connection between what happened there and here, it's between those four niggers and this one." He waved his hand at Parine.

Parine said, "Your Excellency—" and the Bench shook his head at him.

"No, Parine. No more argument. Obviously I am the only one of us who doesn't know what happened at the Committee office. Since neither of you wants to enlighten me, I can't rule on your motion." He rapped his knuckles on the table. "I'm finding you both in contempt. I'll charge you each half a day for wasting my time and trying my patience."

Tanuojin's head snapped up. "I resent being called a liar."

"I resent being lied to."

Parine hurried forward. His flushed face clashed with his yellow vest. "Your Excellency, I consider this a grounds for protesting the conduct of the entire trial."

"Your prerogative, Mr. Parine." The little judge banged on the table. "I'll break for lunch. Until fourteen o'clock. Don't bother to sit, Tanuojin." He walked out the little door in the wall behind his table.

Parine said, "I've never seen such bias in a court of this rank." Among his staff, papercases snapped closed in a series of reports like gunshots. Tanuojin's eyes closed. He put his head back, his hands at his sides, tired.

"I see a few of the raiding party are missing," Parine said.

"Yes," Tanuojin said, "but now we have General Gordon, white boy, and General Marak and Cam Savenia and you are going to wish we didn't."

Paula went around the table to the door to the judge's office and knocked.

"Come in," Wu-wei called.

She turned the latch. Wu-wei was standing at the desk on the far side of the small half-round room. He said, "Oh. Mendoza. Come in."

She crossed the room. On the wall behind him were three or four Japanese woodcuts of women bathing and combing their hair. The little yellow judge sat down behind his desk.

"I'll warn you, Mendoza, the past two days' experience has not inclined me toward your people."

"Don't blame us for the ambush at the Committee office." She nodded at the woodcuts. "Those are beautiful. Are they originals?" The black and white studies were of the style called "the floating world," delighting in the mundane.

"Yes," he said. " 'Ambush' is rather a suggestive word."

She looked from the prints to the smooth face of the judge. "Yes, ambush. Dick Bunker is in jail on a charge of forgery in that sector. He'll tell you what happened." She went back out to the courtroom.

Tanuojin had gone. She stopped, surprised: Saba was sitting in the chair his lyo had been using. She crossed to the other of the big armchairs.

"Where were you? Not at prayers."

"You two didn't seem to need me." He looked around the courtroom. Even in recess the audience still packed the gallery chairs. They sat eating lunches they had brought, a hundred faces moving around mouthfuls of food. Saba said, "Is he hotted up at me?"

"He's yours, not mine. I don't know what he thinks."

"What has happened? Are you still going through the maneuvers with this cockspur lawyer?"

"Yes, here. The big events are all outside the courtroom." She told him about the fight at the Committee office and General Gordon's confession. "So we are acting as if we have the tape. To see how that makes Parine jump."

"A fight. Was he hurt?"

"Momentarily." She nodded past him toward the big doors at the back of the courtroom. "Here he comes."

Tanuojin walked down the aisle, his men at his back, ignoring the hisses and insults of the crowd on either side. He swung the gate open, gave Saba a brief angry look, and came over to Paula, in the other armchair.

"Get up."

She stayed in place as long as she dared, about fifteen seconds, and gave up the chair to him. Saba was looking off in another direction. While she brought a straight chair from the wall to the space between the armchairs, Parine led his staff down the aisle, his chest puffed round under the sunlight-yellow vest, the heavy raised heels of his shoes tap-tapping on the floor. The bailiff stood up.

"Please rise for the Bench."

Paula stood. Everybody else but the Styths got up in a clatter of feet and chairs. Abruptly, Saba straightened onto his feet. He tapped Tanuojin on the shoulder.

"Get up. I outrank you."

Tanuojin threw him a look white with temper. He put his feet under him and stood. A mutter ran through the audience, swelling to a roar of comment, and a few people clapped. Wu-wei sat down behind his table. Parine went forward, bristling.

"Your Excellency, this is rank theatrics—"

Paula sat. She glanced at Saba, who was smiling. Wu-wei said mildly, "First you complain when they don't stand, now you complain when they do. Bailiff, read the case."

The bailiff read the case. Paula could hear the nervous click of Tanuojin's claws on the arm of his chair. Saba murmured, "It's damned hot in here."

"I know," Tanuojin said. "They've turned the heat up."

Among Parine's staff, a young man stood, a paper in his hand. "Bench, in view of some recent developments, we'd like a twenty-four-hour extension."

The crowd groaned. Tanuojin leaned forward. His shirt clung to his back. "So you can change your lie?"

The Martian gave him a harried glance and turned back to the Bench. "Your Excellency—" Parine brushed by him, headed for Tanuojin.

"We have three twenty-four-hour extensions on demand, by right." He glared at the Styth, still in his chair. "Learn the law, black boy."

"Don't push me," Tanuojin said. He got up, his head turning

toward Wu-wei. "They waived their right to extensions when they set a limit to the time."

"Maybe by your backwater laws," Parine said. His face was red as a kettle. "But here—"

Tanuojin jerked around to face him. Parine's voice clogged up. They stared at each other an instant. Saba barged in between them. He got Parine by the arm and swung him around. Paula took her fingers out of her mouth. Parine in a flashy show of strength flung off Saba's grip.

"Your Excellency—"

Saba put his broad back between the lawyer and the judge. "Are you going to let him drain our time?"

"I'll keep the time, Akellar," Wu-wei said. "I'll grant Parine's extension and extend the case. Akellar?" He looked past Saba at Tanuojin.

The tall Styth got up out of his chair. He was hot; his face shone with sweat. "Do whatever you want. Keep us here until we cook." He strode toward the rail.

"Tanuojin," Wu-wei said. "If you walk out I'll find you in contempt."

At the railing, Tanuojin wheeled around to face him, but his furious gaze went to Saba. He spun and marched out of the courtroom. His men trailed him. The crowd booed him thunderously. The bailiff rang her bell, trying to quiet them.

Wu-wei said, "We'll stand in recess until ten tomorrow."

Parine was watching him expectantly. The little judge closed his workbook, and the Martian leaped forward.

"Your Excellency, may I remind Your Excellency of the contempt charge—"

Wu-wei's round yellow face turned up. "I'm not finding him in contempt, Parine, I see no reason to do something that won't work." He stood, gathering his notes, and left.

Parine glared at the judge's back. He and Paula exchanged a barbed look. Saba took her arm. They went down the aisle, through the crowd. A small woman hovered before them, her gray hair decorated with blue plastic birds. "Thank you," she said to Saba.

He smiled at her. Paula looked at the packed rapt faces of the crowd. Unnoticed, she followed him out to the corridor. In the tail of her eye, something moved toward him, a hand, a gun—when she turned, her nerves shivering, it was only a camera.

"I hope you know what you're doing," she said. Crosby's Planet seemed to be fraying Tanuojin's nerves even worse than hers.

"Watch me," Saba said. He went off across the plaza.

. . .

Hedges shielded the broad meadow of the park from the streets all around it. The plastic grass was flushed with artificial sunlight. She walked across the lawn, past the fountain. Two boys were throwing a ball back and forth. A brown and white dog ran between them, barking. David was climbing around in the fountain, fully clothed. She watched him scramble up the water spout. His shirt bellied out, full of water. His black skin shone.

"Mendoz'!"

Sril was sitting under a tree. She plopped down next to him on her stomach. Crumpled papers surrounded him, smeared with mustard and minji sauce. She gathered them up.

"I see you're keeping fed." She found an ice-cream stick and skewered the wrappers to the ground. The spongy plastic turf tore reluctantly.

"That's all I do. Every time I go off watch, Tanuojin comes out with something else for me to do."

"Go on. I'll take care of David."

He rolled up to his feet, still crouched, his eyes on her face. "Thanks, Mendoz'. Can you loan me some money?"

She gave him the money in her pocket. "Thanks." He went off at a trot.

She sat on the ground, pulling at the grass. As long as she did not look up, she could pretend she was alone. The park was insulated and the sound of the nearby streets and traffic did not reach her. She put her chin on her hands, thinking with longing of Matuko's cold twilight and the lake shore.

"Mama."

David was shaking her. She had fallen asleep. She sat up. He was soaking wet; his shoes squelched. She kissed him.

"Are you having a good time? You know, you can take your clothes off by yourself any time you take the notion."

"I like being wet." He held his sodden shirt out from his stomach with both hands. "I climbed all the way up. And look." He pointed down at the ground and turned in a circle, demonstrating his shadow. "Watch." He jumped, watching the shadow. He smiled at her. "It's black, like me."

She took hold of his chin. His eyes were not round or black: dark brown, they tipped at the corners. But he looked like Saba, with Saba's flared jaw and wide indulgent mouth. She stood up.

"Let's go get an ice cream."

They started across the sunlit grass of the park. In the middle, near the fountain, stood a little ice-cream cart. David ran ahead of her toward it. A dog loped past Paula after him. The child stopped, and the dog veered toward him. The little boy screamed.

"Mama!"

Paula burst into a run. The dog reached him one step ahead of her and knocked him flying onto the grass. Wheeling, the big dog snapped at him. She grabbed David in both hands and hoisted him up.

The dog snarled at her; its broad head narrowed like a wedge. It jumped for the child in her arms. She flung out her hand to ward it off and its teeth sliced her forearm. David was screaming. The dog began to bark at her, crouching over its flattened forelegs, and jumped at her again. She dodged it while it wheeled, and ran toward the nearest tree. The dog caught her skirt in its teeth and held on.

David's arms around her neck were throttling her. She pulled at his hand, trying to catch her breath. The park people stood watching, as if at a show. The dog dragged her one step forward, and she yielded an instant. It let go, ready to spring at the little boy screaming in her arms, and she ran to the tree three steps away.

"David—climb into the branches—"

He clung to her, his breath catching in sobs. The dog prowled around her. She boosted her son up to her shoulder, and he climbed into the tree above her. She put her back to the trunk and faced the dog. Her arm hurt to the shoulder. She could not gather her strength. The dog circled under the trees, its gaze fixed on the little boy above it; the light caught glowing in its eyes, pale as amber. She moved to stay between it and David. From the far side of the park there was a long shrill whistle. The dog ran away over the grass.

"David. Come down."

"No—"

"Come down. It's gone." She could not lift her arm. She had to take him somewhere safe before she collapsed. On the path nearby the mass of watching people loosened and began to flow away along the walks, losing interest. David was lowering himself out of the tree. He dropped to meet his shadow on the phony grass. His face was smeared with tears; his nose was running.

"Mama—"

She took his hand. "Hurry." As fast as she could move she led him up the green slope to the gate.

In the crowded street beyond, she stopped, confused, her lungs working for breath. David pulled her on and she followed him. Her head began to pound. The streetlights hurt her eyes. When they reached the moving stair she stumbled.

"Mama, are you sick?"

The moving stair carried them down into the pit of the Planet. Someone behind her jostled her and her knees gave in and she caught herself against the rail sliding by. She was going to fall. Her feet were a mile below her.

"David—"

The street flew upward toward her, the steps sliding away into the floor, and she held her breath and walked forward onto the solid ground. "David." She sat down on the floor in the street, her back to a wall. "Where is the hotel? Do you know?"

Promptly he reached his arm out and pointed. He tugged on her hand. "Come on—it's not far."

"Go find Papa." She shut her eyes. She felt herself tumbling over headlong although she had not moved. "Go find Daddy. Find Daddy." Her eyes opened, swimming. David was gone. A passage of hundreds of legs scissored past her along the street. The floor was warm. She could not get up. The warmth was blood. Someone passing kicked her. She doubled her legs up to her chest. Another hard blow struck her.

"Paula."

She was lifted up into the safety of his arms.

"So help me, if I'd reached her five minutes later they'd have trampled her. These people stop for nothing."

She took the warm cup in both hands and sipped tea. On her forearm the scab of the healed wound was peeling away. David scrambled onto the couch beside her and leaned on her. Saba came out of the kitchen with a bottle of champagne in one hand.

Over his shoulder, he said, "If I were any smarter I'd take *Ybix* and go home."

Tanuojin filled the kitchen doorway. He was eating a sugar-nut. The rest of the crew was out hunting the dog. Paula gave her cup to David. When he had gone into the next room, she said, "That was no accident. Somebody waited until Sril was gone and set that dog on us and called it off after David was safe. It must have been trained. It didn't attack me at all, just David."

Saba drank deeply from the bottle. "You wanted to see which way Parine would jump." He turned toward his lyo, in the kitchen doorway. "I suppose you're against going after him, now?"

"Saba, that's what they want, to force the judge to jettison the case."

"At least then we could get out of this place," Saba said. He tramped into the bedroom.

That night the police came to the hotel saying they had gotten an anonymous warning the Styths' rooms were bombed, and made them clear the suite for nearly an hour while a squad of bomb experts went through the place. Paula sat in a booth in the back of the hotel bar,

David asleep on her lap, while Saba drank whiskey and Tanuojin drank water.

"I haven't gotten a full sleep since I've been here," Tanuojin said, on her right.

Saba yawned. He lifted his glass, half-full of Scotch. "This place is strange. Besides all the people and the cameras and all that. It's haunted or something, the whole Planet." Paula leaned on him, her head on his shoulder, and shut her eyes.

"Parine thinks it is," Tanuojin said. "That's what they're hunting for now, downstairs, General Gordon's ghost."

Paula opened her eyes again. She had not thought before that the bomb threat was anything other than a nuisance. Saba said, "I guess he believes we have that tape."

The waiter came up silently and took their empty glasses and put down new ones, filled. David whimpered in his sleep. Paula closed her eyes.

"Do these things ever start on time?"

"I think it's against the law," Saba said.

Paula sat down in the straight chair. On the far side of the courtroom, Chi Parine and his assistants were talking in a knot. Today the little Martian lawyer wore a black suit, a brilliant red jacquard vest, red and black high-heeled boots.

"Please rise for the Bench."

The spectators massed behind the railing stopped their roar of conversation. Everybody got up. Wu-wei came out of the little door in the back and sat, and they all sat. The case was read.

"Your Excellency," Parine said. He strode forward, puffed up. He reminded her again of Machou. "Due to considerations of interplanetary security, the government of Luna is withdrawing the charges—"

His lips went on moving, but the crowd buried his voice in a bellow. Tanuojin leaped up onto his feet. The bailiff's bell clanged steadily through the thunder of voices. Paula glanced at Saba.

"All this for nothing," she said.

"Not quite."

Wu-wei's smooth face was smiling. He patted at the air with his hands, and the crowd began to quiet down. The bell stopped ringing.

"Yes, Parine," the judge said. "You're withdrawing which charges?"

Parine said, "All of them, Your Excellency. I want to point out that we're doing this only because the case was leading into very sensitive security matters."

Tanuojin put his hands on his belt. "You mean you can't deal with Styths in this court."

Wu-wei laid his forearms flat on the table. His eyes shifted from Parine to the Styth.

Parine said shortly, "What we're saying is that due to considerations of—"

"There's no universal law in your Universal Court if you can't handle Styths." Tanuojin swung around to face Wu-wei. "We are part of the same Universe."

"Indeed we are," Wu-wei said. "What has happened here, in and outside my courtroom, has helped me understand the incident at Luna very well."

"We're talking from different premises," Tanuojin said.

"Maybe. But at the moment you are standing in my premises." The judge smiled at his antique pun. "I have a verdict, which I will give in a moment."

Tanuojin whirled around toward Paula. "How can he give a verdict if they've withdrawn the charges?"

"Your Excellency—" Parine bounded toward the Bench, tipped forward on his high-heeled boots. "Your Excellency, I protest this rash decision to render a verdict without any evidence."

"I have evidence," Wu-wei said. "I'm not blind, and I'm not incapable of reasoning, or I wouldn't be here in the first place. The *Ybix* incident was part of a whole field. This trial has been another aspect of the same field. This isn't the place to comment on people who aggravate the natural tensions between races and individuals for their personal ends, however grandiose, and I won't do that. The *Ybix* incident was a practical exercise. General Gordon made a misjudgment, to which he was helped by a variety of people not even on trial here and for which he has suffered. Certainly neither of the two ships destroyed at Luna would have been shot down if not for *Ybix*'s presence, but *Ybix* had been there for nearly 240 hours without a problem, and therefore I conclude that without General Gordon's miscalculation, the incident would not have occurred. I am holding *Ybix* responsible for one ship and General Gordon for the other. The eight men who died in the ships cannot be brought to life again by any piety or wit in this courtroom. They were soldiers and carried guns, and men who use force can't object if it's used against them. As for the rest of the charges, Mr. Parine of Mars ought to remember when he makes up cases that simple is best. Since Luna brought the case here and then withdrew it, Luna will pay the court charges." He tapped his fingers on the tabletop. "As for *Ybix*, the trial ought to be punishment enough. Are there comments?"

Paula was watching Tanuojin's face. His mouth shut tight, the corners hidden under his mustaches. Wu-wei nodded to him.

"There's a difference between law and justice, you know, which it might profit you to discover. This court is ended." He got up and left the room.

Saba put his hands on the arms of his chair and pushed himself up onto his feet. "He's an anarchist. What did you expect?"

Tanuojin was staring at the judge's door, his hands on his hips, and his elbows cocked out. He said several coarse words in Styth and made for the rail. The Martians were putting away their papers. Chi Parine had his back to Paula. She followed the Styths out. Behind their backs, she finally allowed herself to smile.

The Interplanetary Hotel, where Sybil Jefferson was staying, was plainer and smaller than the Palestine. People sat reading in the chairs scattered around the lobby, in among the banana plants and the racks of hourlies and candy. The Styths sauntering into the hotel cut short all talk and turned every head in the room. Paula kept a tight grip on David's hand. Whenever he saw a dog, he wanted to kill it, provided Saba was there. They went through an air door into a curving hallway.

"I don't understand why we're coming here," Tanuojin said.

"She did us a favor," Saba said. The walls of the hallway were painted with stylized jungle plants and flowers. David lagged, and Paula stopped to let him look. The two men went on around the curve.

David cried, "What's that?" He rushed to the wall, reaching for a monkey coyly painted among the leaves.

"It's a monkey. Something like a kusin."

Saba came back around the curve, picked David up, and hauled her off by one arm down the hallway. "I told you not to bring him." She turned her arm out of his grasp. They went into a bright room opening off the inside curve.

Tanuojin stood on the far side of a pair of bright yellow couches, squinting in the glaring light. Saba put David on his feet. Jefferson crossed to meet Paula. She wore a tomato-red tunic and red pants; she looked like a fireplug. "Mendoza," she said, "don't scold, I'm having the lights turned down. Hello, Akellar." She folded over at the waist, eye to eye with David, and her voice rose to a falsetto. "Well, hello! I know who you are."

David blinked at her, his mouth open. Saba said, "He doesn't speak the Common Speech." The child edged toward him, reaching for his father's hand. Paula looked beyond Jefferson at the three people sitting on the couches. Abruptly the lights dimmed to a half-glow.

David had Saba firmly by the hand. The big man told him Sybil's name. "This is the woman your mother worked for, before she came to me."

"Here," Sybil said. "I'll bet I can do something you can't do."

Paula, behind her, could not see what Sybil did, but David shrieked with laughter. "Mama, look!" Jefferson straightened, turning her head. Her right eye was white and blind as an egg. David let go of his father and gripped Jefferson's arm.

"Do it again!"

Jefferson chuckled. Paula said, "Sybil, you are gross."

"Come meet my guests." Sybil crooked her arm through Paula's. She smelled like milk. "We were just talking about the Akellar's extraordinary grasp of law."

"For a Styth," Tanuojin said.

All three strangers were members of the Council, a man and a woman from Luna and a man from Venus. Paula began to see Jefferson's purpose in bringing the Styths here. She shook a series of hands and introduced the Council members to Saba, using all of his titles she could remember. Jefferson brought them each a tall fizzing glass.

"Where did you study law, Miss Mendoza?" asked the Councilwoman from Luna.

Paula shook her head. "Nowhere. I did a flash reading on the way here." She watched David, who was following Jefferson around. "Yekka is the lawyer."

"It was quite a display, too," said the man from Venus, hearty. "Chi Parine is no amateur."

Tanuojin never even looked in his direction. "I have a good memory," he said to the empty air.

Saba held his glass out to Paula. "It was a piece of theater. Bring me another of these."

"Yes, too bad you were playing to the wrong audience." She gave him her glass and went around the couch to the table against the wall where Jefferson had gotten the drinks. On a table covered with a white cloth were several rows of plastic bottles. She fished ice-balls out of a bucket. Jefferson came up to her side and took a package of biscuits from the back of the table.

"Thank you for coming, Mendoza."

"Thank Saba."

"Your son is his image." Jefferson poured salted biscuits into a hotel dish and went off across the room. Tanuojin was still refusing the attentions of the Venusian and the Lunar woman. Jefferson stood talking to Saba and eating biscuits. The half-light buried the edges of the room in shadows. Paula filled two glasses with ice and whiskey and took them across the room and gave one to Saba.

"Have a cookie," Jefferson said.

"Where is David?" She looked around the room for him.

"Leave him alone," Saba said. "Ever since that thing with the dog you've been all over him." He fished an ice-ball out of his glass and ate it.

"You've got fourteen others."

The third Council member, the man from Luna, took the last of Jefferson's biscuits. "Does he play chess?" He nodded over his shoulder toward Tanuojin. Elaborately unimpressed, he looked up, up at Saba. "What's an Akellar?"

Jefferson turned to Paula. "What dog?"

Paula sipped her whiskey, her eyes on Tanuojin. "Nothing." Thin as a withy, the tall Styth leaned against the wall, thumbing his mustaches flat. The Venusian's hearty voice boomed.

"Actually, strangely enough, the best schools in the system are on the Earth."

"Why is that strange?" Tanuojin said. Jefferson raised her head, her pale eyes sharp.

"The anarchists have no respect for education," the hearty man said.

"Maybe that's why their schools are so good," Tanuojin said.

The Venusian fished cigarettes out of the pocket of his tunic. His hands busy, he said, "Is that some kind of joke?"

Tanuojin was facing him, but his white eyes glanced toward Jefferson. He slid his hands under his belt. "The anarchists have respect for nothing. They'll do anything they have to do to keep the rest of you dancing in their act."

Saba said, in Styth, "Why don't you shut up?"

Tanuojin straightened away from the wall. "You know why we're here—she's trading on—"

"Just shut up when you're in her place drinking with her and eating with her."

"I'm not—"

"I am."

Tanuojin slouched against the wall, sulky, his head to one side. Next to Paula, Sybil Jefferson looked from Styth to Styth, keen as a fox. Paula realized she understood them: she spoke Styth. The Venusian's match clicked into a little burst of flame.

"It's a riddle," Saba said to the Venusian. "Unfortunately riddles don't translate very well from one language to another. What is that?"

"Cigarettes," the Venusian said. He held out the package. "Have one?"

Saba went over to the couch and the Venusian showed him how

to smoke. He maneuvered the cigarette in his claws, fascinating the Lunar woman, who was slightly drunk. Paula looked for David.

Beside her, Jefferson said, "They couldn't have done better if they'd been coached."

Tanuojin was over at the bar, his back to the room. Paula said, "That won't work too often, Sybil."

"Just once," Jefferson said.

"Where's Mitchell Wylie?"

"He left the Planet. Apparently for security reasons." Jefferson moved around to put her back to Tanuojin, ten feet away. "What happened?" Tanuojin was watching them. Paula kept herself from a shrug, a movement of the hand, anything that might signal him.

"The obvious. Parine tried to ambush us. Dick tripped, for once."

"What else?"

Paula raised her eyes again, over the fat woman's shoulder. Saba caught her glance and held his glass out. She stooped to catch David as he passed her.

"Here. Take this to Papa." She gave him the glass in her hand.

"What else happened?" Jefferson said, when Paula straightened.

"I just told you, Sybil."

"Why, suddenly, is Richard oracularly vague on the subject of Tanuojin?"

Relieved, Paula smiled at her. That settled her suspicions. "Ask him," she said, and went off to make herself two more drinks.

In the morning, on the way to the entry port to leave for home, she bought an hourly. The Council had reconsidered the question of Venus 14 and withdrawn the order to send a peacekeeping force in to settle the chronic civil war in the giant dome. Paula folded the hourly and put it in her jacket pocket. At the entry port, eighteen or twenty people were marching up and down with ribbon banners, calling the Styths names. A vitriolic anti-Styth pamphlet she took from one of them had been printed by the Sunlight League, and wore their emblem in the upper right-hand corner of the cover: a radiant star.

VRIBULO

The air of the Empire's heart-city smelled like grease. The darkness made Paula uneasy and she stayed close by Saba in the street. She kept having the feeling that someone was following them. Her ears hurt from listening behind them through the roar of the city. They went along the crowded street toward the mid-city gate, where they were to meet Tanuojin.

He was standing just outside the door, Marus and two others of his watch behind him. As usual he and Saba met with an embrace. Paula turned to look up and down the street. People in Vribulo walked faster than in other places. The free locks of the Vribulit clubbed hair swayed like tails behind them. All she saw in one direction was a mass of hurrying backs and in the other a mass of hurrying faces. Tanuojin sent his men to the Barn, and he and Saba and Paula started across the city to the Akopra.

"Isn't your Akopra House finished yet?" Paula asked him.

"Yes."

She was walking between them, breaking into a jog now and then to keep up. "Then why go to this Akopra, if they're so bad?"

"They may have somebody I can use."

She tucked her hands into the muff. It had been Illy's but Illy had given it to her as a homecoming present. They turned into a lane between high buildings, and behind them a man shouted something. She glanced over her shoulder. A knot of men was coming after them. She grabbed Saba's arm. He and Tanuojin stopped. Another pack of Styths was blocking the narrow way ahead of them. One of these walked forward. His shirt was spangled with bits of metal. His face looked as if it had been cut to pieces and sewn back together again.

Saba shoved her. "Get out of the way. Run."

She backed away from them. The man with the scarred face stopped; she knew it was Ymma, and his ruined face was Tanuojin's work.

Saba said, low, "Keep moving." He lunged at Ymma.

The two packs of men rushed together, like two hands clapping. Paula ran to the fence along the alley, looking for a way through them. Their reek made her heart pound. She could not see Saba or Tanuojin in the fighting. Sliding along the wall, she headed for the street. An arm hooked around her neck. She was hoisted off her feet, the crooked arm strangling her. She wrenched around and slid out of the grasp but someone else caught her.

"Hold her—"

She squirmed uselessly in a pinion grip. A hand yanked her head up by the hair. Someone snarled in her ear. "Watch. This is what happens to people who defy us." She bit her lip to keep from crying out. Ymma's men clogged the alleyway. Five feet from her they had Saba down on his knees, with his belt around his chest pinning his arms down. He was rigid, coiled; if they had let him go he would have shot up like a spring. Tanuojin lay on the ground. Ymma and two of his men were kicking him. She whined, and the hand in her hair twisted so hard tears ran down her cheeks. She heard bone crackle; she saw Tanuojin's eyes close. They went on trampling him long after he began to bleed. At last Ymma stood back, signaling to the other men to stop.

Saba said nothing. He raised his head and gave Ymma an instant's glance and turned his gaze back to Tanuojin. Ymma gave a sharp order. His men surged off along the alleyway. They carried Paula with them, out to the street, tucked like barter under one arm. A hand pressed stifling over her face. She fought for breath. Abruptly they dropped her and ran off along the street.

She gained her feet again, gasping in the rancid air. All along the street, people wheeled to watch Ymma's men run by. She went back into the alley. Saba knelt beside Tanuojin. On the ground behind him lay his broken belt. The ground was covered with blood. Tanuojin's head lay in a great puddle of it. She squatted down and put out her hand toward him, and Saba caught her arm.

"No. Don't touch him. Find out where Ymma goes."

She got up and trotted back to the street. Ymma and his men were nowhere in sight. She loped up the street in the direction they had gone, looking down the side streets. The thick stream of passers-by slowed her. Ahead, near the curve, where the street turned up, she saw a dozen men all traveling together, and she quickened her step.

In the dark she could not tell from such a distance if that band was Ymma's or not. They turned into a side street, and she ran through an alley and climbed a fence and jumped down into another trunk street, which brought her much closer to them. Now she could see the bits of metal on one man's shirt, and she went after them at a flat run.

Above her head Upper Vribulo stretched like a roof in the darkness. On the black lake half a mile from her a boat floated upside down; its bow light gleamed on the water. Ymma and his men walked up the curve toward the lake shore and turned to follow it. She realized where they were going. She went along another street, keeping them in sight on the curved wall of the city, and followed them that way down to the rAkellaron House.

They circled around to go in through a side door, avoiding the Barn. She was tired, and she had never been inside the House. Warily she went up to the door. The building loomed over her, large even for Styths. She went in the door and saw Ymma and his men at the far end of a long dim hallway, going through another door. When they had all disappeared, she ran down the length of the hall, her feet pattering on the stone floor. That door opened on a stairway.

She was afraid to go farther. The stone walls around her chilled her to the bone. She went back outside and waited awhile, to see if anyone came out, but no one did. After about half an hour, she went around the House to the Barn.

Saba was in Tanuojin's office, sitting on the desk drinking whiskey. He watched her come in and shut the door.

"How is he?" she said.

"He's bad." The big Styth set his bottle down. "He's still bleeding. I didn't think he could be hurt that bad any more."

She went to the desk and took the bottle. "Ymma went to the House." The liquor burned her throat.

"Damn him." Saba slapped his knees. "I knew he wouldn't dare do that without help."

"Is Machou behind it?"

"Probably."

She drank another gulp of the whiskey. "What's going to happen?"

"I'll call Ymma down, next watch, and get Machou on my back, and Tanuojin won't be there to step in for me. I'll end up six places down the rank, if I'm lucky. And kicked to pieces."

He took the bottle back and drank, full-throated. She watched the level of the liquor fall. He was afraid, and his fear made her cold. She went through the office to the little room.

Tanuojin lay on his back in the bed, wrapped in the blankets. He was profoundly asleep. His face was swollen shapeless. Saba came in past her and bent over him.

"He's stopped bleeding." He took her by the shoulder and turned her around. "Come on."

There were two time meters on the wall of the middle room of the office, one for Yekka and one for Vribulo, which read forty-two minutes into the low watch. She hadn't even heard the bells ring. She walked up and down the room past the computers.

"There has to be something we can do."

"Yes. I can tear Ymma apart, before they maul me."

She wheeled around toward him, her temper rising. "Stop talking as if it were certain. There has to be some way we can come out of this on top."

"You don't have to fight."

"If I did I wouldn't give up before it even starts."

He pushed a stack of tapes off the top of a cabinet and sat down on it, staring at her down his long aristocratic nose. She heard the pulses banging in her ears. Her fist was clenched. Finally she looked away. "All right. I'm sorry."

"If you help me maybe we can do something."

"What?"

"Go into the House and look around for me. See who's in this."

She gathered her breath. "I will."

"Good girl," he said. "I'll go stir up the flocks."

. . .

The steps up to the front of the House were like ledges. Her legs began to ache before she was halfway to the porch. The broad expanse of concrete was nearly empty of people. The double doors into the House stood open. She went into an entryway, blinking in the dark. The wall on her right glinted. Twelve feet high, it was covered with Styth letters set in gold into the stone. She realized that was the Gold Wall, decorated with the names of the rePriman.

She was wearing slave clothes, a white scarf tied over her hair, and the two men standing guard just inside the entryway never even looked at her. She started up the steep stairs. Saba had told her to go to the third floor, the Prima Suite, where Machou lived. Two men passed her, coming down, one of them Ymma's man. They ignored her. The stairs ended at the third-floor landing. Even before she opened the door she could hear the roar of voices in the hall of the Prima Suite.

It was packed from wall to wall with men. Half of them wore the red chevron badge of the Uranian Patrol. Machou was captain of the patrol. She hung back, her breath stuck in her lungs, until she saw there were slaves among them. She went slowly in among the Styths, catching snatches of their talk. Several doors opened off either wall of the long, straight hallway, but the men all kept glancing at the first door on the right, so she knew that was where Machou was. They sounded impatient to leave. She wandered among them, watching the door they all watched. One of the other slaves suddenly leaned over to look her in the face. She turned away from him and he went off. Nervously she followed him away with her eyes.

The door behind her burst open, and she wheeled around. The patrolmen around her straightened to stand at respect, their arms at their sides. The man who came into the hall also wore the red chevron. Over his shirt a gold filigree collar hung, covering his shoulders and chest. He was flawlessly handsome, as beautiful as Illy. She looked him over, admiring him. From the room he had just left came Machou's harsh voice. The door shutting cut it off.

She glanced around her at the white, moving slaves. The one who had remarked her was talking to another slave, and both of them turned and looked at her. She went hastily out of the Prima Suite, following the handsome man down.

She stayed one flight above him. He stopped on the second-floor landing to meet somebody. Higher on the stair, she went to the rail and leaned out, trying to see who it was. All she could see of him was the top of his head and his gold covered shoulders.

One of them said, "Matuko is out tearing the place up. I take it Ymma did his part?"

The other answered, "Yes—he says. You know about Tanuojin's little kink, don't you?"

"I saw him cut to the bone once, and he never bled a drop. Are you fighting Saba?"

Over her head, the door opened, and feet clanged on the landing. She went on down the stairs, through the several patrolmen waiting in the handsome man's train. Absently, they shifted to let her pass through them. She went by the two men standing face to face on the platform where the stair turned corner. The second stranger was older than Saba; he stood with his head thrust forward.

The handsome man was saying, "I know what I can do, and I can't whip Saba."

"Even with Ymma to soften him up?" the other said.

"Ymma will only give him exercise. He's new back from space, he'll be in perfect condition. He's strong as a motor anyway. I don't think we timed this very well."

She was by them and no longer heard him. Higher, on the stairs above the landing, a voice called sharply, "Stop that slavewoman!" She broke into a run, going down the stairs two and three steps at a time. The sentries were dozing. She got through the door onto the open porch just ahead of them.

In the open they could not catch her. She reached the Barn out of breath. Saba was lying on his bed in the back room of his office, his arms behind his head. Paula shut the door.

"I'm glad you finally decided to come back," he said.

"Who is in the patrol, very handsome, a fancy dresser—" She took off the slave's clothes. "Much taller than you, but lighter?"

His head turned toward her. "Younger than me? Bokojin. The Illini Akellar. I can beat him."

"That's what he says." Her satchel was under the bed, and she opened it and took out her robe. "Another one, stocky, older than you, who carries his head—" She thrust her head forward on her shoulders.

Saba watched her from the bed, his head pillowed on his arms. "That's Leno. Illy's brother, Merkhiz. I can't beat him."

Illy's brother. He did not look like her at all. There was a blanket folded over the foot of the bed. Paula took it and sat down in the chair between the window and the chest of drawers. "Bokojin said you'd be in perfect shape." She opened out the blanket.

"Maybe. The trouble with being strong is you never have to learn the tricks. Leno knows every trick there is. You can sleep with me. Don't you trust me?"

"There isn't enough room."

"Maybe I could take Leno, if I didn't have Ymma to scratch first. I can't wait to get my hooks into him, that son of a bitch."

"How is Tanuojin?"

"Not good."

She pulled the edge of the blanket over her head. The chair was hard as a shelf, but she had no wish to sleep. She rested her head against the back of it. A siren wailed loud along the street below the window and slowly died away. Her legs hurt from climbing stairs. She missed David, whose routine ordered her life in Matuko. Ymma had broken Tanuojin's body, maybe his mind, maybe all their ambitions: savaged in an alleyway.

"You were right," Saba said. "We must be crowding close to Machou."

"You can't get out of fighting Ymma."

"No." He rolled onto his stomach. "Oh, I could, I guess. I could let him go by without revenging Tanuojin. Would you like me to do that?"

"Yes."

The sound he made in his throat was like a muffled laugh. He turned the back of his head to her. "You'll do anything." His loose hair slid over his shoulders, wavy from being clubbed. His back flexed.

"I got in a fight with Leno, once," he said. He was facing the wall. "In Colorado's. Before I married Illy. He stretched me out in about fifteen seconds."

"That was a while ago. He's older than you are. What about Tanuojin? Can he help you?"

His head swiveled around again, directing his eyes toward her. "If I took him in there, in me?"

She nodded. Her hands and face were cold.

"I've thought of that. But he won't be well. It's too dangerous. It's dangerous enough for him when he's sound."

"Could he help you?"

Saba propped himself up on one elbow and reached for the crystal lamp on the window sill. He switched it on. The light sprang into the room; she blinked, dazzled. He put the lamp on the floor midway between them.

"He knows half again as many tricks as Leno. But it could kill him. If he leaves his body it will start to bleed again."

Paula held her legs out to put her feet into the warmth of the lamp. Leno was the Prima Cadet, second only to Machou. If Saba defeated him, Saba took his place. He had to win, whatever it cost him. She wiggled her toes in the glow of the lamp.

The broad porch of the House teemed with people. Paula went through the short entry, with its glittering wall of gold names, and down the hall on the first floor. The hall like a tunnel caught the voices of the men standing thick around the double doors at the far end. She followed a short white figure through the smaller slave door to the left.

She came into a large room full of slaves. Most of the floor was taken by a great open pit with a railing around it. She squeezed through the packed white shoulders to it. The pit was easily a hundred feet across, circular, its sloping walls ringed with three ledges. The rAkellaron sat there with their aides, scratching and drinking and talking, picking their noses, chewing laksi: the masters of the Empire. She leaned on the rail, her chin barely clearing it, stiff with excitement. She wondered if she were the first free Sun-worlder ever to see this.

Machou sat on the second ledge, a little to her right, deep in talk with the handsome man: Bokojin. Leno was across the pit from her on the first ledge. She could not find Ymma. While she looked around, the double doors banged wide, and Saba came into the Chamber.

The other men all craned their necks to see him, and many stood up. Ketac and Sril trailed him. He went straight down the steps of the pit, past her without noticing her, into the round sandy space at the bottom. Now he saw her; he gave her an intense look. Paula held on to the railing with both hands. The slaves around her were avoiding her. Somehow they always knew who she was. Now Ymma came into the Chamber.

Saba saw him. He went to the rail around the little arena. "Ymma, you know why I'm here!"

Machou waved his hand, and the sentries at the double doors swung them shut. The rAkellaron hushed. Ymma was chewing his tongue. He went along the uppermost ledge to a stretch of bare bench. Machou stood up, and all around the pit, every other man stood.

"This session is open. Matuko, you have some special business?"

"You know about it, Prima," Saba called. "You know about it all."

The Prima sat down. "Are you challenging me, Akellar?" He did not sound worried.

Saba went around the pit toward Ymma. His voice rose in a harsh whine. No one but Paula seemed to notice how much he sounded like Tanuojin. He called, "Come down here, Ymma—I want you, and you know why."

Ymma was still on his feet, although everyone else had sat when Machou sat. In a low voice, the Lopka Akellar said, "I have my rights. He shamed me—"

"So you beat him up in the street?"

Here and there on the ledges someone murmured. Directly below her a man leaned toward another and whispered, "I take it Ymma paid his little debt to Tanuojin?" Ymma was sidling along the ledge to the nearest stairs. Paula sucked in a deep breath, her eyes on Saba.

He glanced over his shoulder at Leno and sideways at Bokojin. Backing across the sand, he gave Ymma the room to come into the arena, and turned so that when Ymma came in through the bottom rail Saba was facing all of them, Ymma, Leno, and Bokojin. Ymma stepped out onto the sand. Saba jumped on him.

The onlookers howled. The slaves around her rushed forward to see and nearly crushed her against the railing. All around the ledges the rAkellaron bounded to their feet. Saba hit Ymma so hard the other man landed on his back on the far side of the sand circle. Leno vaulted down across the bottom ledge to the sand. Ymma curled up, his arms around his head. Saba took two steps and fell to his knees on Ymma's chest. He sprang around to meet Leno.

Leno feinted, and Saba shifted to meet him. They grappled. Paula could hardly breathe. The slaves were pushing her hard against the rail. The cheers and screams packed her ears. Leno tripped Saba down. They rolled over on the sand, their claws hooked in each other's face. Ymma was trying to get up. On his knees, Leno straddled Saba's chest, reared back, and slashed at him with his spread hand. Saba caught his wrist. They strained against each other a moment, motionless, their faces twisted with effort. Abruptly Saba gave way and Leno fell, off-balance. Saba pulled him forward and butted him.

The Merkhiz Akellar collapsed, dazed. Saba heaved himself off the sand and drove his elbow like a hammer into Leno's side, all his weight behind it, and when Leno dropped to the sand struck him again in the same way between the shoulder blades. Merkhiz sagged down slack on his face. Saba sprang up to his feet and backed away, his head turning from Leno to Ymma. Blood streamed along his face. The cheering rolled out deafening from the audience.

Paula elbowed and shoved a way through the slaves to the stair. Machou was on his feet. Everybody was watching him. The Prima turned on his heel and walked up the ledges, through the rail past Paula, and went out of the Chamber. Ketac and Sril went into the pit with Saba. His son gave him a towel.

Paula went down the ledges, stretching her legs from step to step. Saba had seen her. He came up to meet her, took her by the hands, and bent and kissed her.

The uproar died abruptly. Behind her a man swore. Her tongue tasted of copper.

"Take her back," Saba said. Ketac stood one step below him. Paula's head whirled in a sudden giddy rush, and she staggered. Ketac took her by the arm.

"Are you hurt?"

She leaned on him. She had lost her voice. Her throat was numb and her sight darkened. At the top of the steps Ketac lifted her up in his arms.

"Open this door."

He carried her along the hall, through the glitter of the Gold Wall, and out onto the plain. Someone shouted. She rested her head on Ketac's shoulder, exhausted.

"Saba just took Leno and Ymma both in thirty-two seconds!"

A raw-throated cheer grated in her ears. Ketac stopped in a circle of other men. He was talking but she was too tired to make out the words. She felt him walking down the stairs. A cold dark fell over her; he had brought her into the arcade.

She said, hoarse, "Tanuojin." She opened her eyes.

"He's asleep, Paula."

"Let me in there."

When he set her on her feet she nearly fell.

She went through Tanuojin's empty office to the back room. Her strength was seeping away. A cold weakness crept like death along her backbone, freezing her mind numb. She sat down on the edge of the bed. Fresh blood was pooled on the floor under it.

In her mind, his voice murmured, "Make sure it's still alive."

She put one hand over the body's mouth. His faint breath cooled her palm. She bent over him and kissed him. Her tongue and lower lip tingled. His mouth was cold. The life woke in her muscles. She ran her tongue over his lips and down his mouth and into his throat.

He pushed at her with one hand, feeble. She held him, her weight on him, kissing him deep against his will until he rolled weakly over onto his stomach. She straightened. He lay face down on the bed.

"You bitch, Paula."

"You do talk. What if your body had been dead? You were set to take mine. You'd have killed me."

He turned his face to the wall. She opened the door and left him alone.

MATUKO. The Krita Festival

"Why did you wear that coat?" Illy said. "That color makes you look like a little old woman."

Paula glared at her across the covered chair. "If you claw at me, I'll get out and walk."

Illy smirked. She wore pink and orange paint on her cheeks and forehead. Her eyes were like black moons. "You can't. You don't have the right clothes on."

"I can do anything I damn well please."

The chair swayed and tipped to one side. Paula grabbed the frame. Jingling with little silver bells, Boltiko threw back the curtain and squeezed into the front bench of the chair, next to Paula. When she sat, the whole box sagged.

"I wouldn't go out looking like that," Illy said. "Not for help if I were dying."

Boltiko squirmed herself comfortable on the seat. She looked down at Paula and patted her knee. The bells on her sleeve rang.

"Where shall we go first?" Illy said. "To the kundra to have our fortunes read?"

The chair swung up into the air. Wedged between Boltiko and the side of the box, Paula rocked with it, surrounded by the clamor of bells. Everybody in Matuko wore bells during the Krita Festival. The chair-slaves bore them quickly along. The curtains were drawn closed and she could not see where they were going. She reached out to draw the curtain back, and Boltiko slapped her hand down.

"Don't you do that when we aren't covered."

Paula sat back.

"Oh, what a miserable watch I had, last watch," Boltiko said. "I didn't sleep above thirty minutes." She knocked on the side of the chair with her knuckles, and their speed increased to a brisk trot.

Illy giggled. "I could tell you a couple of remedies for that." She smiled at Paula.

"Sometimes I think if it weren't for the children," Boltiko said, "I'd go somewhere and die. And then see who would miss me."

The chair sped down a slope. Outside the muffling curtains, bells rang, and music sounded, among laughter and voices. Illy was staring at Paula.

"Tell her how awful she looks in that coat, Tiko."

Paula leaned forward, reaching for the curtain. "Put this thing down." Boltiko struck at her fingers, but the slaves heard her and the chair stopped.

"Oh, Paula," Illy called. "Just come to the kundra's—"

Paula jumped down out of the chair to the street. The slaves lifted it again. She heard, above the two arguing voices of the wives, the sharp bang of Boltiko's fist on the box. The chair swept off, swaying, its curved roof streaming ribbons in its wake.

She was in the street near the lake market. The passing crowd pressed by her on either side. Ahead, in the market, gaudy tents replaced the merchants' stalls. She wandered through the little carnival, going from tent to tent. Some sold pala-cakes or liquor, and others offered entertainments. She stopped behind a wall of Styth backs to watch a girl in a demure long dress dance on a platform to the music of a ulugong. Inside, Paula supposed, she took it off. In the open front of the next tent, surrounded by the upturned faces of children, a red bird climbed up a rope and rang the bell at the top.

A huge paper-and-paste mask swayed toward her, held up on a long stick above the heads of the crowd, the face painted white and the leering open mouth blood-red. There were other masks up and down the street, and prizes later for the best. The false faces symbolized the Moon-people, the first American colonists of Uranus, who according to the legends had been driven out or massacred by the hero Krita. The bells were part of that myth, too: Krita's bell had brought the colonists to their deaths. She walked along among the crowd, enjoying the circus feeling. The colonists had abandoned Uranus when the Three Planets Empire broke up, not because of Krita's bell and knife, but the Styths would never believe that. It was part of their lives, their faith. Although Saba was of another house entirely from the ancient hero, one of his titles was Kritona. She stopped at a stall to buy a pala-cake and went on, looking for David.

"Hold these." David took the white grass garlands off over his head and stuffed them into her arms. Ducking under the rope, he trotted down the street to the starting line of the race. The people around her were eating pala-cakes and making bets. Paula stuck her frozen hands in her sleeves. David grinned at her from the starting line. He was missing three front teeth and his smile was like a tunnel through his face. Something brushed down her back.

"Paula. What are you doing here?"

It was Ketac. She looked up at him behind her. A broad braided ribbon hung around his neck.

"What's that?"

"I won it throwing knives."

The crowd roared and surged forward against the rope. A dozen boys raced down the street toward her. David was leading; David had won. The people around her raised their arms and shook their bells, rattle-rattle like little tin leaves, and cheered.

"Aren't you glad he won?" Ketac said.

"It seems to me you're all winning everything."

"That's because we're the best family in Matuko."

David jogged up to her, hardly out of breath. Another garland hung around his neck. The people around him leaned out to touch him. They thought it good luck to touch a winner. Paula held out the wreaths, and solemnly he decorated himself in his awards.

Ketac pulled on the peak of her hood. "You should stay in the chair. You'll get lost."

"How can I get lost? Somebody always finds me."

They went off toward the crowd. David strutted around, collared in grass, calling to his friends in a new deep voice. Paula ran her hand over his smooth head. They went down toward the lake. A little parade of the paper masks passed them, held up on poles.

Ketac left them. David wandered off into the crowd. Paula went slowly down the hillside street. She looked up at the lake, in the roof of the bubble. They were racing boats there; most of the race involved fighting from one boat to the next to knock the oarsmen into the water. She watched one boat roll over, presenting its long white belly to the air. Heads bobbed around it.

Pedasen was part of a small crowd watching a stick-puppet show near the White Market. She went up beside him and took his hand, and he startled. She smiled at him. The puppets declaimed in falsetto voices from the cut-out stage. The eunuch stroked her palm with his fingertips. When the play ended they walked away toward the lake.

"You ought to be in the covered chair," he said.

"Illy teases me. I don't know how Saba bears her, she's that nagging."

He swung their linked hands back and forth. "You're more like her child. Or her little sister." Through the tail of his eye he glanced at her. "You could always give her up."

David ran up to her, streaming his white grass garlands. Pedasen moved away from her. His fingers slid out of her grasp. Her son bounced around her.

"Mama, buy me a poppet. Buy me a pala-cake." He towed her along by the hand through the White Market. The Martian merchants had joined with whole hearts in the spirit of Krita, raising all their prices 10 per cent.

"When is the Kritaloi?" Paula asked. The ceremony was the climax of the festival.

Pedasen came after her, his hands in his tunic sleeves. "At three bells." David scowled at him and moved between her and him.

"What's he doing here?"

"He lives here," Paula said.

David shot an angry look over his shoulder at the slave. "Come on. I'll show you the poppet I want." He ran off down the street ahead of her.

"I knew he'd get like that about me," Pedasen said. "He's a black, no matter what you do."

A parade of Krita masks bobbed toward them. They passed the shop that sold illusion helmets. The street was sprinkled with bits of paper, mushed pala-cakes, ribbons, and grass. David turned and jogged back toward her, the grass like an Elizabeth ruff over his shoulders. Ten feet from her, a mob of little boys leaped on him.

They screeched. Their arms milling, they fought in the street. David kicked and struck at them; he was smaller than the smallest of them. Paula rushed in among them. They were tearing off his prizes. Her fingers in David's belt, she pulled him out from under three other boys, and they turned on her. David struggled in her arms. She held him tight against her while the other boys slugged her and kicked her shins. In a moment they raced off.

Ketac said, "What's going on?"

She let David go. His cheeks were slippery with tears, and he thrust her violently away from him with both hands. Bleeding scratches striped his forehead. His flags were gone. He shouted, "I don't need you—I can do it—" Crying with rage, he wheeled on Pedasen. "You didn't even stop her—" He ran off into the crowd. Paula bent and rubbed her sore ankle.

"Are you hurt?" Ketac asked her. Pedasen was going away.

Paula shook her head. "He's too little to fight." Her throat felt tight, and her eyes burned.

"So are you," Ketac said.

Along the shore the men stood in rows, shoulder to shoulder, clapping their hands. The beating rhythm and the bells made Paula's head throb. She put her hand on the covered chair beside her. Below her, beyond the mass of people, Saba walked into the water. Dakkar and Ketac followed him. The water purled around them. Saba went in to his waist and turned to face the shore. He took off his belt and his shirt and gave them to Ketac. The pale metal of his order swung across his chest. Dakkar held out a sheath, and Saba drew the curved knife out of it. He slashed an X in the black water before him and carved an X deep in his forearm. Paula jerked. Blood streamed down his arm. He plunged it into the lake. The people let out a great breath of a cheer, shaking their sleeves of bells, waving their belled hats. Ketac gave his father a piece of cloth, which Saba wrapped around his arm, and he put his clothes on.

"He bled quite a lot," Illy said, inside the chair. "A good omen."

Paula swallowed the bad taste in her mouth. Saba walked out of the water. His people cheered in voices half-drowned in bells: "Krita! Krita! Krita!" David came around the chair toward her.

"When I grow up, I'll be brave as Papa."

Paula turned away.

Saba told Illy that he was taking *Ybix* out on another long mission. All Paula's usual means of spying on him failed to discover where he was going. To keep her from working out their target from the kind and amount of supplies they laid in, he had Tanuojin outfit the ship from

Yekka. She went to Yekka herself, on the bus, but before she could learn anything Tanuojin caught her and sent her back to Matuko.

Ybix took the men away. Ketac stayed in Vribulo, as Saba's pitman, and Dakkar, the prima son, ruled Matuko. Paula knew that Dick Bunker would arrive in Styth as soon as the Committee found out *Ybix* had left. She told Ketac to watch for him.

VRIBULO

The mid-city gate was massed with people. Paula got off the bus in a tide of other passengers from Matuko and fought through the people trying to board to go on to Yekka, the next stop. Most of these were Yekkit farmers, with empty baskets on their shoulders, going home from the markets of Vribulo. She ducked a swinging elbow and slid between two fat veiled women toward the street.

"Paula." Ketac came across the chipped tile floor. Two slaves carried a handtruck past her, and she went by it to meet him.

"I brought a chair," he said. "What's this all about?"

"Where is he?"

Ketac took a firm grip on her arm and maneuvered her toward a side door. "I found him coming in, as you said, but he got away."

"He—"

"Easy. I caught him again, I have him in my room. He's a slippery little nigger."

The clear doors to the street had white X's drawn on them, to keep people from walking through them. Outside, in the crowded street, a chair sat on its stump feet, the slaves who carried it squatting at the poles. Ketac hurried her inside. She sat facing forward, and he sat opposite her. The chair bucked up into the air, back end first, and sped away.

"How long has he been here?" she asked.

"Only three or four watches. You were right, he came in from Yekka."

The drapery of the chair enclosed them like a cloth room. She opened the front of her coat. "Good. You did a good job."

"If Machou gets a smell of him, I'll have to give him up. You know that."

She nodded. The chair hurried along, rolling from side to side. Ketac sat deep into the bench across from her, his head back against the fabric wall. She said, "Have you heard anything from *Ybix*?"

"No, nothing."

Saba had been gone over three hundred watches. She rubbed her fingers together, wishing she knew where they were. The chair tipped steeply forward and she pulled the curtain open enough to see out. They were going down the hill around the foot of the lake. Pale blue grass grew along the street, the leaves shaped like swords.

"We'd better walk from here," she said.

"Why?"

"If you don't want Machou to know I'm in Vribulo." She leaned out of the chair. "Stop here." The slaves stopped, panting. She put her hood up and fastened the cloth across her face. Ketac helped her down to the street.

They went into the Barn. Dick Bunker sat on the bed in the back room of Saba's office, his hands and feet yoked together. A Styth stood guard over him. Paula sent that man out and shut the door.

"Hello, junior," he said. "Do I owe you for this?"

She sat on the foot of the bed where she could reach the yoke on his ankles. "I told you not to come back here." She jammed her thumb against the spring tab in the side of the white plastic yoke. It would not budge. "I can't open this."

"I thought you didn't believe in force. This is the second time you've gotten me arrested." He moved his feet out of her range. His eyes glinted; he was angry. She sat back and looked him over. He looked much the same as ever, graying, but still slight and dry.

She said, "My sense of territory is highly developed."

"I was coming to Matuko when I finished here."

"How long have you been in Styth?"

"Awhile." His thin shoulders rose and fell, casual. "I lose track of time here."

Then the Committee had known *Ybix* was leaving before she broke orbit. Their spies were probably all over Styth, in every White Market. She looked around the room. The washbasin stuck halfway out of the wall, a dirty towel draped over the edge, and Ketac's used clothes covered the chair. The wall over the battered chest of drawers was scribbled on. She went to look. Most of the scribbles were women's names with checkmarks after them. A scoreboard.

"What's going on in the Middle Planets?" she asked.

"The more it changes. Venus 14 is enjoying its third government in two years, or was, when I left, who knows but they're on their fourth by now, and Mars is threatening to send the Army in. Mars had their mid-term elections last summer, and the Newrose coalition lost. Cam Savenia was elected First Secretary of the Council."

Paula turned around, startled. He nodded. "Check. She's all for sending the fleet to Venus 14, she wants the Earth to admit all the Interplanetary Police apparatus and hold elections to the Council, she wants to null the Styth truce and cut off the trade between Mars and the

Styth cities. She has a monomania about Saba. Never heard the name Tanuojin. Thinks Saba is plotting to take over the Universe. Fortunately, if Newrose has no majority, neither does the Sunlight League, and Dr. Savenia, I'm pleased to say, is no master of nuts and bolts politics."

"No—she's an actor on the stage of life."

Bunker smiled at her. "Her opinion of you is baroque. Jefferson can handle her. So far. Somebody took a shot at General Marak."

"Who?" She opened the top drawer in the desk, exposing a clutter of weapons, tapes, and small junk.

"I think the Sunlight League, but I hate them, so my opinion doesn't count."

"What do they think of you?" The other drawers held clothes. She went to the rack in the wall and looked in among Ketac's shirts.

"What are you doing?" Bunker said.

"His mother will want to know how he's living. What's of interest to the Committee in Vribulo?"

"Your friends seem to be—"

"Don't call them that."

"I'm using the word in the Styth sense. They seem to be rising to new heights."

She knelt by the bed and slid her hand under the mattress pad. Bunker was watching her sleepily. She said, "Saba is the Prima Cadet now, yes. I wouldn't call that particularly high." Deep under the mattress, her fingers grazed something long and flat. She tickled out a packet of papers.

"That depends on your ambitions, doesn't it?" he said. "What you call high. Which is something I'd be interested to know."

She slit the seam on the packet with her thumbnail and unfolded it. Inside was a coded message and a white card punched with holes and lines. She pressed the seam closed again and rammed the packet back under the bedpad.

"That certainly looked like the key for a photo-relay," he said.

She stood up, frowning. Ketac was lying; he had heard from his father. That meant *Ybix* was coming home. She sat down next to Bunker's feet, her mind busy with arithmetic. Certainly in that amount of time they could have gone no farther than the Asteroids.

"Is there anything else you want to tell me?" she asked.

"Something I want you to tell me. Who are you working for?"

Her gaze snapped up toward his face. "Anybody who will pay me. What kind of a question is that?"

Bunker leaned toward her, his body rolled into a ball. "Junior, I don't know what you've talked yourself into. What I know is you are cheek to cheek with two men who shoot holes in the Universe as a matter of routine."

She wiped her hand over her mouth, staring at him. Finally she called, "Ketac!"

The door creaked on its hinges. Ketac stepped in across the threshold. He had been listening to them. She waved at Bunker.

"Take him to Yekka. There's a boat leaving in ten hours for Mars. Put him on it."

"Why should I—"

"Damn it, Ketac," she said, "don't run me over. Get rid of him before Machou finds him." She brushed past the young man into the next room.

MATUKO

When she left the bus in Matuko three strange men closed in around her. They hustled her off across the city to Dakkar's compound, in the Tulan, the rich district. Dakkar was sitting in a chair under the biggest bilyobio tree in his yard. When she went up before him, he stood, swelling his chest with breath. She knew him little. He had his own family, and he and Saba disliked each other, so he seldom visited his father's compound. He gave her a cold imperious stare.

"I can't place you," he said. "You don't fit in. You aren't a wife, you aren't a slave, you live with him but you aren't kindred. I don't like things that don't fit in, it makes me nervous. Why did you go to Vribulo?"

"It's a nice ride," she said.

"My father told me specifically to know where you are, all the time."

She set her teeth together. "Well, that's where I was. Vribulo."

"You show me respect, woman."

She raised her head. In the two-story house behind him, a window screen moved: someone watched them. Dakkar sat down in his chair. All around the curl of his ear little red stones glittered.

"Ask your brother," she said. "I was with him the whole time."

"My brother," he said, contemptuous. "The next time you leave Matuko I'll have you arrested."

"May I go now?" she said. "Akellar."

"Go."

. . .

She went back through the Varyhus toward Saba's compound. One of the men who had taken her to Dakkar followed her, making no attempt to stay hidden. In the little market between the Varyhus and the Lake District she stopped to buy a drink of water. The slave vendor recognized her.

"Out spying, nigger?" he said. "Sneaking around for the blacks?" She dropped the money and the cup into the street and walked away.

Several watches went by. Illy and David took up her energy. Illy's constant demands had rubbed Paula's feelings to callous. For the fifteenth time she made up her mind to break off the affair. As usual she decided to wait until Saba came back, which would muffle the explosion. David fought in the street, in the yard, with his brothers, with strangers. He was always battered. She wondered if he knew about her and Illy. With no warning, Dakkar had her dragged off across the city again.

He was sitting in the same chair where she had last seen him, as if he had not moved in twenty watches. Now there were three other men standing around him. When she was before him, he said, "Two watches ago a pack of slaves murdered an old man, down in the Varyhus. What do you know about it?"

"Nothing," she said, impatiently.

"Do you recognize this dirt?" He flicked out his hand, and the man on his right gave her a holograph: a pale slab-jawed face.

"No," she said. "I don't think I've ever seen him."

"It won't do you any good to lie."

She held the holograph out to his aide. Saba's son scowled at her. Her temper was burning short. "I'm not lying," she said.

"These street-dirt kicked and beat an old man to death." His right hand on the arm of the chair flexed, unsheathing his claws. "You were seen talking to that slave in the Varyhus market."

"Oh," she said. "The water vendor. I don't know anything about him."

"There are half a million slaves in Matuko, and you talked to that one just by coincidence?"

"If you ask the slaves, Dakkar," she said angrily, "you'll find they don't like me any more than you. Why don't you leave me alone?"

"I can make you talk," he said. He made a gesture, and his soldiers took her off behind the bilyobio tree. She stood uneasily watching Saba's son while he signed a document and read a tape. He would not dare hurt her, or even threaten to hurt her. After a while two more of his men brought Pedasen into the yard.

Her stomach knotted. She sank her teeth into her lower lip. Dakkar straightened.

"Take them inside."

. . .

She reached her house again in the low watch, lay down across her bed, and cried. When she ran out of tears and sobs, she rolled onto her back. David was standing at the foot of the bed. She sat up.

"Did I wake you up?" She wiped her eyes on her hand. Her throat was sore.

"Where were you?" He climbed over the foot of the bed toward her. The old white bedshirt he wore had been Saba's: it was filthy. "What happened? Where you hurt? Why were you crying?"

She shook her head. "I'm all right." His hands were scraped and swollen from fighting. She took his wrist, cold to her touch.

"Why were you crying?"

She shook her head again. Taking his hand in both hers she kissed his palm. "They killed Pedasen." She began to weep again. He tugged on his hand and she freed him.

"Who killed him? Who?"

"Dakkar." She rubbed her eyes dry.

"Why are you crying? He was just a slave."

Her eyes felt bathed with salt. She wiped her face on her sleeve. In the end, Dakkar had believed her, but by then the eunuch was dying.

"He was a slave," David said. "He didn't mean anything."

"I'm sorry I woke you up," she said. "Go back to bed."

He sat on the foot of the bed, watching her soberly with his strange long eyes. His hair was sprouting like bristles over his head. She said, "Don't you care? He lived here. He loved you since you were a baby."

His gaze flinched away from her. Suddenly busy, he picked at the cover with his fingers. He had no claws yet; he still used the flats of his fingers. He muttered, "My father wouldn't care," watching his hands.

"Go back to bed, David."

Whenever she slept with Illy, she dreamt that Saba walked in on them. One watch she woke with a start and smelled a hot metal reek and saw him standing at the foot of the bed.

"Get up and put your clothes on," he said.

Illy was still asleep, her arm around Paula's waist. Paula shook her hard, to wake her. Saba grabbed the bedcover in both hands and yanked it flying away.

"I said get up!"

Paula scurried off the bed and gathered her clothes. Illy raised her head. "Saba!" She sat upright, thrusting out her hand toward him. "Saba, wait."

He unbuckled his belt. Paula was pulling on her dress. Her

clumsy fingers jammed the slide closing. Illy cried, "No—Saba, listen to me. It isn't what you think."

"Go over to your house and wait," he said to Paula. He doubled the belt up in his hand.

She went out through the sitting room to the door. Behind her the belt cracked and Illy screamed in pain. She burst into a run out the door and across the yard. A man waved to her from the Manhus steps: Sril. She went into her house through the kitchen. The kusin was drinking from the hose. At her sudden entrance it darted under the table.

David was asleep. She stood on the threshold of his room watching him. She could not bear to lose him. The boy slept on his stomach, the cover bunched in his right fist. The back door slammed.

She went down to the kitchen again. Saba was half-sitting on the table, his arms crossed over his chest. The kusin had gone.

"That's a low point, even for you. How could you do that to me? I thought you cared about me."

She shut the door into the hall, so that David would not waken. Saba had his temper back. He watched her cross the kitchen and draw a cup of water to loosen her throat. The kusin had left the window over the hose slightly open. She shut it hard.

"What did you do to Illy?"

He came up behind her. "She did it to pay me back, didn't she? For chasing around."

She put the cup down on the counter. Pedasen's frightened face appeared in her memory. Illy's frightened voice. He slouched against the counter beside her, his elbow bracing him up.

"Why are you so white, Paula? You think I'm going to whip you too, don't you?"

"No," she said, evenly.

"How long have you been debauching my wife?"

She turned on him, ready to blast him, and the hall door sighed. She and Saba in unison turned toward David, coming into the kitchen. The long shirt hung rumpled to his knees.

"Papa!" He leaped up into Saba's arms. "When did you get back? Will you take me to *Ybix?* Will you take me for a ride in *Ybicsa?* Pedasen died. I whipped Itak and made him eat mud." Saba boosted him up in the crook of his arm.

"Say good-bye to your mother."

She gripped the edge of the counter in both hands. Her heart began to thud. David twisted around in Saba's arms. "Good-bye. Where is she going?"

"To Yekka. She'll be back before you miss her."

She looked away, relieved. David said, "Can I go too?"

"I thought you wanted to ride in *Ybicsa?*"

"Yes!"

With David riding on his arm, the big Styth went to the door. Paula said, "What if I refuse?"

"Don't make it harder for me, Paula." He shouted out to the yard for Sril. She stared at his back. She could refuse. But she did not want to be around him. David squirmed out of his arms and came down the room to Paula.

"Will you call me on the screen? Just to me and nobody else?"

She nodded. Sril stood in the doorway. Saba gestured at her. "Take her to Yekka."

The trip was stormy. She was sick all the way from Matuko to Vribulo, the midway stop. Drenched with sweat, she sat in the compartment drinking tea. Sril gave her a towel and she mopped her face. The bus swayed and lurched along in its course.

"Thank you," she said. "I feel awful."

"You'll never make a Styth, Mendoz'."

She emptied her cup of the sweet tea. The bench was slippery. She had to hold the grip in the wall to keep from landing on the floor. But she felt better, her stomach steadier than before. Sril stretched his feet across the aisle to the opposite bench, his arms spread out across the back of their seat.

"How did your mission go?" she said. She put the cup into the clamp on the wall.

"Perfect. We took about four hundred slaves. Everybody on the Asteroid who didn't die."

"Terrific," she said, glum. The only Asteroid he could mean was Vesta; Ceres, the only other of the minor Planets so densely populated, was on the far side of the Sun.

"The Man took *Ybicsa* down over the base and pulled off every attack-craft they had, and *Ybix* went in and blew up the satellites. I hit three out of three shots. Of course The Creep put me in the green window, I couldn't miss."

She leaned against the wall of the compartment. Illy's scream sounded in her memory. But it was Pedasen she longed for. The bus lurched and she jumped. Sril put his arm around her, holding her fast, and she moved over against his side.

"Did you and the Old Man fight?" he said. His hand grazed her side. She shut her eyes. Gently he stroked her side and her shoulder. "It looks odd, he comes back and an hour later you're going." His palm curved over her breast.

"Sril," she said. "Switch off."

His hand left her. The bus lurched along toward Yekka.

YEKKA

Yekka was bright as an Earthish afternoon: the pala fruit was ripening. The whole city rang with the sizzling music of insects. Kasuk, Tanuojin's elder son, met her at the city gate, and Sril got back on the bus to go home. Kasuk took her across the green city to the Akellarit compound. Remembering he was shy, she made no effort to talk to him. He looked nothing like his father. A heavyset young man, with broad plain features, he walked slightly stooped, his eyes on the ground. In the compound yard, she looked first for the bilyobio tree that grew near Tanuojin's window. It was sprouting again.

Tanuojin was in the public room of the main building, giving orders to a row of his men. The walls, like much of the compound, were half-paneled, glossy dark on the bottom and flat white on top. The ceiling was held up on square dark pillars. Paula stopped to look at a postboard near the door. Under a permanent heading for his Akopra, which he called the Black Company, was a list of times and dances. They were doing *Capricornus* in a few watches. She began to be pleased she had come, even without David; she liked Yekka.

"I'm supposed to read the book to you," Tanuojin said, behind her. His crew had gone. He cuffed her. "Didn't I tell you to stop doing that?"

"Frankly, I don't remember that you did."

"Tell him I gave you the book." He walked away across the hall toward the far doorway. When she did not follow he threw her a hard look, and she trotted after him.

"You took Vesta," she said, in the corridor.

"It was a damned stupid move. The Martians went back again as soon as we left." He pushed her ahead of him into the room where Saba slept when he was here. "You stay here."

"All the time?" She looked up at his face, arm's length above hers.

"You can go anywhere you want, I don't care. I don't see how he has a right to call you loose. At least you didn't do it with a man."

She went over to the narrow bed and climbed up to sit on it. She was sweating under her heavy clothes; this was the warmest she had ever been in Styth. Tanuojin leaned against the side of the door, his long dished profile toward her. One mustache lay over his shoulder. He said, "While you're here, you can do something with me."

"Oh." The skin quivered over her shoulders. "What?"

He came into the room and shut the door. "I'll show you."

. . .

"Who have you done it with? Anybody else but us?"

"Just you and him. Who else is there?"

She lay on her side on the bed, between Tanuojin and the wall. The light from the ground outside shone up through the window behind her onto the ceiling. There was a krine in the room somewhere, the Yekkit insect, sawing out its violin screech. "Is it different with him than me?"

He rolled onto his back and folded his arms behind his head. "What do you think? You're entirely different people. Your memory is older than his. You know things in different ways than he does." He was sleepy; his eyes half-closed.

She wondered how long they had shared the same body: an hour, perhaps two hours. The krine was coming closer. Now she could see it on the floor, a thumb-sized transparent worm with wings.

"What do you do?" she said. "What does it feel like?"

"I don't do anything. It feels like what you feel like. That doesn't help, does it? So why don't you stop asking questions?"

"I don't understand why you're so kinked about it."

"I'm tired of being treated like a freak."

She propped her head on her fist. Through the neck of his shirt she could see his collarbones. The krine's voice stopped.

"You know the treaty is ending soon," she said.

Tanuojin's eyes opened, shell-white. His eyes had gotten several shades paler since she had first met him. He said, "We talked about that on the way back from Vesta. You should have asked that man from the Committee what they're going to do."

"I'd rather talk to Jefferson. You know what he said to me—Bunker?"

"Yes." His thin lips split into an unpleasant smile. "They think you're double-dealing with them. Nobody trusts you, Paula. Except that slave. And you got him killed."

Her nerves jumped. She held back the hot remark seething in her throat. His smile broadened with malice. She thought, *He knows everything I think,* and opened her fist.

"The Committee needs a counter to the Martians. This time, given the right conditions, we could arrange something with them that would make the Vesta raid look like crude piracy."

He shut his eyes. The smile still curled his mouth. "What conditions? That Saba becomes the Prima?"

"Well, yes."

"He won't do it. We talked about it, as I said. He doesn't think he can whip Machou, and he won't try without a good reason."

"This is a good reason! The two of you could—"

"The three of us could get in a lot of trouble. The last time you talked us into one of your maneuvers, I nearly died."

"Because it worked."

Almost under the bed the krine started to shrill. Tanuojin sat up. "That damned fly." He held out one hand, palm flat. "We don't want the same things, Paula. I use you, and you use me." The krine leaped onto his hand. He threw it out the window. "But we want different things."

"All I want is what's possible."

Monstrously tall, he straightened up onto his feet, stretching. "We'll see what's possible." He went out. She folded her arms behind her head, satisfied. They had already talked about the treaty, even about the advantages of making Saba the Prima; it would breed in their minds. She yawned, pleasantly sleepy.

"Rasputin was a false prophet," Tanuojin said. They had come to the gate out of his compound.

"He was a genuine blood-stauncher," she said. "And he was very hard to kill."

"I'm not a mystic. He tried to predict the future."

"When was that? That isn't so."

"He did predict that he wouldn't be able to save the Tsarevich the next time he was in danger. Didn't he?" The Styth turned the key absently in his hand; he was going to the powerhouse at the end of the city. Paula frowned up at him. She wondered if he had taken his knowledge of Rasputin out of her head.

"He wasn't necessarily referring to the Ekaterinberg massacre. Maybe it was practical—the Tsarevich was sickening and the next time Rasputin wouldn't be able to stop the bleeding."

"Where are you going? I don't like not knowing where you are."

"To the White Market. For a present for David."

Without a farewell he turned and walked off along the narrow pathway. His follower Marus went after him. Paula started across the city toward the White Market.

The ringing tuneless insect yell of the krines rose from every patch of grass. The warmth and the brilliant light made her high-spirited. She reached the stream and followed it down through an orchard. The pala trees were pruned into symmetrical fans, like Jewish candlesticks. Babies hung in sling-cradles from the lower branches while their mothers went up and down the rows picking fruit.

The stream branched into a dozen narrow fingers trickling through the dense grass. She crossed a marshy meadow toward the place where the ground broke off in a long ledge and the many branches of the stream roared off in waterfalls and ran on toward the distant lake. Taking off her shoes she waded across two fingers of the stream. A green fish bit her heel. She sat down on the far bank and put her shoes on.

In spite of the harvest, the White Market was busy as usual. Ten or a dozen Styths were crowded around the window of the illusion shop, looking in—they thought it impolite to go into a store if they were not buying anything. Their eagerness for Martian things put her off. She wanted to protect them from the Martians who would steal whatever they could, stencil images of Capricornus on an undershirt if it would sell. She was trying to work out a treaty in her mind to ally the Empire with the anarchy, since the anarchists would accept the Styths without trying to change them. Sometimes she felt the same urge to protect Tanuojin and his dangerous gifts; she used that to remind herself that many of her impulses were stupid.

She went into the toy shop. In among the board games and dart sets she found a long black rocket, put it down on the floor, and pushed the trigger in the base. With an explosive crack the rocket shot up into the air and disappeared behind the next rack of toys. A Martian shopkeeper hurried up to her.

"I'm just seeing if it works," she said.

"It works. Everything works." He smiled at her, his hands together. "Aren't you the wife of the Matuko Akellar?"

"No. I'm not. I'm Paula Mendoza." She went down the aisle to get the rocket.

"That's what I meant," the Martian said, coming after her.

"Then say what you mean."

The rocket was sticking nose-first into the floor. She pulled it out and straightened its needle-snout. The Martian hovered behind her as she crossed the shop to the counter.

"Mrs. Mendoza, I wonder if you'd consent to talk to—to listen to— That's fifty-five dollars."

She paid him. His soft fingertips tapped over the keys of the computer terminal. "If you'd listen—"

"I'm listening with both ears. You haven't said anything yet."

He pulled the lid down over the terminal keyboard. "We have a complaint. About the Akellar."

"Tanuojin?"

"Yes. Maybe, if you'd hear us out, you could help us."

She snorted, disbelieving. "Well, I'll listen. What is it?"

"Come with me."

He took her three doors away to a little Martian lunchroom, covered with an awning against an imaginary sun. The shopkeeper made her sit at a round table and rushed off.

He came back with a small platoon of other men—all the traders were men; they clustered around the table, all eyes fixed on her. She was drinking a hot mixture of milk and pala fruit. She moved the glass away.

"They are selling slaves in the native bazaar," said the toyman.

"How long have you been here? Half the people in Styth are slaves. Complain about something I can change."

"These people are Martians."

"Oh." She leaned forward, her elbows on the table. Sril had said they had taken over four hundred prisoners from Vesta, which was a Martian colony. "Oh. I see."

"Naturally we abhor any kind of slavery."

The white Martian faces made a circle around her. She said, "Yes, I'm sure. Now, it was almost nine years ago I wrote your contract, but it seems to me there was a clause in it about your staying out of the native market."

"These people are suffering horribly!"

"Well, I'll do what I can, which will certainly cost you a lot of money. Are you ready for that?"

The pale faces changed. The toyman, sitting opposite her, glanced at the men on his right and left. He leaned toward her. "This isn't a money issue. This is a question of common human decency."

"To Tanuojin it will be strictly a money issue."

One of the other men muttered, "That black bastard."

"How much?" the toyman said.

"I can't say. Depending on the condition of the slaves. Yekka is a bad market for slaves, they're a luxury here." She took the rocket she had bought and went out of the lunchroom.

The local market was on the far side of the bubble. She went there in the next middle watch. The Martians from Vesta were caged on either side of the central lane of the market. There were thirteen old people and five children, all under two years. None of the Styths in the market was showing much interest except an old woman who was trying to coax the terrified children up to the bars to give them sweets. Paula went back toward the far end of the bubble.

A high fence surrounded the city powerhouse, near the tail of the city. Tanuojin's man Marus was at the gate, and he let her in. The block-shaped windowless powerhouse hummed. When she went in through the door, the hum increased to a steady roar. From the outside the building was only one story, but she came in to a ledge around a pit eighty feet deep. The two engines in it were round and smooth, like silos, and gave off the even thunderous roar. Far below her, a man walked around the nearer barrel into sight, saw her, and went back. She found the ladder down into the pit.

Behind the engines, Tanuojin was standing over a little desk, and another man was sitting behind it writing on the treated surface with a stylus that had a long cord coming out of the butt end. The noise was so intense it was like hearing nothing. Paula looked up at the engines towering above them.

The men did not try to talk over the noise. They wrote messages to each other on a little workboard. Tanuojin scribbled something and gave it to the man at the desk, who nodded. He took a slotted computer key out of the top of the desk and gave it to Tanuojin, who put it into his sleeve. Paula followed him up the ladder and out of the powerhouse.

In the yard, he pulled two rubber plugs out of his ears. Paula's head buzzed. He turned toward her, his mouth open, and she said, "What were you doing?"

"Turning down the radiation. Stay out of there, you'll go deaf."

They went out the gate. Marus came along after them, staying ten feet behind them, like a wife. Paula looked down the city. It seemed as bright as before; she supposed it would slowly fall dark.

"Then the pala harvest is over?"

"Yes. Did you go to the Martians?"

"They don't like you down there."

He bent and took her wrist. They walked on toward his compound; after ten or twelve strides he let go of her, throwing her wrist back at her.

"You meddle, piglet."

"You have eighteen slaves you can't sell. The Martians will buy them. What's in the way?"

"You stay out of my business. If you want to work you can scrub floors."

She veered off away from him. All thorns and no rose. Kasuk was coming toward them along the path at a lope. Tanuojin stopped, and the young man ran up to them.

"Pop, there's a call for you from the Fleet Office. They're holding."

Tanuojin went off at a fast walk along the path. After he had gone a hundred feet he broke into a run, his son behind him. Paula looked over her shoulder at Marus.

"What do you think that's about?"

Stoop-shouldered, the big man came up beside her in his slouching walk. "I don't think, Mendoz'. I just do as I'm told." They went down the path toward the compound.

The window of her room in the compound opened on the yard. She sat on the ledge playing her flute and watching the vast green city fade into its bright twilight. About midway through the watch the toyman from the White Market came in through the gate, crossed the yard to the main door, and there met Marus who took him into the house. She played a jig. After half an hour the toyman left again. His face was fretted. She was tempted to call to him, to find out how much Tanuojin wanted for his slaves, but there was a knock on her door.

"Mendoz', the Akellar will see you."

Tanuojin was in the hall, eating his high meal. His sons waited behind him to serve him. Paula stood on the far side of the table from him, waiting for him to decide to recognize her presence. He ate fast, hardly chewing or savoring anything, as if someone might steal the food out of his mouth. He had grown up an outsider in a flock of children. Kasuk took his empty plate away to the side. He drained his cup and Junna, the younger son, filled it again from a pitcher.

"We're going to Vribulo in eight watches," Tanuojin said. He sat back, his hands on his stomach.

"To Vribulo," she said. "Why? Have you talked to Saba?"

"Not yet. He'll call this watch. The fleet is awarding us each a flag. For taking Vesta." Kasuk brought a pala fruit and a knife.

"What's a flag?" she said.

"The highest award in the fleet. An automatic promotion, among other things. Like money." He split the fruit in two. She made a face; she was tired of the sweet, damp, greenish meat. He picked the seed out with the tip of the knife. "We're trading you, too."

"You mean I'm going home?"

"That's right."

"You told me the Vesta mission was a failure."

"Propaganda. It's the first time any Styth has mastered an Asteroid. But the Martians took it back again. Psychological warfare, it's all worthless. Usually the result's just the opposite of what you expect."

She laced her fingers together behind her back. "How much are the Martians paying you for those slaves?"

"I told you to stay out of that," he said. "Get out."

VRIBULO

The crews of the Styth Fleet overflowed the plain of the House. They stood on the steps and in the street, blocks of men in long gray shirts, arranged by height, standing rigidly at respect. Paula was shivering with cold. She stood with *Ybix*'s crew beside the front doors to the House. She pulled her coat tighter around her.

Saba and Tanuojin stood square as brackets twenty feet in front of her. Beyond them, Machou was reading in a roaring voice from a long citation.

"Salute!"

The thousands of identical figures swung up their fists. "Styth! Styth! Styth!" She folded her arms. Their singlemindedness bewildered her. Machou came up to Saba. He hung a black sash around Saba's neck and over his left shoulder.

"If you keep doing this, Matuko, we'll have to invent a new rank for you." He and Saba shook hands.

"Thank you, Prima."

Machou draped the flag over Tanuojin's shoulder. They stared past each other, they did not shake hands. The fleet shouted the salute again. Their commanders dismissed them. Machou and the rAkellaron came up to surround Saba and Tanuojin, congratulating them. *Ybix*'s crew broke their ranks. Paula stayed where she was, beside the high metal-bound door. All this for six feet of black cloth.

Marus laid his hand flat between her shoulders, and she went obediently across the plain toward Saba and Tanuojin. The spectators rushed over the steps, crowding around the new heroes. Small among them, she was jostled off her feet. Marus thrust one arm out straight to fend off the mob. She walked under his armpit, closed in by huge people, seeing nothing but their backs. Marus led her to Saba.

He stood talking to Machou, with Tanuojin a few feet away. The crowd surged around them, and hands thrust out toward them. Saba shook one hand after another, paying no attention, his eyes on Machou. She hung back from the Prima. Someone stepped on her foot, and an elbow worked her away from Saba.

Marus pushed her. She went into the shelter between Saba and Tanuojin.

"What are you doing?" Tanuojin said.

"I'm being stepped on."

Marus spoke to him, and he moved off a few steps, stooping to hear, his hand covering one ear to keep the racket out. Saba turned around. A broad hand reached toward him at her eye-level, and he shook it briefly. To Paula, he said, "Are you going to act decent from now on?" Three more hands appeared out of the crowd. He twisted toward Machou, pumping arms. In the roar he had to shout to be heard. "Anarchists, you know, they have the morals of—"

A hand shot past her toward him, a white-skinned hand full of a small black gun. The clamor drowned everything. She heard no shots. She grabbed the arm by the wrist. Someone screamed. The gun arm yanked back and pulled her after it into the mob. She clung tight, left her feet, was dragged into the thick of people suddenly running or trying to run. The body attached to the arm struck her. Its white face screamed at her, a red mouth hedged with teeth, the sound lost in the howl of the mob packed around them. Marus heaved the Martian gunman up away from her. She lost her grip and fell. Through the running legs she saw Saba lying on his stomach on the pavement.

Machou stooped over him. "He's dead!"

A screech went up around her. She scrambled toward Saba. They would trample him. The mob trapped her in their midst, shoving back and forth. Tanuojin brushed past her. She struggled after him, and at the edge of the crowd someone caught her and held her by the arms.

Tanuojin knelt; he bent over Saba, and his lips moved in Saba's name. Blood stained the broad black sash across the dead man's back. Paula whined in her throat. Tanuojin pulled his lyo up into his arms, Saba's head against his shoulder, rocking him back and forth. *Ybix*'s crew was around them, driving the crowd back. She heard Tanuojin's voice: "Saba—Saba—" Calling to him. It was Machou who held her so tight her arms hurt. Tanuojin's hand pressed flat over the blood splash in the dead man's back.

"Saba!"

Saba moved. Paula gathered her breath. Machou's grip eased on her arms, and she edged away from him. In Tanuojin's arms, Saba turned his head and groaned.

Paula was trembling from head to foot. She cast a look at the hundreds of people waiting and turned to the Prima. "You said he was dead."

"He was." Machou's voice was suddenly reedy, his gaze unblinking on Tanuojin.

Ketac broke through the ring of *Ybix*'s crew and knelt beside his father. Tanuojin slumped down on the blood-splattered pavement. His skin was gray around the eyes. Exhausted, he was helpless. She fisted her hand in Machou's shirt sleeve and wrenched his attention around to her.

"He wasn't dead. You were wrong."

The Prima struck her hand away. "That freak."

Ketac was lifting Saba cradled in his arms. She went over to Tanuojin and stooped, her hand on his shoulder. "Can you walk? We have to get out of here." Around them were thousands of people, all watching them. She helped Tanuojin up, one arm wrapped around him, and hurried him after Ketac down the steps.

Saba had been shot through the heart. While Paula was taking his clothes off, in the back room of his office in the Barn, a crowd gathered outside: she could hear their shouts and the tramp of their feet. Ketac came in with a pack of bandages.

"Is he badly hurt?"

"He'll be all right," she said. She ripped open the package and unrolled three inches of bandage.

"What happened out there, anyway?" Ketac said. "Who shot him?"

"I don't know, Ketac. Go away, you're bothering me."

"Do you need help?"

She shook her head. Swinging the washbasin out of the wall, she turned on the hot water. Finally Ketac left her. Saba was out cold. She washed the small hole in his chest and the gaping hole in his back, and picked out the black fibers the bullet had carried into the flesh. The wound was scabbing over when she put the bandage on. She covered him with blankets and left him to sleep.

Sril and Bakan were throwing a bone for money on the desk in the front office. The front door was shut. Still she heard the bellow of hundreds of voices in the street beyond and a crackle of something breaking.

"How is he?" the two men said, in unison.

"He'll heal." She went to the door, and Sril dashed over to stop her.

"Don't go out there."

"What's going on?" She pulled his hand off the door and unlatched it.

Armed men paraded up and down the arcade between the offices and the street. Most of *Ybix*'s crew was massed around this office and the last one in the row, Tanuojin's. In the street facing them people swarmed thick along the foot of the rAkellaron House steps. Many of them carried sticks and handfuls of street shards. More men joined this mob with every moment. Their voices rose in a throaty roar; she could not make out the words.

"It's getting worse," Sril said.

She went to the window in the other wall of the front office. That street was empty. "What's going on?" A howl outside brought her around, every hair stiff. Bakan was still sitting at the desk. He turned the knobbed bone over in his claws. Sril slapped a credit chip down on the desk.

"Doubles."

Paula walked the length of the room. "What's going on out there?"

"Who knows?" Bakan said. "Whatever happened up on the steps last watch, it was strange. People don't like strange things."

Something struck the outside of the door. She twitched. Sril said, "Sit down, Mendoz'. There's nothing to do, even for you."

She walked around the room. The racket of the crowd, growing louder, sawed on her nerves. Ketac came in through the inside door and shut it behind him.

"Has there been any word from the House?"

Bakan shook his head. The bone rattled on the top of the desk, and Sril yelped; he had won. Paula sat down in the chair by the window.

The mob swelled larger through the watch, packing the street and crowding through the arches of the arcade. Fights broke out here and there. At one bell, Leno came down from the House, his bullet head set forward on his shoulders. The man who had shot Saba had confessed: he was an agent of the Sunlight League. Leno went away, but the mob stayed. Their noise kept Paula awake. She sat at the front desk while Ketac slept in the chair before the window and Sril and Bakan walked aimlessly around the office.

"Why don't you sleep?" Sril said to her, deep in the low watch.

"I can't." Her elbows propped on the desk, she pressed her fingers flat to her cheeks. Outside the mob was chanting something she did not want to hear. "That damned Machou."

He glanced at Ketac, sprawled across the chair. Bakan was in the next room. Sril sat on the edge of the desk. "You think Machou is driving this?"

"You don't see him down here stopping it, do you?"

"Because of what Tanuojin did?"

She raised her head. The chant pierced her hearing: "Kill, kill, kill," growing louder. Sril bent down, his voice at a murmur.

"He brought Saba back again."

"Don't talk about what you don't understand." What she did not understand. Whenever she thought about what had happened on the porch a strange exultation swelled her, that drove out fear. The mob voice thundered. She went to the door. Sril reached it first and opened it; Ketac, rubbing his eyes, went after him into the arcade.

The mob surged along the street. Clubs waved in their fists. In an archway Sril was surrounded. Bakan rushed past her out the door, saw, and plunged back into the office. Seizing the first chair he came to, he lifted it over his head in both hands and ran down to the edge of the crowd. A steady banging reached her ears. They were breaking down Tanuojin's door. Bakan held the chair before him with the legs out horizontal and forced his way into the crowd. They yielded, their hands up. A man in the forefront lost his footing and fell and Bakan walked over him. In the arch Sril had his back to the pillar, fighting off people armed with sticks. Bakan reached him. Together they cleared the arch. Other men ran by Paula's doorway to help them. She saw Ketac down near Tanuojin's door.

At a dead run, Leno passed her with a dozen of his men streaming along behind him. They formed a line and thrust the mob back into the street. Stones and filth pelted the cordon of men.

Leno roared, "Drive those fuckers back!" Half the line broke rank and rushed into the crowd, scattering the mob ahead of them. Paula yanked the door shut.

In the relative quiet she heard a new sound, a low whimper from another room, and went through the office to the back bedroom. Saba had wakened. He was crying with pain. She sank down on one knee beside the bed, afraid to touch him.

"Saba."

"My head." He turned his head from side to side. "My head is killing me."

The mob yell rose again to a hysterical pitch. The noise made him sob, his head rolling back and forth. She brought him a cup of water but he could not drink. The door in the next room banged open. Tanuojin came into the room. The black sash hung crumpled across his chest. He sat on the edge of the bed and put his hands on his lyo.

Paula went back to the doorway. Tanuojin helped Saba sit and fed him the water from the cup. He said something too softly for her to hear, and Saba nodded. She went into the computer room. On the walls the analog decks blinked in panels of red and green. Ketac and Sril packed the next doorway, watching.

"How is he?"

Tanuojin came out of the bedroom. "He's good. He's better than I thought." He put his back to them, facing Paula. "There's too much going on here. I can't take it, I'm spinning my wheels, I have to get away. Can you take care of him?"

"I'll take him back to Matuko," she said.

"Keep him quiet. Don't let him do anything at all." His head turned slightly toward the men in the doorway. The strange joy swelled in her again, so close to him. She put her hand on his chest.

"Go back to Yekka. I'll call you when we're in Matuko."

"Don't bother. I'll keep track of you." He turned and walked out of the room.

"I could fly my own ship."

Paula kept hold of the grip in the wall of the compartment. The bus bounced and swayed along in its course toward Matuko. Saba walked in two steps the length of the compartment. "Why can't I fly my own ship?"

Sril coughed into his rolled hand. "The Creep said—"

"What is he, my mother?"

Sril and Bakan, sitting opposite each other, passed weighted looks across the compartment. Saba dropped down on the bench next to Bakan. To Paula, he said, "When are you going to ask me about Illy?"

She glanced at Sril. "Will you bring me a drink of water?"

"Yes, Mendoz'." He and Bakan filed out the door. The bus lurched and the door shut with a crash.

"I divorced her," Saba said. "I sent her back to Merkhiz. First I whipped her backside so bad she probably stood the whole way."

"Did you enjoy it?"

"Enjoy it. How could you do that to me? I'd never catch her in bed with Tanuojin."

She tightened her fingers around the grip. Her stomach heaved with the motion of the bus. "How is David?"

"He's fine. Boltiko has care of him." He put one foot against the side of the bench to brace himself. "That doesn't bother you? About Illy."

"I'm glad she's gone. I was going to end it anyway."

"How long were you lovers?"

Her throat was sweet with nausea. She stiffened against his curiosity. "I'm going to be sick." She staggered onto her feet. He called Sril to take her down to the slave toilet in the back of the bus.

MATUKO

Without Pedasen she had to do all the work in her house by herself. She hated the other slaves, who hated her, and would not let them inside her door. If something broke, Sril or Bakan fixed it for her, but usually the floor was crunchy with grit and cobwebs hung from the ceiling.

She was going around the front room wiping the dust off the flat surfaces when David came in. His upper lip was split and swollen; he had been fighting again. Her chest tightened with short temper and she threw the rag down.

"You know, I'm beginning to forget what you really look like."

He climbed onto the swing couch. His narrow slanted eyes were stony. "Maybe I just won't come back ever again, maybe you'd like that better."

"I'd like you to broaden your interests."

"It's your fault."

"My fault."

"Because you're a dirty nigger."

She started down to her heels. Her son leaned toward her, his head stuck forward. "You aren't my mother. You're just a dirty old slave. My real mother was a Styth, like everybody else's mother."

Her face flushed with heat. Her hands were trembling and she chafed them together hard. "Your mother is me, whether you appreciate it or not, and if it weren't for me, you wouldn't be here living this easy life with the leisure to beat people up." His hostile eyes shifted. Now he was staring over her shoulder. She said, "If it hadn't been for your dirty nigger mother, your clean Styth father would have sold us both for slaves long ago."

"That isn't true!"

He flew out of the couch toward her, his fist raised. She swiped his hand aside. "Don't you touch me, you little brat—" He was not small; he was already nearly her height. "All you can do is fight."

"I hate you. And you aren't my mother." He raced down the hallway. The back door slammed.

She took her notebook to the kitchen, where it was warm. Too jittery to work, she sat at the table drawing on the scarred white top with her stylus.

"Paula?" Saba shouted, in the front of the house.

She raised her head. He came heavy-footed down the hall and tramped across the kitchen to the far side of the table from her. "What's the matter with you? Why did you tell him I'm going to sell him?"

David lingered in the doorway behind him. She laid her hands flat on the table. "The shining knight to the rescue."

"Look." Saba gestured toward the boy behind him. "The other boys tease him. Maybe he should live with Boltiko."

"No." She rushed up onto her feet. "No."

"You dirty nigger kundra," David said.

Saba let out a half-spoken oath. He got the boy by the arm, whirled him around, and spanked him. David squawked. Paula's wobbling legs put her down hard on the bench. Saba dropped him, and David threw a furious glance at him and bolted.

"That was edifying," Paula said. Her throat was tight.

"I hope so. That's what you're supposed to do, not threaten to sell him." He sat on the end of the bench and reached for her notebook. "He has to learn to fight sometime. Look how small he is. He'll never get anything without fighting for it."

"He says—" she cleared her throat, "I'm not his real mother."

He laughed. The notebook was open before him; the pages were covered with the cursive script of the Middle Planets, which he could not read. He tapped the lone Styth symbol on the page: the major Sa she used short for his name. "What's this?"

"Notes. For a new treaty with the Committee."

"What makes you think I'll want a new treaty?" He looked her curiously in the face. "You can't take Vida with you, if you go back to live in the Earth."

"Item," she said. "You need money. As usual. Item. The quickest way to get money is to go to the Middle Planets. Eureka. You'll get a new treaty."

"Item." Saba shut the notebook. "If you go back to the Earth, you'll be just little Paula Mendoza again, but here, you do what nobody else can." He leaned on his elbows over the table, his black eyes at her. "Stop scaring Vida. If he didn't love you, you wouldn't matter to him." He went out the hall to the front door.

YBIX. Watch logs L19, 271–M19, 469

Sril played the ulugong with his eyes shut, beating out the round mellow notes with the heels of his hands. Paula turned around. Some of the pornographic posters on the walls of the Tank had been there since her first voyage. One woman, life-sized, her legs spread wide, had been chewed by darts into gaping holes that finally made her modest.

"Mendoz'," Sril said. "Go get your music-stick."

"I left it in Matuko."

"Damn. Why?"

She made no answer. David had demanded the flute, to keep safe until she came back. The Go set was in the cabinet under the hatch, and she took the grid out of its clamps and the box of pebbles out of the cubbyhole. She looked around for someone to play with.

"Kasuk. Play Go with me."

Tanuojin's son was just coming in the hatch. "What?"

"Play Go with me."

"I don't know how." He scrambled across the Tank toward her, still awkward in the free fall. She dodged fluently out of his way.

"I'll teach you."

"It had better not take effort." He watched her put the grid before her in the air and shake the pebble box of stones. "I don't believe in effort."

She taught him the game. Sril's soft bell-like music played in her ears. Already she missed her flute. Bakan and Marus came into the Tank and threw darts. They had only reached cruising speed during the high watch, five hours before, and the crew were still settling into their routines.

"Where is *Ebelos*?" she asked Kasuk.

"Off our bow. You can see her from the window in the Beak."

Ebelos was Leno's ship. Machou had insisted the Merkhiz Akellar go with them to the Earth for the new treaty conference. Tanuojin had tried to argue around it. Paula suspected Dick Bunker's influence in Machou's sudden interest in the Middle Planets. She set a pebble on the board. Kasuk played slowly, thoughtful, his eyes on the board. Shorter than Tanuojin, heavyset, he seemed painfully shy.

"Kak." His brother Junna dove through the hatch. His hair was growing out. Sometime during the mission he would be clubbed. "Gemini says—"

Kasuk's head turned, and the rest of his body followed, rolling straight. "Pop said you shouldn't come in here."

"Gemini says you're supposed to memorize the interact codes and get on the spark to *Ebelos* and confirm," Junna said.

Kasuk looked at her. "I have to go."

"I heard him."

The young man doubled over and swooped away to the hatch. To Junna he said, "He told you not to come in here," and went out without waiting for a reply. Paula herded the pebbles into the box. His eyes on the posters, Junna loitered in the middle of the Tank.

Sril said, "What's wrong? Isn't Diddums-widdums allowed to look at cunts?" The other men laughed. Junna's eyes flashed. He swung around toward them, rope-thin, gawky, and caught a faceful of jeers.

"You'd better leave fast, Diddums, before those cracks attack."

She put the Go game away and went out. All down the corridor she could hear them teasing Junna and his furious replies.

Without her flute, she had nothing to fill the hours when her friends were on watch. She sat in the Beak, trying to make out the planets among the stars. Saba knew hundreds of the stars by name. The red flame of the Sun burned near the edge of the window. *Ebelos,* Leno's ship, was long and hump-backed. She flew below *Ybix,* sometimes above her, just close enough for Paula to read the markings on her hull. She wrote a letter to David, to send when they reached the Earth, and she daydreamed.

When she went to the library in the high watch she found Tanuojin in there with Kasuk. In the hatchway, she said, "Do you mind if I come in?"

"No." Tanuojin had a workboard on his knee and was writing on it and did not look up. She went past them into the back of the room.

The books were all kept in niches, their tails out. She went along reading the titles written on the butt ends of the tapes.

Behind her, Tanuojin said, "So if a body absorbs energy—" his stylus scraped on the worksheet, "its mass is increased by the amount of energy, *E*, divided by light squared." She found an old book of legends and took it out.

"Are you listening to me?" Tanuojin said sharply.

She turned. Kasuk mumbled something. He lowered his eyes; he had been looking at her. Tanuojin knocked the workboard aside.

"Why do I waste my time on you? You'll never amount to a half-pitch."

She started toward the hatch. Kasuk beat her through it. The workboard floated toward her, and she caught it.

"Damned stupid brat," Tanuojin said.

"He's very good at Go."

"Whenever I try to teach him something he drifts off into that dream world of his."

She held the workboard out to him, and he took it and shoved it into a rubber clip on the wall. He avoided her eyes. "Go away, Paula."

She left, the book of legends in her hand.

She and Saba lived in the same cabin. She slept during the high watch and he slept during the low watch. Just after one bell, while he was getting undressed and she was dressing, she said, "What kind of a sailor is Kasuk?"

"Fair. When he pays attention."

"Why is Tanuojin so hard with him?"

"Why are you so easy with Vida?" He plunged head-first into the wetroom. The round door swung idly. His voice sounded through the open hatch of the dryer in the wall below the wetroom. "It isn't that he's hard, he expects too much."

The wetroom hissed. Paula unhooked the bed from the wall and shook it out. The thick furry nap attracted dust. Glistening wet, Saba came through the dryer into the open room.

"He's smothering him," she said.

"Jesus," Saba said. "Ever since the crumb was a baby, whenever he's fallen down and scratched his knees, Tanuojin's been right over him, giving him hell and healing him up. What do you expect?" He shook his hair back, floating in the air. Paula fastened up the front of her overalls. He said, in another voice, "I could use some help getting to sleep."

"I'll find you some sweet music in the library." She went up the tubular room to the hatch into the corridor.

"What, you only fuck women now? That's bad for you, Paula, it gives you diseases."

"You'd know."

"Maybe you've given it up entirely, like Tajin."

"You've destroyed my trust in men." She wheeled over the latch in the round doorway, swinging her body the other way as a counter. Saba was wrapping himself in the bed.

"I'm surrounded by celibates."

She laughed. "Dream."

Ahead, above the hazy sprinkling of the Pleiades, which the Styths also called the Net, great Jupiter was slowly becoming visible. The Sun lit only a crescent shape along her flank. Every few watches Paula went into the Beak to see the giant and the little pearls of her moons. They would swing around Jupiter for the energy to reach the Earth.

When they had gone nearly two hundred watches from Uranus, *Ebelos* split a crystal in her heart engine, and both ships decelerated back to spacepoint. Paula spent the time in the wetroom, being sick. *Ebelos*'s engines were built in a single train. When one failed, they all failed, and in the course of slowing down, three more crystals cracked. *Ybix* coupled with her, belly to belly, sealed to her with an elastic web. Leno's crew was brought into *Ybix*, and Saba, Tanuojin, Leno, and his second officer crowded into Saba's cabin and spread out charts of *Ebelos*'s engines.

The lights were so dim Paula saw the men only as vague shapes. The cold made her shiver. They had turned the life systems down to save energy. Someone lit a crystal lamp. Saba turned, his face white in its light.

"That's my wife, who does not clean up." He batted a floating book tape away from him.

They put the lamp under the chart and leaned over it. Paula moved along the curved wall. The chart of lines and circles and colored dots looked like a choreograph.

Tanuojin said, "We're falling into Jupiter's influence. How long will this take?"

"Six hours," Leno said. He wore a pressure suit; his arm was ham-sized. His finger moved over the drawing between him and Saba. "We'll have to start here. Unscrew the hood and the hood mounting, set the ancillary crystal, take out this coupling, set the two behind it, and replace the coupling and set the crystal in its head. Reset the timing. It needs two engineers and someone to hold the lamp and the tools."

Saba's head bobbed. The light shone on the curve of his cheekbone. "You and I can do it."

Leno turned to his second officer. "You're dismissed. Go get some sleep."

"Yes, Akellar."

Another man had come in behind the others. She could not see who it was. He gave something to Tanuojin. The tall man swung around, his face turning into the light. "You'd better do this a little faster than six hours. We'll reach primary Jupiter in five." He left.

Leno was rolling up the chart. Paula went down the room, into the warmth of the crystal lamp. Saba said, "I need a volunteer from my watch, to go in with us."

Near the hatch, in the dark, the other man said, "I'll go." It was Kasuk.

"Good," Saba said. "Get into your suit."

Leno clipped down the ends of his chart and fit it into a tube. When Kasuk had gone, he said, "You know, Saba, I wouldn't expect this even of you."

"Expect what?"

"If *Ybix* were Yekka's, he would have run behind me, when my engine failed, until I blew out my ship, or paid his ransom, or turned my ship over to him—whatever he wanted."

"Tanuojin is one of the best officers in the fleet."

"I didn't deny that. One of my own friends wouldn't jeopardize his ship for my sake."

Saba said, "Are you coming to your point?"

In the pressure suit Leno looked two times Saba's size. He said, "I think I've passed it."

"Let's go." Saba turned toward Paula, above him in the dark. "Tell Tanuojin I'm taking Kasuk with me."

"Hurry, will you? I'm freezing."

"Don't worry."

Jupiter made the space around her seethe. The two ships slipped deeper into the turbulence. The seal between them cracked and broke, and they drifted apart. Saba, Leno, and Kasuk were stranded in *Ebelos*, floating away toward the giant Planet. Paula went to *Ybix*'s bridge. It was mobbed with men. The radiation from Jupiter jammed the communicators. There was no way to reach the men in *Ebelos*.

Tanuojin, in the cage, sent *Ybix* chasing the other ship. When he tried to couple with her, *Ebelos* wobbled and rolled away. He pursued, and the bigger ship sheared toward *Ybix*, and he had to pull *Ybix* up so hard Paula ran her head into the wall.

"We can't do it," someone said, behind her: one of *Ebelos*'s crew. "The old dragon's burned a couple more."

Paula shook her head, dazed. Sril's arm slipped around her waist. "Hold on, Mendoz'."

The darkened bridge was faintly lit by the green cube of the holograph. The images of the two ships were bright yellow. The radiant Planet was interfering with the sensors and the images began to flutter. She put her hand on Sril's arm. *Ebelos* broke into three separate pieces in the map and each piece shivered into a dozen outlines, out of register.

Tanuojin put his hand out of the cage. "Bakan. Throw a schema of the Jovian fields into the holograph."

Sril muttered in his throat. In the holograph the images of the ships had dissolved into hazy blurs. Suddenly *Ybix*'s kite shape was surrounded by a ring of identical images. If *Ebelos* hit her, she would break *Ybix* in half. But now *Ebelos* was sailing in her own crowd of ghosts. Paula rubbed her eyes. Junna had come in beside her.

Bakan said, "I have the field schema." A three-color diagram appeared in the holograph, showing the curving space of Jupiter. The multiplying images of the ships sailed through it. A blue curl brushed one of *Ebelos*'s ghosts, without effect, and touched another in the ring. The ship rolled over, and the seven different pictures of her blurred and ran in confusion.

"Marus," Tanuojin said. "Bring her up to zero-eight."

Paula's eyes hurt from trying to follow the chaos in the holograph. *Ebelos* seemed to be rolling over onto her back. Tanuojin gave Marus a stream of orders in a voice without inflection. The incoherent light that seemed to be *Ybix* settled toward one of the images of *Ebelos*. She wondered how he knew which was which.

"It's no use," a strange voice murmured, over her shoulder. "He can't do this."

Paula was leaning on Sril, her hand fisted in his sleeve. He gave her a slight hug. He heard them. The low voices whispered behind her.

"*Ybix* can't support this many men too much longer."

"What's her capacity—eighteen?"

"Look how he's wasting energy."

Junna flung his head back. He and Paula were within arm's distance of each other. His eyes shone. With one hand he raked back his thick floating hair. The blue and orange fields lapped and made a whorl of space that intersected the map cube. There were eight things that looked like *Ebelos*. Three of them fell through the whorl and went on with no change, but the fourth hit the shifting helix of the fields and rebounded. Sril let out a hoarse gasp.

"Marus!" Tanuojin cried. "Reverse—eight-zero. Now! Pick her up, damn it, if you drop her I'll kill you."

"He'll kill us all," the strange murmur said behind her. "We have to grab this ship."

Paula got hold of Junna's hand. He gave her another desperate look and turned his face back toward his father in the cage.

The schema of the fields, which came from the computer inside the ship, was the only steady image in the map. *Ebelos* was a long blur that filled half the cube, and *Ybix* was in many parts, sparkling like a star. Tanuojin was staring at the cube. He gave Marus orders and faithfully Marus did his bidding. A piece of *Ybix* moved down through the orange toward *Ebelos*. The colors of the fields deepened as the Planet's gravity compressed the space around it. *Ebelos*'s blurred mass passed across the intersection between the orange and the blue. Her many images rolled head over tail. Paula's eyes burned from trying to make sense out of the map. She rubbed them with her free hand. Junna's fingers were clamped around hers so tightly she could feel the papery new growth of his claws. She thought of the tumbling men in *Ebelos*.

Ybix reached the intersection. There was a thump like something hitting the padded wall. Paula's ears stopped up. She felt a sharp deep pain in her diaphragm.

"Marus," Tanuojin said. "Now hold her. Hold her. Let the field bring her up to us."

The map was a streaming blur of colors. Sril muttered, "I can't see a thing." Paula's nose was bleeding; she went cross-eyed at the fog of blood in the air before her.

"Bakan," Tanuojin said. "Tell the docking crew to be ready with the new seal."

Nobody spoke. She was holding her breath. Her temples throbbed.

"Now! Throw it on!"

Bakan shouted, "They've got the new seal."

The crew thundered up a cheer. Tanuojin shouted, "Clear the bridge. Marus, put all the spare energy in the ship into the seal. Junna, take Paula to red-three."

Junna flung his arms around Paula. "I knew he would do it." He followed her toward the hatch. "I knew it all the time." His voice was fresh with relief. She went back to her cabin and shut herself into the wetroom.

THE EARTH. November 1862–March 1865

"Hot Jesus Christ," Leno said. He was leaning across the seat in front of her, his cheek flattened against the window. Paula moved into the corner of the seat. If the air bus bounced, he would land in her lap. The other Styths were plastered to the windows on either side of the bus. She stretched her neck to look down the aisle. Saba was in the cockpit, talking to the pilot. She could not see Tanuojin.

She folded one leg up before her. Out the window, thick smoke shrouded the wing of the bus. The sky split. Miles beneath them, red and ocher in the sun, gouged with canyons, the mountains spread across their path. A brown river looped through the humps of the ridges.

"What are they made of? Are they solid?"

"Rock," she said. "Like moons." On the far side of the mountains, the funnel-chimneys of smelters sent up plumes of red smoke. The dense air closed around them again. The bus bucked up and down. Beside her head Leno's claws sank into the foam cushion.

Kasuk dropped into the seat next to hers, on the aisle. "This place is mad. Everything curves the wrong way."

The bus danced through a crosswind. Paula ducked under Leno's arm, bending closer to the window. The clouds thinned. Now they were swept away again. The bus soared over the whitened crest of a mountain. A banner of snow blew off the peak.

All around her, the Styths yelled, delighted. Kasuk said, "Does anything live here?"

Paula said, "Insects. Lichens." She put her hand on the window sill. She had forgotten how bright the Earth was.

"What's that white stuff?" Leno pointed.

"Snow." She used the word from the Common Speech. "Frozen water."

He frowned at her. "Frozen water is ice."

"Snow is water that freezes into crystals and falls from the—" She stared at him, startled. There was no Styth word for sky. "From the upper air," she said, lamely.

Kasuk said, "All this is natural? No one made it?"

"The Sun made it," Leno said. "Everything comes from the Sun."

They were flying toward the Western Sea, red with pollution. The shore was encrusted with robot factories. Feathers of thick smoke streamed past the window. Kasuk leaned over her shoulder.

"Can you imagine flying here? This layer is so thin, and I'll bet you couldn't even get a ship into that layer down there." He pointed to the ground.

Behind Leno, Tanuojin said, "Saba has flown over twenty hours in this Planet."

Paula looked up past the Merkhiz Akellar's thick shoulder. "Not in a Styth ship."

"No. Your friend Jefferson is meeting us in New York. We're

staying in that same place we stayed before. That square house with the short beds."

New Haven house was the only place where the Committee could put up eighteen people. She turned to look out the window.

Kasuk said, "Paula. Does anything live here?"

They were flying over the brown scummy water of the sea. Patches of oil-eating weeds made islands below them. She said, "That's alive. There are sharks. Fish, gulls. Snakes." She turned to look between the seats for Tanuojin. Junna had hauled him to a window at the back of the bus. He stood with one hand on his younger son's shoulder, holding him away. She put her nose against the window again, looking for something else to explain to them.

Sybil Jefferson met them at the entry port. When the Styths walked out onto the broad ramp down to the ground, a swarm of people with cameras and recorders rushed to surround them. The three rAkellaron withdrew into the shell of their men. The cameras whirred. Jefferson hurried around threatening and cajoling. Paula went to the rail. No one paid any attention to her. She looked out over the city. The autumn air was bright and crisp, the grass champagne-colored, the wood toward the south sorrel and yellow and earth-brown. She put her hands on the rail. She had forgotten or never realized how life teemed here. Everything below her was moving, every leaf, every stem of grass, the birds and all the people stirring. A woman in a white coat was walking away from the building, off across the grass. Paula straightened. The woman turned a corner and disappeared.

"Mendoza," Jefferson called. "Are you coming?"

Sybil had shooed off the picture men and voicemen from the hourlies. With the Styths she was going down the ramp. Paula followed them.

Jefferson pattered along beside Saba. "You see, Akellar, you're celebrated men."

Paula went to the rail, searching the ground below them for the woman she had just seen. Tanuojin walked beside her, Sybil Jefferson just beyond. Paula reached across him to pluck at Jefferson's sleeve.

"Jefferson, I saw Cam Savenia just now. What's going on?"

"Savenia." Saba stopped where he was. Leno was going on several feet ahead of them, gawking at the city, and did not seem to be listening. Jefferson kept on walking.

"Was it Cam?" Paula said.

"Possibly," the old woman said. "The Council wanted to send her as an observer, but we talked them out of it."

Tanuojin walked in between her and Paula, and his hand dropped onto Paula's shoulder. "Who did they send?" he asked. Paula pulled his hand away.

"Caleb Fisher," Jefferson said.

They were coming to the foot of the ramp. Saba walked on Jefferson's far side. Tanuojin grasped Paula's wrist, his touch cold as metal. She knew who Caleb Fisher was: a Council member for Mars, once a minister, she thought a defense minister. She said, "Is he a member of the Sunlight League?"

"Ask him." Jefferson's lips curled into a stiff smile, but her blue eyes looked angry. "Since you're so full of snappy questions."

They went into the parking lot. Tanuojin and Saba circled off into the dark behind a row of cars and stood talking. Jefferson sorted out the rest of the Styths among three Committee buses. Paula leaned against the door of a yellow three-seater car with the Committee emblem on the roof. Kasuk came over to her.

"Is this where you lived before?"

"Yes." She watched Leno's men line up at the steps to the biggest bus.

"It's beautiful."

"So is Styth," she said.

"But in another way."

Jefferson came around the rear end of the three-seater. "Mendoza, we were trying to ease them gently into the notion of the observer."

"You could have warned me," Paula said. "I'd have known how to act." She touched the arm of the young man beside her. "Jefferson, this is Yekka's prima son, Kasuk."

"Hello," he said. He put his hand out to Jefferson, changed his mind, and drew it back. Jefferson had already reached to shake it. She lowered her hand, but Kasuk, with a Styth's sense of protocol, stuck his out to her again. Finally they connected, Jefferson looking much amused. Kasuk stood head and shoulders over her. He said, in a false voice, "We are all—"

A shout cut him off. Paula slid past him. At the bus Sril faced Leno's towering second-in-command. He pushed the Merkhizit, and the taller man shouted, "You little worm," and jumped on him.

Kasuk took a step toward them. Paula caught his sleeve. Sril and the Merkhizit tumbled over the paved ground, and the other men roared. They rushed out of the bus to watch. Bakan leaped out the door. Midway between the fight and Paula, Junna stood fixed in his tracks. From two directions, Saba and Tanuojin and Leno ran up and scattered the men away.

Jefferson said, "Did I err in the programming?"

"You did," Paula said.

In the midst of the Styths, Saba had Sril by the arm. The small man's face was bleeding. He shouted, "You should have heard what he said about *Ybix*, and after we saved them, too."

Leno turned away. "I'll never hear the end of that." Tanuojin glared at him. "Your crew's got a big mouth."

Kasuk moved again, and Paula tightened her grip on his sleeve. The bus swayed back and forth. Saba was herding the crews of the two ships up the steps. His fists on his hips, Leno thrust his blunt head forward at Tanuojin.

"Don't get me angry, Yekka. I'll cut you into twenty pieces."

"I don't think you can count that high."

Kasuk laughed. Saba came out of the bus and burst between the two men, driving them apart. "Let's get out of here."

Jefferson said. "What was that all about?"

Behind Saba, Tanuojin shot a vicious look at Leno. The Merkhiz Akellar sneered at him. "Nigger eyes." Tanuojin turned his back. Paula let go of his son's shirt.

To Jefferson, she said, "Two pegs trying to fit into the same small hole. Where is R.B.?"

"Sitting under the bodhi tree."

Saba came up to them. "I'm sorry," he told Jefferson. "It won't happen again."

"Is it safe to divide them by family?" Jefferson said.

Paula pulled open the door to the yellow car. "You drive," she said to Saba, and scrambled across the row of seats to the far side.

"When do we meet this Fisher?" Saba asked.

Paula was staring out the window. They had just left the dome behind them for the thick yellow smoke of the open air. The homing beam blinked blue and red on the dashboard in front of Saba.

In the seat beyond him, Jefferson said, "There's a meeting Friday morning. Tomorrow."

"Are you sure it was Dr. Savenia you saw?" the Styth asked, in his language.

Paula shrugged. "She was pretty far away, and her back was to me."

"I'm not sitting down with anybody from the Sunlight League."

The air outside was so dense it turned the window into a mirror. She twisted around in the seat to face him. "Why? And why do you automatically assume Sybil doesn't speak Styth? And that this car isn't wired? She does It is."

He glanced at Jefferson. The old woman picked up her handbag, popped it open, and rummaged in it. Paula said, in the Common Speech, "I don't suppose you've given us separate rooms?"

"There isn't enough space." Jefferson fed herself a mint. "Unless you'd take the closet. With the queens and skeletons?"

"I could be bounded in a nutshell. But I think I'd like a window. Where's the meeting?"

"At our New York office. I was looking forward to seeing your child again."

"The last time we brought him it was a disaster."

"Such a charming little boy. He reminded me of you."

"He isn't little any more." They were talking past Saba, and she could not see much of Jefferson at all. She crooked one leg under her. Surrounded by the opaque yellow mist, the car seemed to hang still in the air. Saba reached forward under the steering grips and turned down the heat.

"Children do grow up," Jefferson said. "After all, it's been ten years since you left. Ten years would change anybody." The old woman sucked her candy, her soft white cheek hollowed. "Is he a Styth or an anarchist?"

Paula's hand rose to her face. Sybil was no longer talking about David. "Neither."

"In between?"

"Neither." She glanced at Saba's profile. "He doesn't listen to anybody but himself."

"That's reasonable," Jefferson said. She ripped the paper away from the roll of mints. "Have a sweet?"

"No, thanks."

"Akellar?"

Saba's gaze slid toward Paula. "Sure," he said. He reached for a candy.

Caleb Fisher was short and slight, his sparse hair combed across his dome of waxy head. His mustache hid his upper lip. To Paula's surprise, all three Styths shook hands with him. Afterward Fisher looked as if he wanted to wipe his fingers off. They sat around the long table in the Committee meeting room, with Jefferson at the end and Michalski in the corner taking notes. Dick Bunker was not there. Paula had not seen him since their arrival on the Planet. She knew he was watching.

Jefferson said, "We've been very satisfied with the Mendoza Treaty. It's worth noting that there wasn't a single violation of the truce in the whole ten years, not by either side."

Fisher's little gray toothbrush mustache quivered. Paula watched him through the tail of her eye. In a salesman's voice, Jefferson was recounting all the virtues of the Mendoza Treaty. Paula guessed Jefferson had been caught out on a thin branch, to have Fisher forced on her. Paula was willing to let them make her out the hero. Now Fisher was leaning across the table.

"Miss Jefferson, I have to insert one small comment."

Paula raised her head. "I thought you were an observer."

"I am."

"Then observe, and keep the comment in back."

In the big chair on her right, Saba put his hand out to quiet her. Fisher's mustache jerked up like a curtain from his little teeth. "This negotiation is in the interests of the Council. I am here for the Council." He straightened up, looking at Saba. "Maybe there have been no technical violations of the truce, but the past ten years, the years of this much-acclaimed Mendoza Treaty, have been the bloodiest between the Styths and the Middle Planets in centuries. Only fifteen months ago there was an awful raid against a Martian colony in the Asteroids—civilians, women and children—carried off into an unspeakable life of slavery."

"I have no treaty with the Martians," Saba said.

"We have a right to insist on minimum standards of human decency."

Paula shoved her chair back and walked away across the room. There were no windows; book racks like honeycombs covered the walls. At the closet door, she tried the latch. It was locked. Saba said, "What's your minimum standard for murder?" His voice had a short-tempered edge. In the next chair Tanuojin sat picking at his claws, his eyes on his hands. Around the corner of the table from Jefferson, Leno looked bored: their observer. He could barely speak the Common Speech.

Fisher said, "I beg your pardon."

"I'm talking about the Sunlight League," Saba said.

"The Sunlight League?"

"Sure." Saba's hand struck the table. "It's too bad we didn't bring some pieces of the man you sent to murder me."

"We are not responsible for the actions of private citizens."

The air smelled bitter. Behind the Styths, Paula watched Tanuojin's long hands flex. Jefferson was scratching her throat, her pale eyes on Fisher.

The Martian said, starchy, "We will not accept a new treaty that does not settle the issue of slavery. That's absolutely fundamental."

"I'm not treating with you," Saba said. "I'm treating with her." His hand jerked toward Jefferson. While he talked his hand moved every few words in clipped gestures.

"You're treating with the Council," Fisher said.

"I wouldn't lower myself."

"That's enough," Jefferson said.

Fisher snapped up onto his feet. "I will not—"

"Fisher."

He turned toward her; the strings showed in his neck. "I—"

"Fisher," Jefferson said, "sit down."

Meekly Fisher took his place again. The old woman said, "In the interests of progress, suppose we all go and have lunch, and when we come back this afternoon try to talk like people with wits and objectives and not like little boys in a sandpile."

Fisher was still watching her, and when she stood he stood. Paula went back to her chair for her jacket. Around her the Styths' chairs growled and the big men got to their feet. Jefferson, busy with her purse and her candy and scarf, her eyes lowered, was giving no opening for conversation. She headed for the door.

"Don't touch me," Fisher snarled.

Paula looked up. Tanuojin was moving away from him.

Saba went out the door. The rest of the Styths followed him. Leno and Tanuojin reached the door simultaneously and bristled at each other. After a moment Tanuojin let Saba's cadet go first. They went down past Paula's old office to the way out into the park. Paula squeezed between Tanuojin and the wall.

"What did you find out from Fisher?"

His shoulders moved. "Nothing." He stretched his legs and went ahead of her out the door to the gulley.

When Paula went back into the building, she found Jefferson in her office, her fingers going like hammers over her typewriter. The bare white walls of the office were stained in streaks, like watermarks. The only thing hanging on them was a long calendar behind the desk. Jefferson looked up from her work.

"Oh. Mendoza. I thought you were Michalski and my diet biscuit." The old woman rolled her chair away from the typewriter. "Sit down. Have you eaten?"

"We just had lunch."

Paula sat down sideways in a straight chair. She took her jacket off and draped it over the back. Jefferson said, "Where are your companions?"

"Out in the park cooling off. This will never get us any place as long as Fisher is there."

"Caleb Fisher is no problem."

"Not to you, maybe. What did he do, murder his mother and bury her in your backyard?"

Jefferson daubed at her bad eye. Her hair was mushroom-white. She looked old. The door opened for Michalski carrying a cup of coffee on a little tray, which he put on Jefferson's desk. A white plastic heat-folder steamed beside the cup.

"Mendoza," he said. "You've really gotten bad-tempered. There's a message for you on the board in the waiting room." He went out. Jefferson was tearing open the heat-folder. A hot biscuit rolled out onto the tray.

"I'm on a diet." She nodded at the biscuit. "Now they say my heart will have to be replaced. They're turning me into a robot piece by piece. We won't get anywhere unless the Styths are reasonable."

"They're reasonable," Paula said. "As long as it profits them."

"What do they want?"

"Everything. You might as well give it to them, it will make them easier to handle."

Jefferson chuckled. She broke the biscuit in half and scattered crumbs across the desktop. "You like to talk in code, Mendoza. Rather like a Styth. I don't entirely accept your proposition that you're a new kind of creature." She ate a mouthful of biscuit, burped, and patted her chest. "All this shooting at people does have to stop."

Paula hung her arm over the back of the chair. "We need a universal truce."

"The only people we're having any difficulty with are your clients, dear girl."

"Right. So we will arrange a universal truce, and let Saba enforce it."

Jefferson munched her biscuit. Her bad eye was tearing. Slowly her head began to nod. "Ingenious. I like that, Mendoza. Have you discussed it with them?"

"In a manner of speaking." Certainly Tanuojin knew. He and Saba had been happy to see her off to this meeting; they wanted to talk alone.

"You gave me to think you want something for yourself."

"I'd like to be recognized."

"In what form?"

"I'm the only link you have with the Styths. I'll stay that. Keep Bunker out of Styth, and stop trying to make contacts behind my back."

"Have some coffee." Jefferson reached for her cup.

"No, thanks."

"What about the Styths? Do they recognize you?"

"I'll need your help."

"How?"

Paula said, "We'll get to that." She looked around the stained walls of the room, thinking of Bunker again. "I want rank. My own means and place to live, free of either of them. The right to have my son inherit from me." She felt Bunker hiding somewhere, watching.

Michalski came in again, saying, "Jefferson, two-thirty." He popped out without pausing. Paula stood, picking up her jacket.

"You're busy, I guess."

"My dear, you can't know. Is there anything else?"

"Give me a listening device. Just an ear, not a transmitter. Something I can hide in Saba's clothes."

Jefferson opened a drawer in her desk and took out a three-inch plug like a large book plug. She pulled a wire out of the top. "This will stick to any metal surface." She pushed the wire back into the plug. "Turn to zero to erase and to ten to play."

"Thanks." Paula took it. The white band around the plug was marked with numbers. "I'll see you in half an hour." The afternoon meeting started at three.

That session was a repeat of the morning's, except that Saba walked out. Tanuojin followed him, and Leno unfolded his arms and uncrossed his legs and stood.

"Is there some reason we're here?"

Fisher gave Paula a sullen, furious look. "You whore," he said, in a low voice. His gray mustache bristled, and he stalked out the door. Leno looked down at her.

"He sounds like Machou."

Paula followed him into the hall. Fisher was disappearing into the waiting room midway along it. "Merkhiz, you know all the right words." Michalski had said something about a message. She went down to the waiting room, where Fisher stood among his aides, having his coat put on and his papercase handed to him.

The message board was just inside the threshold on the wall.

> Paula: if you ever come back, I'm living in the Nikoles
> Building, Room 68, Green Wing. An Chu.

She took the slip of paper off the board and put it in her pocket.

The Styths had gone back to the air cars. Just as she joined them, Leno took off in the two-seater, his second-in-command in the passenger seat. The car hovered overhead a moment and swooped off toward the wall of the dome. The sun was setting and the domelight was coming on. Saba leaned against the door of the yellow Dutch car.

"Why did you leave?" she asked him.

"I'm getting a headache."

"Do you want me to drive?"

Tanuojin came around the car to her. "I'll drive."

They got into the car, Tanuojin in the middle seat, and started toward the East Lock. Below them the lights of buildings glowed through the trees. The heat was off and she began to shiver and reached behind the seat for a car blanket. Saba pressed his hands to his face.

"Can't you help him?" she asked Tanuojin.

"Not while I'm flying." He turned to Saba on his other side. "Shall I stop?"

"I'll be all right." The big man moved in the cramped seat, his legs bent into the space under the dash. "Is there any place you want to go while we're here, Paula? Anybody you want to see?"

She shook her head. She would see An Chu later and look for Tony. They were coming to the lock. The orange light was flashing; somebody was in the shaft ahead of them, perhaps Leno.

"What about your father?"

"My father is dead. Are you trying to get me out of the way?"

"Isn't that nigger-mean," Tanuojin said. He turned to Saba. "Do you know her father killed himself?"

She stared out the window, angry. Saba said, "No." His voice was taut. Beyond the window the clear wall of the lock was glowing intensely blue. White arrows flashed in the glare. Tanuojin bumped twice going through the dogleg. Saba winced at the second light contact with the wall.

"Watch where you're going."

"Let me drive," she said to Tanuojin, "and you can help him."

"No," they said, in unison.

They flew through the smoky night. A light rain began to fall and Tanuojin turned the blowers on. The lights on the roof of the car shone white on the cottony mist. Saba doubled over, his head in his hands. His breath whistled in his throat. Paula's muscles were kinked with tension. She made herself relax. Tanuojin shook his head. She frowned at him.

"What's the matter?"

"My head hurts. Can I land here?"

"Yes." She bent down and felt along the floor for the switch. The lights on the skids came on. Through the spy window in the floor she could see the ground.

He set the car down on a flat mud plain in the slagheaps. The barren blades of hills stood around them. The rain fell steadily. The ground under them was firm and they had a full pack of oxygen. Paula switched the lights off.

"We can stay here awhile. A couple of hours."

Neither of them spoke. She looked out the window. The rain tapped on the roof over her head. She did not want to think about her father. She had been thirteen when he died. The rain sluiced down the windows, heavier than before, and she looked at the skids to make sure the ground wasn't washing away under them. She thought of the listening device in her pocket. The two men with her were as close to her as brothers, but she could not trust them. She had trusted her father. Lonely, she stared out the window. Tanuojin pushed her.

"It's getting worse. Take us back."

She changed places with him and drove them back to New Haven.

The wire was sticky. She laid the belt across the top of the chest of drawers, in front of the mirror. In it she could see Saba still asleep in the bed behind her. The windows were heavily shaded. The wire was invisible in this light. She pressed it under the rolled edge of the buckle.

She went out to walk in the wood and got lost. Dark came. She found the stream and followed it through thick trees and brush, but it seemed to take her nowhere familiar. Thrashing her way through a thicket she came up against three strands of wire. She stopped, breathing hard. Ahead of her lay an open field, pale blue in the domelight, that sloped up on her right into an arm of the birch wood. The stream shone through the trees below her. In the distance was a group of buildings she recognized: Halstead's. Relieved, she climbed through the wire and crossed the field toward the roadhouse.

Both the Committee cars were parked on the roof. She went in the ground door. Although it was a weekend night, the long L-shaped room was half-empty. Farmers took no days off. Kasuk sat at a front table playing Go with an old man in bib overalls. Two or three other Styths drank among the dozen people at the bar. She went over to watch Kasuk play, but just as she reached the table the old man stood up.

"I quit. I know when I'm beaten." He wore no shirt. His shoulders ended in knobs, his beard hung in thick yellow twists like yarn. "What will it be?"

"Another beer," Kasuk said. He saw Paula and got to his feet, eager. "Hello. Will you play?"

The old man went to the bar. She shook her head. "No, I want to go home. Did you come down here alone?"

"My uncle is here someplace." He scanned the room. "So is my brother. I wonder where they went."

Paula was picking burrs and foxtails out of her clothes and her hair. "Well, drive me home, and then you can bring the car back."

"My uncle has the key."

The old man returned with three liter steins of beer. Paula tried to pay him for hers but he refused the money. They sat at the wooden table drinking while Kasuk swept the Go pebbles into the box and shook them through the sorting screen.

"Play with me," he said to her.

"I'm tired. I've been out lost in the wood for five hours." She licked beer foam off her upper lip. "Where is Tanuojin?"

"Back at the house."

She raised the stein and drank a long swallow of the beer. Kasuk folded the grid. Her curiosity was sparked. Kasuk was telling her a lie. Tanuojin would never allow his sheltered younger son to go off to a drinking dock; therefore Tanuojin was gone.

Kasuk was staring over her head toward the door, and she twisted around on the bench to see. A girl in a brick-colored jacket slipped into the half-lit room and crossed it to the bar. Kasuk said, "That's the woman my uncle was talking to."

The old man put his stein down. "One more game, sonny?"

"Sure."

Paula gulped the rest of her beer. "If Saba comes in again, hold him for me." She went out the front door to the yard, spread with the pale blue light. Around the three buildings of the Halstead complex the grass was clipped short, but a hundred feet away the high straw sprang up, crackling dry. She walked slowly out past the barn and the guesthouse. The wind was cold. On the high ground behind the bar, she came on Saba, Junna, and two girls sitting on the ground passing a little bone pipe around.

"I thought I saw you go in," Saba said. "Where have you been?" He was not wearing the belt with the wire; he was not even wearing a shirt.

"I forgot that it gets dark here." She sat down beside him. The girls were much nearer Junna's age than Saba's. One handed her the pipe. "Which car did you bring?" Relieved, she saw the rest of his clothes on the ground beside him.

"The three-seat."

"Give me the keys," she said, "so Kasuk can drive me home." She sucked on the pipe. The fire was out. She passed the pipe to Junna.

"I'll take you." Saba got up, stooping for his shirt and belt.

One girl had struck a match. Junna bent to light the hashish. His heavy hair hung over his shoulders. The two girls were watching him, solemn. Their youth made them all similar. Saba went off through the high grass, slinging his belt around his waist. Paula ran to catch up with him.

"Uncle Saba," Junna shouted, and Saba wheeled; he kept walking, backward now. Junna cried, "Will you come get us?"

"Walk," Saba shouted.

"Hey!"

Saba laughed. He turned front again. Paula jammed her hands in her pockets. She wished she knew where Tanuojin was. There was a ladder up the side of the tavern, and she went around the corner of the building to it.

"I take it you feel better?"

He climbed up the ladder after her to the parking lot on the roof. "I feel top."

The yellow Dutch car was parked in the center of the roof. The door was locked. She watched him try the keys; he was in a very high mood, and she guessed he had smoked a lot of the bhang.

"Where is Tanuojin, while you're out educating his sucklings?"

"He took one of the other cars out."

It was a bad lie, since she could see the only other car available to him from where she stood. He swung the door up and she slid across the three seats to the far side. Saba got in next to her, behind the steering grips.

"You never told me your father killed himself."

"No, I never did."

"How did he do it?"

Slumped in the seat, she put her head back and looked out the clear roof. He started the car. They rose in a looping spiral into the air.

"Are you cold?" he said.

"I'm hungry."

"Why did your father kill himself?"

"Oh, Christ. He left me a letter. I kept it for years, I finally burned it. He said he was afraid of losing his mind. He was afraid of being helpless. He left the dome, and the pollution killed him. I wish Tanuojin had kept quiet about it. I didn't know he knew."

"How old were you?"

"Junna's age."

The car was settling down over the tops of trees. She sat up, thinking about what she could have to eat. She put her father and his flight out of her mind. He landed the car and they went into the darkened kitchen, smelling of roast pork.

"Give me something to eat." He sat down at the table and propped his feet on the other chair. "It must have been hard for you, what your father did."

She opened the cold drawer and took out a sack of milk, a bowl of apples, and a cheese. "Don't be fatuous."

"I'm making a point."

She put the food down on the table between them. He straightened to reach the apples, taking his feet off the chair, and she sat. The room was too dark for her to see his face. He said, "I've been thinking about this all watch. He was an intelligent man, your father, you've told me that, but being intelligent didn't save him, or you. That's what drove him crazy."

"He wasn't really crazy."

He drank milk. The domelight threw an elongated reproduction of the window onto the floor.

"There's only one thing in life," he said. "To do whatever comes to you as well as you can. That's what honor is, the perfect image, the ideal life. Anarchists have no sense of honor. That's why they can kill themselves like that."

She ate cheese. "Your father was murdered."

"He didn't desert me. Your father abandoned you."

The hallway door creaked, and Leno came in, his feet scraping on the floor. He and Saba made half-worded noises at each other. Paula reached for the sack of milk. Everybody with any intelligence sometimes was afraid of going crazy. Leno took another piece of cheese and a loaf of bread and went out the back door into the yard.

"My father did not desert me."

"Maybe it doesn't look like that to you, but that's what I'm getting to. These people here can live like this, without wars and feuds and governments, because they give up the most important things in life. There are debts people owe each other out of the fact of nature. Just common humanity. The anarchists refuse them. They're not real people, they're just shells of people."

She poured milk into a glass. She was the only anarchist he knew well.

"You have to make a choice," he said. "Actually you made it a long while ago but you have to face it now."

"What are you talking about?"

"Jefferson and the Committee have never done anything for you. You and I and Tanuojin, we belong to each other. Fate, Karma, whatever you want to call it, something brought us all together because we need each other."

"What if I call it chance?"

"Nothing happens by chance."

She wiped her mouth on her hand. "Everything is by chance. The readiness is all." He gave an exasperated shake of his head. She took an apple out of the bowl in the middle of the table. What he had said burned in her mind and made her angry. He was always trying to steer her into something. She took another apple and left her chair.

"I'm going to bed."

"Stay here and keep me company," he said.

"Go find Tanuojin," she said. "Talk to him." She went down the hallway to the stairs.

. . .

She woke late Sunday afternoon. Saba lay asleep beside her, naked. She found his belt and pried the wire loose and went down to the kitchen, where she had hidden the plug half of the device.

The recording was flawless. The voices were precise and there was no background noise at all. Sitting in the meadow, she listened to Saba collect his nephews to go to the roadhouse.

"Where's Paula?"

"I don't know," Kasuk said. "I haven't seen her. Do you suppose she's all right?"

"If you do see her, remember, she isn't to know about Tanuojin."

Then he had already left, before she put the wire on Saba's belt. She tore up a handful of dry grass. The cook's old white cat was creeping around the side of the barn. The daws shrieked and fought in the spread branches of the elm tree. She listened to Saba and a strange girl pick each other up at Halstead's. They hardly spoke; they never even exchanged names. It was the girl who suggested they go outside. Hollow people. Another strange female voice said, "Want to smoke some hash?"

"Sure," Saba said.

Junna said, in a whisper, "My father will find out."

"Do you want to look like a baby to those girls?"

She listened to him talk about the debt owed to common humanity. Lying down in the grass, she spread herself out to the late sun. The birds scrapped in the elm tree. On the far side of the house someone shouted. She thought about David. She could call him on the Committee's photo-relay. He would like that, a message all the way from the Earth just for him. The tone of the birds' racket changed. She raised her head. Tanuojin was walking under the tree toward the back door.

Sitting up, she scanned the last few centimeters of the wire and put it through the plug to erase it. He vanished into the house. She went after him, left the plug in a kitchen drawer, and caught up with him on the stairs.

"Where have you been?" Carefully she stayed out of his reach.

He was fighting the will to yawn. His eyelids drooped half-closed. "I got lost in the trees." At the top of the stairs he turned left to his room and she went right, to go back to Saba and replace the wire on his belt.

Paula sat sideways in her chair, cleaning her fingernails with a toothpick. She had stopped listening to Fisher a long time before. He had brought two other Martians with him and the room was stuffy from too many people. Beside her, Tanuojin pulled himself up straight in his chair and slung his right leg over his left, jittery in the close quarters.

"I keep telling you," Saba said to Fisher. "I'm not here to talk to you. I'm here to talk to her." He nodded toward Jefferson. "Now, you can shut—"

Fisher's nostrils flared, yellowish. He turned to the old woman at the end of the table. "Do I have to put up with this?"

Saba said, "Shut your mouth, or we will talk where you can't hear us, and you won't know anything." The big Styth's hands thumped the arms of his chair. He wagged his head at Paula. "She does my advance work. If you want some arrangements with me, talk to her."

The Martian stood up straight off his chair. "You insufferable, arrogant barbarian." His aides ranked themselves behind him. "I demand an apology."

"I don't apologize to niggers," Saba said, and Fisher started for the door.

"Wait." Tanuojin caught his arm. Fisher's eyes glittered. In a sweeping gesture he threw off Tanuojin's hand and rushed out the door. His aides followed him.

Leno grunted. "I don't understand any of this."

Paula dropped the toothpick on the scarred top of the table. She looked behind her at the closet. Jefferson took out her false eye and wiped it on a cloth.

"Officially, we are supposed to be negotiating for the Council."

Saba put his hands behind his head. "I can't see why we should maintain your fictions." Tanuojin sauntered around the edge of the room. Leno had started up, thinking the meeting was over, but now he settled down again.

"I can see how you would consider it a fiction," Jefferson said. The eyelid fluttered over her empty socket. Tanuojin had wandered around behind her. "We need some organization, and at present the Council serves. Don't touch me, Yekka."

Tanuojin's long face narrowed. He came slowly past her toward Paula. Saba said, "You can't be our friend and the Martians'."

"I am nobody's *friend*." Jefferson slipped the eye back into her face. "I am certainly not your *friend*."

Paula planted her elbows on the arms of her chair. "He means ally. Don't get caught on semantics."

"I'll avoid it. You may lord it over Fisher, Akellar, but you still are only representative of part of the Empire—one small part."

"The rest of them will follow me. Most of them. Just as they did with the crystal trade."

Tanuojin stood behind Paula's chair. His cold fingers moved down her cheek to her throat. The touch of his claws sent a shudder through her. Saba and Jefferson discussed his influence in the Empire.

The old woman was well informed, and a master of such talk: she had him on the defensive within moments. Paula leaned forward, away from Tanuojin's hand.

"Jefferson, stay on the line, will you? It's to your advantage to make him look like the Emperor."

"To maintain your fictions?"

"Life follows art."

Jefferson laughed. Leno was staring at the wall, his face slack with boredom. Saba said, "You have Fisher in your sleeve. You can control what the Council hears about this." He gave Leno an oblique look. "We'll keep up your face in front of Fisher and talk behind him." He pushed his chair back. Leno jumped out of a doze. "Tomorrow."

Jefferson said, "As you wish, Akellar." Her voice was velvet. Everybody stood.

Paula went out to the hall, and Tanuojin came after her. "What did you tell her about me?" He smacked her between the shoulder blades.

"Nothing. She guessed from the way you've been pawing Fisher. What's going on?"

"You really think you can play her against us?"

She looked behind them. Saba was coming after them down the hall, giving Leno an edited version of the talk with Jefferson. Tanuojin went ahead of her out the door. She put her jacket on.

"They are my children," Tanuojin said. "I'm sick of the way you meddle with my children."

"Tut tut tut," Saba said.

"Junna is still a little boy! The next he'll be taking morphion—" His voice rose, and Paula took the tape plug out of her ear and turned the volume down. She put her feet up on the frayed arm of the couch. None of the Styths was awake yet. A flat blade of sunlight pierced the curtained window opposite her, yellow with dust motes. In her ear Tanuojin and Saba differed sharply about Junna. She picked at the threads on the worn couch cover.

"You and Paula, you both take your crumbs so seriously."

"You're such a hypocrite."

She heard her conversation with them in the car going down to New York, and the meeting with Jefferson and Fisher. Something was missing. She had expected to hear something between them when Tanuojin got back from wherever he had gone. Glumly she realized they had talked about that before Saba put his clothes on.

"We're just trying to get rid of the pinch-faced Martian," Saba told Leno.

The time meter on the wall read ten minutes to noon. At four they were due in New York again. Stacks of bound hourlies cluttered the floor. She sat up and rested her feet on a bundle. In her ear the plug played back the maddening small talk of the trip from New York to New Haven. Maybe she should wire Tanuojin. Plant a homing device on him in case he went somewhere else. That was desperate. She wondered what they would do when they found out she was spying on them.

"What about Fisher?" Saba said. "Did you reach him?"

"When he's angry he's clear as water. He saw Savenia over the rest-days, it's all set up. I'd love to know how much the old woman knows."

"Paula must have told her not to let you touch her."

"No. She figured that out for herself. Or Bunker told her."

"Does Paula know? About the coup."

She went taut as a wire. Tanuojin said, "No. Not yet."

"I don't like treating her as an enemy."

"Part of her is everybody's enemy. You heard her tell Jefferson that she's only interested in what she can get for herself. The bitch. After all we've done for her."

"I also heard her call me the Emperor."

"That's how she sells it to you. It sounds a little different when she's talking to Jefferson."

"Naturally. Did you check on *Ybicsa*?"

"Saba, we can't go back and forth every watch between here and the ship. I hid her in a ditch. Nobody will find her. The League is planning to spring the coup the day we leave. They'll arrest the Committee first, and then they'll take us. All we have to do is let them destroy the Committee, and then we step in and save the Earth from the Martians. What could be simpler?"

She yanked the plug out of her ear. Everything fitted. She should have made sense of it before, when Saba was telling her she had to choose.

She sat down on the couch and made herself think about what she would do. There seemed very little choice. The League probably thought they could pull off their plot without enlarging it into a war, and Tanuojin thought he could contain everything in a counterplot. There was too much involved, too many rearrangements, too many people. The coup would spread like bursting atoms. It would stop only when it had brought everything else in the system into a balance with itself. She went down the hall to the library, where the videone was, and called the Committee office in New York.

Jefferson took a long time to answer; or Paula imagined that she did. Paula stood over the cabinet banging her fingers on the screen. The red and white holding pattern on the videone screen split apart to show her Jefferson's face, tinged green.

"Yes, Mendoza. I—"

"I can't chat," Paula said. "The Sunlight League is mounting a coup against the Committee and the Styths. Saba and Tanuojin know about it and intend to use it to wipe you out and grab the Earth."

Jefferson's eyes popped round as a Styth's. "The League. Who?" She leaned forward into the screen, and the green color increased in her cheeks: she looked dead. "Fisher and Savenia?"

"I don't know anything more," Paula said. "I'm going up to talk to them—they can help you if they want to."

"Mendoza, wait."

She went out to the hall and up the stairs. The house was quiet enough that she could hear the whisper of the upstairs hall curtains billowing over the open windows. The bed in her room was empty. She went back around the corner to Tanuojin's room.

They were both there, Tanuojin before the closet putting his shirt on, and Saba lying on his back across the bed. She threw the tape plug at him. "You have one hell of a gall talking about honor." She slammed the door.

Saba caught the tape. He sat up on the bed. Tanuojin was staring at her with an intent look on his face. She turned on his weakness: Saba. "You pirate. You're no better than your father. You're a cheap, sleazy politician, just like Machou."

"Don't listen to her." Tanuojin reached his lyo in one long stride. Saba put the tape into his ear.

"Has she told anybody else?"

Paula looked beyond him at Tanuojin. "If this is all you can do with your mind, you should do it for money in a carnival."

His heat flared. He pulled back one arm to hit her, and Saba caught him. There was a knock on the door. Paula backed away from the bed. Her head was pounding as if she were feverish.

"What is it?" Saba shouted.

Sril answered him through the door. "Akellar, that fat old woman is on the box downstairs."

"Jefferson," Paula said. "Who I told. Talking about choices. What are you going to do?"

Saba still sat on the bed; he looked back over his shoulder at Tanuojin, and she saw in their faces that their minds were set. She started toward the door.

"You can do it without me."

Saba grabbed her arm. "They'll kill you." He pulled her around bodily and pushed her toward Tanuojin. "Send her back to the ship."

"Akellar," Sril called.

"I'm coming!" He thrust her into Tanuojin's grasp and went out the door.

Tanuojin twisted her arm up behind her back and hoisted her over to the unmade bed. "I brought something for you all the way from Yekka, in case this happened." He let go of her, and she took her throbbing wrist in the other hand. He swung a straight chair down in front of her. In his other hand was a plastic hand-yoke.

"Tanuojin, don't do it. You'll lose everything. You can't manage a war."

He pulled her arms through the slats in the back of the chair. "I'm not doing anything. It's nigger eating nigger, just like in the books." He snapped the yoke onto her wrists.

"Ouch." The inside edges of the yoke were knife-sharp. The tight fit pinched her.

"Bleed." He went out. The door shut. She heard the key turn in the lock.

She put her head against the back of the chair before her. In the hall, Sril called some question. Her wrists throbbed in the yoke. She straightened, lifted the chair up on her forearms, and carried it over to the window.

From here she could see the backyard, the barn, and the meadow. The Dutch car was parked beneath the window. The bonnet was tilted up, and Leno bent over the engine. Kasuk walked across the meadow. Her wrists were numb. There was a springtab in the side of the yoke. Her fingers would not reach it, and when she pressed it against the wall, the knife edges of the yoke slit her skin. She cocked her arms up and bit the tab, without result.

Saba spoke in the hall. She turned toward the sound of his voice. No one came in. She took the chair once around the room. The sunlight streamed in the window and stretched across the floor. Leno was still working in the car's engine. The yoke cut into her wrists. If she broke the back of the chair she could at least free herself of that. She laid the chair down on its side, one end against the bedframe, put her foot on the middle slat, and kicked it out.

Her numbed arms pulsed, swelling up fat, and she sat down a moment to get her breath. A man laughed in the hall outside her door. She stood up again, holding her arms out carefully to balance the yoke. Below the window, Leno slammed the bonnet down on the car. Grease covered his hands. The cook's white cat was trotting across the meadow toward the trees. A daw flew at it, shrieking, and the cat broke into a gallop. The bird harassed it into the trees.

The door opened behind her. Tanuojin circled the foot of the bed toward her. He kicked the broken chair aside.

"You could get out of anything."

She stood with her back to the window. The late sun hit his chest. He said, "Saba has Jefferson half-convinced you misunderstood us. I want you to tell her you did."

She shook her head. "It's a mistake."

"It isn't a mistake. Listen to me. You call yourself an anarchist." His hand shot toward her into the sunlight, palm up, his claws like hooks. "Then when you come to the crunch you get stuck on some damn rule about being peaceful. This is where we take it all. Are you going to let some idiot weakness about a little bloodshed keep you out of it?"

"What do you know?"

He shouted at her, "I know I need you and you're letting me down."

"For my own reasons." Her fists were clenched. Her wrists hurt. Her whole body shivered with anger. "I'm doing what I want, not what you want, not anybody else—"

"Because you're a coward."

"Who is a coward? Why do you do everything you do, your whole life, everything—because you're afraid— Hit me." She watched his hand cock back. "Go on, big man, show it off. You're down on your knees to that Empire, and I'm not, so you have to beat me down to your level."

She was watching his hand, expecting him to hit her, and to her surprise he lowered it. He said, "One last time, Paula. Join us."

She turned back to the window and looked out. Her arms hurt. She felt his presence like a pressure against her. Finally he went off around the bed toward the door. Halfway there he stopped.

"You'll beg me to take you back, Paula. When this is over."

She ignored him, and he left. She went once more around the little room. Everything was over, her whole life for nothing. He might revenge himself on David. Saba would protect his son. Dark was coming. The colors faded out of the room. Her eyes strained in an ashen darkness. The Styths' world. She had to get away, she could not live with them any more. The floor rippled under her feet. A wave of heat struck her and carried her into the wall.

A sheet of light blasted her eyes. She dragged herself back to conscicusness. She was lying face down on a burning floor. Flames crept toward her along the seams of the floor. Her lip was burned when it had touched the wood.

She pushed herself up on her hands and knees. The walls were burning, and the bed. No use trying the door. She staggered up and went to the window. The curtains burst into flames. The heat made her eyes itch. When she touched the window frame her hands shrank from the heat. The bedtable was beside her, with its lamp and clock. She swept them off the tabletop and picked it up and threw it into the window. The glass burst outward. The curtains had burned to nothing in an instant. She put her head out the opening in the window.

It was Saba's voice. "Paula! Jump! Hurry!"

Her dazzled eyes could not find him in the dark below her. She put her feet up on the window sill, flinching from the heat, and launched herself into the outside air. He caught her.

The cool air bathed her face. She turned her head away from the fire, still uncomfortably close. Saba took the yoke off her wrists. Somebody was screaming.

"What happened?" Kasuk said, behind her. "Where's my father?"

"Somebody just bombed the house," Saba said. "I haven't made up my mind if it was the Committee or the Sunlight League."

"Where is Tanuojin?"

"In the barn. There's seventy bricks of fuel in there. Go help him."

The young man raced off. Paula raised her arms, scored and welted from the yoke. The fire crackled in her ears. Saba knelt beside her.

"Was it the Committee?"

She shook her head. The whole house roared with the fire; its rippling orange light brightened the meadow back to the trees. She stood. Leno ran up, his arms pumping.

"We have all the ships safe. And the fuel. The shed is burning now, that's a hot fire."

"We have to call *Ybix* and *Ebelos*. My scout's parked in the desert. We can meet the big ships halfway here. You and I and Tanuojin."

Leno stuck his hands on his hips. "I'm not leaving my crew here."

"We can pick them up in a watch and a half. Leno, we have to get off the Planet. If they catch any of the three of us, no one has a chance."

Paula stood watching the house burn. Her face was tender. In a stream four or five men raced around the edge of the heat ball. Sril led them.

"Mendoz'. Somebody said you were in there when it blew up." He turned toward Saba. "Akellar, *Ybix* is all here and sound."

"They got the cook and the cat." Saba swung around. "Kasuk!" His hand closed on her wrist. She gritted her teeth. Her torn skin stung at his touch. Kasuk came up, smelling of smoke.

"You take care of her," Saba told him.

"Yes, Saba."

Saba went off through his men. He was gone in a moment. She

backed away from the heat of the fire. The Styths' faces glistened in its light.

"Come on," Kasuk said softly. "This is dangerous, standing around here. Junna!" He touched her shoulder, and she went obediently out of the crowd, into the dark, the two young men flanking her.

"Do you know where to meet *Ybix*?" she asked.

Kasuk glanced behind them. They reached the wood. The flickering light from the fire poked its long fingers ahead of them among the trees.

"I know one thing, which is not to stay around here."

Junna said, "Where did Gemini go?"

"To *Ybix*. Tanuojin brought *Ybicsa* down on the Sun Day."

A web broke against her face. She scrambled down a short rocky slope through a screen of brush. The roar of the fire dimmed away. Now she heard the soft, particular voices of the crickets and birds around her. Her eyes ached.

"It's so open," Junna said. "I feel so left open here."

Behind them another thud of an explosion bumped in the air. There was a clatter of sharper noise. Kasuk caught her arm.

"Guns. We need someplace to hide."

A hot Styth cheer went up, bloodthirsty. Junna cried, "They're fighting!" He started back through the trees.

Kasuk pulled her into the curve of his left arm and got his brother by his right. "They're asking to be killed. We have to hide. Paula, where can we hide?"

She wiped her scalded face. Cold and dark: a cave. "Halstead's. The Underground." She had no idea how to find the roadhouse on the ground.

"Kak," Junna said. "They're fighting back there. I'm going back."

"Listen to me," Kasuk said. His voice was intense. "Papa told me to watch you. He's gone now, he's a thousand miles away. If you're hurt, he can't heal you, you might die." He pushed his brother ahead of them into the wood.

They went on through the trees. She could not keep up with them at a walk. When they reached the edge of the wood and came out to a cornfield, the two Styths broke into a trot. They ran through the stubble of the corn. When she fell behind, Kasuk came back for her.

"Run." He took her arm and half-carried her along. They jumped a narrow stream at the edge of the field and ran down a steep open slope.

An air car was coming toward them, its white running lights flashing. Kasuk plowed to a stop. He pushed her away and disappeared into the dark.

"Junna!"

She stood still, panting. The air car was circling toward her. A blinding light glared in her face. A voice shouted down at her.

"Stay where you are! Put your hands over your head!"

A long shape burst up from the ground and caught the air car's rear skid. The light reeled off away from her. A gun clattered. Paula took two steps back. The car lurched over, Junna clinging to the skid. The light wheeled in a circle. Kasuk jumped out of the dark. He met the car in mid-air and brought it down nose-first. He tore open the cab door. The gun rattled again. It sounded like a toy. Junna stood beside her, his chest beating in and out. Kasuk came toward them.

"They look like Martians to me. They have uniforms on."

They went down the field. At the edge of the trees was a low stone wall topped with a strand of wire. They climbed over it into the wood. Kasuk's shirt was torn along his side. He held her by the arm, helping her run, and when she flagged, he picked her up and carried her. They crossed another field and a stretch of ancient paved roadway. Ahead, a sign glowed white in the domelight: Halstead's.

"Be careful," she said.

He stopped and put her down on her feet. Junna was just ahead of them. The windows glowed with light. On the far side of the yard was a small barn.

"There," she said. "That's where they cool their beer. It's an old station on the Underground." Inside the tavern a burst of music played.

The barn door was open. They went single-file into the dark. The horse nickered in the corner. The barn smelled of hay. Paula went to her left.

"There are steps, somewhere—"

"Here," Junna said, ahead of her.

Her feet groped down slippery stone steps. A dank cold blew into her face. Mildew. A wet echo rebounded back to her from below. She bumped into a wall. Her outstretched hands touched boxes stacked higher than her head. She went down another flight of steps in the darkness. Under her feet the ground was smooth and wet. She began to shiver.

"It's running like a river," Kasuk said. His voice boomed hollow ahead of her. "There's a tunnel—Paula, where does it go?"

"All the way to New York, if it isn't blocked."

Junna said, "What's going on? Kak, shouldn't we stay where Papa left us?"

Paula walked forward into the dark, feeling her way with her feet. Something brushed her hip. Groping on the wall, she found a cold metal rail along the wall.

"Junna, stay here with her." Kasuk was passing her in the dark. "I'm going to look around. I'll be right back."

Above her, several yards away, a patch of gray light shone an instant and faded. She closed her eyes, useless in the dark. Junna touched her.

"We should stay where Tanuojin left us."

"No," she said. "Kasuk is right, we'd just be killed."

"Is this a war, now?"

"Yes. I guess so." Just like in the books.

"Who are we fighting?"

"I don't know, Junna."

"Are you afraid?"

"I'm cold."

He moved; she expected nothing; a moment later the heavy clammy material of his shirt surrounded her. Her skin shuddered at the contact. It slipped down her back and she clutched at it.

"Aren't you—"

"No," he said. "I'm not cold. It's nice in here."

She put the shirt on, shivering, and moved around to warm it. Her feet slipped on the slick tile floor. Kasuk had been gone a long while.

"We need a torch. Maybe there's something to eat here." She found the steps again and started up, and Junna caught her arm.

"Stay here. You heard what my brother said."

"But—"

"Do as he said. He has two stripes, and you're just a woman."

She stood breeding arguments suitable for the adolescent mind. A wedge of light pointed across the barn from the door. Kasuk's broad shape came through it and the light thinned and disappeared.

"We have to get out of here," Kasuk said. He came down the stairs past them. A narrow beam of light shot from his hand, glistening on black water stretching off as far as the light reached. "There are ships all over the sky, and the people in the house are all listening to the box. Something is going on."

Up over their heads, a dog began to bark. He shone the torch along the walls and ceiling of the tunnel, overgrown with weed. They went down to the cold water. Along the edge it lapped barely to her ankles, but when Junna walked toward the center he fell in over his head. Kasuk held the torch down at his side. Junna swam toward them.

Paula stooped and dipped her hand in the water. It tasted brackish but not polluted. Something splashed away from the light ahead of them. The red beads of its eyes gleamed at them. Above them, on the surface, the dog was barking steadily.

"What is this?" Kasuk asked.

Paula said, "It was an underground railroad, all up and down the coast."

"You said it goes to New York."

"Hundreds of years ago. Before the island sank. Who knows where it goes now?"

He aimed the torch beam at the far end of the cavern. The light glanced off the narrowing walls. The water swirled into the black mouth of the tunnel. A wave broke in a ripple of foam.

"Come on." He took her arm.

"Kasuk. I can't swim. You go. Leave me here. I'll be all right—"

A dull thud sounded like a thunderclap somewhere above them. The floor trembled under her. Her knees quaked. The water leaped along the walls of the cave. Kasuk said, "There, you see? Hold on to my back. Junna, stay behind me." Paula put her arms around him, her cheek against his back, and he dove into the river.

She breathed deep and shut her eyes. The cold water closed over them. She raised her head into the air. Kasuk swam strongly under her. The light was gone. The air smelled of wet rot. One hand on the neck of Kasuk's shirt, she let him tow her through the water. She heard the current rushing loud along the tunnel walls, and they were swept along in a close roar of water. Kasuk straightened and switched on the torch.

"Hold this." He gave it to her over his shoulder. "Junna?"

"Here," his brother called, behind him.

Kasuk swam on his stomach down the tunnel. Paula aimed the light ahead of them. The walls were massed with velvety weed. Thick curtains of it hung down from the ceiling. She ducked her head.

"Watch out!" Junna cried, behind them.

The river swelled. Paula clutched the torch. The water lifted them up and crashed them into the wall. Greasy water filled her mouth and nose. She lost Kasuk. Her head broke the surface of the water and she gasped for air. She held the torch with both hands. The water leaped around her, booming on the walls of the tunnel. The light of the torch glowed in a green band under the water. Kasuk reached her. She flung her arms around his neck.

"Don't strangle me." He caught her hands. "I have you."

Junna swam up to them. "What was that?"

Paula changed her grip to the back of Kasuk's shirt. He took the torch. "Another bomb. Maybe the drinking dock, that was close. Let's go."

They swam off. The river swept them through the tunnel. Junna went on before them, his hair sleek, diving under the surface and popping up again like a water-puppy. They could not reach New York this way. Somewhere ahead, the air would turn foul, the tunnel would collapse, the roof fall in, they would drown in the dark.

"There's light ahead," Junna cried.

Kasuk switched the torch off. Ahead, an irregular patch of light shone into the tunnel through a hole in the roof. Paula sighed.

"It's another station." The air was clean. They were still inside the dome. Kasuk swam toward the light. Her feet struck the shelving ground, and she let go of him. She walked out of the water. Through the break in the tunnel roof, she could see the domelight. Kasuk grabbed her arm.

"Where are you going?"

"Kasuk—" She turned toward him, her hands on his arms. "Let me go. I have a chance here."

He wiped his hand over his face. "How far is it to New York?"

"Ten hours. Eight. Depending on the current."

"Good. Then we can make it."

"Kasuk! I'll drown!"

"You heard what Saba said. I may be stupid, Paula, but I know what he told me." He turned to Junna. "Watch her. I'll be right back." He looked up at the hole in the roof, ten feet above them, crouched, and jumped. Swinging from the lip of the opening, he muscled himself up and out of the tunnel.

Paula went into the shallowest water. "We'll all die," she said to Junna.

The boy sank down on his hams in the water. "Papa will save us. He always does." His hands played over the water. In his voice was the cheerful courage of someone who had never been afraid.

In the distance, up on the surface, a dog began to bark. She looked around the tunnel. There was nowhere to go. The opening overhead was too far for her to reach. It darkened, and Kasuk swung down through it. He had a coil of rope around his shoulder and a jug of milk in one hand.

They sat in the shallow water and drank the milk. Outside, the dog barked steadily. Kasuk wiped white foam off his mouth and his young mustaches. "You hear that? They'll come through this city with packs of those things. We have to get out of here."

She knew he was right. They tied the rope around their waists, five feet of slack between Kasuk and Paula and twenty feet between Paula and Junna, and she looped her arms around Kasuk's neck and they swam into the dark.

The tunnel closed in tight around them. They came to a sheet of plastic thrust down through the ground, a foot thick: the wall of the dome. Kasuk dove under it. The air on the far side stank. The light glanced off patches of foam on the walls. The white crusts thickened to nests of round bubbles hanging just above the water. It buzzed. A million wings quivered all over the walls. Wasps zipped back and forth in the air.

"Take a deep breath."

She filled her lungs and he dove. They tore through the water. It streamed over her face. They shot to the surface. The bubbles and the boom of wings lay behind them. They swam on. Bare rock walls lowered down around them, encrusted with salt. Her throat began to hurt when she breathed. Her mouth was full of a bitter numbing taste. Kasuk swam in a kind of breaststroke, silently, his hands only occasionally breaking the water. The light hung around his neck, shining through the water. A reek of gas clogged her nose. Her lungs refused it. She locked her fingers in his shirt, dizzy. Putting her head down close to the water, she drank the rotten air.

The two Styths swam steadily. In places the current carried them faster than they could swim. Once she lost her grip and was yanked away from Kasuk. Junna caught her before she could scream. She climbed back onto Kasuk's shoulders. Her head pounded.

Her eyes itched and streamed. The poisonous air clawed at her lungs. The water rose in the tunnel until they scraped their backs against the rock roof. The walls widened abruptly. They were swept into the cavern of an ancient terminal.

Kasuk switched off the light. The terminal was not completely black. Through a wide crack in the roof, she could see the night sky. Far up there, Luna showed, silver-white. They swam into the black tunnel and he switched the light on again.

Wings fluttered past her. Something bobbed against her in the water, crawled along her side and leaped away. She kept her eyes closed against the stinging air. Her throat was raw. She licked her lips and her tongue began to itch.

"Kasuk—Kasuk—" Just beyond the light, Junna choked and gasped for breath. Kasuk spun around, grabbing for him. She clung to his shoulders. The boy gagged; he vomited; mucus streamed from his nose. He was dying. Kasuk pressed his mouth to his brother's and breathed into him. Paula laid her head against his back. Something bumped her. Tore at her cut wrist with its teeth. She struck at it, whining, and it darted away, green in the flashlit water.

Kasuk said, "Can you breathe now?" His voice was hoarse.

"Yes," Junna whispered. "Better."

Her teeth chattered. The fish was back, swarms of fish, nibbling at her arms, swimming into the deep sleeves of the shirt. She fought them off. Kasuk slid his arm around her.

"Should we go back?" he asked.

"I don't know."

"How close are we?"

"I don't know."

Junna swam beside them, his lips near the surface of the water, sipping off the air where it was least poisonous. Kasuk reached for him.

"We can't stop now."

They swam on. When Junna began to drag at the end of the rope, Kasuk lashed him and Paula to his back. The light went out. He carried them on through the dark. His strength amazed her, his measureless endurance. She clung to him in a half-delirium. If he had dived to the bottom she would have drowned rather than leave him.

He dragged them on and on through the tunnel. She swallowed water and heaved it up again. Her head reeled. She clung to Junna with one arm. The current whirled them around in a dizzy eddy. Kasuk hit something solid and held tight. She raised her head. Her eyes were swollen almost shut. They had come to a fork in the river. The wild current, leaping across a bar of concrete, was dragging them into the left-hand channel. On the right, overhead, another stream thundered straight down twenty feet to meet them. Kasuk dragged them to the right side of the tunnel. With them hanging on his shoulders he climbed hand over hand up the weed-covered wall, through the roar and the flying spray of the waterfall, into a cold sunlit layer of sweet air. She gulped it into her aching lungs. Kasuk pulled them through a crack in the earth out to the surface. They lay on cold stones and slept.

She woke up shivering. Her mouth tasted foul. His black skin rough with gooseflesh, Junna slept curled up beside her. Kasuk was gone.

High above her the sky was brilliantly sunlit but she lay in deep shadow on the floor of a gorge. The steep slopes on either side were overgrown with brush and wiry pine trees. The air tasted fresh and delicious. They were inside a dome; the only dome it could be was New York. She sat up, looking for Kasuk. She still wore Junna's shirt. The boy stirred in his sleep, his length doubled up on the ground, and his hair caught with leaves. There was a stream running along the foot of the far wall of the gulley. She climbed down through rocks to the inch-deep water and drank from her cupped hand.

Above her the brush rustled violently. She stood. Kasuk was climbing down the slope, a dead swan hung over his shoulder, one long wing trailing.

"Let's eat."

"That?" she said, uncertain.

He stepped across the trickle of water and went up through the jumbled boulders toward his brother. She followed him. When she sat down beside him, he was tearing open the swan's belly with his claws. Its long neck stretched out over the ground, the feathers rumpled. The swan had fattened on eelgrass and popcorn and children's lunches. The raw meat made her gag. The Styths picked out the bird's heart and liver, packed in congealing yellow fat.

"Kak," Junna said. He hooked his arm around his brother's neck. "You saved our lives."

Kasuk was using a swan feather to pick his teeth. He pushed Junna away. The younger boy turned to her. "Didn't he?"

"Yes," she said. "You saved both of us."

His heavy shoulders lifted and fell. "I just kept thinking about my father. I couldn't let him down again. So it was really my father." He grabbed Junna by his shaggy hair and shook him. "Go keep watch. Make sure nobody sneaks up on us."

The boy raced off. Paula's eyes followed him in his headlong run across the gulley and in among the trees. The swan's broad wings sprawled around her, the feathers broken. Kasuk wiped his hands on the grass.

"My father told me to protect him. I'm just dragging us deeper. Can we leave the dome?"

"You'll need an air car," she said. "But I'll be damned if I'm going with you."

"Saba told me—"

"I don't care what he said. I'm telling you what I'll do."

He made a little harried gesture, avoiding her eyes. A flap of his torn shirt hung down over his stomach. His chest was massive, his shoulders like a beam. His strength was perfect. He wore no scars from fighting, no killing marks.

"I have to follow orders," he said.

"I can only help you if you let me go."

"Then I'll have to get us out by myself."

The smell of smoke reached her nose. She said, "Which way is the lake from here?"

"Out there." He pointed behind them. "There's fighting here, too—what's going on?"

"Here comes your brother."

Junna was bounding down the slope, tall as a young tree, scattering stones and dirt on ahead of him. He jumped across the stream and ran up to them. Scratches decorated his body; he was naked.

"Cover yourself up," Kasuk said.

"Why? She doesn't care. I'm hungry again. When will Papa come? Will we start fighting when he gets here? There are fires up there, and people shooting guns."

"What's going on?" Kasuk turned to Paula. "I thought the Martians were just attacking us, but there aren't any Styths up there."

"The Sunlight League is staging a coup against the anarchy."

"To kill us," Junna said.

She bobbed her head, her gaze on Kasuk. He said, "What does Gemini have to do with it?"

"Everything."

Junna raked at the ground with his claws, his head bent. "Papa knows what he's doing."

Kasuk said to her, "Then I can see why you don't want to go back. I won't take you back."

"Kak!" Junna cried. He grabbed his brother's arm. "Who will protect her?"

Kasuk scrubbed his face with his hand. He crooked his fingers in the neck of his shirt and pulled at it. "I wonder what's happening to the rest of the *Ybix*."

"Kak!"

"Shut up. I've made up my mind." He looked at Paula. "Can you get us an air car?"

"I'll try," she said.

Night came. The domelight did not shine. She made her way toward the middle of the dome. A siren raised its hound-voice ahead of her. In the dark she had trouble finding a way through the trees. She skirted the east edge of the lake. Faint moonlight gleamed on the water. The swans were all roosting in the high grass near the head of the lake. As she crossed the open ground between the beach and the wood, near the hourly stand, a shot cracked out.

She sprinted into the cover of the trees. Another bullet followed her, whining like a hornet. She stopped beside a tree. Her ears strained to hear. The wood was full of sounds. The brush crackled behind her. Leaves rustled. The wind rose in a low call that lifted the hackles of her neck. In spite of the cool, she was sweating.

She went on, trying to keep silent. Twice she saw lights moving in the trees ahead of her. An air car droned above her. The wind made the branches dance. She went around the edge of a meadow. On the far side, four little deer grazed, their tails busy. Through the trees she saw a building burning like a torch, crackling, sending up a thick roll of smoke. The bright yellow light spilled into the wood and gave pebbles and ferns and bits of twig shadows ten feet long. She circled a great pit, still smoking, where an underground building had been blown up.

She heard more gunshots. The woods ended. She trotted across the south end of the campus. The place looked different in the dark. The air hummed with cars. Three or four searchlights swung back and forth over the uneven ground. She went into the shadow of the turret of a university building. Voices sounded, coming toward her. Several people passed by, arguing. She ran across the campus into the mouth of the gulley where the Committee office was.

The smoke around the building made her eyes itch. On the hillside to the north, a mob of people was gathered. She heard the rattle of a gun. The door to the building was open.

The waiting room was jammed with rubble. The back wall ended halfway up to the ceiling. The place had been bombed. She stopped in the smashed doorway. The floor of the hall was covered with broken glass. She went down through the darkness toward Jefferson's office. An overturned desk blocked the way. She crossed the slippery spill of papers beyond it. Jefferson's door was unlocked. She opened it slowly inward.

The room was dark. A little light came from the window. She touched the inside wall, hunting for a light switch, and the wall crumbled away under her fingers. She went toward the window and tripped on a piece of the shattered desk.

Something clicked behind her. A thread of bright light shot past her, shining on the edge of the ruined videone. Dick Bunker said, "Junior, I knew you'd come here, sooner or later."

She turned one hand up against the light. He was sitting on the floor behind the door. She saw him only for an instant; he switched off the torch and the dark covered them.

"What happened?" she asked.

"The Martians are rescuing the Earth from the Styths. As you can see, the Committee is considered Styth. You aren't alone, are you?"

"Yes."

"I don't believe you, Paula, you aren't that stupid."

She sank down on her hams, her feet under her, her arms around her knees. He would know where to find a car and how to smuggle Kasuk and Junna out of the dome. She rubbed her nose, itching from the smell of smoke.

"How did the League find out we knew about the coup?" she asked.

"Jefferson told them."

"Jesus. Why?"

"To bring them on before they were ready." His voice speeded up into a snarl. "I was hoping they'd account for the Styths, but that fool Savenia can't do anything well."

She caught the glint of light on his hand torch. She was beginning to make out his shape in the dark. She groped over the floor around her, over shards of split plastic, the shell of the videone screen, and sat cautiously down on the litter.

"Where's Jefferson now?"

"I don't know. The Central Committee had a meeting. What we

always do in times of crisis, talk. It lasted five minutes, we voted the strike notice in three and disbanded the Committee in two."

"Strike," she said. "You've called a general strike?"

"What else are we supposed to do? There are three thousand Martians in New York and New Haven alone. It's too late to talk them out of it."

She pursed her lips. Bunker moved, the trash grating under him. He said, "Your two pigs escaped."

"Yes. I have Tanuojin's two sons with me. I have to get them out of the dome. Will you help me?"

"I hate the Styths."

"Don't be so emotional."

"Find your own way home."

"I'm not going. I've had enough of the master race." Now she could see him passing the torch from hand to hand. His sweater was ripped at the elbow and his white shirt showed through.

"Then why help them at all?"

"One of them is honest."

A dull explosion sounded outside the building and something fell off the wall. The floor heaved under her. She flung one hand out, startled. She had to get out of here.

"Do you think a strike will work?" she asked.

He shook his head. "I don't know. Nothing will ever be the same again, that's sure. You have your revolution, junior."

"Help me get Tanuojin's sons off the Planet."

"Why should I? They're no better than the Martians. Why help a pack of Fascists?"

"The debt owed to common humanity."

He squinted at her in the darkness. "What?"

"Insurance."

"You are baroque."

Another bomb rumbled in a long explosion, farther away than the first, and the window behind her rattled. She said, "Put Tanuojin in your debt. You may need that someday."

"For what?"

"Don't be obtuse. You know what he can do. He's getting stronger. The more he does, the more he's capable of. I need an air car."

"The Committee cars are all in the entry port. The League holds that, and the locks."

"The Manhattan boat."

"What?"

"Why not? The tourist boat to the underwater dome." She shivered. The broken window breathed cold air down her back. "They love water."

"Maybe. I can . . . I have a key to the lower lock." He opened the door. "Come on, junior."

She followed him out to the corridor. He walked with a limp. The hall reeked of char. "They're down at the southern end of the dome, in the park, near the wall." Carefully she picked a way over the rubble blocking the hall. "Can you whistle?"

"Yes."

She taught him *Ybix*'s recognition code. "Remember, everything you tell them, Tanuojin will find out." She stumbled on the pile of papers and nearly fell. Bunker let her go first down the hallway past the overturned desk. She put one hand on the wall for balance.

"Go right," he said.

Innocent, she went in through a door, and he slammed it shut on her. She whirled. Her shin collided with a chunk of plastic, and she fell. The lock clicked in the door. She slammed against it.

"Dick!"

Silence. She shook the latch. The room was totally dark. She stepped on trash. Stooping, she ran her hands over the littered floor. Books, and a bookcase, and a jumble of wires half-melted into a clump. The meeting room. She brought an image of it into her mind. There were no windows and only the one door. In the table, somewhere, was a switch to unlock the door. On her hands and knees she crawled into the depths of the room and found the tabletop, lying on the floor, its broken legs under it.

Another bomb exploded, so close the building trembled. She felt carefully along the underside of the table's edge. Maybe Kasuk would develop a vicious streak and take Bunker along with them to *Ybix*. Hunting for the switch, she occupied her mind with the various things the Styths would do to him for doing this to her. She found a switch and pressed it. A light flashed on in the ceiling and exploded. The wrong switch. While she was searching for the right one the door burst open. A blinding torchlight glared in her face.

"Stay where you are! We are government police. Put your hands up."

She turned her back to the light. Her eyes hurt. Grim, she raised her hands, surrendering.

"Out." The gun jabbed her in the back.

She climbed out of the air car. She had paid no attention to where they were taking her. They were somewhere in the north of the dome. She stepped down into a plaza in the middle of three tall buildings. Banks of light shone down from the roofs, flooding the place with a blue-white glare. The soldiers pushed her forward. Other people swarmed around her. She was so tired she staggered.

She was coming to a scaffold. A crowd gawked around it, shading their eyes from the blazing lights. She slowed, her eyes on the carcasses that hung upside down from the frame. There were four of them. One was Sril. She stood staring at him, ignoring the men around her and their orders. The gold wire had been ripped out of his nose. Her eyes swam and overflowed with tears.

They took her into the nearest building. She wiped her eyes but they filled again instantly. She wondered how long it would be before she was hung up beside him. The soldiers hustled her along a wide carpeted lobby and through a door.

"Yes," Cam Savenia said. "That's Mendoza."

The Martian woman came down the long office toward them. Her fair hair was smooth as metal over her head, her mouth was painted on. "You said Bunker wasn't there."

"No, Dr. Savenia. We posted a guard."

"Go look for him. I don't want that particular specimen out loose." Cam waved impatiently. She wore white gloves, buttoned at the wrist. "And find out how she got into this dome. It must have been the air bus. Check into it."

Paula stood in the center of the room. At the far end was a desk, and heavy matching wooden chairs were ranged along the walls: an office. The doors behind the desk probably went to a private vertical car. The soldiers left, and Cam sauntered back toward Paula. Her trousers and tunic were white, like a uniform.

"There must be something we can say to each other," she said.

Paula gave her a hard look. She was too tired to argue. Cam circled her. "Your big hero won't rescue you. In two hours half the Martian Army will be here to blast *Ybix* and *Ebelos* into another Universe." Cam struck her hard in the chest with the flat of her hand. "Do you understand? You are through."

A stream of soldiers came into the room, their feet loud on the floor. Cam turned, crisp, to meet the little fat man in their midst. "General Hanse. You're right on time. Have you heard from the Army?"

The fat man stared curiously at Paula. "Still two hours out, doctor, we can only go so fast." Paula looked into his glittering little eyes. He was only a few inches taller than she was. He said, "Who's that?"

"General Joseph Hanse," Savenia said. "Meet Paula Mendoza. Late toady of the Styth Empire."

Paula sat down in the big soft chair behind her. Her stomach was gripped with hunger. She felt wrung up to the breaking point, ready to scream. Their voices sawed back and forth over her head.

"What are you going to do with her?"

"Put her on trial," Cam said. "Get a full public confession, and execute her."

Paula lifted her head. The front of Cam's white coat was buttoned in gold. "I'm hungry."

"You'll live," Cam said.

The fat man waved, and a soldier hurried up with another chair. The general sat. He took a stick of candy from one pocket and a long brown cigar from another. He gave the candy to Paula and licked off the cigar.

"How well do you know the Matuko Akellar?"

"I worked for him for ten years."

"General," Cam said, "she's my prisoner."

"Worked for him. How?"

"She was his whore," Cam said.

Paula stripped off the candy wrapper and bit into the flat chocolate. "Kind of a lawyer, I guess."

"Kind of a traitor." Cam planted her fists on her hips. "What do you think you're doing?" she said to the little fat man.

Hanse stuck the tail of his cigar into his mouth. A soldier sprang forward to light it. The general and Savenia measured each other. If they had been Styths they would have been starting to smell. Savenia said evenly, "We have an agreement, remember?"

More people were crowding into the room. Cam sidled away from Hanse, her head rising. "Good. You got him."

Three of her gray-jacketed police were leading Richard Bunker down the room. Paula crowed.

"Enter the Grand Fink, attended by constabulary."

His hands were tied, and a yard of rope connected his ankles together. He ignored her. The policeman beside him said, "We caught him at the excursion boat terminal—he'd sabotaged all the boats."

Bunker said to Cam, "You told me if I delivered Mendoza you'd let me go."

"A promise to an anarchist," Cam said, smiling. Before the ragged man she stood spotlessly white and clean. "Especially to you." She looked at the police. "Was he alone?"

"Yes."

Paula licked chocolate off her fingers. Then Kasuk was gone. She thought of Sril again. If he was dead Bakan was surely dead. As she would soon be dead.

Bunker was looking at the floor. He shot a murderous sideways glance at Cam. His trouser legs were wet to the knees. Cam swaggered around him toward Paula.

"He'll talk. He'll tell us where they all are, from Jefferson on down. Mendoza is mine. We made an agreement. I handle the civilians and you handle the military."

"Exactly," Hanse said, genially. He sat down again, his knees spread to accommodate his great melon of stomach. "She's necessary for military intelligence. She probably knows half their general staff."

Savenia's cheeks were patched with red. "She's a criminal. She—"

"I'm not exactly letting her loose," Hanse said.

"Neither am I."

A man in a brown uniform brushed through the crowd, stopped before Hanse, and stuck out one arm in salute. "General, the Styth Manta is maneuvering very close to the dome." Hanse went at top speed out the door.

Paula sank down into the yielding chair. Now that she saw a way out of it, she began to be frightened of dying. Cam bent over her.

"Don't get your hopes up, baby. You're done."

Behind her, Bunker murmured, "The Bearded Lady of the Sunlight Freak Show."

Cam turned around and slapped his face. Paula blinked. "I thought that went out with girdles." Bunker had not moved; the only sign he had been hit was the faint mark on his dark cheek.

"Shut up," Cam said, and went away down the room.

"Why did you listen to her?" Paula said to him. "She'll kill you."

General Hanse came back down the room, trailing a little plume of cigar smoke. "They've made another rendezvous. If Luna would cooperate we could gun down the bastard when he stops dead in the air like that." He huffed at Cam, whose back was to him. He pointed at Paula with the cigar between his fingers. "You speak Styth?"

"Like a Styth," she said. She could not resist robbing Cam. She stuck her chin out at Bunker. "So does he. If you need corroboration."

Hanse swung around, interested. "Oh?"

Cam hurried down the room. "I'm serious, General. I need these two for propaganda purposes."

"Do you need the Army?" Hanse said. He planted the cigar between his teeth. Cam's face settled. He nodded to Paula. "Lock them both up."

The Martians gave her pills, weighed her, bandaged her arms, bathed her like a baby, and locked her into a small room on the sixth floor of the same building. She slept. She dreamt of Sril and woke up crying. She paced around the room, thinking of David. He was safest in Matuko. She would never see him again.

The room was equipped with a bed, a desk and chair, and a little washroom, so she expected to stay there awhile. The window was of triplex glass and did not open. Down below, many floors below, crowds moved along, ropes of people, like one animal, never stopping. When night fell the glow of fires lit the dome with brilliant rippling orange light, fading to black and shooting up again, fiery, like an aurora.

The following day and for days and days thereafter, from early morning until well after dark, men in uniforms brought her lists of questions and taped her answers. Most of the questions were military: they wanted to know where the Styth cities were, how they could be attacked, how *Ybix* was laid out inside, what her crew was. Sometimes she had no idea what they were talking about. She told them the truth, except when they asked about Saba's assassination; then she said they had shot the wrong man. Her door was locked and a guard posted outside. The men who sat on the far side of the desk reading questions at her never spoke to her personally—never even said hello to her. The woman who brought her meals didn't talk at all. Once the guard outside her door made some careless remark to her while an interrogator was leaving. The next hour he was gone and a stranger there who would not look at her.

At night the dome was a great display of light, flickering here and there, red to yellow. The room was sound-proof. She could see the crowd churning below the window, but she could make no sense of what they did, she couldn't even see if they were anarchists or Martians. Whenever the interrogators left her alone, she looked out the window, trying to see what was happening.

One morning while she was drinking her coffee, General Hanse came in. She turned her back to the window and put her cup on the sill. The fat man settled himself in the chair by the desk.

"Well, you look a lot better than you did."

She went around her chair and sat down, the desk between them. His wide cheeks rolled down to his chin. When he leaned back the chair creaked. He said, "You've been very forthcoming. I guess it hasn't been easy on you, the last week, but you've passed the test. Bunker corroborates practically everything you say." He took a flat leather case from his jacket. "Do you mind if I smoke?"

"Yes."

With the cigar halfway out of the case, he paused, his moist eyes unblinking. Finally, he took out the cigar and got a clipper from his pocket. "That's too bad," he said, with genuine regret in his voice.

"What do you want?"

He said, "I want to know what the enemy is going to do. That's simple enough." He lit the cigar, puffing his cheeks full.

Paula rocked her chair back on its hindlegs. She knew who her enemy was.

"Are you married to him?"

"To who?" she said, startled. "To Saba? God, no."

"But you did bear him a child."

She stared at his pear-shaped face. "He gave me my son. That was ten years ago."

"Dr. Savenia says he's the motive force behind the Styths, but you and Bunker both seem to think it's this—Tan-you-gin—"

"Tanuojin," she said. "Four syllables. Accent on the antepenultimate. They're a matched pair. Tanuojin does the long-range thinking."

"That isn't what Dr. Savenia thinks."

Paula lifted one shoulder in a shrug. She didn't care if he believed her. His questions baffled her. They had nothing to do with what she knew would be happening in Styth. Maybe he did not know what to ask.

"Well," he said, "we have the psychological advantage, at any rate—they have to come to us."

Sharp in her memory, Tanuojin's voice sounded, denouncing psychological tactics. She moved her chair back and forth. "Can I get out of this room? Walk somewhere—in the park?"

"No."

"I'm—I hate being cooped in."

"We're afraid someone might try to do you some damage."

"Damage," she said. "Who?"

His round body bulged his uniform out in tires of fat. "Another anarchist, perhaps. There's been a certain bitterness. Although you people are submitting pretty tamely." He took out his cigar case and removed a thick brown finger from it. "You know—" He wagged the cigar at her. "You screwed yourselves. You made such a fetish out of peace, and then when the bite came, you couldn't even defend yourselves." He peeled the plastic wrapper off the cigar and licked it all over. With almost no effort she saw it as a thin brown penis. He stuck it in his mouth. "I can see being shy of irrational force, but rational force is what holds a community together." He lit the end of the cock in his mouth.

She covered her mouth with one hand to hide her smile. He put the light-stick down beside the ashtray.

"You know, I don't understand you." He set the cigar down on the dish. "You're an intelligent, pretty woman, you know your way around—what's the attraction in a tribe of primitives who paint their faces and pound their chests?"

The cigar was smoking in her face. She thrust the dish aside. "Have you ever met a Styth?"

"I've seen them."

"Talked to one?"

"I don't speak the language." He put his round shoulders back against the chair. "I'm told they smell bad. Their bodies certainly do."

She circled her hand over the desktop. "They have scent glands in their necks that open when they get angry. Or sexy. It has an aphrodisiac effect after a while. Do you belong to the Sunlight League?"

"I'm not interested in politics. You didn't answer my question. How did a woman like you ever get involved with the Styths?"

She rocked the chair back and forth, her eyes on him. "Oh, I'm noted for cultivating the lower orders. I even know some Martians."

His mouth closed up tight. She said, "Don't rub me up, General."

He reached for the cigar and tapped off another round of ash. "I'm trying to make this more pleasant for both of us."

She made a nasty sound with her tongue. He fooled elaborately with the big cigar, watching his hands. "You know, Dr. Savenia has some interesting ideas about what to do to you and Bunker. When—" he smiled at her, cherubic, putting the cigar in its dish, "if I ever release you to her."

"Fine." She leaped up out of her chair. "Torture me. Kill me. The Earth is dead anyway, and you killed it." She knocked the ash and the cigar flying. "You and the Sunlight League."

The fat man's jaw was clamped shut. His jowls hung loose over his jawbone. She went away to the window. The crowd below carried signs and waved flags. Hanse shouted, "Rodgers!"

A young man came in, cracking to his salute like a spring straightening. Hanse pointed to the dish and the smoking cigar. "Pick that up."

The impeccable soldier gathered the cigar and the ashtray and reassembled them on the desk. Hanse said, "Captain Rodgers, this is Paula Mendoza."

Paula turned her head. Rodgers glanced at her. "I'm pleased to meet you, ma'am."

Hanse said, "Captain, I want this place kept clean. Go arrange it." Rodgers left. The fat man's chair wheezed. His eyes were fixed on her.

"Yes, General. You were just threatening me."

He scratched his rolled chins. "I wasn't threatening you, honey. You're being very useful." He pried himself up out of the chair. "Keep it up, and we'll get along." He went out.

When Hanse had been gone about half an hour, Captain Rodgers came into her room again. "I can see you need some behavior training." He took her down the hall to an empty room and tied her up, her knees crooked around a length of pipe, and her wrists fastened to her ankles. She lay alone in the dark room for a full day. When he came back and untied her she could not stand. He dragged her back to her own room and left her. She rubbed and worked her legs for hours until she could walk again.

Rodgers seemed to be in charge of her. He brought papers and supervised the rare appearances of the maid. He hardly ever spoke to her. Periodically he took her down to the little room and tied her up and left her. Once he hung her head-down from the ceiling. Her meals came at irregular intervals, with now and then a day when she went unfed. Although he pulled her hair he never beat her. She thought he was afraid of leaving marks.

One night a knocking on her door woke her. She rolled over in her bed.

"Yes?"

"Please dress, Miss Mendoza. You're wanted downstairs."

"Forget it. I'm tired." She buried her head in her arms.

"Miss Mendoza." Rodgers banged on the door. She put the pillow over her head, but he went on hammering. Finally she got up and put on clothes: a long dress. All the Martians would give her was dresses.

"All right, I'm coming." She picked at her hair with her fingers.

They went down to Cam's vast office. Sleek as an otter, Cam herself sat behind her desk, smoking a cigarette in a plastic holder. General Hanse was talking to a group of his own people. Paula walked down the room. There was a tall statue opposite her, a young man made of stone; a six-foot acrylic poster hung on the wall beside it. She looked slowly around the room, startled. On the wall on her side of the room was an illuminated initial from Kells. Rodgers touched her arm, and she sat down in the chair he indicated.

Dick Bunker was coming in the door. She yipped, delighted: he was wearing a uniform. Three of Hanse's khaki soldiers followed him down the far side of the room.

"Paula," Cam said. Rodgers tapped her shoulder again. She went up to the desk. There was a little gold cherub beside the ashtray; it looked old. Probably it had been converted into a cigarette lighter. Cam leaned back in her swivel chair. She was smiling, her mouth red with paint. General Hanse beside her looked rumpled. She held out a medal on a chain.

"What does this mean?"

Paula lifted it by the chain. It was the medal of the order of the Supernova; on the back in Styth characters was Sril's name and the name of Matuko and a saying: *"I flower where I bleed, rose without thorns."*

"Did it come in the mail?" she asked. She put it down on Cam's desk.

"What does it mean?"

"Somebody considers you responsible for the death of a Styth. It means they'll take vengeance." She looked from Cam to the fat general. "Which of you got it?"

Hanse wheeled toward Cam, leading with his jutting chin. "Satisfied, Dr. Savenia? You brought us all here just for an audience for this."

Cam smirked at him. They started to argue, and Paula backed away from the desk. Bunker was standing in front of the marble statue. She went across the room to him.

"Look at this," he said. "She's looting the Earth."

The statue was almost six and a half feet tall. Its smile and magnificent body reminded her of Kasuk. She turned back to the other anarchist.

"Why are you wearing that cowboy outfit?"

He moved one shoulder to indicate Hanse and Savenia. "She tried to detach me, so he drafted me into the Army. I'm a major, which is one higher than that plastic captain you came in with. What did that medal mean?"

"I'm not sure."

"A message to you, maybe."

"Maybe." Hanse was coming toward them, his face oiled with sweat. Clearly he had lost his argument with Cam. Paula moved away.

"Are you getting along all right?" Hanse said. His little eyes gleamed. "Rodgers is treating you well?"

"Very well," she said. "A perfect gentleman, Captain Rodgers. The flower of Martian manhood."

"I'm going to Luna for a few days. We've had a tempting offer from some friends of yours." He was watching her intently, unblinking. The creases of his face were marked in talcum powder. "The Styths have two flag officers of mine they're willing to exchange for you."

"You're going to do it?"

"I need those officers. You're outstaying your usefulness. As much as I enjoy our conversations."

She turned her face away from him. That was what the medal had meant. Her hand rested on the desk and she beat her fingers on it. She would go back to Styth with nothing, at their mercy, like a slave. Sold like a slave. Hanse stood, his uniform jacket bulging over the pad of his stomach.

"If everything on Luna goes as I expect it will, I won't be seeing you again—we'll exchange off Ceres in an Earthish month. I'd like to feel we parted friends." He put his hand out to her.

Paula bounded out of her chair. She felt too large for her body, a scream coming up from the gut, a bursting rage. "Get out." She looked around for something to throw. Hanse, scrambling, was already at the door, calling for Rodgers. She threw the ashtray at him. He went out fast and the door slammed.

She was not ready for Rodgers; she barricaded her door with the desk. They spent two hours taking the door off the hinges. She went three or four times around the room, which she knew now inch by inch. When Rodgers came in she was sitting on the bed, resigned. He hauled her down to the little room and tied her up to the wall so she could neither sit nor stand straight and left her. The worst was waiting for him to come back.

Slumped against the wall on her throbbing legs, she thought with alarm of the exchange Hanse was planning. The Styths wanted her back because of what she knew about the Middle Planets. Hanse certainly realized that. He would never send her to them in any condition to serve them. Her half-bent knees gave way and she fell, hit the rope that fastened her arms to the wall, and jerked them almost out of her shoulders. Grimly she pushed herself back up to a crouch. This was all Hanse's idea, so she would complain and he could rescue her from Rodgers and make her trust him. She closed her eyes.

The first thing she saw in Cam's office was the large painting by Jacques-Louis David of Marat, dead in his bath. The oil hung directly over Cam's desk. Paula stopped near a chair to the side of the room, looking around, while other people filed into the room. On the paneled wall beside her a dragon-robe was spread out like a pair of scarlet wings, feathered in gold thread. The room was cluttered. Pictures hung thick as scale from the walls. Here and there among the living people statues stood. Paula sat down in the chair behind her. Surrounded by soldiers, she rubbed her fingers nervously together, her eyes on the painting of the dead revolutionary above the desk.

The wall below it split open. Cam came out of her private lift. Two trim young men followed her. The soldiers in the room straightened rigidly to attention. Cam was neat as a mannequin. Her hair gleamed. An aide held her chair for her. She spoke to him, sitting down, and he laughed at what she said.

"At ease, gentlemen."

In unison they relaxed. Paula looked curiously around at their scrubbed, shaven faces. In their midst Bunker stood with his jacket unbuttoned, his cheek blurred with beard. Cam folded her hands together.

"He defiled the uniform, putting you into it."

Behind Paula, Rodgers muttered, "In she goes."

"Are you drunk?" Cam said to Bunker.

He shuffled his feet. "Slightly." He glanced up at the clay-colored corpse on the wall above her. "Not enough."

"You're a disgusting little man."

"Thank you. I was hoping you'd appreciate my modest efforts."

"Cut his balls off," Paula said. "Make him walk the plank."

Cam swung back and forth in her chair. "It makes me sick to see him in a Martian uniform."

"Shall I take it off?" He pulled one arm out of the sleeve.

"You're out of uniform," Cam said, "for which you'll spend the next five days in solitary."

Paula cheered. She clapped her hands together three or four times, the only sound in the crowded room. Cam threw her a hard look. "Do you want to join him?"

"Then we wouldn't be in solitary," Bunker said. He shrugged into his jacket.

"Complete solitary," Cam said. "In the closet. No food, no water, no lights. No liquor." She sat back, smiling. Bunker said nothing. Alert, Paula settled deep into her chair, watching him, thinking about what he had just done. Cam's gaze swung toward her. "Why aren't you cheering, baby?"

"I hope you got me down here for some purpose," Paula said. "Other than making an ass of yourself, which is less entertaining than it used to be."

"Rodgers, the same for her. Five days."

Rodgers was standing behind Paula. He said sharply, "Doctor, you're going to put them together?"

"That's what I said. Put them both in the closet. Maybe they'll tear each other to pieces."

"That's immoral. General Hanse—"

"Joe isn't here," Cam said. She took a sheet of clear paper from her desk and held it out to one of her aides, who brought it up the room to Paula. Cam was lighting a cigarette. She said, "Read that, Paula."

"You're crazy," Paula said.

Cam smiled at her. Her lip-paint was the color of venous blood. "Six days in the closet." The aide was holding the paper out to Paula, who ignored it. Bunker was paying no attention to any of this.

"Seven days," Cam said.

Rodgers said, "You can't put them in together, for Christ's sake, it's immoral."

Cam gave him an instant's angry look. She stared at Paula. "Eight days."

Paula took the page. Around the room, the men stirred, commenting to each other, impressed by Cam's techniques. Paula turned the plastic around. The message was in Styth. When she read it, her heart quickened.

"It's a declaration of war," she said. "How formal."

"Read it," Cam said.

"To Mars, by the rAkellaron. We have warned you in many ways to submit to us before justice brought you into its course. Now you have violated the Earth, our mother, and wakened her children dead even in dreams. If you resist us, we cannot say how you will suffer, only that you will suffer." She handed the page to a soldier, who took it to Bunker.

"What tripe," Cam said.

Bunker was reading through the paper. "I don't follow this *dead even in dreams.*"

Paula was chewing the skin around her thumbnail. "The old heroes. You know they're all descended from heroes." Krita was ringing his bell again. It was a stronger declaration than she had expected: very strong.

"It sounds as if they're committing the whole Empire."

"Yes."

"They double-crossed you," Cam said to her. She tapped a cigarette on the desk, her holder in the other hand. "They're using you as an excuse. I told you that bastard would do this. Why the hell didn't you listen to me?"

Paula got up. "Come on, Rodgers. The dark is more edifying." She started toward the door.

"Paula! Get back here until I dismiss you." Cam bounced up onto her feet, poised behind her desk. At the door, Paula wheeled.

"I dismiss you." She snapped her fingers at Cam and went out the door. Someone caught her by the arm: a soldier.

"Let her go," Rodgers said. He pushed her on across the hall.

"Dr. Savenia—"

"Dr. Savenia is a civilian." Rodgers hurried her into the vertical.

They went up three flights in silence. Beside her Rodgers stood with his hands clasped behind him, his feet exactly eighteen inches apart. He took her down the hall to the little room.

"I'll call General Hanse," he said. He shut the door on her. The lock turned over.

She had never been here before without being tied up. There was little to explore. Three strides across by four strides down. The room was without windows. While she was walking around it, the door opened and Bunker was put in with her. The door shut and the light in the ceiling went out.

"Is this place wired?" she said, in the dark. She sat down with her back to the wall.

"I don't think so." His voice passed her, going down the room. "Why couldn't you keep out of this?"

"You gave me to Hanse, you can help me get away."

"It won't be easy. Probably impossible, in fact. You'd be better off staying here."

"Have they been working you over?" she asked.

He made an indefinite sound. For a long while they sat in the dark without saying anything. Finally, he said, "I would love to pay them back. More than anything. I'd pass up getting away to pay them back."

"I'd sooner get away."

Another silence fell. She got up and walked up and down the room, trailing her fingers over the wall. The seamless plastic felt cold to the touch. There was no way out but the door. Maybe she had misjudged his intentions. Maybe he had no way to escape. She sat down but in a few moments she started to pace around the room again.

"Don't step on me," Bunker said.

She went around and around the room in the dark, avoiding him. Her mouth was dry with thirst. For eight days she would get no water. Finally she sat down in a corner. Hours seemed to pass, or maybe just minutes. Bunker got up and went down the room to the door. He returned to his place against the wall opposite her.

She managed to doze. He shook her awake.

"Let's go. The guard's left for a few minutes."

Muzzy with sleep, her heart pounding, she followed him to the door. She could hear a faint metallic click, like a combination lock being dialed, and then the door opened. The bright light hurt her eyes. They went into the long empty corridor.

"Hurry." He took her arm and pulled her along, and they ran down the corridor, past the vertical and past the door to her room. The guards were all gone. Many of the overhead lights were out. It seemed to be late at night. At the end of the corridor was a door marked EXIT. Bunker led her through it onto a stair landing.

"Sssh." He put his finger to his lips. The stairwell was painted glossy gray. She looked up overhead, up the stairs, and went to the rail and looked down.

"Which way?"

He started down. She took her shoes off, to keep from making noise, and went after him. The stair treads chilled her bare feet. They passed another door, marked with a big red 5.

Below them, voices sounded. The hollow of the stairwell distorted them so that she could not make out the words. Bunker stopped. She went by him, cautious, down past the door marked 4, and he came after her. On the third-floor landing she put her head out over the railing.

On the next landing down was a table, with three men sitting at it. She held her breath, disappointed.

"Hey, did you hear this one?" said a man on the landing. "How do you tell when an anarchist is lying?"

She raised her head. Bunker was on the steps above her. She shook her head at him.

"You got me," another Martian voice said, below her.

"His lips are moving."

There was general laughter. She climbed back away from it, and Bunker turned and preceded her. At the third-floor landing, he pushed the door open onto the corridor where Cam's office was.

"What—"

He beckoned her after him. The corridor was dark except for a single light over the vertical doors. Her feet sank into the deep carpet and she stopped to put her shoes on. Bunker went ahead of her to Cam's door, fastened his magnetic key to the lock, and bent to fiddle with it. He had given up on escaping and was going for his revenge.

She went at a trot down the hall to the vertical. There had to be some way out of the building. She could not take the vertical down for fear of meeting someone else, but there was certainly some other way. A chime rang over her head, and she jumped. The vertical arrow flashed. Someone was coming to this floor. She sprinted back down the hall to Bunker, who was just sliding Cam's door open. They went into the office.

"What are you going to do?" She made sure the door was locked again. The office was dark, but as she spoke Bunker turned on a light midway down the room.

"I didn't ask you along," he said. He circled behind Cam's big desk to the big wheel-file against the wall.

Paula looked up at Marat, hanging on the wall over the door to Cam's private lift. The wound in his chest was like a mouth, like his slack mouth. Bunker was trying to open the drawers of the file with his key. She sat in Cam's chair and tried the desk drawers.

They were unlocked. She yanked them out and turned the contents over in a heap on the floor. When she tipped over the deeper drawer on the bottom shelf, a mass of photographs and slides fell out, and a little white egg rolled after. She picked it up.

"Dick."

He turned, and she held Sybil Jefferson's eye under his nose. He sucked in his breath. When he put his hand out to take the eye, she closed her fingers over it and put it in her pocket.

Bunker pushed the file box. "I can't open this. It must be important." He gave the box a savage kick.

Paula took the cigarette lighter off the desk and knelt by the pile of papers and film on the floor. "They killed her." She held the flame to the edge of a photograph.

"That's your diagnosis, is it?" He punched the call button on the vertical several times with his thumb.

"You need a key for that, too."

The flames caught and ran over the heap of papers. The holographs burned better than anything else, and she took one by the corner and torched the rest. Bunker was pushing and rocking the waist-high round file cabinet.

"I have an idea. Help me."

She helped him push the box up onto two legs. It fell over onto its side and he caught it before it toppled onto its back.

"Now."

The door of the vertical slid open easily, exposing the empty shaft. They propped open the door with a chair and pushed and groaned and heaved at the file box until it rolled like a wheel between the wall and the desk toward the vertical. Paula's fire was beginning to light the carpet. She rushed around ahead of the file, pushed the chair through into the shaft, and held the door open, and Bunker guided the rolling file through the gap. It crashed below. Bunker leaned after it. He braced the door open.

"Look what happened."

She put her head over his shoulder out into the shaft. The file had broken into the car parked in the basement of the shaft. Bunker stretched his arm toward the back wall and caught a heavy cable hanging down from the darkness above. He yanked hard on it to test it. The fire leaped crackling in a burst toward the ceiling. Paula wrinkled her nose at the smoke. Bunker swung himself into the shaft, clinging to the cable, and climbed down hand over hand.

An alarm bell in the ceiling clanged. Bunker was scrambling through the hole torn in the roof down into the vertical car. Paula wrapped her hands around the cable. Using her leg around the cable to brake herself, she slid down after him.

Voices sounded in the room she had just left. She jumped down into the vertical car. The floor was covered with loose film. Her feet slipped out from under her and she landed on her backside.

"Hurry up. I can't see."

She went after Bunker out of the car, into a vast darkened room. She could tell by the sound his voice made that it was large but not empty, and she smelled dust and cardboard and guessed it was a storage basement. Now, about twenty feet away, she made out a faint gray oblong. A window. She grabbed Bunker by the sleeve and towed him through the room toward it. They met a wall of boxes and climbed over them. Two or three alarm bells were ringing insistently overhead.

She put her hand out and touched the wall. The window was arm's length over her head. She felt over it for a latch. Bunker put his arms around her legs and boosted her up so high a spiderweb draped itself over her face. She found the latch and the window swung open. They crawled out to the cool open air.

"Put that thing away."

She cupped her other hand over the false eye. "I keep thinking we ought to do something with it."

They were walking toward the west wall of the dome. All the trees in the park had been cut down, and the ground was cluttered with stumps. It was like a wasteland. No birds sang and all the animals were gone. She sat on the edge of a gulley and slid down the bank. A cascade of dirt and stones followed her to its foot.

The Martians would probably find out almost immediately that they were gone. Sooner or later Cam's police would catch them again. She thought of Jefferson, who had been caught, and drew her left hand out of her pocket. Opening her fingers, she looked down at the false eye.

"Here." Bunker snatched it out of her hand. His arm cocked back and he flung the thing off into the dark, out of the gulley.

"What did you do that for?"

He went off at a fast walk along the floor of the gulley. An air car droned across the dome over her head. Red lights flashed in the sky. At the end of the gulley was a house built back into the hillside. A row of garbage bins flanked it. As soon as she and Bunker approached, a dog began to bark inside the house. The garbage bins were head-high. She climbed up onto the edge of the first one and dug out a moldering sack full of squeezed oranges and coffee grounds.

"Where did you get that key?" she asked Bunker.

He leaned over the edge of the bin and groped around in the heap of garbage. "I made it. They gave me an electronic typewriter."

She turned half an orange inside out, ate off the pulp, and threw the hull back into the bin. "To write letters? Did you write their correspondence? You don't know the language very well. What was this exchange about?"

"The Styths have two pilots Hanse thinks he needs. He offered them money but they aren't having any."

"Who mentioned me?" The dog was barking steadily in the house. She found a heel of soggy bread and bolted it down.

"Nobody in my hearing. The Styths said they wouldn't take money but they might consider meat. Their term. And henceforth in this matter Hanse could communicate in the Common Speech. That was the last I heard." He jumped down and went to the next bin. "Here. You can use this." He dragged something large out of the bin: a heavy coat, missing one sleeve.

They ate until they were satisfied and went on. Without trees, the land looked strange, flat, naked, vulnerable. Bunker led her along at a fast walk. There was no wind and the air smelled dry, dusty, and bitter. They came to a building scooped hollow like a grave. The below-ground floors had been bombed out.

"Well," Bunker said, "so much for that." He sat down heavily on the ground.

Paula went to the edge of the pit. She guessed he had lived here. The destroyed building gaped below her. She sat down next to Bunker and put her arm awkwardly around his shoulders, and he raised his head.

"What are you doing?"

"Don't you find it comforting?"

He snorted up a laugh. "Junior, comfort maketh the mind dull."

Day was coming. The eastern wall of the dome shone with fresh light. Her arm hung around his neck. He resisted; he would not rest on her. She took her arm away and buried her hands in her lap.

They sheltered in the ruins, in a forest of melted plastic drippings. She woke with the sunlight shining in her face. Bunker lay beside her. He had her shirt open down the front; his hand cupped her breast. She put her arms out to him.

"That was nice," he said, after. "I kept telling myself the first thing I'd do when I escaped was get laid."

Paula picked black chunks of grit off her clothes and out of her hair. "Do you want to stay together?"

"I hadn't thought about it. Do you?"

She sat up, spreading out the coat he had found in the bin. It was stained and torn, a long heavily lined man's coat with a notched collar. "For a while, at least. Until we find out what's going on here."

He stood to pull on his pants. His body was thin and bony, his chest sprinkled with crisp hair, graying like the hair on his head. "All right," he said. "Let's go."

By daylight the whole dome seemed changed. Nothing was left of the wood but the stumps of trees. She could see from the ridge near the old campus all the way across the lake to the yellow hills south of the water. Everything looked much smaller. Many of the buildings had been blown up and packs of dogs drifted around the middle and south of the dome. The only birds she saw were crows.

Tony Andrea's building was still lived in. She left Bunker digging through a trash can at the edge of the meadow and went cautiously in the side door. There was a big poster on the wall at the foot of the stairs reading: WORK IS LIFE. The floor was dirty and black handprints marked the walls around the doorways. She knocked on Tony's door.

"Who's 'ere?" a woman called, behind it.

"I'm looking for Tony Andrea."

"Who?"

Paula backed away, looking up and down the hall. At the far end she saw another poster: HELP THE STATE—COOPERATE! In red paint across it and part of the wall beside it was scrawled: STRIKE—STRIKE—STRIKE. The woman behind the door called, "Who's 'ere?" Paula went away.

She remembered An Chu's message and went down the dome to the Nikoles Building. It was underground; she was shy of going into a place with so few ways out. At last she went down into the guts of the building and found the corridor where An Chu had said she was living. She could not remember the number of the apartment. On the corner of the green corridor was a list of the tenants. She stood before it, reading through it, without finding An Chu's name. While she was looking down the list for the third time, a woman's voice said, "Can I help you?"

She wheeled around, her hair standing on end. It was a tall, black-haired woman, too dark to be a Martian. Paula swallowed. "I'm looking for An Chu."

"Who?"

The closed space around her suddenly pressed tighter on her mind. She turned down the corridor. The woman cried, "Wait!" Paula broke into a run. She reached the stairs and went up into the open day.

They went off along the edge of the drying lake. There seemed to be a boundary of a sort, at the head of the lake, cutting the dome in half. South of this border, no building stood intact. Here and there a tree still grew, its branches fuzzed with leaves just unfolding from buds. The lake shore was scummed with dead weed. She saw no animals until just before dark, when a brown dog began to trail them.

"Dick."

"I see her," he said. He gestured at her. "You go that way."

They split up. The dog followed Paula. Patiently she led it along the shore, moving slowly, careful not to look at it too much. Bunker circled around behind it. Paula sat down on the mud beach. There was a thick yellow froth in the water at the edge of the lake, like soap. The lake smelled of rot. The dog slunk toward her, until about fifty yards from her it lay down on its belly, its ears flat to its head. Under its rough dun-colored hide its ribs looked round and sharp as wire hoops. When she moved, it leaped up, its tail curled between its legs. Its dugs hung down along its belly. Paula settled on her hams again. She was painfully hungry. The dog watched her from the weeds, its head on its paws.

Bunker crept up on it, but he made some sound, and the dog bolted away. The man retreated, and the dog paused, its ears pricked up. Paula swore.

"Come on," Bunker said. "Let's walk it down."

Her legs were already sore. She got up and went after him. The sun was setting. They followed the dog into the darkness. It ran in short bursts ahead of them, galloping out of reach, turning to watch them, dashing away again when they got too close. About an hour after dark, they lost it in the gulleys south of the lake.

Paula was too tired and hungry even to complain. They slept in the shelter of a sheer hillside, shivering. Three or four times during the night air cars flew overhead, waking them. Once a searchlight sliced through the dark around them, and they huddled against the cold ground, their heads buried in their jackets, until it left. Before dawn hunger drove them out again.

Crisscrossing the ridges and notched hills below the lake, they divided up, moving along on parallel courses three hundred feet apart, searching for food. She chased a gray snake along a dusty hillside from tuft to tuft of grass. The air was smoky yellow. The dry ground gave up an odor like an empty husk. Her thigh bones ground in the sockets of her hips. Her mouth was filmed and gluey.

In the late afternoon Bunker shouted on the far side of a gulley. She scrambled down the steep bank, knocking loose a shower of small stones and dirt, and ran toward his voice. He was on his knees digging into the bank of the ravine. His arms were gray with dirt.

"I knew that mutt had a den up here somewhere." He scooped dirt away. "Watch out—she'll be back." He plunged his sleeve down over his hand, reached deep into the hole he had dug, and took out a squirming black puppy.

Its yips were small as rabbit sounds. Paula straightened. The brown dog came running along the floor of the ravine. Paula charged it, shouting, and the dog veered off. Its stained teeth showed. Bunker was taking pup after pup out of the den. Their squeaks brought their mother forward, snarling. Paula moved between her and the den. She snatched a long branch off the ground. The dog faced her, its ears flat, and growled.

"Don't take them all—leave her a few."

"Paula Pityheart." He took off his jacket and wrapped the puppies up in it. "Let's go." He slung the wiggling bundle onto his shoulder. When Paula moved, the dog darted past her and rushed into its den. Paula and Bunker went down the gulley to the open ground, made a fire, and roasted five puppies.

Day after day, from the first light to the last, they searched for food. Some days they found nothing at all. Paula fell sick, but she dared not stop hunting even for an hour. One resting while the other tracked, they walked down wild dogs and foxes. In the bombed-out buildings they cornered rats. They went north again, past the head of the lake. Paula dug sacks of rotting garbage out of the trash bins. They broke into an apartment but found nothing to steal except water. Even the clothes in the closets were as shabby as their own. As the lake dried up and turned foul, good water was nearly as scarce as food, until they found the narrow opening into the underground river, whose water was sweet. One evening, while she was rummaging through a garbage can outside the Nikoles Building, someone called her name.

She ran. The voice screamed, "Wait!" Twenty strides away, at the corner of the building, she turned to look back, ready to run again. A small figure was walking after her.

"An Chu." She took a step forward. Maybe it was a trap. A smile spread across the other woman's round face. She put out her hands, and Paula rushed toward her.

"I knew it was you—Jennie said it was somebody with brassy hair—"

Paula hugged her tight, her face against the other woman's coarse black hair. Her throat thickened. She could say nothing. An Chu babbled in her ear, "We've been looking for you—Willie thought he saw you once—" An Chu held her tight, one arm around her shoulders, one around her waist. "Where are you living?"

Paula stepped back. "In the . . ." She nodded toward the south of the dome. She cast a look around them, to be sure they went unwatched.

"In the open?" An Chu took her hands. "Are you hungry?"

"I'm starving."

"Come with me."

Paula followed her down the long side of the building, but An Chu did not go through the door. She hooked her arm through Paula's arm. "The hourlies say you're dead." She squeezed Paula's arm against her, smiling wide. "The Dragon Lady of the Styths. I took the hourlies around to everybody I knew and told them who you really are." They passed the end of the building and went into the open. The evening was warm. Mosquitoes buzzed around her face. High overhead, the red lights of an air car flashed off and on. An Chu glanced up casually and walked Paula in a circle.

"Aren't you living there?" Paula asked.

"Yes—we all are, Willie and Jennie and I. Jennie's the only one who's official. You can't have an apartment unless you have a job-card. You don't get a job-card unless you work. With everybody on strike, that's hard. Jennie works in the dome-maintenance crew. We decided she could, since it's for our sake as much as the Martians'." She looked up into the sky. "He's gone. Hurry." Stooping, she pulled up a round piece of the turf. Paula climbed into the hole in the ground.

She slid feet-first along a steep lightless tunnel, smelling of clay. The curved wall was slippery under her hand and a protruding root lashed her face. At the bottom of the slide she came to rest against a plastic wall. An Chu came after her. She reached over Paula's shoulder and tapped on the wall. It slid open. Paula climbed through into a long room hollowed out of the dirt beside the wall of an underground building.

"Who are you?"

She stood, facing a strange man, fair-faced, with long yellow hair. An Chu crawled after her into the narrow room. "She's Paula Mendoza. I told you we'd find her."

The only furniture in the room were two cots against the outer wall and a big old breakfront cupboard opposite. An Chu opened the wing-doors and took out a loaf of bread and a chunk of cheese.

"Here." She gave them to Paula. "This is Willie Luhan. He's my friend, mine and Jennie's."

Paula sat down on the cot and sank her teeth into the cheese. Her stomach clenched with yearning. An Chu said to the yellow-haired man, "She's been living in the open. She can stay with us."

"It's fine with me," Willie Luhan said.

"I'm not alone." Paula tore off a piece of the bread and stuffed it into her mouth.

"Who's with you?" An Chu asked. She brushed back a strand of her black hair. It was much longer than Paula remembered.

"Dick Bunker. He was on the Committee."

"We don't know him."

"I know him."

An Chu pressed her fingers to her cheeks, her gaze turning to her friend. The man scowled. "Nobody comes in here unless we know him. That's our rule. We have to do it that way, you see."

Paula wiped her mouth on her arm. The taste of the cheese lingered on her tongue. "Then I'll stay out there with him."

The two people before her looked at each other again. Willie licked his lips. His wide face was troubled. An Chu nodded to Paula.

"Bring him."

. . .

"I have to get to Vancouva," Bunker said. "Isn't there any way at all?"

"I'm sorry." The woman spoke with a Martian accent. "Unless you have travel papers from the dome secretary, I'm not authorized to sell you tickets. If you'll just—"

Only her head and shoulders showed above the back of her chair. Paula slid through the door behind her. There were three or four other people in the office waiting room, on the far side of the partition, and she dropped to her hands and knees to keep from being seen.

"But my wife is there," Bunker cried. "I have to get there. Can't you see that?" He gestured dramatically with both hands. "I have to!"

"Well," the woman said nervously, "I can't do anything about that, I'm sorry."

Bunker launched into his passionate lie. Her eyes followed the wide movements of his hands. Paula sneaked up behind her and lifted a card-folder out of the shoulder bag hanging on the woman's chair.

In the corridor outside the travel office, Martian soldiers stood talking, rifles on their shoulders. Paula went past them, her head down. She wore An Chu's clothes, even An Chu's shoes, which pinched her feet. A lunch cart rolled toward her, and a soldier called out to the man pushing it to stop. The Martians gathered around the cart. There was an hourly stand against the wall between Paula and them. She took the card-folder out of her pocket and thumbed a dime from the coin slot. She bought an hourly. The Martians were buying hot rolls and minjis from the cart; the pusher clicked change from the machine on his belt. She dropped the hourly and stooped among the Martians to pick it up, and thieved two handfuls of rolls off the bottom shelf of the cart.

Outside, the loudspeaker on the corner of the building was playing high-spirited marching music. She walked along the side of the building, past the line of people waiting to get into the travel office. Bunker had waited nearly two hours for three minutes of diversion. The ground was scattered with discarded hourlies. She threw away the one in her hand.

Bunker caught up with her at the end of the walk. From habit they went along twenty or thirty paces apart, not talking. An air car buzzed overhead; on its side was the blue star of the government. They went down through the waste land toward the Nikoles Building.

An Chu lit the candle. The ends of the narrow room stayed in deep shadow. The little door that led to the underground building was open, a square cut in the wall, through which Paula could see the pipes and canisters of the garbage-eater under Jennie Morrison's kitchen sink. The flat beyond was one small room, only a little larger than the secret room. The square of plastic that covered the door between them hung on the wall over it, and An Chu pulled it down and fastened it in place. Bunker pulled the stolen job-card out of the plastic folder.

"You got one," An Chu said. "How?"

"Stole it," Paula said. "The Martians are awfully easy targets." She took the hot rolls out of her jacket and put them on the sway-backed cot.

"Do you have a magnifying glass?" Bunker asked. He sat on the head of the cot and peeled the plastic wrap off a hot roll. Paula ate a ham minji.

An Chu gave Bunker a pocket magnifier from the cupboard. She pushed the wing-door shut, sat on the bed, and took a roll out of its wrapping. "Meat. Wonderful."

The folder lay open on the cot. While she ate the minji, Paula looked through the cards in the plastic windows. Bunker held the magnifier up to his eye and the job-card into the light.

"The green cards are for women, the white cards for men?"

"Green for civilian women, white for civilian men, blue for soldiers, red for Martian topshots." An Chu sat on the bed beside Paula. Paula found a pocket in the back of the folder and took out three dollars. It was worthless; all the paper money was worthless.

A sharp knock banged on the door to the kitchen. Kneeling, An Chu unfastened the square cover from the wall and leaned it up against the foot of the cupboard. Jennie Morrison crawled into the secret room. Paula hardly knew her. She wore a bright green dress with her job-card pinned to her collar like a badge.

"I was stopped on the way here. They're searching everybody." She saw the food, the empty wrappers scattered on the bed. Her voice rose. "You've got food! What have you been doing—holding out on me?"

"Relax," Paula said. She handed her a minji. "We just got back from the north."

Jennie ripped off the wrapping. "And you ate it all. I do all the goddamn work—you people just sit around all day—"

"Shut up," An Chu said. Bunker with a single ferret look at Jennie dropped to hands and knees and vanished out the hole in the wall.

"I'm going up in the head." Jennie sat down on the bed. Her mouth was full of minji. "I know you all hate me because I'm working."

"Nobody hates you."

"You're half-right," Paula said. "You're going up in the head."

Jennie gulped food. "This is my house."

"That's my minji."

"Shut up," An Chu said to her.

Bunker forged a job-card and ration tickets for Paula, and she took them up to the public dispensa, across from the government building, stood in line, and brought back two loaves of bread, a pound of rice, a pound of dried vegetables, a gallon sack of milk, a pound of maxibeans, half a pint of oil: a week's ration for a civilian woman. She and An Chu stowed the food away in the secret room. In the apartment, Bunker sat hunched over the table, the reading light aimed at the paper inches from his eyes. She went up behind him and watched him draw the curlicues on the upper-right-hand corner of a ration ticket.

"Don't look over my shoulder."

She moved away from him. An Chu was slicing bread on the counter at the kitchen end of the room. Paula went up to her.

"I have some honey," the other woman said.

"Great."

Bunker finished his work. He brought the sheet of blue ticket paper over to Paula. "There's a man on the red wing who has a white card he'll give me for twenty ration chits." He reached for the bread. "Did you get meat?"

"They don't have meat."

An Chu spread a thin film of honey on a thin slice of bread. "Only the Martians get meat. The red cards and the soldiers. You need special tickets."

The blue sheet was divided into two rows of five ration slips each. They were perfectly drawn. He used An Chu's thick hairs for his brushes. Paula said, "You're wasting your talent, rat, they hardly even look at them, they just tear them up and throw them in a box."

He was biting into a slice of bread. "You're eating, aren't you?" His eyes were puffy, and his fingers stained with ink.

"I bought an hourly." She took the folded sheet from her hip pocket. "Not a word in it about any fighting." An Chu took it.

It was late in the afternoon. Paula could hear the people moving back and forth in the apartment above them. She got the paper shears from the desk and carefully separated the tickets. Bunker rubbed his eyes. "The other page is in the desk."

Paula opened the desk drawer and took out the second sheet. Like the other, this was perfect, ten identical tickets; even the hairline flourishes on the capital letters were exact. She sat down and cut the sheet out. Stacking the tickets, she decked them neatly on the floor.

"Thanks," he said, and took them from her and went out the door.

"He doesn't talk much," An Chu said. "I don't think he likes me."

"He never talks to me, either. It could be worse if he did, like Jennie. If she loses her job, can we stay here?"

"I don't know." An Chu fingered the worn mat flooring. Paula watched her Aztec profile. "There's some dirty talk about rounding people up and sending them to work camps."

"That's just rumor. There aren't enough Martians to do that." She would not go back to jail. "What about Tony Andrea? Do you know where he is?"

An Chu raised her head. "Tony was arrested right away. They all were—all the known people like that. Especially writers. And you know Tony. He never shut up."

"No, he wouldn't." She remembered him vividly, his bright blue eyes, telling her she had sold her soul. She went into the secret room, alone.

She removed her job-card from her collar. The name on it was Stella Dominac. While she stood thinking of Tony, the door behind her rasped back into the wall, and Bunker came in and sat next to her on the cot. He thrust a white card at her. The photograph had already been sliced off the surface. She ran her thumb over the raised numbers.

"The description's not even close." Hair: Black. Eyes: Hazel.

"I'll fix it." He rubbed his eyes. She put her arm around him and kissed his cheek. He turned his face toward her so that their mouths met.

"You taste like honey."

"Try me."

Standing up, he started to take his clothes off. She lay back on her elbow. She liked seeing him naked. An Chu looked in the door and shut it. In the gloom the light on the wall cast shadows over the floor like hiding places.

"I wish I had something left to surprise you with," he said. He peeled off his shirt and lay down beside her, and she put her arms around him.

The cold made her shiver. She shifted from one foot to the other, her hands jammed in the pockets of An Chu's overcoat. Above the fur collar of the coat just ahead of her was a head of hair as gray as Bunker's, molded into sleek curls. She had been standing in line for three hours and she was still only halfway to the door. The walk was carpeted in hourlies.

STRIKE ENDS IN JOHANNESBURG
PRODUCTION JUMPS 18% IN JANUARY
LIGHT SKIRMISH IN THE ASTEROIDS
SAVENIA CELEBRATES BIRTHDAY

She rocked back and forth on her heels. Across the plaza was the government building, where she had been jailed. The white trim around the windows was freshly painted. The scaffolding before it carried a brotherhood poster, three stories high: a white hand clasping a brown hand. She wondered what they had done with Sril's body. Thrown it on the garbage heap. Every time she came here she saw Martians she knew going in and out of the building. Once General Hanse passed within fifty yards of her. She hid behind her hourly.

LIGHT SKIRMISH IN THE ASTEROIDS

Mars Combined Forces has destroyed two Styth cruisers
in a three-hour battle near Vesta.

The people around her chafed their cheeks with their hands and blew out plumes of white air. "What's holding things up?"

"You know I had to wait five hours this week to have my hair done?"

Paula leaned against the wall behind her. The line moved sluggishly forward into the mouth of the building. Probably the dispensa clerks were checking each ticket through a scanner. That had baffled Bunker at first, until he discovered that the Martians used the same metallic ink to print hourlies. They had a connection with the hourly men. A file of soldiers marched by in their dark winter uniforms. Their white gloves swung mechanically in time.

"Halt!"

She stiffened. The soldiers had stopped ahead of her, along the line. The ringing voice of their commander was shouting something. She leaned out to see. The soldiers stood shoulder to shoulder facing the line of civilians. Their commander and another man stood between the two groups. The other man held up a piece of blue and white cloth.

"This is the flag of the Martian Republic. Now it's also the flag of the Earth. It represents all of us—our solidarity against enemies, our faith in ourselves and the future. To salute—" The officer wheeled smartly. His right arm snapped up, palm flat, toward the flag.

"You will now salute the flag."

Paula drew back against the wall. Her heart pounded. She looked back along the line. Above the fur collar, the silver-haired head turned. "Now, what's this all about?"

The soldiers and the man with the blue cloth were moving slowly down the line, stopping to let each person salute. Paula gripped her hands together.

"Salute the flag!"

"Why?" a girl's voice asked.

"She's an anarchist. Take her in custody."

Paula burst out of the line, running away from the soldiers down the string of waiting people. Someone shouted. She ran close to the line; they would not shoot into the crowd. A hand snatched for her and she eluded it. A man raced past her, fleeing. Her foot slipped on a loose hourly and she fell. A bullet whispered past her ear. People screamed. She leaped up, dodging between two buildings. The little metal whisper hummed by her again. She ran around the corner of a building. Something hit her like a hammer and knocked her flying. She rolled over and over, leaped up, and ran on. People shouted, somewhere behind her. Her hip began to hurt. Through the screams behind her she heard the clatter of gunfire. She limped away into the wasteland, panting.

Some while later their building was raided. She and Bunker, Willie and An Chu sat for hours in the tunnel. It was freezing cold. She laid her cheek against Bunker's shoulder and closed her eyes. Once they heard Jennie Morrison screaming. Finally, just before dawn, they crept down into the secret room again.

Jennie was gone. The apartment was wrecked. The desk had been smashed and the cupboards and counter pulled off the kitchen wall. The wall between this and the next apartment had been broken out. The man who lived there was gone too.

An Chu leaned on Willie's shoulder and cried. Paula took her jacket off. The healing bullet wound ached in her backside. She and Bunker went out to the hall.

All up and down the hall the doors to the apartments were broken inward. She went along the hall, looking into the rooms. In some of them even the mat flooring had been ripped up and the floors cracked open. No one was there. Paula wiped her hands on her sleeves. So they had done it, rounded everybody up and taken them away. Bunker went ahead of her toward the stairs. She turned back to Jennie's room.

Willie paced up and down the room, his arms swinging. "This proves it. We have to get out of here."

"Where?" Paula said. Bunker returned, and her shoulders sank an inch with relief.

"The people hidden under the floor in 73 are still here," he said. "And the two women who live in the broom closet. I guess the police just didn't bother to look in there."

Willie walked past them, his strides quick as a soldier's. "I'll kill them. I'll smash hell out of them, if I can just get my hands on them." He brandished his fists.

An Chu came in from the secret room with a cup of water. "What are we going to do about Jennie?"

"We have to get out of here," Willie said.

"We can't leave," Bunker said to Willie. "Not right away. They'll be watching to see if anybody bolts." He slid under the sink to open the secret door.

Paula and An Chu followed Bunker into the narrow room. The smell of mildew grew strong just inside the door. An Chu dropped down onto the cot she and Willie shared, her face tipped up to Paula's.

"We have to find out where they've taken Jennie."

At the end of the room, Bunker turned around. "No. There's nothing we can do for Jennie now."

"When we find her we can decide what to do," Paula said. Her left buttock throbbed deep in the wound. Willie Luhan was stalking down the room, his fists still clenched tight.

"You know, I think you're a coward," he said to Bunker.

"I think you're an idiot," Bunker said. He went head-first out of the room into the ruined building.

An Chu straightened, her hand on Paula's arm. "They took dozens of people. It won't be that hard to find them."

"I'll help you," Willie said. "I know where I can get a gun."

Paula's hand pressed against her bad hip. She went to the bucket for a drink of water. It was nearly morning. They would have to wait until night to look for Jennie. The pain in her hip nagged her. She was going nowhere with Willie and his gun. Of all the people she knew, the only one she needed was Bunker. He would not help her, and he was right. She hunched her shoulders.

At a lope she crossed the close-cropped lawn to the next building, An Chu behind her, and sat down in the lee of the wall. An Chu raced up beside her. Paula wiped her hand over her face.

"This is impossible."

An Chu muttered something. There were four buildings in this complex, all above ground, rising six or eight stories above the trim lawns. Down the hill, Paula could see a section of the wire fence that separated the buildings and grass from the barren wasteland. A light came on in the building she was sitting against.

"We aren't doing this right." She got up. Her hip had stiffened and when she put her weight on it she nearly fell. She led An Chu the length of the building to the door. It was locked. She pressed her nose to the window. Inside was a hall, and along the wall a row of vending machines.

"We need an hourly."

An Chu pushed her out of the way to look. "They won't say

where they took them in an hourly." She rattled the door. Paula turned, casting around the lawn for loose paper.

"Listen." An Chu clutched her arm. "Is that about us?"

Somewhere nearby a siren moaned up toward a whistling shriek. Paula moved away from the building, toward the dark. Another siren joined the first, and another, and another, and suddenly one on the roof before her, so loud she jumped a foot.

"Come on." Limping, she started down the hill toward the fence. The grass was even as pavement under her feet.

The sirens screeched up to a high note and stuck there. An Chu beside her broke into a trot. She glanced back.

"Watch out!"

Paula wheeled. A searchlight snapped on near the building they had just left. An Chu whispered, "Run!"

"No." Paula grabbed the other woman's arm and held her. She faced the searchlight's blinding eye. The sirens' high scream needled her ears. Two indistinct figures ran down the gentle slope toward her.

"Stay where you are. Put your hands up."

Paula raised her hands. She called, "What's going on? We're trying to get home."

Two Martian soldiers reached them. One carried a heavy automatic pistol. The other slapped his hands down Paula's sides.

"All right. Where's home? You know you're half an hour past curfew."

Paula gave the address on her identification. She took the white job-card out of the collar pocket on her jacket to show the soldier. The searchlight went off; the round eye of the lamp faded slowly through yellow to brown to black. An Chu stood rigid while the soldier groped her up and down. Suddenly the sirens too were turned off. The silence rang like the aftertone of a bell. The soldier with the pistol looked up over his head at the dark dome.

"False alarm?"

The other man was reading Paula's card, luminous in the dark. "What are you doing all the way—" He raised his head. High overhead there was a boom.

"Come with us. Run." He grabbed Paula's arm and dragged her across the lawn at a dead run toward the nearest building. The other man and An Chu raced after them.

Another boom sounded, nearer, like a crash of thunder. The echo rolled off around them. The sound hurt Paula's ears. The soldier opened a sloping basement door and pushed her toward a flight of steps leading down into the underground floor. She looked back. Far down the dome, beyond the fence, there was a sudden great spark, blue-white, like a giant star, gone in an instant. The soldier thrust her down into the basement.

"Attention," a wall speaker said. "Your attention please."

The dark basement was crowded with people, packed together body to body. The man behind Paula directed her through the room. His hand torch flashed a narrow light ahead of her. She stepped over legs and bodies sprawled over the floor. Two people squeezed apart to make room for her.

"Paula—"

She caught An Chu's hand and pulled her after her. There was room for only one of them to sit, and they stood, An Chu in front of Paula. The soldiers were gone.

"Attention. We are experiencing a meteorite barrage. There is no need for alarm. Please remain quiet and obey your building commandos."

"Meteorites," An Chu said. "What do they—"

"Sssh." Paula slid one arm around An Chu's waist. Her hip hurt and she shifted her balance to the other leg. The door was behind them, ten yards away: twenty people away. Wait. Under her feet the floor vibrated. The people around her talked in low voices. The soldier who had brought them still had her job-card. He might be checking it. The sirens began to howl again.

"Attention. Your attention please. The all-clear is sounding—"

The crowd got to their feet in a sudden relieved roar of voices, their feet loud, reaching for coats and children. Paula shoved An Chu forward.

"Hurry."

They worked their way through the shifting mob toward the door. The ceiling lights came on, dazzling bright, drawing a gasp from most of the people in the room. Between Paula and the door a man helped another into a coat. He had been sitting on an hourly, which clung to his backside. In passing, Paula removed it. She bundled it in her fist and followed An Chu to the door. They slid out to the cool night air and ran down the gentle slope toward the fence.

RAIDS BREAK SABOTAGE RING

> Government Police have arrested over a thousand anarchist terrorists in raids that broke the back of a dome-wide subversive organization.

"Over a thousand," Paula said. Even allowing for official exaggeration, that meant hundreds of prisoners. There were very few places in New York large enough to keep hundreds of people. Even after the immigrations of the past months, the Martians did not have enough men here to guard hundreds of prisoners in small groups: they all had to be together. Paula swept a look around them. They were walking along the side of a hill, outside the fences of the Martians. Dawn was coming.

"How's your butt?" An Chu stuffed her hands in her jacket pockets.

"It's all right."

"They don't expect anybody to believe that was meteorites," An Chu said.

"They do have meteor storms on Mars," Paula said. "The air's that thin." She folded the hourly. A dry ridge of hillside rose up ahead of them, beyond a forest of tree stumps four feet high. She swung around the foot of the hill.

Climbing the gentler slope beyond, she smelled smoke, and when she reached the crest of the hill saw a ruin, still burning, on the level ground beyond. She stopped. An Chu caught up with her.

"What's the matter?"

Paula was staring at the ruin. It had been bombed out long before; the old walls had sagged almost to the ground. Someone had bombed it again last night. An Chu said, "That must have happened during the raid. Then it's the Styths, isn't it?"

Paula went on without answering. With masers, they could bomb inside the dome, and they obviously had some way of finding buildings, although without distinguishing inhabited places from ruins. She thought nervously of Bunker in the building near the lake and went faster down the hillside.

The wound in her cheek itched. She hoped that meant it was healing. Limping after An Chu across the barren wasteland, she thought wryly of what Tanuojin had said; she wished for him now, with his doctor's hands. An Chu ran off over the crest of a hill, out of sight.

The night was much warmer than the one before had been. The dust made her nose itch. They had spent an hour talking over the whole dome and the places where the Martians could house hundreds of prisoners. There was only one: the entry port on the northwest wall. She rounded the hillside and a dry wind brushed her face. An Chu dashed up to her.

"Look what I found."

She had half an overripe melon, lightly peppered with coffee grounds. They ate it while they walked. The sweet juice ran down Paula's chin and she caught it on her fingers and licked it off. They crossed a stretch of low ground that had been bulldozed flat, as if for a new building. Paula looked south. The dome stretched off below her, spotted with islands of lights. The sirens began.

"Again?" An Chu put her head back to look up.

"Come on," Paula said. "This will make it easier—they'll all be indoors."

They went on side by side toward the west wall of the dome. The sirens' hound-voices rose and fell, reached their high note, and stayed there. The first crash boomed in the peak of the dome. The thunder radiated out like a wave. Paula found herself walking at top speed in spite of her bad hip.

Another, louder bang sounded. Suddenly, just ahead of her and a hundred feet off the ground, there was a silent explosion of light, blue-white, brilliant as a sun. It was gone at once. She stopped, her breath caught in her lungs, An Chu beside her. They were near the top of a hill; to the north was another complex of buildings. The booming in the dome grew louder and the reports closer together. Another star burst at ground level between the two women and the buildings. For an instant the buildings, the land, the dead stumps of the trees were printed on Paula's eyes like a photographic negative. The blackness that fell afterward was like being blind. Another boom echoed through the dome and a few seconds later another light shone, and one of the buildings to the north exploded into a stalk of flames.

Paula turned and ran down the hillside. Her ears rang. The thunder rolls of the attack came so fast they blended into one long crash. The light-bombs burst with every stride she took. An Chu ran beside her. The grass broke under Paula's feet and a sharp dry stalk jabbed her in the leg. Dazzled by the bombs, her head throbbing from the racket, she ran straight into a heavy wire-mesh fence.

The attack ended. The sirens of the all-clear began to moan. Paula and An Chu climbed the fence and dropped down onto the smooth clipped grass of a Martian lawn. Limping, Paula jogged toward the dome wall, just ahead of them beyond a building. Voices sounded, and people began to spill out of the below-ground floors onto the grass. The lights in the building came on. Paula and An Chu went unnoticed in the crowd; they sneaked down into a basement to hide for the day.

An Chu found them a banquet in the garbage: soggy bread and apple cores and four containers with beans and vegetables still clinging to the bottoms. They drank from a public fountain and spent most of the day in the basement of the building, in behind the cleaning machines. After dark they started along the wall of the dome, going north, to find the entry port.

It bulged out of the side of the dome, taller than any building, about fifteen minutes' walk from where they had spent the day. The wire fence surrounding it was strung on rubberized posts. Five feet inside this fence was another fence, higher, also insulated.

Paula sat down. Her backside hurt more than yesterday and she knew it was infected. "That must be where they are."

"Is it electric?" An Chu put her hand out.

"Touch it and find out."

"Why are you in a mood?"

Paula looked away. Now that they had found Jennie, there was nothing to do to help her. She got up and went on along the fence, limping. The blank wall of the entry port rose up beyond the second fence. She could see people walking on the ramp over her head, perhaps sentries. One leaned on the rail a moment and she saw the barrel of a gun on his shoulder.

"When the Styths raid again," An Chu said, "we can try to get in."

Paula rammed her hands into her pockets. Every time her left foot hit the ground her whole left side ached. She had to remember that and compensate for it. The fence curved away from them and she bent her course to follow.

"Hey! Stop where you are!"

The shout struck her like a bullet. She sprinted dead away from the fence, toward the darkness. The lawn spread out before her. An Chu passed her ten feet to one side, her arms pumping.

"Stop or I'll shoot!"

Paula's hip threatened to give way. She could not run. She dropped down flat on her face on the ground. An Chu kept running. A gun fired a burst of shots. An Chu fell to her knees. Other people were hurrying after them across the grass. An Chu struggled onto her feet. The gun rattled again and the woman fell and lay still.

A man with a gun ran by Paula, and she got up. People crowded toward An Chu where she lay on the grass. Paula went in among them. The anarchist was dead; the spray of bullets had cut her like an ax. A tall man behind Paula said, "Weren't there two of them?"

Her hands in her pockets, she walked away from the clot of people. Behind her voices rose, and the gun went off again in a sudden burst. There was no place to hide. She kept herself from running, which would surely give her away, and tried not to limp. The gun rattled again, far back there. Shooting at Martians. Something huge and vague loomed up ahead of her. She put her hands out and touched cold net.

The fence. She leaned on it, her face against it, damp on her cheek. She had no strength left to climb it. Her fingers crooked into the mesh. Up. Her left leg refused to move. She flung one arm up over her head and took hold of the fence. Up. The air sang with the shrill yell of a siren. Like krines only louder. She dragged herself up the fence, her toes jammed into the meshwork. Throwing her arms over the top, she hung there, out of strength. The sirens screeched behind her. Her left leg dangled uselessly. She squirmed up and across the top of the fence. The barrage began. The lights seemed to burst inside her head, exploding in her eyes. Blinded and deafened, she struggled her body over the fence and let go and fell. It did not hurt when she fell. The ground quaked under her. She gained her feet and shuffled away into the wasteland.

She came back to the Nikoles Building in the daylight and stayed out in the park until night rolled over the dome. Her face was hot and her mouth parched and she could barely walk on her bad leg. After sunset she crept into the tunnel and slid down to the hatch into the secret room.

Willie answered her knock. "Paula!" He helped her out of the hatch. "Where have you been? Where's Ana?"

"She's dead." Paula lay on the cot. Her lips were cracked with thirst and fever.

"Dead," Willie said.

She rolled her arms around her head. Her whole body hurt. He gripped her forearms and shook her. "What happened?"

"Let me alone."

He shook her harder, back and forth, until she moaned. "What happened? Where did you go?" She was getting sick to her stomach. Her head was spinning off her neck. She slumped into a thick dark exhaustion.

When she came back to waking, she was lying on the floor, thickly wrapped in blankets. The only light in the room was the greasy dip-lamp burning in a chink in the dirt wall. She moved, untangling herself from the blanket, and knocked over a cup of water beside her. There was a patch of tape stuck to the inside of her elbow.

"Dick?" she said.

At the end of the room, something stirred in the dark. Bunker came down toward her, past the cot where Willie was asleep. "What happened?" He picked up the overturned cup.

"Jennie's in the entry port. You were right. There's nothing we can do."

"Then why did you try?"

"The debt owed to common humanity."

"You keep saying that. What does it mean?"

"Ask Saba. It's one of his dicta."

"Then it's meaningless. Give me your arm."

She held her arm out toward him, and he ripped the tape patch away. On the pale field of skin at the crease of her elbow were several small pinpricks of blood. He took another patch out of its paper folder and stuck it to her arm.

"No," she said. "It means something to him. To An Chu, maybe even to me. We couldn't let Jennie go without trying."

"It doesn't mean much to An Chu any more."

That was so. And what they had tried to do certainly meant nothing to Jennie Morrison. He smoothed the patch with his thumb.

"What's on this tape? Where did you get it?"

"Antibiotic. While you were out playing cowboy with An Chu I broke into an apartment building. During a raid."

"I'm thirsty," she said.

"The water is where it always is."

She went the length of the room, limping hard to show him how hurt she was, although her hip felt much stronger. The water was cold. She drank two cupfuls and went back. Willie slept like a child, the blanket snug over his neck. The dip-lamp flickered in the draft of her passing. An Chu's blanket-coat was slung over the foot of the cot. Paula sat down with her back to the wall, beside Bunker, and folded her knees up to her chest.

The glossy mud of the lake was cracked and dry. Paula swiped at the stinging insects buzzing around her head. She was moving at a fast walk toward the ruins on the lake shore, three shells of houses half-buried in thorn bushes. There had been no rain in the dome since the coup. With the trees and animals gone and so many more people living here, the whole environment had changed. She climbed up a steep slope and went in among the walls of the ruins.

Here it was hot, even hotter than outside, and the bloodsippers and no-see-ems attacked her in clouds. She looked quickly over the snares she had set. A half-dead bird was tangled in the net trap; she killed it. Something bigger had sprung the other snares and eaten the baits and she reset them.

East of the lake the land flattened out. The grass here was full of snakes. She ran toward the north, holding the binoculars with one hand to keep them from banging her chest. The flats broke into a rising hillside. She walked up to the height, sat down on a tree stump, and focused the binoculars on the nearest of the Martian settlements, about a mile away.

The eighteen buildings of the complex were surrounded by a mesh fence over twenty feet high. The grass was jewel green. Dick, who went there all the time, said it was plastic turf. The glasses showed her children playing kickball, a woman in a sun-chair with a pad over her eyes, a dog sleeping in the shade. She looked in the windows of the building. The man on the third floor had almost finished his water color. She watched the Martians for nearly an hour. When dark fell she went back across the lake to her building.

Outside the tunnel hatch she pulled out most of the bird's feathers, gutted it, and put the innards in her bait-jar. When she went down into the hidden room Bunker was there with three people she had never seen before. She put the bird on a spit.

"This is all of you?" Bunker said to his guests. "Just you three?"

"How many more do you want?" the strange woman said.

Paula took the bird out to Jennie Morrison's empty flat, where she had dug out a fire pit, and lit the fire. Through the open door she could see the people in the hidden room. She pretended not to be watching. She had eaten nothing but meal for two days and had no interest in sharing the meat.

"Give me ten days to steal the car," Bunker said. He stood. He wore no shirt and sweat glittered on his washboard chest. The other people rose.

"If there's anything we can do," the woman said. "Any way we can pay you for your help—"

"I'm not doing it for you, I'm just hurting Savenia."

Paula went into the room to get a drink of water. It irritated her that he spent days helping strange people leave the dome. With a lucifer match she lit the dip-lamp in the wall.

"When you get outside," Bunker said, "you'll have to dodge the Styths."

Her back to them, Paula muttered, "Tell them Paula sends her love."

"What?"

Bunker escorted his clients out through the flat toward the stairs. Paula took her clothes off. The heat made her hair frizzy. Her skin was rough with insect bites. She washed with a towel and a pan of water.

"Have you seen Luhan?" Dick said. He came into the room and slid the door shut.

"Not in days."

The water in the pot was murky. She threw it out and poured fresh water to wash her face with. Sitting on the cot, she combed her hair. "How many of these people do you think escape from the Martians and the Styths both?"

"Very few."

"Maybe none." She watched him walk the length of the room. His gray beard grew like wool along his jaws. Dropping down beside her on the cot, he scratched her back.

"We ought to move," she said. She squirmed to bring other parts of her back under his fingernails. "I'm getting a bad feeling about staying here."

"You're superstitious."

"We've been here too long. You bring half the population of the dome in, everybody knows where we are. You should put out a sign. *I'm saving the world, apply here.*"

"Savenia has a reward out for those people."

"She probably has a reward out for us. And it wouldn't surprise me if Saba and Tanuojin have money out for us."

"All right." He scratched her shoulders and down her arms. "We'll move."

"Good."

"After I get these people out of the dome."

Paula woke up with a jump. Something was crashing against the apartment door. Beside her Bunker thrust himself up on his arms.

"Raid." He left the bed like a bird from the limb.

The door crashed open. A bright light stabbed into the room. Paula scrambled across the head end of the cot toward the darkness. Men rushed into the room, surrounding her. She lunged for the door, tripped, and fell on her face halfway across the threshold. A boot tramped on her hand. She was hauled up by the arms to her feet.

In the white glare of a hand torch, Bunker stood with his arms gripped behind him and a rifle across his neck. Three men held him. He looked frail. His muscles were strung like wires along his bones. The men around him wore no uniforms, although on their upper arms there were red armbands.

"You're the forger?" Another man stepped between Paula and Bunker.

"Who are you?" Bunker said. His voice was hoarse.

"My name is Han Ra. I'm the chief of the Red Army. We fight the Martians. If you're anarchists, you'll join us." He was taller than Bunker, and lean, with a wild yellow beard and hair like a mane hanging down over his back.

"I don't join anybody," Bunker said.

"You have an air car. Where is it?"

More men crowded into the room. The third man was Willie Luhan, with a rifle in his arms.

"Where is the air car?" Han Ra said. He whipped a long knife out of his belt and aimed it at Bunker's chest. Dick took a breath; his chest swelled as if to meet the knife.

"Don't hurt him," Willie cried.

Han Ra laughed. He ran the tip of the knife down Bunker's breastbone. "Where is the air car?"

Bunker said nothing. Paula was standing on tiptoe, her arms crooked painfully behind her. She glanced at Willie Luhan again, caught him looking at her, and gritted her teeth, and he brushed by the man in front of him and went to Han Ra.

"You told me you wouldn't hurt them."

"I want that car. What about her? Does she know?"

"Yes, but—"

Han Ra drew his arm back and drove the knife into Bunker's belly. The slight man went down bonelessly to the floor. He made no sound. Han Ra swung to Paula, the knife bright in his hand.

"Where is it?"

Willie clutched his arm. "No. Don't hurt her. I—I know where it is. I was lying before. Keeping it for myself." His eyes glistened. The glare of the torch shone on his face and the wild bearded face of the Red chief. "Don't hurt her, for god's sake."

"Come on," Han Ra said. He squatted to go through the door. The man with the hand torch followed him. The darkness they left behind in the room swarmed with men.

"What about her?" someone called, behind her.

"Leave her. She's a woman. What can she do?"

They left her. Passing by, the last to go knocked her carelessly to her knees. She went after them to the low door and shut it and crept back to Bunker lying on the floor.

"Dick." The room was utterly dark. Her hands groped over him. He was rigid, doubled up in a knot on his side on the floor, and for a moment she could not feel him breathe and thought he was dead. Her fingers slid over the skin of his ribs and down and touched the slime of blood.

"Paula."

"Wait." She scurried off around the room. "Just a minute—I'll get a light—" She banged into the end of the bed so hard that for a few steps her leg would not hold her. Feeling over the wall she reached the dip-lamp in the chink by the cupboard and lit it. The medical patches were in the old cupboard. She knelt beside him and pasted one square to each of his elbows.

"Paula."

"Don't talk." She yanked the bedcovers off the bed and wrapped him in a blanket. The dip-lamp made the room stuffy in a moment.

"Get out," he said. His voice wheezed.

"I won't leave you."

When he breathed in, his breath whistled. "Stupid bitch. Both of us. Get out. Luhan. Doesn't know. Where. The air car."

"Oh."

He closed his eyes. His skin looked black in the feeble light. She tore pieces from the second blanket and made a bandage over the slit in his belly and fastened it with a nail. He tried to help her move him but he could not even stand. She dragged him up the tunnel. Every few yards she stopped to rest, and while she rested held him tight in her arms to keep him warm. By the time she reached the surface, he was unconscious.

The warm night was unusually windy. The long slope led away from the mouth of the tunnel toward the lake. She laid him carefully on one blanket and pulled it by the edge down across the grass. The wind rustled behind her and she started so hard she went cold, thinking it was Han Ra coming back.

A hundred feet from the tunnel, the slope broke off in a sheer fourteen-foot drop, like a bite taken out of the hillside. She hid Bunker in the shadow at the back of this notch and returned to the secret room. All their food was hidden in a hole dug out of the wall behind the bed. She put it into a sack, took the sack and some rope out across the wasteland to the only tree in the area, and hoisted it up to the high branches, away from dogs.

Bunker was where she had left him: awake now. She felt of the bandage. It was so full of blood it squelched when she touched it.

He whispered, "Tools. Fire." His voice sounded as if it were rising through water.

"I'm afraid to leave you here. It's too close to the tunnel." She bundled him up again in the blankets. There were only three or four hours left until daybreak. His eyes were closed and she thought he was asleep again, but when she lifted him with his arm around her neck he pushed with his feet, trying to help. She took him off over the gentle hump of the next hill and down into a narrow gulley whose sandy bottom yielded under her feet.

When she had found him a soft shelter she went back at a run to the tunnel. On the slope, she stopped still. Above the tunnel, near the crown of the slope, was the flat turret of the building's gatehouse. A light shone through it. While she watched it faded out. She went at a jog up to the gatehouse and looked in the door.

She could see down the stairway, and the light was just disappearing away along the corridor that led to Jennie's flat. Quietly she followed it. For the first time, she remembered she had no clothes on. Her bare feet made no sound on the slick plastic floor. Ahead, the light bobbed along; the people carrying it were one dark moving thing, now and then a head and shoulders silhouetted against the ball of light before them. They went into Jennie Morrison's old flat, and Paula went into the next one.

There was a hole blasted through the wall between this place and Jennie's. Chunks of plasticrete and shelving littered the floor. She stepped carefully over a sink basin.

"They're gone," someone said loudly, in the next room. "That bitch got him out."

"I told you to do for her."

"We'll find them."

She put her hand on the wall and looked through the hole into Jennie's flat. The low doorway under the sink was open wide and the light shone out from the secret room. Long shadows passed back and forth through it: the legs of the men walking past the light. They were looting the place. She backed up a step into the ruined apartment behind her, stooped, and in the rubble found a piece of plasticrete she could lift.

"We could use this cupboard for firewood," one of the raiders said. "I wonder how they got it in here?"

She threw the chunk of building stone at Jennie's kitchen wall. At the thud someone yelled.

"What's that?"

Paula was hurrying through the darkened apartment, gathering up pieces of stone. She went back to the hole and threw the debris against the wall around the low doorway. Something crumbled and a shower of dust fell like hail.

"Hey! Who's that? What's going on?" A head poked out the doorway, and she flung a stone that came nowhere near him and he ducked back.

"Get away or we'll shoot!"

She leaned against the wall in the dark room, listening to them. When no more rocks fell around them, they began to talk in low whispers, and suddenly three men burst out of the doorway. A gun went off half a dozen times, like thunder in the closed space, and the three men raced out Jennie's door and down the corridor, taking their light with them. Paula went into the secret room. Bunker's tools, matches, the last of their clothes, and the dip-lamp were all piled on the bed. She wrapped them up in her winter coat and lugged them up the tunnel to the wilderness.

From where she was sitting, she could see the whole lake. Three people were coming toward her along its edge. It was strange how even now that the lake had no water in it at all and the mud was dried firm as concrete, people walked along the edge instead of across. Habit. They saw what they were used to seeing. Paula sat cross-legged in the lee of the ruined building watching the three people come on.

The woman led them. Paula had seen that of the three of them the woman was the boldest. The two men followed her trustingly. They reached the big boulder that marked the southernmost tip of the lake and turned to walk along the edge of the meadow, following the curve of the next hillside. Paula stood up.

Instantly the man second in the line saw her and tapped the woman on the shoulder and pointed. Paula waved to them. They broke into a run toward her. Paula waited until they were nearly on her and went off past the ruin. They fell in around her.

"Where is your friend?" the woman said. "We were expecting him."

"He's busy."

Beyond the ruin where Paula had waited for them the land was broken into ridges where the grass still grew thick and there were still many trees. Narrow defiles separated the ridges, their beds made of round stones. She led these people down a twisting gulley, past the place where she and Kasuk and Junna had come into the New York dome, two years before. At the mouth of this gorge, she went between two old trees and into a cave in the hillside. The cave was lined with polished tile. It was an old terminal on the Underground. A big blue arrow on the tile pointed into the gloom; a sign above it read INDEPENDENT LINE. The air car was parked against the opposite wall.

"Fantastic." One of the men rushed to it and pried the bonnet up.

Paula put her hands into her pockets. So near its mouth the cave was light enough to make out the strange woman's broad-nosed, pleasant face. She said, "Do you hear that?" and wagged her head toward the rear of the cave. The roar of the underground river came from the darkness.

"It sounds like water," the woman said calmly.

"That's how you get out. This car isn't amphibious, so you have to be careful about getting it wet. Follow the river there downstream until you come to the waterfall. Then you go upstream. About fifteen miles up there's a hole in the roof of the tunnel."

The woman was smiling at her. In the same placid voice, she said, "You and he are the last ones, you know. Every free anarchist has gone."

The two men were climbing over the air car. One called, "This is super-check, Kadrin." The woman waved her hand at them.

Paula said, "If you're smart, you'll go when it's light out. After dawn. The Styths don't like bright light."

"Thank you," the woman said.

"Don't thank me. I don't think you're going to make it. There's nothing to thank us for."

The woman laughed. She clapped Paula on the arm, as if Paula had made some tremendous joke, and went to join her friends. Their voices rose, excited, as they explored the car. Paula went out of the cave. She stopped in the gorge, still hearing their voices behind her, and listened awhile.

"There was something snuffling around outside," Bunker said. "When I woke up."

She crawled in beside him and lay down. Her hair caught on the thorny brush above her. Carefully she freed herself. In the thicket, their latest hiding place, there was just room enough for him to lie on his back and for her to lie on her side next to him. The water bucket stood near his head. She drank a cupful of water.

"How do you feel?" she asked.

"It hurts like hell."

She could barely see his face. Dawn would come in less than an hour; she was tired, and she put her head down on her curved arm. He had his hands pressed to his belly.

"I'm beginning to know what Saba meant," she said. "About the debts between people. There must be something. There has to be something people do for each other besides prey on each other." The thorny brush smelled bitter, and her teeth were full of gritty dust. She wiped her face with her fingers. "Something we owe each other."

"Where did you go?"

"To take those people to the air car. Kadrin and her friends."

"Oh. I didn't recognize the mood."

"They won't get away. The Styths will get them if the Martians miss them. Why should they even bother?"

"Oh, junior, come on."

"What do you mean, come on?" Her throat felt tight.

"I mean you're a little old to be searching for the meaning of life."

Rebuked, she lay still, her head on her arm, and watched while he crooked his arm up over his head and felt for the cup and dipped himself up some of the water. He did not drink it, but rinsed his mouth with it and spat it out.

"There must be something," she said.

He made a sound like a laugh. She thought his eyes were closed.

"Why did you join the Committee?" she asked. "If not to help."

"I like to watch people."

"A spectator? You make a pretty lively audience."

"Not an audience," he said. "A witness."

She did not understand the difference. She lay still, listening to the sounds around her. Something little scurried through the dense brush of the thicket. Mouse. She would eat him if she caught him. Far away a dog howled. Probably that had snuffled around the thicket, waking Bunker. She wondered if he had been frightened. A witness. It meant something exact to him, a word from his private language. She had lived as close to him as she had without learning even that much about him; after so long together she knew him as indistinctly as she saw him in the darkness. There was no bond. There was no debt, only the longing for one, for some connection, some common understanding. It was all a lie, like hope and love and faith. She reached for the cup again, to get herself some water.

In the late afternoon, she went up to the elm tree, climbed into its branches, and lowered the sack of food she had cached on a rope over a high fork. While she ate bread and the last of the rotten meat, she looked through the branches. There were three or four people walking around on the mud of the lake. In the middle a man was digging with a shovel. She knew them all; they lived in three or four caves in a gulley about half a mile south of her thicket. She could just see the glittering metal fences that ringed the nearest Martian compound. The foul meat made her stomach churn. She climbed down to the ground and circled around the thicket, keeping watch for Han Ra's men. In a ditch, near another elm tree, Willie Luhan lay dead on the ground.

She did not go near him. His face and hands were half eaten away. The putrid smell was strong. She wondered what had killed him. His jacket was gone, his shoes gone, his legs inside his ragged trousers swarmed with feeding insects. She went back fast to the thorn thicket, to Bunker. That night the Styths bombed the dome from sundown to sunrise.

She went up to the Martian compound and caught a fat little dog, throttling it with her hands. She also found an hourly.

OPERATION DUNKIRQUE

> In the most ambitious mass operation ever undertaken, the Combined Services today began to relocate the populations of sectors endangered by Styth raids.

To her surprise, Bunker laughed. He lay back, one arm curved under his head. "Well, junior, put it in the pot, maybe it will flavor the dog." He held out the other hand in the air. A spider crawled over his thumb.

"They're giving up," she said bitterly. The spider reached the end of his thumb and paused, confused. "They're running and leaving us to take it in the face. How can you let that bug crawl on you?" The spider was groping cautiously over his hand.

"I am intimate with every insect in this bush, which is your fault for bringing me here."

She sat under the elm tree, looking across the dome. Dawn was coming. Up toward the north, two points of yellow light glowed in the darkness: the fires of Han Ra's men. If the Martians left, they would take the dogs, her main source of meat. She would not steal from Han Ra's people and the people who lived in the caves, for fear of bringing them down on her. Bunker was stronger, the hole in his belly had closed, and soon he would be able to help her. Her feet were cold. She went back down the slope to the thicket and crawled in beside him.

The dawn made the air above them white, each leaf of the thicket sharp against it, like a woodcut. They fell asleep in the ripening day.

The terminal pond at the Manhattan dock connected with the ocean. In spite of the drought it was full. Paula and Bunker climbed over the sagging fence to reach it. The wall of the dome came down just beyond it, streaked with condensation. Paula went to the sandy shore of the pond. The three buildings on the far side had been blown up, and the water was clogged with the wreckage.

Bunker took off his jacket and stepped out of his pants. He dropped his shirt onto the heap of his other clothes. He felt of the water with his hand, stuck one foot in, shivering, and jumped into the pond.

Paula gathered his clothes. At the edge of the pond she stood leaning over the water trying to see down to the bottom. Bubbles broke the surface. Far down there, she had no idea how far down there, was the boat he was fixing. A great shining gobbet of air burst up out of the water. That was the hatch opening. The boat's environment still worked, and he could stay down there nearly ninety minutes before he had to come up again and fill the air tank. She waded in the shallows, her trouser legs rolled up, hunting for turtles and crabs which were safer to eat than mussels.

Bunker brought the boat's air tanks up and filled them. Night was coming. Paula made a fire to cook the four little green crabs. Bunker's pump chugged; it ran on fusion cells he stole from the Martians and broke nearly every time he used it. Little waves slapped on the pond shore, mimicking the great ocean just beyond the dome wall. She split the red backs of the crabs with her knife.

They ate in silence. She sucked the meat from a crab's spidery leg. Bent over the fire out of the cold, his beard ruddy in the light, he ate crabmeat and wiped his fingers on his sleeves. There was an aftertaste in the back of her mouth. Probably tomorrow she would be sick to her stomach. Far up the dome, a siren began to whistle.

Paula got up and kicked apart the fire. They sat side by side in the dark listening to the alarm. The barrage began, first the thunderous boom and then the silent, blinding explosions of light, coming faster and closer together until her ears and eyes were clogged and she could hear and see nothing any more, as if the whole world had vanished. Bunker put his arm around her shoulders. She pressed her face against his neck.

The gash opened like a mouth in the floor of the ravine, lipped in mossy concrete. A dead tree stood over it. She unslung the coil of rope from her shoulder and knelt down. The underground river roared in the cavern below. She put two stones into the skin bag and lowered it down through the gap in the ground.

Behind her, the sirens whined; they had been crying all morning, all the night before, the day before that, without an attack. She paid out the rope, holding it looped around her wrist to keep from losing it when the bag struck the flying water below. She squatted down and pulled the bottoms of her trousers over her half-frozen feet. Her cracked and bleeding toes were more important than the distant sirens. The rushing river caught the bag and flung it out to the limit of the rope. She held on tight. More than once she had lost the whole apparatus down the river, and they were hard to make.

Hand over hand, she reeled it in a little, to see if the bag was full, and let it down again. When the weight convinced her, she began to draw it up. The rope was soaked and bitter cold. Halfway up, it snagged. She tugged. There was nothing down there to foul it. Puzzled, she jerked on the rope, and it yanked back, flying out of her hands.

She leaped away, bounding down the ravine. At the edge of the open ground, she wheeled to look. Her hair stood on end. A huge man was dragging himself up through the cleft. He wore a heavy helmet over his head, but his arms were bare and black as tar. She turned and ran.

She went toward the lake at a steady lope. Her feet were cold and bruised and she began to limp. She glanced over her shoulder.

The Styths were swarming up out of the ground, spreading over the ravine. She turned forward again. Her feet banged on the cold ground. There was no place to hide. She swerved across the dead lake. Just as she reached the far side, an explosion burst in the ground behind her. They were widening the way in.

She went down into the gulleys and hills between the lake and the southern end of the dome, looking for Bunker. When she could not find him, she ran north, stopping every few moments to walk and catch her breath. In the middle of the dome, near the ruins of the campus, two Styths caught her.

She was too tired and footsore to be afraid, only glad they did not rape her. They made her run and laughed when she fell. Half-dragging her, they took her north to the plaza in front of the government building, where already hundreds of other prisoners were gathered. She lay down in the dirt near the steps of the dispensa and slept.

She woke and went through the mob. Most of the prisoners were Martians. They sat on the ground or stood leaning on one another. Their pale faces were stained with dust and tears. The small children screamed. No longer hunting the other anarchist, she wandered around the plaza, too frightened to sit still.

Styths ringed them. She recognized none of them. Her feet hurt. She sat down to rest, but her nerves drove her on again, around the plaza in circles. The afternoon dragged past. More people crammed into the space, until she could hardly move. Taller people surrounded her and she could see nothing.

"You will divide up by sex," a Styth voice shouted, in the Common Speech. "The men will come this way. The women will stay here."

All around her the people cried out, and the mob stirred. Paula sighed. She wiped her face with her hands. Maybe Bunker had not been taken. The air car was almost finished; maybe he could escape.

"Now," the Styth voice said, "all you pigs take your clothes off."

The women raised their voices in a yell. The men had been sifted out, and the crowd was much looser than before. Paula sat down cross-legged, her hands in her sleeves, watching them move restlessly around her. They refused to obey, and the Styths closed in around them. Catching one woman by the arms, they stripped her naked. They laughed and pulled on her breasts and jabbed her in the crotch. Paula lowered her eyes. She was afraid of being raped. Around her the other women were silent.

"Take your clothes off, or we'll take them off."

"But it's cold," a girl murmured, behind Paula. They began to shed their clothes. Their pretty white blouses fluttered to the ground. Some of them tried to keep on their underthings but the Styths made them remove those too. Paula sat still, her hands in her jacket sleeves.

"Tanuk," a Styth called. "The dark one here isn't stripping."

The Martian women around her muttered in their throats. They closed in around her, stooped, and clutched her and kicked at her. Paula rolled up in a knot, her arms over her head. The women tore at her clothes. A foot thudded into her side. Blood ran into her mouth. The women cursed her, shrieking, and ripped at her heavy jacket and trousers.

"Get away!"

She curled into a ball, swallowing blood. The women backed away from her. She sobbed for breath. Her chest hurt. She was hauled up by the front of her jacket. She looked up at a blurred black face. He had something in his free hand: a photograph.

"Maybe. It could be." He spoke to her in Styth. "Are you Paula Mendoza?"

She said nothing. She closed her eyes, stiff with the pain in her chest and side. He lifted her up. "Call the Akellar."

He took her into a little room on the first floor of the government building, sat her down in a big leather chair, and brought her a mug of hot meat soup. While she was drinking the soup, the Lopka Akellar came into the room. His face was a patchwork of little scars.

"That's the one," he said. "Do you remember me, Mendoz'?"

She stared at him, unwilling to speak the other language. He glanced at the man behind him. "Send to the Prima that we have his wife."

"The Prima." She put the cup down, startled.

"Saba is the Prima now. Machou tried to block him on the war action."

She looked in another direction. Ymma left her alone. She moved stiffly around the room. The door was locked and there were no windows. Her side hurt. Aimlessly she paced around the room. She drank the rest of the soup and sat thinking about Bunker and trying idly to reduce to an aphorism the fact that she was always well fed in jail and starved when she was free.

After some time Ymma came back and took her out to the verticals. "If you won't go willingly, I'm supposed to carry you."

Her feet hurt. The corridor was crowded with Styths. The overhead lights had been shut off. At the end of the dim busy corridor the outer doors shone pale with sunlight. She stopped, drawn like a moth, and Ymma pushed her. She had not been indoors in months and the closed spaces made her hunch her shoulders.

"We took London last watch." He led her into the first vertical car. "So' Bay the same watch as here. If we had more men we could have them all at once."

"What happened to the Martian Army?"

"Since we won Luna, they have no base. We were flying them around the Sun anyway. The Creep isn't a bad strategist, you know. Not a bad strategist at all."

She wrapped her arms around her. The language was exotic in its inflections and order and accents. The car stopped and the doors slid apart. She stayed where she was. Ymma stood watching her from his ruined face, his black eyes like wells. She went out to the dark hall.

Half a dozen men were lined up against the far wall. She went past them into a broad, dim room. The windows were covered in black paper. Saba was sitting on the desk, talking to Ketac.

She stopped, and her hands fisted at her sides. Saba was graying. On his wrist was the iron cuff of his rank. He and Ketac turned to face her; she glanced at his son and stared at Saba, her jaw clenched with anger.

"Go on," Saba said to Ketac. "We have to hurry this up."

Ketac paused as he approached her, maybe to say something, changed his mind, and went out. Saba came after him, his hands on his belt.

"What's the matter with you? You should be thanking me. You'd be down there being sorted and numbered if we hadn't gone out of our way to save you."

"To save me!" She felt swollen with rage. She said, "You have it screwed around a little." Wheeling, she started for the door.

"Where are you going?"

"Down out of your way."

He caught her arm. "Listen to me, damn you!"

Her breath whined in her throat, and her temper snapped. He had hold of her arm. She clawed at him with her fingernails, first his hand, and when he wrenched her around and flung his arm around her waist she lunged at his face, her arms milling. He picked her up, pinning her hands. He was carrying her somewhere, through a doorway. She struggled around in his grip and sank her teeth into his face. He wrenched free. Skin tore in her teeth.

"Paula—Pauliko—I'll number you—"

She twisted hard, corkscrewing back and forth, and rammed her arm into his chest. They fell lengthwise onto a bed. Kicking and elbowing him, she fought free at last and lunged away, and his weight landed on top of her.

All her wind rushed out of her. Her head whirled. He was pulling her jacket off. His breath was hot on her face. His heavy odor filled her nose and mouth. He took his hand off her to unbuckle the belt of his leggings and she jerked one arm loose and raked at his bleeding face with her nails. His arm crooked around her throat. She tried to bite his hand and got a mouthful of thick armor-shirt. He pinned her under him again, face down.

"You'll like it, Paula." He was panting. "You always liked me best." He pulled down her pants and shoved himself into her.

She yelled. His whole hot weight buried her. Every time he moved it hurt. She bit her lips, her eyes squeezed shut. Stinking and hot, he groaned in his climax.

He moved away from her, his harsh breathing loud. She turned over onto her back. Her legs and groin were stiff with pain. He was watching her. The deep moon-shaped bite on his jaw bled in a stream. She got her feet under her and attacked him again.

"Hey!" He caught her. They fell off the bed onto the floor, and she landed on top of him. He was wedged between the bed and the long chest of drawers against the wall. Snarling and crying, she scratched his eyes. He heaved himself up and threw her bodily across the room. The wall hit her. Dazed, she pushed herself up on her arms. He bolted out the door and she heard the lock turn over.

She sat on the foot of the bed, her chest heaving. A deep bleeding scratch ran across her belly. Her thighs were smeared with his slime. She cried out and scraped at the greasy skin with her nails, tearing at the only part of him she could reach.

She slept in the bed. When she woke up there was a pile of women's clothes on the chair. She picked up a long white sleeve and the fabric snagged on her roughened fingertips. The door was still locked. She went into the little washroom connected to the bedroom and took a shower. She dried herself off and went out to the bedroom. Tanuojin was sitting on the bureau, joined at the back to his reflection in the mirror.

"Oh," she said.

"You're scrawny as a chicken's neck," he said. "I'm surprised he still wanted you."

His eyes were pale as lamps. She put on the white dress, which hung around her like a sack, and hunted among the other clothes for a belt.

"How is Kasuk?" she asked, bent over the chair.

"My son is dead."

Her head flew up. Her lips made a round, soundless word. She flung the clothes in her arms aside. "What was it—an honorable sacrifice? Did you kill him in your war?"

"Yes, he died in the war. There was no way to avoid it. Even you have to see that all this came out of the mouth of the past."

She sat down on the bed. Her fingers laced together in her lap. She thought of Kasuk's blind adoration of him.

"I need your help."

Her gaze snapped up to him. "No." She went past him to the door.

The room beyond was crowded with a tall forest of Styths. When she came in, their talk hushed, their heads turned toward her, round-eyed. She went through them toward the door, dwarfed among them.

"Akellar," a man said, behind her, "Pert' is asking to surrender."

The bedroom door clicked shut. Tanuojin said, "Call the Prima. He's in *Ybix*."

She went out the door. Leno stood in the middle of the hall, a swarm of men around him. "If I have to deal through The Creep—" She brushed past them toward the vertical. The familiar people unnerved her. She felt herself sucked into that world again, that life.

She went down the hall to the rank of verticals. No one came after her or tried to stop her. They were letting her go. The call button on the wall between the double doors of the verticals was blinking on and off and she put her back to the opposite wall to wait. A steady stream of Styths walked by in both directions. She tried not to understand their talk. It was still hard to realize that Kasuk was dead. The war ate him. The vertical doors on the right slid back and a flood of men strode out toward her. She waited for them to pass. One was still shaven. A boy. Smaller than the others. A shock ran through her to her heels. She said, "David?" His narrow brown eyes turned on her. His mouth opened. He put his arms out to her, and she rushed into his embrace.

Naked, joined by ropes from neck to neck, the Styths' captives squatted in the cold. The air reeked of their bodies. Her skirts caught in her hands, she passed the rows of women, sorted by age, the rope wearing their shoulders raw. All but the youngest children had been taken away from them. She tried not to look at their faces. An old woman passed her, carrying a bucket of water with a ladle in it, and in the lines the prisoners' voices rose, crying for a drink.

She reached the men and stopped, her shoulders slumped. There were thousands of them, fair heads, dark heads, bald and furry. She would never find Bunker among them, even if he were there. A Styth was coming toward her. She started along the first row of men, and the guard caught her by the arm.

"Where do you think you're going?"

She pulled on his hand. "Send for Tanuojin."

He grinned at her. A long scar indented his cheekbone. "Send for Tanuojin. This one is funny." He shook her arm, lifting her half off her feet. "Who do you think you are? Where did you get these clothes?"

"I'm Paula Mendoza."

He let go of her. "Oh. I'll call up top." He went off at a long-striding walk. She started along the row of captives.

They were nearly all Martians, their hair clipped short in the military fashion. They sat or lay in the dirt, their heads down, and did not look at her as she passed. Their expressions frightened her and she stopped looking at their faces. The stench was making her sick to her stomach. Halfway along the row she passed two men shoveling the waste and filth into buckets. On one round white back there were deep scratch marks like ruts. She began to hurry.

The next row was of old men. She started on to the string beyond until she remembered that Bunker was gray-headed. She knew he was not old but a Styth might think so. She went along the line. Halfway along the row a scrawny old man lay curled on the ground. His flesh was white as cheese. His open eyes were glazed and unseeing. His hands were already stiff. On either side of him other old men sat, their heads turned away. She stepped across an iridescent stream of piss. The hem of her skirt was heavy and wet and scraped her bare feet. She went along the third string, still without finding Bunker. The fourth row was of adolescent boys and she skipped over it to the fifth.

Bunker was sitting on the ground halfway along the row. His eyes were closed. He seemed to be asleep. She squatted down beside him.

"Dick."

His head rose, his eyes opening, and to her surprise he smiled at her. "I thought it was probably a waste of time to worry about you, junior. What happened?"

"Somebody recognized me," she said. "Dick—" She held out her hands to him. He took her wrists and pressed his face against her palms. It was so like the Styth gesture that she drew back, and he let her go.

"What will they do now?" he said.

Her ears caught the drone of an air car. She looked around the sky for it, then stood up. The air car was hovering down above them. Ten feet over her head Tanuojin swung out the door and dropped to the ground beside her. He gave a humorless yelp of laughter.

"Richard Bunker." He put his foot on Bunker's shoulder and knocked him on his back.

"Let him go," Paula said.

Tanuojin looked down at her from his towering height. "Why?"

"You said you wanted my help. Well, I'll help you, if you let him go."

He pulled his catfish whiskers straight. "It's no use, Paula. There's no place to go. When I'm done here, we'll blow up the dome, and we'll blow up all the others as soon as we can get the people out." He kicked Bunker again, and the anarchist got up onto his feet. "If you want him," Tanuojin said, "take him. I'll give him to you."

Bunker's neck was rubbed raw by the rope. He said to her, "Come with me. What kind of a life will you have with them?"

"Later," she said. "When I'm finished with him."

Tanuojin made a scornful sound in his chest. He pulled the rope off the anarchist's neck, and Bunker started down the row of prisoners. After a dozen strides he broke into a run. Paula watched him until he was out of her sight. Tanuojin stood beside her like a tree. Slowly she went back toward the buildings in the distance.

She went with Tanuojin down to the third level of the cellar. In the vertical, he took her suddenly by the hand, and the unexpected cold touch startled her and she snatched her hand away from him. The vertical car boxed her up. She felt unable to breathe.

"What's the matter with you?"

"Don't touch me," she said.

The car settled to a stop, and the doors began to slide apart into the walls. He glanced at them and they shut again.

"Oh," she said, "that must be useful."

"Are you going to cooperate with me?"

She hunched up her shoulders. "I said I would." She refused to look at him.

He opened the doors with another look and they went into a narrow gray corridor. The concrete floor was icy to her feet. A guard let them in a metal door to a wide room. The only lights were on an I-beam suspended from the center of the ceiling. The floor under her feet shone with wax. It was painted with red circles and alleys: a games floor, a gymnasium. The walls were lined with Martians. Tanuojin's fingers closed on her wrist.

"Bring a light," he said to the guard. He held her arm doubled in his grip. Against her will she felt the cool pleasure of his touch. With the guard carrying a light before them, Tanuojin led her along the rank of Martian prisoners against the wall.

"Who do you want?" she said to Tanuojin.

"Just look at them and let me do the thinking."

She went on along the row of prisoners, staring into their faces. Some of them she had seen before, at Cam's and Hanse's meetings. At the end of the first row was Captain Rodgers, his uniform crisp, his buttons shined, his feet exactly eighteen inches apart.

Their eyes met; she remembered the things he had done to her and her cheeks went hot. His wet lips parted. Before he could speak Tanuojin let go of her and grabbed the Martian by the front of his uniform. Rodgers squealed. Tanuojin threw him flat back against the wall and his head hit the concrete with a thud. He sank down, limp, against the base of the wall. Paula went away across the gymnasium.

Tanuojin came after her. His hand gripped her again. She said, "You're no different than he is."

"You made me do that." He stooped to talk into her ear. "You did that."

"You have an excuse for everything, don't you? Don't talk to me. It makes me sick to talk to you."

"Saba's right. You're hysterical." He pushed her toward the next row of prisoners. "Who is that?"

Against the wall stood a line of women, medics, in white uniforms. Paula scanned their faces. The third from the end was Cam Savenia.

Tanuojin said, under his breath, "I thought so." He nodded to the guard. "That one. There's a room up on the sixth floor all ready for her." He let go of Paula.

The guard took hold of Cam's arm. Her face went dark with rage. "You swine." She shouted at Tanuojin, her eyes flashing. "You dirty black dog. You can do what you want, but you can't break me. You can't break me!" The guard hauled her away bodily. Tanuojin laughed, his hands on his belt. He kicked the heels of his boots against the floor.

"It's the same room they kept you in," he said. Paula left.

The prisoners were gone. The barren hillside stretched down toward the lake. A haze of dust stood in the air. Three or four buildings, ruins, rose among the forest of tree stumps. The dead pan of the lake was cracked and dry as the surface of a moon. She stood there trying to remember what it had been like before the war, green and alive, a free world.

The Styths were still claiming that they fought to save the Earth from the Sunlight League, but the last anarchists were mixed in with the Martians in the slavepens, and the Earth was wasted, and the war was not over. Hanse had escaped with most of the Martian Army. Saba was in a hurry to take his base of operations to Luna, which he could defend. Paula was going with them. She was unsure why; she had some vague tangled thought that she could make them feel her rage. And she was afraid to die. Bunker was somewhere in the ruined dome, maybe dead already. Unwitnessed. Her son was calling her. She went back up the barren slope toward the government building.

LUNA. Martius–Averellus 1865

"I don't understand," David said. "Why aren't you living with me and Papa?"

Paula opened the rattan cabinet on the wall. Inside were two shelves of bottles. "What does Saba say?"

"He says you're crazy."

"I'm crazy."

She took out a bottle of gin. Behind her, two men brought more furniture into the room. She had the whole suite to herself, three rooms, pretty as a hotel. Ketac came in, directing the workmen around. She poured gin into her glass and filled it up with limon-woda. Luna was stocked with the spoils of the Earth. It was like being in jail again.

"Paula," Ketac called. "Come see what I found you."

She went down the long room toward him. His attentions made her suspicious. He had spent the morning putting carpet down and now he was unpacking a large box. He set a big yellow ball on the table and held it with one hand to keep it from rolling while he fished in the carton.

"See if you can find the base."

David had followed her. He stood with his hands behind him, his forehead grooved. Paula took a plastic foot out of the box and Ketac put the yellow ball on it.

"It's not to scale," he said. He took a handful of smaller balls out of the box and tossed them up into the air. They flew toward the yellow ball and swung into orbit around it. Paula murmured. It was a magnet-driven model of the Middle Planets. The Earth and Luna passed her, turning around and around each other, painted with their surface features.

Ketac said, "There's been some kind of change in the Council. Not by force."

"An election."

"Whatever. Now they're asking us for peace terms."

Paula said, "Those bastards," under her breath.

"The Prima will need your advice."

She gave him a sharp glance. Then that was why he was here. His long ugly face was aimed at the model. She reached for her glass on the sideboard along the wall. "All right. Tell him I will."

His head nodded. The men were bringing a big backless couch in the door, and he went to tell them where to put it. David came up beside her.

"I don't understand," he said stubbornly.

"Don't act like a baby."

"Don't you love us any more?"

"David, I'm not playing this little heartbreaker game with you. If Saba is putting you to it, you're a fool, and if not, you're a sadist."

His face stiffened. When he was angry he looked younger, a little boy again. "I hate you," he said.

"At least that's honest."

He ran out of the room. The wrong man's son. She looked down at the model, Mars was spinning toward her, busy in its coils of moons. She batted it across the room. Unharmed, it flew back to its orbit around the yellow Sun. Ketac had gone. The workmen banged chairs into each other. Deep in her thoughts, she watched the model turning. Suddenly she knew someone was staring at her, and raising her head she saw Tanuojin behind her.

"What are you doing here?" he said. "I thought you were planning an elegant suttee in memory of your lover."

She turned back to the model. "Impractical."

"Maybe you just have a short memory."

"Oh, no, my dear. I remember everything."

The workmen sprang to attention. Saba was coming in, trailed by a procession of men, Leno and Ymma, their aides, David, Junna, and half a dozen others. Paula moved away from Tanuojin, up to the middle of the room, where she could see them all. Leno stood before the big chair on her left, waiting for Saba to sit down. Paula leaned against the waist-high bookcase that ran the length of the wall.

"Who is Alvers Newrose?" Saba said. He sat down on the backless yellow couch, and the other men lowered themselves into their chairs.

"He's a Martian politician," Paula said. "He was Council First Secretary before Cam Savenia, I don't know what he is now."

"Can I trust him?"

"Probably not." It was strange to be talking so civilly to him. She wished she had scratched his eyes out. She said, "Jefferson liked Newrose. She dealt with him by preference."

"What happened to her?"

From the end of the room by the model, Tanuojin said, "Savenia had her shot."

Saba stood up again, and all around the room the lesser men shot to their feet. He paced around the low couch. "This Newrose is coming here to talk. If we can get the Council to surrender, we can handle the Martian Army on our own time."

"They won't surrender," Ymma said. The overhead lighting made grotesque shadows on his hacked face. "Not while their fleet is still out. Will they?"

"They saw what we did to the Earth," Saba said.

"Where is the Martian Fleet?" Ymma asked.

Leno was standing behind his big chair, his hands on its back. When he leaned his weight on it, he nearly tipped it over. "Scattered around in the first and second rings of the Asteroids. I sent eighteen ships to scout them out." His mustaches, braided with silver, trailed down over his chest.

"We'll have to fight them anyway," Tanuojin said to Saba. "Why do you bother with this Newrose? Let him wait. When we've beaten their fleet, the Martians will go down on their knees to us, where they belong."

"That could take forever." Saba went back to the couch. David stood at the head of it, attending him, but now he left Saba and came across the room to Paula's side.

"They have to go back to their base sometime," Ymma said. He leaned against the wall, a few feet away from Leno.

"Obviously they have bases in the Asteroids," Saba said.

Beside Paula, David murmured, "Are you still angry?"

"No," she said. She put her hand on his arm, relieved at his friendliness. The men were arguing. She watched her son's face. "I still love you, David, but there's nothing between me and him any more."

"That isn't what he wants," he said, stubbornly. "That doesn't have to be so."

"If you really want to find the Martians," Tanuojin said, in the middle of the room, "don't send Leno to look for them."

Paula's attention snapped back to the Styth Council. Leno strode up the room. "What did you have in mind, Creep?"

"Shut up," Saba said. He palmed Tanuojin roughly on the shoulder. Leno's blunt head was thrust forward, and he came straight up to Tanuojin.

"I'm sick of—"

"I said shut up," Saba said. "The meeting's over. You're all dismissed." He went up between Leno and Tanuojin, one hand on Tanuojin's arm, but his face to Leno. "Just get me some approximate idea where the Martians are."

Leno was swollen with temper. He and Tanuojin glared at each other over Saba's shoulder. The other men were filing out. Paula turned to David again.

"It is so. You'd better accept it, because that's how I want it."

"Mother—"

"Vida," Saba said, and the boy wheeled. Saba nodded at the door. Leno had gone. "Go with Merkhiz, in case he has messages for me."

"Yes, sir," David said. He went out of the room at a trot.

"Stay away from Leno," Saba said to Tanuojin. He gave his lyo a shove for emphasis. "How are you doing with Dr. Savenia? Can she help us with Newrose?"

"She's coming along."

"Bring her here. Let me see her." Saba nodded at Junna, behind his father. "Go get her."

Tanuojin began, "No. I—" and his head turned, his gaze went to Paula. "All right." He nodded to Junna. "Go fetch her here."

Paula folded her arms over her chest. She was about to be the object of a demonstration. Junna left. Saba wandered around the room, looking at the illusion pictures on the wall. He came up beside her, so close she was uncomfortable, but she did not move away. She was not afraid of him.

"Any word from Vribulo?"

Tanuojin shook his head. "They are being very, very unconcerned. You know Machou."

The door slid open and Marus came into the room. "Akellar."

Cam Savenia walked past him. Paula wheeled. It had been ten days since Tanuojin had found her. She still wore white: loose trousers and a tunic. Paula had never seen her without makeup before. Her face looked peeled.

Tanuojin stood with his hand on Saba's shoulder. Cam went into the middle of the room, beside the couch, her arms at her sides.

"Dr. Savenia."

She raised her head. "Yes, Akellar."

"Look at that woman there." Tanuojin pointed at Paula. "Do you know her?"

Paula met Cam's blue eyes. Cam said, "Yes, she's Paula Mendoza."

"Who is she?"

"She's an anarchist." Cam's voice was perfectly even. "She betrayed us. She's corrupt. Perverse. I hate her. I wish I could kill her."

"No," Tanuojin said. "You're wrong. She is a Styth. She's the Prima's wife. Sometimes she's bad but she follows the law."

"I follow the law," Cam said.

"Then tell me who she is."

Cam's wide eyes stared at Paula. "She is Styth. She is good. She's the Prima's wife."

Paula went around the couch. Taller by half a head, Cam turned to face her. Paula said, "You remember Dick Bunker, Cam. Don't you? Who is he?"

Cam's lips parted. She looked uncertainly at Tanuojin.

"He's dead," the Styth told her.

Cam said, monotone, "Richard Bunker is dead."

Paula jabbed her chin at Tanoujin and Saba. "Who are they?"

Cam's hands clasped together. "Do I have to talk to her?"

"Answer her, Dr. Savenia."

"He is the Prima. You're my friend. You know everything."

"That's right."

"Who is he?" Paula said.

"My friend."

"What's his name?"

"He's my friend."

"Do you know his name?"

"He's my friend."

Paula stared at the pale womanly face above her. Cam would not look at her. Her hands hung at her sides.

"Would you like to go to Mars?" Tanuojin said.

"Yes." Eagerly.

"You'll have to do just as I say."

"I will."

"Good. You're a good girl. Marus. Take her back."

Marus took Cam Savenia out the door. Paula let out her breath in a sigh. Her hands were trembling.

Saba said, "She'll have to do better than that."

"Don't worry." Tanuojin paced away. "She'll be right, before Newrose sees her. She's come a long way. You didn't see her at first."

"It's vicious," Paula said. She sat down on the end of the couch.

"Why? She's happy now. She doesn't have to think, she doesn't worry. She isn't afraid. She's on the right side, that's all she cares about."

"How long would she stay like that?" Saba said. "If you weren't there?"

"I'll always be there. In her mind."

Paula scrubbed her palm over her face. "What mind does she have left?" She was glad David had gone.

"She never used it that much. She's always done as she was told. That's why it was so easy to—" Tanuojin's eyes closed. "Re-educate."

Saba paced around the room. "I don't see that she'll be much use." He went down to the model. Her gaze followed him. Tanuojin didn't frighten him. His hair was gray as iron; he looked tired.

"Besides," Tanuojin said, to Paula. "She's a woman. Her prime function is centered somewhere much lower than her mind."

"She wasn't much of a woman."

"Because she's not like you with that guillotine between your legs?"

Saba wheeled around. "Damn you, I've had enough of your filthy mouth. You're dismissed."

"Saba, I—"

"Get out of this room!"

Tanuojin's long legs carried him fast out of the room. Paula let out her breath. Saba came slowly up the room from the model.

"I've had the feeling you've been avoiding me," she said.

He reached the couch and sat on it, his legs straight out before him. "Did you want my company?"

"No. Why did you tell David I'm crazy? Tell him you raped me. Maybe you can fit it into the lecture on honor."

"You started that."

She could not remember where she had bitten his face. The wound was gone without a scar, Tanuojin's work, keeping him perfect. His sleeve half-hid the cuff on his wrist.

"Look, Paula," he said, "you have to help me."

"Help you," she said, surprised. "To do what?"

"With this Newrose."

"Oh? Shall I hold him while you hit him a few times?"

"Damn you, I'm asking you for help. Why do you have to fight me all the time?"

"Bah."

"You don't give a damn about me any more, but you could do this for Vida's sake. You don't want him to be killed, do you?"

"Why did you bring him, anyway? He's too young to be here."

"He wanted to come. When we found out you were still alive, he wanted to come rescue you."

She was clenching her fists. She had to keep calm, to stay uninvolved, but talking to him made her angry. She loosened her hands on the edge of the shelf where she was perched. "How did you know I was alive?"

"Tanuojin had a dream about you."

"And you trusted that. From so far away?"

Saba made a gesture with his hand. "What does time and distance mean to him? It was the watch before we fought Machou. He was ready for anything."

She imagined the Chamber, boiling with voices, the scent of rage and blood, the excitement: not just a pit fight, but a fight for the Primit cuff. Saba watched her from the couch. He was too large for the furniture, too tall for the room. He belonged in his cold city, not here. But he was stuck here, in Tanuojin's war that could go on forever. His shoulders looked as broad as the door. She had been crazy to fight him; he could have killed her with one hand.

"Do you like being Prima?" she said.

"I'm getting used to it."

"I don't understand what you want me to do."

"Talk to Newrose for me. You're the only person I trust who knows the Martians. I'll support any reasonable settlement of the war."

"Give me an earnest."

"What?"

"How many anarchists are there up in those slave cars?" The pens of prisoners were in a high orbit over Luna.

"I don't know. It should be easy to find out."

"Let them go back to the Earth. Give them a dome."

He straightened his mustaches. "I can't."

"One dome!"

"I can't do that. Tanuojin is right, the Planet breeds anarchy."

She slid off the shelf to her feet. "You don't want my help very much."

"I'll separate them out. We'll let them go to Mars and Venus." Smoothly he said, "When you settle the war for me."

Finally she said, "All right."

"Come down to my trap for the high meal—we can talk over the small things."

"Yes."

"I'll send Vida for you." He went out.

Alvers Newrose was a short man with an egg-shaped, hairless head. He smelled of lavender. A small group of his aides followed him into the room where Saba was to meet him. From the far end of the room Paula watched the Martians arrange themselves around Newrose, and the Styth escort draw back to the walls. She went toward the man from the Council.

"Mr. Newrose?"

"I'm Alvers Newrose."

"My name is Paula Mendoza."

They had not known she was here. One of his aides made an undiplomatic gasp. Newrose's watery pale eyes blinked. He held his hand out. "I'm pleased to meet you. I've heard a lot about you from some of your colleagues on the Committee."

She let him pump her limp hand. Ketac announced the Prima, and Saba came in, alone. He took the big chair at the head of the room. Paula led Newrose up to him. Even sitting, Saba was taller than the Martian. She said, "Prima, this is Alvers Newrose, First Secretary of the Interplanetary Council."

Saba looked him over at leisure. Proper and composed, Newrose did not speak. He would say nothing until Saba was formally introduced to him and he was certain he was talking to the right man. The Styth said to Paula, "Tell him as long as he's in Luna he is under my protection."

She translated it, watching Newrose for any sign that he spoke Styth. She said, "This is the Prima Akellar, the Matuko Akellar, Saba, Kritona, the Guardion, the prima General of the Styth Imperial Fleet."

Newrose started to offer his hand but stopped, without embarrassment, when he saw Saba would not take it. The Martian inclined his head in a shadow of a bow.

"I hope our mission here will be fruitful and of advantage for everybody concerned."

"You tell him," Saba said, "that the only advantage he can hope for now is ours."

"Give me a chance to translate."

"He knows all about me, he knows I understand him, look at him."

Newrose was watching them, his face bland. She said, "I don't think he speaks Styth."

"I don't think he speaks anything that I speak."

Ketac was standing in the doorway. Saba got out of his chair and Newrose backed away a stride to give him room; his eyes followed the big man up. Saba waved to his son. "Mind him." Without another word to Newrose, the Prima left the room.

Paula grunted. "He isn't a diplomat." Ketac advanced toward her, and she took his arm and brought him face to face with Newrose. "Mr. Newrose, the Prima's son will attend you." Leaving them together, she went out after Saba.

"They're stalling," Saba said. "Newrose is just here to gain time for the Martian Army."

Paula sat down on the edge of the bed. There were eight rooms in his suite, but this was the only place they could talk in private. Everyplace else was given over to his aides and officers. She said, "I wish Tanuojin had been there."

"I'm trying to keep him away from Leno."

He went restlessly around the overcrowded room. She fingered the shaved nap of the bedcover, thinking of Newrose. All the furniture in the room, the bed, the three padded chairs, and the sideboard, had been picked for size, not design. Nothing matched, not even the colors. He opened the sideboard and took out a bottle.

"I don't have any of that glue you drink or I'd offer you a drink."

"Never mind. I'm going back to my room." She went to the door. "I'll see you at dinner."

A dogleg corridor led through his suite to the trunk corridor. It was jammed with Styths. She went in among them. In their midst was a tall redheaded girl, saying, "But I have to see him. Please—"

The girl was at least twenty years younger than Paula. An aide of Newrose's: she recognized the fiery hair. Her one-piece suit, of some metallic cloth, was cut out over the stomach and most of the back and the holes filled with net. Paula said, "What is she looking for? Or am I silly to ask."

The Styths' faces were broad with their smiles. Ketac sat on the table at the mouth of the small corridor. He said, "She says she wants my father." The other men laughed.

The girl clutched Paula's arm. "Please—I have to see the Prima."

"Did Newrose send you? Let go of my arm."

The girl's fingers opened but her hand rested on Paula's forearm. "I just have to meet him. I know I can change his mind about us." She was six inches taller than Paula and had to bend to talk to her. Paula looked around. There were no other Martians; she had come alone. Paula looked past the fluffy red head at Ketac.

"Go ask him if he wants to see her."

"Thank you." The girl gripped Paula's hand. "I can—we may save the Middle Planets." Her hand was slick. The Styths were all trying to see through her clothes. Paula freed herself from the moist grip. Ketac came back.

"He says to send her in."

Paula nodded to her. "Go on. It's the last door on the right."

The girl reached for her again, and Paula avoided her grasp. "Please," the redhead said. "Come with me."

"It'd be an inhibiting factor."

"But I don't speak their language."

Paula let herself be drawn up the narrow corridor, away from the Styths. "I think you might. Anyway he's bilingual." At the door, her hand on the latch, she turned, admiring the smooth skin of the girl's net-covered belly. It would be fun to tease him. She opened the door and let the girl in ahead of her.

"Prima, now they're sending you virgins."

He was standing near the foot of the bed. The girl went toward him, her hand out. "My name is Lore Smythe. I'd like to talk to you."

"Talk." He took her hand, not to shake it, and smiled at her. "Why would a pretty girl like you want to do something that boring?"

Paula leaned over the back of one of his stuffed chairs. "You are so subtle."

He nudged Lore Smythe toward the sideboard. "The liquor is in that cabinet." His head swiveled toward Paula. "I thought you were leaving."

"She thinks she'll need an interpreter." Paula smirked at him.

"Good-bye, Paula."

"Not even a stirrup cup?"

"Miss Mendoza," Lore Smythe said, in a new sharp voice. "Stay where you are." Paula and Saba turned in unison toward her. In her hand she held a gun.

Saba lunged toward her and the gun snapped. Paula heard the thunk of the missile hitting him. He fell on his face and rolled over. A short clear dart stuck up out of his left chest. He clawed at it once and his hand slid limp to the floor.

"That was stupid," Paula said. Lore Smythe pointed the gun at her.

"The rest of the shots are all killers," the redhead said. Her voice was different than when she had been pleading to see him. "And I don't have any orders to bring you back alive."

"Is Newrose behind this?"

Lore's full mouth curled with contempt. "Newrose." She stuck two fingers down into the front of her metallic suit and took out a small blue piece of plastic. "Here. This is a thumblock, you see? Put it on him." She threw the plastic at Paula. Too light to carry far, it landed on the brown tile floor midway between them. Paula stooped to pick it up, and Lore Smythe circled behind her to the door. She heard the lock click.

"That's narcolepta in the dart," the redhead said, in her hard, crisp voice. "It will drip into his system for the next twenty hours. By then I'll have him halfway to Mars."

The thumblock was shaped like a figure-of-eight. Paula went over to Saba's body. The girl called, "Don't get between me and him. And don't try to pull the nail out—it's long, and it's barbed. Hurry up."

The dart's clear three-inch barrel stuck up straight out of his chest. Blood tinged it pink at the needle end. Paula circled behind him and knelt. She touched his cheek and his throat. His skin was cool, but not cold. He was only asleep, then, not knocked out.

"This will never work," she said. "They'll kill all three of us before they let you take him to Mars."

"Just thumb him."

His left arm lay half under him. She pulled it free. "Do you want me to tie his hands behind him or in front?" Surreptitiously she took a fistful of his shirt under his armpit and tugged, which tilted the dart toward her.

"Unh—"

"Have you tried this on any real Styths? You know they're much stronger than we are. Him especially."

Lore's eyes narrowed. Her cheeks were flushed. "Just do as I tell you." She waved the little gun. Its narrow barrel was longer than its body. "All I have to do is pull this trigger, lady, and in thirty seconds you'll be dead."

There was a knock on the door, and the redhead wheeled, the gun aimed at it. The latch moved up and down. While Lore was watching the door, Paula tugged once on the dart. It was fast in his chest. The pink color was spreading in the drug. He traded a drop of blood for a drop of narcolepta. The knock sounded again.

"Papa."

"David," she called, alarmed. She was afraid to speak Styth to him; Lore might think she was calling him in. "Come back later. We're busy."

The Martian turned toward her, her blue eyes direct above the gun. "That's right. Put that lock on him. Take his arms behind his back."

Paula reached across him for his right arm and hauled him up onto his side, his back to Lore Smythe. His wrist seemed cooler, his pulse slower. She had to hurry.

"Be careful when you roll him over," the Martian girl said. "Do it slow and you won't run that nail through his lung."

Paula stepped around him, between him and Lore, to turn him onto his stomach. She brought his hands behind him and took a tight grip on his shirt. When she rolled him slowly onto his stomach, just as his chest turned onto the floor, she wrenched on his shirt to tilt the dart. For an instant the dart braced him up. She leaned on him and heard a tiny splintering crack, and he lay flat. She crossed his thumbs behind him and bound them with the plastic bridge.

"Back off," Lore said, and she moved away across the room. The redhead went cautiously to him and pushed him with her foot.

"He doesn't look so big now, does he? Not so big at all." She kicked him. Bending, she pulled on the bond on his thumbs. "Good, you did it right."

"That's my motto," Paula said. "If I can't do it right, I don't do it at all." She folded her arms over her chest.

"You think you're funny, don't you? You think you're tough." Lore kicked him again.

"I admit I'm not that brave, to kick him when he's tied up and unconscious." A thin trickle of fluid seeped out from under him, running across the floor. She tore her eyes away from it. "You think you're brave enough to kick me, Lore?"

Lore turned toward her, the gun aimed at her face. "I don't have any orders about you at all. You're supposed to be dead. I can do anything I want with you." She strode up to Paula, waggling the gun, and took another thumblock out of her silvery clothes. "Turn around."

Paula turned her back. "You won't make it out of this room, Lore. You might as well give up."

The girl's sweating hands fastened on Paula's wrists. She wrenched her arms behind her. Paula said, "By now they know everything that's happening here."

Lore was hooking Paula's thumbs together. By the quality of her grunt Paula knew she had the gun in her teeth. She said, "The place is wired, Lore."

"I don't believe you," Lore said. She stepped back. "These barbarians aren't that sophisticated."

"This is Luna, remember?" Paula faced her, her arms fastened painfully behind her back. "Everything is wired."

"You're supposed to be dead," Lore told her. "You made a lot of trouble for us."

"The Sunlight League."

"That's right."

"You know Dr. Savenia is here." It took effort to keep from looking beyond the redheaded girl at Saba. Frantically she kept talking. "Only I doubt you'd know her now."

"She goes with me too," Lore said. She tipped the gun up at Paula's face. "Maybe I'll take you, if you cooperate."

"I'd sooner eat dirt."

The cold barrel of the gun pressed under Paula's chin. "Oh, you think you're so tough." The gun pushed her head up.

"You won't know Cam." Paula's tense muscles throbbed. Her arms began to hurt from her thumbs to her shoulders. "She's had a Styth education. She isn't—"

Behind Lore Saba heaved himself up onto his knees. The redhead saw him. She wheeled, the gun swinging toward him, and Paula lunged into her. With a flat crack the gun fired into the floor. Saba blundered up onto his feet. Lore thrust Paula off and raised the gun again and Paula dove into her. She heard the nasty snap of the gun firing again. Lore struck her in the neck and she fell, but before Lore could turn Saba crashed into her.

The gun sailed off and Paula on her knees scrambled after it. Saba was still only half-conscious. He tripped, and Lore got away from him. She raced for the gun. Paula dropped stomach-first across it. Lore was panting. She wrenched at Paula, grabbing for the gun pressing into her stomach. Saba stumbled toward them. Lore dodged. She came up against the bed and tried to duck past him, and the Styth knocked her down and fell on her.

Paula rocked onto her side. She brought her knees up to her chest and dragged her cramped arms around under her feet. Lore Smythe lay still on her back. Beside her, Saba was trying to sit, his head wobbling. Paula went over to him and helped him get up.

"What's going on?" he said, muzzy.

"You are a champion." The dart was gone. On the front of his shirt was a damp stain. "I forgive you every rotten thing you've ever done. How do you feel?" Sliding her joined hands under his shirt, she found the wound in the heavy muscle of his chest. Part of the barbed needle was still stuck in his body.

"I feel . . ." He shook his head. His eyes were not focusing well. "She shot me."

"She was about to shoot me, and with me it would have been permanent. Do you have any scissors?"

He blinked at her. She held up her hands and he blinked at the thumblock. He wagged his head down the room. She went past the bed to the washroom. On the glass shelf below the mirror was a pair of clippers. When she came out, the bedroom door was shaking under a heavy pounding knock.

"Prima!" It was Ketac.

"It's all right," she called. "Wait a minute." She knelt behind Saba. The clipper blades were shorter than the thumb-bridge. She hacked at the tough plastic.

"She shot me," he said.

"She shot you with a drug. She's from the Sunlight League."

"Paula," Ketac roared. "Let me in."

Saba's head swung toward the door. "Stay the hell out!"

Paula bore down hard with both hands on the clippers, her teeth clenched, and the tool bit through half the thumblock. "Unh. She was taking you to Mars. I guess to ransom the Middle Planets. Cowboy stuff. All Fascists are romantics." She struggled with the clippers.

Lore Smythe groaned. He flexed his arms, and the half-severed lock broke. On his hands and knees he went over to the Martian girl.

"Don't—save her to question," Paula said.

He put his hand on Lore's throat and choked her. When she was dead, he came back to Paula and unfastened the lock on her thumbs.

"Damn Newrose." He pulled her hands apart. "I told you he was fake."

"He didn't have anything to do with it."

He touched his chest, and she caught his hand and held it away from the wound. "Be careful. There's a piece of the needle broken off in there."

He ground the heel of his hand into his eye and shook his head. "It's still no good. Newrose."

"Think about it, Saba. We have a hook in him now—we can pressure him now."

"I don't see the use."

"You will when you wake up."

Lore Smythe lay on the table, covered with a red blanket. Paula sat down in one of the three chairs before it, her back to the body. The only lights in the room were the two ceiling lamps near the door, and this end of the room was plunged in shadow. The Styths moved past her like shadows. Tanuojin went behind her to the table and pulled back the blanket.

"I wish you hadn't killed her."

"Don't blame me. He did it."

Ketac and David came single-file through the door. Ketac said, formal, "The Prima." Saba walked into the room, and David ran up to arrange a chair for him.

"I'm telling you, this Martian is hoaxing us." He sat down. "This won't do any good." Ketac and David hurried around bringing him a cup, putting a little round table beside him, turning out one lamp that shone in his eyes and turning on another. Junna came in to serve Tanuojin.

The tall man walked around the room, his hands on his hips. "If he really didn't know about this Leaguer woman, maybe we can use it to get something out of him."

Even if Newrose had known, Lore Smythe could be a tool. Paula hoped he had not known. She began to devise ways of talking the Styths into treating with him even if he had engineered the whole plot. Tanuojin was prowling along the wall. Saba said, "Sit down, will you. You make me nervous."

Tanuojin had found the wall switch, and he clicked it on. The whole wall lit up, one great illusion picture: a moonlit cliff, at its foot the night-blue ocean rolling in to boil its white surf among the rocks.

"There should be sound," Paula said.

He touched another switch, and the sound came on, soft, the growl of the surf. Saba said, "What is that?"

"These people live in a fantasy," Tanuojin said. He walked up the room toward his chair.

"Where is Newrose?" Paula asked Ketac.

"In the next room."

"Let him wait," Saba said.

Tanuojin slouched in his chair. "Everything here is an imitation. In Mars, too. They left the Earth, but they took it with them in their heads. They couldn't make anything new or real where they went. But they forgot the Earth, too—when they came back, they had forgotten how to live there. They destroyed your city out of sheer ignorance of how it worked."

Paula was chewing on her fingernails. Everything depended on Newrose. "Your way is just as much an illusion as theirs."

Saba made a loud, contemptuous noise. Tanuojin said, "My way works."

"It's all in your mind," Paula said.

Saba raised his hand to Ketac. "Go get Newrose."

"You need a shovel," Tanuojin said to her. "There's only one law."

"There is no law." She stood and went behind her chair, her eyes on the door where Newrose would appear. "You glorify your superstitions into laws, just like the Martians." Newrose came into the room, Ketac behind him. She raised her voice and spoke to him in the Common Speech.

"The Prima has called you here on a very serious matter, Newrose."

He approached them, squinting in the dim light, his face bland. "Then I wonder why I was kept waiting for nearly thirty minutes."

"I warn you," she said. "Anything you say may strike back at you. David, turn on that light." She pointed at the lamp over the table. "Come here, Newrose."

He circled Saba's chair to the table, his smooth egg-face sucked thin with uncertainty. The light came on. He put one hand up, dazzled. She pulled him by the arm another step closer to Tanuojin and threw back the red blanket.

His jaw dropped. He leaned toward Lore Smythe, her white throat mottled with bruises. "But—what—" Paula flung the blanket over the dead woman.

"She tried to murder the Prima."

"Oh my God," Newrose said. "Oh my God."

Tanuojin left his chair and walked to the other end of the room. Paula nodded to David, who shut the light off. In the dark Newrose obeyed her touch like a child, moved into the center of the room, and stood. He said, "I assume you have proof of these charges." His voice was higher than before.

"We have the gun she brought, the dart she shot at him—several darts, in fact—and the wound." The wound was gone. They would not need it. Saba was watching him, his chin on his fist. Tanuojin came back toward them.

"He didn't know," he said, in Styth.

"I can see that." Saba tapped her arm. "Tell him about the Sunlight League."

The League's name was almost the same in the two languages; Newrose recognized it and said, "Was she from the League?"

Paula nodded. He made a little gesture with one hand, palm up. "I didn't know. Her credentials were quite in order. She had the highest recommendation—"

"Fortunately as usual the League misjudged the Prima."

Newrose turned toward the big Styth in his chair behind her. Low, he said, "You have my wholehearted congratulations on your escape. I trust the wound isn't serious?" His voice sounded stronger. To Paula, he said, "If you'll allow me, I'd like to go collect my—"

"Oh, no," Paula said. "Not yet. You'll talk to your party, and who knows how many of them are Leaguers?"

"I can assure you—"

"You can't assure us of anything, Newrose. You didn't know about her, you say. Even if that's true, which we doubt, you're nothing better than a Trojan Horse for the League."

Tanuojin said, "Shall we introduce him to Dr. Savenia?" He crooked his finger at Junna. "Send Marus for my poppet."

Newrose frowned at Paula. "Now, Miss Mendoza—"

She cut him off with an abrupt shake of her head and turned to Saba. "Do you want to talk to him yourself?"

"Yes. You translate it."

"I—"

"Just do as I say." He rose, looming over Newrose, and gave the Martian his finest autocratic look. "We aren't afraid of the Sunlight League. Even if she had killed me, I'm unimportant, only Styth is important, and Styth is immortal."

Newrose was collecting himself; he squared his shoulders. The hiss of the surf ran under Saba's voice and Paula's voice translating. The Prima said, "We have our honor to consider. If we deal with you for the sake of expediency and lose our honor, we fail even if we succeed."

Newrose inclined his head. "I'm sure we can make some agreement that serves everybody's interests."

Paula glanced at David, who stood beside the wall, watching his father. His smile showed in the faint light from the illusion wall. She straightened her gaze. "I don't think they have much respect for your honor."

Marus appeared in the doorway. "Akellar, I have Dr. Savenia."

Tanuojin thumbed his mustaches back. "Send her in. Paula, tell this nigger who I am."

"Newrose," she said, "this is the Yekka Akellar, Tanuojin, the Prima's lyo, the cadet general of the fleet." She nodded toward the door. "You know Dr. Savenia."

"Of course," Newrose said.

Cam walked down the room toward them. She wore a gray tunic over a long black skirt: probably Tanuojin's choice; he took a gruesome interest in every detail of her life. Her face was perfectly drawn. Before Saba she dropped to one knee, bowing her head.

"Prima."

Saba said nothing. He despised her. She rose and crossed to Tanuojin and bowed from the waist. Newrose watched her, his damp lips parted.

"Hello, Cam," Paula said.

"Paula," Cam said, coolly. "You look very well." She turned to Newrose, whose gaze had been fastened on her since she had come in. "Hello, Alvers. I understand you're here to negotiate a surrender."

Newrose coughed. "I'm not . . . I don't think we've settled what we're negotiating."

"Of course it's a surrender," Cam said, in an irritated tone. "What else can you do? The Styths are our genetic superiors—our natural masters. It's the will of history. What else can we do?"

Paula leaned on the back of her chair. Newrose scratched his nose. "You seem to have changed your opinions, doctor."

"I recognize my mistakes."

Tanuojin said, in the Common Speech, "Dr. Savenia, you can take Mr. Newrose around while he's in Luna."

"Thank you, Akellar. I'd like that."

Saba said, "Paula, tell him we'll send for him again later. And get her out of here." He leaned past her toward Tanuojin. "Can you reach him? What is he thinking?"

"No—just at the beginning, when he saw the dead one, he shed it like a scent."

Ketac and Marus were ushering out the two Martians. Paula went around her chair and sat down. She put her elbows on the chair's arms.

She went up to the surface of the Planet. In an ancient room there, outside the artificial gravity, she sat looking up at the Earth. Blue and brown, it shed its soft reflected light toward her. A blinking red beacon passed by in the high distance. She guessed it was a slavepen. The room was built in a crater. Around it the toothed walls rose, jagged and airless. She sat watching the Earth, until Newrose came to meet her.

Cam Savenia was with him. While Newrose was settling himself across the table from her, Paula said, "You can go, Cam."

"The Akellar—"

"This isn't the Akellar's meeting."

"As you wish," Cam said, sulky. Her feet rang down the treads of the ladder into the dark below. Paula sat down.

"She tells him everything. Even what she forgets."

"You seem fond of riddles." Newrose opened his papercase and laid out a pad of notepaper, styli, his pencase on the table before him. She picked up the pencase and snapped it open.

Inside the case a clear button with a tiny coil of wire in its heart was fastened to the lining beside one hinge. She broke it out of the case with her fingernails and slid the case back over the table to him. Newrose looked troubled. His small hands pattered on the tabletop.

"What's happened to Dr. Savenia?" he said.

"Nothing she didn't do to herself." She laid her forearms on the table. "You know, Newrose, you need a settlement of the war now. If the war continues, the League will destroy everybody."

"The League," he said. "What about the Styths? They seem to do an ace job of destruction."

"That's up to you, isn't it?" She reached for his styli. "Actually, you've caught them at a good moment. They might be willing to end the war now, before they take so many prisoners they glut the slave trade."

"Slaves," he said, rigid.

She made dots on the table with a stylus and connected them with straight and curved lines. "Surely you aren't going to protest on principle, Newrose? After all, there were work camps on the Earth all through the war." The stylus scratched on the tabletop.

"I can't believe you support the Styths," he said. "After what they did to your Planet."

"Therefore I must support you?"

"I'm your own kind, Mendoza," he said, earnestly.

"My kind." She watched her hand making scribbles.

"Whose side are you on?"

She raised her head. "Did you know Richard Bunker?"

"Yes, of course."

"And Sybil Jefferson?"

"Naturally."

"I'm on their side."

"They're dead."

"That's why I am on their side."

"Another riddle."

"I'm their witness," she said. "I'm the last witness to what happened down there, what you want to forget, and the Styths want to forget." Her hands were shaking. She spread them out flat on the table, over her scribbles. A bump pressed against the palm of her hand. She sat back, her anger broken, and picked Newrose's spy device up in her fingers.

"But you're working for them," Newrose said.

"Oh," she said. "I have learned to forgive my enemies." She dropped the plastic button onto the table again. Where there was one cheat there would be two. "I am a practical woman, Newrose."

"Will they let you go back?"

That struck her; she gave him a single swift glance and reached for the stylus again. He leaned across the table toward her.

"No," he said. "Of course not. But we would. If the Earth were under our control."

"Are you trying to bribe me, Newrose?"

He tilted back in his chair, and his white hands folded themselves into his lap. "These people are savages, you know. When you're of no further use to them, they'll turn on you. You're just as inferior as we are to them."

She had to laugh at that. Putting the stylus down, she pushed it and the spy button across the table at him. "I'll see you tomorrow, Mr. Newrose." She climbed down the ladder into the Planet.

The floor around the swimming pool stood an inch deep in water. The hard walls of the room reflected back the racket. Paula leaned against the doorjamb, watching. Naked, glistening, David rushed along the side of the pool and jumped in among the other men. The water slopped up over the rim of the pool. Ketac and another man were wrestling, their bodies coiled together; while they fought to drive each other under the water they laughed.

Saba came in the door beside her. "What are they doing?"

"Killing each other."

One hand on the top of the door, his weight slouched onto one leg, he watched his crew in the pool. "You'll have to finish with Newrose by yourself. The Martian Fleet is regrouping. We have to go meet them."

She gathered her breath, her eyes turning toward the pool, looking for David. The boy shot up out of the water, caught the edge of the bottom diving board, and swung himself onto it.

"It's too bad he's so small," Saba said. He put two fingers in his mouth and whistled. All around the leaping surface of the pool the Styths' heads turned. He called, "Report to the ship in two hours. My watch on watch." He went off through the dressing room, splashing through the puddles. Paula moved away, to let the naked men out of the water.

Newrose said, "Then we're all alone here."

"*Kundra* is still here. Ymma's ship. The man with the scarred face." She leaned back in her chair, her eyes on the clear ceiling. The sun was setting. In the mid-heaven the Earth shone in half-phase. "Twelve Styths, eighteen of your people, and me." She leveled her gaze at him. "What did Tanuojin tell you?"

The Martian's pink cheeks sucked hollow. "We talked for two hours. I should say he talked for two hours. The conversation ranged from the superiority of Styths to the superiority of the Styth Fleet to the superiority of the Styth legal system. I was unimpressed. Frankly, I think he suffers from some kind of mental disorder."

Paula hooted with laughter. The tabletop was still covered with the marks she had made during their first meeting. She rubbed her hands over it. "If you can diagnose it, Newrose, do let me know."

"Probably he came away with no good impression of me," Newrose said.

She turned sideways in her chair. Up overhead, through the clear roof, she could see the blue Earth. Above it were the stars of Scorpio's tail. Paula said, "I've been thinking about what you said, the other day."

"Have you? I'm glad to hear that."

"What if I did help you? Where would that take me?"

Newrose pulled his chair closer to the table. "Isn't this interesting? Now you seem to have changed your heart."

"Tanuojin is gone," she said.

"Ah."

"I can see why you don't trust me." She glanced up at the Earth again and back to Newrose.

"I want to trust you," he said.

"Suppose I were to give you a proof? Could you get me out of Luna?"

"When?"

"As soon as possible."

Newrose's pale eyes gleamed. He said, in a taut voice, "Well, that depends."

"Suppose you were to get me to Mars," she said, "and suppose I were to take the Styth codebooks with me?"

The Martian's throat worked in a swallow. His gaze never left hers. "Yes. I can see why you'd have to get out of Luna. Under those circumstances." His hand rose toward his face. "You can do this?"

Feet crashed on the metal treads of the ladder just below them. She stood and lost her balance and nearly fell. Ymma came up through the hatch in the floor. He shot a fiery look at Newrose, still sitting.

"Get him out of here."

She nodded at the Martian. "You'd better go." He looked sharply from her up to the hatched face of the Styth and climbed away down the ladder. Ymma scowled, all the creases dented in his cheeks.

"I just got a message from Tanuojin. The Martians ambushed them—we lost twelve ships in thirty-two seconds."

She thought unwillingly of David, floating in the metal bubble of the ship. "I don't know anything about fighting," she said, and went away down the ladder.

. . .

At six in the evening by the clock, most of the lighting in Luna dimmed out, signaling the beginning of the artificial night. Newrose and his staff were quartered on the fourteenth floor, where Paula also lived. She took a current book of codes and went down the empty corridor to Newrose's suite. She knocked on the door, and Newrose himself opened it.

"Miss Mendoza," he said. He sounded surprised. Backing up, he held the door wide. "Come in."

Paula went into the room. It was too warm and too bright for her, and she felt closed in. One of Newrose's aides sat on a candy-striped settee under the illusion window. He stood up when he saw her. Down a dark hallway opening off the room, she heard Cam Savenia's voice.

"This is an unexpected pleasure," Newrose said, smiling.

Paula gave him the codebook. "Here. To prove I'm honest."

Newrose said, "I never doubted it."

Paula laughed. She glanced at the entrance into the hallway. Cam Savenia came out of it and stopped.

"Hello, Paula."

"What are you doing here?" Paula asked.

Newrose came up between them, still smiling, and patted Paula's arm. "Stay and have a drink with us."

"I'd better not." She turned toward the way out, her eyes on Cam. "You shouldn't let her in here, Newrose."

Cam flushed. Newrose said, "Oh, well." Paula went out of the room.

In the corridor, she walked down about fifteen feet from the door into the shadows and waited. After a few moments Cam came after her. Paula fell into step beside her.

"You heard what the Akellar told me," Cam said. She stopped to light a cigarette. "I'm on your side now, remember?" The matchlight made a mask out of her face. She flicked the match off down the corridor like a firefly into the night.

"What have you found out?" Paula asked.

Cam started off again, long-legged. "Newrose came back from your meeting looking happy as a clam. You must be working on him. Not that I ever doubted you would."

They went around a corner and into the trunk hall. The night lamps on the walls were replicas of old-fashioned street lamps, hanging on curved brackets over their heads. Paula said, "Is Newrose in touch with anybody off the Planet? Like Hanse, for example?"

Cam's eyebrows rose. "Not that I know of. Do you think he is? What are you trying to do?"

"I have an intuition." They had come to Paula's door. She stopped and reached into her sleeve for her key. "There's been a battle.

General Hanse has won. Not decisively, but well." She pressed the face of the key into the patch above the doorknob.

Cam's expression stayed calm, almost placid. "When will the Akellar be back?"

Paula shrugged. She let her door slide open. Cam sucked on her cigarette. The red coal followed her hand through the dimness down to her hip. "I don't feel exactly right when he isn't here. I don't know what I'll do when he goes back to Uranus."

"Maybe he'll take you."

"He says he has work for me in Mars."

Paula studied her a moment, wondering what the work might be. Cam's cigarette made its arc upward toward her mouth. She breathed out smoke and said, "You might be right about Newrose and Hanse. I think the Martians know about this battle."

"Oh?"

"It accounts for something one of them said. Aren't you going to invite me in?"

"Not in a million years."

"What's the matter, baby?" Cam said. "Can't stand the competition?" Paula went into her suite and shut the door.

Midway through the artificial night Newrose woke her, pounding on her door. "Hurry," the Martian said. "We haven't much time." He hustled her off along the trunk corridor. She glanced behind them down the empty hallway into the darkness. Their steps sounded hollow here. Newrose took her arm and led her into a vertical car.

The car was supposed to be dead. The panel beside the door was missing and the instrument plate showed bare, its surface etched with circuits. Newrose took a key from his pocket and pressed it to the plate. The car climbed toward the surface, past the thirteenth floor where the Styths lived, up through layers of uninhabited space where the environment was supposed to be turned off. She wondered how many miles of tunnels there were under Luna's surface. Hundreds. She looked at Newrose, smiling all over his face.

"Good news," he said. "There's been another battle. Hanse has won again. We're beating the hell out of the Styths."

"*We*. Do you like Hanse?"

"I can reason with him," Newrose said. "Unlike the Sunlight League. Or the Styths."

The car stopped at the sixth floor. They went out onto the vertical apron. Several corridors fanned away from them. One was lit by spots of light running off into the distance and Newrose took her off along it.

Every few yards a power torch was stapled to the wall at shoulder-level. They passed a pile of rubble that smelled of char.

"The Styths never took all of Luna," Newrose said, hurrying along. "Just the surface and the nerve center on the thirteenth floor. The life support systems. Then they turned off the oxygen everywhere else."

"Tanuojin," she said. "He's an economical man. Then what are we breathing?"

"Local emergency supply."

Ahead a box torch glowed on a crossbeam. She knew about the battle for Luna. Kasuk had died here. The broken wall bulged into the corridor and Newrose went ahead of her through the narrow gap. Paula glanced behind her. She thought she saw something moving in the dark.

The air turned cold. Under her feet the floor was buckled and she had to watch to keep from tripping on the plastic waves. They went through a door, down a hall, through another door. She had lost her way. They crossed a stretch of darkness where her ears told her the walls left off and vast space stretched away around her. Newrose took her up a short flight of stairs and into a small room.

"We can't promise to get you off the Planet right away, but the Styths will never find you here."

She looked around the tiny L-shaped room. Another Martian sat at a table under the ceiling lamp, playing cards scattered before him. In the foot of the L was a box with a screen like a videone: a photo-relay. On the panel above the screen a green light was burning.

"The signal is through," said the man playing cards. "That book she gave us is authentic."

Newrose smiled at her. Paula shook her head at him, exasperated. "You should have checked that before you brought me here."

"I trust you," he said.

"Then you're naïve." She opened the door to the corridor again. From the darkness Ymma came past her into the room.

Newrose's man gave a muffled cry and stood up. The Styth loomed over them all. In the taut silence, another Styth walked in from the corridor and went straight to the photo-relay.

His hands on his hips, Ymma said to Paula, "Are they signaling Hanse?"

"I don't know. Maybe Mars." She was watching Newrose's face harden into an expression of outrage. The other Martian sat down with a thump. She said to Newrose, "Who are you calling?"

On his domed forehead a film of sweat appeared. He said, "I should have listened to the people who told me you were treacherous."

She turned to Ymma again. "He didn't even check the book. He isn't very good at this. And he says there's been another battle."

"The word came just before I left. We lost another eight ships."

The Styth by the photo-relay said, "Akellar, the transmission beam focuses in Mars."

"You were right about that, too," Ymma said to her.

She faced Newrose again. "You call me treacherous, Newrose. We let you come here in good faith. Even after Lore Smythe, we acted in good faith. When are you coming up to my level?"

Newrose took a white handkerchief from the breast pocket of his tunic, opened it out, and patted his forehead dry. He folded the handkerchief again. "It's your move, Mendoza." With two fingers he stuffed the handkerchief back into his pocket.

"Show me how to get back to the verticals."

They went back through the ruins of Luna. Newrose clasped his hands behind his back. Until they had crossed the stretch of darkness they walked in silence. In the lighted hallway, she said, "You can't cheat, Newrose. You have to do this the hard way."

The lights shone on his face. She smelled char. They were going along between walls swollen and cracked from fires. She was ready to remind him of Tanuojin, who had done all this, but Newrose took out his handkerchief again, mopped his face again, and said, "I'll try to do my job."

"I want an unconditional surrender."

"The Martian Army is winning the war."

"The Styths will win." She slowed to keep her footing on the uneven floor. "Tanuojin will want something impossible, and Saba will do it. If you and I haven't arranged something by then, they'll go straight for Mars, and you and I will have missed our chance."

"What did you have in mind?"

Ahead the corridor led off, banded around with alternate yellow light and dark from the torches. At the end she saw the double doors of the verticals and quickened her steps. "We'll talk about it tomorrow. But it's very simple. You and I are going to rule the Middle Planets."

When she came up the ladder to the surface, Newrose was already in the ancient room. She opened her notebook and put it down on the table. "Sign that."

"I want to know a little more about—"

She slid onto the chair facing him and folded her arms on the tabletop. "Sign it."

"I warn you that if necessary I shall repudiate this agreement."

"Sign it."

He signed the surrender. She turned the notebook around and folded that leaf over. "Good. Now, we have a lot of work to do."

"What exactly are you planning?"

She looked out through the clear window, across the barren floor of the crater to its steepled wall. The sun was still setting; the slow rocking of the Planet on its axis had kicked it up higher than the day before above the rough horizon. "I don't know. Whatever is possible. How much work does the Council do?"

He shrugged. "All the relations between the member governments." His hands were clasped together before him on the table. They opened enough to gesture at her and folded together again in their two-handed fist. "Actually, in practice, the Committee's liaison with us—Miss Jefferson—went between the parties involved and settled everything outside the official meetings. Otherwise there'd be just too much detail."

"How many members?"

"Mars, Luna, the Politburo of Crosby's Planet, the twenty-three governments of Venus. Naturally Mars is the most important member."

She raised her head. "Why?"

"Well, because the Earth—because Mars is the strongest and richest."

"Because the Earth wasn't a member."

"The Committee always kept in close touch with us." His clasped hands spread again, the fingers splayed. "Depending on the personalities involved, the Committee could be very powerful."

She put her pen down. "The Committee ran the Middle Planets."

"Oh, that's a little extreme."

"No. You know what the rAkellaron is. The Council of the Styth Empire? The rAkellaron will take the place of the Council."

Newrose tapped his fingertips together. "Can they handle it? The Middle Planets is a very complex—"

"The rAkellaron as a body is incapable of rising to its feet." She turned. Feet boomed on the rungs of the ladder, and Ymma's head rose up through the round hatchway in the floor.

"They tore them up," he said, in Styth. His face crinkled into a wide grin. "The fleet. Tanuojin just called. They captured three Condors and blew away four more."

Paula let out her breath in a sigh. She closed the notebook. Newrose was watching them, his eyes sharp. She said, "Congratulations, Secretary. Our side won."

He gave her a lick of a glance. Ymma slouched against the clear wall of the room. His shadow fell outside across the dust. "The Creep baited them right down his throat. He kept them winning until they all gathered, and then he wiped them out."

Newrose said, dull, "I should tell my staff."

"Go." Paula nodded to him.

Ymma moved out of his way, still beaming; he radiated a faint bright scent of pleasure. She put the notebook into her papercase. Newrose's pink head sank below the surface into the Planet.

"*Ybix* was in every single fight," Ymma said. "She was the bait. He's all iron, Saba. I wish I'd been there."

"I'm glad you were here," she said. Newrose had signed the surrender with half an hour to spare. She went down into the Planet, to send the message to Saba that his war was over.

The new dress fastened up the back. Between her shoulder blades the slide jammed. She crooked one arm over her shoulder and the other around her side and tried to tease the fastener loose. It was stuck tight. She wrenched at it, her teeth clenched. Abruptly she realized there was someone behind her.

She let out a high, choked yell and wheeled. It was David, laughing at her.

"You didn't hear me," he said proudly.

"No." She turned her back on him. "Fix that, will you?"

He pulled on the slide fastener. Paula watched him in the mirror on the wall beside her. He was already her height, growing burly, like Saba. In this light she could not be sure, but she thought she saw hair on his smooth upper lip. He muttered, triumphant, and ran the slide up behind her neck.

"Where is the Prima?" she said. She buttoned the tight-fitting forearms of the sleeves.

"Talking to that nigger."

"Newrose."

"Why does he bother? We beat them, now they have to obey him, don't they?"

She faced him, reaching for the long black coat thrown across the chair. "Are your mustaches starting to grow?"

"Can you see them?" He rotated toward the mirror. With one forefinger he stroked his lip. She put the coat on, its silky fur collar against her cheek, and buttoned it up the front. When her son turned away from the mirror he was frowning. She straightened his shirt, to be touching him.

"Don't." He pushed her hand away. "Come on—you'll be late."

Her neck and face heated. She went after him into the hall. He was ashamed of her. Her gaze on the floor, she walked fast through the guards around the meeting room. Somebody announced her.

David left her as soon as they entered the long room. The air was freezing. Along the illusion wall the ocean streamed midnight blue up to the thin white curl of surf. Against that background the Styths moved in silhouette. She crossed the room toward the tall stocky shape standing against the ocean.

"Where did you get that dress?" Ketac said. He ran his hand over the sleeve. "Oh. I like that."

She held her arm up so that he could stroke his cheek against the fur. "I looted it. On the sixth level. There were a lot of shops up there that didn't get burned." She glanced down the room after David, shorter than the other men.

Several more men came into the room. They pushed the furniture off into the corners to make space. Their voices rose. Ketac was holding a cup out to her and she took it. The surface was chased with a scrolled ribbon. She held it out to look and decided it was a vase for cut flowers. The cool potent drink tasted of mint.

A loud voice said names, over by the door. Leno and Tanuojin were coming in. Paula lowered the cup. Tanuojin walked first into the room, ahead of the Prima Cadet.

"Well, well," she said. She sipped the icy, minty liquor.

Tanuojin was coming toward her, and Ketac backed off, giving way to him. The tall man said, bad-tempered, "Isn't there anything to drink in here except swill?" He put his back against the ocean, his hands behind him. Ketac went quickly down the wall.

"Hello, Prima," Paula said to Tanuojin.

"Hello, Paula."

The men around the room were standing stiffly at respect. Saba came in. Behind him was Alvers Newrose, almost unnoticed in the dark. Ketac went to attend his father. The Martian stayed by the door, his head moving from side to side. Saba circled around the middle of the room.

"Listen to me. I have some things to get said. The fleet has voted thirty-six promotions, which I will have posted next watch." He was in a very good temper. Paula had told Newrose what to say to him, and apparently he had obeyed her. She watched Newrose peer blindly around the room, looking for her. Saba recited names and ranks in an ascending order. David was not one of them. Of course he was too young even to be a subtenant.

Saba said, "The last three are the best. Ketac, in *Ybix*, goes to a master commander and third watch officer of the ship. Leno, in *Ebelos*, to a general commander." He turned, one hand out, and Ketac brought him a strip of black cloth. "Tanuojin."

Beside her, the tall man shifted his feet. Slowly he went across the room to Saba. The Prima hung the flag across his lyo's chest. "The fleet has only voted two flags since I've been Prima, and both of them to you." He started to shake the other man's hand but instead they put their arms around each other, hugged each other chest to chest. The other men beat their hands together in applause.

Newrose was watching, so his eyes had sharpened in the dusk. Tanuojin came back to the wall next to Paula. Around the room, the aides of the other ranking officers brought them drink and chairs and took their private messages from man to man.

Leno said, "Prima, what word from Vribulo?"

"None," Saba said.

"Nothing at all?"

"Who's dominant in the Chamber?" Saba took a big glass from Ketac. "Bokojin and Machou. The vice commander and the commander of the Uranian Patrol. The only cheers we'd hear from them is if we crashed the whole fleet on an Asteroid."

Paula looked up at Tanuojin on her left. The black sash hung across his chest. His hands were jammed under his belt. She took hold of his wrist. His skin was cold; he did not push her off.

Near the door, Ymma said, "It looks as if the war isn't quite over after all."

"Maybe," Saba said. He held the glass out to David, who held it for him, and gestured to Ketac. "But that's between me and Bokojin."

"And the rest of us," Leno said. The other men murmured loudly in agreement.

"I think I can take Bokojin," Saba said. He pointed toward Newrose, next to the door. In the Common Speech, he said, "This man is the spokesman for the Council of the Middle Planets. The Mendoz' has arranged a peace with him. I told him we only want the honor of the Empire, not revenge. As an earnest of that I'm giving him the Martian general we took prisoner."

Leno said, "What is he giving us?"

Saba made a careless shrug. Ketac came in, with General Hanse just behind him.

Paula straightened. She let go of Tanuojin. Hanse had shrunk by fifty pounds. He walked awkwardly, slowly, not like a man in the dark: as if he were drugged. Tanuojin got her sleeve and pulled her arm behind her and held her. Hanse stopped between Saba and the door. Newrose went to him and spoke to him, touched him, and walked around him. Hanse stood speechless, moveless, unseeing.

"What happened?" Paula said to Tanuojin.

"It didn't work."

Leno had come deep into the room. His jaw stuck out. "What assurances are they giving you?"

"They'll keep the agreement," Paula said. "As long as it's in their best interests."

The Merkhiz Akellar stamped toward her. His gaze swiveled

from Saba to Tanuojin. "Why do you trust her? Didn't she double over on us in the Earth, that time? If you ask me, she's one of them."

Saba had gone off to the side of the room. David was with him. She tugged on Tanuojin's grip and he freed her.

She said, "Leno, I won't say who betrayed who on the Earth. Newrose is a Martian. You know what the Martians did to my Planet." She went toward him three or four steps. Everybody was watching her.

Merkhiz said, "This smells rotten. Why would you help us?"

"Because you're the only people I have left." She stared up at his broad face. "I didn't choose this, Akellar. All my friends are dead, because of you and the Martians."

He said nothing for a moment. His round eyes gleamed. Finally he said, "From what I've heard of this arrangement, they're giving us nothing but promises."

She went past him, making him turn to keep up with her. Now she was facing Tanuojin, past Leno's shoulder, and she spoke to him. "If you want to do it your way, do it your way. They'll fight, you'll have to go from dome to dome beating them down, you'll be stuck here until the Planet comes around again. Let Bokojin be the Prima. I don't care." She turned her back on him and Leno and went over to Newrose.

"What's going on?" Newrose said, low.

"Jabber-jabber." Hanse's slack face hung before her, his skin draped in folds over his cheeks. She waved her fingers under his eyes. "Hanse." She patted his cheek. "Hanse!"

"He's catatonic," Newrose said. His lips tightened, grim.

"Take him out."

Newrose like a nurse led the general away. She stood watching them maneuver through the door. She could guess what had happened. David touched her arm.

"Papa wants to see you." His hand lay on her forearm. "Not all your friends are dead, Mother." His voice trembled.

Tanuojin was leaving, Junna behind him. David tugged on her sleeve and she went to Saba.

"I don't know what happened," Newrose said. His face was rosy from the chilly air. Paula walked faster. Like a little terrier the Martian hurried along beside her. "Hanse can't talk or think, the man can scarcely move."

She led him into the corridor to Saba's suite, lined with Styths. Leno had an office here, too, somewhere. She stopped at the table that blocked the way, and the aide sitting behind it got up and went to tell Saba that she was there.

"What do you want me to do?" she said to Newrose.

"Protest. Whatever they did to him was definitely contrary to all the rules regarding prisoners of war."

"Tsk." The book open on the table was the watch roster. She skewed around to read who Saba was meeting. Tanuojin had taken *Ybix* to the Earth. The aide came back.

"The Prima will see you, Mendoz'."

Newrose stepped between her and the door. "Miss Mendoza, I'm serious about this."

"Newrose," she said, "you are a funny man. I was Hanse's prisoner for six months. I have no sympathy for him." She went past him down the corridor.

Saba was in his bedroom. Ketac let her in. He mumbled at her; his breath smelled foul. She said, "You don't look so daisy-fresh," and went past him into the room.

"I feel awful."

The overstuffed chairs had been dragged back. At the foot of the bed was a table, up on blocks to fit a Styth, where Saba sat eating. David was waiting beside him to serve him. The Prima wiped his mouth on a white cloth. "You see," he told Ketac, "she stops drinking before she makes herself sick. Vida, bring her a chair."

"You were as drunk as I was," Ketac said.

"I am never drunk."

Paula snorted. She climbed up into the chair David brought her. Saba picked over the remnants of his meal, nudged the plate away, and twisted around in the chair. "You have those orders," he said to Ketac.

"Yes, Prima." Ketac went down the room to the door.

When he was gone, she said, "Ketac has done very well."

"I can depend on him. Vida, sometimes, but Vida talks back to me." David was bending past him to pour water into his cup, and Saba swatted him on the backside. "He even talks back to Tanuojin."

"Sometimes he's wrong," David said.

"He's your son," Saba told her. "Down to his bootsoles."

"What happened to General Hanse?" she said. David put a cup down before her. He held the fat-bellied jug in his other hand.

"It's just water," he said.

"I'll suffer."

The boy poured her cup full. Saba was toying with the white cloth on the table. "Hanse. Tanuojin tried to take him, the way he took Dr. Savenia, but Hanse fought, and his heart stopped with Tajin in him."

David put the jug on the table. He seemed uninterested in what his father was saying. She guessed he had been there: Saba took him everywhere.

"It was hell," Saba said to her. "I thought he was gone."

She drew the Earth-sign in the frost of her cup. That was safe.

Even if Hanse got well enough to talk, the Martians would think he was crazy.

"This deal you made with Newrose," he said. "You want the rAkellaron to take the place of the Council. That won't work. You know that, don't you?"

"It isn't meant to work," she said. "It's meant to look good, that's all."

"Then who does the real job?"

"I will."

He slapped the table. His cup jumped. "What about Tanuojin? He doesn't like this arrangement at all."

"He's going back to Uranus, isn't he?" She crossed her legs on the seat of her chair. "Then he'll use Dr. Savenia. You and I can handle him, and Newrose can handle her."

He got up and walked toward the door. Paula reached across the table for his dish. He had eaten all the meat. Cubes of vegetables stood in the pool of red sauce.

"You'll have to go up front for me in the Chamber," she said.

"That's who I am, isn't it? I'm pretty, I smile, I'm everybody's best face."

She used a scrap of potato to soak up the sauce. "What's wrong with you? I thought you liked being the front."

"Sometimes Tanuojin treats me as if that's all I am." He came back to his chair. "You're the only one of us who knows enough about the Middle Planets to make this work."

"It will work," she said. She ate the potato.

"This settlement won't be popular on Mars," Newrose said. He had a scarf wrapped around his head, like an egg-cozy.

"How is General Hanse?" Paula said.

"He's terribly ill."

"He had a heart attack while they were questioning him. The Styths don't know much about medicine."

She was facing the clear wall of the space port waiting room. Out on the flat crater floor a hundred feet away two ships stood in the first two wells of the launching dock. While she watched, the accordion cover of the third well folded back, and another ship rose through it to the surface. That was *Ybicket*, *Ybix*'s new sidecraft. A man in a pressure suit jogged across the gray dust to the ship and disappeared inside the hatch. Paula turned toward Newrose again. Her pressure suit held her arms out away from her sides, like a gingerbread man.

"Just keep watch on Dr. Savenia," she said.

"I thought you said that was settled?"

"I trust Tanuojin about three inches to the mile." She trusted him least when he appeared to give in. He had accepted the Martian Treaty more readily than Leno. It was impossible to surprise him. Maybe he had learned not to waste his time on things he could not control.

"Do you trust the Prima?" Newrose said.

"Under the circumstances I'd rather be hung for a lamb than a sheep."

"Clear the launch area," said the speaker in the corner of the ceiling. In the naked waiting room it boomed. A moment later the same voice repeated the words in the Common Speech. Newrose's eyebrows drew close over his nose.

"I do wish you'd stay here," he said to her.

"What do you mean?" *Ybicket*'s hatch opened and the man in the black pressure suit dropped lightly to the ground. He came at a lope across the launch area toward the waiting room.

"You seem to think I can just pull down a few levers and push the right buttons and make what you want happen," Newrose said. "I can't do that. I can't explain it as well as you can." He looked at her bitterly. "I'm not a diplomat, Mendoza, I'm a garden variety—"

She laughed at him. "Don't worry. You'll do very well." She watched the man in the pressure suit enter the airlock to the waiting room. "Better than Dr. Savenia. Do you know my son?" Pulling off his helmet, David came into the room.

"We have to go," he said to her.

He was flying her to *Ybix*. She introduced him to Newrose and went to take her helmet from the shelf along the back wall. Newrose and her son stood silently side by side, not looking at each other; neither spoke the other's language. She shook Newrose's hand and David took her out to *Ybicket*.

YBIX. Watch logs H21, 969–H22, 336

She opened the hatch to the Beak and rose up into the pyramidal room. Tanuojin was there. The shutter was open. Paula turned around in mid-air, so that the spread of the stars was above her. The Milky Way cut the corner of the window; she could barely pick Uranus out of the thickness of stars below it. The Planet was just entering the constellation Capricorn, sacred to Matuko and Saba's family, the House of Exile. Tanuojin was too long for the Beak room, and his body curved to fit and left almost no space for her. She turned to the stars again. Near the top of the window were two familiar patches of light, like pieces of the Milky Way that had drifted: the Magellanic Clouds. Between them a brilliant star shone. She could not remember seeing it before. But it must have been there; stars did not change.

"That one did," Tanuojin said. "It went supernova during the War."

The star flashed white and green and orange. Out there was something greater than ten thousand systemic wars, but she had no way of knowing what it was. Like the events of atoms, the lives of mesons lasting trillionths of trillionths of seconds, the nova happened beyond her range. She was hung between them, her clocks too slow or fast, her rulers too long or short, so that these things that must all be part of one thing seemed to be unrelated.

Tanuojin said, "Saba always tells me how direct your mind is."

"Who asked you to listen?" She faced him, the nova of his race. "What do you think about?"

"I don't think any more. I just watch." The while he talked to her he was writing on a tablet.

"It must be boring," she said. "Always knowing what people will do next."

"I don't. And it's never boring."

He was making notes on the supernova. The hot star sparkled like a jewel, now orange, now white again. Below it was Uranus. A memory of the dark cities of the Styths crossed her mind, and she thought with longing of the sunlit Earth. She thought painfully of Richard Bunker. Tanuojin was watching her.

"I keep going in circles," she said. She pulled the hatch open and swam out to the corridor.

David's claws were growing in. Saba had stopped shaving his head, and when his hair grew long enough to tie, David would be clubbed. When Paula went to her cabin, her son and his father were there. She went past them to the end of the room where the bed hung on the wall.

"The order of the command is the father's order," David said. "Law grows in the father, generation on generation." His voice was singsong; he was reciting from memory.

"Give me the formula for the oath," Saba said.

There were three hundred formulas, which David had to memorize before he was clubbed. He gave Paula a cutting look and began, "When you tell—"

Saba said, "Not when *I* do it. Say it right."

"But—"

"Don't change the formula."

Paula was taking her clothes off. David's voice rose. "What are you doing in here? You aren't supposed to listen."

She took her sleepdress out of the bin on the wall. "Then don't say it in my bedroom."

"She isn't supposed to hear it," David said to his father.

Saba said to him, "Go feed yourself. We're on watch pretty soon."

David flew out of the room. Paula doubled over in the air and pulled the robe down over her feet. It unsettled her that he was going through this education—that in a few months he would be a grown man. She opened out the folds of the bed.

"I guess he gets his temper from me."

"It's his age," Saba said. "Boys get hot when their claws come in." He went to the hatch. "You taught him to say what he thinks, Paula."

"I didn't teach him to think like a Styth." She yanked the bed out straight and wrapped the wings around her.

Saba laughed. "No, you certainly didn't." Three bells rang, and he left.

In the three hundred and sixty-third watch of the voyage *Ybix* crossed the orbit of Uranus. She slowed, falling into a course around the white Planet, the rest of the fleet behind her. Paula stayed in the wetroom. When she came out there was a note from Saba stuck in the hatch commanding her to the library. Her stomach and the muscles of her arms and legs were cramped so that moving was painful. She dressed and went down to the galley.

Junna was eating protein strips just outside the hatch. He said, "You're supposed to be putting your head together with Gemini."

She punched out blue tablets. "Are you glad to be home?"

"We're a long way from home. There are fifty ships of the Uranian Patrol stacked up around us."

"What?"

The speaker hummed in the wall. "Paula," Saba said, "get down here now." Her sleeves stuffed with food, she went along the corridor to the blue tunnel, where the library was, next to Tanuojin's cabin.

He and Saba were crowded against the lower wall of the library. A little projector threw an eight-inch cube of green light into the other end of the room. She had to go through it to reach the only open space. Yellow shovel-nosed ships floated around her like darts. In the middle of the cube was *Ybix*, huge among the fog of little ships.

"What is this?"

Tanuojin's eyes were shut. Saba said, "They were waiting for us when we fell into orbit."

"Bokojin?"

Under his breath Tanuojin muttered an oath against Bokojin. She looked from him to Saba, whose arms were stretched out relaxed along the curved wall behind him. "What about the rest of the fleet?" she said.

"The patrol has let them dock. This is our war, not theirs." The grainy red beam of the holograph projector ran diagonally across his face.

"We can make it their war," Tanuojin said, without opening his eyes.

"No."

"Damn it, Saba—"

"I told them I wouldn't ask them to fight Styths."

Paula watched the coils of ships around *Ybix*. She tore open a water tube. Uranus lay below them, the crystal heart of the Empire. "What does Bokojin want?"

"It's more than Bokojin," Tanuojin said. "He must have a couple of the others with him."

"What's wrong with you?" Paula asked.

"I'm just tired."

Saba was watching her, his mustaches floating back over his shoulders. He said, "Do you have any ideas?"

"That depends on what Bokojin wants," she said.

Tanuojin reached out and turned the projector off. *Ybix* disappeared. Saba said, "Start talking."

VRIBULO

Huge in the pressure suit, David's arm stretched up above the seat in front of her to a switch in *Ybicket*'s ceiling. She tipped her head back inside the helmet. Behind her Junna was talking in a string of numbers, reading off the navigation signals. *Ybicket* flew down the D corridor toward Vribulo; Paula would meet Bokojin in Vribulo.

The radio crackled. "SIF-16 *Ybicket*, this is Vribulo mid-city gate. We will dock you."

She turned her head. On the curved wall beside her an ax hung in brackets. Behind her, Junna said, "Vribulo, we have orders from our commander not to surrender control of the ship."

"Stand by, *Ybicket*."

"Overflying Vribulo," David muttered.

Junna's voice fell to a ringing whisper. "Are you sure you can fly this jog?"

"I could take *Ybicket* through the Sun."

Paula swallowed. A burst of static rattled out of the radio. "*Ybicket,* this is Vribulo. You may dock your own ship."

The voices of the two young men sounded softly in the helmet above her ears. They guided the ship through the maze of the entry chute. She kept her eyes straight ahead, careful not to look at the hologram. Junna gave directions in a level singsong. She realized she was hanging onto the harness of her seat. The ship banged into the side of the tunnel and she shut her eyes an instant. Junna said, "Steady, little boy."

"Sorry," David said.

Ybicket flew out across Vribulo. Paula sighed, relieved. She wrenched her helmet back and forth until the seal broke. The ship rolled over and descended in a long swoop toward the surface. She looked up. The roofs of houses flew past over her head. People walked upside down in the street above her. *Ybicket*'s secondary engines thundered; she slid forward into the harness. David settled the ship down into the dark gate of the dock. A roof clanged shut over the window. She felt the slap of the anchor hitting the hull under her feet.

David let out a whoosh of breath. He and Junna unbuckled their harnesses. Paula fought with the spring clips that held her into her seat. David came around to help her.

"I'm sorry I hit. In the tunnel."

"I love surprises." She climbed out of the deep broad seat toward the hatch. Junna threw an arm around him, buoyant.

"You did it. I'd never even try it. You're like the Prima, little boy, you can fly anything."

She stood on the dock ledge beside the ship, watching David's face shine at Junna's words. She should have praised him like that. Won that look from him. They came up to the ledge beside her.

When they had shed their pressure suits they went out the front of the dock into the city street. The cold and greasy air struck her; she raised her head, her heart racing. A man brushed by her without breaking stride. His hair hung down his back in the Vribulit club. A siren wailed nearby. Blackened with time, the ancient buildings tilted out over the street. A fat woman came down the alley across from Paula, arguing. Paula looked up at the lake of Lower Vribulo, six miles across the twilit air, bounded in blue grass like surf.

"Mother—"

She went down the street, flanked by the two young men.

"Bokojin could have sent a chair to meet us," Junna said.

"He could have." Bokojin had refused to let either Saba or Tanuojin into Uranus. When Saba suggested sending her to negotiate with him, Tanuojin had shown enough distaste for that to make Bokojin insist. She trotted along beside David, one hand on his arm, looking around. They went through a fish market, gleaming with scales, and a chicken market, white with feathers. The street narrowed to a steep lane cut into steps.

At the top was Bokojin's house. He kept her waiting long minutes at the door, and David fumed.

"I'm not leaving you here alone."

"The Prima gave you orders."

"They didn't know what this was like. You'll need help."

She remembered Tanuojin's closed eyes: he knew what was happening here. She glanced at Junna. Tanuojin's son went down the steps from Bokojin's door to the street. David lingered. His inch-long mustaches bristled. "Vida," Junna called, and the boy said a very colorful oath and followed him.

A few moments later Bokojin's slaves let her into his house. Bokojin, Machou, and two other rAkellaron were waiting for her in a room of blue and green lights, rippling in slow sweeps through the room. The walls were decorated with a network of knotted ropes. When she came in, the four men stared at her, moveless in their chairs, each with an aide behind him like a standard. She went inside the arc of chairs.

"Mendoz'," Bokojin said. He sat with his feet together before him, his knees apart. "The talk was that you were dead."

"I was visiting another life." She looked at Machou on her left and the two men on her right. Even sitting they were taller than she was. Machou looked drunk. To Bokojin, she said, "The Prima is tired. He wants to come home and rest. Why are you putting yourself in his way?"

"We all know Saba," Bokojin said. "He's always had exotic ideas. We want assurances he isn't coming back with any strange notions of walking all over us just because he's taken the Middle Planets."

There had to be more to it than that. She looked at the other men. "How well do you know Saba?" From the fold of her coat she took the Primit cuff and dropped it ringing on the floor.

They straightened in their chairs. Their eyes followed the cuff. Machou leaned forward, his hands sliding off the arms of his chair. Paula backed one step away from the cuff on the floor.

"The Prima says if any of you thinks he can hold that metal, let him take it."

They all stood. Machou took a step toward the cuff. Paula tasted their scents, personal as faces. Bokojin said sharply, "Stand back, Akellar." Machou's head rose, his teeth showing behind his gray mustaches, and his thick shoulders set. Bokojin thrust his chest out.

"Back off!"

Machou shot a fierce look at Paula. "Don't be a fool—you're doing what she wants." He bent to pick up the cuff.

"Leave it," Bokojin said. "Leave it where it lies, Akellar."

Machou's thick throat worked. The cuff lay at his feet. He looked from Bokojin to Paula and back to Bokojin, and when Bokojin advanced a step toward him Machou backed away. He turned and marched out of the room, his soldier behind him.

"Go," Bokojin said to the other men. "I'll tell you later what she says."

Paula tucked her hands into her sleeves. The other two men began to protest, both at once, and Bokojin drove them out. The door shut behind them. Bokojin sat down again. The cuff lay on the floor between him and Paula. His handsome face was taut; his nostrils flared. Paula went up beside his chair.

"Put it on, Bokojin." She leaned on the arm of the chair.

"What is he trying to do?" Bokojin said to himself. She watched his face. He had a thin scar down his cheek. His jaw was finely shaped, almost delicate. It was not a sensual face: sexlessly beautiful.

"Why don't you take it?" She nodded at the cuff on the floor. That was Saba's idea: *Make him put it on.* Like Nessus's shirt. Her fingers grazed Bokojin's knee. "Do you need help? I'll help you."

Bokojin left the chair like a man bolting a trap. His lip curled at her. "I don't take other men's wives."

"I'm not Saba's wife," she said.

"Then you're just a dirty woman, and not worth my time."

She felt the heat flush rise through her throat and cheeks. She told herself she hadn't really wanted him anyway. She sat down in the chair he had just left.

"What do you want, Bokojin?"

"You don't sit down in my presence."

"Tsk. I sit down in the presence of a Prima whose name reaches from here to the Sun."

"My grandfather was the Prima," he said. He stalked toward her. He wore a heavy collar of rectangles linked together: a family emblem, Gemini was sacred to his house. "Saba has been making a loud noise among people who are natural slaves. Let him come back here, where his equals are."

"He is back. You won't let him home."

"Get out of my chair."

She stretched her arms along the arms of the chair. "I like it here. I'll stay."

He was standing with the cuff at his feet. She watched his expression settle. The cuff defended her as if Saba still wore it. He said, "I don't dirty my hands on niggers. Get up or I'll call my slaves."

"Oh, you won't do that." She drew her hand over the smooth arm of the chair, admiring the inlaid decoration. "Not while I'm your only line to Saba."

"Then maybe I should open another—" He wheeled. A man in the chevron badge walked fast through the door.

"Akellar. The Prima is in Vribulo."

Bokojin spat out the same oath David had used earlier, and Paula laughed. He said, "Then arrest him."

The patrolman said, "I'm sorry, Akellar, we can't—there's such a mob around him, you can hear them cheering him all the way up to the House."

"Get Machou—"

"Machou says to do it yourself."

Bokojin's face shone with heat. He wheeled toward Paula. She sat in his chair, the cuff on the floor between them. "Illini," she said, "we are giving you half an hour to get out of Vribulo. That gives you no time to do anything to me."

He took a step toward her. She stayed in her place, watching him. He kicked the cuff across the room and strode out. Alone in the room, she let herself relax. The cuff lay against the wall. She went over to it and picked it up, shining in the blue and green light streaming through the room. She put it on her wrist. Even over her coat sleeve it was too big. She wondered how he could wear it all the time; it weighed so much it hurt her arm. She sat down again in Bokojin's chair, to wait for Tanuojin.

"You agreed to it in the Middle Planets," Paula said, angry.

"That was a long way away. And a long time ago." Leno lifted his hands off the desk. "I've changed my mind." His broad hands dropped solidly to the desk.

Paula glared at him. She went off around his large, empty office, turned on the far side of the room, and glared at him again.

"Don't you give me that look," he said.

She marched back up to his desk, chest high to her. "Or you'll do what?"

There was a long silence while they stared at each other. Paula laid her forearms down flat on the desk. Like everything else in Styth it was too large for her.

"Be realistic," Leno said. Carefully he straightened his braided mustaches. "You aren't one of us. You can't do an Akellar's work. There are plenty of other niggers who will be happy to go between us and the rock-worlds."

"So you don't need me any more."

"You've done your work," he said. "And I honor you for it."

"Merkhiz—"

"You have a lot of enemies."

She left.

The message from Newrose filled eight pages. She read it in the coderoom on the second floor of the rAkellaron House and read it again in her bedroom of the Prima Suite on the third floor. Rereading it made it no sweeter. Newrose was full of gloom. After months of almost Talmudic debate, even his own party had rejected the Luna Agreements, and the Council had voted to stay in session past the date when they were supposed to shut off the lights and go home. Paula balled the thick papers up and flung the wad across the room.

Boltiko had come from Matuko for three watches exactly, to get Saba settled into the Prima Suite. Paula had made her paper this bedroom white. There were six ruby-laser paintings on the walls, streams of color constantly changing. She sat cross-legged on the end of the bed and watched a red line curl and curl across the wall. Just when she had felt safe, her life was breaking apart again. The flying colors on the walls made her nervous. Putting on her coat, she went out into the city, to the new White Market in the Steep Street.

She had arranged this market, the first in Vribulo, worked by free people, not Styths. Morosely she walked around the rings of stalls. This was the only practical thing she had ever done. Gradually it was doing more business. People wandered from booth to booth, and a crowd kept her away from the jewelry, the metalware.

Under a sign advertising fabric a vendor in a long apron was stacking bolts of cloth on a table. Nobody seemed to be interested. Paula stopped and put her hand out toward a shining red silk.

"Not that." Saba pushed her hand away. "That would look terrible on you. I don't think you have any sense of what you really look like." He waved to the vendor, who stooped and brought up more cloth. Paula smiled up at the big Styth, pleased to have company.

"Where is Tanuojin?"

"I just saw him get on a bus to Yekka."

"To Yekka." She straightened, turning away from the cloth. "But aren't you taking the Luna Agreement into the Chamber next watch?"

"I don't need Tanuojin for that. Look at this."

She looked down at the table again. The textured surface of a panel of black fabric drew her fingers. Woven into the material was an abstract design of gammadions, the good luck sign.

"Give her this," Saba said. "And that." He stretched across to reach a bolt of black cloth glinting with silver threads. He faced her again.

"This stuff is Martian fiber, dyed in Venus, shipped in Styth hulls. The Luna Agreements only say the obvious. How can they reject the obvious? There's one system, that's the way the system works."

She paid the vendor and told him to send the cloth to the man who made all her clothes. Everything was twice as expensive as before the war. She clinked the coins in her fist.

"I need a demonstration for the Council. What if three or four ships turned up near Crosby's Planet?"

"When?"

She shrugged one shoulder. "Are you on some kind of schedule?"

"Some kind. I'm getting married."

"Married. Again?" She had to laugh at him. They started on along the ring of stalls. She looked up at his profile. "Somebody told me once how handsome you were. I suppose you still are. Who is the blessed fifth wife?"

"Ymma's daughter."

"Oooh."

"She's prettier than he is."

"I should hope so. When is this to happen?"

"In twenty-two watches."

"In Lopka? Can I go?"

He was walking slowly so that she could keep up; he gave her a long look sideways. "Ymma asked me not to bring you. Or Tanuojin."

"Tanuojin wouldn't go anyway." That rankled. She thought of Leno. "Ymma took my advice in Luna, didn't he?"

"That was different."

"I guess so. I just talked to Merkhiz, and he says he won't support the Luna Agreement unless I resign."

"Oh? Somebody must have gotten beside him."

What Leno said in the Chamber would sway people. She wondered darkly if Saba had already sold her away. Saba stopped to look at a table of plants, each in its ball of dirt wrapped in plastic. She decided to write Newrose as nasty an answer as she could. Saba turned away from the little garden.

"I'll hold the Agreements back out of the Chamber for a while. Come to my wedding."

"I'm not going where—"

"I need you. Somebody has to stand forward for me. It's supposed to be my best friend, but Tanuojin won't do it. He hates Lopka. You do it."

Her gaze flew up toward him. "Stand forward for you? You mean be in the ceremony with you?"

"They'll all be there," he said. "Leno, Bokojin, everybody."

"Hunh." She nodded. "Oh, yes, I will."

Ymma's hacked face hid whatever he thought. He spoke the rote words of the ceremony in a voice without feeling. He and Paula stood facing each other before a bilyobio tree. The wedding guests made a ring around them; beyond Ymma she could see Bokojin, looking angry, and Machou, looking drunk.

They were all men, these guests. The women would be watching from the windows of the buildings beyond, except for one, who sat inside the left-hand of the covered chairs by the bilyobio tree. Paula was terrified of forgetting her answers to Ymma's questions. The ring of witnesses never looked at Ymma; they all stared at her. David was here, too, behind her. Her mouth felt frozen, her lips numb.

"Who are you, coming here as my guest?" Ymma recited. "Tell me your name and your purpose."

She lifted her voice, so that none of them could say later that he had not heard her. "I am Paula Mendoza. I am the Earth Akellar. I come for the sake of peace, for the Prima's sake, to take his wife to him."

Nobody moved. She wondered if they had expected it. Ymma's voice sounded choked. They exchanged another prescription, and he led her to the gorgeous covered chair, worked in filigreed metal.

His daughter looked no older than David. Pretty as a doll, she sat dressed in a robe woven with gold and gem crystal, her eyes shining with fear. Ymma said, "Daughter, go with this man—" and bit his teeth together. After a moment, he said, "With this Akellar, to live under your husband's rule."

The child's name was Melly. She put her hands out, and Paula took them. At the touch the two women looked surprised at each other. Melly's hands were icy cold.

There were three oaths, one for each of the steps to the other of the chairs. Once Melly flubbed her answer and Paula prompted her in a whisper. Except for them the place was silent. Saba was waiting in the right-hand chair. He spoke some words and the child replied, her eyes downcast, mumbling. When Saba put his hands around theirs, Melly almost would not let Paula take hers away.

The bride sat down in the chair beside her husband. Paula backed away, lighter by a burden. She had done it perfectly. For the first time, she realized that she had been frightened of botching a Styth ritual. She shut her eyes, smiling.

. . .

Finally the door shut on Saba and his bride. The wedding guests let out their breath in a gust of noisy conversation. Paula went after some of them down a strange hall in Ymma's house.

Most of the people in the sitting room were still standing up. Slaves brought them liquor. Dakkar and Ketac were talking by the far wall. Paula avoided them. Dakkar reminded her of Pedasen.

"I think we've just been taken," Bokojin said. He tramped into the room. "The *Earth* Akellar."

"Cool off," Leno said.

"I don't care if she hears me." Bokojin was plowing through the mass of standing men toward the banquet table. The crowd yielded to him, third-ranked in the rAkellaron. His voice boomed. "Is Ymma sure this wedding is legal?"

Paula stood just behind Leno. They had all seen her. She went over to the table for something to eat. Bokojin turned away, his back to her. Dishes covered the table: skewered meats, fruit soaked in liquor.

David had come in. She put a sliver of pala fruit into her mouth, watching him cross the room. His shoulder-length hair was too long to keep neat, and to his horror it curled at the ends. He spoke to Ketac, and Ketac bent to listen, turned, and tapped Dakkar on the arm. They followed David out of the room.

Paula ate the sweet fruit. She went through the crowd and down the hall after her son.

They led her into a darkened stretch of hallway, and she lost them. While she was going back toward the wedding party, she heard a sharp stranger's voice through a window.

"Just like a nigger, running for help!"

The window was over her head. It seemed to look over the courtyard. She stood under it, looking up at the patch of barred light on the ceiling. Outside, David said, "They're to watch. I'm tired of getting jumped just when I'm beating the shit out of one of you." Paula walked away down the dark hall.

She went back into the room where the wedding guests were drinking and talking in a din. As she came in, a voice was shouting, "Suppose what would have happened if Yekka had been here," so she knew what the main subject of talk was. At the end of the table there was a pump. She pumped a thin stream of Lopkit beer into a cup. Leno came over to her.

"Somebody brought this for you." He gave her a folded paper.

She put the cup down to open the message. It was from Newrose, sounding desperate. With three Styth ships cruising mysteriously in their immediate space, the Council of the Middle Planets had decided to disband after all, but they still refused to ratify the Luna Agreement. That made no difference, as long as they disbanded. Leno was watching her from his advantage of height. He had read the message. She folded the paper in thirds and put it away in her sleeve.

"Of course they accepted it," Saba said. "I told you I wouldn't have any trouble." They were in his office in the House, and he leaned back in his chair and spread his arms out. "Just the same, I want you to stay out of the Chamber. Unless there's an emergency."

"You don't have to convince me. I have too much to do anyway, to waste my time sitting around with those politicians."

"Good."

She put her elbow on the broad arm of her chair. They had been back from Lopka six watches, but she had seen little of him. He spent most of his time with Melly. "How is your marriage?"

"Ah, Paula—" He smacked his stomach with one hand. "I'm getting old."

"That bad?"

"It's that good. I—" He looked up, beyond her, and his whole face smiled. "Where have you been? I haven't seen you the long watch."

Paula turned. Tanuojin was coming in the door. He had a three-cornered coat over his shoulder. She sat back into the corner of the couch. His height even now sometimes surprised her. He and Saba hugged each other in greeting.

"You're getting fat, being married."

"It's good for me. I've just been telling Paula, you should try it."

Tanuojin snorted with laughter. He glanced at Paula and turned back to his lyo. "You know the probe we sent to Lalande in Melleno's Primat—"

"No."

"Melleno 372. The planetary spectra are coming in now. Come up to Oberon with me and look at them."

Saba went back behind his desk to his chair. "When?"

"Now."

"I can't—I told Melly I'd take her to the Akopra next watch."

"I'll go," Paula said.

Tanuojin flung his arm out. "To the Akopra. Here? Jesus, you'll ruin her taste, if she has any. Bring her down to Yekka. These are the first accurate composition bands we've ever gotten from another solar system. Why wait?"

"Go on. Take *Ybicket*. Vida can fly you."

"I'll go," Paula said again.

Tanuojin gave her a sour look. "With you inboard, it would take a watch and a half just to get there." He turned to Saba, across the desk. "Take her some other time."

"I promised her." Saba shrugged. "Come see me when you get back. Let Paula go with you. She's having another one of her fits."

She left the couch and started toward the door. Tanuojin stayed to argue with Saba. The waiting room, as large as the office, was crowded with men waiting to see him. She lingered a moment, in among the Styths, and Tanuojin came out, looking sullen.

"Are we taking David?" she asked.

"I can't fly *Ybicket* by myself," he said.

Lalande was a Class M star eight light years from the Sun, with a family of twenty-six planets. Under Melleno, the rAkellaron in a rare constructive moment had sent out six probes to nearby stars. Two had failed. Three were still in course, but waves from the Lalande probe had begun to reach the radio-pans on Oberon. Paula strapped herself into the middle of *Ybicket*'s three seats. Tanuojin hooked her suit into the lifeline.

"Don't forget," he said to the front of the cab. "She can't take too much acceleration, even in this fancy suit that eats up all the energy in the ship."

"Yes, I know that," David said.

"Don't mouth off at me, little boy, you won't like it."

"How long will it take?" Paula asked. She looked up at the window, covered with the dark shutter, reflecting a red light winking on a dial on Tanuojin's radio deck. He put the dark helmet over her head.

"Six hours." Round inside the helmet, his voice came from over her head. He and David climbed into their places.

The ship butted down five miles of the chute into the Planet. In the holograph, Vribulo was a fibrous wall to the right of the ship, streaming long threads of tunnel. They left the city and traveled off through the magma. A thick yellow wave rushed on them. *Ybicket* slid in a long swoop down its crest.

"Why did he get married?" Tanuojin said. "He's making a fool out of himself with that baby."

"Let him alone. He's having a good time." The ship rolled from side to side, barreling through a stretch of clear green. Ahead of them lay the Vribulo Stormbank, five thousand miles of turbulence. She remembered thinking once that two hundred kilometers an hour was a breakneck speed. David drove as fast as Saba.

The ship hurtled through the edge of the storm. She clutched her harness with both hands. Her stomach churned. If she were sick inside the helmet they would be all the way to Oberon cleaning up the mess. Tanuojin, navigating, talked steadily in her ears, guiding David through the layers of the storm. His voice was quicker than usual. She changed her mind about his lethargy. He was wound up tight as a set trap: waiting.

The ship bucked and swerved, and she gulped. She had been sick once and they had teased her mercilessly for three watches. Grimly she fought against her nausea all the way to the surface of the Planet, until they escaped into space.

Oberon was the moon farthest from Uranus. One face was always turned to the Planet, but now, with Uranus in its variant season, the Sun seemed to rise and set, instead of bathing one hemisphere in constant light. They reached the observatory in early morning. David set *Ybicket* down on a pad in the landing field and they got out and walked through the light gravity toward the group of buildings. Paula looked around them. Beyond the buildings of the observatory complex, with their clear domed roofs, stood the ruins of ancient houses built by the first settlers of Uranus. They had been stripped down for material to make the laboratory and the spherical houses for the telescopes. Only the foundations remained.

They went into the observatory. Through the clear domed ceiling she could see the black of space, scattered with stars. She unbuckled the wrist straps of her gloves and took them off.

Three or four men in long coats converged on them. Tanuojin greeted one by name and was introduced to the others, who bowed to him. She went slowly across the huge room before her. The floor was inlaid with a schema of the solar system. She walked down a gap through the Asteroids.

The technicians took Tanuojin off to a long bench against the circular wall. A light switched on above it. He swore at what he saw. Paula went over to his side. The technicians backed away, letting her through. The bench had a light in it, and a screen for viewing: a strip of colors was running across it. The colors ran the brilliant clear range of the spectrum. The technicians pointed to different areas and talked about calcium and hydrogen and compounds of oxygen.

She leaned on the bench, her eyes on the stream of colors, the clear deep violet and snapping yellow, pictures of worlds light years away. She glanced around the spacious, circular room. A man in a long coat came in a far door and sat down at a desk on the opposite wall. Her face was stiff with cold but the pressure suit kept her body warm. She looked up through the ceiling into the stars.

"Very good," Tanuojin said. "Good, good, good."

The technicians, all but one, wore white coats; the one wore a green coat, and he turned to the others and dismissed them in an important voice. Bending over the spectra, he pointed to a mass of yellow. "Akellar, let me point out the sodium lines here." His claws were clipped short. Probably they got in his way. On the wall above the bench compasses hung, in several sizes, clear plastic shapes to measure with, clippers with toothed edges. She still had her gloves in her hand and she stuffed them under the strap on her shoulder.

"Those are rho lines," Tanuojin said.

The film stopped moving with a sharp double click. "Some malfunction in the pulse source," the technician said. "We noticed them right away, of course—I thought they'd been removed." He stooped and pulled down the underside of the bench, which swung outward on curved hinged arms. The film ran along it on sprockets. "The probe fixed itself—the interference is just in this series." He shouted over his shoulder and another man came quickly toward them. Paula moved out of the way. Brimming with apologies, they brought in another piece of film and replaced the first.

"The computer reconstructed the series awfully well." The technician pushed the film train back into the bench.

"What's a rho line?" Paula asked.

Tanuojin's head turned. He spread the discarded piece of film out on the bench to one side of the screen. Without the lights behind it the film looked dull. He pointed to a band of yellow. "These spectra show which elements make up the Planet—each of the elements absorbed a characteristic wavelength of the light. These—" his claw tapped a broader gray space, "that's a rho line. Radio interference in the transmission." He went back to the corrected film. "Have any of the photographs come in?" he asked the technician.

"Not yet."

"What are these?" Paula asked. A row of dots ran along the edge of the film under the spectrum.

He was bent over the bright rolling film; he did not take his eyes from it. "Pulses. Rate of emission." He and the technician talked about ferric salts. She looked down at the strip of defective film beside her hand. Those stripes of color bounded her experience. Lalande's light fell mostly in the infra red; people there would see a world invisible to her. Perhaps inaccessible to her. The Styth astronomer was writing down a formula on a pad of paper, explaining something to Tanuojin. Tanuojin nodded. His interest in this impressed her. He was curious about everything. Her gaze fell again to the ribbons of color on the bench by her hand. The rho lines made thick breaks in the loom of colors. She counted the pulses between them.

"It's a message," she said.

The two men swiveled their heads toward her. "What?"

"The spaces between these rho lines," she said. "Four–nine–forty-one–thirty-six. The number of pulses between them." She struggled to keep her voice even; she was filled with excitement. "They're perfect squares, see?"

"Forty-one?" the technician said. He glanced at Tanuojin. "Is she crazy?"

He shook his head. "Sixteen plus twenty-five." Pushing her away, he stooped over the film and counted dots.

The technician said, surly, "It's a dysfunction in the transmitting laser." He scowled down at Paula, a round-faced, smooth-skinned man, who never fought. "What does she know about spectroscopy?"

"Nothing," Tanuojin said. "That way she doesn't get confused by facts." He rolled up the film and shoved it in under the edge of the bench. "You ought to write illusion serials," he said to her. "You have a full-round imagination." He went back to the rolling color band.

Paula retrieved the film and spread it out again. He did not want to believe it, but she did. She counted the pulses between the nine rho lines in the spectra: 4–9–41–36 = 13–16–25–36. Then there were two rho lines missing, mistakes in the mistake. She looked up through the ceiling at the stars, wondering which was Lalande.

"Akellar, I hate to keep mentioning this, but nobody else in the Chamber takes our work seriously—"

"You need money," Tanuojin said. They crossed the complex of buildings toward the landing field. David went ahead of them and opened the hatch into *Ybicket*, standing on her tail.

"We've had to give up some very important work because we just haven't got the equipment."

"I'll talk to the Prima."

Paula stood beside the slender ship, put her hands on the lower edge of the hatch, and hoisted herself up to the opening. In the light gravity it was easy. David helped her across the narrow aisle, now vertical, between the hatch and the middle seat. Inside her helmet she could still hear the technician's pitch. Tanuojin filled the hatchway, blocking out the faint sunlight.

"I'll fly back," he said to David. "You take the kick-seat."

David wheeled around in the drive seat ahead of her. "But—"

"Do as you're told."

"But—Uncle—I can't navigate in the Planet."

"Then this is a good time for you to learn." Tanuojin climbed into the seat with him, and David tumbled out, giving way.

"Paula—"

"Leave me out of it," she said. She leaned forward and groped for the lifeline to attach it to her suit. David climbed down past her to the kick-seat.

. . .

When they got back to the House, Saba was sitting in her favorite chair in the front room of the Prima Suite, writing on a workboard. Paula took her coat off. "How was the Akopra?"

"Terrible."

David came in, still warm under the friction of Tanuojin's pedagogical sarcasms, and Tanuojin after him. Saba put the workboard down. "What did you find out?"

"The films are perfect." Tanuojin unslung his coat. "All twenty-six of them came through, the probe worked perfectly."

"I'll see them when the laboratory sends them down. Have they gotten any photographs yet?"

Tanuojin shook his head. He picked up the workboard from the floor and wound back the surface to read what Saba had written. "I told them not to send the stuff down here piecemeal, to wait until everything is together. They need more money."

"They always need more money."

Paula stood watching them together. She saw what she should have noticed long before. Saba was gray-headed, but Tanuojin's hair was still jet black. He looked no older than he had when she first met him, at the Nineveh, sixteen years before. He was not aging.

"Tell him about your little pink men," Tanuojin said to her. He threw down the workboard. "Wait until you hear this," he told Saba. "You'll like this one."

Melly turned and turned at the far end of the room, dancing. She held out her skirts in her hands, her head to one side. Paula stood in the doorway watching the girl play. Abruptly the Styth girl saw her and stopped.

"Go on," Paula said. "Dance. I like it."

Melly watched her enter the room. Paula's favorite chair had a little step built into the base for her use. She settled herself in the chair, her back to the window. Melly said, "I am not a toy for your amusement, Mendoz'."

"Then don't act like a pompous little lady," Paula said.

The girl's face tightened up, much older when she scowled. Paula laughed. Melly was allowed to go unveiled in the suite, but not outside; Paula wondered if she had ever been outside. She wondered if Melly were pregnant yet.

"My father says I ought to be friendly with you," Melly said. "But I don't see why. You aren't friendly to me."

"I could be."

"You stole my wedding to make into your—coronation."

"I'm sorry. We were a little pressed." She was reminding herself of Jefferson. Uneasily she moved around in the oversize chair.

Melly began to speak. Something she saw in the hall stopped her, and she went to the threshold and made her extravagant bow.

"Prima."

Paula looked out into the hall. Saba was coming into the room. To Paula, he said, "I have a headache—I'm going to lie down on your bed. Make sure nobody bothers me." Melly stood watching him expectantly. He touched her face. "Not now, baby." He went down the hall toward Paula's room.

She climbed down from her chair and ran after him. Going ahead of him into the room, she turned the heat lower and pulled the window shade closed. "What about Tanuojin?"

"He's sick too. Go on, leave me alone."

She went out to the corridor and shut the door. Melly was watching her from the doorway of Saba's room. As Paula came into the hall the bride vanished into the room. Paula went back to the sitting room.

She wrote a letter to Newrose, asking for information and giving him suggestions. They wrote back and forth every three or four watches. The situation in the Middle Planets always seemed desperate. She was beginning to think that was a standing condition of life there.

Just before one bell, she went down to her room. Saba lay on her bed with his head turned away. She walked to the side of the bed. His face was smooth, without any sign of pain. She put her hand on his forehead. He was dead. He had been dead for hours.

She sat down beside him. The room was utterly still. She touched his mouth and the inside of his wrist. With her hand on him she sat still, in the quiet. Finally she went to the door to call David.

The room was so crowded Paula could not see the bed. She backed away toward the wall. Everybody was talking at once. Melly was crying, and Ketac took her away. David stood by the bed like a guard. Paula's face felt tight and stretched. She was still surprised by the death. Tanuojin came into the room.

His hair was down over his shoulders and his back. Sleep rumpled his face. His eyes were intent on Saba. David saw him and grabbed his shirt in both hands.

"Bring him back. Bring him back."

Paula went toward them, elbowing a way through the gaping slaves and onwatchers. His gaze never leaving Saba, Tanuojin thrust David hard away from him, but the young man clung to him, his hands fisted in Tanuojin's shirt.

"Bring him back, you did it before—if you're a god you can bring him back—"

Paula took him by the arm, turning him to face her. "David, stop."

"Bring him back." He twisted to shout at Tanuojin, his mouth open, and she slapped him with all her strength. He ran out of voice. He stared at her, round-eyed, his mouth open and empty. Ketac appeared beside her and took him out of the room. Tanuojin sat down on the edge of the bed. There was nothing he could do; she had known that as soon as she touched Saba. She drove the other people out, to leave him alone with the dead man.

Under the sweet odor of incense she could smell the rotting body. She had been sitting here a watch and would sit here two watches more, Melly beside her shedding tears like a sweat behind her veil, and Boltiko beside Melly, her mouth thin as a seam.

The incense had a woody smell, like cedar. The smoky air and the constant drumming of the rUlugongon had her half-drugged. Her aching eyes dressed each of Saba's sons, standing around the dead man, in a shimmering cloak of light. They were in the entry to the rAkellaron House. Beyond Ketac and Dakkar the Gold Wall rose, spangled with the names of the rePriman. The people of Vribulo were filing through the right side of the double doorway, around the body on its bier, and out the left. From talk she overheard she knew many of them had come from Matuko, and some from other cities, as far away as Ponka on the far side of the Planet.

David stood near the foot of the bier, between two of his tall brothers. He looked like an old man. His cheeks glistened. He was crying again. She looked away from him, made uncomfortable by his grief, made lonely. She had never loved Saba that much. Now that he was dead her circumstances were utterly changed. Her only assets were her influence in the Middle Planets and her relationship with Tanuojin.

Tanuojin himself had been stripped by the death. The highest ranking officer in the fleet, he had no ship, since *Ybix* would go to Ketac. Officially he was ranked only eleventh or twelfth in the Chamber; Leno would be Prima now, who hated him. None of that would get in his way. He had enemies, but she was his only rival.

Sometime in the next watch David went out and did not come back. She was too numb to care where he went. Probably he would be better off away from the sight of his father. Melly collapsed with much exhibition, and was carried out. Paula's eyes throbbed. She was determined to sit there until the end. The steady stream of people passed by. They moaned, or reached out to touch Saba, or put something down by the body. The bier was covered with bits of paper and grass braided into rings, mourning symbols.

She closed her eyes a moment. When she looked Tanuojin had come in. He stood by the foot of the bier. Above the collarless neck of his shirt, a metal chain crossed his shoulder. It was Saba's order medal; she wondered if anyone but her knew he wore it.

One bell rang. The crowd went away. The slaves shut the doors. Boltiko rose, groaning with effort, and stood over the bier. "My boy," she said, in a low voice. She laid her palm against Saba's cheek. "My poor boy." Paula was beside her. The two women turned to each other, reaching out, and took each other in an embrace.

They went up to the Prima Suite. David was not there. Paula poured three fingers of Ponkan gin into a cup and drank it all. The others of the family were wandering around, even Saba's daughters, with their children, their faces unveiled. Ketac sat in her chair, by the window.

"That's my chair," she said, and he moved.

The cold air coming through the window made her feel better, her head clear. Ketac slouched against the wall beside her, one foot propped on her chair.

"Who will be the Akellar now?" she said.

"Dakkar is the heir."

"I think you'd make a better Akellar than Dakkar."

Ketac straightened. He put his foot on the floor. "So do I." He looked around the room. Two of his sisters came in, chattering about children.

"Can you take him?" Paula asked.

"I can try."

"Where? Not in Matuko, that's his ground. You'd better do it here."

"I'm in sack shape," he said. Two more people came into the room, and he lowered his voice. "I'll go to *Ybix*. I can turn the pressure up to double and work up my strength."

"I'll call you when he comes here to claim his seat in the Chamber."

"Good."

She held her jaws together against a yawn. Junna stood just outside the door in the hall. She wondered again where David was. The bland innocence on Ketac's face almost made her laugh. Saba had preferred him to Dakkar anyway, and obviously he had been thinking about it. He did not come virgin to this bridal. She closed her eyes.

. . .

David had disappeared into the city. She knew better than to look for him. Leno was taking over the Prima's offices on the second floor, and his eight wives sent a slave to ask when Paula and Melly would move out of the Prima Suite. Melly was going back to Lopka, her father's city. Paula was busy watching Dakkar and had no place to go anyway.

Tanuojin had gone back to Yekka, but every other Akellar was in Vribulo. Leno proclaimed the first session of his Primat for the eighteenth high watch after Saba was made ash. The wives' slave brought Paula a pointed invitation to move out of the suite. That same watch, Dakkar arrived in Vribulo to claim his father's place in the rAkellaron.

She went down to the second floor, to talk to Leno.

She could not see the door to the Prima's office through the thick press of men around it. She wound a way through them to the open door. The waiting room was jammed. The benches were full of men, and other people stood leaning against the walls between the maps and recognition charts. At the table in the middle, Leno's pitman argued in a loud voice with a man in a patrol uniform. She went around him to the half-glassed door in the back and knocked.

"Who is it?" Leno called. He sounded angry. She tried the latch, which was unlocked, and went into the long room.

Tanuojin was sitting on the bench before the middle window. Leno glared at her from the middle of the room. "You could wait until you're asked." He pulled his belt up over his stomach. Both of them were giving off a marginal reek of bad temper. Shutting the door, she crossed the room, going in between them.

"Leno," she said, "let me stay here. You can open up the rest of the Prima Suite—there's plenty of room."

His lips parted with surprise. Tanuojin laughed. The Prima flung his arms out. "Here. No." He wheeled away, his broad back to her. A dark patch of sweat showed between his shoulder blades. "Get out. I'm busy."

"I have to have someplace to stay." She glanced at Tanuojin. "When did you get back? I thought you were in Yekka."

"Last watch."

Leno loomed over her, his hands on his hips, his blunt head forward. "I told you to leave."

"I have nowhere to go." She raised her eyes to his face, shining with temper. He and Tanuojin had been arguing before she came in. She put that away in her mind to think about later. Her eyes on the Prima's angry face, she said, "I suppose you'll want Saba's presidency?" She turned back to Tanuojin. "I'm sending Newrose a notice of Saba's death—what about Dr. Savenia?"

Leno said, "I'm the Prima now. Why is it neither of you will admit that? You're both insane." He strode off across the room. The three windows across the wall let in the city racket. "I can't keep you here, Mendoz'. And the presidency of the Middle Planets goes with the office of Prima."

"I'll have to look that up," she said. She scratched her nose, staring at his back. It did not work to be subtle with him. "I could go back to the Earth, I suppose. Although without me you'd certainly lose four-fifths of the Empire."

Leno turned. Rather than look at her he faced Tanuojin. The tall man shrugged. "Well, she is the only one of us who knows anything about the Middle Planets."

Leno's shoulders dropped an inch. Paula went to the door. With her hand on the latch, she looked over her shoulder at the new Prima. "You don't have to feed me, I'll eat by myself."

"I'm the Prima!"

"Yes, Prima. Thank you." She went out.

The Fleet Office was in Upper Vribulo. The broad street, patched with blue grass, was lined with drinking docks and sack-houses. She passed a swinging half-door that let out a boom of noise and a rush of odors: beer, Styth, and vomit. A man slept in the high grass in the next alley. The narrow front of the Fleet Office was indistinguishable from the docks and flops around it and she walked past it twice.

The dark, deep room inside smelled of copying ink. A handprinter was clacking behind the high barrier that cut off the back of the room from the front. A line of men in fleet uniforms slacked up against the wall beside a closed door.

"Hey, I love you, let's go next door."

An old man with jewels in his nose came up to the barrier. Paula's head just cleared the top rail. She said, "I want to send a message to a ship in orbit."

"Which ship?" He leaned on the barrier, looking down at her.

"*Ybix*."

"*Ybix* hasn't been answering our signals since the Prima died." He spat past her; she smelled the rich odor of laksi. "Deep sleep to him."

"He doesn't have to answer," Paula said. "Just say that his mother wants him to come home."

The old man's mouth curled thoughtfully. "His mother."

"Just send that message."

"Yes, Mendoz'."

She walked back past the Akopra. A loudspeaker on the porch announced the theater was closed to mourn the Prima. The new

Off-World Market was empty. Green paper banners, the Styth mourning color, hung from the gates of the houses. She climbed the steps to the rAkellaron House and went inside.

She went in through the slaves' entrance to the top rung of the Chamber. Her coat made her uncomfortably warm and she opened it down the front. Half the rAkellaron stood and talked and scratched and spat and bragged on the ledges above the pit. A slave scampered past her with a tray of cups. She went down the enormous steps, her skirts and the heavy skirts of her coat bunched in her hands.

Tanuojin was in his place on the second tier, his arms out straight across the rail and his head down. No one spoke to him. His own aides stayed away from him. She stood beside him. Machou was up on the high ledge, talking to Bokojin. She sat down on the hard bench. Tanuojin did not move.

Leno came down the steps. Behind him was Dakkar, with three of his men in his track. Leno went to his place on the second tier, and Dakkar continued down the steps to the pit. He looked like Saba, a black-haired, slender Saba.

"This session is open," Leno said. "Dakkar, you are in the pit."

Dakkar walked across the sand. "I am Dakkar, Saba's oldest son. I'm dominant in Matuko, and I mean to take my father's place here. Does anybody challenge my right?"

The men on the ledges canted forward to watch him. Leno stood. His mustaches hung down heavy with braid to his chest. Paula looked around the Chamber, surprised. None of the other men were standing up.

"If nobody—"

"I challenge," Ketac said, above her. He came down the steps past her.

She got up onto her feet, her fingers tight around the rail. Several of *Ybix*'s crew followed him. David was not among them. Dakkar crouched. When Ketac stepped into the pit, his brother attacked him.

The rAkellaron roared. All around the rings they leaped up, bellowing. Their hot reek made her stomach heave. Ketac fell and rolled, Dakkar hanging on his back. Even through the screams of the men watching she heard the brothers' snarls. Her heart pounded in her throat. Tanuojin towered over her, banging his hands on the rail. The sand was splattered with blood. Dakkar jammed his knee into Ketac's spine, his hands splayed over his brother's face, bending him backward.

"Kill him!" someone howled. "Kill him!"

Ketac reached over his shoulders. His claws hooked in Dakkar's shirt. Tanuojin shouted so loud she flinched. Ketac dragged his brother down into the sand. He reared up and brought his elbow like a club into Dakkar's face.

Paula let go of the rail. Ketac leaped up, panting, his shirt crusted with sand. Dakkar doubled over, one arm across his broken face. The cheers of the rAkellaron faded, cooling. Ketac held his hands over his head.

"I am the Matuko Akellar. Does anybody challenge me?"

The whole Chamber was on its feet. They let out another buoyant cheer. She was sweating from their heat. Tanuojin sat down, and the other men began to settle. Paula shifted, her heavy coat on her shoulders. Tanuojin called, "How long did it run?"

"Fifty-two seconds," Machou called, hoarse. "He's no Saba."

Dakkar's friends were stooped over him. Ketac leaned on the pit rail. Dakkar put one foot under him and pulled himself up on his friends' shoulders. They were both bleeding, she could not see the wounds, just the red slime on their faces. Ketac spoke to Dakkar, and the taller man nodded. He hung one arm around Ketac's neck. The rAkellaron cheered again, pleased. Paula sat down. Ketac and Dakkar climbed the steps.

Leno stood again. Again, none of the other men stood up in respect for him. The Prima said, "If nobody else has any special business—"

Tanuojin said, "She has a question."

Leno put his hands on his belt. His head thrust forward. "Mendoz', what do you want now?"

Paula stood up. "I'm going to need money."

Across the pit, Bokojin shouted, "What is she doing in here, anyway? Saba is dead. She has no place here. She had no place when he was alive."

Paula looked down at the blood-splattered sand. Three or four men shouted back and forth at each other, and Leno made no effort to order them. She said to Tanuojin, "I thought ten dollars a watch."

"I don't see why we should pay you. Why don't you tax the Middle Planets for it? If you'll be doing their work."

"Because they don't need me," she said. "And you do."

Bokojin was leaning forward over the rail. "This makes me long for the old times when a man's widows burned with him."

A quarter of the round away, another voice rose, clear and mild. "It makes me long for the old times when the servants of the Empire were treated with respect."

"Hear," someone muttered, behind her.

"Are you challenging me, Saturn?" Bokojin roared. He and Melleno's son Mehma traded jibes.

"Every one of you gets some revenues from the Middle Planets," she said to Tanuojin. Down the ring, Leno was playing with his mustaches, his eyes on them. "You need me to keep the arrangements going. In fact, make it twelve dollars a watch."

Tanuojin stood up, and all the other men rose. Bokojin's voice cut off. Tanuojin said, "Give her enough to live on. Eight hundred a turn. Until someone else can take over her work with the slave-worlds."

Leno said, "Done." Tanuojin sat down, and the rest went back to their seats. They talked of other business. Paula slid down the bench to the steps and climbed out of the pit.

Ybix's crew was carousing along the arcade in front of the Barn. She went through them, ducking a swinging arm. Someone shouted her name.

"Mendoz'. Have a drink." Ketac's helmsman poked a jar into her face. While she was pretending to drink he whirled her around again, her skirts flying out. There was a burst of thunderous laughter all around her. She reached the ground, dizzy.

"Mendoz'! Kib, pass her over here."

Kib snatched for her. She dodged around behind him to the door into the Matuko office.

A washtub of beer stood on the desk, and two men had their faces in it. Dakkar slumped in the chair before the window. She thought of Pedasen. Dakkar's face was striped with blood. He looked half-drunk and very gloomy. Probably he had forgotten the slave he had killed. That warmed the revenge, the years she had waited to pay Dakkar back. She went through the file room, where three men were pouring beer and minji sauce over two girls from Colorado's.

Even through the door she could hear the men shouting in the little back room where the bed was. She let herself in among them. Half a dozen of his crew surrounded Ketac in a ring. Small as she was, she stood overlooked behind them. At the end of their rhythmic bellow of a cheer they poured a bucket of beer over the new Akellar's head.

"Paula." Dripping, he pulled her in among them by the arm and put a mug into her hand. "Drink to me. What did you think? It was a great fight, wasn't it."

"I don't know anything about fighting." She was standing in a puddle of beer. She moved toward the window. His hand on her arm, Ketac followed her out of the circle of men. Beer dripped from his mustaches and his shirt.

"Did you see that cross-block? Papa would have liked that."

"Yes, I saw." She looked out the window. In the street an old man with a shawl over his head was straining to see through the next window into the party. Ketac lifted his head and shouted to his men to leave.

"I don't want to interrupt your good time," she said.

He took a towel from a bin in the wall and scrubbed vigorously at his wet hair and face. "Just *my* good time? I couldn't have done it without your help. Why did you help me?"

"I like you," she said.

"You went to some trouble to put me in your debt."

"I need someone to stand up for me in the Chamber," she said.

"You need a husband," he said. He hung the towel over his shoulder.

"Not formally."

"Do I get what husbands get?"

She had to smile at him. She said, "Go lock the door."

When she got back to the Prima Suite, in the low watch, David was in her sitting room. She was glad to see him, but she was used to hiding her feelings from him. She took her coat off and hung it over the arm of her chair.

"Where have you been?"

"Thinking." He came up the room toward her. His hair hung in a wild shag around his shoulders. "Getting drunk. Getting loaded. I—" He made a little gesture with one hand. His long eyes made him look belligerent. He said, "I'm sorry, Mother. I'm sorry."

"Sorry. What for?" He smelled awful. He had not been out of his clothes since the funeral.

"I've spent my whole life fighting over things I can't change. Maybe I shouldn't even have wanted them changed." He made that same motion with his hand, palm up. Asking for something. "So I'm sorry."

She grunted, her eyes following his gesture. To keep from touching him she slid her hands behind her back. "Did you come on this enlightenment in a junk-gun? I wish you'd told me where you were—you could have helped me."

"Helped you. What—" He straightened up to respect, his arms at his sides, looking beyond her. Leno tramped into the room.

The new Prima strode up to her, his face knotted in a scowl. "You and Tanuojin set me up, didn't you?" He glanced at David. "Stand off, little boy, the war is over."

Paula said, "Did anything else happen in the session?"

"Nothing important to you. Yekka wants to see you."

She went to her chair, before the window, watching her son. He was scraping the edge of his boot against the floor. His mustaches were beginning to droop over. She wondered what had happened to him to make him like her. Leno said sharply, "He wants to see you now."

"I'm busy now," she said. She leaned on the carved arm of the chair. "Jesus, Leno, aren't you high-born for a messenger boy?"

He bristled up, his neck swelling. "To hell with you." He marched out, and the door slammed behind him hard.

David was frowning at her. "Mother, he's the Prima."

"He isn't my Prima. I'm my Prima. Come have dinner with me."

He was already moving toward the door. "No. I have something else to do. Can I use your room to clean up?"

"You can live here. Nobody is using your room." She smiled at him. "I'm glad you're back, David."

"So am I, Mother."

While she was walking up the street toward Colorado's, she heard her name called behind her. She stopped and looked back. Marus was jogging down the curved street after her. He veered around a pushcart and reached her, breathing hard.

"The Akellar wants you."

"Later. I'm hungry." She walked off up the street.

"He says it's about David Mendoza."

She went back to him. "What about David?"

"I don't know. The Akellar said I should tell you that."

She hurried back toward the end of the city. On either side of the street were buildings marked to be torn down; she heard children playing in them. They reached the Barn and she went into Tanuojin's office.

David was not there. Tanuojin was sitting at the desk in the front office recording a book tape, a set of earphones over his head. He gestured to Marus to leave. She leaned on the desk, impatient. He turned a switch on the recorder and another on the left earcup.

"What is this about David?" she said.

"Nothing. That was the best way to get you here. I have to talk to you."

Her shoulders sank an inch. For a moment, speechless, she could only stare at him. He took off the headset and put it on the desk. She went out of the office.

He came after her. "I have a tax I want you to arrange in the Middle Planets. Newrose will accept it if it comes from you."

"Get away from me." She was walking as fast as she could, even though there was no way to outrun him. She left the arcade and turned into the street past Colorado's, and he steered her toward the drinking dock. She gave up trying to go anywhere else and went into the vast dark room.

It was all but empty. The blue lights were lit along the pipe-wall and a slave on a ladder was swabbing out a barrel with a mop. Two more slaves raked off the sand. She went into the brightest corner and sat down.

"No," she said to Tanuojin. A slave hovered nearby, and she sent him for her meal.

"It's very simple," he said. "Listen to me before you refuse."

The slave brought her a split dish of beans and leaf, Colorado's staple lunch. She broke the piece of bread in half. "No. I don't like taxes, and I don't work in the Middle Planets for your benefit." She used a piece of bread to shovel up the beans.

He dropped on one knee beside her. "I need that money."

The slave who had served her was back. "Mendoz', Kuuba wants to know if this goes on Matuko's bill."

"Matuko." She swallowed a mouthful. "Why should Ketac pay my bills?"

"Uuh—" The slave touched his upper lip with his tongue. His gaze slid toward Tanuojin.

"You put it on my bill," she said. "You put everything I buy on my bill." The beans were syrupy with red sauce. She ate the soaked bread. Tanuojin leaned over her.

"Don't make me angry, Paula."

"Tsk."

"You don't really think Ketac can take me."

The salad was oily. She ate the crunchy leaf. "Are you going into the pit again? Show off your peculiar talents in front of everybody?" She looked into his face. "Saba is dead now, you're all alone."

His white eyes dilated, round as targets. She saw he was still afraid of the mob. When he stood up, his kneejoint cracked.

"You remember I said once I'd break you?"

"Yes," she said. "Not in those words." She put the dish down. Her fingers were greasy and she wiped them on the sand. Tanuojin started to speak and turned.

David was coming into the great empty drinking dock. He crossed the deep sand toward them. He had washed and changed his clothes, and his long thick hair hung untied down past his shoulders. He reached Tanuojin.

"Uncle, I apologize for what I said. I—"

"I don't care about your diseased half-breed raving," Tanuojin said. Fish-lean, he stood over David by sixteen inches. He said, "You're as bad as your slut-mother. You're white-hearted."

The slaves leaned on their rakes watching them. The kitchen

master put his head out the doorway. Tanuojin pointed at Paula. "Do you know what she's been doing? Saba wasn't cool ash before she was turning up her heels for Ketac at a drunken party."

"Ketac."

David's jaw set tight. He flung her a nasty look. "You Creep," he said to Tanuojin, "I'm surprised your tongue hasn't rotted away."

The tall man gave off a spurt of rage. Both hands hooked in David's hair. "Club it up!" David clawed at him, and Tanuojin swung him around by the hair and dragged him to the door. "It's not just for looks, you see, no matter what you anarchists think." He slung David out the door.

The slaves were motionless, rapt. The man on the ladder had dropped his mop. Tanuojin walked back toward Paula, picking clumps of David's hair off his hands. "You slut. You won't even fight for your own cub."

"He does well enough by himself, doesn't he?" She circled past him toward the door. "Not so much rotted, I think, as pickled." She laughed and went off to the door.

In the next watch, Ketac, Dakkar, and Junna ambushed David on the plain of the House and clubbed him. A crowd gathered to watch. Paula came out on the second-story balcony. David fought them. They wrestled him down on his knees and Ketac wrenched his hands in front of him to give him the oath.

Paula glanced behind her. Tanuojin had come out onto the balcony.

"Did you put them up to this?" she said.

"That's right."

David burst up, his hair flying, and Junna sprawled across the concrete. The crowd cheered, boisterous. Ketac and Dakkar trapped David between them. Ketac was laughing. They forced David down on the pavement.

Tanuojin said, "He's too stupid to know when he's beaten."

Ketac had David's hands stretched out before him. Junna pinned him down by the shoulders, and Dakkar leaned past him to knot David's hair into the club. Ketac shouted the oath.

"Who is the man?"

"Styth," the crowd roared. David made no sound.

"Which is the way?"

"The Sun!"

"Keep faith!" Ketac milled his brother across the cheek with his open hand. Paula twitched.

David bounced onto his feet. His brothers danced away from him, teasing him; Ketac clapped his hands under David's nose. Paula went indoors.

She was sitting on her bed in her room writing to Newrose, and Tanuojin came into the room. She closed her notebook. There was a high-backed chair against the wall by the chest, which he took and turned toward her and sat on. His long legs bent like a spider's.

"Paula," he said. "You are letting yourself in for this. I—"

"Wait. Let me. You are about to tell me how fond you are of me, and you don't want to hurt me or David, but for the good of the Empire . . ." She stood up on her bed and swung the shutter closed over the window, cutting off the noise of the city. "Not with me, Tanuojin."

"Get me that money."

She sat down cross-legged on the bed again. She had the feeling if she took her eyes off him he would change to another form: a poison mist.

"You're in debt already," he said, reasonable. "Leno wants you to leave. You'll have to come to me sometime. Why get me angry?"

"It's good exercise." Ketac had just bought a house in Upper Vribulo. She could live there. She leaned against the wall behind her and folded her arms over her chest.

"You'll regret it." His deep voice rasped; he was beginning to lose his temper. "And you can't live with Ketac. It's already the ripest scandal in Vribulo. You're twice his age."

She laughed. "Well, I'm remarkably preserved." There was a tap on the door, and she lifted her voice. "Yes?"

David came in behind Tanuojin. His knotted hair was already falling loose. He said, "Mother, I need money." His slanted brown eyes flicked at Tanuojin, sitting with his back to him. "Hello, Uncle Tajin."

"Do you want work?" Tanuojin said. But he was watching Paula.

"What?"

She said, "You can work for me."

"What would you pay him with?" Tanuojin said. His hands slid under his belt. He never looked at David. "Vida, I need a pilot. I'm buying *Ybicket.*"

"*Ybicket,*" David said. He came two steps into the middle of the room, circling Tanuojin's chair to face him, and she knew she had lost. "Where is she now? How much are you paying for her?"

"I still owe Ketac four million dollars of it, which I won't have until your mother starts to cooperate. The ship's in Matuko. Can you go get her?"

David stuck his open hand out. "I need bus money."

"Take Junna to navigate for you." Tanuojin gave him credit. Paula sat, watching them, silent. His hair was too fine to stay clubbed.

The side of his face was bruised. Tanuojin said, "Dock her in the number 4-A slip in the mid-city gate. Report to Marus when you're done."

"I'll bring you something from Matuko," David said to her. He left.

"That's the anarchist in him," Tanuojin said. "No loyalty."

"He's Saba's son too." Her voice sounded rough. She coughed to disguise it. Useless.

"I warned you," he said.

Tanuojin went to Yekka. Ketac took her to the Akopra. During the interval between the first two dances, Bokojin came into the box. Ketac greeted him with some pleasure. Paula sat with her back to them, sipping kakine. They agreed to meet sometime indefinitely later and the Illini Akellar went out.

The Vribulo company performed three more short dances, two old, and one experimental. New rAkopran were rare and she watched this one with attention. It bored Ketac, who played with her hand, talked to her, and tried to get her to caress him.

"Come to my house," he said, when they were leaving the theater.

"Not if Bokojin is going to be there."

They went across the lobby, through little knots of people dressed splendidly in long brocaded shirts, in dresses trimmed with metal lace. Ketac took a firm grip on her arm. "How do you know Bokojin is going to be there?"

"You agreed to meet him, don't you remember? Just two hours ago." She went ahead of him out the door. The long blue paper banners hanging on the eave of the porch advertised the next cycle. The street was thick with the people just out of the theater.

"He won't stay long," Ketac said.

"I hate him. Ask him what he thinks of me. I'll see you in the middle watch." She pulled her arm out of his grip, and he let her go. She went down the street toward the corner.

There, in the midst of the crowd, she turned and looked back. Ketac was going off in the opposite direction, toward his house. She trotted after him through the swarming traffic and followed him across the city, staying about forty feet behind him. He was easy to keep in sight, taller than the crowd, his black hair tied sleek among the shaggier Vribulit heads of the other men. Whenever his long stride took him to the limit of her vision, she broke into a run to catch up. He led her through the edge of the slums by the lake and down the Steep Street, cut into broad steps. At the foot of the hill he went through a gate in the wall of his new house. Paula circled around the corner into the next block, ran down the alley, and climbed onto the recycling bin and dropped over the fence into the yard.

The house was built in a hollow square, one room thick all around. In front of each of the windows was a trellis covered with vines, to keep the place private. She crawled between the wall and the vine screen over Ketac's bedroom window. The skirt of the black dress caught on a strut of the trellis and ripped.

Ketac's room seemed empty. She reached in across the deep sill and dragged herself into the room. The torn skirt of the dress tangled in her legs. She got up, pulling the dress off; she wore a pair of overalls under it against the cold.

The bed was on a bench built out from the wall on her left. A blue curtain hung from the ceiling hid it. She looked in to make sure it was empty and tossed the ruined dress onto the pillow. Crossing to the door, she slid it open an inch.

All the rooms opened onto a circular inner yard. Ketac liked to spend his time there, and he was there now, standing at the far end beside the bilyobio tree reading a piece of paper. She pressed her eye against the crack in the door. A slave came from one of the eight rooms ringing the yard and spoke to him, and Ketac nodded. Paula watched him cross the yard toward her. He ambled, looking around him with a proprietor's critical eye, moving a chair and stooping to fuss with a loose flag in the neat grass-seamed pavement. Bokojin came out of the house.

Paula sucked on the inside of her cheek. They met with the little greeting ceremony of their way of life, jibing, punching each other, and finally shaking hands and sitting down. Bokojin sat facing her, his feet primly together.

"Where is she?"

"I let her go back to the House."

"You what?"

"I couldn't very well drag her off in the middle of the street. She doesn't like you. She said she wouldn't—"

A slave brought them a tray with cups and a jug. Bokojin reached for one. Peevish, he said, "Damn it, I left her to you because you said you could—"

"Why are you so high?" Ketac said. He waved the slave away. "I'll handle my mother. You handle Tanuojin."

Paula straightened away from the door and rubbed her eye. She wondered if they were planning a gambit in the Chamber or something more direct. Bokojin said, stiff, "I wish you wouldn't call her your mother."

Ketac laughed. "She'll do anything I say. Don't worry about her." He slung one leg over the arm of his chair. "How is Machou?"

"Drunk. How is he ever? When we've done this, we should get rid of him. He's useless." Bokojin got up, a cup in his hand, and sauntered around the yard, expansive. "The main thing is to put the rAkellaron in order, the way things are supposed to be."

There was a crash inside the house on the far side of the yard. Paula put her face against the slit in the door to see better. Ketac stood and Bokojin's head turned. The door of the far side of the yard flew open.

"Akellar—" A man ran two steps out toward them and pitched forward on his face. Six inches of a throw-stick thrust out of his back between his shoulder blades.

Bokojin gave a loud cry. Three men rushed into the yard. The man leading was Marus, and he had a blowgun in his hand.

Bokojin put his fingers to his mouth and whistled. Ketac took two steps sideways, into the open away from the chairs.

"What is this?"

"You're under arrest," Marus said. He looked from Ketac to Bokojin. Two more of his men came into the yard.

Ketac backed toward the door where Paula watched. "What for?"

Bokojin broke for the door he had entered through, and Ketac sprinted toward Paula. She backed in a rush to the window. In the yard someone shouted. Bokojin whistled again. She climbed over the window sill down into the narrow space between the house and the vinework.

Ketac's slaves clogged the area around the front gate. She went close enough to see through the main door into the house. That room swarmed with armed men. In their midst half a dozen patrolmen stood with their belts strapping their arms down. Someone shouted, "The Akellar is dead!" The slaves around her wailed in chorus. Paula elbowed and wiggled a way through to the gate onto the street. It was shut, and two men stood guard over it, leaning against it. Behind her there was a splintering crash.

One of the gate guards saw her. He grabbed the other man and pointed at her. She slid back among the slaves.

"The Mendoz'! Here she is—"

"Take her," Marus roared, from the house. "She's under arrest too."

Paula went back around the house. Before she reached the backyard she smelled smoke. When she ran around the corner of the building, a fire was burning up the vine screen over Ketac's bedroom window. Men shouted in the room behind it. They were trying to push the blazing trellis away with poles. Ketac was climbing over the wall. In the street a watchman yelled. Everybody chased Ketac. Paula went over the wall and ran the other way.

She took the shortest way back toward the House, cutting through the fields of blue grass along the lake shore. The grass was full of snakes and stinging beetles and she watched her feet. She trotted past a row of little boats drawn up on the shore. A bell began to ring.

When she reached the street again, people filled it, standing in tight groups, although it was deep in the low watch. Several more bells were ringing, all over the city, out of time. A woman leaned out of a tenement window over Paula's head.

"What's going on?"

"The Akellar is dead!"

All around her people screamed and cried, their voices drowning the bells. Which Akellar? They thought it was Machou. Paula slowed to a walk, her hand pressed to a stitch in her ribs. The bells clanged steadily from one end of Vribulo to the other. She turned into the street that ran past Colorado's. People flooded out of a shop. Each carried a crystal lamp. The last to emerge was the shopman, who shut his door and locked it and rolled the shutter down over it. In spite of her fatigue she began to run again. She reached the steps of the House and climbed them, panting. As she reached the plain she noticed that the light was fading. She stopped and looked out across the city. All over Vribulo dark was falling.

She shivered in the deepening cold. If she stayed here she would die, but there was no place to go. The House was deserted. On the stairs she saw no other person, no trace of other people, not even a slave. By the time she reached the Prima Suite, she could see nothing at all. Black night had come. She groped her way to the door. Her memory took her down the hall to her room.

From her window, she could see flecks of light: fires, and the pinpricks of crystal lamps. The bells rang in a clamor, hundreds of bells. Far away a siren screamed, and a mob let up its many-throated roar. The war had reached Vribulo.

Behind her the door opened. She sprang away from the window into the concealing dark. "Mendoz'," Leno said. "You're under arrest."

"What for?"

A hand closed on her arm. "Don't argue with us. We have to get out of here before the gate closes. Mehma—"

"I have her," said the Saturn Akellar, on her other side.

"Wait," Paula said.

Roughly Leno shook her arm. "Don't argue with me."

"I want my flute." She wrenched her arm in his hold. He let her go, and she went back to her bed to find her flute.

The city gate was locked. She stood shivering with Mehma in the dark while Leno went off to find someone to open it. In the next street a building was burning, and cinders and glowing embers showered down around her. She wrapped her arms around herself.

"What am I under arrest for?" She could not see Mehma beside her. His mild voice came from over her head.

"I guess because Tanuojin wants you in Yekka."

"Tanuojin," she said. "I thought so."

The building directly opposite them exploded into a roar of flame. The ground bucked under their feet. Leno rushed up through the dark red glow. "Come on. This is bad and getting worse." He had a key and he struggled with the lock on the gate. The ground was pitching up and down. Paula lost her balance. Mehma caught her. They hurried into the terminal. Mehma left them in the lane between the launching tubes. She went after Leno to the last tube, where his sidecraft waited.

YEKKA

In Yekka the watch was high. Leno took her across the Koup Bridge to the Akopra House, standing in the fields of rellah vines, far from bilyobio trees and people. The city was bright and cold, the grass brilliant green like an Earthish spring. They went through the side door into the round building.

It was dark except for the lights above the stage in the middle. Tanuojin was drawing on the stage with chalk. Four dancers stood behind him. Paula went to the edge of the raised platform.

"Why am I under arrest?"

Tanuojin drew a circle on the floor. "Ketac was plotting to kill me. I think you had something to do with it." He walked slowly around, his gaze on the stage floor, counting his steps, and sank down to make another series of marks.

"You know that isn't true," she said.

The dancers watched her covertly. In their black rehearsal clothes they were nearly invisible in the dark. The stage around him was scrawled with white markings. He said, "About you I never know anything for certain." He waved to the dancers. "Try it like that." He came down off the stage past her and went on into the back of the theater.

Leno had moved over to the door. She could hardly pick him out of the shadows. She followed Tanuojin up the aisle. He sat on the last bench, his hands between his knees, watching the stage. She sat on the end of the bench.

"Where is Ketac?"

"I haven't caught him yet. I will."

On the stage, one dancer lifted another, slow and smooth, their arms straight, their palms flat together. The man in the air curved bonelessly over onto the shoulders of the man who held him, who sank down in the same smooth slow dreamlike quiet onto one knee. She rubbed her eyes. She had slept on the way, in Leno's ship, but she was still tired. Leno came down the aisle, his eyes on the dance. "They're really good. It's amazing, in a place like this."

Tanuojin gave him an oblique glance. He raised his head, his voice pitched to reach the stage. "How does that feel?"

The stocky man who did all the lifting walked to the edge of the stage. "It would be easier if I started facing the other way. Then I could use my strong leg."

"Try it," Tanuojin said. He turned toward Leno. "Mehma went back to his ship?"

"Yes. I didn't know whether you wanted him to go or not."

"That suits me. Go back to Merkhiz. Let the thing burn out in Vribulo, there's nothing we can do."

Paula stood up. The dancers broke out of their pose and clapped each other on the shoulders, pleased. She went down to the aisle and out the door of the theater.

The path led between fields of water. Under the glassy surface of the fields, new pale rellah vines curled like worms. She had never seen the adults, strung up on stakes to be bled. She went on toward Tanuojin's compound in the distance.

Ketac arrived unconscious, strapped into a sled. Paula unbuckled the straps and pulled the blanket back. The long rips in his stomach and chest were oozing with infection.

"Marus did that," Tanuojin said. "He's over-anxious."

She laid her hand against Ketac's cheek. His skin was harsh with fever. Tucking his arm back into the narrow sled, she covered him in the blanket. The sled lay on the floor next to her bed. Tanuojin was sitting across the little white room, in the big chair next to the desk.

"Shall I heal him?"

"No. He'll die if he's lucky."

"Why are you bitter at me?" He thumbed down his mustaches. "The way Bokojin feels about you, I probably saved your life."

She went to the window. At the far end of the yard, David and Junna were coming in the gate. She put her hand out to the warmth of the radiation, her eyes on the two young men, one short and burly, the other slim as a vine.

Tanuojin got stiffly out of the chair, stretching, and crossed the room to the sled. Looking down at Ketac, he said, "Don't let him die. I have a use for him." He went out to the hall and shut the door behind him.

Tanuojin spent most of his time at his Akopra. Paula considered searching his private rooms in the compound but he would have anticipated that. The rioters in Vribulo had set half the bubble on fire, and now word came from Leno that Illini had also gone dark. Bokojin's brothers were fighting over the succession. The Uranian Patrol held most of the city. Paula stayed in Tanuojin's library.

While she was going to her room again, after a watch reading novels, David met her in the hall. He turned to walk beside her.

"How is Ketac?"

"I don't know, I haven't seen him for eight hours," she said.

He lagged behind her to let a man coming the other way pass by. "Tajin should have killed him."

"Don't encourage it. Do you like him?" They crossed the main hall to her room. At the door she stopped and looked up at him.

"He's taught me a lot," David said. "Once I started listening."

"What, for example?"

He shrugged. He was filling out through his chest and shoulders, and his upper arms packed his sleeves. He said, "I'm not going to work for him for the rest of my life, you know."

His solemn look made her smile. "Oh, really?"

"Someday I'll get my own ship. Junna and I. We've talked about it. Actually, we've been talking about going to Neptune. Maybe even beyond."

She thought, He's like me. She unlocked her door and went into the white room beyond.

The sled was empty. She looked around, startled, and saw Ketac sitting on the window sill. "Oh," she said. "Do you feel better?"

He wore no shirt. The purpling half-healed wounds ran like a flag across his chest. David was behind her on the threshold, and he and his brother paid each other a long fierce look. She bent over the empty sled.

"Help me get this out of here." She picked up one end of the sled.

David took the other end and they carried it out to the hall. He propped it up against the wall, out of the way, for a slave to take. He said, "Now he's going to sleep with you, is that it?"

"That's right."

At the end of the hall, the outside door opened, and Junna came in. He was tall and thin, and for an instant she thought he was Tanuojin. David called to him. She went into her room again.

Ketac was still sitting on the window sill, looking out at Yekka. Paula shut the door and latched it. He said, "Why am I here?"

"Because you're a stupid ignorant idiot." She took the chair from her desk to sit beside him.

"You were there, weren't you? At my house. I found your dress. How much did you hear?"

"Enough."

He was avoiding looking at her. On his chest the puckered wounds ran from his right shoulder to his navel. She said, "You thought that was your plot, didn't you? That was Tanuojin's plot, Ketac, he has been waiting for this chance since before Saba died." She leaned toward him and said into his face, "You did this."

He shed a rising heat. His hands pressed against the window sill. Turned away from her, he said out toward Yekka, "Why didn't he kill me?"

"He needs *Ybix*."

He made a sound in his throat. She looked around the little room. The white walls made it bright. Tanuojin could hear her; he knew everything she did and thought, so there was no use trying to surprise him.

"Are you done tongue-whipping me?" Ketac said.

"Bah."

"Will you help me escape?"

"No."

"Come on, Paula, we've been friends for a long time." He swiveled to face her and took hold of her hand. "Tell me what to do."

With her free hand she took his fingers from her wrist and held them. "Not escape. You have to make him do what you want." She laced her fingers with his. "I'll help you do that."

The Akopra was dark. She stood still a moment, blinking her eyes clear. On the round lit stage, four dancers climbed on each other. She looked around the back benches until she found Tanuojin and went along the curved wall toward him.

"Shut up," he said. "I'm watching this."

Obediently she watched while they moved through the third design from *Capricornus*: where Capricornus met his lyo. The bench was hard and she sat restlessly. A young man she had never seen before stood off to one side of the stage. When the figure was over, she said, "What are you going to do about Ketac?"

Tanuojin thumbed his mustaches down, his eyes on the stage. "Leave him to me."

"What are you going to do?"

He raised his hand and made a gesture, and the young man at the edge of the stage went into the middle and took the place of another dancer. Tanuojin settled down again. He said, "The same thing I did with Dr. Savenia."

"He's not like Cam," she said. "And you haven't got the time to do it right. You'll kill him."

He made a sound in his chest. Slowly the four men on the stage began the same design over, this time with the new dancer as Capricornus. Paula watched, her attention caught by the young man's fiery gestures.

"He's going to be good," Tanuojin muttered.

"He's going too fast."

"I'll teach him better."

The young man stood on his hands on the hands of the stocky dancer. She watched the muscles flex under his tight black sleeves. Tanuojin said, "What's your idea about Ketac?"

"Do it through me," she said. "He'll accept it from me."

Spinning, the young dancer flipped up onto his feet on the floor-man's shoulders. He lost his balance for an instant and wobbled and the floor-man caught his ankles. Paula leaned back against the wall behind her. Tanuojin was watching her, his fingers entwined in his mustaches.

"In the low watch," she said. "He's still a little weak. He'll be easier to handle. I'll take him to bed with me, and when he's asleep, you take him through me."

He nodded. On the stage, the dancers had finished. He waved to them, and they left the stage and came toward him.

Paula said, "I'll be there to get you out if anything goes wrong."

Tanuojin nodded again, watching her. The dancers stood in the aisle on his far side. He turned his head. "What's your name?"

"Kapsin," the new dancer said.

"You can stay for fifty-one watches on trial. Don't try that flip again until you know what you're doing. You could have killed him." He faced Paula again. "Do you know, Paula, I think you have a good idea."

Paula settled back against the wall. He had jumped at it. She had expected him to. She listened to him lecture the dancers on the art of Akopra.

. . .

Ketac went to bed with her. The ruts in his chest and belly were like seams under her hands. When he was asleep, she rose from the bed and opened the door. Tanuojin came in. He left his body in the chair by the desk, and she took him to Ketac.

In his sleep, Ketac knew her kiss; he stirred, his mouth soft under hers, willing. She took his hands. He did not waken, even when she drew back, sitting beside him, her eyes on his face.

Tanuojin said, in Ketac's voice, "Be careful. I'll wake him up."

She held Ketac's hands. He stiffened, and his eyes opened, shining with terror. His mouth moved but said nothing. His chest heaved.

"Ketac," she said. "I'm here. It's all right, you'll be all right."

His hands closed painfully over her fingers. She bit her lip. "Just relax. It won't be for long."

Ketac's lips moved again. His long body flexed under the blanket, and his eyes shut. She pulled her throbbing hand free of his grip and worked her fingers and gasped at the pain in her knuckle.

"Take me, Paula."

She bent down and sucked him out of Ketac's mouth. Ketac lay still in the bed, asleep again. Her throat was numb. She crossed the room to the chair where Tanuojin's body slumped and breathed him coppery back into his own flesh.

Tanuojin straightened; he touched his mouth with his hand. "You're right. He'd have died if I'd had to force him."

Cold, she went back to the bed and sat down, pulling the blanket around her. Tanuojin came over and touched Ketac's face.

"He's stronger than Saba."

"Go away and let me sleep," she said.

He went to the door. "Now we'll see who wins." He left. She lay down next to Ketac again.

Ketac would not talk about what had happened. Paula walked beside him along the stream. She expected him to be angry that she had helped Tanuojin do it, but he seemed not to care. She took his hand. In the high wild grass along the stream-bank, krines sang in reedy voices.

Finally he said, "Why didn't you tell me?"

"You wouldn't have believed me."

"Have you done it?"

She nodded, her eyes on the sleek water. Stopping, she put her hand into the stream. "Will you help me against him?"

"Against him?" He stood beside her, kicking at the grass with one foot. "What can I do against him?"

"That depends on you," she said. "You have to know what he is, but when you do, there are possibilities." She sat down on the grass. The water rippled and went smooth again: a passing fish.

"What is he? He isn't just a man."

"I didn't mean it that way."

"He's more than a man. Why do you want me to help you against him—what are you trying to do to me? It's blasphemous to defy him."

She let her breath out, defeated again. Certainly Tanuojin was listening. Maybe she could not resist him. On the far side of the stream, the path ran down through the waste fields toward the Koup Bridge. Someone was walking along it. It was Kapsin, the young dancer, another instrument of Tanuojin's will. She turned her face away.

In the low watch David and Ketac and Junna flew *Ybicket* to *Ybix*, in high orbit around Uranus. Paula could not sleep. The pillow smelled faintly of Ketac and she got up and sat by the window. The door opened, and Tanuojin said, "*Ybicket* is docking."

She put on two pairs of overalls and a jacket. All she was taking with her was her flute. They went down through Yekka to the city gate, on a platform over a field of rakis beans. There was a freighter in the main loading pod. A small crowd had gathered along the glass doors to watch it unload. Paula and Tanuojin went to the next pod, where *Ybicket* lay in her harness.

David came along the catwalk toward them. "I have to replace a crystal. The captain of that freighter has a message for you."

"How long will it take?" Tanuojin said.

"I'm half done. About an hour."

Tanuojin bobbed his head once. He went out of the dock to find the freighter's captain. Paula watched him go. David said, "Sit in here and talk to me while I do this."

She climbed into *Ybicket* after him. The instrument panel in the front of the cockpit was tilted up on its hinges, showing the guts of the drive system packed into the nose. She sat in the drive seat, where she could watch. David lay on his back on the curved floor and slid under the raised panel.

"Give me that tube of glue." He waggled his hand at her. She bent down and put the squeeze-tube of glue into his fingers.

"Why did you take him back?" he said.

"Who, Ketac?"

"I don't see how you could go from Papa to that."

She ran her hand over the diamond-seamed upholstered seat. "There's a lot you don't know."

"Are you fighting with my uncle?"

"I don't call it fighting. You know I'm a pacifist."

The wrench slid out across the sloping floor of the ship. The handle was pierced with holes for his fingers, spaced to keep his claws out of the way. She heard him counting under his breath. Finally, he said, "Do you need help?"

That surprised her. Her face was cold and she turned up the collar of her coat and slid her hands into her sleeves. "What if it meant helping Ketac?"

"Oh, there's no saving Ketac," David said. "He belongs to my uncle, eyes, hooks, and paranoia. I'll help you."

She raised her gaze to the hatchway, where Tanuojin stood. "Come put your suit on," he said. She stood on the seat and stepped across the ship to the hatch and up to the dock. The locker door was folded back against the wall and Tanuojin was taking out his black pressure suit. Her special suit hung in the rear of the locker. "Here," he said.

He gave her an order medal. She looked down at it, frowning: the symbol cut into the surface was the triple star.

"Whose is it?"

"Bokojin's, I guess."

She put the medal on the locker shelf and took out her suit. "The whole patrol is in the star."

"Pretty much."

Stooping, she lifted the heavy shoes over the lip of the locker. In the ship, David called, "I'm finished."

Tanuojin said, "There aren't five ships in the chevron as fast as *Ybicket*, and they don't know when we're leaving." He pulled his suit over his shoulders and sealed the front together. "Put your helmet on, we have to launch hard." He took his helmet out of the locker and went over to *Ybicket*.

She clumped after him, lifting her feet high in the thick-soled shoes. Inside the cocoon of the ship, Tanuojin was bent over the radio deck in the kick-seat. He said, "You fly her. I can handle both guns from back here." She licked her lips. Her stomach fluttered unpleasantly. She would probably be sick; she was always queasy, flying in the Planet. David took her hands and helped her into the middle of the three seats.

Paula stuffed her hands into the gloves. David went out of the ship. She pulled the straps tight around her wrists. In the seat behind her, a metallic click sounded and an electric whine undulated louder up and down. When she put the heavy dark cylinder of the helmet on, the whine was painfully loud through the speakers above her ears.

"Can't you turn that off?" She held the helmet at arm's length away from her ears.

David swung himself into the ship and pulled the hatch closed.

"There's nobody for miles on the scan," Tanuojin said. The piercing noise stopped. She lowered her helmet onto her head.

The launch nearly knocked her cold. She rested her forehead against the helmet, groggy. The green glare of the holograph shone over the front of the cab. Her suit was rigid as a shell around her. Above her ears, Tanuojin's voice came out of the helmet.

"Take her down an M."

"There's a reef—"

"Stoop under it. Somebody's coming."

The ship rolled down into a dive. Paula swallowed the sour taste in her throat. Her eyes watered. Smoothly *Ybicket* swung into a wide rising curve.

"Where are they?" David said, in the top of the helmet.

"I think we lost them. Take her up again to—"

A sheet of white light flashed in her face. She could not breathe. She lost consciousness.

She woke up with a start, her ears ringing, alive. The ship was streaking through the magma. Her pressure suit was flexible again. She said, "David?"

Nobody answered. Her hands slipped on the helmet, and she pulled off the gloves. The helmet was jammed. She wrenched it back and forth until the seal popped. The air of the cockpit was icy cold. In the dark, she could hardly see; opposite her seat the wall seemed to be crumpled inward. She said, loudly, "David," and unsnapped her harness and unhooked her suit from the lifeline.

The ship hurtled along, yawing slightly from side to side. The radio chirped behind her. She scrambled out of her deep seat forward to David's seat.

He was slumped against the side of the ship. The green light of the map cube shone on the side of his face. Blood coated his face. It had burst from his eyes, from his nose and mouth. She felt along his throat for his pulse. Her head hurt as if a vise were screwing down on her temples. He had no pulse. She tore open the front of his pressure suit and his overalls underneath and thrust her hand in to his skin. His head tipped forward onto his chest.

"David."

On the instrument panel behind her a yellow light flashed. Something hummed. She pulled David against her, stroking his hair, his head on her shoulder. He smelled of blood. Behind her the hum turned to a beep.

She let him down again, cradling his head against her arm, easing him down against the black quilted seat. When she turned around, the yellow light made her squint. She wiped her mouth on the back of her hand. The control deck was divided into three panels, a sheet of dials on the left, four levers in the middle, buttons and switches on the right. The levers flew the ship. She squeezed down into the seat beside David and took hold of them.

When she pulled the outside levers down, the ship turned over completely and dumped her on her head. She put one hand on the ceiling and pushed the levers up again, and *Ybicket* righted. The ship was tearing like a bullet through the Planet. The beep and the flashing light unsettled her. She took the inside levers and drew them down, bracing herself in case the ship pitched, and slowly *Ybicket* raised her nose and began to climb. The beep fell to a hum, and after a moment the hum stopped, and the light blinked off.

She let go of the levers. The ship was still going terribly fast. She glanced at the holograph; the magma around them was clear green. The foot pedals were hidden in the dark under the instrument panel. She groped down along David's legs to the floor. His feet were jammed down on the pedals. She pulled them back and made his knees bend and put his shoes on the floor.

The ship slowed. She sat back, watching *Ybicket* in the map. The narrow ship was climbing. The heavy sludge of hydrogen slowed her. Now another light glowed on the console. A wave lifted the ship and threw her backward. Paula lay back on the seat and put one arm around David.

The patrol would be looking for them. She had forgotten about Tanuojin. She climbed back through the ship, one hand on the wall. At the waist, the ship's wall bulged in, the skin rippled. She had to squeeze past into the tail of the ship.

Tanuojin was folded forward over the radio deck. Like David he wore no helmet. She pushed uselessly at him. The ship rocked over a wave. She climbed into the back of the kick-seat, slid her hands under his arms, and heaved him upright.

He had not bled. His head flopped back against her shoulder. She put her hand over his mouth. His breath grazed her fingers. He was alive, deeply unconscious, inside healing himself.

She pushed him off. Her head beat painfully hard. It was impossible to think. If she waited long enough, he would waken, do the thinking, and fly the ship. Another wave laid *Ybicket* over on her side and swung her stern around. Paula crawled out of the seat. His helmet was still in the clamps on the ceiling. She fitted it over his head, in case the patrol found them, and straightened his legs and pulled him upright in the seat, fastening the harness around him to keep him there.

Ybicket lay dead still in the magma. Paler green eddies lapped her hull, nudging her over sideways. Paula unsnapped David's harness. If he had worn his helmet, he might not have died. She cranked the back of his seat down as far as it would go and dragged him over it into the middle seat.

She had to sit down. Her head was splitting. Something was wrong with her. She lay down beside David, her cheek against his cold cheek. The console was humming again, and another light burned. She put the back of the drive seat up and sat in it.

She moved the levers. The ship would not answer. She stretched her feet down toward the pedals. When she sat on the very edge of the seat she could reach them with her toes. Cautiously she pushed them down. Nothing happened. That was what the light meant: *Ybicket* was stalled.

She had seen Saba start the engine. She pressed the green button on the right panel and pushed down the pedals. The ship bucked violently. She moved the four levers up all the way and tried again, and this time the light went off, the hum stopped, and the ship moved slowly forward. When she stepped harder on the pedals, *Ybicket* gathered speed.

The radio behind her crackled. "Pan-patrol. This is H.C. All ships in sectors C-42, C-43, C-44, D-42, D-43, D-44, report in."

She wondered where she was. Pulling down one outside lever turned the ship around. She did not want to go back, she had to keep going away from Yekka. She experimented with the other levers. When the ship dove below a certain level, the yellow light came on again. She fought off the ache behind her eyes. There was something wrong with her. Carefully she took the ship down just to the level where the yellow light flickered on and off. Maybe she could crawl under the patrol.

"Pan-patrol. This is H.C. Mark this craft. SIF-26 *Ybicket*, three-man scout, Matuko-built, engines IQ, two guns fore and aft. Damaged. If sighted, report, intercept, take in tow, or destroy."

She put her arm over her aching eyes. Her face was cold.

"H.C., this is 214. Do you have a last-reported on the mark?"

A blast of static blurred the voice. She watched the dials, decided that the long thin one on the top of the panel was the speed gauge, and pumped the pedals to teach herself how to read it.

"214, this is H.C. The mark was sighted Yekka plus 160, C-43, bearing 8-8-5, axis minus 38° Yekka, speed 1500. We hit her head-on with a compression bomb, the crew must be point-operable."

Ybicket reared up. Paula caught the seat harness with both hands, felt the ship falling over, and grabbed for the levers. The map showed a moving yellow ridge forcing the ship back on its tail. She pushed the middle levers up. Nothing happened. The pounding in her head grew louder. She stamped down on the pedals and pulled the levers down, and the ship rolled over. She fell out of the seat and climbed back into it, clinging to the harness with one hand. The reef passed overhead. Without her feet on the pedals, *Ybicket* was slowing, and the stall light began to flicker. Paula pushed the levers this way and that and got the ship righted.

She pulled the harness over her shoulders. The reef had turned *Ybicket* around. She was moving back toward Yekka. Paula pressed one lever and one pedal and swung the ship in a loop turn. She had to watch the holograph. If a reef caught her the wrong way it would wreck the ship. The harness kept slipping off her shoulders. The yellow light was blinking on and off. She wondered where she was going. The radio crackled behind her. Here and there in its random noise a word sounded, meaningless.

Daffodil-bright, a reef jutted up in the magma ahead of her, moving in the same direction as *Ybicket*. Paula pushed the levers around and steered the ship over it. Her damp palms slipped on the steering pins. The vise closed on her head. She slumped down into the seat. She could push the levers down and dive into the Planet, take David down into the heat and pressure that would make nothing of him and her. She ground her fist into her eyes.

The radio gave another burst of static. *Ybicket* bucked in a cross-current. She was getting sick to her stomach. Her eyes were sore. If she died, it would not matter that David was dead. Tanuojin belonged in the deep Planet; it had made him and it could kill him. That thought settled her mind. She was not finished with Tanuojin. She had not kept his secrets for so long to kill him now, with his work undone.

She turned *Ybicket*'s nose up and stamped on the pedals. Straining to reach, her legs ached along her calves and the backs of her knees. She held herself on the front of the seat by her grip on the levers. In a round dial on the left-hand panel, a red needle sliced across the numbers. The ship bucked, slid along a wave, and rolled back. The left lever was jerked out of her hand. She snatched for it. The ship lurched. *Ybicket* was falling back into the Planet. She hit a surging pale green wave and bounced up again, tail-first. Paula rammed the pedals down. She had to go faster now, flying against gravity. Her stomach rolled half a turn behind the ship. She pulled the levers and got the ship nose-up again. *Ybicket* raced through a clear patch of green.

"D-61, D-61, identify."

Paula glanced back at the radio. A light flashed on it. She stepped hard into the pedals. *Ybicket* surged upward. The speed-gauge needle climbed steadily. Paula watched the map. A faint green cone of a wave streamed back from *Ybicket*'s bow.

"D-61, you're outside the corridor. Identify or we will notify the patrol."

She laughed, pleased to know he was not the patrol. She

wondered where the corridor was. At least she was out of the traffic. Something bright yellow and long and hairy appeared in the top of the map. The image sharpened into a thick string cutting diagonally across the cube. She guessed it was a city mooring.

"D-61, D-61—"

The ship hit another wave. This time she kept hold of the levers. It was hard to judge the angle. The wave broke sharp against the ship's hull and knocked her sliding. Now she was headed in another direction. Paula steered around a yellowish mass like a mountain floating in the magma: a lump of something frozen. She was going so fast *Ybicket* left a visible rippled wake.

"D-61, this is UP-115, identify and heave to. You are outside the corridor." The voice sharpened. "Damn it, heave to or I'll shoot!"

There was no sign of another ship in the map. *Ybicket* raced straight up. Paula braced herself against the edge of the seat. In the limit of the holograph another long string appeared. She wondered what city it was. They might not shoot if she kept close by the moorings. Two men shouted at her at once in the radio.

She passed the city within holograph range, a great yellow wall that went on for long miles beside her, encrusted with hairy growth. Another ship flew across her course. She headed *Ybicket* straight for it. She rammed the pedals down as far as she could reach. For a moment the ship hovered there ahead of her, but the city was just behind her; the craft could not shoot and reeled away. She hurtled past, going steadily faster.

The cab filled with a lemony sunlight. She glanced through the window into a fog like dirty wool. The light grew brighter. The ship answered differently to her touch on the levers, tender as an egg on a table. She was bobbing in the harness, nearly weightless. *Ybicket* flew up through the thinning clouds. She crossed into black space.

She put her helmet and gloves on and went back to stuff Tanuojin's hands into his gloves. He was still sunk in sleep. She groped over the radio deck, found the light, and switched it on. In its glow she could read the tags on the buttons. The one on the left was marked ID and she turned it on. She swam back to the drive seat. Just as she reached it, a blow struck *Ybicket* with a flash of white light.

The shock threw Paula head-first into the seat. Someone was shooting at her. She squirmed around, reaching for the levers. The ship was streaking down toward the white Planet. When she pulled the levers, she moved herself and the controls stayed still. She had to learn all over again how to do it in free fall. The ship began to roll over as she fell. Paula thrust the pedals down and forced the levers down, clenching her teeth, and still tumbling the ship leveled off.

Another light exploded in the window overhead. There were no other ships around her. They were shooting from the cloud-white Planet or from a moon. *Ybicket* was rolling over and over. When Paula pushed the outside lever to steady her, the spin quickened. She tried other combinations and stopped the roll but *Ybicket* dropped her nose again and dove toward Uranus. Far above her, there was another explosion.

"*Ybicket, Ybicket,* this is *Ybix,* answer."

The voice roared through the helmet above her ears. She could not work the radio, so she said nothing. *Ybicket* was plunging down. The Planet filled the window. The levers were frozen. The ship ran into something that flung it sideways. Paula hit the wall. Her helmet banged her head. Her eyes went in circles. When she came back to herself, Ketac was shouting at her.

"*Ybicket.* I'm taking your controls. Let go."

"I don't know how."

"Paula!"

She swam back to the drive seat. The lifeline had uncoiled after her like a white worm and snaked into its housing under the seat. Ketac said, "Push the auto button. The red button under the safety hood on the right of the instrument panel. Do you see it? What are you doing in the drive seat?"

Her head hurt unbearably. She lifted the metal hood on the right side of the console and punched the red button there. Ketac was shouting at her. She crawled into the harness and shut her eyes.

Her eyes opened. Around her the Mylar walls glistened. A stopwatch floated about a yard away from her face, rocking slightly back and forth. She was in *Ybix,* in Saba's old cabin in *Ybix,* wrapped up in a shaggy bedrug. She unfolded herself from its warm laps.

The time meter read the middle of the low watch. Shivering, she went around the room gathering her clothes and dressing. While she was in the galley taking a protein strip and blue and white chalk tablets out of the food machine, a crewman swam into the hatch and told her that Tanuojin wanted to see her. He was in the library. She went up to the blue corridor, traveling slowly in the free fall.

Ketac was perched on a stool pulled out from the wall, between her and Tanuojin. He grabbed hold of her hand. "Have you ever flown *Ybicket* before? Who let you do that?"

She swung the hatch closed behind her. Inside the round room, its curved wall coated with book cells, the three were crowded together. Tanuojin said, "The vulgar belief is that Vida's ghost flew us in." He crooked his arms behind his head. "The fleet is here," he said to her. "And Mehma's Saturn Fleet."

"They came when you called," she said. She turned her arm, and Ketac let go of her.

Tanuojin said, "Something has to be done. The whole Empire is falling apart."

Ketac took hold of her again. "There's only one power in the system that can bring Styth back to order now. And that's Tanuojin."

"Go on," Tanuojin said to Ketac. "I'll talk to you later."

Ketac went past her, spun the hatch wheel, and dove out into the corridor. In the expanded space of the room Paula let herself stretch out. Tanuojin said, "I'm calling a session of the rAkellaron in Vribulo in eleven watches. The fleet's small craft can dominate Vribulo, no matter what the patrol does. The Chamber will elect me head of the Empire for my lifetime. Leno is my deputy in Uranus. Mehma is my deputy in Saturn. Ketac will be head of the fleet."

She wondered how long he would live. When she was random dust, when Ketac's grandchildren were old men, Tanuojin would rule. She said, "Congratulations."

"You can help me."

"I helped you. I got you here."

"More than that."

"What's more than your life?"

The wall buzzed. He put one arm out, and a narrow drawer among the cells of books slid toward his fingers. "You refuse to admit that I'm right." His voice was brittle. He took the earphones out of the side of the drawer and turned a switch. On the panel inside the drawer a red light flashed on and off. "Tanuojin," he said, into the mouthpiece. Leno's voice rasped in the speaker. She left.

VRIBULO. A Hundred Watches Later

Vribulo was full of people standing in lines, like the Earth during the coup. The city seemed much brighter than before. She walked along the street that led past the lake, Junna beside her holding his stride short to match her pace. Down a lane she saw block after block of blackened concrete and plastic rubble. The air smelled of acetone.

"We executed the last of the patrol last watch," Junna said. He steered her around a line of people toward the next street. A long lock of his hair hung down unclubbed over his ear. "Every city in Styth has sworn obedience to my father."

"You don't sound pleased."

"I don't know, Paula, everything is changed. I don't know what will happen now. The oaths are all different—he made them up, who knows what they really mean?"

She took the loose lock of his hair in her fingers. "What's this?"

"That's for Vida."

They were coming to the Steep Street, leading down past the head of the lake to the rAkellaron House. She had followed Ymma along this street once, years ago, after Ymma had kicked Tanuojin half to death: long ago. She had thought of David all the while she had spent in *Ybix*. She had dreamt of him, his face glowing with blood, his body burst. Sometimes in the dreams he had bled fire. He was always dead in these dreams. She said to Junna, "I know what that means. What happened to his body?"

"My father can tell you." His tone warned her: something bad.

He took her up to the Prima Suite. In the white front room, half a dozen men were sitting, Leno, Mehma, and other rAkellaron. When she came in, they all stood up. It was like them; when she had been one-third of a Prima, they would not have done that.

"Where is Ketac?" she said to Junna.

"I don't know. I'll get him." The tall young man left. Her favorite chair was still in its place and she took it, and the six aristocrats sat down. She did not want to talk to them. Turning in the big chair she stared out the window at Vribulo.

After a while Marus came in. He gave something to Leno, who left, and said, "Mendoz', the Akellar wants to talk to you."

She followed him across the hall. At the threshold of Saba's old room, the back of her neck began to tingle. She rubbed it with her fingers, wondering what it meant.

The two windows on the far side of the room let in oblongs of light onto the ceiling. All along the blank walls were piled boxes of film and books and paper. Marus came in behind her. She touched the back of her neck again. Tanuojin came in from the next room, and the tingle grew stronger. He handed a paper to Marus.

"Give that to Mehma. Tell the others to come back in a watch."

Paula looked around the room. It was still painted light yellow, Boltiko's choice of color. There was no furniture except the table below the windows and a sling chair pushed away under it. Marus left, and she swung around to face Tanuojin.

"What did you do with my son's body?"

"He was burned." Tanuojin sauntered away from her toward the table. His back to her, he hitched his belt up with both hands. His shirt hung loose from his shoulders; he was much thinner. "I thought better of bringing you down for the ceremony. It got very emotional. People took him for a symbol. You don't like ceremonies anyway."

"No," she said, angry. "Especially not when they're arranged for your purposes. Damn you, that was my son you used."

"He always wanted to be a hero." He propped his elbow on the table and leaned on it, sideways, facing her. "You are getting old, Paula. Old and hidebound."

"Well," she said, "we all get what we deserve." She put her hand to the back of her neck.

"You still think you can revenge the anarchy."

"I don't have to," she said. "You are my revenge."

He shook his head at her. "I think too many people have died on you."

She looked around the bleak room again. All the decoration was in his mind. There was nothing in here she wanted, and the rustle of her nerves bothered her. She went out to the corridor to find Ketac.

MARS. August 1870. Tanuojin's Empirat

The lobby of the Nineveh was dimly lit. Shadows hid the edges of the room. Paula sidled away from Ketac. The Styths were pressed tightly together. In this strange place they were all shedding a faint cold fear. At the staircase, the five or six Sun-worlders stood neatly posed like mannequins. Alvers Newrose stepped forward to greet Ketac. Behind him Cam Savenia's face was white as pipe-clay.

"We are honored to receive you," Newrose said. His head was cocked back toward Ketac's, a foot and a half above him. "Our first business must be to express our grief and the grief of all the Middle Planets at the death of Saba. He was as just an overlord as he was terrible an enemy. We don't expect to see his like again."

Paula chewed the inside of her cheek. Around the broad, dim lobby, the unlit display cases like mirrors reflected back the people massed around her. Ketac was making a stiff little speech in answer to Newrose's stiff little speech. She circled between two men to the door.

Tanuojin was already in the corridor beyond, looking out at the gardens through the glass wall, his hands on the rail. She went past him, reading the numbers on the room doors.

"Why did you do this? Why here?" She found 110 and put her thumb on the white patch. The door slid back into the wall. The lights in the room beyond came up overbright. After so long with the Styths, the bright light dazzled her. She found the wall switch and turned them down. There was no aquarium.

"To remind myself how rich these people are." Tanuojin came in behind her.

"Savenia doesn't look any different," she said.

"Leave her alone. I'm tired of your sniping at her."

She went into the next room. The bed was draped in a black fur cover. The lime green carpet made her hungry. She stretched her arms out. After so long in *Ybix* she welcomed these expanses of space and color.

"The older I get," he said, "the more I hate that ship." He walked around the room. She twisted to reach the hooks on the back of her dress.

"Undo this for me, will you?" She turned her back to him. The dress opened down to her waist. She shed it and went into the washroom.

The walls were glossy white. The hot water of the shower needled her skin. A row of push buttons ran across the tiled wall above faucets. She pushed one and the middle nozzle sprayed white suds over her. She revolved in the stream, pressed other buttons: perfume, deodorant, body finisher. The back of her neck tingled.

"Come in—try this. You could have it installed in *Ybix*."

There was a deep Puritanical mutter behind her in the doorway. The panic in her nerves subsided. He had gone away. She rinsed herself clean of the cosmetic mud and odors and dried herself in the warm air blower by the sink.

When she went back to the big green room, Tanuojin was lying on his stomach across the bed. "Watch."

She sat down beside him. He held his hands cupped before him. After a moment, a big red poppy appeared on his fingertips, its brilliant petals cupped around the black center. She touched its papery soft edge.

"Are you making it up?"

"No. It's in the garden." When he talked, the flower shivered and faded. She bent down to sniff it, but there was no smell. Maybe poppies had no odor.

"I'd be more impressed if you were making it up."

In the next room, Ketac's voice sounded, loud. "Bring me something to eat. A real spread. For her, too. And some liquor. And—" He strode into the room, saw Tanuojin, and stopped, coming up to respect, his head back. Paula slid off the bed and went to her bags for her robe.

"Are you eating here?" she said over her shoulder.

Tanuojin nodded at Ketac. The poppy was gone. "Yes. Call Alvers Newrose here. And Dr. Savenia."

Ketac relaxed, his feet apart. "When?" There was a blowgun in his belt.

"Whenever they're ready."

She pulled the white fur robe down over her head. "See if they have any decent whiskey."

Ketac went to the door and talked through it to his aides in the sitting room. She tied a belt around her waist and groped around the sides of her bag for her comb.

"I want to go to the Earth," she said.

Tanuojin lay back on his elbows. "There's nothing left of it. It's a desert. Red sand."

"Maybe you could make up some trees for me."

"I have too much to do."

"Ketac can take me." She sat down on the foot of the bed. Her hair crackled from being washed. Ketac went past her to the bathroom, giving no sign he heard. He would do whatever Tanuojin said. Through the half-open door she saw him turning on the shower.

"Do they still have the women?" He threw his clothes out onto the bedroom floor.

"Probably. It's the same old Nineveh." She glanced at Tanuojin behind her on the bed. "Down to and including Cam Savenia."

"Paula—"

"Your deputy in the Middle Planets."

He kicked her. In the shower, Ketac let out a yell. He had found the cosmetic bar. She rolled onto her feet and went to the bathroom door and stood watching him lather himself. He was too large for the shower; he had to stoop to put his shoulders under the spray. The white soap washed down his body.

"Newrose is coming." Tanuojin went to the other door. She turned. Ketac got out of the shower, and the roar of the air blower started. Tanuojin was standing in the doorway to the next room, his head bent to clear the lintel. Paula looked quickly through her bag for her shoes. She heard Newrose's knock and went barefoot behind Tanuojin into the sitting room.

Junna let Newrose into the room. His egg-shaped head was smooth and pink, his face babyishly bland. He knelt down before Tanuojin and put his right cheek against the floor beside the Styth's boot.

Paula murmured. She went back into the bedroom.

"Well?" Ketac said. He stood at the closet, half into his leggings.

"He did it." She bounced down onto the bed. "I'm getting old. Betrayed like a gull by Alvers Newrose."

He was bent over to lace his boot. "Do you mind if I take one of the whores?"

"Do what you want."

He got out a red shirt, stitched with gold in his kite-shaped emblem. In the next room, there was another knock. Cam Savenia was making her entrance. Paula stayed to watch Ketac dress. She knew Cam would perform the *kutal.* Ketac sat on the bed next to her.

"How do I call the slaves?"

There was a console built into the night table at the head of the bed. She took the receiver off the cradle. Beside it was a row of buttons. One was marked PERSONAL SERVICES. She said, "Are you having a party?" When she pressed the button it flashed red.

"Marus and Tibur and I."

A clerk answered into her ear. She said, "Hold on, please," and put her hand over the receiver. "Not here," she said to Ketac.

"Upstairs." He reached for the receiver. She got up. For a moment, unused to the gravity, she nearly fell over. Carefully, she went into the next room.

They had swung the couch over perpendicular to the fireplace, and Tanuojin sat in the corner, his head propped up on his fist. Junna stood on the hearth, and Marus, his hands behind him, leaned against the drapery-covered windows behind him. Two junior officers were bringing a white service cart in the door. Paula veered around them to the fireplace.

Newrose stood before Tanuojin, talking about Mars. Cam Savenia waited behind him. Paula glanced at her and their eyes caught. Simultaneously they looked away. The two Styth lieutenants turned up the lid of the service cart to uncover a drawer of bottles and glasses.

Newrose said, "Will you be staying on Mars the whole mission, Akellar?"

Tanuojin stretched out his legs, long as rope. "She wants to go to the Earth."

Savenia glanced at her. "The Earth isn't much of a tourist hell these days."

Paula took the empty glass from Ketac. On her way to the couch she gave it to the aide by the serving cart. "I like to go in circles." She sat down on the soft-cushioned couch at the far end from Tanuojin.

The aide brought her glass. Junna came along the back of the couch to give it to her. Newrose backed away two steps from Tanuojin, bowed, and went behind Savenia to Paula's end of the couch. His hands disappeared behind his back.

"We just heard today that you've lost your son as well. You have my deepest condolences."

Tanuojin said, "Don't do that." He was talking to Savenia. She stopped in the act of fitting a cigarette into her holder. Her gaze swung toward Paula. She put the cigarette back in the case and the black holder back into her pocket. Tanuojin looked at Newrose.

"You saw the demograph?"

"Yes, Akellar." Newrose wet his lips. "I hope we can change your mind . . . convince you to change your mind."

Tanuojin drank water. "Go on. Give me your speech."

Newrose gave Paula a quick beseeching look and faced him again. "The people of the Middle Planets are used to a high—perhaps an unnaturally high material standard. What you propose is nothing less than a conversion of the whole society to slave labor." Newrose tilted forward slightly from the waist, intense. His voice was low. "Akellar, we've avoided serious trouble here because the Prima was wise enough to preserve the continuity of our traditions and institutions. If you attempt this, there will be resistance, perhaps violence. The work of the last several years will be lost." His gaze went to Paula again.

Tanuojin stretched his arm along the back of the couch toward her. His eyes never left Newrose. His voice was deeper than usual: pontifical. "I don't have a choice. Junna—"

His son circled around the couch, a spherical star map in his hands, and put it on the floor at Tanuojin's feet. Tanuojin turned it around in its bracket until Lalande was on the top.

"This is Lalande. There are twenty-six Planets here, iron, calcium, plutonium, uranium, gold, argon, salts—everything we are starved for now."

"Also life," Paula said. "With a prior claim to its worlds."

"You believe that because you want to."

Newrose's cheeks shone. He stooped beside the dark blue globe. Tanuojin gave his empty glass to Junna. "The Martians build the best hulls. We design the best drives. Sometime in the next year—Uranian year—we'll break the light barrier. After that we can go to Lalande."

Newrose straightened up, his eyes on the Styth. "That's impossible. The speed of light is the absolute speed limit."

"There are no absolutes," Tanuojin said. "There are no limits."

"But—"

"We have to do this. It's the purpose of life, to grow. The only way is for everybody in the system to work together. If there's resistance, I can deal with that."

Newrose said, "Yes, sir."

"You can go."

"Yes, sir." Newrose backed up three steps. His egg-face was white. He left the room. As he went out, two hotel waiters in white coats rolled another serving cart in the door past him, and the two lieutenants went to take it from them.

Tanuojin said to Savenia, "Have you worked it out?"

Savenia looked significantly at Paula. He said, "She's not involved any more." Junna brought him a dewy glass of water.

"I have everything," Cam said. "Names and addresses, meeting places, even their hideouts and escape routes. I can jail fifty thousand dissidents in two days."

"Good."

The two lieutenants were setting out the food in the serving cart. Paula stretched her neck to see. A roast chicken lay in a dish in the middle of the top tray surrounded by vegetable flowers and cranberry sauce. Her tongue ran with water. Savenia said, "What about Newrose, Akellar?"

"I'll handle him. He may still cooperate. You can go."

Cam bent from the waist, a marionette bow, and backed away. Paula rubbed her hand over her eyes. She felt sorry for Newrose; she hated Cam. Lowering her hand, she looked around the room. The furniture was upholstered in gold brocade. The walls and floor were shades of brown. In the hearth, behind a pile of plastic logs, a cylinder of crinkled foil turned under an orange light to simulate fire.

Tanuojin said, "Ketac, where is the Earth?"

"About thirty-five light seconds behind Mars."

The aides brought the cart of food around beside the couch. Junna served his father. Ketac came around the knot of people by Tanuojin and sank down on his heels beside Paula.

"You're sure you don't mind?"

"Just don't wake me up when you come in."

He kissed her hand and her cheek and stood up. The fancy red shirt hissed when he moved. "Akellar—"

Tanuojin nodded, put his head back, and said, "Marus, you can go." The big man followed Ketac out. Paula was still barefoot, and her toes were cold. She went into the bedroom and found a pair of Ketac's socks. When she came back into the sitting room, everybody was gone but Junna and Tanuojin.

"He never makes himself that pretty for me." She went to the cart. The chicken was neatly sliced. She put a piece of the brown skin into her mouth.

"Newrose is still your thing," Tanuojin said to her.

She tried eating cranberry sauce with her fingers and switched to a spoon. Tanuojin came up to the cart to feed. Junna followed him. They stood around the roast chicken and the pots of gaily colored vegetables, eating.

"He'll believe anything you tell him," Tanuojin said.

"Don't you ever get tired of thinking, Papa?" Junna said. "There must be something more important than thinking."

"Why don't you tie up your hair like a man?"

Junna flicked back the loose lock of his hair. He was Tanuojin's height and build, supple, bonelessly graceful. His father had been that way once. Now Tanuojin was stiffening, slackening, as he used his body more and more only to carry his head around. Paula ate meat. The Emperor walked away through the room, his back to her. She imagined him in his final phase, a great soft brain resting in a chair.

"Why do you want to go to the Earth?" Junna asked her.

"It's my home."

"You mean you want to stay there?"

"She's crazy." Tanuojin sat down in a corner of the couch.

Paula wiped her hands on a white napkin. Junna frowned at his father, one hand on his hip, his body curved like a bow. He turned to her.

"I'll take you."

"You stay out of this," Tanuojin said.

"Why? She's your oldest friend. She saved your life. Vida died for you. Why shouldn't I help her?"

The Emperor settled into the couch, one arm across the back, his head down. "Is that your substitute for thinking?"

Paula hung the white napkin over the handle of the cart. "He'll take me himself," she said to Junna. She went back for her glass, on the floor beside the couch. "Sooner or later."

Junna was scowling at Tanuojin. Paula held out her empty glass, and he took it and went to the cart full of drink.

"Sooner or later," Tanuojin said to her, "you'll do as I say."

She went to sleep alone in the wide cool bed. Presently she woke, or seemed to wake. The back of her neck crawled with nerves. Tanuojin stood beside the bed. His eyes were like mirrors. She felt unable to move, as if in a dream. He lay down on the bed next to her.

"Paula—" He took her face between the cold blades of his hands. "Pauliko, now you submit." She thought, *It is a dream.* His narcotic touch lulled her. She closed her eyes. His mouth touched her. A dream. He disappeared. Silence and darkness closed around her. Restless, she tried to waken. Her mind was scattered. She struggled to think. It was no dream; Tanuojin had her.

She collected her mind, floating in a black emptiness like deep space. Without her senses she was confused and could not decide what was actually happening, or what she should do. Perhaps nothing. Other people panicked and fought uselessly until they died or were too tired to resist. If only she could see, she would have something to hold on to. She strained to see.

A green world spread out around her, trees and meadow grass yellowed with sunlight. That was her imagination. She could go in there and rest. With an effort she wiped it away. The black blindness fell around her again. She had to keep away from that trap of telling herself what to see. She organized her mind to use her eyes.

A light flashed so bright it dazed her. Her mind stopped, stupid, in the grip of a gray after-image. It faded. She mastered herself again, encouraged; she must have almost broken out, to be driven back like that. She pitched herself against the dark.

This time the brilliance shattered her. Five or six of her circled aimlessly around each other, like voices talking at once, all numb. What happened? *Give up,* one voice said, loudest. *Give up. Give up.* She was lost in the midst of herselves, helpless. Two brushed together, saying the same thing, and she made them lap and fit together. Several after-images of the light flash hung around her. As she formed her mind together again all the images blended into one, and she focused on that. The cogent loud voice telling her to give up faded away. That was Tanuojin. She fastened her attention on the after-image, dying in the black.

The image was not featureless, like the first time. In it she saw white on white a doorway, another room. A roll of light showed in the background, the bright false fire in the hearth of the sitting room of her suite.

The dark closed over her. She rested, hoarding her strength. All her selves had melded again, and she could not find the seams between them. This time she had to keep trying, she could not let him drive her back. She gathered herself up and went forward into the dark.

Suddenly, without the blast of light, the corridor of the hotel lay before her. A Styth coming toward her stopped and saluted her. She relaxed, triumphant. The corridor was darker than before, and the colors strange, muted to halftones, the shading between dark and light more distinct than she was used to. It was a Styth image. Styths saw that way; he was tricking her. She refused to see what he was feeding into her mind, she forced it to dissolve.

The light struck her, dazzling, destroying her. In the sheet of light figures moved. She strained toward them. The light pierced her, merciless, she was glass, she was sheer to the brilliance, and she passed through into a dim room, where a white Martian face hung before her, concerned, mouthing words she could not hear.

She was in some other part of the hotel. The Martian, looking reassured, went out a side door. She had no physical control over the single eye she occupied, and it blinked and she was blind. Not the same dark as before: blood tinged the eyelid. When the eye opened, Newrose was there in front of her.

He talked, smiling all over his pink face, and she apparently answered him. They passed into another room. On the left was a plush stuffed couch and on the right a desk. She went straight between them to a window and stood staring out over the garden, one story below her. She could see nothing of Newrose; she might as well have been blind again.

She needed to hear. She reached out, struggling to hear. Newrose's voice sounded faintly somewhere behind her, and she snatched for it. It was a bait. She was thrown back. Like a knife the black fell across her sight. The sound was gone. She was locked tight in her mind again.

He was in here with her. It was her body. She had done it wrong, the first time, stupidly attacking the dominant, most disciplined sense. She had to move fast. Collecting her will and her concentration, she flung herself out along all her nerves.

Feeling sprang alive in her hands and feet and along her back, spread over her face and her belly, running hot like blood under her skin. She shut her blind eyes and doubled up, falling. Her cheek and hip hit the yielding floor. Her stomach clenched in a cramp. Something clawed at her, deep in her body. She almost weakened. She nearly yielded. Gasping for breath, she struggled to hear, and sound burst alive in her ears.

"Miss Mendoza—" Newrose squeaked. "I'll get help."

"No! Leave me alone."

She blinked, panting. Her guts and belly were knotted, like the fierce cramps of labor. The light hurt her eyes. She forced herself to see. The floor stretched away shiny past a pair of modish two-tone shoes. Over there was the couch. She pushed herself up to her knees and the claws ripped her as if he were trying to tear a way out through her stomach. She could not straighten. Newrose held his pink hands down to her. His eyes were round as a Styth's. She shook her head at him.

He spoke to her. She paid no attention. Putting her feet under her, she lurched up and staggered to the couch. Her muscles fluttered with weakness. Her mouth tasted of copper. The jagged edge slashed her stomach. She wiped her drooling mouth on her hand.

"Shall I bring you something?" Newrose danced around her. "Water? A little brandy?"

"No." Her strength was ebbing. A long pain stabbed into her lungs. She pressed her arms against her body, where her prisoner gnawed her.

"Please," Newrose said.

She got up onto her feet and started toward the door. Her lungs were burning. She wondered if he could save himself by killing her. Newrose came into her way, and she brushed by him to the door.

"You have to help me." Newrose pursued her across the anteroom beyond, past his startled aides rising like puppets off their chairs. "I need your help."

She threw him a wild look. Her throat was closed; she could not speak even if she had wanted to tell him anything. Her breath burned going down. She went out to the hall.

"Miss Mendoza!"

Her knees were buckling. For a moment her lungs froze and she could not breathe, and she nearly panicked. She leaned against the glass wall of the corridor and made herself calm and insisted on breathing and the air crept down her swollen throat. The glass before her was fogged with the breath leaving her. Out there lay the gardens. She started down the hall toward the stairs.

Twice on the steps she fell, and the second time she rolled all the way to the bottom. She nearly lost consciousness. Lying in a knot at the foot of the stairs, her face against the floor, she felt him rising through her, ready to seize her as soon as she weakened, and she throttled him down again. This time it was easy. He was tiring. She got to her knees and pushed herself up to her feet and went across the corridor to the door.

The gardens spread off toward the thick fence of the trees along the golf course. The colors of the flowers were drowned in the blue domelight. The air chilled her cheeks. The pain seemed to be gone, or she was numb to it, but her body felt as if it were melting away. She could not lift her feet, she dragged them along, plowing through the beds of poppies, the peonies and wildflowers.

No, he said, in her mind; not a voice but a thought. *Go back. Take me back.*

She blundered on through the heavy branches of the deodars to the edge of the sweeping lawns of the golf course. Behind her someone shouted her name: she thought it was Ketac. She let her body down to the ground, her dense flesh like mud, all the feeling gone, and shut her eyes. If she died, he would die.

No. Don't. No.

Her will had kept her alive, and she could will her death. Freed of her nature she would reach across the Universe, she would instantly be home.

Tajin, she thought, *you made a mistake.* He still needed her for shelter. He was her child, her beast, the unimaginable future, which she had nurtured and protected until he was strong and his course was inevitable. She thought, *We are finished with each other.*

Please, he said. *I'll do anything you want.*

Ketac shouted again, closer. She turned her head to answer.

"I'm getting rid of her."

She raised her head, coming awake in a start. She was lying on her bed, alone, with her clothes on. She could not remember anything beyond the moment when Ketac found her lying on the grass. The door to the next room was open and voices came through it: Junna's now.

"You can't kill her, Pop."

Sliding off the bed, she went to the open door and stood on the threshold. The back of her neck hummed. Ketac was directly in front of her, his broad shoulders blocking her view of the room. He said, "I don't see how you can even think of killing her."

"She's malicious," Tanuojin said. "And she's perverse. Whatever I think she believes the opposite, to spite me."

Paula went by Ketac and stood between him and the wall. Junna faced Tanuojin, who was sitting on the couch. He was excited; the measure of it was that he did not notice her.

"She's your friend," Junna said.

"She has never been my friend. We have always hated each other."

Ketac was staring at her. She said, "I'm thirsty. Bring me a glass of water." Tanuojin had seen her. He was unexcited. He was simply refusing to look at her.

Junna said, "You can't kill her, Papa, she hasn't done anything wrong."

"I said I would get rid of her. I didn't say I'd kill her."

Paula looked down at his head. Studiously he avoided her glance. He could not help but see her in his mind. Ketac came back with a cup of cold water. She went back into her bedroom to change her clothes.

THE EARTH

Red sand blasted the window. Paula glanced down at the holograph, in which *Ybicket* was flying through a blizzard of green lights. She tipped her head up again toward the window. Junna said, in the drive seat, "Do you have a temperature for the geosphere?"

"About 30 degrees at the bottom margin. There's a change in density up ahead in the gas that looks like a clearing. Bearing course plus 72." Tanuojin pushed the radio deck up and pulled out the scan on its hinge from the wall.

Ybicket swooped into a shallow gliding descent. They flew out of the dust storm. Paula stood up in her seat to see. The sand was rippled like a washboard into red dunes. Against it the hard blue sky blazed with sunlight. The light glared on a lake ahead of them.

"We're about three thousand feet above the geosphere," Tanuojin said. He was in the kick-seat navigating. "Where are you leveling off?"

"Pretty soon. You should feel the ship. She's really hoopy, but the gravity's like the deep Planet."

"Saba used to say flying in the Earth was more risky than fighting."

"Over there." Paula pressed her nose against the window. "Down over the lake." Ahead, the sun caught on a jagged glassine edge at the shore. They flew low over the choppy water and passed the broken shell of a dome, rising a thousand feet above them. Sand was drifted like a tide along its sheer flank. Sand was filling the lake.

"Alm'ata," Paula said.

Junna took the ship up steeply over the ring of mountains. They flew on above ridges of high rock, bleak as iron bones. The window was cold against her cheek. The two Styths complained of the bright sun and put their helmets on. They passed the ruin of another dome. Night covered them. Paula sat back. She looked up at Luna like a silver mask in the sky.

"Go around to the light side again," Tanuojin said. "Paula, put your helmet on."

They climbed and raced around the Planet into the day. Junna took them along a northerly coastline. Paula looked out over the shore, deeply embayed, into the hills in the distance. The air along the horizon was brown with dust. Below the ocean laid an edge of foam along the narrow beach.

"Junna, take her down," Tanuojin said. "At the water's edge. Do you see that lump of mineral down there? Sit down, Paula."

The needle ship dropped its nose toward the ground. She sat down, craning her neck to see over the bottom edge of the window. Below, the water foamed along a strip of beach. A boulder broke the surf, weed streaming green along its base. The ship upended smoothly and settled down on her tail, so that Paula was lying on her back in the deep seat. Tanuojin climbed up next to her in the vertical lane between the seat and the wall.

"Watch out for the radiation," he said to Junna.

Paula got to her knees on the flat back of her seat. Junna swung the hatch out, and a burst of cool fresh air swept in over her face. A bird shrieked just outside. The sunlight was brilliant. Tanuojin took her by the arm and helped her to the hatch and lowered her down to the sand of the beach.

The air smelled of salt. It was warm, and she pulled open her pressure suit. Two brown gulls were floating in the air above the ship. Junna ran off along the line of the breakers, away down the beach.

"Here." Tanuojin handed her flute to her in its case.

She pulled off the sleeves of the suit. "Why is the air fresh here?"

"All this grass is making the oxygen." He waved his hand toward the inland. On the dunes blades of sawgrass sprouted out of the loose sand. "But it's only this stretch. Twenty miles that way the air's foul again." He nodded down the beach after his son. "Ten or twelve miles the other. Three miles inland." He stood over her while she tugged her feet up out of the boots of the space suit. "There's sweet water, and if you work, you can find enough food to live. But you don't get off this beach until you realize where your place is."

She stepped out of the pressure suit. "You'd better call your son before he swims to China."

Tanuojin looked up. Junna's head bobbed in the ocean, forty feet beyond the breakers. His pressure suit and uniform lay in a heap on the wet sand. Paula took her flute and walked away along the beach. She stopped once and looked back. Tanuojin stood there staring down at the sand at his feet. He would not look at her. Perhaps he could not. She turned and went on her way.